Praise for *The Roll of the Drums*

"*Roll of the Drums* is a well-written novel centered around an Amish family and their tight-knit community during the Civil War."

Interviews & Reviews

"This historical romance is a thoughtfully crafted love story. . . . It reads like an intricate tapestry of love set against a counterpoint of evil."

The Historical Novels Review

"A heartfelt Amish novel. . . . Complicated, charming, and sweet, *The Roll of the Drums* is a great read."

Urban Lit Magazine

Praise for *The Sound of Distant Thunder*

"Twenty-year-old Jonas Weaver can't resist fighting the evil of slavery by joining the War Between the States. Off to the army he goes, despite strong objections by his family, his Amish church, and his sweetheart, Katie Stuckey. When Jonas's letters stop coming, Katie has to face something from her past she has tried to ignore. Jan Drexler's *The Sound of Distant Thunder* combines historical research with compelling characters to create a memorable story of love in the time of war."

Suzanne Woods Fisher, bestselling author of *Anna's Crossing*

"In *The Sound of Distant Thunder*, the sweetness of young love, the conflict and sorrow of the War Between the States, the wisdom of couples long married, and the cost of making a stand for what one believes are blended into a story that kept me turning pages. The way Jan Drexler's Amish characters spring to life off the page will leave readers wanting to know more about the people in this Amish community. For sure and certain."

Ann H. Gabhart, bestselling author
of *These Healing Hills*

"Faith, family, and freedom are tested by the crucible of war in this haunting love story of a gentle people whose lives—and hearts—are disrupted by the sound of distant thunder. Historically rich and rare, this is a unique glimpse into a nation divided that both captures the mind and nourishes the soul."

Julie Lessman, award-winning author of The Daughters of Boston, Winds of Change, and Isle of Hope series

"In a beautifully woven story, Jan Drexler once again gives her readers a true look at the struggles of faith, hope, and love facing families, churches, communities, and a nation during a time of turbulence."

Ruth Logan Herne, award-winning author

SOFTLY
BLOWS
the BUGLE

Books by Jan Drexler

Journey to Pleasant Prairie

Hannah's Choice

Mattie's Pledge

Naomi's Hope

The Amish of Weaver's Creek

The Sound of Distant Thunder

The Roll of the Drums

Softly Blows the Bugle

SOFTLY BLOWS *the* BUGLE

JAN DREXLER

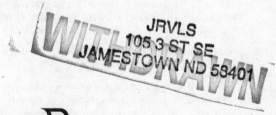

Revell

a division of Baker Publishing Group
Grand Rapids, Michigan

Published by Revell
a division of Baker Publishing Group
PO Box 6287, Grand Rapids, MI 49516-6287
www.revellbooks.com

Printed in the United States of America

Library of Congress Cataloging-in-Publication Data
Names: Drexler, Jan, author.
Title: Softly blows the bugle / Jan Drexler.
Description: Grand Rapids, Michigan : Revell, a division of Baker Publishing Group, [2020] | Series: The Amish of Weaver's Creek ; 3
Identifiers: LCCN 2020005245 | ISBN 9780800729332 (paperback) | ISBN 9780800739232 (hardcover)
Subjects: LCSH: Amish—Fiction. | GSAFD: Christian fiction. | Love stories.
Classification: LCC PS3604.R496 S67 2020 | DDC 813/.6—dc23
LC record available at https://lccn.loc.gov/2020005245

Scripture used in this book, whether quoted or paraphrased by the characters, is taken from the King James Version of the Bible.

This is a work of historical reconstruction; the appearances of certain historical figures are therefore inevitable. All other characters, however, are products of the author's imagination, and any resemblance to actual persons, living or dead, is coincidental.

The author is represented by WordServe Literary Group.

20 21 22 23 24 25 26   7 6 5 4 3 2 1

To the Morning Coffee Circle at Greencroft Manor IV in Goshen, Indiana: thank you for welcoming me into your group a few times a year and sharing your stories. I always enjoy your insiders' look at growing up Amish.

Soli Deo Gloria

Wherefore seeing we also are compassed about with so great a cloud of witnesses, let us lay aside every weight, and the sin which doth so easily beset us, and let us run with patience the race that is set before us, looking unto Jesus the author and finisher of our faith; who for the joy that was set before him endured the cross, despising the shame, and is set down at the right hand of the throne of God.

Hebrews 12:1–2

1

Life and knitting. Each one goes along smoothly, needles and events gliding against each other to form a seamless whole, until the day you look back and see the one missed stitch that has affected the entire fabric.

Elizabeth Kaufman dropped the ruined sock into her lap and closed her eyes, leaning her head against the back of the rocking chair on the shaded front porch. A bird sang somewhere above the roof, its fluid call carrying through the quiet afternoon air like an autumn leaf falling. It rose, then paused. Rose again, then swooped down only to end on a high trilling note.

A shriek from inside the house brought an abrupt end to the birdsong. Katie Stuckey's feet pounding on the stairway and more shrieks brought Elizabeth to her feet, her knitting falling to the porch floor.

"He's coming!" Katie slammed the wooden screen door

open and grabbed Elizabeth's arms, spinning her in a circle. "I saw him from the window! On the road!"

Katie jumped off the porch and headed down the lane toward the road, leaving Elizabeth breathless and alone on the porch.

"Who?" Elizabeth called after her, then laughed to herself. Who else could it be? The long-awaited day had finally arrived. After three long years of serving in the army, Jonas—her brother and Katie's intended—was home.

It was a happy day, for sure. Elizabeth picked up her yarn and needles and went into the house. She added more ham and water to the pot of beans cooking for their dinner. Then she mixed up a big batch of cornbread, knowing *Mamm* would have many mouths to feed today. As soon as Jonas's letter had come telling them he was returning home, Mamm had started planning the celebration. They hadn't been sure which day to expect him, but they knew it would be sometime this week. The whole family hung in expectation, but as anxious as Elizabeth was to see her brother, she would let him have some time alone with Katie first. She would arrive at the home farm in time for supper.

When the cornbread was finished baking, she wrapped the dishes in towels and placed them in the back of the pony cart. As she hitched up Pie, a sudden longing to see Jonas swept over her. She hadn't been close to him since she married Reuben, but her life was different now. Jonas was her little brother, and he was home. Had the war changed him?

She hurried Pie along as quickly as she dared with the pot of soup sloshing in the back. As Elizabeth crossed the stone bridge into the yard of her parents' farm, Jonas stepped out of the door to meet her. She jumped from the cart, not bothering to tie the pony, and ran to her brother. He lifted her in strong arms.

"Welcome home, Jonas," she said into his ear.

He set her down and looked into her eyes. "How are you?"

"As good as can be, now that you're back." She pulled back slightly. "You are home, aren't you? You don't have to return to the war?"

Jonas grinned, looking more like the boy she remembered. "Mamm asked me the same thing. *Ja*, for sure I'm home. I've been mustered out. The army doesn't want me anymore."

Katie appeared behind him. "Come in, Elizabeth. Jonas brought a friend home with him."

Jonas propelled her toward the door. "I left Aaron in Mamm's hands, the poor fellow."

A lean man sat at the kitchen table, a spoon halfway to his mouth. Jonas had been right. Mamm had dished up a bowl full of chicken and noodles for the stranger, and he had already finished most of it. He put his spoon down when he saw Elizabeth and rose to his feet.

Elizabeth forced herself not to stare as the man grabbed a pair of crutches and hobbled toward her, one trouser leg pinned up at the knee.

"Aaron Zook," he said, thrusting a hand toward her. "Jonas told me about his family. I'm guessing you must be Elizabeth."

Stunned, Elizabeth shook hands with him. Her thoughts swirled. Aaron spoke in Englisch. He wasn't Amish.

"Ja . . . Yes," she stammered. "I'm Elizabeth."

His lower face was covered with a long red beard and

mustache, but underneath she could see hollow cheeks and pale skin with a gray cast. His welcoming smile stopped at his mouth, not reaching his shadowed eyes. The expression in those dark blue eyes reminded her of the man she had been trying so hard to forget.

"Aaron and I met in the hospital where I was stationed in New York," Jonas said, grasping his friend's shoulder.

"Were you a medic too?" Mamm asked.

Aaron's smile disappeared as he turned away from Elizabeth. "No, ma'am. I was a wounded prisoner. A Confederate soldier."

Elizabeth's head swam. A Confederate soldier, just like her husband, Reuben, had been. She took a step back as Aaron went on.

"Jonas saved my life in more ways than one, and I owe him a great debt. With my family and property gone, I had no reason to return to Tennessee. Jonas suggested I come here to Ohio with him before I move on."

"You're welcome to stay as long as you like," *Datt* said.

Elizabeth took another step back. What was Datt thinking, inviting this man to stay?

"I'd like that," Aaron said. "I'll work for my keep. Don't worry about that." He patted his right leg. "I don't let this slow me down much."

"We'll talk about that later," Datt said. "Our older son Samuel will be here with his family soon, and his oldest boy has gone to tell Jonas's other sisters that he's come home. Today is a day to celebrate."

Elizabeth slipped out to the porch, then leaned against the wall, her heart pounding. Somehow, she would have to

12

join with the rest of the family in welcoming Aaron to the community. Swallowing hard, she closed her eyes, dread seeping into the place that had held such joy only moments ago.

She shook her head, trying to clear it away.

He isn't Reuben. He might not be anything like Reuben.

She wiped the dampness off her upper lip and rubbed her palms on her clean apron. If Aaron Zook stayed in Weaver's Creek, nothing could be right again.

The house was crowded, noisy, and hot. Aaron's head pounded with the strain of being pleasant, the flat tones of Yankee talk mingled with the harsh Pennsylvania Dutch words Jonas's family and friends used among themselves, not realizing he could understand only some of what they said.

Finally, supper was over, and Aaron slipped out of the house. He needed quiet. Peace and quiet.

The porch off the kitchen was crowded, too, but folks moved aside for him as he hobbled through. The sun had gone down, leaving an orange glow in the western sky. Aaron went toward the outhouse, then swung past it and ended up at a board fence. A dark meadow faded into the dusk, a horse standing nearby was a black shadow against the night sky. Aaron leaned his crutches against the fence rail and grasped the post, glad for the breeze that cooled his hot skin.

Frogs croaked. Aaron closed his eyes. An early owl hooted from somewhere to his left. The voices he had left behind were faint, then someone laughed, the sound rising above the others for a brief moment.

Footsteps in the grass behind him. Aaron turned to see Jonas. Ever since they had met in the hospital after one of the many battles in the Siege of Petersburg in October, Jonas had been the one to keep Aaron's path straight. But it wouldn't be long before they would go their separate ways. How did he ever come to be friends with a Yankee?

"Are you feeling all right?" Jonas rested his arms on the fence rail next to him.

"You aren't a medic anymore."

Jonas gave a soft chuckle. "It has become a habit." He rolled his shoulders. "It feels good to be home, but . . ."

Aaron let the silence grow between them. He sighed. "It isn't what you remembered?"

"It's still home, but not much has changed. It is as if the war didn't happen at all."

"But the war changed you." Aaron let his mind go back to the angry, fiery young man he had been, hot to kill any Yankee he could find after a scouting party shot Grandpop and left him to die with his blood seeping into the Tennessee land he had loved. "Both of us. War will do that."

Jonas looked out over the meadow. "You're right. We've both seen things that Katie and my family can't fathom. And I don't want to tell them. I don't want Katie to know how terribly cruel men can be."

"Do you still think war is wrong?" Aaron looked at his friend. "Your side won. The Confederacy is dead."

"And the slaves are free." Jonas bowed his head. "But the cost . . . The cost is so great. I was willing to give my life so others could be free, but when I think of how many others paid the ultimate price, it grieves me." He passed a hand over

14

his face. "Yes, I believe war is wrong. I pray that our country will never be in another one."

After a few minutes of silence, Jonas changed the subject. "What do you think of my family?"

Aaron let a smile tug at the corners of his mouth. "You described each one perfectly. Except your sister Elizabeth. I wouldn't have been able to choose her out of a crowded hog wallow if I didn't hear your mama say her name."

"Elizabeth is different than I remember, but she didn't spend much time with the family when her husband was alive."

Aaron leaned on the fence post, easing the weight pressing on his good leg. "She's a widow?"

"Mamm said Reuben was killed at Vicksburg."

"I thought you said that the Amish don't fight."

"Reuben wasn't Amish."

Aaron shifted again to ease his aching leg. Elizabeth was a puzzle, but he wouldn't be around long enough to sort it out. Jonas, on the other hand, was home. He had often talked about his plans on their journey west, and his doubts.

"Did you talk to your pa about getting married?"

Jonas turned and leaned back against the fence, facing the house. "I mentioned it, but Datt didn't know how the ministers would handle the situation."

"I don't see what the problem is. She's your girl, ain't she? Just up and marry her."

"I have to join the church first. I can't get married until I do."

Aaron turned and leaned his back against the fence post. Someone had lit the lamps in the house and warm golden light spilled into the yard through the windows.

"I don't think I'll ever figure you out. What does joining some church have to do with marrying Katie? They can't tell you what to do. It isn't like you're still in the army."

"It's the way we live. I've always been part of the church, but to be baptized and become a member means that I am committed to being part of the community. And we don't allow members to marry before they're baptized."

"You've got your life all planned out, then, just like you said. You'll join the church, build your house, marry Katie, and have a passel of youngsters."

"One step at a time. The first thing I need to do is find out if I'll be allowed to be baptized after being in the army." Jonas turned toward him. "What do you intend to do? Will you stay around here for a while? Or will you head west like you keep talking about?"

Aaron shifted again, trying to ease the strain of bearing all his weight on one leg. He missed the silence of the Tennessee woods and the cabin Grandpop had built when he finally settled down after leaving Pennsylvania as a young man, but that peaceful home was gone forever. Burned to the ground by Yankee scum. They had eradicated his past as thoroughly as they had destroyed his future. But they hadn't succeeded in taking his life. His thoughts shied away from the ravenous black pit of death.

Aaron grasped at the dream he had held fast during the long nights in the prison hospital. "I heard the West is open territory. No one to get in your way."

"I heard the men talk about that too. It sounds pretty lonely." Jonas's eyes reflected the lamplight from the house. "It would be mighty hard for a man to build a home out there."

"Some men do better alone." Aaron glanced at Jonas. "You want to be part of this community, with your folks and your girl. That's what you want. But I've always been on my own, taking care of myself most of my life. I'm itching to hear nothing but the sound of the wind in the trees again."

Silence fell between them. The owl in the woods hooted. Frog song echoed from the creek. Somewhere on the other side of the pasture, a bull complained in the darkness.

"A healthy man with two sound legs might be able to survive on his own," Jonas said, his voice quiet. "I worry that you won't. It hasn't been that long since you nearly died from blood poisoning."

A familiar flare of anger at his situation rose in Aaron's chest. "I won't let a missing leg stop me."

Jonas chuckled, his face hidden in the darkness. "I don't imagine you will."

⌒

"Lydia, did you hear about Young Peter Lehman and Margaret Stuckey?"

Elizabeth froze as Salome Beiler's voice drifted into the front room from the kitchen. She was Bishop Amos's wife, but where Amos had grown in his tact and wisdom since becoming bishop a couple years ago, Salome was as thoughtless in her comments as she had ever been.

"I know they've been keeping company." Mamm's words were quiet. She never liked to listen to Salome's gossip.

"I heard a wedding will take place this summer."

Mamm didn't answer and Elizabeth continued tidying up the front room.

"Isn't it about time your Elizabeth married again?" Salome's voice took on the wheedling tone that set Elizabeth's teeth on edge. "She's been a widow far too long."

"I'm not concerned," Mamm said. "The Good Lord knows what Elizabeth needs, and he will provide."

"Now that she has repented of her unfortunate marriage to that outsider and has joined the church, my Levi might consider marrying her." Salome sniffed. "The Good Book instructs widows to marry, and your daughter has many good childbearing years ahead of her."

Elizabeth sank into the chair she had just straightened. The front room was empty now that nearly all the community had returned to their homes. The night was growing late. Elizabeth longed for her own bed and a good night's rest, but Salome had insisted on staying while Mamm cleaned the kitchen. Elizabeth wouldn't leave when there was still work to be done, but with Salome in the kitchen, Elizabeth was stuck unless she wanted to face the gossip head-on. Surely the woman knew that she was in the next room, able to hear every word of her conversation. But that had never stopped the busybody before, and it wouldn't now.

"Abraham and I will let Elizabeth make her own decisions concerning her future." Mamm's voice had an edge to it that told Elizabeth she was trying to hold her temper.

Salome grunted. "You should have reined that girl in years ago, before she ran off and married that reprobate. If she was my daughter—"

"She isn't your daughter, Salome," Mamm broke in.

Another grunt. Elizabeth leaned over far enough to see Salome cut another slice of cornbread for herself, then smooth the dish towel over the pan on the table. Mamm was facing the window and didn't see part of tomorrow's breakfast disappearing.

"I think Amos is ready to leave." Salome's chair scraped across the wood floor as she rose from the table. She stood, tying her bonnet. "I'm happy for your sake that Jonas is finally home," she said, moving toward the back door. "The past three years haven't been easy for you with your son off in the outside world, doing who knows what."

Mamm pressed her lips together as she moved a chair out of Salome's way. "*Denki*, Salome. We are very thankful to have him home with us again."

Elizabeth joined Mamm in the kitchen as Salome left. Mamm took a handkerchief from her apron waistband and wiped the perspiration from her forehead.

"That woman." She turned back to the sink to finish washing the dishes while Elizabeth picked up the dish towel. "Every time she visits, I'm happy to see her go. But then I have to repent of my uncharitable thoughts."

"She is horrible," Elizabeth said, drying a plate and setting it on the shelf above. "I don't see why you let her talk to you that way."

Mamm sighed, then smiled at her. "Now you need to repent. Salome isn't horrible. I don't think she knows how hurtful her comments can be, but she can be caring and helpful at times."

"All right. I'm sorry. But she's as prickly as a porcupine." Elizabeth wanted to add more to her description of Salome but didn't. Even though the woman was part of their community and the bishop's wife, Elizabeth couldn't forget the years Salome had acted as if she didn't exist, only because she had married outside the church.

"Salome did bring up a valid concern, though." Mamm didn't look at her as she immersed a stack of bowls in the dishpan. "It's been two years since Reuben died. Have you thought about marrying again?"

Elizabeth swallowed, her mouth suddenly dry. Even though Reuben had left to join the Confederate army nearly three years ago, she still had nightmares about him. She couldn't imagine willingly putting herself at the mercy of another man.

"I am content now, Mamm. I don't really want to marry."

"What about children? A family?"

Elizabeth's head pounded. She forced herself to pick up the next bowl to dry and watched her hand rub the dish towel over the wet surface. She had never told Mamm about the baby she had lost. That baby would have been five years old now, nearly the same age as her nephew Ezra, Gideon and Ruby's son.

"I don't think the Good Lord wants me to have children."

Mamm was silent as she finished washing the bowls and turned to the big pot Elizabeth had brought the ham and beans in.

"We never know what he has planned for us."

Mamm's voice was soft, but sure and steady. Elizabeth wished she could have even half of her mother's faith, but she was sure her future didn't hold the pleasures of a family and her own little ones. The Good Lord might bless others in that way, but not a woman like her.

After the kitchen was cleaned up, Elizabeth said good

night to Mamm and took her empty pot out to the pony cart. Datt had seen her coming and was hitching up Pie. Jonas's friend Aaron sat on the edge of the porch, his crutches next to him. He scooted away from the steps as Elizabeth went down them.

"It was nice to meet you, ma'am," Aaron said.

With the light from the kitchen window behind him, he didn't look as much like Reuben as Elizabeth had first thought. His words were drawn out and slow, nothing like the Englischers Elizabeth was familiar with.

"Thank you." Elizabeth paused, trying to think of what Mamm would say to him. "I hope you feel at home in Weaver's Creek."

"Yes, ma'am, for the time I'm here."

"You don't plan on settling here, then?"

Aaron rubbed his leg, the one that ended just above his knee. It was an unconscious motion, as if the leg often pained him.

"I don't know yet what I'm going to do."

Datt tied Pie to the hitching rail and took Elizabeth's pot from her.

"There's a place for you here," he said, setting the pot in the cart. "There is always room for a Zook in the community."

Aaron didn't answer. Elizabeth untied Pie's reins as Datt went back to the barn.

"Wait." Aaron rose and took a step toward her. "What did your father mean? Is there something special about my last name?"

"It's a common name among the Amish. Datt meant that you would fit in here easily, if you wanted to."

"Grandpop was raised in Pennsylvania. He never had a good word for his Amish family."

"Then you are Amish."

He shook his head. "I'm not Amish. I'm not anything."

"But if your grandfather's family was Amish, then—"

Aaron pushed back on his crutches, turning toward the porch steps. "I'm not Amish. I don't care what Grandpop's family was."

He swung up the steps and into the house, leaving Elizabeth standing alone with Pie. She stroked the pony's neck, then climbed into the cart and started for home.

She had thought Aaron was just another man like Reuben when she first met him, but Reuben, as hard as he was, never let her see any weakness. Reuben couldn't admit any vulnerability. But in her brief conversation with Aaron, she had caught a glimpse of a sad and lonely man.

2

On Monday morning, Aaron stayed behind in the barn while Jonas went to work with his father and brother. The men would spend the day walking behind the harrow or cultivator as they drove teams of horses back and forth across the fields. A man needed two good legs for work like that.

It was no good feeling useless, though. Once he was alone, Aaron found a broom to sweep out the aisle in front of the horses' stalls where some grain had spilled. He leaned on one crutch and grasped the broom with his other hand, but the result was an awkward drag of the bristles through the dust.

Ineffectual and helpless. The familiar feeling had dogged him day and night for the last eight months.

Setting his crutches firmly under his arms, Aaron grasped the broom with both hands and pushed it from right to left, creating a satisfying track in the layer of dust and grain. Several sparrows that had been picking at the grain scattered, fluttered between the barn rafters, then settled on the barn floor again, well out of reach of the broom.

"That's right, little birds." Aaron moved to his left, set the crutches, and prepared to make another sweep. "Stay out of the way. I'm armed and dangerous."

Two of the birds hopped closer as he grasped the broom again, then flew away as he set the bristles for the next pass. But he reached too far and lost his balance. He remembered to twist his body to take the impact on his shoulder and rolled in the dust. He ended up facedown on the dirt floor, his crutches careening in opposite directions as he fell. The birds flew up to the rafters in a flurry of fluttering wings and panicked cheeps.

Aaron rose up on his elbows and brushed the dirt from his beard. He wasn't going to lie here feeling sorry for himself. No one had witnessed that dunderheaded move. He reached for the broom and leaned it against the stall gate. Next, he grasped the crutch that had fallen near his head, then used his foot to bring the other crutch close. Setting the crutches upright, he pulled himself up until he stood again, his arms quivering from the exertion. He wiped the sweat from his eyes and started again.

He put the crutches in their places under his arms and put his weight on his foot. Once he got his balance, he picked up the broom again. Little sweep. Adjust the crutches. Little sweep. Adjust the crutches. This simple chore was going to take all day. The birds peered at him from above, waiting for another chance at the spilled grain.

What he wouldn't give for a rifle and a day tramping through the western Tennessee woods. Alone and free. Dependent on no man.

With two good legs.

Adjust the crutches. Sweep.

"Is my datt in here?"

The woman's voice startled him as it echoed in the empty barn and he took another dive onto the dusty floor, landing on his shoulder.

Groaning, he rolled onto his back. Elizabeth stood over him, a frown on her face.

"Are you all right? I didn't mean to surprise you."

Aaron frowned back. "I lost my balance, is all."

"Let me help you," she said as she reached for one of his crutches.

"Leave it." His voice sounded harsh to his ears. Like Pa's voice. He took a breath and started again. "Leave it. I don't need your help."

Elizabeth stepped back. He picked up the broom and leaned it against the stall gate, then the crutches, one at a time. He sat up, then pulled himself to a standing position again, looking away from the young woman's face. Her soft and vulnerable face.

"Your pa's working in the fields with the others." Aaron leaned on his crutches as rivulets of sweat ran down his back. "What do you need?"

She chewed on her lower lip. Aaron stared at the floor to keep from meeting her eyes. In the short few weeks since he had left the hospital, he had learned to avoid eye contact. Most folks either looked at him with pity or revulsion, and he couldn't take either one. Especially from a woman as fine as this one.

"Something got into our henhouse last night and I need to close off the hole it made."

"You lose any chickens?"

"Four." She glanced at him, then lowered her gaze to the floor as if the sight pained her. "Whatever it was only carried off one and left the rest behind."

"Probably a weasel. They kill for sport."

She nodded. "That's what I thought. Or maybe a fox. And it will come back again if I don't get that hole closed off."

Aaron drummed his fingers against the handles of his crutches. If he had two good legs, he'd know what to do. Fixing a hole in a chicken coop was easy.

He gazed out the barn door, then at the woman beside him.

"How far is your house?"

"Just up the road a piece, less than a mile. An easy walk—"

Her voice broke off as she glanced at his crutches. Her face turned pink as Aaron gripped the handles to hide the exhausted shaking in his hands. Elizabeth's eyes narrowed as she continued to stare at his leg.

"Maybe I should wait for Datt or Jonas."

Aaron's face burned at the dismissive tone of her voice. "I can do it. I don't need both legs to fix a chicken coop."

A frown brought her pale brown eyebrows together. Her eyes reminded him of Ma. He looked away again.

"I can't ask you to do it. You might hurt yourself."

Hurt himself? All thoughts of her vulnerability fled at that challenge. He would fix her chicken coop if it killed him.

Aaron tilted his head toward the back of the barn where the wagons were stored. "We'll drive Jonas's wagon. And I'll need to borrow some of your pa's tools."

Doubt still filled her gaze, but she gave a swift nod. "I'll tell Mamm we're taking the horse and wagon. Datt keeps his tools in the workroom over there."

He found the tools he needed, and using one crutch, he was able to carry them to the spring wagon. Elizabeth wasn't back from the house yet, so he let himself lean on the wagon wheel long enough to get his breath back.

Maybe Jonas was right. Heading into the wilderness of the West was hard enough for a man in good condition. Somehow, he'd have to learn to use his one good leg and build up his strength at the same time. Starting with the chicken coop.

By the time Elizabeth returned, her expression still wary, Aaron had retrieved the crutch he had left in the workroom and managed to bring in Rusty, Jonas's driving horse. The harness had been beyond his ability, though.

"Couldn't you find the harness?" Elizabeth asked.

"I was just getting to it," Aaron said. He started toward the wall where the harness hung on pegs. He might be able to get it down, but he knew he didn't have the strength or balance to toss it onto Rusty's back. His shoulders ached just thinking about it.

"Mamm said you might have trouble with the harness." Elizabeth stepped past him and lifted it off the hooks. "I can do this."

"I can't stand by and let you do the work."

She glared at him. "You think I can't harness a horse?"

He glared right back. "You seem to think I can't."

She shifted the weight of the harness in her arms and walked toward Rusty. As she tossed it onto the horse's back, the straps tangled, leaving a messy heap. Rusty turned to look at her.

But she had gotten the awkward weight up there. That was more than he could have done.

Aaron watched her pull on one strap, and then another, but the horse's back was above her head. She was such a short little thing that she couldn't see what she was doing. That didn't stop her, though. She squared her shoulders and tried again.

"Do you want some help?"

Those firm shoulders slumped, then she nodded. "I guess I could use another pair of hands. I can't seem to get it straight. This horse is much taller than my driving pony."

Aaron went to Rusty's off side. He would need two hands for this task, so he leaned his crutches against the post behind him. His good leg was aching from the unaccustomed work already, but it held him up as he straightened the harness and arranged the straps so Elizabeth could fasten them from the other side.

By the time Elizabeth had backed Rusty into position in front of the wagon, Aaron could hardly stand. He put the crutches into the wagon, then readied himself for the jump and pull up to the wagon seat. Elizabeth was climbing onto the seat from the other side, so if he failed to make this jump, she would witness everything. He grasped the handles Jonas had installed on either side of the wagon seat and jumped up, trying to make the clumsy maneuver look as smooth as he could.

But he couldn't stop panting once he reached the seat and twisted himself around to face the front. His face burned, but was it from exhaustion or embarrassment? From the corner of his eye, he could see Elizabeth's frown.

What he didn't expect was her question.

"How long has it been since you lost your leg?"

"Eight months." Eight long months of constant pain and bed rest.

"So you're still getting accustomed to it."

"I suppose so." Aaron leaned his crutches against the seat and rubbed his bad leg. "The trip out here took more out of me than I thought it would."

"Have you ever thought about getting one of those wooden legs? I saw a soldier in Millersburg with one a few months ago. If he hadn't been limping, I never would have noticed it."

A wooden leg. Sure, he had seen them. The men who had gotten them looked whole again. The muscle on the side of his jaw began to twitch.

"Union soldiers can get them from the government, but they won't give them to us Rebs."

Elizabeth picked up the reins and clucked to Rusty. She was silent as they drove over the stone bridge and onto the road. Then she turned to him again.

"Why do you have to have someone give you one? Why not make your own?"

He stared at her, ready to say . . . what? One of the other prisoners in the hospital had talked endlessly about how the Federals owed the Rebs something for leaving them crippled like this, but he knew Washington didn't owe him anything. He was a casualty of war, that was all.

Aaron turned away from her and stared into the trees. A

casualty that left him only half a man. The war had stripped him clean, but he wasn't going to crawl into a hole and wait to die. Elizabeth's suggestion rang in his ears. Why not make his own leg? Then nothing could stop him from standing on his own two feet.

"One, two, three . . ." Katie counted the chickens as Elizabeth scattered cracked corn for them.

"I think you counted the red one twice." Elizabeth tossed an extra handful of corn toward the little reddish hen that was her favorite. The chicken had a distinct personality and always made Elizabeth smile. She was glad Prissy, as she secretly called her, had survived the marauder.

Elizabeth recounted the chickens in the yard as Katie went into the henhouse to count the ones still sitting on their nests. Elizabeth counted the flock three times and then joined Katie inside the little building.

"How many did you find in here?"

"Eleven," Katie said, reaching under a brown hen for the next egg.

"That makes twenty-five. They're all here again today."

"Whatever Aaron did to fix the hole in back, it has worked." Katie ignored the next chicken's complaints as she took an egg from her nest. "What do you think of Jonas's friend?"

Ignoring Katie's sidelong look, Elizabeth searched through the empty nests for eggs.

"He's all right, I guess."

"He's a single man." Katie got to the end of her row of

nest boxes and turned toward her. "I thought you might be a little more interested than you appear."

Elizabeth reached for another egg, but her stomach was quivering. She couldn't tell Katie why she would never be interested in any man. Not even her own sister Ruby knew the whole story.

"You know I don't plan on marrying again. Being a single woman suits me. I'm very happy."

Katie didn't seem to hear her. "Aaron Zook is an honest, hardworking man, according to Jonas. His missing leg doesn't keep him from helping around the farm."

"But there are some things he just can't manage with his crutches, like walking behind a plow or cultivator."

"That's true. But he repaired our henhouse, didn't he?"

Elizabeth gave in as she put the last egg in her basket. "You're right. He's a hard worker and pleasant enough to be around. But that doesn't mean I'm going to marry him."

"You don't have to marry him," Katie said as she fastened the henhouse door and led the way toward the house. "Just be willing to see the possibilities. Who knows? You just might fall in love."

As she said this, Katie twirled around to walk backwards up the path, grinning at her. Elizabeth met her irresistible happiness with her own smile. Katie had endured many months of waiting for Jonas's return from the war and she deserved the happiness that spilled from her like clear water from a pump.

"All right. I'll be open to what might happen."

"You never know what the Good Lord might have planned for you."

Elizabeth worked to keep the smile on her face. She might have made her peace with the church, but God was another matter. She didn't dare to think about what God would do to her after the years she had spent living a life outside of his will.

After the morning chores were done, Katie went to her sister's house while Elizabeth started toward the home place to spend the day with Mamm in her garden.

It was good to see Katie laughing again. Much had changed while Jonas had been gone. Katie's father had passed on, then in the autumn of 1863, her mother had also died. Since the news had come of Elizabeth's husband's death at Vicksburg, both friends were single and alone. And with her sister Ruby's marriage to Gideon Fischer, Elizabeth had left her husband's old, dark cabin and come to live with Katie. The two enjoyed each other's company in the pleasant little house in the Stuckeys' woods.

But with Jonas's return, Elizabeth's life was changing again. She had felt sorry for Katie during the long separation from Jonas, but whenever she considered the full and vibrant future Katie looked forward to with Jonas's return, self-pity closed in.

How she hated feeling sorry for herself! For sure, her marriage had been a mistake, but now she was free of Reuben. She shuddered, remembering her life before Reuben went off to join the Confederate army. The dingy cabin, the horrible odor of stale alcohol, the fear . . .

Elizabeth blinked her eyes, forcing the threatening tears away. Reuben wasn't part of her life any longer. That time was in the past. The war was over, Jonas was home, and life could get back to the way it was before the war.

She was free and content, wasn't she? And she meant to stay that way.

As she reached the road at the end of the lane, Elizabeth was surprised to see Jonas and Datt at the clearing across the creek where Jonas had planned to build a house before he had gone to war.

Jonas saw her and waved, so Elizabeth walked across the log bridge.

"Are you starting on your house again?" she asked. Aaron sat on a bench, out of sight of the road. If she had seen him earlier, she would have called out in Englisch, but Aaron didn't seem to notice her.

"It's about time to finish Katie's house, don't you think?" Jonas said as he met her at the end of the bridge. "We're figuring out how much lumber to order, and Datt has some ideas for changes to my original plan."

Datt smiled at Elizabeth, his tender look reminding her of the closeness they had shared before her marriage. "I had thought that Jonas and Katie would live in her house to begin with, but it turns out that there will be another couple using that house."

Elizabeth's stomach turned. "You mean the house Katie and I are sharing now?"

"You haven't heard? Katie's brothers decided that Young Peter Lehman should have it when he marries Katie's niece Margaret this summer. But you don't need to worry about where you live. Your Mamm and I always have room."

Swallowing, Elizabeth attempted a smile. "That's all right. I'll move back to my cabin. There's no reason to have it sitting empty, and I will enjoy living closer to Ruby and her family."

"Do you think it is wise for you to try to manage one hundred sixty acres on your own?" He stroked his beard. "If you want my advice, I think you should sell the farm and move home. If you want to live on your own, we can build you a house near ours."

Jonas grinned. "You could build near the woodlot and be our neighbors. Katie would like that fine."

Datt looked around the clearing as if he was measuring the space. "But first we need to make these changes to Jonas's plans. His original thoughts are fine for a young couple just starting out, but they'll want a larger house as their family grows."

"Have you talked to the ministers then?" Elizabeth asked.

Jonas shook his head. "Not yet, but I have confidence that they will give permission for us to marry."

"What will you do if they say you can't join the church?"

Her brother's face darkened. "I'm not sure yet, but we'll do something. Katie and I have waited long enough to get married, and I don't want to let anything stand in our way."

Datt's frown told Elizabeth how he felt about that idea. "We'll see what happens. Just don't be too quick to act."

Elizabeth glanced at Aaron. They had been speaking Deitsch during their conversation. He hadn't been listening but was examining a piece of wood about two feet long. He put one end on the ground, then stood next to it.

"Does that one look like it might work?" Jonas said in Englisch, walking over to him. Elizabeth followed.

"It might." Aaron sat again and handed the piece of wood to Jonas. "It's a solid piece of oak. I'll need to form some sort of socket in the top."

A wooden leg. Aaron was making a wooden leg. Elizabeth glanced at his pinned-up trousers.

"You'll want a cushion too," she said. "The man I saw in Millersburg had a pad between his leg and the wooden one."

"Elizabeth is right," Jonas said. "And you'll need a harness to fasten it on. A couple of the members in our community are harness makers. Perhaps they could help you design something."

Aaron's face took on a hopeful look that banished the empty expression in his eyes. Perhaps he needed nothing more than a goal and a plan to be useful.

"Harness makers? Grandpop taught me a little bit about working with leather, and I'd be beholden to them if they could teach me how to make such a thing."

"Dan Zook and his brother Ephraim run the business together along with their farm," Datt said. "Who knows? You might be related to them."

Aaron glanced at Elizabeth. "One of the many Amish Zook families? I don't think you'll find any of my relatives here."

"What if you did?" Jonas asked. "You don't have any other family. It would be a blessing to find someone to belong to."

Aaron's face closed again, making Elizabeth curious. It was possible that Dan and Ephraim Zook were related to him, but Aaron didn't seem interested in them at all. Was he so determined to remain independent that he'd even deny his own family?

3

Aaron looked forward to a quiet morning by himself on Sunday. After breakfast he went out to the back porch. The sun was coming up behind a covering of gray clouds. It would rain today.

The family was getting ready for church and their usual routine was hurried. Jonas came out on the back porch, dressed in black trousers and a snowy white shirt. He smoothed his hair down before settling his black straw hat on his head.

"You're not coming?" he asked as he tugged on the ends of his sleeves to smooth the creases.

"I'm not much for church going," Aaron said, easing back farther in the chair. "Haven't since Ma passed on. I'll just stay put." He didn't tell Jonas that he intended to go back to bed as soon as the family was gone.

Jonas peered closely at him. "Are you all right? You've been working pretty hard the past few days."

Aaron resisted rubbing his stump. "I'm a bit tired. Those

months in the hospital took more out of me than I thought they would."

"I've heard that a man can lose more strength by lying in bed than anything else. But you came pretty close to death a few months ago. You need to build up your stamina. Give it some time." He leaned against the porch rail, dusting it with his hand first. "I wish you'd change your mind about staying home this morning. Spending the day worshiping the Lord might be just what you need."

Just what he needed? A sudden memory of Sunday mornings by Ma's side at their country church at home brought moisture to his eyes. Aaron rubbed it away. He was tired, nothing more.

"Y'all eat there?"

"Sure. After the services we eat together. Not a big meal. In the summer it's usually cold roast and bread, along with pickles and other such things. And desserts, of course. Usually pie."

Aaron's mouth watered even though he had just finished breakfast.

"But the preaching is in German," Jonas went on. "You probably wouldn't understand too much of it."

"Grandpop made sure I understood German. He used it enough that I picked it up. I can make out most of what y'all say."

Jonas stood up, dusting off the seat of his trousers. "It sounds like you're talking yourself into coming to church."

"I don't have fancy duds to wear." Aaron glanced sideways at Jonas's clothes.

"These aren't fancy, although they are special for the

Lord's Day. But you're a visitor. No one will expect you to dress like us."

Aaron ran his fingers through his beard. It might be worth sitting through the preaching to get to the meal. If he stayed here, he'd have to rustle up his own grub. And it wouldn't be as if he didn't know anyone there. He had met most of the community at Jonas's welcome-home party.

"I'll go with you." Aaron ignored Jonas's grin.

"I'll hitch up the spring wagon."

A number of folks had already arrived at the farm just past Elizabeth's and Katie's house when Jonas drove the wagon into the yard. Abraham and Lydia had insisted on walking, and Aaron saw that there were only a couple other buggies.

"Where's the church building?" he asked Jonas.

"We don't have one. We meet in homes, like the Amish have always done. Each family in the community hosts the church service twice a year. Today it's Karl Stuckey's turn."

Aaron looked for faces he knew and saw Elizabeth standing with some other women. Katie nodded to Jonas and smiled.

"We'll wait out here until everyone has arrived," Jonas said in a quiet voice. "We use the time to prepare ourselves for worship."

He led the way to a group of men standing off to the side. The group was a subdued contrast to the other night. No one spoke more than a quiet greeting.

Just after Abraham and Lydia had joined the gathered community, another buggy arrived. The horse was black and spirited, but the man driving the shiny rig held the reins with confidence. He pulled the horse to a stop in the middle of the crowd. Abraham stepped forward.

"Welcome, stranger. Can I help you?"

The man smiled. "The name is Solomon Mast." He flashed a smile at the crowd. "New in the area. I just bought the old Patterson place and moved in this week from Lancaster County in Pennsylvania. Neighbor Amos Beiler told me where the community was meeting for worship today, so I thought I'd join you."

Aaron's feet didn't move as the men around him stepped closer to the newcomer. The man's voice plucked at his memory, taking him back to a night in Virginia, smoke hanging in the dark air between the tents of the camp. He shook his head. It couldn't be the same man.

"You're welcome, brother," Abraham said. "We are just about to go in to worship." He signaled behind him and one of the older boys ran forward to take the horse and buggy to the barn.

"Denki," Solomon said. "I look forward to getting to know all of you."

As the man's gaze scanned the crowd, he paused when he saw Aaron. His eyebrows lifted as if questioning his presence, and he met Aaron's gaze. Instead of the open, honest expression Aaron had come to expect from Jonas's family and friends, Solomon Mast's face tightened, his eyes narrowing and his full lips pressing into a thin line. Then, as if a towel were whisked away, the smile returned, and the man's gaze continued around the gathered group. Had it been a look of recognition? Or only surprise at seeing a non-Amish man in the group?

Then Jonas nudged Aaron. It was time to go into the house. Rows of benches lined the large open room with an aisle between them. The women and young children sat on one side and the men on the other. Aaron and Jonas took their seats on the back bench, while Solomon Mast followed Abraham right up to the front. Aaron frowned. They might both be visitors, but Solomon showed the stark difference between them. He acted as if he belonged here and Aaron did not.

Elizabeth helped serve the fellowship meal after church, but her thoughts were on today's visitors. Solomon Mast had appeared in their midst like a fresh breeze on a warm day. He sat with the ministers and Datt for the first seating of the meal, and his voice rose above the other conversations.

"The Patterson farm is eighty acres," Solomon said, answering someone's question. "It's good land, but less than forty are tillable at present. The rest is poor and stony, but it will be useful for grazing cattle."

Elizabeth carried a bowl of sauerkraut to the table and set it down in front of Bishop Amos. Solomon smiled at her, making her the center of his attention for a moment. Elizabeth felt her cheeks grow warm as she moved down the table to place a second bowl in front of Jonas and Levi Beiler at the other end. Aaron sat with them and smiled his thanks to her.

The conversation at the other end of the table continued.

"Do you have a family, Solomon?" Preacher Amos asked.

The man's face grew downcast. "Sadly, no. I am a widower. My wife passed away and our only child perished with her." He paused as the other men expressed their sympathy. "But it has been several months since her passing, and I am ready to start again. That is why I moved here to Ohio." He glanced at Elizabeth, then turned his attention back to the men. "This is a new beginning for me in a new community. I must thank you for your kind welcome to a stranger."

"Are you in need of any help on your farm?" Gideon Fischer, Elizabeth's brother-in-law, asked.

Solomon shook his head. "Patterson had already done the spring planting, and he sold me the equipment and livestock along with the land and buildings."

"I hadn't realized Abel Patterson was planning to sell out," Gideon said. "I spoke with him a few weeks ago."

"He told me he had decided to go back to New York to live with his son. I met him in the land agent's office in Millersburg where I went to inquire about land for sale." Solomon smiled at the men around him, his white teeth gleaming. "I suppose you could call the meeting the Lord's providence. We settled the matter there and then."

Elizabeth went to the kitchen to fetch another plate of bread. When she came back, the men were still discussing Solomon's business.

"Gideon, is it?" he said, turning to her brother-in-law. "You said you had spoken to Patterson recently. Does that mean that we're neighbors?"

"My farm is nearby," Gideon said, "but Elizabeth's land is between us. She owns one hundred sixty acres, eighty on the west side of the Berlin Road and eighty on the east side." He nodded toward Elizabeth as she set the bread on the table. "This is Elizabeth Kaufman."

Solomon turned his warm smile on her. "Elizabeth, I am happy to meet you. So, you and your husband will be my closest neighbors."

Elizabeth felt her cheeks warming again. "My land is your neighbor." She couldn't keep from returning his smile. "I don't live on the land, and my husband has passed away."

"We will have to become better acquainted, then."

"I'm sure we will." Elizabeth turned and nearly ran for the kitchen. Her sister Ruby, Gideon's wife, and Millie Keck, Salome Beiler's married daughter, were there, along with Mamm. All of them stared at her.

"What is wrong?" Millie asked, jiggling one of her twin babies in her arms. "You look as if you're running away from a wolf!"

Elizabeth laughed at the image Millie's words portrayed. "Don't be silly. I was just thinking of something, that's all."

"I saw you talking to that new man." Millie rocked the fussing baby back and forth. "Where is he from? What is he doing here?"

"Girls, we don't want to gossip," Mamm said, slicing another loaf of bread.

"He was very open about his business as he spoke with the men," Elizabeth said. "He has bought Abel Patterson's farm and intends to settle here."

"And his family?" Ruby asked.

"There is no family. He's a widower."

"That is interesting," Millie said, grinning. "A widower in the community. I'm sure he'll be looking for a new wife."

"He can look all he wants," Elizabeth said, reaching for Millie's son. He settled in her arms and stared up at her, his fist in his mouth. "There are plenty of young single women for him to court, between our community and the neighboring ones." She smiled at the baby and touched his nose. "Which baby is this one, Millie? I can't tell them apart."

"That's little Amos. But don't think you're going to change the subject. What about Solomon Mast?" She sighed. "I can see the wedding now."

"What wedding?" Ruby asked, laughing at Millie's dramatic expression.

"When Elizabeth marries Solomon, of course." Millie laughed along with her. "Don't you think they belong together?"

Elizabeth handed little Amos back to his mother. "Don't be silly. I don't even know the man. Save your wedding plans for someone else."

"I think they're well suited, with his land right next to hers," Millie said as Elizabeth escaped out the door. She didn't wait to hear Ruby's reply.

When it was the women's turn to eat, Elizabeth found a seat at the table between Mamm and Ruby. As the men had finished their meal, they had drifted toward the barn where they could stand out of the light rain and visit. Some were admiring Solomon's buggy as he pointed out the red-painted details on the undercarriage. He laughed often and even the soberest of the men joined in. Such a contrast to Reuben, who would never gather with any of the men in the neighborhood except Ned Hamlin.

Aaron and Jonas had not made themselves part of the

group. They sat together on a bench under a tree talking with Gideon, but Aaron's attention wasn't on either man. He was watching Solomon. Solomon didn't seem to notice, but then Elizabeth saw him glance in Aaron's direction. His handsome face paled, then he shifted his stance so that his back was to Aaron. Aaron frowned, still staring at the group of men, fingering his long red beard.

What was that all about?

Levi Beiler took a deep breath of the fresh evening air as he stood at the top of the hill, just before the road dipped into the Weaver's Creek valley. The afternoon showers had moved on, leaving cool weather behind for the rest of the Lord's Day.

He often stopped in this spot near Elizabeth Kaufman's old house to enjoy the beauty of the farms and woods with the creek winding through like a thread. Tonight, the creek was golden as it reflected the lowering sun, and off to the east a rainbow graced the sky. A familiar longing twisted his heart, though he barely noticed it after so many years. If only . . .

Levi shook his head. He had no reason to be discontent. At twenty-three years old, he finally had a comfortable, respectful relationship with Father. And the farm was doing well enough to support his parents and himself. Millie, his younger sister, was married and happy. At least, he assumed she was. Any woman would be happy, as busy as she was with her six-month-old twins.

Most satisfying of all was the freedom he now had to

study the scriptures and other church writings to his heart's content. Father even discussed what he was reading with him on occasion.

No, he had no reason to be discontent, except that a man should have a partner. Adam had Eve. Father had Mother. Jonas had his Katie. If only there was someone he could share the joys of this life with. Even though Paul had written that it was better for a man to be alone . . . except he also wrote that it was good to marry . . .

Levi started down the hill. He mustn't forget his errand. Solomon Mast's appearance at the church meeting this morning had taken everyone's attention and Levi hadn't been able to have his talk with Abraham.

He found the older man alone in the barn, finishing up the milking.

"It's an easier job now that you only have one cow, isn't it?" Levi leaned on the top rail of the cow pen.

Abraham glanced at him, then picked up the pail of milk and poured it into a can. "It is. I've tried to convince Lydia that we don't need even this one, that we could get our milk from Samuel, but she won't hear of it." He patted the cow on the rump and sent her back out to the pasture. "What brings you by?"

Levi grabbed the milk can and followed Abraham to the springhouse between the barn and the house. "I wanted to talk to you about the next ministers' meeting this afternoon at church, but I didn't get an opportunity. It's going to be in Wayne County again this year."

"I had heard," Abraham said, closing the springhouse door after Levi set the can in the cool running water. "I also heard that the last two meetings, in Pennsylvania and Indiana, were dominated by the change-minded faction."

"That's exactly right. That is why as many conservative leaders as possible are meeting here in Holmes County the week before the general meeting in July."

Abraham's gaze was piercing. "It sounds like they're ready to pit one side against the other. That isn't a peaceful way to solve the differences."

Levi followed Abraham to the porch. "Even though many hold out hope that there can be a reconciliation, I don't see how there can ever be the unity we've enjoyed in the past. The change-minded faction is determined."

"So are the traditionalists." Abraham settled into a chair and Levi joined him. "I hate to see it, but these controversies have been brewing for many years."

"Sometimes I think a schism in the church is inevitable."

Abraham sat silently for a few minutes, then heaved a sigh. "You'll be going to this meeting?"

"I'll go to both of them with Gideon. I want to observe, even if I'm not allowed to vote on the issues. I'm curious to see how the change-minded group accepts our position."

"You think they will object?"

"The conservative leaders want to state our position in a unified way and present it in written form so that their meaning can't be mistaken." Levi rubbed the perspiration off the bridge of his nose. "But I'm afraid the change-minded ministers won't pay much attention to them. They dismiss their brothers as old fashioned and afraid to try new things."

"We will have to wait and see how it plays out." Abraham

rose from his chair. "The end is in the Good Lord's hands, and he knows best."

A thump sounded from inside the house, followed by a pause, then the sound of the kitchen door opening. Jonas came out on the porch, along with his Englisch friend. As Abraham went inside the house, Levi greeted Aaron with a nod. He had been surprised but pleased to see the stranger at the church meeting this morning.

"Aaron," Jonas said, keeping his Deitsch slower and more distinct than usual. "This is Levi Beiler. You've heard me mention him."

"Several times." The man grinned as he shook Levi's hand. "I remember seeing you at the church service this morning."

"Did I hear your last name is Zook? You must be related to Dan and Ephraim."

Aaron's grin disappeared as he shook his head. "Not that I know." He sat on the top step, resting his crutches on the edge of the porch.

Jonas laughed and clapped his hand on Levi's shoulder. "Everyone who meets him asks him that. I think it would be good if we found out that Aaron was related to the Zooks here. It doesn't matter who you are, knowing you have family around is important."

Aaron rubbed the stump of his leg.

"You don't have family back home?" Levi wanted to pull back the words as soon as they were out. He didn't know this man well enough to prod him with a personal question like that.

Jonas lowered his voice. "Aaron's father and grandfather died during the war. He has no one else."

Levi moved to the porch steps and sat next to Aaron. "It would be good for you to find out if you have family here. Dan told me his father is coming to Ohio for the ministers' meeting next month. He lives in Lancaster County in Pennsylvania but will be moving the rest of the family out here to live near Dan and his brother, Ephraim. He might know if you have any family connections."

"I don't know. I might not be here next month." Aaron had switched from struggling to speak in Deitsch to Englisch.

Levi glanced at Jonas.

"I thought you had decided not to go west," Jonas said.

"Yeah, well, I haven't decided for certain yet." He picked up a pebble from the step and threw it out into the twilit drive. "I'm not sure I'm ready to put down roots anywhere." He picked up another pebble and rolled it between his fingers. "Every time I stop moving, memories catch up with me."

"Those memories will fade eventually," Jonas said. "I've heard that men can recover from the effects of war."

"Not when reminders show up when you least expect them." Aaron tossed another pebble. "Like that Solomon Mast this morning. He reminds me of someone. Someone I'd rather forget."

In the east, the evening star shone in the darkening sky. Fireflies blinked on and off in the meadow while silence followed Aaron's words.

After long minutes, Jonas sighed. "Promise you won't head west until you've healed," he said. "It hasn't been long enough since your injury for you to recover fully."

Aaron looked down. Levi followed his gaze to the pinned-up trouser leg. He had always admired Jonas and they had been good friends, but Jonas had traveled through a valley with Aaron that he couldn't imagine. Perhaps it would be best if the stranger just moved on like he said he wanted to. A friendship this close with a non-Amish fellow could pull Jonas further away from his home than the war had.

The most important task for Jonas right now was to join the church and get on with the life he had planned with Katie. He needed to put the war and Englisch ways behind him.

4

After the Monday morning chores were done and Katie had gone to visit her sister-in-law Lena, Elizabeth tied her bonnet strings under her chin. Ever since Datt had told her that Young Peter and Margaret would be moving into this house she was sharing with Katie, Elizabeth had been restless. It was true that she was welcome at Mamm and Datt's house and could easily move back into the bedroom she had shared with Ruby as they were growing up, but she had left nearly fifteen years ago now. Would it be so bad to move to the log cabin where she had lived while she was married? She hadn't been back since she left to set up housekeeping with Katie after Margaretta had passed on nearly two years ago.

Leaving the laundry to finish drying on the line, Elizabeth walked down to the road. But as she passed the home farm and turned up the hill leading toward Reuben's farm, her steps slowed. Perhaps she would stop and visit with her sister Ruby first. After all, she would be passing the Fischers' farm.

Elizabeth interrupted her thoughts with a quick shake of her head. She would visit with Ruby after she took a look at the cabin. It was no use putting off the unpleasant task once she had determined to do it.

She hurried past the lane leading to Ruby and Gideon's house and climbed up the hill. When she could see the cabin, she stopped, forcing herself to look closely instead of turning her head away like she usually did when she passed this way. The walls leaned farther into the slope than she remembered, and the roof was covered with moss. She took a few steps closer, putting a trembling foot on the overgrown path that had once led to the front of the cabin. The door hung open. One of the leather hinges had finally rotted through. Walking up to the door, she pulled on it gently and it swung open a bit farther. The table was still in its place but was littered with dirt and half-eaten pinecones. The bed frame in the corner was bare, the ropes that had once held the mattress hanging loose. The rest of the cabin was in shadow and a rustling noise came from the darkness in the far corner.

The last time she was here, Ruby had been with her, helping her pack her things to move to Katie's house. Ruby had always filled the cabin with life and light, but now the old memories had crept back with the neglect. Elizabeth's head throbbed as her mind ran in a direction she couldn't bear, and she backed away, pushing the heavy door closed with all her strength. She clasped her stomach. She wouldn't get sick. She wouldn't. Reuben was dead. She was free.

She took a deep breath and walked around to the back of the cabin. Her garden was overrun with weeds and the chicken house had blown down in a storm. It must have happened last winter, because she remembered it was there the last time she had seen the cabin, her home for so many years.

Not home. Home was a place of love and joy, where folks made you feel welcome. Reuben's cabin had never been her home. Elizabeth turned her back on it and headed down the hill to Ruby's.

Five-year-old Ezra and his two-year-old brother Daniel were in the shaded front yard playing in a sandpile, but when Ezra saw Elizabeth, he ran to her.

"Guess what we're doing," he said, his feet planted in front of her as if he dared her to try to walk past him. "Guess."

"Only if you give me a hug first."

Elizabeth opened her arms and he fell into them, squeezing her waist in a hard, quick hug, then pulled away. He took her hand, tugging her toward the sandpile. Elizabeth longed to hold him close, but he was never still long enough to satisfy her. Every time she looked into his face, she wondered . . . had her child been a boy? Would he have been as active and full of life as her nephew?

"We're building a farm," Ezra announced before she could make her guess. "Daniel is building the lanes and I'm planting the fields."

The boys had plucked leaves from the surrounding bushes and Ezra had planted them stem down in neat rows. Daniel's lanes wobbled between the fields, wherever he pushed his piece of wood to make a flat road.

"It's a fine farm." Elizabeth knelt at the edge of the sand. "What crops are you growing?"

"That's corn, and that's oats, and that's barley, and that's wheat." Ezra pointed as he named the fields. "We're going to plant beans next. Then there will be a meadow and Daniel will put his animals in it."

Daniel looked up. "Cows and horses." He stood up. "I get them."

Both boys ran toward the house. Elizabeth followed them, letting herself into the kitchen. Ruby looked up from rolling out a piecrust on the kitchen table.

"I thought I heard someone talking to the boys. What brings you this way today?"

Elizabeth sat at the table and watched Ruby roll the dough with short, sure strokes. "I went up to the farm. I thought I might be able to fix up the old cabin to live in, but it's a mess."

Ruby finished rolling out the crust and eased it into a pie plate.

"You never liked living there alone," she said as she lifted the plate and cut the overhanging edges of dough. The spiral fell back to the table.

"I know, but I need to find somewhere to live. Katie and Jonas will be married soon, and the Stuckeys have planned for Margaret and Young Peter to live in Katie's house after their wedding."

"So, you need a house." Ruby fetched a pan from the stove and poured the red fruit filling into the pie.

Elizabeth took a deep breath. "Rhubarb?"

"With strawberries." Ruby checked the oven's temperature. "It's Gideon's favorite." She gathered the dough scraps into a ball and started rolling out the top crust for the pie. "But back to your house. You won't really move into that old cabin, will you? Talk to Datt. Perhaps we could build you a new house on your farm."

"Datt suggested selling Reuben's—" She stopped herself. "My farm. He says I can move in with the folks, or they could build a house for me on the home farm."

"That sounds like a good solution to your problem." Ruby positioned the top crust over the pie and settled it into place.

Elizabeth watched as her sister put the pie in the oven and brushed the flour off her hands, as confident as Mamm in every motion. She was happy.

The thought was startling. Elizabeth's mind went back to the days before Ruby and Gideon married. Her sister had been pleasant enough to be around, but she hadn't been happy. Marrying Gideon had given her a husband to love and a ready-made family. The arrival of Baby Lovinia almost a year later had given Ruby even more confidence, but now it was combined with a joyful peace that Elizabeth watched with envy, tinged with fear for her sister. She knew what men could become when they thought no one was watching.

"I don't want to give up my independence," Elizabeth said, pushing those thoughts aside and giving an answer Ruby would approve of. "If I sell the farm, I won't have anything of my own. I'll go back to depending on Mamm and Datt again."

Ruby poured a cup of coffee for both of them and set one in front of Elizabeth before sitting down.

"There's nothing wrong with that, is there?"

"You're the one who always told me a woman should be able to support herself."

"And I still think that." Ruby stirred some honey into her cup. "But being able to support yourself and doing it when it isn't necessary are two different things. You're a widow, but you don't have to be alone. If you don't want to move back to the home farm, you could get married again."

A sick knot twisted in Elizabeth's stomach, but she put a smile on her face. "Who would I marry?" She forced a laugh. "I'm not going to grab a man off the streets in Millersburg."

Ruby laughed with her. "Nothing like that. But there's Levi Beiler. He's still single, and definitely ready to get married."

"He's a lot younger than I am. Besides, I doubt if Salome wants me for a daughter-in-law." Elizabeth shuddered, remembering the tone of Salome's voice when she had mentioned that very thing to Mamm not too long ago. But Salome had been right to let the idea go. She would never be good enough to satisfy that woman.

Ruby tapped her forefinger on her lips, thinking. "Aaron Zook is single, and any friend of Jonas might be a good prospect."

Elizabeth pressed her lips together and shook her head. "If I ever marry again, my husband will have to be a member of the church. I'll not make that mistake again."

"Perhaps Solomon Mast is the answer. We need to get to know him better, but he seems like a good Amish man. Solid and secure."

Elizabeth turned her cup between her hands. The warmth felt good on her suddenly chilled fingers. Solomon was handsome and outgoing, but he probably wouldn't look twice at a woman like her. She certainly wasn't the new wife he would be looking for.

"He'll most likely snatch up some pretty young girl. I don't think he'd be interested in me."

Ruby sipped her coffee. "I'll keep looking. There has to be a man out there for you somewhere."

Elizabeth reached across the table and took Ruby's hand. "Don't. I'm not planning to marry again. I don't ever want to be at the mercy of another man."

"Not all men are like Reuben," Ruby said, her voice low. "There are good men too."

Elizabeth's eyes filled as Ruby squeezed her hand. She didn't deserve a good man.

~~~~~

By Wednesday, Aaron had the wooden leg fashioned to his satisfaction. He smoothed his hand along the straight length, checking for any stray splinters. It still looked more like a piece of wood than a leg, but it should do. He had hollowed the top like a bowl to give his bad leg a secure rest, then he had whittled the remaining log down until it resembled a peg. Carving an actual leg with a foot had been his first vision, but that was beyond his skills. And he appreciated one advantage to this design. It was lighter than if he had tried to duplicate his missing limb's shape.

Since the day was overcast and drizzly after a night of heavy rain, Jonas had offered to drive him to Dan Zook's in the afternoon. The cool, damp air made Aaron's leg ache.

"I'm happy you will finally be getting to know Dan," Jonas said, breaking the silence of the quiet drive.

"I didn't meet him at church, did I?"

Jonas shook his head. "They had some illness among the

children in both families last Sunday." He grinned. "But I told him about you, and he's convinced that you're related to each other."

"I doubt that we are. Grandpop told stories about a brother, but no other kin."

"So, you don't know your grandfather's family?"

"Never met them, and from his stories about his pa, I'm not certain I'd want to."

"Family is important." Jonas leaned back in the wagon seat. "Even when I was out East with the army, I knew my parents and the rest of my family were keeping me in their prayers. And home . . ."

His voice faded. He swallowed and then continued.

"Coming home wasn't to see the buildings and the farm, but to see the people. Katie, of course, but also my parents, my brother and sisters, the church family. That's what makes a home." Jonas turned the horse onto another road that angled toward the east from the one they had been on. "I know you lost your house in Tennessee, and your father and grandfather. That makes it even more important to find any other family. What if Dan turns out to be a cousin you never knew you had?"

Jonas's words brought back memories of the events that had propelled Aaron into joining the army. Grandpop had been killed trying to defend his home and property from a Yankee raiding party, and then Pa, never in his right mind since Ma had passed on, had been killed early in the war, taking a foolhardy chance trying to avenge Grandpop. With their deaths, the last vestige of home was destroyed. He was alone and adrift in the world.

Aaron pulled his mind back from the edge of that dark abyss. "My family is gone. Clinging to some imagined sense of attachment to a stranger isn't going to change that."

"But what if it isn't imagined? What if it's true?"

Aaron snorted. "They're still strangers, ain't they?"

Jonas whistled a bar of "Dixie," then grinned at him. "They're only strangers until you meet them."

The roof of a large barn rose above the trees, and before long Jonas drove the horse into the barnyard. The house was nearly identical to the Weavers' home, painted white to match the barn. A garden had been planted between the house and the road, and across the farm lane was a smaller building that matched the barn and house, with a sign over the door. The words were German, but Aaron recognized the name. It was the same as his own. His mouth went dry. Knowing there were other Zooks around was one thing, but reading his name on the sign . . . he couldn't deny that it felt good to see it.

A tall man that looked close to Aaron's age came out of the shop to greet them. He spoke to Jonas in Pennsylvania Dutch, his words running together too quickly for Aaron to follow, but his eyes often drifted to Aaron as he spoke. Those eyes . . . they were Grandpop's eyes.

When Dan spoke to Aaron, it was in Englisch. "Jonas tells me you know some harness making."

"A bit. My grandfather taught me how to repair our mule's harness when I was a youngster, but not much else."

"Come into the shop. We'll see what we can do."

Jonas took the wooden leg and they both followed Dan into the harness shop. Aaron breathed in the various scents of leather, tannin, and neat's-foot oil. Scents that were sharp and familiar. If he closed his eyes, he could be back in the barn in Tennessee, watching Grandpop work the oil into the old mule's harness.

Dan motioned for Jonas to set the wooden leg on his workbench. "Let's see what we have here."

He examined the leg, using his hands to explore every inch from the supporting saddle to the peg leg.

"That's fine work. Not a splinter anywhere." Dan looked at Aaron. "Did you have any ideas about how to hold it on?"

"I modeled this after one I saw while I was still in the hospital. The man had a cloth belt with laces that fastened around his leg above the knee, then leather straps on either side sewn to that. The straps were fastened to the wooden leg near the top."

Dan nodded. "We have a piece of canvas we can use for the belt, and the leather straps should be easy enough. Will you be able to work on it with me so we can be certain it fits properly?"

"How long do you think it will take?"

"A few days." Dan started sorting through a bundle of leather scraps, then grinned at Aaron. "It will give us an opportunity to get acquainted and figure out how we're related."

Jonas returned home, leaving Aaron with Dan as they got to work. As Dan talked, his face was animated. Every expression reminded Aaron of Grandpop, as if he were with a younger version of the man who had raised him. The man who had refused to talk about his father but had entertained the young Aaron with tales of his boyhood escapades during the quiet winter evenings by the fire.

"Tell me what you know about your Zook family," Dan said as he sorted out straps that were approximately the same length. "Where do they live?"

"Grandpop said he grew up in Pennsylvania, but I don't know if any of his family still lives there. He had no brothers or sisters."

"Do you know where in Pennsylvania?"

"All I know is that it was in Lancaster County, but it was a long time ago. Grandpop was near ninety years old when he was killed, and he said he left home when he was barely old enough to grow a beard."

Dan took an awl from his workbench and started tapping out the stitching guides along the edge of the leather. Aaron took a second strap and another awl and followed suit.

"*Dawdi*—my grandfather—was about the same age as him, then. He passed on last fall." He measured out some thread and started coating it with beeswax. "My datt and stepmother still live in Lancaster County, but in his last letter Datt wrote of moving out here now that Dawdi is gone. He would know more than I do about the Zook relations. We'll have to ask him when they arrive next month."

"So, you and your brother moved out here together, but your father stayed in Pennsylvania. What made you decide to move to Ohio?"

"We had heard about the good farms out here and talked about making the move, but then Datt married a widow with her own children, and Ephraim and I decided it was time to head west. Tobias and Elise, our stepbrother and stepsister, needed Datt's attention after being without a father for several years." Dan took his strap and Aaron's and started sewing them together with the waxed thread. "We've been here for six years. The land is better than the farm in Pennsylvania, and we've got a good Amish community here, so Datt decided to join us."

"You must be a close family." A memory trickled into Aaron's mind. A mother. A father. Grandpop. Happier times.

"I suppose you could say that," Dan said, concentrating on his stitching. "We write every week even though we haven't been able to visit the rest of the family since we moved out here." He grinned at Aaron. "It will be good to see them all again."

Aaron watched Dan finish the seam, his strong hands tightening each stitch before going on to the next one. In profile, the resemblance to Grandpop was even stronger. It was possible they were related, but what difference would that make? Dan didn't need him. He had a family that he loved. He didn't need a tagalong shirttail cousin trying to fit himself into a home here.

He would move on when the time came.

⁓

Solomon Mast rose early on Friday morning. After two days of steady rain, he frowned at the clear light of sunrise as he stood on his front porch with a cup of black coffee in his hand. The rain had kept folks home and had given him time to plan his next move. The better weather might bring unwanted callers.

Patterson had built his house on the highest point of his land, giving Solomon a good view of the valley to the south and the creek that wound past the tidy farms. Weaver's

Creek, they called it. He drained the cup of coffee and grimaced at the bitterness. He spat out the coffee grounds that had been mingled with the last mouthful.

When he had stopped by the land office in Millersburg earlier in the month, he had spent hours examining the map of the county and had settled on German Township because most of the farmers were Amish. Solomon liked the Amish he had run into since he left the Shenandoah Valley two years ago. They were as peaceful as the Mennonites he had grown up around, but much more placid. Like sheep, they didn't act until the entire community agreed on a matter. And like sheep, they were trusting of anyone as long as he acted like one of them.

Sunday, his first introduction to the folks of Weaver's Creek, had gone well. They had been friendly and accepting, just as he had expected. They welcomed him as one of their own, but he hadn't missed the clucks of disapproval when old Abraham Weaver had inspected the red trim on his new buggy.

"Buggies are new around here," he had said, "but that red trim stands out. You say it's allowed in your old district?"

Solomon had painted over the glossy red paint with dull black on Monday morning.

He sat in Abel Patterson's willow rocking chair and leaned back, his gaze on the land across the Millersburg Road. Hearing that the farm belonged to the widow Elizabeth Kaufman hadn't surprised him. He had learned that information at the land office. But finding out that she was young and lovely was a welcome bit of information he had tucked away. He had taken the Patterson place because of the widow across the road, and her beauty just made his plans more desirable.

Settling back in the rocking chair, Solomon rested his heels on the porch rail. The widow's land was one hundred sixty acres, divided into two parcels. Added to the eighty acres he got from Patterson, he was on his way to a respectable-sized farm, but just a small place compared to Abraham Weaver's holdings. The number of acres in the Weavers' names had turned his gut into a twisting mass as he had traced the borders on the map. He needed that land. It should be his. It would be his. His heels thudded on the porch floor as he stood to get another look at his neighbor's land.

Patience. He batted at the word as if it were a wasp circling his head. Patience? He had no time for patience. The land was his.

He took a deep breath, his gaze still on the land across the road. No mistakes this time. Move slow. Don't rush. Make them trust you.

Movement on the road to the east of the Patterson place drew his gaze. A spring wagon pulled by a single horse. A young man and an older woman. He watched the horse turn into his farm lane.

"Callers." The very thing he had expected when the morning had dawned so fine. He turned around and cracked open the front door. "Dulcey!"

The young woman appeared in the hall leading to the back of the house, her dark skin blending into the shadowed interior of the house.

"Get yourself down into the cellar and stay put. Someone is coming and I don't want them to see you yet."

The girl disappeared like a shadow and Solomon closed the door. He shook his arms, letting his hands hang loose for a moment, then took a deep breath. As he let it out, he stepped into the man his visitors expected to see. Well-to-do Amishman Solomon Mast, new to the community and pleased to be part of it.

The young man driving the rig had a fair complexion with pink skin that looked prone to sunburn. The woman with him looked old enough to be his mother. Solomon searched through the faces in his memory. Sally? Sarah? Not quite.

The woman waved to him as the young man brought the wagon to a stop at the bottom of the porch steps.

"I'm glad we found you at home," she called, rising to her feet before the wagon came to a complete halt.

With the sound of her grating voice, the name came to him.

"Salome Beiler, isn't it?" Solomon stepped off the porch to help her step out of the wagon. He glanced at the driver. "And Levi? Did I remember correctly?"

Salome's smile was broad. "You did. Levi is my son. I wanted to call on you earlier this week, but the weather didn't allow it."

"Won't you come in? I have coffee on the stove."

"Ach, *ne*." Salome waved him off. "I know you're living alone, so I brought some things over for you." She signaled Levi and he jumped down from the wagon and brought a basket from the rear. "Only a few baked goods and a pot of soup. Just enough to give you some of the comforts of home."

"I appreciate it," Solomon said, reaching for the basket. The fragrance of freshly baked bread drifted through the morning air.

"Levi can take it into the kitchen for you." Salome peered around him to the front door. "And it wouldn't be any trouble for me to fix a fresh pot of coffee for you."

"That won't be necessary," Solomon said.

As he took the basket from Levi, Salome slipped past him and started up the porch steps.

Levi gave him a sheepish grin and shrugged his shoulders. "Very few folks find it easy to keep Mother from extending hospitality when she sets her mind to it."

Solomon fought to keep his face pleasant. "What a charming trait, and so appropriate for a woman of her position."

At Levi's raised eyebrows, Solomon mentally gave himself a kick. No Amishman talked like that. He took the basket into the house, Levi following him. Salome was in the front room.

"Abel Patterson left all of his belongings?" she asked.

"He was in a hurry and sold it all to me." He pushed past Salome, hoping Dulcey had followed his instructions and left no evidence of her presence. "The kitchen is this way."

As he set the basket on the table, Salome took charge. Whisking off the covering towel, she brought out two loaves of bread, a pie, and a covered iron pot wrapped in a cloth. She unwrapped the pot and set it on the stove, then stirred the morning's fire and put more sticks on to bring it up. She moved the coffeepot to the front of the stove and opened the lid, peering into the dark interior.

"Tsk, tsk." She shook her head and poured the remainder of the contents into the slop bucket. "I'll make some fresh coffee and we can visit while we have some pie." She turned to Solomon. "I hope you like peach pie. I made it with some preserves from last summer. Now sit down and we'll have a nice visit to get acquainted."

Solomon's smile was genuine as he took a seat at the kitchen table next to a resigned Levi. He might not have wanted callers this morning, but Salome Beiler was just the type of person to give him the information he needed without even realizing what she was doing.

He gave Salome his most charming wink and picked up his fork as she set a plate in front of him. "Now then, tell me all about my new neighbors." He cut the point off the triangle of pie. "Start with the Weavers."

As he listened to Salome talk, he savored the sweet peach syrup and flaky pie crust. Yes, Salome was a perfect fit for his plans.

5

A week after his first day of working with Dan Zook, Aaron strapped on his new wooden leg, ready to begin his new life. He stood next to his bed, testing the weight on his leg. The stump was still tender, but the pad Lydia had made for him helped distribute the pressure. He took a step, adjusted the laces on the cloth foundation, then took another careful step. Finally, he straightened up, stretching to his full height.

He grinned, catching sight of himself in the small mirror hanging on the washstand. He looked normal again. After nearly a month in Weaver's Creek, eating Lydia's good cooking and working outdoors, he was gaining strength. His color was better, his cheeks ruddy above his red beard rather than pale. The new leg would take some getting used to, and he'd need to use a cane to help with balance for the rest of his days, but for the first time since that fateful battle near Richmond, he could look himself in the eye.

"You look like a man again," he said to his reflection,

keeping his voice low. "And from now on you'll act like a man, not a wounded animal."

He took a step closer to the mirror, but a sharp pain stopped him. The stump was still too tender to put his full weight on it for very long. With a sigh, he grabbed his crutches and went downstairs to breakfast.

"I hope you won't mind being on your own today," Jonas said as they went out onto the porch after the meal. "I'm meeting with the ministers this morning and Datt's coming with me."

"Are they going to decide if you can join the church or not?" Aaron stopped and adjusted the laces again. It would take some time to get used to this contraption.

"They'll discuss it. They have some questions to ask me, and I hope they'll decide to let me join. Everything is at a standstill until we hear their decision."

"What if they decide against you?"

Jonas shook his head. "I hope it doesn't come to that."

"What work needs to be done?" Aaron tapped his new leg. "I'm able to do much more now that I have this."

"Before this meeting was scheduled, I was going to fix a broken board on Katie's porch. Do you think you could do that?"

"No one could do it better." Aaron looked up the road toward the house Katie and Elizabeth shared. "I'll have to drive up there."

"The horse and wagon are available, and the tools are in the workshop. Do you need help hitching up Rusty?"

"I think I can do it." Aaron had a flash of memory of the last time he tried to harness the horse. "But stick around.

I'll try to do it myself before you leave and let you know if I need help."

As Jonas went back into the house to finish getting ready for his meeting, Aaron went to the barn, using his new leg as much as possible instead of the crutches. If it were anyone but Jonas, he would never ask for help, but Jonas was different. He had seen Aaron at his worst, when he had been near death and delirious with fever but hadn't abandoned him. In fact, their friendship had grown stronger.

Rusty was standing just outside his stable door in the morning sunshine and came right away when Aaron called him in. Through the door, Abraham's bull stood in his pasture. The big animal grazed with the sun on his sides, absorbing the morning rays.

Aaron patted Rusty's neck. "You know you'll get oats when I call, don't you?" He poured a cup of oats into his feed bin and fetched the brush.

His new leg held him up well enough as he groomed Rusty, and Aaron reveled in the new strength in his arms as he lifted the harness from its place on the wall and carried it to the horse. He had to walk slowly, but he kept his balance during the few steps between the wall and where he had tied Rusty, even turning around without falling.

Aaron had settled the harness on Rusty's back and was beginning to buckle the straps when Jonas came into the barn.

"It looks like you're doing well without my help," Jonas said, standing off to the side while Aaron worked.

"The new leg makes a big difference," Aaron said, reaching under Rusty's belly for the final strap and fastening it. "I can keep my balance and use both hands at the same time. I think I'll need help with the wagon, though."

Once Rusty was hitched to the wagon, Jonas fetched the toolbox and some lumber from the workshop while Aaron boosted himself onto the wagon seat, adjusting his jump to accommodate the weight of the wooden leg. Jonas stowed the toolbox in the back and Aaron clicked his tongue at Rusty. As the horse headed out of the barn, Aaron fingered the lines in his hands. He hadn't driven in nearly a year and he had missed this live communication with the horse through the reins. He drove across the bridge and turned onto the road.

The drive was pleasant with the early morning sun low enough that the shadows were still fresh with the night's cool air. Birds sang in the trees and Aaron spied a wild turkey hen with her brood scurrying across the road ahead of him.

A tune came to him. It was a hymn from his childhood, long forgotten until he had heard the boys in the camp singing it around the fires at night during the war. He hummed it for a few bars, then whistled it as Rusty turned into the drive leading to Katie and Elizabeth's house. The tune stuck with him as he hopped down from the wagon seat and tied Rusty to the hitching rail. He pulled the toolbox from the back of the wagon and carried it to the porch, using one crutch for balance.

The front door opened. Aaron had hoped it would be Elizabeth to greet him, but instead it was Katie. When she saw him, her smile turned to a disappointed frown.

"I thought Jonas was going to fix the porch."

"Sorry," Aaron said. "Plans got changed so you're stuck

with me." He grinned at her. "I know that isn't as much fun for you."

Katie blushed, her pink cheeks turning red. "What is Jonas doing that's more important than fixing our porch?"

"He said he had a meeting with the ministers this morning." Aaron set the toolbox on the porch next to the broken board. "I guess he thought that was important enough."

A happy smile covered her face. "That's for sure. I had hoped they would meet this week. We've waited a long time."

"Are you sure Jonas is worth it?" A familiar, nearly forgotten, teasing note colored his voice.

"Of course, he is. That doesn't make the time pass any faster, though." Katie's smile didn't fade as her gaze went past him, down the drive toward the unfinished house on the other side of the creek. "I'd wait my whole life for Jonas if I had to."

She stood there, unaware of him or anything else, lost in her thoughts. Jonas had told Aaron about Katie, but until he came here and witnessed the bond the two of them enjoyed, Aaron hadn't realized how strongly Jonas's life was tied to her. Yes, to the farm, his family, and the community too. But Katie was Jonas's home.

As Katie went back into the house, Aaron got to work. He pried up the broken board, then hammered out the nails and straightened them. Going back to the wagon, he found a board the right size and tested it on the porch. A little trimming, then some sanding, and the new board would fit right in.

Humming as he worked, Aaron sat on the top step of the porch. Without thought, the words to the song formed themselves and he sang softly, remembering Ma's voice singing this same hymn.

> "Rock of ages, cleft for me,
> Let me hide myself in thee . . ."

Aaron stopped, the board in one hand and the sanding block in the other. This little house surrounded by pines reminded him of the cabin where he had grown up. Had Ma called upon her God when she was in her final affliction, that terrible day when she breathed her last? He let the sanding block rub along the grain of the board, continuing the song.

> "Let the water and the blood,
> From thy wounded side which flowed,
> Be of sin the double cure;
> Save from wrath and make me pure."

Grandpop had never called upon the Lord, but Ma had spent hours holding Aaron on her lap, teaching him about her Lord Jesus Christ and what she called his saving grace. The same Lord who had abandoned her to her fate and Aaron to a life without her.

He pressed his lips together and rubbed harder.

"Don't stop singing."

The voice came from behind him, but he recognized it. Elizabeth had come out onto the porch and he hadn't heard her. He was losing his soldier's awareness.

"I got to the end of the verse," Aaron said, not looking at her.

"Then sing the next one. It's a lovely tune." She sat on the step next to him.

He turned the sanding block and started the next verse.

> "Not the labors of my hands
> Can fulfill thy law's demands;
> Could my zeal no respite know,
> Could my tears forever flow,
> All for sin could not atone;
> Thou must save and thou alone."

"That's a beautiful thought," Elizabeth said, sitting with her chin in her hand watching the trees at the edge of the yard. "The words are talking about Jesus, aren't they?"

"Probably. It's a song my mother liked to sing."

"So, you sing it to remember her?"

Aaron nodded. "It's about all I remember of her." He turned his mind to the memories of her last day and night as she gave birth to the sister he had never known. "She passed on when I was a youngster."

"But she believed in the Lord?"

"I suppose she did. She tried to teach me, but it didn't stick. Didn't help her much, either."

"Why do you say that?"

Aaron ran his hand along the new board. No splinters. He'd give it a coat of paint, then nail it into place after it dried. He looked at Elizabeth, who still waited for an answer to her question.

"Where was her God when she was in the agony of child-birth? Where was he when she cried out to him for help? Nowhere. She died and that was it."

Elizabeth's face was thoughtful.

"You're not going to argue with me?"

She shook her head. "How can I?" Her voice dropped to a whisper. "He turned his back on me too."

Elizabeth rose from her seat with a jerk and disappeared into the house. Aaron's sanding block slowed, then stopped as he turned to look after her. Grandpop had always told him that the Amish were high and mighty, bragging about their special place in God's eyes, but Elizabeth didn't seem to be like that at all. Her whisper . . . maybe he wasn't meant to hear it . . . but her whisper betrayed a brokenness as deep as his own.

<hr/>

Levi slipped in the front door of his family's home and sat in a chair near the door, close enough to observe Jonas's meeting with the ministers without interfering.

"There has been no precedent on this issue that I can think of," Wilhelm Stuckey said as he opened the meeting. "Jonas was not a baptized member of the church when he took up arms, nor did he join the army out of a sense of discontent or anger."

"But he did join the army, something that goes against the deepest ingrained teaching of the church. Jesus Christ himself showed us the way to live, and loving our enemies is paramount." Father paced as he spoke, just as he did when preaching on Sunday mornings, his left hand fisted behind his back and his right hand punctuating his sentences in the air.

Abraham Weaver leaned back in his chair. Gideon, the third minister, sat with his fingertips steepled beneath his chin, his eyes closed in thought. Jonas perched on the edge of his chair, looking from one man to the other as they discussed his fate.

"The precedent exists," Gideon said, his eyes still closed. His voice was strained, and Levi felt the anguish he was experiencing at deciding Jonas's fate. "During the American Revolutionary War, members of the church that supported the rebellion against the established government never rejoined the fellowship of the church."

"But that doesn't address Jonas's case." Wilhelm looked at Father with a hard gaze. "I say that if he can assure us that he didn't act in a war-like manner while he was in the army, then we should welcome him into fellowship."

Father, silent for once, stared at Jonas, then resumed his pacing.

"Amos, what questions would you ask him?" Abraham's voice stopped Father and all the ministers looked at him. "What would satisfy your requirements?"

"First of all," Father said, taking his seat, "we need to be clear about whether his actions ever harmed another man."

All three men looked at Jonas, who didn't meet their gaze but stared at the floor.

"There were times when I was required to fire my rifle. However, I aimed above the soldiers' heads and didn't intentionally kill or wound any man. I can't say that the bullet spent itself without causing harm, but I'm not aware if it did so."

Wilhelm cleared his throat. "So, you did not knowingly take the life of any man, but you were involved in fighting a battle?"

Jonas nodded. "Before I was transferred to the medical

corps, I was in several battles as a soldier. I found a way to make myself useful by treating the wounded and pulling them from the heaviest part of the fighting. Then, at the Battle of Fredericksburg, I was captured by the enemy."

Father stopped his pacing and faced Jonas. "Jesus taught that sin is not only in the committing of a deed, but also in the contemplating of the deed. During these battles and after you were captured, what thoughts filled your mind? Did you hold animosity toward your fellow man?"

"No. I felt . . . pity. Remorse at the situation I was in. Horror at the evil that overtakes men during a battle."

Levi saw a slight shudder pass through Gideon, the only other one in the room who shared Jonas's experiences. Gideon had told Levi of the part he had played in the war when he had been forced to work as a teamster. He had also told him about the agony he experienced when his inaction caused the death of a young soldier.

Gideon addressed his question to Jonas. "Was there ever a time when you could have prevented an act of violence, but didn't?"

"Not that I know of. I tried to save the wounded, Federals and Rebels alike."

Father resumed his pacing. "If I have the facts clear, after you were released by your Confederate captor, you were transferred to service in the medical corps, where you spent the rest of the war in acts of mercy. Is that correct?"

"For the remainder of the war I served in field hospitals and most recently at a hospital in a prisoner of war camp. I did my best to bring comfort to the wounded and dying."

"But you were still a member of the army."

Jonas nodded, his eyes on the plank floor beneath his feet.

Clasping his hands together, Father turned to Abraham and Jonas. "If you would wait outside, we will discuss this matter among ourselves."

Jonas led the way out of the room and Levi followed him. Abraham brought up the rear as they walked to the shaded area in front of the barn, out of earshot of the discussion taking place inside the house.

Abraham sat on a bench near the barn door and leaned against the wall. The late morning air was warm and humid.

"What do you think, Datt?" Jonas asked, keeping his gaze on the house. "Do you think they will support me?"

"I can't say." Abraham stroked his beard.

Levi's thoughts drifted back three years to the night Jonas had left to join the army. Had his friend's actions been foolish? Perhaps. But he had kept his brother Samuel from suffering a worse fate.

"What will you do if they refuse to bring you into the fellowship?" Levi asked. They both watched the house for any sign of a conclusion to the deliberations.

"I've had a lot of time to think about this," Jonas said. He sat next to Abraham on the bench. "For three long years I've wondered what would happen today. If they decide against me, I will still marry Katie. We'll join a Mennonite church, or a Dunker congregation. We would still be part of our families, just not the church."

Abraham laid a hand on his son's knee as if he could call him back. "Don't forget that Katie has joined our church already. Would you have her turn her back on her membership vows?"

Jonas drew both hands over his face. "I hate to put her in the position of deciding between me and the church, but it's up to the ministers now."

"Ne." Abraham patted Jonas's knee. "It's up to the Good Lord. We will pray that the ministers listen to him."

A bumblebee buzzed in the clover near the barn door. It stopped on one purple flower, making it sway up and down, and then moved on to another, landing heavily. Levi watched it search each part of the blossom for the nectar within. By the time the bee had flown away to a new hunting ground, the front door opened, and the three ministers came out.

Levi followed Jonas across the barnyard, then fell back to keep pace with Abraham. He searched the three faces. None of them met Jonas's gaze as he walked toward them. They stood on the porch, no one talking.

They caught up to Jonas at the foot of the porch steps. Father glanced at his fellow ministers, then at Jonas.

"We have decided that we need more time to pray and discuss this matter. We will also confer with other ministers from around the country next month when they gather for the ministers' meeting in Smithville. Until we come to an agreement on our decision, Jonas is welcome to continue worshiping with us as he has always done."

So, there was dissent among the ministers. Jonas's shoulders slumped.

Levi stepped close to Jonas. "Everything will turn out all right."

The other men said their farewells and left, the Stuckeys in their spring wagon and Abraham and Gideon walking home together. The two paused on the road, waiting for Jonas to join them.

"You think it will?" Jonas's face was stony. "No decision at all is worse than refusing to let me become a member. Now everything will be delayed more weeks before they decide against me."

"You don't know what the final decision will be."

"Don't I?" Jonas scrubbed the back of his neck with one hand. "I knew the night I left to take Samuel's place in the draft that this would be waiting for me when I came home. If the church wants to turn me away, Katie and I will be all right. We'll find a community that will accept us. But this isn't the way I wanted our lives to be."

Levi swallowed the lump in his throat. "Don't do anything rash. Wait until the ministers make their decision."

Jonas sought Levi's gaze and held it. Years of friendship stood between them, shimmering like heat rising from the barn roof on a hot summer day. Levi fought the urge to grasp Jonas's arm. To hold him fast, pull him back from the edge.

"I'll wait." Jonas rolled his shoulders. "I need to do everything I can to stay in the church for Katie's sake."

He gave Levi a nod, then turned for home, joining Abraham and Gideon on the road.

On Friday morning, Elizabeth and Katie left the house early to help Mamm in the big garden at the home farm.

"I love our little house," Katie said. "The pine trees whisper in the wind, and the shade keeps the place cool in the summer. But there isn't a sunny place anywhere."

"No spot for our own garden, that's for sure." Elizabeth kicked a stone to the side of the road. "But you Stuckeys have that big garden for the family, and our family has this one." She grinned at Katie. "I guess this is the year that you are part of the Weaver garden."

Katie blushed. "By harvesttime Jonas and I hope to be married. I'm glad to be able to put up what garden produce I can before then."

"And we're glad to help you." Elizabeth smiled at the friend who was like a sister already.

Mamm was hard at work with her hoe when Elizabeth and Katie arrived.

"Is Ruby coming today?" Elizabeth asked, stopping to train a stray bean stalk onto the trellis Mamm had erected when they planted the beans last month.

"She said she'll be down later. Roseanna brought word that she is pickling eggs this morning, but she'll come down when she's done."

"Pickling eggs?" Katie took a hoe from the pile Mamm had brought out to the garden. "Her hens must be laying well."

Elizabeth picked up her own hoe and started at one end of the corn row. The little shoots were almost hidden in the weeds that had sprung up since last week. May was always the month to fight weeds in the garden. By June the plants would be tall and full enough to shade the ground beneath them and keep the weeds from growing as well. She worked steadily as Mamm and Katie visited, but she didn't pay attention to their conversation. The combination of the bright sunshine, the earthy odor of the garden, and the call of the red-winged blackbirds along the creek transported her thoughts to many childhood days of hoeing weeds. She had hated the task then, but now that she was older, it was a joy. A quiet respite from the busyness of life.

A movement on the other side of the pasture fence caught her attention. It was Datt's bull, Samson. Datt had raised him from a calf, but Elizabeth hadn't seen him for a long time. Datt had been keeping him in the far pasture, away from the cows. This spring the bull had grown to his full size and looked like a brute instead of the sweet yearling she remembered.

"Mamm, is Samson supposed to be in that pasture?"

Mamm shaded her eyes and watched Samson walk along the fence as if he was looking for a weak spot.

"He must have broken through his fence again. Abraham needs to sell him. We have no need for a bull, and he's getting too big for the men to handle. I'll let your datt know he got out again at dinnertime."

The bull raised his head and looked in their direction.

"Here comes a visitor," Mamm said, turning to see what Samson had noticed. "It looks like Solomon Mast."

"Is Datt in the barn?" Elizabeth put her hoe down. "I'll go fetch him."

"Ne, he's out in the fields."

Mamm dusted off her hands and walked to the farm lane and Elizabeth joined her. Solomon drove his horse over the stone bridge and into the farmyard and smiled at them as he pulled his horse to a stop.

"Good morning, ladies." He touched the brim of his hat.

Elizabeth looked at her feet to keep from staring. The

various Amish communities had different customs, but she had never heard any Amishman greet anyone like that.

"Abraham is out today," Mamm said. "You'll find him if you follow the farm lane west along the creek."

Solomon stepped out of his buggy. "I didn't come to see Abraham. I had hoped to find Elizabeth here."

"Me?" Now she didn't worry about staring. Solomon's face was as pleasant as she remembered, with dark eyes set wide and a ready smile. White teeth gleamed above his beard.

"Do you mind? Perhaps we could go for a little walk?"

Elizabeth wiped her hands on her apron, sure that garden dirt clung to them. "I'm busy right now. The garden needs to be hoed."

"Katie and I can get along without you for a few minutes," Mamm said, turning back to her work. "Take your time."

"Well then." Solomon indicated the lane leading along the creek past the house. "Shall we?"

He set the pace, walking slowly between Elizabeth and the creek. She strolled next to him, waiting for him to begin.

"I hear that you are a widow."

"That is right."

"And you have heard that I lost my wife a few years ago."

Elizabeth glanced at him. "I have heard that."

"I thought"—he caught her gaze and smiled—"that since we're both alone, perhaps we should learn to know one another, to see if we're compatible."

"You are very new in the area. We don't know you yet."

"That's true. But I wanted to see how you felt before any other beau has a chance to snatch you away."

He wiggled his eyebrows as he said this, and she laughed.

"I don't think there is any danger of that. I don't intend to marry again."

Solomon stopped walking and grasped her hand. "Perhaps I can change your mind."

She held his gaze. His eyes were clear and open, his smile friendly. Elizabeth pulled her hand from his grasp and continued along the lane. "Tell me about yourself. Where did you live before you came to Ohio?"

"In Lancaster County, in a small community outside Ephrata. I settled there soon after my wife passed on, but after two years I still hadn't found the right woman to share my life, so I decided to try farther west."

Elizabeth watched his profile as he spoke. His voice had caught when he talked about his wife passing away, but he showed no other emotion.

"Why did you choose Weaver's Creek?"

"Because of Abel Patterson. He had a farm to sell and I was looking. The situation was providential."

"Providential?"

He smiled. "God's providence. All good things come from God."

Elizabeth stopped at the gate in the fence between the farmyard and the wheat field. Feathery green growth covered the field, undulating in the gentle breeze. She had heard that phrase before, that all things come from God. Good as well as bad. Was it God's providence that brought Solomon Mast to Weaver's Creek? Could it be that God was giving her a second chance to make a marriage that was pleasing to him?

Across the field, coming toward them along the lane, Aaron drove the farm wagon. Solomon opened the gate as he approached. Aaron drove through, then pulled the horses to a halt.

"Solomon Mast, isn't it?" Aaron asked. He made no move to climb down from the wagon seat.

"That's right." Solomon stepped close to Elizabeth, close enough for their shoulders to touch. "I recall seeing you at the meeting on Sunday, but I don't think I heard your name."

"Aaron Zook. I think we might have met before," Aaron said, his voice hard. "A few years ago? In the Shenandoah Valley?"

Solomon chuckled. "What would an Amishman be doing in the Shenandoah? We have no communities there."

Aaron's eyes narrowed and Elizabeth felt Solomon stiffen. Why was Aaron being so rude?

"I need to get to my work in the garden," she said. "Are you going back to the barn, Aaron?"

He shook his head, but his gaze didn't leave Solomon. "Abraham needs to borrow a tool from Gideon, but I can give you a ride back to the house, if you would like." His blue eyes shifted from Solomon to Elizabeth and softened. "You needn't walk if you are in a hurry."

Elizabeth glanced at Solomon. She didn't want to abandon him in the middle of their walk. "I'll go back with Solomon."

Aaron slapped the reins on the horse's back and went on, but twice he turned around to look at her.

"That was a strange question for him to ask." Solomon took her hand and tucked it around his elbow as they started walking back toward the house. "He doesn't seem to be Amish. Where is he from?"

"Aaron is from Tennessee. He and my brother became friends during the war."

His arm tightened under her hand, but his face was calm and relaxed. They were nearly back to the house and Solomon's buggy.

"I hope you've given some thought to my proposal. I think we could become very good friends." He untied the black horse from the hitching rail. "Shall we go for a drive on Sunday afternoon? Just the two of us?"

Elizabeth shook her head, her hands growing clammy. She took a step back. "It wouldn't be proper. I mean, to ride in your buggy alone with you." She had learned her lesson many years ago. Before they had been married, Reuben had always urged her to come with him alone, but a woman alone with a man was too vulnerable.

A frown appeared for a second, so briefly that Elizabeth couldn't be sure she had even seen it.

"You are right, of course. Perhaps you have a friend or a sister who could accompany us?"

Bells clanged in Elizabeth's head. She shook them away, but the warning persisted. Would the memory of Reuben always affect her this way?

"I wouldn't want to leave the fellowship early. Maybe . . ." She licked her lips. "Maybe another time."

She turned and strode toward the garden, searching for her abandoned hoe through clouded eyes. What was wrong with her? Solomon was a good man, a member of the church, friendly and solicitous . . . Her hoe struck deep into the packed dirt and ripped out a dandelion. And that was the problem. She didn't deserve a man like him.

6

On Sunday, Aaron slipped into the back row of benches just in time for the service to start. Jonas had already taken his seat near the front next to Levi, but Aaron didn't want to draw attention to himself by thumping up the aisle. Folks stared at him enough as it was.

He looked around the room as the first hymn started. The congregation sang slow, drawn-out songs in a chant that sounded nothing like the hymns Aaron had heard before, and the words were in high German rather than the Pennsylvania Dutch he was more familiar with. He hummed along, not bothering with the words as he tried to identify the folks he knew from the backs of their heads.

On the women's side he found Elizabeth's sister Ruby easily. Her red hair floated in light tendrils around the edge of her kapp. Next to her were her daughters and Lydia. Samuel Weaver's wife, Anna, was next with her daughter. Aaron had seen them often at the Weavers' farm. And then came Elizabeth, sitting very still, her eyes closed as she sang, her expression a slight frown, as if she was concentrating on the words.

The singing ended and the song leader announced the next hymn, *Das Lobleid*. This was the one he was beginning to learn since the congregation sang it at every worship service. The song was a praise to God, and Aaron let the words surround him, singing along when there was a phrase he remembered. He watched the back of Jonas's head five rows in front of him. Jonas would nod as one word, which followed several notes, ended and the next one began. It was just enough of a cue to allow Aaron to keep up.

But then at the third verse, the man sitting three rows ahead shifted in his seat, blocking Aaron's view. Aaron frowned and tried to lean to the left, but he was between two strangers and couldn't move far enough. All Aaron could do was wait until the other man shifted again. He stared at the back of the man's head. Straight black hair, smoothed against the head with the imprint of the hat band visible . . . Every thought of the church service and the song fled Aaron's mind. He had seen that head before. He blinked.

"Got any more information for me?" the lieutenant had said. The night was dark, the air filled with the smoke of a hundred campfires.

"Sure enough." That voice. Smooth as if it had been run through a grease bucket. "The Yankees are in Winchester, but they're gettin' ready to come this way."

"How about the provisions?"

"The Dunkers have banded together to hide their stores." The voice chuckled. "But I know right where they are, just a few miles from Staunton. I can show you on the map."

Coins clinked together as Aaron looked around the tent flap. The lantern in the tent showed the spy clearly, but only the back of his head. His straight black hair, shining in the light, smoothed against his head with the imprint of the hat band visible . . . a man dressed in the plain clothes of the farmers in the valley. He held out his hand and the captain dropped the coins into it.

The song ended and Aaron blinked again. As the leader called out the number of the next hymn, Aaron stared at the back of the head. Solomon Mast's head. But why would an Amishman have been in the Shenandoah Valley during the war? And why would he sell information to the army? He had to be mistaken. It couldn't be the same man.

After the services were over, the men arranged the benches for the fellowship meal. Aaron found a place at the table between Jonas and Dan Zook. Ephraim sat across from them.

"When do you expect your father and the rest of the family to arrive?" Jonas asked Dan as he buttered a thick slice of bread.

"Datt wanted to be here in time to attend the early meeting before the ministers' meeting begins next week," Dan said. "So, we expect him any day now."

"Does he have a place to live?"

"Dan and I have their house nearly built," Ephraim said. "Between us, we have more than enough farmland for all three families."

Levi sat down on the other side of Jonas. "We will certainly welcome them to the community. Will it be your parents alone, or do you have younger brothers and sisters?"

"Datt remarried several years ago," Dan said. "Our stepmother was a widow and brought her two children to the family." He looked at Ephraim, his eyebrows raised in a question. "Tobias was eighteen when they married, if I remember correctly."

Ephraim nodded. "And Elise was fourteen. So, they are twenty-four and twenty now."

"And both of them are coming to Ohio?" Levi asked.

"That's what Datt indicated in his last letter," Dan said. "I thought Tobias would be married by now, but from what Datt says, he's anxious to establish his own home out here in Ohio." He chuckled. "It sounds like he'll be looking for a wife."

"Is your father a harness maker, also?" Aaron asked, concentrating on the Pennsylvania Dutch words.

"He's the one who taught us the trade," Dan said. "I was thinking that it might be good for you to keep learning. You already know quite a bit about it, and it is a skill that you don't need both legs to do."

Aaron took another slice of bread and laid a piece of ham on it. "I don't know. The community isn't large enough for so many harness makers. Besides, I'm not sure how long I'll be around here."

Ephraim pushed his plate away and leaned across the table toward Aaron. "Even if you don't stay in Weaver's Creek, the harness trade is one you could do anywhere. You should learn from Datt while you can. He has a lot of experience that he'll be happy to pass along."

Taking a bite of his sandwich, Aaron let Ephraim's words settle in. He had never considered that he would be a tradesman. He had spent the years before the war hunting, fishing, and trapping. He had always planned to go back to that life once the war ended, but that was out of the question now. Even in the settled hills of western Tennessee, he would find it impossible to make a living with only one leg. He'd be at the mercy of every bear and panther in the forests, and even more so in the West. He'd heard tell of giant bears out there with grizzled shoulders that could kill a man with one swipe of their paws.

A trade would provide a living, if he could stand being in a workshop all day long. And he enjoyed the feel of leather between his fingers. Dan had said he had a talent for stitching even seams. He had felt welcome and at home in the harness shop when they were constructing his wooden leg. It was something to think on.

The men's conversation continued without him as the others prepared to leave the table to make room for the women and children. Solomon Mast got up from his seat at the end where he had been sitting with Bishop Amos and Abraham. Instead of accompanying the other men outside, Solomon made his way toward the kitchen. He leaned against the doorframe, talking with the busy women in the crowded room. Whatever he said made the women laugh, and then he stood aside to let someone through—it was Elizabeth. Her face blushed pink as she went past him, her hands full of clean plates and a smile on her face.

Solomon watched her walk away, and his gaze caught Aaron's. His smile widened, then he looked back at Elizabeth's figure. Aaron's eyes narrowed. In any other place, he would accuse Solomon Mast of taking liberties with a woman, watching her like that. But the Amish had different ways. Ways he wasn't familiar with. Perhaps if two adults were courting, the man was freer to show his attraction in public, asserting his claim.

Somehow, that thought left a sick feeling in Aaron's stomach.

"Solomon Mast is watching you." Millie's voice held a teasing lilt. She was washing the dishes after the fellowship meal while Elizabeth and Katie dried them.

Elizabeth frowned as she dried the cup in her hands. "You must be mistaken. Why would he pay any attention to me?"

Katie nudged Elizabeth with her elbow. "Because you're a young widow and he's a widower. What could be more normal than the two of you becoming a couple?"

Elizabeth glanced behind her. Solomon smiled when he saw her looking, his expression warm and friendly. She turned back to her friends.

"Nothing is going to come of it. He's becoming acquainted with the people in the community, that's all."

Millie giggled. "I think he wants to become acquainted with one particular member of the church, and that's you. Don't look now, but he's coming this way."

Katie grabbed a dry dish towel and concentrated on wiping the next cup while Millie suddenly started scrubbing a plate. Elizabeth felt the warmth of someone close behind her.

"Would you care to take a short walk with me?"

Solomon's breath stirred the hairs on the back of her neck, causing Elizabeth's stomach to flip. She turned around and took a step back as he towered over her. His dark eyes twinkled as he smiled at her, and the scent of something rich and woody played in the air between them.

"I . . . I have to finish drying the dishes." Elizabeth concentrated on the snowy white front of his shirt. "I can't leave the work to Katie and Millie."

"Go ahead," Katie said, taking the forgotten towel from Elizabeth's hand. "We're almost done. Millie and I can finish up."

"You have no excuse then." Solomon stepped aside, indicating that she should lead the way.

Elizabeth kept her gaze on the floor in front of her as she made her way through the front room of Wilhelm Stuckey's house and out into the yard. From the comments she overheard, all the women noticed what was happening. A creeping red heat started at her neck and went upward.

"Where does this path go?" Solomon asked, pointing to the trail through the pine woods.

"It goes to our house. The one Katie and I share."

"Was your husband one of the Stuckey family?" Solomon strolled beside her along the dirt trail.

"Ne. I live with Katie Stuckey. At least I do until she and Jonas marry."

"Then you'll live there alone?"

Elizabeth glanced at Solomon's face, but only saw mild curiosity.

"I'm not certain where I'll live yet. The Stuckeys are giving the house to Young Peter Lehman when he marries Margaret Stuckey later in the summer."

"You own a farm, don't you?"

"My husband owned the farm that borders my father's

and brother's land. I had thought of moving back to the house there."

"That old cabin?"

"You know the cabin?" Elizabeth stopped and looked at him. "So, you knew I owned the farm all along."

Solomon chuckled and kept walking, forcing her to catch up. "I admit it, I asked your brother-in-law about you. But only because I was curious about my neighbor. You wouldn't consider living in that cabin in the shape it is now, would you?"

Elizabeth shuddered. "I don't think I could live there again even if it was in decent shape."

"You didn't enjoy living there?"

His eyebrows were raised, but his question sounded more like a comment. How much about her marriage would she divulge to a stranger?

"My husband was difficult." As Solomon nodded in understanding, Elizabeth decided that was all the explanation he needed. "Datt has talked about building a new house for me, but he wants me to live on the home farm, closer to the rest of the family."

The path opened into the yard of the little house she shared with Katie. Solomon strolled past the chicken coop and the clothesline.

"So, this is the house you live in now?"

"Ja, with Katie." He stood in the center of the yard, his hands clasped behind his back, looking at the house. Was he waiting for an invitation to come inside?

"It's a fine little house," he said, walking around to the front. "Well built and solid. The log walls are quaint." He stepped onto the porch and turned around to watch the chickens scratching in the dirt along the path.

Elizabeth waved a hand toward one of the chairs. "Would you like to sit down?"

He smiled and a wave of relief washed over Elizabeth. His smile meant he was happy and enjoyed being with her. Could it be that he would choose to court her? She had never been the center of any man's attention, except Reuben's.

"Do you mind if we sit here and talk?" Solomon took off his hat and fanned his face. "We were interrupted the other day."

Solomon sat in Katie's rocking chair near the door and Elizabeth slid past him to take her seat in the corner of the porch. He leaned back in his chair and pulled on his coat to straighten it.

Once he was settled, he smiled at her again. "How long were you and your husband married?"

Elizabeth's mouth went dry. "Reuben and I were married for almost thirteen years before he passed away."

"No children?"

The memory of that young life stirring under her heart brought tears to her eyes. She looked away from Solomon and blinked them away. "We weren't blessed in that way."

His eyes narrowed briefly. She had said something wrong. He would leave if she couldn't steer the conversation back to a more positive topic.

"I suppose you're right. Some couples never do have children." He rocked in the chair. "I've gotten the feeling that your family thinks it was a good thing when your husband didn't come home from the war."

"He . . . Reuben . . . wasn't Amish. My family didn't approve of my marriage."

"But you're a member of the church?"

"I wasn't baptized when I married him. That came later, after he was . . . gone."

Solomon leaned forward in his chair, a warm smile on his face again. "You had said you don't intend to marry again when we talked before. Is there anything that would change your mind?"

Elizabeth forced herself to look into his eyes. Open, friendly, serious. There was nothing in his manner or his speech that reminded her of Reuben. Life with him would be gentle. Predictable. The way an Amish couple was supposed to live. She pushed her caution away and let a smile pull the corners of her mouth up.

"I don't know. Perhaps, if I got to know you better."

Solomon's smile turned into a satisfied grin. "That's easily done." He took her hand. "I think you are a lovely example of what a fine Amish woman can be, and I think you will make the perfect wife for me."

Elizabeth's heart pounded as he stroked the back of her hand with his thumb. He knew about Reuben—it seemed he knew as much about her as her own family did—and he was still interested in her. She caught her bottom lip between her teeth and searched his face. Perhaps he was the man she should have married in the first place. She smiled into his brown eyes.

"I would like to spend time with you, to get to know you better."

His grin widened. "Wonderful. Tomorrow? You can come

to my house and see where you will be living. We'll have a picnic lunch on the front porch."

"Where I'll be living?" Elizabeth withdrew her hand, the caution coming back with full force. "I didn't say I would marry you."

"Not yet, you haven't." Solomon rubbed his hands together. "But you need to see what I can offer you. Please come tomorrow, sometime in the morning."

Elizabeth paused. Up until she met Solomon, her mind had been closed to the possibility of a future marriage. Closed to putting herself under the power of a man again. But here he was, the man of her childhood dreams come to life. She pushed past that warning bell again. Solomon would be a son-in-law her parents could be proud of.

"Ja," she said, smiling at him once more, "tomorrow will be fine."

As Elizabeth stood to walk back to Wilhelm Stuckey's place, Solomon took her hand and threaded it through the crook of his arm. She was slender and quiet. Not nearly as meek as he would wish, but that would come in time.

Meanwhile, she was coming around. Agreeing to come to the house tomorrow was a stroke of luck. They would be alone, but it was too soon. Too early to press his advantage. That was the mistake he had made back in Pennsylvania. That girl had been just flirtatious enough to fall easily into his hands. As the only child of wealthy Amish parents, she would inherit everything from her father. But his error had been to assume the girl's parents would be eager to marry her off once they learned she had been compromised.

Elizabeth, though, was as cautious as a doe in an open meadow. He had to be careful not to frighten her away. From what he could tell from the talk about her dead husband, she had reason to be reticent. That was all right with him. He only had to win her trust and she would be his.

"Isn't that beautiful?" Elizabeth had stopped in the path, her hand still in the crook of his elbow, looking into the pine branches above them. Solomon looked up but didn't see anything. Was she daft?

"What did you see?"

"Didn't you hear it?" Elizabeth resumed walking, still watching the branches above them. "It was a cardinal calling."

"Sorry." Solomon stroked the back of her hand. "I was paying more attention to you."

She blushed at that. This woman wasn't used to compliments. Solomon filed that information away.

"We're almost back to Wilhelm's farm," she said. "Denki for the walk."

"We don't have to end it so soon." Solomon kept her hand tucked in close. "It's still early. Is there another path we can take?"

"Maybe another time. I don't want to miss visiting with my friends. I will see you tomorrow, close to noon."

He let her hand slip away. When they reached the edge of the farmyard, Elizabeth started walking faster, leaving him behind as she hurried to join the other women. One glance behind her told him all he needed to know. She regretted leaving him.

Solomon watched her until she disappeared into the group of women and he couldn't distinguish her kapp from the others. Amish women all looked the same, except that Elizabeth was pleasant to look at all around. Walking away was especially enjoyable as her skirt swayed with every step. Yes, he could get used to that.

"Well, my fine fellow," he said under his breath, "you've lucked into a good spot here. A willing widow, one hundred sixty acres of land nearly yours, and more to come."

He scanned the groups of folks resting in the shade while they visited. A crowd of children played a game close to where the women had gathered, their laughter piercing the afternoon quiet. Solomon made his way in the other direction toward a group of men that included Abraham Weaver. Elizabeth's father. He needed to get on the old man's good side.

Nodding to Gideon, Solomon took a seat next to him, one that the one-legged man, Aaron, vacated when Solomon entered the circle. Solomon felt the other man's stare as he hobbled to the edge of the group and leaned against a tree, but he chose to ignore it.

"Well, Solomon, are you getting settled in?" Abraham asked. Several of the other men leaned forward to hear his answer.

"Without any problems." Solomon included the whole group in his smile as he spoke to Abraham. "The house is in fine shape and the livestock are in good health."

"Abel sold his livestock to you as well as the farm?" one of the men asked. Solomon thought he might be one of the Weavers.

"The farm equipment, also. He didn't want to take anything with him, and it saved me from having to search out the necessary items." Solomon kept his voice calm to smooth over the suspicious wrinkles on a few of the foreheads. "He was traveling by train, so he only took his clothes and other personal things."

"I still think it's strange that he didn't stop at our place to say farewell," the younger Weaver said.

Gideon shrugged his shoulders. "He must have been in a hurry. Or perhaps he stopped by when you weren't home."

Solomon jumped in to stop the speculations before they went too far. "He told me that he received a telegram and had to act quickly. Most likely, he didn't have time to say goodbye to his neighbors."

That Weaver, Solomon thought it might be Samuel, still looked suspicious, so he changed the subject.

"The corn looks to be growing well." He nodded toward one of the older men. Lehman, if he remembered right.

The man took the bait. "Ja, for sure. It's a fine year for corn. Growing well and leafing out already."

"Don't start building new silos yet," said another man. One of the ministers. "Take heed, lest you fall into the error of counting your bushels before they're harvested."

"Come now, Amos," said Abraham, "let's enjoy a good crop while it lasts. If it keeps up this way, we'll have plenty of work to groan over come harvesttime."

The other men chuckled, and Solomon joined in.

"How is Abel's crop doing?" Abraham asked Solomon. "He purchased a new seed drill last year and was hoping it would increase his yield."

Solomon made a mental note to examine the machinery in the barn and try to figure out which one was a seed drill.

"The corn looks good to me," Solomon said. "The seed drill must have worked the way he wanted it to."

Silence followed his statement, then he remembered.

"Any one of you is welcome to borrow it next spring, come planting time. It's there and waiting."

The men murmured their thanks, then the subject changed to breaking horses and Solomon relaxed. He noticed movement out of the corner of his eye. Aaron was making his way around the outside of the circle, then stopped when he got to a tree in Solomon's line of sight. He hadn't met this man before he came to Weaver's Creek, as far as he knew. Solomon stared back, trying to fit the man's face into his memory, but he would never have forgotten that dark red hair and piercing blue eyes. Eyes that watched every move he made.

Solomon shifted in his seat so he wasn't looking directly at him, but Aaron shifted again so that he could see him out of the corner of his eye. This was irritating. If the man knew him, that could be the end of his plans. But he had never been to Ohio and had never been in an Amish community except the one in Pennsylvania.

Could it be that this man had seen him in Virginia? Solomon pushed the thought out of his mind. Impossible. Even if he had, nothing could be proven. It would be one man's word against another's.

But the one-legged man still stared at him as if he could see right through him. Solomon shifted again. He would have to confront the fellow, find out what he knew, and then take care of it.

7

As the afternoon drew to a close, Aaron was relieved to see that Solomon left with the rest of the families. A few of the young people stayed behind to prepare for something Jonas called a Singing.

"It's for the singles to get to know each other and have fun together," Jonas said. "Sometimes young folks come to our Singing from other districts or we go to theirs. We look forward to it."

"Will you be going?" Aaron noticed that the young men staying behind were quite a bit younger than either he or Jonas.

"Ne, not me. I'm too old. And besides, I've already found my Katie."

Jonas looked across the farmyard to the house where Katie was saying goodbye to her friends. Elizabeth was with her, empty dishes in her hands. Abraham and Lydia had already left, walking down the lane toward the main road.

"I suppose we should be going," Aaron said. "I can walk all the way, but I'm slow. You can go on ahead of me."

"I won't leave you behind, but I'm going to walk Katie and Elizabeth home first. Come with us, and then we'll walk back together from there."

During the short walk along the path to the cabin in the woods, Katie and Jonas fell behind, leaving Aaron and Elizabeth to lead the way. Giggles drifted in the late afternoon air from the couple behind them, and Elizabeth grinned.

"I hope those two are able to get married soon," she said. "Katie is miserable on the days when she can't see Jonas. Is he the same?"

"Not that I've noticed." Aaron was using only one crutch and had to concentrate on each step. "Although he does look in the direction of that house he's building more than he needs to."

"Katie tells me she acts that way because she's in love."

Aaron had no response. Being in love was far outside of his experience. The women he had known never lingered in his mind.

Elizabeth stopped in the path, looking into the branches where a cardinal was calling, establishing his territory to all who could hear.

"Isn't that lovely?" she asked.

"One of the prettiest calls in nature," Aaron said.

They both listened for another minute, then Elizabeth walked on, humming to herself.

"Have you ever been in love?"

Aaron glanced at her. "What?"

"I was just wondering. When a man falls in love, is it the same for him as when a woman falls in love?"

"I wouldn't know."

"Well, a woman in love spends all her time thinking about the one she loves. She imagines talking to him and what she will say, and she tries to understand everything he's doing and saying." Elizabeth plucked a dandelion that was growing along the path. "Take Katie. She does nothing but talk about Jonas. Their house, their plans, if he needs his hair trimmed, what he ate for dinner, what their wedding will be like. You would think she has no other interests in the world."

Aaron longed for the companionable silence he usually enjoyed when he was with Elizabeth.

She continued. "And a woman will also speculate about new men that she meets, wondering if he might be the right man for her."

"Do you mean that Katie is thinking about someone else?"

Elizabeth laughed. He couldn't remember hearing her laugh before. "Katie would never do that."

They had reached the house, and Elizabeth led the way around it to the front porch. She skipped up the two steps, then sank into the chair nearest the door with a sigh. Aaron watched her. She couldn't be talking about herself. The sick feeling in his stomach was beginning to act like an old friend. Elizabeth was smiling, looking at . . . He turned his head to follow the direction of her gaze. Nothing. She was smiling at nothing.

Women.

"I'm going to start for home. When Jonas gets here, tell him I'll see him there."

Elizabeth nodded absently.

Aaron picked his way down the lane toward the road. It was a gentle slope, but he hadn't mastered going downhill yet. Even with the crutch helping him, he was unsteady. He was nearly to the main road when he caught a whiff of tobacco smoke. He stopped as Solomon Mast stepped out from behind a tree.

"I thought you'd come this way," he said, his voice friendly. He extended his right hand. "I'm not sure I caught your full name."

Aaron took his hand. Where Aaron's hand was hard and sinewy from working in the harness shop the past few weeks, Solomon's was as soft as a clerk's.

"Aaron Zook."

"I'm sure you know I just moved to the area from Lancaster County." He stepped closer to Aaron. "I've noticed you watching me. Are you trying to warn me away from Elizabeth?"

His eyes narrowed as he spoke, and he watched Aaron's face. Aaron kept his expression neutral but watched Solomon's eyes in return.

"I thought we might have met a few years ago, in the Shenandoah Valley."

The other man's pupils widened, although nothing else in his expression changed. "I've never been to the Shenandoah. Isn't that in Virginia?"

"Yes." Aaron switched to Englisch. "I was there with Heath's division during the war."

"You're not Amish, then? I didn't think so." Solomon's Englisch words echoed with the soft, rolling accent of the Blue Ridge.

Aaron adjusted his crutch. "Your voice betrays you. I know a Virginian when I hear him."

Solomon chuckled. "You have a good ear. My family was originally from Virginia, but when our Amish community dwindled, my parents moved to Pennsylvania. That was many years ago, when I was still a boy."

Could Aaron have been mistaken? The voice, the manner, even the tobacco scent all told him this was the spy from the Shenandoah Valley, but he had never seen that man's face.

Solomon's smile remained, but his expression grew hard. "So, what is a non-Amish Zook doing here in Ohio?"

"Jonas Weaver is a friend. I came this far with him."

"You have no interest in his sister, then?"

"What if I did?"

The smile widened and the voice lowered. "I'd tell you to move on. You have no place here. You're an outsider that will never be part of the community." He pulled a pair of fine leather gloves from a pocket inside his coat. "On the other hand, I am the perfect husband for Elizabeth. I will be able to support her well, and she will have a good standing in the church with me as her husband. None of the folks here can claim the kind of heritage I can. Especially you."

Aaron's fists clenched.

"And if you try to tell anyone I said any of this, I will deny it. Think, Aaron Zook." He reached over and tapped Aaron's forehead. "Who will they believe? A war veteran who is only half a man, or me, a successful farmer and member of the community?"

Solomon tipped his hat to Aaron, then walked away to the horse and buggy he had left waiting on the main road.

Solomon's words echoed in Aaron's mind with the beat of the horse's trotting hoofs. *Half a man. Half a man.* That's exactly what he was. Half a man who would never be able to support himself or . . . He threw the crutch on the ground.

Or find a woman who would ever look at him with anything but pity.

Before Ruby left for home on Sunday afternoon, Elizabeth had made her promise to spend Monday morning with her. Mamm had agreed to care for the little ones, and Elizabeth set out with the pony cart on Monday morning to pick up Ruby and take her along to Solomon's house.

She hadn't slept at all the night before. The memory of Solomon's deep brown eyes twinkling at her warred with her better sense. One minute her imagination would have him embracing her with the gentle, protective comfort of her feather bed, and the next she would be fighting off his attentions in the nightmare that often visited her dreams. Then she would sit up in bed, sweaty and nauseous, unable to go back to sleep until she had woken up fully, paced around her small bedroom, then crawled back into bed for another fitful hour or two.

"It's just silliness," she said to herself as she turned Pie onto the stone bridge. "I'm letting my imagination take me places that I don't belong."

The pony shook his head and trotted faster when he saw the open barn door.

"Not today, Pie." Elizabeth turned him toward the hitching rail in front of the house. "No lounging in Datt's barn for you."

Ruby slipped out of the kitchen door before Elizabeth

could tie the pony to the rail, waving Elizabeth back into the cart.

"Mamm has little Lovinia occupied for the moment," she said as she took her seat. "If the baby sees me leave, she will cry until we are out of sight. This way, all she knows is that she's with her *grossmutti*."

"And she has the other children to keep her company, too." Elizabeth backed Pie away from the house, then turned him toward the road again.

"You never told me where we are going today. If we're going into town, I'll need to stop by the house and get my shopping list."

Elizabeth shook her head. "Not that far. It would be too much for Pie." She paused. Now, in the light of day, it seemed silly to have asked Ruby to come with her. "Solomon asked me to come to his house this morning and have lunch with him."

"Are you certain I'm not going to be in the way?"

"Not at all. I know better than to be alone with a man." Elizabeth forced a smile. "What would Salome say?"

That brought a laugh from Ruby. She knew how Salome's rumors spread, better than most others. Elizabeth's hands grew sweaty on the reins. Ruby would also understand that Salome's rumors weren't the only thing she was cautious about. She had learned her lesson about putting herself in a compromising position with a man.

"I'm glad we have these few minutes alone," Ruby said as Pie walked up the slope past Reuben's old cabin. "I want you to be the first to know, after Gideon, of course."

Elizabeth shook herself out of her morose thoughts. "What is it?"

"I'm expecting another little one, sometime before Christmas."

Ruby had blushed a bright red and her face shone. Elizabeth was happy for her. Really. She gave her sister a hug, letting go of the reins. Pie's walk slowed as he reached the turnoff at the top of the hill.

"That is wonderful news, Ruby."

Tears blurred her vision. She fumbled for the reins she had dropped and started Pie off again, down the road toward Millersburg and Abel Patterson's place, Solomon Mast's new farm. But Ruby knew her too well.

"I know—" Ruby broke off and put an arm around Elizabeth's shoulders. "I know you wanted your own children with Reuben. I'm sorry that he died before—"

"Don't." Elizabeth interrupted her sister. "Don't even think about it. That is all in the past." She took a shuddering breath, then tried to smile. "It's all right. Maybe someday I'll meet someone, or maybe not."

Maybe Solomon . . .

Ruby spoke Elizabeth's thoughts out loud. "Maybe Solomon Mast is the one for you. He couldn't stop watching you yesterday afternoon."

"That's why I wanted you to come with me today. Sometimes I think he might be a good husband, but I don't trust my own judgment. And I don't trust myself alone with any man. I don't want to end up with another Reuben."

"Solomon isn't anything like Reuben." Ruby squeezed her shoulders again. "And I'll keep you from being charmed into doing something you don't want to do." She grinned. "Solomon is very good looking, isn't he?"

"Too handsome for me. Why would he even look at me twice?"

"Because you are a very beautiful woman. Both outside and on the inside, where it counts."

Elizabeth drew a shuddering breath again as Abel's big brick house came into view. Ruby knew her as well as anyone could, but she didn't know about the black pit of sin and despair that hid itself from her family and friends. If anyone knew, they would hate her. Cast her out from the church and their lives. But if she was lucky, no one would ever know. Especially Solomon Mast.

"Look," Ruby said, shading her eyes with one hand. "Solomon is on the porch waiting for us."

Elizabeth shook her head. "Waiting for me. He doesn't know you're coming."

"Well then, I will be a nice surprise for him." Ruby didn't look the least bit worried.

When Elizabeth drove up to the hitching rail on the gravel drive, Solomon met them at the bottom of the porch steps. It could have been only in her imagination, but she thought she saw a frown cross his face. But when he caught Pie's bridle and looped the reins over the rail, he was smiling at both of them.

"Welcome to Fairacres," he said, extending a hand to help Ruby out of the cart, and then Elizabeth. "I didn't expect to see you, Ruby. I thought you would be busy today tending to your little ones."

"Mamm is happy to take care of them this morning so I could accompany Elizabeth."

"You didn't need to go to the trouble." Solomon smiled

at Elizabeth, his eyes twinkling, just like in her dream. "We would have gotten along just fine on our own."

As Solomon led the way up the steps, Ruby said, "I didn't know Abel Patterson had named his farm."

"I had that privilege." Solomon stopped on the top step and let his gaze sweep around the farm, finally resting on Elizabeth. "The countryside around here is very fair, and I thought my farm should reflect that."

Ruby, standing behind Solomon, caught Elizabeth's eye and raised her eyebrows. Elizabeth knew what she was thinking, that naming a farm was a fancy thing to do. But she supposed Solomon knew best.

"After all," Solomon said as he led the way to some willow chairs on the wide porch, "once Elizabeth and I marry, we will join our farms together. My eighty acres added to her one hundred sixty will create a grand farm, and one worthy of the name Fairacres."

"I haven't yet said that I will marry you," Elizabeth said. She sat next to Ruby in a willow seat large enough for two.

Solomon's smile didn't change. "That will come in due time. You will soon see that my ideas are good for both of us."

A young woman in a simple dress with a handkerchief tied around her head came out of the house carrying a tray. Her skin was darker than any person Elizabeth had ever seen, even among the few freed slaves that lived in Millersburg.

"Thank you, Dulcey," Solomon said in Englisch. "You can set the tray here on the table. And as you can see, I have an extra guest for luncheon. Bring another plate and silverware."

The woman didn't look up but put the tray down and fled back into the house.

Elizabeth exchanged glances with Ruby again.

"Who is Dulcey?" she asked.

"She is my housekeeper and cook. I found her in Millersburg, and since she was looking for a job, I brought her here."

"She doesn't look very happy," Ruby said.

"She has had a hard life." Solomon's face grew sad. "She was born in the Deep South. Mississippi, I think. How she ended up here I don't know. But until the end of the war, she was a slave."

The woman came out to the porch again with the plate and silverware, then started laying out the items for a picnic, setting three places and bowls of cooked minced chicken with slices of bread, cold potatoes, and strawberries. A covered basket came last, with the mouthwatering scent of fresh biscuits rising from it. She turned to go back into the house, but Ruby stopped her.

"Aren't you going to have lunch with us, Dulcey?"

Dulcey glanced in Solomon's direction, her gaze still lowered.

Solomon chuckled. "Dulcey will be happier in the kitchen, won't you?"

Dulcey nodded and disappeared. Once she was gone, Solomon bowed his head for the silent prayer. After a very short time, before Elizabeth had finished her own prayer, she heard the clank of a spoon in a serving dish. Solomon was helping himself to the food.

"Once we're married," he said, "Elizabeth won't have to tie herself down with dull chores. Dulcey will take care of everything."

Elizabeth had been reaching for the glass of water in front of her, but at Solomon's words, she stopped.

"We Amish don't employ servants, Solomon. Surely you know that. Dulcey would be a great help with the house-work, but I wouldn't think of letting her do it all. I would work together with her. We could become great friends, I think."

Solomon's smile only grew wider. "What a kind thought. With everything you say, I am more convinced that we are meant to be together." He beamed at Ruby. "I know I have much to learn about living in your more conservative district, but I intend to make my home here, with a lovely wife by my side."

He turned his gaze to Elizabeth when he said the last phrase, and her heart melted. This man was nothing like Reuben and seemed to have her best interests in mind. Could she get used to living in such a big house, with a hired woman to help her? Her mind flitted ahead to children filling the house, days spent working by Dulcey's side, and Solomon coming home in the evening, caressing each of the little ones on the head and leading them all in family worship after their supper. Perhaps Dulcey would also find a husband who could work on the farm. Their children would fill the house to bursting. How blessed could she be?

"What are you smiling about, my dear?"

Elizabeth focused on him, her imaginary life still very fresh in her mind. "I was just thinking about how beautiful the weather is today."

Solomon reached over and took her hand in his. "It is a perfect day, isn't it?"

Clouds moved in on Monday afternoon, providing a re-spite from the bright late-May sunshine, but not the heat. Aaron wiped his arm across his sweaty brow before he grasped the end of the beam he and Jonas were lifting into place. This one was the center beam and the support for the attic loft Jonas was putting in his house. He and Jonas held it in place as Abraham slid the support post under the center. When they were finished, Aaron sat on an upended log in the middle of Jonas's future kitchen to catch his breath.

"It's beginning to look like a house," Jonas said, step-ping back and looking up toward where the rafters would be placed next. "There were times when I never thought I would finish this house."

"I always knew you would finish it." Abraham took a drink of water from an earthenware jug and passed it to Aaron. "Even when the first house blew down in the storm, I didn't give up hope. You're a man who finishes what he sets out to do."

Aaron passed the jug to Jonas and looked around the spacious ground floor of the house. Jonas had often told him that thoughts of Katie and their unfinished house were what kept him going through the long nights in the army hospital. He had to agree with Abraham. Nothing would stop Jonas once he set his mind to something.

"What about you, Aaron?" Jonas sat on a pile of sawn lumber and took a drink of the cool water. "You aren't still thinking of going west, are you?"

Aaron shifted on his seat, easing the pain in his leg. Jonas was known for following through on his plans. Could he do any less? "It's what I've been planning, ever since my home was destroyed. With nothing to go back to, I figured I'd head out that way once the fighting was over." He rubbed his leg. "I never figured on this, though."

"I wish you would decide to settle here," Abraham said as he sat next to Jonas. "You fit in well, and there's always work for a skilled harness maker."

"I'm not sure I'm what you'd call skilled."

"Dan says you have a natural talent. It's a good, steady job for a man looking to make a home somewhere."

He could always settle in some little town out where no one had ever heard the name Zook. Out where it didn't matter if you were from Tennessee or Pennsylvania. Out where a man's worth was based on what he could do, not who his kin were.

Aaron rubbed his leg again. The muscles cramped every once in a while, and he didn't think anything of it, except that out west his leg would be the first thing folks saw. Everywhere he went, he would have to prove himself. Something a whole man wouldn't need to do.

"Why is Mamm taking care of Ruby's children today?" Jonas asked, taking the conversation past where Aaron had dropped out of it.

"Ruby is spending the day with Elizabeth. Lydia said Elizabeth told her Solomon Mast had invited her to see his house and farm."

"Is he thinking about courting her?" Jonas asked.

Aaron looked from Jonas to Abraham. "He can't," he said. "He isn't—" Aaron stopped himself. Solomon just

114

might be Amish. Just might be who he said he was. "He isn't the right man for her."

Abraham leaned his elbows on his knees. "He appears to be a good Amish man, in spite of a few unusual ways. But he's trying to fit into the community. I heard that he asked to be considered for membership in the church."

Aaron's insides coiled, but he had no evidence for his suspicions. It was his word against Solomon's, and he might be wrong. But if he was right, Elizabeth had no business being near him.

"I just have a bad feeling about him, that's all." Aaron took another drink of water. If Solomon was the man Aaron suspected him to be, Elizabeth needed to be warned, and he was the only one who could do it.

After supper, Aaron walked up to Elizabeth's house. All afternoon he had waged a war with himself, what he should say to her and how. He had no claim on her. Nothing gave him the authority to put his stick in her fire. If she wanted Solomon to court her, he couldn't say anything about it. But he'd give warning to anyone about to step into a rattler's nest, whether he knew them or not.

He was being a friend. That was all.

Elizabeth was sitting on the front porch working on something with her knitting needles, rocking and humming to herself. The same song Ma had always sung about the Rock of Ages. She hadn't seen him yet as he stood in the evening shadows under the pines. A soft wind blew through them, sounding like the sea on the Virginia coast, catching Elizabeth's kapp strings. As he watched, one blew over her shoulder, but she didn't notice. She kept rocking and knitting, the evening sun landing on her face every time the chair went forward. He didn't blame Solomon Mast for wanting her.

He continued toward the porch steps until she finally saw him approaching.

"Is that you, Aaron? I didn't see you coming."

"You were busy wool-gathering."

"I was thinking about my day. I saw that a lot of work got done on Katie's house. Did you help Jonas today?"

"Ja, I did." Aaron tried to think how he would say what he needed to say in Pennsylvania Dutch but gave up. He switched to Englisch. "I heard you and Ruby went to Solomon's this morning."

Elizabeth gathered up her knitting and put the needles and yarn in a basket at her feet. "Solomon invited me to see his house and farm. It's a lovely, large house."

Aaron tapped his crutch on the hard-packed earth studded with gravel. "So, you liked his place?"

"It's still very Englisch. Abel Patterson left all of his furnishings, and they're quite fancy. Too much for my taste, but Solomon likes it. He says all the houses back East are filled with upholstered furniture and pictures on the walls."

Aaron snorted. "Not all of them."

"Solomon also said that I could choose which things to keep and which to sell after we're married."

The percussion of mortar fire wouldn't have left him more numb than her statement did. "Is he . . . is he courting you?"

"He wants to." Elizabeth looked beyond him to the dark blue sky between the pine branches. "I haven't told him he could yet."

"Don't let him. He isn't the man for you."

Her gaze skewered him in his place. "What does it matter to you?"

"It doesn't." Aaron pulled on his beard. Why did it matter? "Except you're the sister of my friend, and I want to look out for your welfare."

"And you think I'm in some kind of danger?"

The image of Solomon's smiling face yesterday afternoon flashed through his mind. The face might have been pleasant, but the man's voice held a threatening edge. He knew what kind of man Solomon was, but he had no evidence, and without proof, Elizabeth would never listen to him.

"You might be. Solomon might not be the man he appears to be. There's something about him."

Elizabeth laughed. "Are you sure you're not just jealous?"

"Why would I be jealous? That would mean that I think of you as more than my friend's sister." He couldn't meet her eyes.

"I meant that you're jealous of Solomon. He is everything you're not. He's an upstanding member of the community, a successful farmer. He has property and a house—"

"And I have nothing."

Elizabeth stood, picking up her basket of knitting. "You have what you have. But Solomon belongs here."

She went into the house, leaving him standing there, the words she didn't say hanging between them.

"And Solomon is a whole man." He said the words softly, but he couldn't keep the bitterness out of his voice. "A whole man with a home to offer any woman that appeals to him."

He turned and started the slow, halting walk back to the Weavers' farm, making his way down the lane and onto the main road. Elizabeth was right. He didn't belong here. Nothing was more obvious. He should pack up tomorrow and head west. Head toward whatever was waiting for him out there. Except . . .

Elizabeth had lit a lamp inside the house and a light gleamed through the pine branches. He couldn't leave. Not as long as Elizabeth was in danger. He might not be the man for her, but he'd die before he saw her wed to Solomon.

8

On Wednesday, the last day of May, thirty-four men from Amish communities as far away as Indiana in the west; Ontario, Canada, in the north; and Somerset County, Pennsylvania, in the east began arriving in Holmes County. Levi met the train in Millersburg and drove the men to the farm where the meetings would be held. The mood of his passengers was solemn but determined.

"They can't ignore us this year," one man said, a minister from Elkhart County in Indiana.

"If they don't listen to our needs, I see a split in the church coming." The second man was close to Father's age, with curly black and gray hair framing his round face.

A tall man Levi recognized from the first meeting that had been held in Wayne County three years earlier shook his head. "I don't know why those who want these changes don't join the Mennonites or form their own church. Why do they have to make all of us accept their modern ideas?"

Then the man sitting next to Levi on the wagon seat, a

man older than anyone Levi had ever seen, gripped the top of his cane. He turned as far around as he could to address the ministers in the back of the wagon.

"We must remain true to the old ways. If we stray, we stray from God himself." He faced front again and tapped Levi's foot with his cane. "You listen to what I say, young man. We can't leave God behind in the quest for progress."

"I agree," Levi said. "The church must hold on to Scripture, above all."

The old man nodded with satisfaction and rode the rest of the way in silence.

On Thursday morning, the first day of discussions began. Levi stood outside the crowded house with Jonas and Aaron, trying to hear the proceedings. But even though he listened as closely as he could, he only heard every third or fourth word that was spoken in the meeting. Finally, he gave up and sat on the porch step next to Jonas.

"What do you think they'll decide?" Jonas asked.

"They've already decided it. They want to write down their position in an official paper to present at the ministers' meeting next week. Right now, they're discussing who should be the one to do the writing."

Aaron chuckled. "The more men there are to discuss something, the longer it takes."

"There's someone else coming," Jonas said, looking down the road. "An emigrant wagon."

The three of them walked to the road to greet the newcomers.

"We're looking for Weaver's Creek," the driver said.

"You're nearly there," Levi said. "Keep going down this

road about three miles. Is there someone in particular you're looking for?"

"Dan and Ephraim Zook."

"You must be their father. They've been expecting you." Levi reached up and shook the man's hand.

"I'm Casper Zook. This is my wife, Rosina." He lifted the cover of the wagon. "Come on out. There are young folks out here you'll want to meet."

A young man about Levi's age pulled back the wagon cover and jumped out. "Name's Tobias," he said, then he reached up to help a girl out of the wagon. "And this is my sister, Elise."

She was beautiful. A shy smile, blue eyes, and a dark red dress that was neat and clean in spite of riding in an emigrant wagon. Levi swallowed. Then she glanced at him and her cheeks grew pink. She looked away again and that lovely face was hidden in the depths of her bonnet.

Jonas stepped forward. "I'm Jonas Weaver, and my friends are Levi Beiler and Aaron Zook."

"Zook?" Casper looked closely at Aaron. "You don't look much like any of the rest of us Zooks."

Aaron's face was as red as his beard. "I was told that I take after my mother's side of the family. They were Scotch-Irish."

Casper's eyebrows rose. "Scots-Irish? Not Amish? I'd like to hear your story when we have more time, but right now I'd like to see my sons. Can you direct us to their farms?"

Levi glanced back at the house. He hated to leave, but nothing much would happen today, and he couldn't let this opportunity to get to know Elise better slip out of his hands.

"I can show you. I need to get home, and the Zook farms are on the way."

Jonas nudged his arm with an elbow. "Why don't you ride with the Zooks? Aaron and I can follow with your spring wagon." He grinned and shifted his eyes toward Elise and back at Levi.

"We'd be pleased to accept your help," Casper said. "Come on up here and take the reins."

Levi climbed up to the tall seat of the wagon and lifted the reins. The tired horses shook their heads as if to say they thought they had gone far enough.

"It's only a mile or so to Ephraim's farm." Levi started the horses, conscious of Elise standing in the wagon bed, looking out between him and her datt . . . close enough to touch. He swallowed.

"The boys have written about their life here. They praised the fertile soil, the rolling hills, and the strong community." Casper watched the scenery as they traveled along the road toward the Zooks' farms on the northern edge of the Weaver's Creek district. "That's one reason we decided to come out here to join them."

"I'm glad you came." Levi swallowed again. "I mean, we're glad you're here. Dan and Ephraim are welcome members of our community. They're becoming well known around the county for their harness making."

"So, tell me about this Aaron Zook. Where is he from?"

How could he explain the situation?

"Jonas worked in a hospital during the war. Aaron was one of the patients there and came home with him after the war was over."

122

Casper fingered his beard. "So, Aaron was a soldier?"

Levi nodded. "He wasn't raised Amish and joined the army when the war started. He said he did it after his father and grandfather were both killed in the fighting."

"Zooks fighting in that terrible war." Casper shook his head. "I wouldn't have believed it, but many strange things have happened during the last years."

Tobias, standing in the wagon bed next to his sister, said, "Look! That has to be Ephraim's barn. It's exactly as he described it in his letters."

"That's right," Levi said. "We're almost there. Dan's is just beyond it, down the road."

Casper leaned forward and Levi jiggled the horses' reins to get more speed out of them. They picked up their pace, and as soon as they turned into Ephraim's lane, Tobias jumped out of the back of the wagon and ran toward the house. Levi pulled the wagon to a stop in the farmyard, and Casper climbed down, then helped Rosina. Levi jumped down from the seat and went around to the back of the wagon, hoping he wasn't too late.

Elise stood in the back of the wagon with an expectant look on her face. When Levi came close, he held out his arms, and she grasped his hands as she dropped to the ground. He held her hands in his for the briefest of moments, and she looked up at him, her blue eyes mirroring his own. The same shade of blue. She smiled, then went to join her mother. Levi's hands tingled as the spring wagon drove up.

"Levi." Jonas tapped his shoulder with the buggy whip. "Are you all right? Or have you been bitten by a bug?"

Aaron grinned, sitting next to Jonas.

"It's nothing." Levi started to climb up into the seat of his spring wagon. "We'll let the Zooks get on with their reunion."

"Wait a minute." Jonas stopped him. "She's looking at you."

Levi frowned. "It isn't fair to tease me."

"I'm not teasing. Look behind you."

He turned, expecting to see the Zook family ignoring everyone but themselves, but Jonas was right. Elise was watching him until she saw him look. Then she ducked her head, her face hidden again by her bonnet. A roaring started in his ears. He had heard of someone falling in love at the first glance at a pretty face, but he had always thought that was just silly girls' chatter.

He had been wrong.

~

The Sunday after the Zook family arrived was a non-church day. Aaron enjoyed the relaxed off Sundays, but Ma had taken him to church every week, down in the hollow where the preacher lived next to the sawmill. Even though Jonas had tried to explain the value of the fellowship time and rest the community enjoyed on these quiet days, Aaron still had the feeling they should be in church. Maybe it was the memory of that fiery preacher's voice, echoing in the little frame building. Whatever the Amish believed, Aaron knew that Tennessee preacher would find fault with neglecting the meeting two Sundays a month.

On the other hand, he enjoyed the relaxed atmosphere of the farm after the morning chores were done. The family lingered over breakfast, and then Abraham read from his big Bible. The language was high German rather than Pennsylvania Dutch, but Aaron could now understand most of what was read after weeks of being immersed in the language. On this Sunday, Abraham read the Twenty-Third Psalm. Aaron was surprised that he remembered the words in Englisch and could recognize them in German. He must have been no more than five years old when Ma helped him memorize those words, but he hadn't thought of them much since she passed away.

Afterward, he joined Jonas and Abraham on the front porch. The side porch was where Aaron sat most often, right off the kitchen and mud room. The front porch seemed to be saved for summer Sundays. Facing north, it was shaded all day long, with the westerly breezes ruffling the leaves of the morning glory vines Lydia had planted to break up the afternoon sun's rays.

Abraham dozed in his chair woven from willow twigs while Jonas fidgeted in the seat next to him.

"I'm going to see what Katie is up to today," he said as he finally rose.

"I wondered what was taking you so long."

Aaron grinned as Jonas gave him a playful slap on the shoulder on his way to the porch steps. As he headed toward the lane that would lead him across the stone bridge toward Katie's house, Aaron relaxed in his chair.

Stretching his leg out in front, Aaron's eyes closed as he listened to the bees buzzing in the flowers. He couldn't remember such peace. Not since the war started. Rest. No worries. Nothing to tug him away, nothing to hold him back.

His thoughts drifted to Elizabeth. Should he worry about her? She seemed so vulnerable when it came to Solomon. She was like a dove, unaware and unafraid, being stalked by a fox.

That thought pulled his mind out of the drowsy place it had gone, then the buzzing bees and gentle breeze lulled him back until Lydia opened the front door.

"Abraham." Her voice was soft, reluctant to wake him up.

Aaron sat up just as Abraham lifted his hat off his face. "Ja, what is it?"

"We have visitors. The Zooks are coming."

Abraham stretched as he rose from his seat, then went to greet the Zook family. Aaron followed, curious about these relatives who weren't really related. Sharing the same last name with Dan and Ephraim had come to feel ordinary while he had been working with Dan in the harness shop, but the thought they might be family was just wishful thinking.

He stood back as Abraham greeted Dan and Ephraim and their families and was introduced to Casper and Rosina, and Rosina's children, Elise and Tobias. Lydia stepped forward then, inviting the women to join her in the kitchen. Dan's and Ephraim's children ran off to play in the little house near the barn that Abraham had built for his grandchildren. The men followed Abraham back onto the porch, and Aaron leaned against the porch rail as the men sat in chairs.

Half listening to the conversation, Aaron watched the Zook men. They looked like any other Amish fellows, and certainly nothing like him. But they also looked a lot like Grandpop with their round faces and wide-set eyes. The mannerisms were similar, too, giving Aaron the feeling that

126

they could have been sitting on the front porch of Grand-pop's cabin in the Tennessee hills.

Then Dan turned to him. "How is your new leg doing? Does the harness work the way you wanted it to?"

"Ja, for sure it does." Aaron showed where the harness was strapped onto his leg outside his trousers. "The details you suggested, like using soft leather for the side next to my leg, work fine. It doesn't slip at all."

Casper was closest to Aaron and leaned closer. "That's fine stitching. Dan, is that your work or Ephraim's?"

"It's Aaron's. He knows quite a bit about harness making."

The older man looked up at Aaron. He was about the same age as Pa had been when he died.

"Who taught you, son?"

"My grandpop. He did harness making off and on, whenever someone would pay."

"And you're from Tennessee, you said."

Aaron nodded, wondering what the man was thinking.

Casper looked at his sons, then back at Aaron. "There's a story in our family, about my datt's brother. Years ago, back before the second war with England, Datt's brother had a row with his father and ran away. He was never heard from again."

Abraham leaned forward. "That's a tragedy. What do you think happened to him?"

"We never knew. My father, Heinrich was his name, had been very close to his brother as they grew up. He told me that there was something about him that was worrisome. He was a rebellious child, and it only grew worse as he got older. He got so he was against everything the family stood for—their faith, the work they did, even eating together as a family. He was only sixteen years old when he left home."

"I've never heard this story, Datt," Ephraim said.

"By the time I married, and you boys came along, we had stopped talking about him. I think the memories just hurt my father too much. I know he never forgot his brother, though. I was named after him."

Aaron's mouth went dry. The reason for Casper's story began to become clear.

"Did anyone ever try to find him?" Abraham asked.

"My grandfather never stopped looking for him. At first, they thought he had gotten lost in the forest. There were some that said the Indians had taken him captive." Casper ran his hand over his face. "There was even a report from a trader that he saw a young man living with an Indian tribe in western Pennsylvania, and the description matched Datt's brother. To my grandfather's death, he hoped that his son would return."

"You think," Aaron started, but he couldn't think of the Pennsylvania Dutch words. He started over in Englisch. "You think your father's brother might have ended up in Tennessee."

"Now that I've met you, I think so. He knew harness making, and he could have a grandson about your age."

He swallowed. "Grandpop's name was Cap, not Casper."

Casper smiled. "That's a short name for Casper. My grandson is called Cap." He stood. "And your father's name?"

"His name was Henry. Grandpop said he named him after his brother."

"Henry is the Englisch way to say Heinrich. He named his son after my father." Casper's eyes filled with tears in spite of his widening smile. "It couldn't be, could it? That we would find the answer to the mystery here in Ohio?"

Dan grinned. "The evidence seems to point that way. What do you think, Aaron?"

Aaron ran his hand over his face, suddenly aware that it was the same gesture Casper had made a few minutes ago. Talking with him . . . it was as if Grandpop had come back to life as a younger man. "It sounds like it could be possible. I never thought Grandpop's family in Pennsylvania would still remember him."

"Remember him?" Casper shook his head. "You never forget family. No matter how long it's been since you've seen them. Uncle Casper's place in the family has been empty for years, but now we have an answer."

"The Lord works in mysterious ways," Abraham said, his smile as wide as Casper's. He called into the house for the women to join them.

Once Rosina heard the story, she walked over to Aaron and pulled on his shoulder until she could reach his cheek. She kissed it softly. "Welcome to the family, Aaron."

"Almost like the Prodigal Son," Dan said, shaking Aaron's hand.

It was too much. Aaron reached up to wipe away the tingle that Rosina's kiss had left, but she stopped him.

"That's a mother's kiss, young man. And a mother's kiss lasts forever."

He heard an echo in his memory. Ma, happy to see him and pleased with the results of his first hunting trip with Pa.

She had taken his face between her palms and kissed him on the cheek. He felt too grown up for that and wiped it away with his hand.

But Ma had laughed. "A mama's kiss lasts forever. No wiping or washing will ever make it disappear."

She had been right. He could still feel that kiss. He grinned at Rosina, and then at Dan. He didn't know what to say. But he knew—knew in his heart—that Casper must be right. All the pieces fit. This was the family Grandpop had left behind so long ago.

Then Ephraim hugged him, laughing. "Look at you! You'd think you never had a family before."

Aaron returned Ephraim's hug, then hugged Tobias before Casper wrapped his arms around him in a tight, strong grip and held him, as if to make up for all the lost years.

Ephraim was right. He had never had a family like this before.

9

"Did you hear the news?" Katie asked.

It was Tuesday morning and Elizabeth was ironing the dresses they had washed and dried the day before while Katie folded the rest of the laundry.

"Only that the ministers' meeting has started. Several of the men from our district have gone up to Wayne County this week."

"Not that. The news about Aaron and the Zooks."

Elizabeth shook her head in reply, concentrating on ironing out a stubborn wrinkle.

"It turns out that Aaron is a long-lost cousin of theirs."

Giving up on the wrinkle, Elizabeth placed the iron back on the stove to heat again. Katie was quick to share every rumor she heard, especially if it sounded like good news.

She smiled at Katie's earnest face. "How can they know if they are related or not? Are you certain this isn't just more gossip?"

"I heard it straight from Jonas, and he heard the story

from his father. You know Abraham wouldn't spread any news unless he is sure it's true." Katie pulled the basket of dish towels closer. "Jonas said Aaron's grandfather was the brother of Dan and Ephraim's grandfather. Aaron's grandfather left home when he was still a boy, and the family never heard from him again."

Elizabeth picked up the second iron and tested it. Just right. She tackled the wrinkle again. "And they think Aaron's grandfather is that boy? How do they know the two were brothers?"

"That's what is so wonderful about this whole story. Dan and Ephraim's grandfather named his son after his brother who had run away, and Aaron's grandfather named his son after his brother too. The family names are what told them that Aaron belonged to them."

Elizabeth put the iron back on the stove and adjusted the skirt so the next wrinkled section was ready to work on. Aaron was a difficult person to learn to know, but she had seen the wistful expression in his eyes when he spoke of his mother, as if he missed having a family in spite of acting like he didn't need anyone. What did he think about the idea of belonging to the Weaver's Creek Zooks?

A knock on the front door interrupted her thoughts. Katie went to answer it, and Elizabeth heard her talking to someone. She moved the coffeepot to the front of the stove to prepare for their visitor, but Katie came back into the kitchen alone, carrying an envelope.

"It was Mr. Stevenson, from the sawmill. He had been to Farmerstown and he said Mrs. Lawrence asked him to deliver this letter for you. It had been waiting at the post office for a few weeks, waiting for someone from Weaver's Creek to fetch the mail. He said it looked important."

Elizabeth took the envelope and sat in a chair at the table. It was larger than any envelope she had ever seen and had official-looking printing on it.

"Hoben, Williamson, and Turner. Attorneys at Law. Vicksburg, Mississippi," she read aloud, then looked at Katie. "What could it be? Why would a lawyer contact me?"

Katie sat across the table from her. "You won't know until you open it." Her eyes glowed with excitement. "Maybe it has something to do with Reuben. Wasn't he in Vicksburg when he passed away?"

Elizabeth turned the envelope over and smoothed the sealed flap. Katie was right. It might have something to do with Reuben, or the new wife he had married during the war, or the son they had had together. Touching the letter brought life to her memories. Unwelcome life. What would opening it bring?

"Don't you want to know what it says?" Katie drummed her fingers on the table. "It might be good news."

"It could also be bad."

"You won't know until you open it."

Katie handed her a knife and Elizabeth slit the envelope. She took out the letter and unfolded it. The script was large and bold, and at the bottom was a notary's seal embellished with gold.

"It looks official." Elizabeth tried to make out the Englisch words, but the writing was too different from the German script she was familiar with.

"What does it say?"

"I'll have to find someone who can read it. Perhaps Datt can."

"Abraham went to the meeting with the rest of the men." The coffeepot started boiling and Katie rose to pour two cups. "Do you think Aaron could read it?"

"I'm not sure." Elizabeth recognized her own name but couldn't make out the rest of the writing. "Solomon could. He seems to have more experience with Englischers. He could read it and also tell me what it means."

Katie grinned. "Are you sure you aren't just making an excuse to see him again?"

Her face heating, Elizabeth folded the letter and put it back in the envelope. "Of course not. I just think he might be the best person to ask. I can't wait too long, either. That gold seal means that the letter is important."

The letter's weight pulled at Elizabeth's mind as she finished the ironing, fixed a small lunch for the two of them, and cleaned up the kitchen. What could it say? Letters like this one changed folks' lives.

Reuben had received one several years ago, soon after they were married, and had taken it to a lawyer in Millersburg. The lawyer said Reuben had inherited some money from his father in Philadelphia.

Elizabeth gave the kitchen shelf a final wipe with the dish towel before rinsing it in the last of the rinse water and hanging it up to dry.

That money had been enough to pay the mortgage and then some, Reuben had said. She never found out what happened to the rest of it, but that letter changed Reuben . . . for a time. He was kinder and easier to live with until the following winter when the money was all gone. Then he had blamed her for spending it, or hiding it, but Elizabeth suspected he had lost it at the gambling house he frequented.

She stopped, tapping pursed lips with her finger as she considered. Should she go to a lawyer in Millersburg first like Reuben had? If Datt was home, he would advise her. But all the men had gone to the ministers' meeting, except a few. Solomon was the only Amish man she could think of to ask.

Was it proper for her to call on Solomon alone? Katie had gone to Lena's after lunch to help the Stuckey women prepare for Margaret's upcoming wedding, and Mamm had gone to Wayne County with Datt. Ruby wouldn't be able to go with her in the afternoon during the children's nap time. She could go by herself. It wouldn't hurt anything. And she wouldn't be alone with Solomon, not with Dulcey there.

The sun wasn't far past its noon zenith when Elizabeth had hitched up and was on her way. The letter crinkled from its spot in her waistband, reminding her of the importance of this errand. All was quiet in the farmyards she passed, and she kept Pie at a trot until they started rising out of the valley. She slowed him to a walk until they crested the top of the hill.

She watched Solomon's house grow out of the surrounding fields as she approached. Pie shook his head and she loosened her tight grip on the reins. He had sensed her sudden misgivings.

"You can trust Solomon," she told herself. Pie's ears swiveled to listen to her voice. "He has always been kind to you. Besides, Dulcey is there. You won't be alone with him."

The red brick house seemed taller than before, leaning

toward her as if it were a cat welcoming a mouse to dinner. She shook her head, clearing her vision. It was just a house. There was nothing for her to fear.

She tied Pie to the hitching rail and walked up the wide porch steps. She lifted the iron knocker on the door and let it fall with a sharp tap. After a moment, Dulcey answered the door.

"Hello, Dulcey." Elizabeth smiled in a way that she hoped would let the young woman know she wanted to be friends. "Is Solomon at home? I need to speak to him about something."

Dulcey didn't meet her gaze but backed away to let Elizabeth into the hall.

"Masta Solomon, he's in the study. I'll fetch him straightaway."

Dulcey knocked softly on a door that led from the hall, then pushed the door aside and slipped into the room. Elizabeth looked around at the tall seat with hooks for hats and capes, the table with a vase of flowers on it, and the narrow carpet in the center of the floor. She wondered when Solomon would dispose of Abel Patterson's fancy furnishings to make the house more comfortable. She missed the simple lines of her parents' home.

Muffled voices came from the room Dulcey had called the study, then the doors slid open and Solomon walked through, a smile on his face.

"Welcome, Elizabeth. This is a surprise."

Elizabeth pulled the letter from the envelope and handed it to him. "I received this letter today but had trouble making out what it says. I hoped you could help me."

Solomon glanced at the letter, then at her. "Why don't we go into the front room to discuss this." He gestured for her to lead the way.

Elizabeth went into the dim sitting room. The shades were drawn against the bright afternoon light, and the room was crowded with furniture. She sat on a chair with a horsehair seat and waited for Solomon to read the letter all the way through.

His expression changed from interest to a frown, then he looked at her again.

"This letter says there is a woman in Mississippi who is claiming ownership of your land."

"You mean my husband's land."

"This letter says that Reuben Kaufman is the husband of Melanie Kaufman. This law firm is making inquiries on behalf of Mrs. Kaufman and her young son." He laid the letter on the table next to Elizabeth's chair and looked at her, his eyes narrowing. "I had understood that you are the widow of Reuben Kaufman, but this letter claims that you were his sister. What is the truth, Elizabeth?"

A familiar sense of helplessness washed over Elizabeth. It was as if Reuben were alive, accusing her of her sins from across time and space. She swallowed, then took a deep breath. *He is dead. He is dead. He can no longer harm me.*

Elizabeth stood, reaching out to him as if her touch could convince him of the truth. "My husband betrayed me by marrying this other woman while we were still married. But I am Reuben's widow. He must have never told this woman in Mississippi that he was married to me, and she assumed I was his sister."

Solomon turned his back on her and stared out the window that was obscured with lace curtains. His rigid back told her everything she needed to know. He didn't believe her.

———

Solomon straightened his shoulders, aware that the woman behind him was scrutinizing every movement. Had she lied to him? If she had, then the entire community had agreed with the story.

His mind tried to tie the evidence together with this new information, but it didn't make sense. According to the county land records, the land was owned by Reuben Kaufman's widow Elizabeth. Elizabeth was the daughter of Abraham Weaver. It was the first step in his quest to gain control of the valley.

But now there was another claimant.

Solomon clenched his fist. Another silly woman thinking she could claim his land. The answer was clear. He needed to confirm that Elizabeth's ownership of the land was secure and immovable.

"This other claimant." He turned back to the woman standing in the center of his sitting room. "Were you aware of her?"

Elizabeth nodded. "Someone came to the farm with the news of Reuben's death. He had assumed I was Reuben's sister since Reuben had married this other woman in Mississippi." Her face grew pink and she rubbed the end of her nose in a gesture that reminded him of a young child. "I didn't correct him. I was—" Her cheeks flamed red. "I was only relieved to hear that Reuben wouldn't be coming home."

Solomon read through the letter again. "It will be simple enough to clear this up. We will send a copy of your marriage certificate to this lawyer, and this woman's claim will be worthless."

"I don't have a marriage certificate."

"You must. When you get home, look among your things."

She shook her head. "I don't have any papers."

Was she lying again? Or was she just stupid?

"You have the deed to the farm, don't you?"

She shook her head again. "My husband didn't tell me anything about his business, and I never found any papers. No deed, no marriage certificate. Nothing."

Solomon threaded his fingers together. Shaking her senseless as he longed to do wouldn't achieve anything. "Then we will look for them. You will search your cabin, and I will pay a visit to the county courthouse in Millersburg. You must establish your ownership of that property or all our plans will be ruined."

Elizabeth chewed on her bottom lip. "What plans?"

He smiled in the way that he had learned disarmed people and gave him what he wanted. He took both of her hands in his.

"Our marriage. Our future. Our family's future. Uniting our properties will help us provide for generations to come."

She blushed, her eyes turned down and a smile on her lips. His smile stretched wider. He had found her weak spot. A family. Children and grandchildren. He could ask anything of her now.

Taking a step closer, he released one hand and lifted her chin with his finger. "You know I lost my dear Anna in childbirth along with our child. I look forward to being blessed with a house full of children."

"I had heard that you still grieve for her, and I can . . . imagine the pain of losing your child, also. Reuben and I were . . . we never had . . . children."

Her voice caught, betraying her emotion, and the thrill of easy prey coursed through him as her eyes glistened. Unrequited longing. Her hopeful expression fed his instincts.

He licked his lips. "But first, before we can move forward with our plans, we need to establish that you are the rightful owner of your farm."

"Reuben's farm."

Her soft voice barely registered in his hearing. He chose to ignore it.

Solomon took her shoulders and steered her toward the door. "You go and search the cabin. Men hide important papers in strange places sometimes. Perhaps he hid them under a stone in the fireplace or in the loft. Check everywhere they could be hidden."

"I will." She turned to look at him. "What will happen if we don't find them?"

"Don't worry about that. I'll take care of everything." He pushed her into the front hall. "You just look in the cabin."

She frowned, making her even prettier. "What should I do if I find them?"

He patted her back. "Bring them to me. I'll take care of everything. But don't say anything to anyone else. This lawyer may have an agent working here, and we don't want them to learn information that would put us at a disadvantage."

Her frown softened into a puzzled look. Pretty and naive

enough to trust him. His favorite type of woman. "You can rely on me, Elizabeth. I have experience with these matters and I only have your best interests at heart."

She gave him a nod as he prodded her closer to the door that Dulcey held open for her.

Elizabeth grasped Dulcey's free hand and spoke in Englisch. "Thank you, Dulcey. I look forward to visiting with you sometime. I would like to learn to know you better."

Dulcey didn't answer but closed the door as Elizabeth walked out to her cart.

"What was that all about?" He glared at Dulcey.

The skinny girl backed against the door, still holding the knob with one hand. She shook her head.

Suspicion left a metallic taste in his mouth, feeding his need for release.

"Have you talked with her before?"

Dulcey shook her head, her eyes tight. "No, Masta, not once. I don't know why she spoke to me like that."

Solomon reached for the buggy whip he kept in the umbrella stand next to the door. His heartbeat pounded in his ears, strong and steady. He could already see the welts the whip would bring on Dulcey's bare legs. Red stripes, each one crossing the other until the blood flowed freely in rivulets against the dark skin.

"You must have encouraged her. Smiled at her?"

He stepped closer and Dulcey's knees buckled, casting her prostrate on the floor in front of him.

"I swear, not once. I don't never look at her."

Solomon reached down to lift her skirt above her knees, exposing the evidence of previous days and weeks of satisfying his lust for blood on her. Then a thought crossed his mind and the whip dropped from his hand, forgotten. Elizabeth's interest in talking to Dulcey could be used to his advantage. He grabbed the slightly built girl's arm and lifted her to her feet.

"I have something for you to do." She was shaking and flinched when he reached to straighten the kerchief on her head, his hand gentle. "I want you to talk to Elizabeth the next time she visits. Invite her into the kitchen for coffee. Offer her something to eat."

Dulcey cast a sideways glance up at him. "Why?"

"She'll tell you things she would never tell me. Ask her about her farm and her life. Find out everything you can and then report to me."

His servant didn't answer but looked at the floor. He shook her, still holding her by the arm.

"Do what I say, or you'll end up back in that saloon where I found you. You remember what that was like, don't you?"

She nodded.

"Now go and lay out my regular clothes, and make sure you've brushed my coat. Then hitch up the buggy. I need to go to Millersburg."

As she disappeared up the stairs, Solomon picked up the buggy whip and put it back in its place. Dulcey would obey him. She was always compliant.

⁓

Late Tuesday afternoon as Aaron was walking home from Gideon's farm, he heard a cart coming behind him on the road. He glanced back, preparing to make his way to the edge of the graded dirt track, but then saw Elizabeth turn her pony cart into her farm. He changed direction and headed up the hill, using his new cane to steady his steps. Whatever Elizabeth was doing at the old cabin, she might need some help.

By the time he arrived, the pony was tied outside the cabin. Aaron walked to the door and looked in just in time to see a ceiling beam give way in a shower of dirt and old leaves.

"Elizabeth!"

"I'm all right."

Her voice came from the loft above, or what was left of it.

"What are you doing up there?" Dust filled the air in a cloud, obscuring everything.

Elizabeth coughed. "I'm looking for something and thought it might be in the loft." She coughed again. "What brings you here?"

"I saw you turn into the farm from the road and thought you might need some help."

The dust started settling and Aaron picked his way through the debris covering the floor. Elizabeth was standing on a second beam, keeping her balance by holding on to the rafters. He leaned on his cane.

"It looks like you might need some help getting down. How did you climb up there?"

"There is a ladder. It was leaning against the beam that fell."

Aaron found the ladder under the broken beam and pulled it out. Setting his cane aside, he maneuvered it upright and leaned it against the remaining beam. Elizabeth grasped the top, then started down.

"How did you avoid falling when that beam gave way?"

Elizabeth reached the floor and tried to wipe the dust from her skirt. "I was between the two beams when I heard it crack. When I jumped toward the wall, it fell, but I had reached the second beam. I'm glad it didn't break too."

Aaron looked around at the old cabin. He had seen some shacks in west Tennessee, but not many in as bad shape as this one was.

"You used to live here?"

Elizabeth looked around at the mess, crossing her arms with her palms cupping her elbows. "It was in better condition then. After Ruby and Gideon married, I moved into Katie's house. I thought about moving back here once, but I've realized that even a good cleaning wouldn't make this a place I'd want to live in."

"You could tear it down and build a new house here."

She snorted. "It needs to be burned down."

Another cloud of dust rose up as part of the beam settled farther toward the floor.

"We should get out of here. Something else may fall."

"Not until I find what I'm looking for."

"I can help. What is it?"

"Some papers. I've never seen them in here, but Solomon said they must be somewhere. This is the only place Reuben could have kept them."

Aaron grimaced at the mention of her husband. Jonas had told him little about Elizabeth's marriage, but from the information he did give him, Aaron knew he wouldn't want to meet the man.

"What kind of papers?"

Elizabeth shifted her gaze away from his, chewing on her

bottom lip. "Solomon didn't want me to tell anyone, in case the lawyer in Mississippi finds out. But I could use your help." She shrugged her shoulders. "I'm looking for the deed to the farm, our marriage certificate. Important documents."

Aaron's stomach twisted. Why did Solomon want her to find papers like that? And what did a lawyer have to do with it? But he wasn't going to leave her alone to look. Another part of the old cabin could fall down at any time.

He waved away the swirl of dust motes hanging in the air between them. "Did he keep the papers in something? Like a leather pouch or a metal box?"

"I don't remember ever seeing them, but he did have a metal box. He never let me see what was in it."

"But you don't know where he kept it."

She shook her head. "The only time I saw it was—" She bit her lip. "I was sick, and he thought I wasn't watching him, but I still don't know what he did with it."

"I have some time this afternoon. I can help you look."

She hesitated. "You won't mind? As you can see, it's going to be a dirty job, and we might not find anything."

"Let's start at that corner and work our way around."

Aaron prodded at the dry chinking between the logs in the corner while Elizabeth pulled the bed frame away from the wall.

"So, Solomon suggested that you look here?"

Elizabeth peered up the cold chimney. "He said he would look through the records at the courthouse in Millersburg, but he thought Reuben would have kept the papers here."

"Why is Solomon looking for them?"

"Because of the letter." She was standing on the floor of

the fireplace with her head inside the chimney and her words were muffled.

"What letter?"

She stepped out of the fireplace and started examining the mantel. "I received a letter from a law firm in Mississippi asking about any property Reuben might have owned in Ohio."

"Why would a southern lawyer be interested in Reuben's property?"

Elizabeth coughed again. "Let's go outside for a few minutes while the dust settles."

Aaron grabbed his cane and followed her into the bright afternoon sunshine. She drew a bucket of clear water from the well and they both took a drink, then sat on a bench someone had placed in the shade of a tree long ago. Elizabeth sighed deeply and gazed at the cabin.

"My husband was a cruel man." Her voice was even. Flat. As if she were telling him about the weather.

"Jonas told me a bit about him."

"Reuben joined the Confederate army early in the war and was in Vicksburg for more than a year. While he was there, he married another woman. They had a son."

Disgust for this man Aaron had never met rolled over him in a wave. Both Grandpop and Pa had taught him that women were to be protected, nurtured, and cherished. Women were strong and capable, but their job of bearing and raising children made them even more precious. The thought of this man turning his back on Elizabeth . . . Aaron resisted the urge to take her in his arms and settled for laying his hand on top of hers.

"I'm sorry."

She looked at him, her eyes wide. Tears glistened in the corners.

"You believe me?"

"Of course. Men can be stupid creatures, only thinking of themselves. If it had been me . . ." He let his words trail off. If Elizabeth had been his wife, he would have done everything in his power to come home to her.

"I took the letter to Solomon because it was written in Englisch. I got the feeling he didn't believe me at first. In fact, he insisted that I had to find a certificate of marriage to prove that I was Reuben's wife."

Aaron's jaw clenched. "You should have brought it to me. I could have read it for you."

She pulled her hand out from under his. "I didn't think you would be able to read it. The script was very fancy, and the letter was full of long words I couldn't make out. I knew Solomon had had dealings with the Englisch and he would know what to do."

"Solomon isn't the man you should be going to for advice. Abraham will be home in a few days. Wait to see what he says."

"I can't wait that long. The letter took several weeks to arrive. I know the lawyer is waiting for an answer." She chewed on her lower lip, still watching the cabin. Finally, she looked at him, a smile on her face. "I had better start looking for those papers again. Solomon thinks they are very important."

"Did he say why?" Aaron rose to follow her back into the cabin.

"He said we needed to prove that I am the rightful owner

of the farm, although I don't know why he is so insistent. If this other woman needs money to support herself and her child, I would give the property to her. It doesn't mean anything to me. If Solomon and I marry, we could live very well on his farm."

Aaron halted as Elizabeth continued into the cabin. Marriage to Solomon would be the worst mistake of Elizabeth's life, if he was right about the man. As bad as Reuben had been, Aaron knew Solomon would never give Elizabeth the life she longed for. Men like that never considered anyone else when they made their plans.

10

Elizabeth found herself standing near Salome Beiler on Sunday morning before church. It was pleasant weather on this second Sunday in June and people lingered outside Simeon and Hannah Keck's house, waiting for the service to start.

"Tsk, tsk, tsk," Salome said, shaking her head. "I never thought I would see a minister act like that."

When Elizabeth saw what Salome was looking at, she covered a grin with her hand. Gideon had purchased a buggy for his family and had driven it to church. The black sides shone in the bright sunlight.

"We all voted on whether to allow buggy driving on Sunday, Salome," Mamm said from the other side of Elizabeth. "For families with several children or for older folks, driving a buggy makes it possible for them to attend the church meeting. Too many stay home when the distance is too far for them to walk."

"I didn't vote for it." Salome crossed her arms.

"No one at the meeting objected." Mamm's voice was

strong and steady. Elizabeth admired her for keeping her temper, even in a disagreement with Salome.

"I knew everyone was against me."

"Solomon Mast drives a buggy to church, but I've never heard you complain about him."

Salome sniffed. "Solomon Mast is different. He is a good Amishman."

Elizabeth kept her gaze on the ground. What would Salome think if she knew that Solomon had practically asked her to marry him? Elizabeth stifled a giggle. She might be speechless, given her opposing opinions of the two of them.

"We are equal in the eyes of God." Mamm's voice held an edge, as if she was warning Salome to watch what she was saying.

"Ja, ja, ja." Salome started walking toward the house. "I know, Lydia. You needn't bring it up again."

Mamm chuckled softly.

"What was that about?" Elizabeth asked.

"I decided that the way to stop Salome's thoughtless comments was to remind her that she is no better than anyone else." Mamm smiled. "It has made bearing her company more pleasant."

Elizabeth followed Mamm toward the house, falling behind a little as she watched the buggies arrive. Solomon hadn't driven up yet and Elizabeth hoped he wasn't going to miss the worship service. Finally, just as she reached the door, she saw his black horse turn into the farm lane. She had only seen him once since he had asked her to look for the documents proving her ownership of Reuben's farm.

When he learned that she hadn't found them yet, his frown was enough to bring a quick apology.

"I'm sorry. I'll keep looking."

"See that you do." His voice had growled. "We don't have anything to discuss until you find those papers."

"I won't stop until I find them."

Then he had caught her chin in one hand, grasping it hard enough to leave a red mark. "I know you won't."

He had patted her cheek and gone into the house to talk to Datt.

Elizabeth hadn't liked how hard he had held her chin, but he didn't know how strong he was. That was the only problem. Solomon would never deliberately hurt her.

She slipped into her place on the bench next to Ruby and her family just as the first hymn was announced. While they sang, Solomon walked in and took the last spot on the bench on the men's side, directly across the aisle from her. He didn't look her way but opened a copy of the Ausbund and joined in the singing. As the service progressed, Elizabeth tried to catch his eye, but his gaze remained on the front of the church.

After two of the sermons were done and Gideon was rising to deliver the third one, Ruby leaned over to whisper, "I need to take Lovinia out to change her. Would you watch the boys for me?"

Elizabeth nodded and held her arms out for Daniel. He climbed into her lap, sleepy as they drifted toward the end of the service. Ezra took his mother's place between Roseanna and Sophia and watched his father.

Gideon started his sermon.

"I will be speaking on the twelfth chapter of Hebrews, the first and second verses."

The pages of the Bible rustled in the quiet room as he turned to the passage. As Gideon read the verses, Elizabeth heard them as if they were birds' wings beating a soft thrum on her heart. When he reached the phrase "the sin that so easily besets us," she thought of how a crow will struggle to fly away from the smaller birds that attack it when it comes too close to their nest. She knew what it was to be beset by sin. Nothing had ever been able to remove that dark stain. She could almost feel the sharp beaks picking at her, attacking her, never letting her forget.

Then Gideon read, "'Looking unto Jesus, the author and finisher of our faith.'" Elizabeth didn't hear the rest of the verse. She had heard about Jesus all through her life, but had she ever looked to him?

Gideon finished reading and closed his eyes for a brief minute. When he opened them, he talked about the stain of sin and how there was nothing in one's own power that could remove that terrible curse. Elizabeth found herself nodding in agreement.

Then Gideon said, "But there is an answer. God has provided the way for you to be free of your sin."

Elizabeth leaned forward over Daniel's sleeping body, but his next words were lost when Ruby came back and pushed past Elizabeth to take her own seat. After Ruby had sat down again, holding a sleeping Lovinia, Elizabeth happened to look across the aisle and caught Solomon watching her. He nodded at the sleeping boy in her arms and smiled.

A warm wave of delight washed over Elizabeth and she

returned Solomon's smile. His message had been clear. He liked seeing her with her nephew in her arms. Solomon turned back to the front of the room and Elizabeth leaned down to kiss Daniel's sweaty forehead. Someday, perhaps soon, she could be holding her own child in her arms. A child that was wanted and loved, not rejected by his father.

She stroked Daniel's cheek, dreaming of that day, until Gideon's voice stopped speaking and the ministers stood to close the service. Whatever she had missed of Gideon's sermon didn't matter anymore.

After the fellowship meal, Levi joined the other men standing in the doorway of the large bank barn. The doors were swung wide at both ends of the building and the gentle breeze cooled the shaded bay. The rafters in the open haymow tossed the men's voices back to them in soft echoes.

"What did you think of the ministers' meeting last week?" Simeon asked. "I wanted to go, but I had a cow about to calve and couldn't leave."

Abraham lifted his eyebrows. "A heifer?"

"Healthy as I could ask for. She's out there with her mamm now." Simeon pointed out the far door at a brown cow and calf in the meadow. The calf was nearly hidden by the tall grass.

Gideon leaned against the doorframe. "The meeting went like I expected."

"You mean they ignored us," Caleb Lehman said. "The tradition-minded men had drawn up a fine document stating our views and they didn't even discuss it."

"At least they read it," Levi said. "I never expected it would be discussed."

"It's as if they mean to drive us out of our own church," Gideon said. "I fear the split that started in Indiana will spread to the rest of the communities."

Casper Zook pulled at his beard. "The change-minded folks are the ones leaving and they will never come back. They're adopting new worldly inventions as fast as they can."

"Photographs and lightning rods," said Caleb.

"Holding political office," Simeon added.

"Building churches and holding Sunday schools," said Solomon.

"What is so bad about Sunday schools?" Aaron asked. He looked around at the men. "Other churches have them."

"Sunday schools are acceptable if they are done carefully and don't take the place of the parents' instruction," Abraham said. "My main objection to them is that they separate families when the children are still at a tender age. But we don't adopt changes only because other churches have. We are called to follow God's direction, not the world's. And especially not the churches of this world."

The men were silent for a few minutes. Levi watched the folks gathered in small groups in the shaded yard behind the Kecks' big farmhouse. The children played a game of tag while their mothers watched. Older women sat in a circle under the biggest tree listening to something Lydia was telling them. The older boys huddled near the pasture where the horses were grazing, furtively glancing at the group of older girls gathered at the kitchen door.

Levi grinned. Not too long ago, he and Jonas and the others would be pretending to watch the horses while keeping a close eye on the girls. Now most of their group were married as well as those girls. He and Jonas were the only bachelors left from their group of friends, and he hoped Jonas wouldn't remain unmarried for long. Father and the other ministers had discussed his situation at the end of the ministers' meeting in Wayne County. Levi hadn't heard the results of that discussion yet, but Father needed to tell Jonas what they decided before anyone else did.

His gaze slid over to the group of young women, many of them girls when he and Jonas had idled their Sunday afternoons away with the fellows. Some were married, some not. None of them had children old enough to play tag with the others. It didn't take long for him to find Elise. She sat next to Millie, with one of the twins on her lap. She laughed at something Millie said and her face was as joyous as a lark's song. Even though her smile wasn't aimed at him, it found a target and wound itself around his heart.

"What do you think, Levi?" Gideon asked.

Levi felt his face heat as the others waited for his answer.

"I'm sorry. I missed what you were talking about."

"Too busy watching the scenery," someone said, and the others chuckled.

"What will you do if the change-minded faction decides to leave the church? Should we try to force them to stay?"

He cleared his throat. He wasn't asked to share his opinion very often. "You can't force someone to go against their conscience, even if you think they're wrong. If we try to force them to remain united to us, the only result would be discontent and complaints. I think we should approach their decision the same as when an individual leaves the church. If they are sinning, we need to shun them until they repent." Levi wiped the trickling sweat from his forehead as the men nodded in agreement. "But I'm not convinced that they are sinning. We have a difference of opinion regarding certain things, but those things are contrary to our traditions, not the teaching in the Bible."

"Even when they take photographs?" Solomon crossed his arms. "Isn't that a graven image?"

"I've heard some say that," Levi said. He spoke carefully so he wouldn't be misunderstood. "I don't think a photograph is breaking the second commandment. When you read through the commandments in the Bible, it is clear that God is forbidding us from worshiping idols, especially images we might try to make of God. But a photograph or an engraving, capturing a moment in time in a visual way, is innocent. It is only the sin in our own hearts that is a danger when we are tempted to use it as an object of our worship."

Perspiration prickled on his back as he looked around the circle of men. He had never spoken at such length before in a group like this, with men listening who were older and wiser than he was. Their faces were thoughtful. Some were nodding in agreement.

"Well said, Levi." Casper Zook smiled at him. "That was a prudent answer and one we should remember. The change-minded group are still our brothers in Christ, no matter what we may think of their actions."

The conversation continued as Levi left the group. The sight of Elise's face . . . had it given him the courage to speak his mind like that? He searched for her among the women, but the seat next to Millie was empty.

He walked down to the house to get a drink and found her next to the well. She was trying to pump some water for herself and hold the cup under the waterspout at the same time.

"Can I help you?" The question sounded silly to his ears. Levi nearly ran back the way he had come.

Then she smiled at him. "If you pump it, I'll fill the cup and we can both have a drink."

He worked the handle until the water began to flow. It filled the small tin cup to the brim and spilled over onto the grass at their feet. She laughed and his heart squeezed.

"Are you enjoying your new home here?"

She nodded and handed the cup to him. "The other girls are very friendly. I've been invited to stay for the Singing tonight, and Datt has said I may." She smiled. "I hope you will be staying also."

Levi smiled back. He was too old to go to the Singing and hadn't attended for several years. But if Elise was going, he wouldn't miss it.

"Only if I may walk you home afterward."

She blushed a pretty shade of pink. "I would like that."

He handed the cup back to her. "Then it's all arranged."

Their fingers met around the cup and she dropped her gaze to the ground.

"Elise—" Levi stopped. What should he say? He didn't know her well enough to ask if she felt the same as he did. "Elise, I hope no one else will ask to take you home."

She looked at him again. "Even if someone else does ask, I'll tell him he's too late. I'm already walking home with the finest man in the church."

Levi's face burned, but it was worth all the embarrassment to hear her say those words.

⁓

Even though no work was done on Sunday, certain chores were necessary. Aaron had started doing the Sunday evening chores a few weeks ago to give Abraham a rest, and he found he enjoyed it. Taking over the Sunday evening responsibilities was little enough compared to what Jonas and his family had done for him.

He took the stool from its hook on the wall and placed the milk pail under the cow's udder. She was an old cow and used to the morning and evening routine. She turned to look at him as he milked, strands of hay sticking out on each side of her mouth.

"You're all right, Bossy, you know I'll take good care of you."

The milk pinged in the pail until he had milked enough to cover the bottom. Aaron leaned his head against the cow's flank, taking in the comfortable fragrance of fresh milk and sweet hay. Even the odor of manure couldn't overpower the pleasant aromas of the barn but settled underneath it like a rich foundation.

The barn cats had heard the sound of milking. One twined itself around his ankle while the others sat in a circle, watching him. They knew he would pour a little fresh milk into a pan for them when he was done, but a few sat up on their haunches, begging for an early taste. He aimed one of the teats in their direction and squeezed. The big gray cat was an expert and caught the entire stream in its mouth. The black-

and-white one tried to bite at the milk and ended up covered with white drops. Aaron chuckled as it quickly cleaned its face before the drops disappeared.

He stopped in surprise. When was the last time he had laughed? The cow stomped a foot in protest, and he started the rhythmic milking again. He hadn't felt this comfortable and settled since . . .

Aaron thought back. Not at all while he was in the army. Every day he had lived in anxious fear that death would strike without warning. That the next artillery shell or musket ball heading his way would be the last one he would ever hear—if he heard it at all. And during the long days between battles, he lived as the other soldiers did. Bitter, angry, and hungry. Cold in the winter and hot in the summer. Nothing brought joy, even though he had tried nearly every diversion available.

Even the weekly church services he attended failed to satisfy his longings. He had sat in the back, in the shadowy edges, watching the preacher's face lit by a half-dozen campfires circling him. He had gone for the music. The hymns the men had sung reminded him of home. The home he had known before Ma died.

Closing his eyes, Aaron let his cheek rest against the soft flank as if it were Ma's bosom. If he listened closely, he could hear her singing to him. But when he opened his eyes again, it was still all gone. Destroyed. He was the only one left.

Not the only one. He smiled. The Zooks had taken him in as if they had known him from the time of his birth. Even though none of them had known Grandpop, they had accepted him for the old man's sake, and for Casper's father's sake. Both men gone, but their memories lived on in their descendants. Aaron whooshed out a breath. It was hard to get accustomed to, but he had a family. Dan and Ephraim were his cousins. Their children were part of him, carrying on a legacy he only knew from Grandpop's stories.

Grandpop had never returned home to his family, but Aaron had that chance. He could plant himself among the Zooks and others from the church, if he wanted to.

That was the problem. What did he want? He couldn't go home, and he couldn't see what was ahead. Anything beyond now was a shadowy haze.

He finished the milking, poured the cats' milk into the pan, then set the pail next to the door, covered with a towel and ready to take to the springhouse.

Leaning against the doorframe, he watched the sun lowering into a bank of clouds in the west, lighting the sky with colors so vivid he longed to grasp and hold them. The children were playing near the barn in the little playhouse Abraham had made for his grandchildren. Ezra and Daniel chased each other in and out while the older ones tried to catch the fireflies that were beginning to appear as the twilight cast its glow.

Aaron's breath caught. This . . . this was what he wanted. Not a western town where he would be a nameless stranger. Not a world where every day was a fight for a few pennies to survive. He wanted a life with a family. With children who hunted for fireflies, and a wife . . . He swallowed, casting his gaze back into the barn where the horses waited for their supper. A useless dream. No woman would marry half a man. The shadowed interior of the barn revealed the same future he saw for himself. Nothing. No answers anywhere.

The horses were gathered at the back door of the barn,

waiting to come in for their evening feeding. The team of big draft horses needed grain, even after a day of rest. Tomorrow would bring another long day of work for them. Aaron undid the clasp that held the gate closed and then started pouring the measures of grain into their feedboxes. One for each horse.

The children's voices grew louder. At first, Aaron thought they were playing a different game, but then he heard the shouts for help. He dropped the grain scoop and hurried outside. When he saw five-year-old Ezra in the pasture with Abraham's bull, he ran for the fence, thrusting himself forward with his good leg and pivoting on his wooden peg. He scrambled over the fence and dropped on the other side.

The bull didn't look his way. The beast must have broken through the fence again. His attention was on the boy in front of him. Ezra stood about ten feet away from Samson and too far away from Aaron. The big beast shook its head and grunted.

"Ezra." Aaron kept his voice calm as he slowly got to his feet. "Don't move."

"I didn't know Samson was in this pasture," Ezra said, his voice quivering. "I thought it was empty." The bull raked at the ground with one hoof.

"Don't talk." Aaron swallowed, watching the bull. "Just stand still."

Aaron took a slow step toward the boy. The animal cast one glance his way, the red eye rimmed with white. Aaron stopped and licked his dry lips. Ezra was frozen in place, his gaze locked on the bull. He had to make sure the boy would be able to follow his directions.

"Ezra, look at me."

The boy pulled his gaze away from the bull and turned a pale face toward Aaron.

"Can you take a step backward? Just one step. Very slow."

Ezra lifted his left foot and put it behind his right heel. As he moved, the bull grunted again and tossed its head.

Aaron tried to judge the distance between him and Ezra. He only had one chance, and when he acted, the bull would charge. Just beyond Ezra was a shallow depression in the ground. That low spot was his only chance to save the boy. Aaron tightened his muscles, ready to jump.

"I'm going to save you, Ezra. Don't worry. Just stay where you are."

Movement off to the side distracted him. The other men, racing from the house. The bull saw them, too, and bellowed. They wouldn't reach the pasture in time.

The big animal dug his hind feet into the turf, propelling himself forward, and Aaron leaped, running at full speed. He grabbed Ezra and rolled into that hole, covering the boy with his body.

The ground shook as the bull overran them. As it passed over the depression where Aaron pressed their bodies as close to the ground as he could, a blow hit Aaron on the back of the head as strong as the percussion explosion of artillery. He crouched over Ezra, using his body as a shield. The bull would turn at the end of his run and come back.

Aaron glanced up and saw the horns flash in the last light of the setting sun. Flashing like the fire from the Yankee artillery. A roaring bellow split the air just as he heard the explosion. It was the last he knew.

11

Elizabeth volunteered to sit with Aaron on Thursday. She had avoided the task all week, but Mamm and the others were making cheese in Anna's dairy at Samuel's house across the road. With Solomon's interest in her at the top of her mind, she wasn't sure she could keep from talking about him during the work frolic, and she wanted to keep these new feelings close to her heart for now.

She wrung out a cloth in the basin of cool water and replaced the warm one lying across Aaron's forehead. Her biggest job was to keep the stubborn man in bed when he was awake. The bull's hoof clipped the back of his head as he had crouched over Ezra, protecting him, and Mamm said the best way to recover from an injury like that was to rest for at least a week, perhaps more.

Whenever he was awake, Aaron insisted he was ready to work, but Mamm was firm, and Elizabeth trusted her judgment on injuries and illnesses. She resisted smoothing the vertical line between his eyebrows, evidence of the pain he was suffering.

In the weeks she had known Aaron, becoming acquainted with him and even becoming friends, Elizabeth had never taken the time to look closely at him. He didn't appear like the Amish men she knew. His face was lean, his cheeks hollow. His hair was as wiry as his beard and hard to tame. Mamm had cut it shorter than Aaron had been wearing it to make caring for him easier, and now it looked more like an Amishman's simple cut. But his beard and mustache were thick and long. And red. As red and hairy as Esau in the Bible.

She removed the cloth and replaced it with a new one, pushing his hair off his forehead. She stroked it again. It didn't feel as wiry as it looked. It felt soft, like a lamb's woolly coat. She paused. Was his beard that soft? Or was it coarse like Reuben's had been? Her fingers curled in anticipation. No one would know if she felt it. She was alone in the house with the sleeping man.

Letting her hand drift down to his chest, Elizabeth took the edge of his beard between her fingers. Not as soft as the hair on his head, but still—

A rough hand caught hers and she looked up to see Aaron's blue eyes watching her. She snatched her hand back and buried it in her lap.

"You're awake."

His mouth twitched in a smile. "I'm awake."

Elizabeth's face was burning. "How long have you been watching me?"

"Long enough. I was dreaming that Ma was waking me up in the morning, but when I opened my eyes, it was you."

A memory from long ago flashed through Elizabeth's mind: her mother stroking her hair to awaken her in the morning. She had forgotten that in the intervening years. How many mornings had Mamm gently woke her in that way? Yet she had turned her back on her loving family, thinking she knew best. She shook her head to dispel the memories.

"How are you feeling?"

"Like I'm tired of staying in this bed." Aaron glanced at her. "I'm sorry. It isn't your fault I'm here."

"How can I help you?"

"Tell me what's going on outside of this room. Is Ezra all right?"

"Ja, he's fine. The bull isn't, though. Datt says he won't have an animal on the farm that's a danger to anyone."

"He shot it, didn't he?"

"Just before it was going to run over you again." Elizabeth closed her eyes, but that didn't erase the image of the bull running down Aaron and Ezra. "I'm glad you weren't hurt any more than you are."

"What else? How is Jonas?"

"He had his meeting with the ministers. They're going to let him join the church."

"And that means he can marry Katie, right?"

Elizabeth grinned. "I'm so happy for them." She looked at the clock. It was almost noon. "Are you hungry?"

He stretched, his long arms reaching above his head. "Hungry and thirsty. I'll go down to the kitchen and get my dinner."

"You will not. Mamm says you're not well enough to go

downstairs yet." She straightened the light blanket covering him. "I'll slice some bread and cheese for you."

"Is there any of that summer sausage left?"

She smiled. His hunger was a good sign that he was improving. "I'll bring some of that too." She started toward the door. "Don't try to get out of bed. Mamm wants you to stay there."

"I have to get out of bed, but I won't leave the room. Just be sure to knock before you come back in."

By the time she had fixed a plate for each of them and took them back upstairs, he responded to her knock with a grunt. When she opened the door, he was sitting on the edge of the bed, wearing a clean shirt and loose trousers. Drops of water sparkling in his beard told her that he had washed up, but he leaned his head into his hand.

Elizabeth watched him for a moment. When he didn't move, she adjusted his pillows and helped him recline on them. The pillows were stacked so he could sit up enough to eat without choking, but he could rest his head back whenever he wanted. Then she lifted his good leg up onto the bed next to the stump of his other leg and covered him with the blanket up to his waist. His eyes remained closed.

"Aaron," she said, sitting on the chair next to his bed and picking up his plate, "eat something. It might make you feel better."

He opened his eyes and reached for a slice of bread. As he chewed, he leaned back and stared at the ceiling.

"Did you overestimate your strength?"

Aaron attempted to nod, then winced. "I was all right until I bent down to pull on my trousers. I've spent enough time being sick and crippled since I was wounded last year and I'm tired of it. All I can think is that if I just make myself get out of this bed, I'll work through the pain."

"If you try to work now, you'll only make the injury worse. You know that. Mamm says you need to rest until Saturday, then you can get out of bed. But no strenuous work for several days after that."

He took another bite of his bread. "You said Ezra is all right. He wasn't injured?"

"Not hurt at all, thanks to you. He has promised he will never go into a pasture without looking to see what animals are there first." She picked up her own slice of bread and laid a piece of cheese on it. "You were very brave. You could have been killed."

"I'm not brave. I just knew I couldn't stand by and watch that bull run the boy down without trying to do something."

"But you risked your life. Not many men would do that, especially men with . . ." She let her voice trail off.

"You mean because I'm only half a man?" His voice was bitter. Caustic.

"That isn't what I meant. Just because you're missing a leg doesn't mean you're not a man. You proved that when you saved Ezra. But your missing leg would have given you a good excuse to do nothing."

His eyes narrowed. "I only did what needed to be done."

Elizabeth broke a piece of her cheese in half. "I don't know many men who would have seen it that way, except perhaps Solomon." Surely, he would have leaped into the pasture to rescue a little boy.

"Do you believe Solomon would have tried to save Ezra?"

He stuffed the crust of his bread into his mouth. He spoke around the food, his words muffled. "Somehow, I don't think so."

Elizabeth took a small bite of her bread, chewing it slowly. Of course, Solomon would have, her mind protested. But she turned in her chair so Aaron couldn't see her thoughts as they flitted through her mind and across her face. She had to admit that she couldn't imagine Solomon running to intercept that bull the way Aaron had.

"I hope Solomon would have rescued Ezra. He's a good Amishman and would risk himself for those of the community."

Aaron set his plate aside, one slice of bread left uneaten. "Do you really know him, Elizabeth? Is he the kind of man you want to spend time with?"

She snapped her head in his direction. She had never spoken those ideas aloud, but they had played at the back of her mind.

"You've seen the kind of man he is," she said. She took a deep breath remembering the look in Solomon's eyes when she told him she hadn't found Reuben's papers yet. Was she trying to convince Aaron, or herself?

Aaron reached for her hand and she tried to pull it out of his grasp as she set her plate down.

"I have seen the kind of man he is." He tightened his grip on her hand and pulled her closer. "I've met him before. He denies it, but I know I saw him in Virginia during the war."

"That can't be true. He is from Pennsylvania."

"I couldn't forget his voice, his stance, and his veiled threats. He's a dangerous man." He dropped her hand and rubbed his head along his hairline like his headache had suddenly grown worse. "I hate to see you ruin your life with him."

Elizabeth pressed her lips together. Aaron Zook had no right to talk to her this way. She held her fist to her mouth as her chin started quivering. And what he didn't know was that her life was ruined anyway.

"You don't know what you're talking about. Solomon is . . . is a good man." She hiccupped. "He is Amish and—"

"And I'm not." Aaron's voice was bitter again. "He's a whole man and I'm not. He's a wealthy landowner and I'm not." He glared at her. "If you don't want to listen to me, then go away. I don't need your company. I promise I won't try to get out of bed."

He slumped down under the covers and turned his back to her.

Elizabeth picked up the plates and walked to the door. As she turned to close it behind her, she looked at that hard back again. He knew nothing about Solomon. She slammed the door and went down the stairs to the kitchen.

~

Aaron was feeling good the next Monday but still took Jonas's advice to hitch up the horse and wagon rather than walk to the Zooks' harness shop. He chuckled to himself as he tossed the harness up onto Rusty's back, remembering the first time he had tried to harness the horse alone. He had his strength back, he was steady on his feet. Or foot. And his headaches had dwindled to a reasonable level.

On Sunday afternoon, a week after the incident with the

bull, most of the community had stopped by the Weavers' farm to see how he was faring. He had sat on the back porch, Ezra close by his side. The little boy didn't seem to notice Aaron's missing leg as he listened to the adults talk about bulls and how dangerous they could be. Everyone seemed to have a story about a run-in with a bull, and every one of the men shook Aaron's hand, thanking him for his heroic action.

By the end of the afternoon he still didn't feel heroic, but he felt welcomed like he had never felt before. Except for Elizabeth—and he couldn't reckon why it bothered him so much when she ignored him. She hadn't come to visit him or her parents since Thursday when she had refused to listen to his advice about Solomon Mast.

Only that wasn't his name. Aaron had spent the hours through Thursday afternoon and evening searching through his memory, and that name wasn't one he recognized. He had even started doubting that he had the right man again, until the name slipped into his consciousness. The spy in the camp when Aaron was in the Shenandoah had been called Simon Miller. Rumors had been that he was a Mennonite farmer who helped both sides destroy the rich farms up and down the valley to prevent their enemies from living off the land.

A waste of resources, for sure, but the generals had all said it was the way to win a war. That might be so, but it still didn't change the fact that all the officers, even a captain like himself, knew that Simon Miller was a snake. A useful spy, but not a man to be trusted.

Then late on Thursday night while lying awake with that pounding headache, Aaron had remembered another rumor that had circulated around the camp when they were in the same area as Simon Miller. The rumor of a predator who attacked girls and young women among the Mennonite and Dunker farms and small towns in the southern Shenandoah Valley. Folks had speculated that the man could be one of the soldiers, but Aaron had been tempted to connect that rumor with the spy. The thought that Solomon Mast could be that man made his blood run cold, but he blamed his imagination. No girls or women had gone missing since Solomon had moved into the Weaver's Creek area. He had dismissed the thoughts and tried to sleep.

Solomon was still on his mind when he turned the horse into the Zooks' farm lane and pulled to a halt outside the harness shop. He had been here often since Casper and the rest of the family had moved to the area, and he knew Dan's boy Cap would be watching for him.

He was right. The ten-year-old had seen him coming and ran from the house to greet him.

"I thought you'd never get here."

Aaron used his cane to steady himself after climbing down from the wagon seat and tousled the boy's hair. "I'm here right when I told your grandpop I would be." He started toward the horse's head to tie him to the hitching rail. "What are you up to today?"

"I'm going to hoe the garden for Mamm. She says the weeds are about to overrun everything and steal all our food."

"Then you have an important job, all right."

Aaron started to tie the lead rope to the rail, but Cap took it from him.

"I'll put Rusty in the pasture for you. *Grossdawdi* says you're going to be here all day."

"Thank you." Aaron grinned at the exasperated look on the boy's face. "All right. In Deitsch. Denki, Cap."

Aaron walked into the harness shop. Just as he expected, Casper was already at the workbench, cutting the strips of leather needed for a set of harnesses from a tanned cowhide.

"Where can I start?" Aaron asked.

Casper finished the strip he was working on and pushed it off the worktable onto a pile of others.

"This harness has been ordered by an Englischer in Berlin. He wants it double strength for his driving carriage. I've already dyed the leather black, and next we'll need to measure the lengths of the straps and sew them together." He turned to a large paper tacked to the wall with the various parts of the harness listed, their measurements, and the number needed next to each one. "We'll work off this list. As you finish each piece, you can mark it off with the pencil there. Start wherever you have a mind to."

"Will Dan and Ephraim be working on it, too?"

"They're in the tanning shed, getting hides ready for the next project after this."

Aaron started sorting through the pile of straps for the sizes he needed. "What's that project?"

"A set of horse collars. Have you ever made one?"

"It will be something new for me. I hope I'm around long enough to learn how to make them."

Casper picked up his knife and rotated the cowhide to the side he wanted. "Why wouldn't you be here?"

"Ever since the war, I thought I might go west. There are a lot of opportunities out there for a man who needs a fresh start." Especially a fresh start away from Elizabeth Kaufman.

If she still thought Solomon Mast was a good choice, he would have to move on.

The older man worked silently for a few minutes while Aaron measured the straps and trimmed them to the right size.

"What do you think you will find out there that we don't have here?"

Aaron shaved a jagged spot on the edge of the leather until it was smooth. "For one thing . . ." He stopped, trying to think of what had drawn him to the West when he had heard the other southerners talking about it, other than a place to escape from the memories. "For one thing, a man won't be judged by which side he fought for in the war."

"Do you think we judge you?"

"Ne, but an Englischer might."

"What else?"

"I could establish my own business there, build a home, and start a family."

"It's hard to start a new business from the beginning." Casper finished with the hide he had been working on and slid another one from the big table where they were stored onto his work surface. "Why not work here with us?"

"I couldn't do that," Aaron said, turning away from Casper as he selected the right size awl from the rack above the bench. "The three of you have a family business. Tobias should be the next man you take on."

"Are you saying you can't be part of it because you aren't one of my sons?" Casper dropped his knife on the table and walked over to Aaron. "You are family. You're one of us."

Aaron turned the awl between his fingers, still not looking at the man who was Pa's cousin. He had been playing at belonging in this family. They had been gracious, going along with it. But now they were talking about a business, not a family reunion. As much as he would like to stay and be part of this community, he hadn't been born to it. Belonging wasn't something he could claim.

"I need to make a home for myself." He looked at Casper. "I don't really belong here, you know that. I'm an Englischer. An outsider."

Casper kept his gaze on Aaron's face, the wrinkles around his eyes softening into a look that was the same as one Aaron had seen on Grandpop's face many times. The look that was willing him to understand.

"A home. That's what you're looking for? A place to belong?"

The sweetness Aaron had felt as he stood in the doorway of Abraham's barn last week flooded his senses. A home.

He nodded.

"You won't find it out west. You won't find it anywhere you go looking for it. Home is right here. Now." He spread his arms to take in the workshop and everything beyond it. "Home is with these people and in this place." He poked his forefinger into Aaron's chest. "Where God is, that's your home. And he is where you are."

Aaron stared at his feet, thinking. If Casper was right, then . . . "I don't need to go anywhere?" Saying it felt good. "I'm already home?"

Casper nodded. "That's right. Because home isn't a building, or a farm, or a business. It's where you belong. The place where God has brought you to and with folks who love you." He took a step closer to Aaron. "Do you want my advice?"

Aaron nodded.

"Stay here. Join the church. Learn to know us better and be part of our family. We'll help you build your own house, your own place on Zook land. Then find the right woman to marry."

Casper's words described a dream that danced in the air just beyond his reach. "Did you forget that I'm not a whole man?"

Casper laid his hand on Aaron's arm. "No man is whole when he is by himself. All of us are broken on the inside until we find our place with God—broken, sore, and weary. Your brokenness is visible, but the solution is the same as it is for any other man. God will make you whole."

Aaron couldn't speak.

Casper patted his arm, then went back to his worktable. "Think about it, son. I would hate to see you leave us to chase a dream that you'll never catch."

Picking up the awl and a hammer, Aaron started the slow process of marking the stitches in the leather. As he worked, a song Ma used to sing formed itself in his mind.

> *Come, ye sinners, poor and needy,*
> *weak and wounded, sick and sore.*

That described him for certain and sure. He couldn't remember the next line, but it had something to do with Jesus curing all those ills, like Casper had described. A whole man.

He hummed the tune as he continued his work, and another line came into his memory.

> *If you tarry till you're better,*
> *you will never come at all.*

The awl wavered and he dropped the hammer onto the workbench. The last eight months he had been waiting until he was healthy again. Waiting until he was back to normal. Waiting until he was better. A better man than he was now. But too much had happened. He had seen too much. The brokenness would never heal itself.

If you tarry till you're better,
you will never come at all.

⁓

Elizabeth stood in the old cabin on Reuben's farm on Wednesday morning. With the beam lying on the floor, chinking pried out from between the logs, and dirt and debris everywhere, it was no longer a place anyone could live. The best thing that could happen to it was for lightning to strike and burn it down.

She turned in a circle, looking for any spot she might have missed. Aaron had taken a methodical approach the day he helped her, examining the walls inch by inch, while she had gone from place to place, searching everywhere she thought Reuben might have hidden the box. Behind the bed, inside the fireplace, in the kitchen cabinets. But it hadn't turned up for either of them.

Perhaps there was a place for the box higher up in the chimney than she could reach. Walking over to the fireplace again, her shoes thumped against the wooden floor. Then one footstep sounded different. Elizabeth tried the spot again, stomping her foot on it, then stomping on the floorboard next to it. The first spot sounded hollow. It had been underneath the bed until she had pulled it away from the wall.

As she knelt on the floor, trying to pry the board loose with her fingers, Elizabeth imagined the look on Solomon's face when she finally brought him the papers. He said he hadn't been successful in Millersburg. Either Reuben had never filed their marriage certificate, or it had never existed. More than anything, she wanted to prove to Solomon that she could be the kind of woman he thought she was. Honorable, truthful, faithful. A good Amish wife.

Before the floorboard gave way, Elizabeth had broken two fingernails. But no matter. When she lifted the board out of its place, she found a square hole dug into the dirt beneath the floor. And in the hole was a dull, rectangular metal box. She snatched it from its resting place and took it out into the morning sunlight. This was it. This was the box she had seen in Reuben's hands the night she lost her baby. Her hands shook and she whooshed out a breath along with the lingering threads of the painful memory. That was in the past. This box held the key to her future.

She pried it open. The box was full of paper. On the top was money. Elizabeth lifted the stack of bills out and counted it. Nearly one hundred dollars, all in Confederate money. Useless to anyone now.

Underneath the money were folded documents. As she opened the first one, she could tell it was the deed to Reuben's one hundred sixty acres, with an additional paper declaring that the mortgage had been paid in full. The second document was faded, but legible. A marriage certificate, stating when she and Reuben had been married. At the bottom was another paper, the letter Reuben had received after his father had passed away. She kept the marriage certificate and the deed but placed everything else back in the box. After she returned the box to its place under the floorboard, she started off for Solomon's house.

As she drove Pie up the hill, she dusted off her skirt as well as she could. Solomon wouldn't want to see her in such a state, but he was anxious to see these papers. She couldn't take the time to go home and change her clothes.

Solomon must have seen her coming. He stood on the top step of the porch watching her drive toward him. His face wore a frown, but that wouldn't last long once he saw what she had.

As she pulled Pie to a halt at the hitching rail, she waved the folded documents. "I found them!"

She had been right. His face opened into a wide smile as he bounded down the steps and gave her his hand to help her out of the buggy.

"I'm so glad, my dear. This is the deed?"

Elizabeth nodded as she brushed a cobweb off her sleeve. "And the marriage certificate. I came over as quickly as I could after finding them."

"Come in. I assume you have not had lunch yet?"

She shook her head and let him take her arm as they went into the house.

"I'll ask Dulcey to fix a meal for you. Perhaps the two of you could eat together in the kitchen and become better acquainted."

Dulcey stood at the kitchen door, smiling at Elizabeth.

"I would like that very much." She smiled back at the woman she hoped would be a good friend and companion.

"Take your time and visit all you want. After I look through the papers you brought, I have some work to do in the barn, so I won't disturb you."

Elizabeth followed Dulcey through the swinging door into the kitchen.

"It will just take a minute to fix your lunch, Miss Elizabeth."

"Just call me Elizabeth, please. And I'll call you Dulcey. If we're going to be friends, then we shouldn't let formalities stand in the way."

"No, Miss."

Elizabeth gave up. "I can fix my own lunch if you tell me where things are."

"Oh, no, Miss. I can't do that. You set yourself down and I'll do it." She hesitated. "And I'll fix enough for the two of us so we can eat together?"

"For sure we should eat together. How can we visit if we don't?"

Dulcey worked quickly, slicing some cold chicken and arranging it on two plates with a dish made from peas with a creamy sauce. She also put a plate of sliced bread on the table and two glasses of water. Then Elizabeth bowed her head for her usual silent prayer, but Dulcey prayed aloud.

"Dear Father, Lord of all of us. Hear our prayer of thanksgiving for this meal you done given us, and for the life you done given us, and all. In Jesus' name, Amen."

Then Dulcey started eating, not looking at Elizabeth once.

Solomon had said they should visit, but Dulcey looked so nervous that Elizabeth didn't know how to start.

Finally, she asked, "How did you come to start working for Solomon?"

Dulcey looked startled, then glanced at the door before she answered. "Masta Solomon found me working in . . . in Millersburg. I wasn't happy in that place, so he offered me this job."

"Do you enjoy working for him?"

"Oh, yes, Miss. Masta Solomon is a fine man. Always treats me well." Dulcey's hands shook as she took some of the peas on her fork. "And you? Masta Solomon says you is widowed?"

"Yes, I am. My husband was killed in the war."

Tears welled in Dulcey's eyes and she rose from the table. She walked over to the swinging door but didn't open it. She stood as if she was listening. When she came back, she took Elizabeth's hands in her own and leaned close to her.

"You are a nice woman, Elizabeth."

Dulcey's voice was a whisper so low that Elizabeth had to lean closer to hear her.

"So are you. I know we'll be good friends."

Dulcey shook her head emphatically. "No, Miss. No. You need to go away from here. Don't ever come back. Masta Solomon, he ain't the kind of man you think he is."

Elizabeth looked into the young woman's eyes. They were filled with tears.

"I trust Solomon. He's never given me any reason not to."

"You listen to me. I was married, but I lost my man during the war. He may be dead, he may have just run off. But after emancipation, I had nowhere to go. You understand? Nowhere. I had to eat. I went from place to place, following that North Star to the land of promise I heard tell of all my life, but when I got across the river, nothing was different than in the South. Freedom don't fill no stomachs. I found a job in a terrible place, but I didn't starve. I did what I had to in order to survive."

Pulling her lip between her teeth, Elizabeth stood on the brink of that whirlpool spiraling downward, leading to that dark pit. She knew. Oh, she knew what a woman would do when she had no other choice.

"I understand." She turned Dulcey's hands in her own and squeezed them gently. "I know exactly what you mean."

Dulcey's smile was grim. "Masta Solomon, he found me there. Said he had work for me if I would take it. He don't pay me like he said he would, and he beats me some, but I eat and I got a dry place to sleep." A tear escaped from one eye and rolled down her cheek. "But I can't do what he wants me to do now."

Elizabeth's stomach twisted. The Solomon Dulcey described couldn't be the man she knew . . . or thought she knew. He would never beat a woman, would he?

"What does he want you to do?"

"He wants me to find out things about you to use against you. He wants you to tell me things you wouldn't tell anyone else."

"Why?"

A thump sounded from beyond the kitchen wall. Dulcey jumped in her seat, her eyes wide.

"I daren't say, Miss. Just tell me something, please." Her

voice had dropped to a soft whisper again. "Just tell me something he don't know."

Elizabeth's mind raced. Dulcey was frightened of Solomon, that was clear, but Solomon wasn't as threatening as Dulcey seemed to think. Elizabeth knew him well enough to know that. Solomon was nothing like Reuben had been. The poor woman must have been badly mistreated by her master when she was a slave and expected that same treatment from Solomon, but what could she do to help?

Suddenly, the words of Gideon's sermon came into her mind. *"God has provided the way for you to be free of your sin."*

She smiled, thinking she finally knew what Gideon had meant.

"Dulcey, God will help you and me. He will set us free."

She would be free from the memory of those sins that beset her by exposing them. She wouldn't hide Reuben's sins from the world anymore. She swallowed, hesitating. What would the other church members think of her if they heard?

But if she never told the secret, how would she ever gain her freedom from Reuben's hold over her?

"Tell Solomon that my husband caused our child to die before it was born because he thought he couldn't be its father."

Dulcey gripped her hands even harder. "Oh, my Lord, oh no."

"Reuben was a cruel man and a drunkard." Elizabeth could no longer see Dulcey's face because of the tears in her eyes, but she clung to the other woman's hands. "I've never told anyone this, Dulcey. It's a secret I thought I would take to my grave, but Reuben doesn't deserve for me to protect him anymore. You can tell Solomon that. If he thinks he can use it against me somehow, then let him."

"That is a terrible thing to keep hidden. It's the kind of thing that eats at your soul."

Elizabeth shuddered. Dulcey had described it exactly. Her soul had been eaten away, but no more.

"Do you think the Lord will help you now?" Dulcey's tone was that of a woman clinging to a slim thread of hope. "After all you been through, do you think he'll help you find peace?"

Elizabeth blinked away the tears and looked into Dulcey's face. "I'm certain he will. And he will help you too." What had Gideon said? "Turn to Jesus, Dulcey. He's the only one who can help us."

12

After months—years—of trying to walk through hidden, muddy trails, Aaron finally felt like his life was back on course. Talking to Casper on Monday had shown him that the Zooks didn't think of him as an unwanted tagalong cousin but saw him as part of the family. As they had continued working day after day on the order for the harness, Casper had talked about where they could build Aaron's house, and where his forty acres would be. Dan and Ephraim had purchased a one-hundred-sixty-acre quarter section when they came to Ohio, but Casper didn't want to farm anymore. The harness making work was enough for him, so he was glad to pass on his forty acres to Aaron. Eating with the family during the noon meals, he felt a sense of belonging he had never experienced before.

In the days since then, his path had been clear. He grinned as he fed grain to the horses in Abraham's barn on Saturday morning. Nothing was better for a man than knowing what he wanted out of life and how to achieve it.

Suddenly a forkful of hay fell out of the haymow and onto his head.

"Watch what you're doing!" He pulled his hat off and brushed bits of hay from the brim, his shoulders, down his front. He looked up to see Jonas's head through the opening.

"I didn't know you were there." Another forkful of hay dropped into the manger. "You need to make some noise while you work."

Finished with the hay, Jonas came down the ladder.

"You knew I was graining the horses," Aaron said, tossing some chaff in his friend's direction.

"But you usually whistle or something. Why are you so quiet this morning?"

Aaron put his hat back on and rolled his shoulders to try to dislodge the hayseeds and chaff stuck to his back. All thought of horseplay had disappeared with Jonas's question.

"What would you say if I stayed around Weaver's Creek?"

Jonas leaned his pitchfork against the horse stall. "You mean you've changed your mind? You don't want to go west anymore?"

He paused, sifting through the empty promises his plans had held. "I'm not sure if I ever really wanted to. During the war, it seemed to be the only way I could start my life over."

"I think that is wonderful." Jonas's grin was sincere. "We'd love to have you stay here. There's plenty of room."

Aaron looked at the floor. "That isn't the plan. The Zooks have offered me a place on their farm and as a harness maker. I'm learning a lot from Casper."

"A home?"

A sweet thrill ran through him at those words. He hoped

it would never feel too familiar. "A home. A house, a trade, a family." His throat squeezed at that last word. He had lost the only family he knew and now God was healing that broken place.

Jonas laughed with delight and slapped Aaron's back. "The next thing you'll tell me is that you're going to become Amish."

Grinning, Aaron returned Jonas's gesture. "I start meeting with Gideon for membership instruction next week."

Jonas turned serious. "Do you mean it?" He gazed into Aaron's face. "You do mean it! We'll become members at the same time, then. The ministers said I can start my membership instruction as soon as it can be arranged." He returned the pitchfork to its place on the wall and took down the mucking rake. "The only thing left for you is to find a wife."

As Jonas went into the back of the barn to start cleaning the cow's pen, Aaron walked to the doorway of the barn, the same place he had stood on the day Ezra wandered into the bull's pasture. The same feeling overwhelmed him, but this time coupled with a certainty that he would find his dream. Somewhere, there would be a woman who could overlook his missing leg.

He ran his hand under his shirt collar, brushing out particles of hay. None of the women he had known before he was wounded would have done that, though. The thought of one of those—he shook his head at the man he had been—one of those saloon girls living here in this peaceful setting was impossible. No, whoever he married would have to be a special woman. One who could see beyond the man he used to be, beyond his wounded exterior, to the man he was becoming.

Movement on the road caught his attention. It was Elizabeth, walking across the bridge toward the house. On her way to see her family. He watched her sure gait, her slim figure looking barely larger than a child's at this distance. He didn't have to be close to see the warmth in her eyes and the way those crinkles appeared around them when she laughed. But she was vulnerable. If only she would listen to him. If only she would let him . . . An ache started in his chest and spread to his shoulders, his arms, down to his fingers, causing him to clench his fists. He wanted to protect her, but she had turned her back on him, setting her cap for Solomon Mast. He couldn't think of marrying a woman whose dreams were so different from his. Just like the other women he had known, what a man appeared to be on the outside was the only thing that mattered to her.

He grabbed the other mucking fork from the wall and entered the nearest box stall. He couldn't change her and couldn't change the past. But—

Pausing, his load of soiled straw midway to the wheelbarrow, the truth hit him with the sifting thoroughness of a forkful of hay, filling every pore of his being. He loved her. He loved Elizabeth. He loved that exasperating, stubborn, willful, beautiful woman. Dumping the load into the wheelbarrow, Aaron let that knowledge take hold.

But what could he do? He couldn't force Elizabeth to love him. She had her sights set on someone else. With gritted teeth, he thrust the fork in the horse's bedding once more and tossed a load into the wheelbarrow.

Her love would be a precious thing to earn, but Solomon—Simon Miller—would only use her and throw her away.

187

Somehow, he had to find evidence to prove what he knew was true and convince her to trust him.

And if Simon Miller acted first, before Aaron could prove who he really was?

Aaron leaned on the fork and wiped his sweating brow. He would need to stick close to Elizabeth so he would be there to protect her. She might resent him. She might even refuse to let him near her. But at least she would be safe.

~

By Saturday, Elizabeth no longer cared who knew about the terrible secret she had held close for so long. As she walked to Mamm's house, an elusive breath of joy blew through her. She wasn't looking for pity, although that would be the reaction of some of the women. She refused to speculate what Salome's opinion would be. The most important thing was to tell Mamm before any hint of a rumor reached her. Then, if Solomon decided to use her secret against her, at least he wouldn't take Mamm by surprise.

Mamm was in the kitchen pulling fresh loaves of bread from the oven. Elizabeth took in a deep breath of the homey aroma. She had known Mamm would be baking this morning, just as she did every Saturday.

"I need to put the pies in the oven next," Mamm said as Elizabeth came in the kitchen door, "and then we'll sit down together for a chat."

Elizabeth pumped water into the big cast-iron teakettle and set it on the hottest part of the stove. While it was heating up, she took the jar of tea from the cupboard.

"What brings you by this morning?" Mamm put the last pie in the oven and sat at the table.

"I have something to tell you." Elizabeth got two mugs from the cupboard and set them on the table with the teapot.

Mamm smiled. "It must be good news. I haven't seen you look this content for a long time."

"It isn't good news. It's something I should have told you a long time ago."

Elizabeth joined Mamm at the table. It would be several minutes before the water was hot enough to brew the tea.

"So, it isn't something about Solomon?"

"It's about Reuben."

Now that the time had come, Elizabeth wasn't certain how to begin. Mamm sighed as if she was preparing herself.

Elizabeth put her hands on the table, lacing her fingers together. She concentrated on the way each finger curved around the one next to it. "Several years ago, I found out I was expecting a baby."

"Ach, Elizabeth. You never told me."

"I . . . I couldn't. I knew Reuben should be the first to know." She looked at her mother. "Isn't that right?"

Mamm nodded. "For sure. Your husband should have been the one to hear the news before anyone else."

"But when I told him—" Elizabeth bit her lip as tears welled in her eyes. "When I told him, he didn't believe me. And then he accused me—" She took a deep breath, willing her voice to remain steady until she had told the whole story. "He believed that he couldn't be the child's father. That someone else must have . . ."

She swallowed. No more words would come. The teakettle

started grumbling and Mamm rose to pour the hot water into the teapot to brew.

"So, Reuben didn't believe he was the father of your baby?" Mamm took Elizabeth's hands as she sat at the table again.

"He caused my baby to miscarry." The words rushed out. "I couldn't tell you. I was too ashamed and too scared."

"When you were married to him, I was afraid that he might have mistreated you. I felt like we had lost you and we didn't know what to do. How to reach out to you. But it sounds like your life was much harder than we imagined."

"It wasn't your fault. I could have come to you at any time . . . but I told myself that you wouldn't want me since I had turned my back on you and the family." Mamm started shaking her head and Elizabeth went on. "I know that isn't true. I should have come home as soon as I knew the terrible mistake I had made. But I didn't, and my baby paid for it with his life."

Mamm was silent as the clock in the front room ticked away the minutes. Finally, she spoke. "You can't blame yourself for what Reuben did. If he were still alive, I would have a hard time forgiving him for how he treated you and your child. But why are you telling me this now?"

"Because someone else knows about it." Elizabeth drew a deep breath. "I decided that I wasn't protecting anyone but Reuben by keeping that secret, but by burying it, I was reliving that horrible time over and over again. I wanted to be free."

"The truth shall set you free," Mamm said, a faint smile on her trembling lips.

Uneven footsteps on the back porch told Elizabeth that

Aaron was on his way in. She wiped any remaining tears with the edge of her apron and Mamm rose quickly and opened the oven to check on the pies. Aaron paused in the doorway.

"I didn't mean to interrupt anything," he said as he stood with one hand on the doorknob. "I just came in for the pail of slops for the pigs."

Elizabeth forced a smile as he went to the sink and lifted the pail from its spot underneath. He turned to go out again, then paused, looking at her.

"Is everything all right?"

"For sure it is." Elizabeth fought to keep her smile steady. "Why wouldn't it be?"

He glanced at Mamm, standing at the stove with her back to them, then at the still-empty mugs, then at Elizabeth again.

"No reason." He shifted the pail in his hand. "But if there is something wrong, I listen pretty well."

No man had ever wanted to listen to her problems, not since she was a little girl and Datt would take her on his lap. Aaron's offer tapped gently on a closed place in her heart.

"I'll remember that," she said.

After Aaron was on his way to the barn, Mamm came back to the table, a plate of piecrust cookies in her hand.

"I made these for your datt, but he won't miss a few."

Elizabeth picked up one of the diamond-shaped cookies dusted with cinnamon. For as long as she could remember, Mamm had made these cookies from the leftover scraps of piecrust dough on baking day. As she took a bite, the taste of the flaky pastry took her back to her childhood.

"Have I ever told you how sorry I am that I ever looked twice at Reuben?"

Mamm patted her hand. "I always knew the Good Lord would help you find your way through."

Elizabeth took another bite of her cookie. What would Mamm say if she knew about Solomon's intentions? He would be a man her parents would approve of, but Dulcey's warnings rang in her ears. Solomon couldn't be the man his servant had described, but only Dulcey knew what he was like behind closed doors. She reached for another cookie.

Solomon seemed to be the man who could make her dreams come true. He wanted children and was a good Amishman. He was friendly and helpful to everyone in the community. She wouldn't risk losing her chance at a good life just because Dulcey didn't like him.

"I can't get over how Aaron has changed," Mamm said, breaking into her thoughts. "When Jonas first brought him home, I didn't know what to think. He knew nothing about our ways and appeared to be so sickly. But he has learned our language and willingly goes to church with us, and it turns out that he's related to our Zook families."

"But he isn't Amish."

Mamm's eyebrows rose. "Does he need to be Amish?"

Elizabeth shook her head. "I thought you were getting ready to say he would make a good husband."

Laughing, Mamm squeezed her hand. "I don't know who would be a good husband for you, but if Aaron was Amish—if he joined the church—would you consider him for a husband? The two of you get along well."

"I made a promise to myself that I would never marry a man who wasn't Amish. I made that mistake once. Aaron isn't Amish, and I don't think he'll ever join the church. He wants to go west, not stay around here."

"You never know what might happen," Mamm said as she went to the oven to check on the pies.

Elizabeth finished her cup of tea. Solomon might not be perfect, but she could trust him to treat her well. He was the man to help her dream of having a family come true.

She reached for another cookie, ignoring the unsettled thoughts in the back of her mind.

One bothersome thing about Elizabeth Kaufman, Solomon thought as he fought boredom during the first sermon on Sunday morning, was that she was cautious. Too cautious.

He forced his knee to stop bouncing and glanced at the man sitting beside him. Amos Beiler sat with a straight back on his bench, gaze forward, as he watched Gideon Fischer preach, his eyes widening or narrowing, depending on whether he agreed with the point Gideon was making or not. In front of him, Abraham Weaver's head nodded.

Looking across the aisle to the women's side, he let a brief smile twitch his lips as he watched Salome. She had proven to be a better source of information than he had first thought. Thanks to her, there was little he didn't know about the members of the community.

The Beilers' home was too small for Sunday meeting, but they took their turn at hosting twice a year like everyone else. At least the place had plenty of windows on all sides of the house, and they were all open to the warm late-June air.

Solomon stifled a sigh. By the end of the morning, these backless benches would be torturous. But it was the price he needed to pay. A landholding the size he had his eyes on didn't come easy. He watched Abraham's snowy hair rub against the man's neck as his head bobbed. What had Weaver done to acquire his farm? No one achieved the success that he enjoyed without destroying a few lives to get there. Two sections of land, if he included Elizabeth's quarter section. One thousand two hundred eighty acres of prime farmland, and parts of it were still uncut timber. He flexed his fingers.

Old Abraham would die soon, and the Weaver land would be divided. Before then, he had to have Elizabeth's land firmly in his grasp. She was the key to everything.

The chatter he had heard this morning before the services started was unfortunate. He thought he had the information he needed to keep her in line, but for some reason, she had told everyone she knew about it, not only Dulcey.

"A secret," Dulcey had said.

But it wasn't a secret anymore.

He let his eyes drift to the side without moving his head. Elizabeth sat one row in front of him next to some of those tiresome brats. She was lovely, at least. Living with her wouldn't be as painful as it had been with his last wife. The cow. It had been a chore to just sit across the table from her during the few meals they ate together. But when she had started complaining, well, he knew how to put an end to that. It had been quick, and the fact that there had been a child involved made him the object of sympathy for months afterward.

Elizabeth was a better prize. The curve of her neck looked

soft, with fine hairs curling against her tanned skin. The future was a ripe plum ready to fall into his hand, except for her skittishness. He had worked too hard for the privilege of taking her hand, but she had never let him go any further than that. He wouldn't be able to compromise her that way, but he would find another way.

After the meal, Solomon looked for an opportunity to steer Elizabeth away from her friends. Soon, he would have to start weaning her away from them for good. A confidant was a threat to his plans. Finally, she left the kitchen to join the group of women sitting together in the yard. He intercepted her just before she reached the door of the farmhouse.

"I haven't had the opportunity to visit with you this morning." He stood close to her, bending his head toward hers.

"I've been busy."

She backed against the wall and glanced toward the door, but Solomon had made sure to place himself between her and her view of her family and friends.

"I thought perhaps we could go for a drive this afternoon. We need to talk about our future plans."

Then she looked at him, her expression calm. Where was the eagerness most girls showed at this stage?

"We do need to talk. Was the deed in order? And does the marriage certificate prove that I am Reuben's heir?"

Solomon was all too aware of the possibility of others listening to their conversation. "We can't talk here." He gave her his most seductive look, but she didn't respond.

"Let's take a walk, then. We can walk down the road as far as your house, and then back again." She bit her lower lip and glanced toward the door again. "I'll meet you at the end of the farm lane in a few minutes."

Ten minutes later, Solomon paced in the road, waiting. Finally, she appeared and fell into step beside him as they walked down the road. She had taken control of the afternoon, leaving him to catch up. That wasn't how things were going to be, and he needed to show her that now. But how to do that without scaring her off was the problem.

"I wondered if you were ready to set a date for our wedding." He caught her hand in his. "I can't wait until we are man and wife."

He stopped walking and pulled her closer to him, bending his head toward her, ready to catch those soft lips in a kiss. To his surprise, she let him place a quick kiss on her lips before she turned away and continued walking, her arms crossed.

"I'm not convinced we should get married. I've made the mistake of marrying the wrong man once, and I don't want to do it again." She looked at him, her expression hopeful. That was his opening.

"Have I ever done anything to make you think we weren't meant to be together? Just think of the home we will build together." He counted. *One, two, three.* "And our family. The children that will fill our home."

She stopped, then turned to face him, her eyes searching his. "Is that what you really want, Solomon?"

He took both of her hands in his. "A home. A family. You by my side."

Her expression hardened. "I thought you might only want to marry me because I own the quarter section of land next to yours."

She was too smart for her own good. He smiled. "I have to admit, that was one reason why I was attracted to you at first. But now that I know you—"

"If I hadn't found those papers, the deed and my marriage certificate, would it have made a difference?"

Solomon worked to keep the irritation off his face. It was time to use his ace. "There was no marriage certificate."

That surprised her. Her face turned white and her mouth dropped open. "I saw it. I read it. It was in the papers I gave to you."

Solomon shook his head, steadying his sorrowful expression.

"You were mistaken. There is no proof that you were ever married to that Reuben character. Obviously, the man was a reprobate and took advantage of a young girl."

Her face was still white. He led her to a fallen log at the crossroads where she could sit and have a view of the roof of his house. He sat next to her and placed one arm around her shoulders.

"Without the certificate, how will I prove that I own Reuben's land?"

"I've already taken care of that."

Solomon smiled to reassure her. The wheels were in motion. He would own her land as soon as they were married.

"The problem," he said, keeping his voice calm and reassuring, "is that the Amish community thinks you are a moral woman. Foolish, perhaps, but moral. They believe you were in an unfortunate situation, having no idea of the truth."

She shook her head. "The truth is that I was married to Reuben."

"The truth is that there is no proof. I'll give you the benefit of the doubt. Perhaps he lied to you and you believed you were married for all those years."

Elizabeth's eyes blinked several times, her fingers were cold and trembling. Solomon could have laughed. He had her right where he wanted her.

"But I thought that even if a person isn't legally married, that they are considered married after a time?"

"You mean common-law marriage?" When she nodded, he adopted his most condescending tone. "Oh, my dear, do you think the church would consider that to be a true marriage?"

She dabbed at her eyes with the hem of her apron. "What can I do?"

Solomon rubbed her shoulder, then brought her closer to his side. "There is only one solution. We must get married before people start asking questions. You know how damaging rumors can be. All it would take would be for someone to mention something to the wrong person . . ." He let his voice trail off, letting Elizabeth draw her own conclusions.

"I . . . I need to think about this."

Elizabeth stood. Solomon took her arm to walk her back to the Beilers' farm, but she pulled away.

"I'm going to walk home." She took a step back. "Please tell the others I'm all right. Only a bit tired."

Solomon weighed the risk of letting her go against forcing her immediate agreement to their wedding. Elizabeth was cautious. He decided to give her time.

"When can I expect an answer to my proposal?"

She gave him a quizzical look, then shook her head as if

clearing cobwebs from her mind. "I'll let you know in a day or two."

"Until then." He bent to give her another kiss, but she pulled back and walked away from him, down the road toward her home.

Solomon watched her go. He could pursue her. Force her. But his first thought had been correct. Let the rumors about her past start circulating, and she would come to him of her own free will. Chuckling, he turned to walk back to the Beilers' farm and the willing ears of Salome.

13

Aaron had watched Solomon and Elizabeth as they walked down the road. Elizabeth had gone willingly, he could see that, but he still paced between the house, the barn, and the end of the farm lane.

Jonas and Levi were near the barn in the shade, talking with Dan and a few of the other men. He stood with them, not listening to the conversation, then decided to go and look down the road again. Perhaps Solomon and Elizabeth were coming back. But Jonas followed him and caught his sleeve.

"What's wrong with you? I've never seen you this jumpy."

Aaron wiped the perspiration off his nose. "It's probably nothing. Just my imagination."

"Your imagination doesn't make you act like this."

"Solomon and Elizabeth went down the road together a little while ago."

Jonas shrugged. "It's common enough for couples who are courting to go off together during the afternoon. They'll be back."

Aaron glared at his friend. "Who says they're courting?"

"I only assumed they were, if they walked off alone. I know Elizabeth has been interested in him, and it makes sense. They're both widowed, both alone. They're neighbors. Why wouldn't they try to find out if marriage is a good idea?"

Aaron stared at his foot, leaning on his cane. "I don't think Solomon Mast is the man he says he is, but I don't have proof."

Jonas watched him, his arms crossed. "How certain are you?"

"I know what I know. I'm sure."

"Except that your imagination could be making you think things that aren't true."

Jonas could be right, but Aaron was sure he remembered Simon Miller correctly . . . or did he?

Touching Aaron's shoulder, Jonas nodded toward the road. "There's Solomon now."

"But where is Elizabeth?"

Aaron made his way toward Solomon. The other man had stopped near a group of the women who were sitting together in a circle near the house. As he drew close, Katie left the group, heading toward the house.

Aaron stopped her. "Did Solomon say where Elizabeth is? She didn't come back from her walk with him."

Katie fanned herself with her hand, her face flushed. "She told him she was tired and not feeling well, so he walked her home."

She went on past him and Aaron tapped his cane on the ground, watching Solomon. It didn't add up. Solomon hadn't taken his buggy, and he hadn't been gone long enough to go all the way to Elizabeth's house and back.

Heading down the farm lane, he started off after Elizabeth. Solomon could be telling the truth, but the only way to find out was to find Elizabeth.

By the time he reached the cabin that Katie and Elizabeth shared, Aaron was walking slowly, nursing his bad leg. When he saw Elizabeth sitting on the front porch, he was relieved, then disgusted with himself for being so suspicious. He stopped in the shade, resting, until she saw him and waved.

"Aaron, what are you doing here? Come on up and sit down."

He felt each step up to the porch and sat heavily in the chair closest to the door. Elizabeth sat with her feet under her, a glass of water in her hand.

"That looks good," Aaron said, nodding toward her glass. "Could I trouble you for some?"

When she brought it, he took a long drink. The water was cool and sweet.

"Did you walk all the way here from the Beilers'?" Elizabeth asked when he finished. "It's such a hot afternoon. You should have waited until evening."

Aaron turned the cup in his hands. Now that he was here and she was safe, it did seem a bit silly.

"I was worried about you. When Solomon came back from your walk without you, I wasn't sure what happened."

"He didn't tell you I came home?"

"He did."

"But you didn't believe him."

Aaron ignored the frown on her face. "I worry about you."

"There is nothing to worry about. Solomon and I are getting along fine. I know you think he's this man that you met in Virginia, but I haven't seen anything that tells me he's anyone except who he says he is."

"Then why don't you seem happy?"

She shot a look at him. "I'm happy."

Then why the tears in her eyes on Saturday when he saw her in Lydia's kitchen? "I think you're mistaken." He turned his cup in his hands again, watching the droplets of water threatening to fall from its sweating surface. "I think you're telling me what you hope is true, and you're trying to believe it yourself."

Minutes passed. A cardinal called from the tops of the pines. Elizabeth sniffed as if she was trying to keep from crying.

"You don't know anything, Aaron. You're only guessing. Solomon has asked me to marry him, and I'm thinking of saying I will. He can give me everything I've ever wanted."

"If he's a respectable Amishman, solid, secure, and faithful, like you claim, then why do you always look a bit frightened when you're around him?"

She snorted. "You're imagining things."

"You look like you're afraid you'll do something that will displease him. You've seen him when he's angry, haven't you?"

Silence. The cardinal called again.

Aaron steepled his fingers, looking through them to the porch floor. "Do you love him?"

More silence.

"Does he love you?"

"Of course, he loves me. That's why he wants to marry me."

He turned his head, catching her gaze in his own. "It isn't love if you feel like you need to earn it. How many times do you do what he wants just to appease him?"

"You don't know what you're talking about, Aaron Zook." She stood, her fists clenched. "It isn't any of your concern if I marry Solomon or not, and you have no right to question what I'm doing. You aren't my father or . . . or my brother."

She stomped past him to the door, her bare feet thudding on the wooden porch floor. She paused with her hand on the door as if she wanted to say more but went inside, letting the wooden screen door slap closed on its spring.

Aaron rose and started the walk back to Abraham and Lydia's house. She was right. He had been too harsh. But he couldn't stand by and watch her make the biggest mistake of her life.

What would he do if she married Solomon?

He thumped along the dusty lane down to the road.

He would have to watch them on church Sundays. Watch their family grow. Watch her face for signs that she was unhappy. But he wouldn't be able to do anything about it, not once the wedding was over. Until then he had hope she would come to her senses.

But if she didn't . . . If she didn't, he would have to leave. She would be another memory he would leave behind.

Aaron stopped at the trail that led across a log bridge to the house Jonas was building for Katie. The rafters rose above the little willows that lined the creek, and he knew the siding was almost complete. Soon Jonas and Katie would be getting married and he would bring his bride home to this house he had built for her.

How would he explain his leaving to Casper? The man had taken him into his family. They had talked about his future and started drawing up plans for his house. He shook his head, still unable to believe it was true. His house.

Would Casper resent him for running away and leaving behind the family he had so recently found? Would they mourn for him as Casper's father had mourned for Grandpop?

Being part of a family meant making the commitment to stick together through good times and bad. Aaron ground the end of his cane into the soft gravel on the roadside. A real man would face up to the bad and go through it, not run away from it.

He would stay, even though he was helpless to change the course of the disaster he saw ahead for the woman he loved.

Elizabeth didn't sleep well that night. It seemed that every time she sank into slumber, she would hear Solomon's voice again, telling her there was no marriage certificate.

Finally, as the approaching dawn turned the sky outside her window from black to a slightly lighter shade of gray, she gave up. As she got ready for the day, she went through finding the metal box again in her mind. Step by step, she followed her actions in her memory. The Confederate money, the deed to the farm, the letter from Reuben's father. And the marriage certificate. She was certain she had seen it. The writing had been faint. Feathery. Had she put it back in the box instead of taking it to Solomon?

In the kitchen, she built up a small fire in the stove and started the coffee. There was a chill in the air this morning as the weather was changing. Clouds covered the sky she could see between the pine trees, low-hanging and dark. Thunder rumbled in the distance.

She needed to talk to Ruby. Once the thought passed through her mind, it took on an urgency. Her mind was foggy with trying to remember where the marriage certificate could be. Solomon's words swirled in her consciousness, confusing her. He seemed to say one thing and mean another. Did she feel this way only because she hadn't slept well?

Thunder rumbled again, still far away. If she hurried, she could reach Ruby's before the rain started. Her sister wouldn't mind company, even this early in the morning.

Elizabeth scribbled a note to Katie, apologizing for leaving her with the morning chores, and hitched up Pie. The pony sensed her hurry and trotted through the gray morning. The thunder was closer now and Pie put his ears back. He didn't like the rain.

"Keep going," Elizabeth said. "You'll stay dry in Gideon's barn."

Pie swiveled his ears and trotted faster. In only a few minutes they had reached Ruby's house. She drove Pie through the open barn doors where Gideon was bringing the cows in from the pasture for their milking.

He called to her from the back of the barn. "Elizabeth? What brings you here so early this morning?"

"I wanted to talk to Ruby, so I came to help with her Monday chores."

Gideon let himself out of the cows' pen and took Pie's

halter. "You go on in before the rain starts while I take care of Pie. Ruby will appreciate your company. Rainy days always make her a bit gloomy."

Big drops were beginning to fall as Elizabeth ran from the barn to the house. By the time she reached the cover of the back porch, the rain was falling in sheets. Ruby had seen her and opened the door.

"Welcome, Elizabeth! I didn't expect to see you today."

Elizabeth gave her sister a hug, then went around the table to hug each of her nephews and nieces, avoiding their sticky oatmeal mouths. "I hoped you might like some company today. I know how you hate rainy Mondays."

"For sure, I do." Ruby turned back to the stove where a pan of bacon was frying. "I'll have to hang the laundry in the loft, but I can't complain too much about a summer rain. We know the crops need it."

Elizabeth ate breakfast with Ruby and Gideon and their family, enjoying the lively company. Ten-year-old Roseanna took charge of little Lovinia after the meal was over, taking her into the front room to play until her nap time. Eight-year-old Sophia and the boys, Ezra and Daniel, cleared the table, piling the dishes in the dishpan. Gideon stood at the door, watching the steady rain.

"It's eased some," he said, reaching for his hat. "I have plenty to do in the barn, and the boys can help." He lifted Daniel in his arms and handed Ezra's hat to him. "We'll be back in time for dinner."

As they left, Sophia joined her sisters in the front room, leaving Ruby and Elizabeth alone.

"Now," Ruby said as she poured hot water from her

teakettle into the dishpan, "tell me what this is all about. You didn't just come all this way to help me with my chores."

Elizabeth took the bar of soap off the shelf above the sink and started paring shavings into the hot water.

"You're right. I thought we could talk."

"About you and Solomon?"

Elizabeth replaced the soap in its dish. "Are we that obvious?"

"You left the fellowship time after church yesterday and went off together. Then Solomon came back alone. When he said you weren't feeling well, Mamm almost went after you, but Solomon said it was only the heat and you would be all right."

"That's almost true."

"Almost?" Ruby tested the temperature of the dishwater, then pumped some cool water in. "Were you feeling ill?"

Elizabeth opened the cupboard to get a clean dish towel. "I wasn't ill. I just wanted to think over what Solomon and I had discussed."

Ruby began washing the plates. She rinsed each one in the pan of clean hot water and handed them to Elizabeth.

"Are you going to tell me what the two of you talked about, or do I need to pry for the details?" Ruby made a face and Elizabeth laughed.

"I'll tell you because I need your advice."

"All right. I'll try." Ruby finished the plates and reached for the bowls.

"Solomon asked me to marry him."

Her sister grinned and gave her a hug, wet hands and all. "I thought he might get around to that sooner or later."

Then Ruby grasped her shoulders and held her at arm's length. "You don't seem as happy about this as I thought you would."

"I'm just not sure why he wants to marry me."

"Who wouldn't want to marry you?"

"I mean, he is such a . . . well . . . handsome and desirable man. He could have his choice of any woman around. Why would he choose me?"

"Because he loves you?"

Elizabeth dried the rest of the plates while she thought about Ruby's words. He had never spoken of love, only about their future together. "He says he wants a family. You have seen his house. He wants to fill it with children."

Ruby took her hands from the dishwater. "Isn't that what you want, too?"

"Did Mamm tell you?"

"About your baby? She did. I'm so sorry, Elizabeth. I wish I had known."

"I wish you had too. But I didn't tell Mamm what I found out yesterday." She pointed to the bowls still soaking in the water and Ruby started scrubbing them again. "It appears that Reuben and I were never legally married."

Ruby didn't say anything, and Elizabeth waited. She dried the first bowl, and then the second.

"I always thought you were. You said you and Reuben were married in Millersburg."

"I always thought I was too. I'm sure I saw the marriage certificate, but Solomon says it doesn't exist. He said if he and I get married quickly, then no one will worry about whether Reuben and I were really married or not."

"So, you think you might marry him because of that?"

"That's why I wanted to talk to you. Is that enough of a reason to get married?"

Ruby finished washing the dishes and swirled her dishcloth through the rinse water. "Do you love him?"

"Aaron asked me that same question."

"Aaron?" Ruby's brows went up. "You talked to Aaron about Solomon?"

Elizabeth shrugged her shoulders, not sure what to say. "He asked, and I told him about Solomon's proposal."

"What did he say?"

"He doesn't like Solomon and doesn't think I should even talk to him."

"That is interesting." Ruby wrung out her dishcloth and hung it on a bar under the shelf that held the soap. "But what did you tell Aaron? Do you love Solomon?"

"I didn't tell him anything." Elizabeth hung her dish towel on the same bar. "How can you tell if you love someone? I was married to Reuben for thirteen years, and I still don't know if I ever loved him."

"That man killed whatever love you might have had for him."

"If I married for love when I married Reuben, then why should I take that chance again? Don't you think I should marry for a good reason and let love happen later if it will?"

"It depends on the reason. Why would you marry Solomon?"

Elizabeth pulled her lower lip between her teeth. Ruby would understand. She had a good home now, with a loving husband and children, but a few years ago all she had were dreams, just like Elizabeth.

"He could be my last chance for happiness. With him, I could have everything I've dreamed of—a home with a loving husband, and children." Tears filled her eyes. "I can see the fulfillment of that dream in front of me, waiting for me to reach out and take it. All I have to do is tell Solomon I will marry him, and it would be mine."

"But what good is that dream if you don't have love?"

From the front room, baby Lovinia started crying.

"It's time for her nap." Ruby turned to go to her daughter, then hesitated. "Think carefully, Elizabeth. You know what it's like to be married to a man who doesn't love you. Don't make that same mistake again."

As Ruby left, Elizabeth turned to the pile of laundry in the corner of the kitchen and started sorting it. Was Ruby right? Or could she make Solomon love her?

Elizabeth held up a small dress, one of the baby's. She held the little scrap of fabric to her chest. If she could give Solomon a baby—a son—then he would have to love her.

~

On Thursday, Solomon hitched his black horse to the buggy for his weekly trip into Millersburg. Dulcey had brushed the horse and washed the buggy early in the morning, but Solomon still inspected his rig from all sides, rubbing off bits of dust with a rag before he was satisfied. Then he went into the house to dress for the trip.

Dulcey had laid out his town clothes while he was in the barn. Solomon dressed himself in the linen shirt and wool suit. It was a warm day for such attire, but he hadn't been able to purchase a linen suit yet. Patterson had divulged the location of his money, but it wasn't as much as Solomon had hoped, and he was close to the end of it. Soon, though, if his business dealings in the South panned out, he wouldn't have to worry about cash again. That, added to his land-holdings here in Ohio, would provide well for him for the rest of his days.

He put the finishing touches on his attire and combed his hair back. He picked up his bowler hat and gloves and went downstairs. Using the mirror in the hall, he adjusted his cravat and settled the hat on his head.

"Dulcey!"

The young woman came from the kitchen and stood next to him, her head bowed as he had taught her.

"While I'm in town today, I don't want you to let anyone come into the house."

"Yessir."

"Not even Elizabeth. If she comes, tell her you're too busy to visit. I don't want you talking to her unless I'm in the house."

"Yessir."

"What am I having for supper tonight?"

"Cold roast, sliced fine, with pickled beets and cottage cheese."

He turned to glare at her. "Do I look like one of these Amish farmers?"

"No, Masta."

"Then will you come up with an appropriate menu for me?"

"I can roast a ham, but it will make the kitchen awful hot."

The stroke with the back of his hand was swift and hard, knocking Dulcey off her feet.

"I don't care if the kitchen is hot. That isn't my problem. I want the ham, with mashed potatoes and green beans. Cook them with bacon. And I want fresh bread. The toast you gave me this morning was stale."

Dulcey cowered on the floor.

"I'll be back at my usual time, and I expect my supper to be on the table, hot and waiting for me." He nudged her with his foot. "Do you understand?"

She nodded. "Yessir."

As he drove toward Millersburg, he considered the state of his household. He needed another servant. Perhaps a man to be a likely husband for Dulcey. The two could work for him as cheaply as one, and then the farm work would get done without having to soil his own hands. Then as Dulcey's children grew, they could also work in his growing household. The vision pleased him. He would make inquiries in town.

The livery stable he normally used was full, so he drove to the new establishment down the street and made arrangements with the boy for his horse, requesting that the animal be fed, rested, and ready to go by two o'clock. The next stop was the post office. The rest of the Weaver's Creek community used the post office in Farmerstown, but he didn't want his business passing through the hands of the shopkeepers there. He called for his mail and took it to his favorite bench in the shade of the bank on the south side of Main Street. The limestone walls were cool, even in the middle of the afternoon, and it made a pleasant place to observe the business of the town as he read his letters.

Sifting through the envelopes, he saw one from that lawyer who had contacted Elizabeth. His last missive should have been enough to dissuade them from trying to contact her again.

Solomon slit open the envelope and scanned the letter, then shoved it back into its cover. Keeping a pleasant look on his face as he nodded to the businessmen who passed by on the sidewalk, he went over the letter in his mind.

The woman in Mississippi was desperate, the letter had said. She had been cast out of her family when she married Reuben Kaufman and could not return to them with her son. The only resource she had was the property Reuben had mentioned that he owned in Ohio. She needed possession of that property to support herself and her son, and it was owed to her son as his only legacy from his father.

Solomon slit open the next envelope in the pile. Stupid woman. She should have known better than to marry a reprobate like Kaufman. He dismissed her from his mind as he read through the letter in his hands and fingered the check that had been included. The sale of the property he had invested in had gone through, and he and the rest of the syndicate had realized a tidy sum. The next three letters yielded similar results, and Solomon rose from his seat. He would deposit the checks in the bank before he left town. With results like this, he would consider expanding his business ventures in the South. The postwar years might be even more profitable than the last four years had been.

When he returned to the livery stable, the large black man

that had been there before was hitching his horse to the buggy. He turned to greet Solomon when he came in.

"The horse is all ready for you, just as promised."

"Very good." Solomon tossed a dollar coin to the man, then looked at him a second time. Young, strong, and polite. "Are you looking for a job, boy?"

The man's eyes narrowed. "No sir, I'm not."

"Well, if you're ever unhappy with your employment here, I can offer you a job on my farm. I'm looking for a strong young man like yourself. You'd be overseeing the whole place, if you're fit for that kind of work."

The man threaded the reins through the guides on the buggy. "No, thank you. I'm not interested."

"I have a girl working for me. She doesn't have a husband, and I'd like to find a man who would . . ." The man's expression had grown hard. Solomon frowned at him. "I can see you wouldn't suit me at all."

He climbed into the buggy seat and picked up the reins, but the man laid his arm over the horse's back.

"Mister, my name is Elijah Wilson, and I own this livery stable."

He pointed to the sign above the door, inviting customers to come back to Wilson's Livery as they drove out onto the street.

The man continued. "You are welcome to use the services of my establishment as long as you remember that I am a free man. I don't have to listen to any customer of mine talk the way you have to me this afternoon. If you can't respect me and my property, sir, you are not welcome back here."

"You don't need to worry about that." Solomon sat

straight in his seat, looking down on Elijah Wilson. "You will not see my buggy in any establishment owned by a—"

Before Solomon could finish his sentence, Wilson stepped aside and slapped the horse on the rump. Solomon lost the reins and clung to the dashboard of the buggy as the horse jumped, then galloped out of the livery stable and down the road. By the time Solomon regained his grip on the reins and was sitting in his seat again, he had decided that Elijah Wilson was definitely not the man he wanted to hire to work on his farm.

14

Elizabeth woke on Sunday morning feeling stiff and sore. Her head throbbed. Every time she had tried to sleep during the night, the same dream pursued her—the dream of Reuben chasing her, catching her, overpowering her, smothering her. And every time she had woken with a start, sitting up in bed, breathing hard.

Swinging her feet to the floor, she gathered her blanket around her and headed downstairs, following the smell of coffee.

"You're finally awake," Katie said as she pushed a chair away from the table for Elizabeth with her foot. "The coffee has been ready for an hour and you look like you need it. Didn't you sleep well?"

Elizabeth took the pot from the back of the stove where it had been keeping warm and poured a cup. As she sat down, she said, "I'm glad today isn't a church Sunday."

Katie leaned forward. "I heard you dreaming during the night. Was it that same dream about Reuben?"

"I don't know how I can stop them, and they're getting more frequent. Ever since . . ."

Elizabeth's mind went in a direction it had never gone before.

"Are you all right? Elizabeth?"

"I'm all right." She forced a smile and took a swallow of her coffee. "I just remembered something I have to do this morning."

"On a Sunday?" Katie turned to watch her as she took a final swallow of coffee and poured the remainder of the cup into the slop bucket. "You won't miss our picnic lunch today, will you?"

The picnic. Elizabeth had forgotten all about it. Jonas and Katie had invited her to come along with Levi and Elise. She had been looking forward to it so she could get to know the new girl better.

"You'll have to start without me. You're going to that spot on the Beilers' farm, aren't you? The one by the little stream? I'll join you later if I can."

Elizabeth headed back upstairs to get dressed. Those dreams of Reuben had come more frequently ever since Solomon had come into her life, and in last night's dreams, she didn't know if the man attacking her had been Reuben or Solomon. Somewhere in her mind, the two men had become one. Why hadn't she seen it before? Aaron had been right—Solomon was not a man to be trusted. She had to find that marriage certificate. If she found that, then Solomon would have no hold over her.

When Jonas came to pick up Katie, Elizabeth stood on the porch, watching them walk down the lane together under

218

the pine trees. Bitterness welled up, but she shoved it down. Katie and Jonas deserved their happiness. Perhaps someday, her dreams would come true, too, but not with Solomon.

The morning was pleasant for early July. Elizabeth hurried down the road, staying behind Jonas and Katie until they passed out of sight up the hill, going toward the Beilers' farm. As soon as she reached the turnoff to Reuben's cabin, she quickened her pace.

Pulling the door open to let the morning light in, Elizabeth went straight to the loose floorboard and pried it up. The box was still there. She opened it, dumped the papers onto the floor, and sifted through them. The letter from Reuben's father's lawyer, more Confederate money . . . but no marriage certificate.

After she gathered the papers into a loose pile, Elizabeth sat on the floor, leaning against the bedstead. There was no question in her mind that she had seen the marriage certificate. She remembered the faint writing. Her name and Reuben's. The official seal from the notary public. She hadn't imagined it. But where was it?

As she retraced her movements in her mind, a seething restlessness filled her breast. Her feelings might have been muddled by Solomon's handsome face, but now her mind was clear. She had found the certificate in the box along with the deed to the farm. One quarter section of land in Reuben's name, or his heir's. She was Reuben's heir. The land was hers.

The deed and the certificate had both been in her hand when she had driven to Solomon's house. He had taken the papers from her, then she had gone into the kitchen to have dinner with Dulcey.

Where had Solomon gone? Into his study. With the papers.

He had lied to her last week. He had the certificate. Solomon lied only to gain power over her, to force her to marry him quickly.

But why would he do that? Because of the land?

Elizabeth put her fist to her mouth. What about the letter from Mississippi? There was someone else who could claim the land. If the marriage certificate existed, then Elizabeth's ownership of the land was without question. If she married Solomon, then the land would belong to him. So why would Solomon say the certificate didn't exist?

A cloud passed over the sun and a gust of wind blew the door shut, making Elizabeth jump. With last night's dreams fresh in her mind, the shadowy corners of the cabin seethed with memories. She jumped to her feet.

"Never again, Reuben Kaufman!" She shouted the words into the air. "I'm not going to be any man's victim again!"

Elizabeth felt for the matches she had always kept above the kitchen cabinet. There was one match left. She went back to the pile of useless papers she had left on the floor. Her mouth dry, she struck the match and held the faltering flame close to a Confederate bill. The dry paper caught, the flame gaining strength, full of color from the ink. She fed the little fire with more bills, then the letter, then some dried leaves she found on the floor.

Backing away from the growing flame, Elizabeth found more fuel. Old kindling in the box by the fireplace. Pieces of the beam that had fallen. The kitchen cabinet door that pulled easily off its hinges.

The fire took on a life of its own, jumping up to lick the

leg of the bed, spreading across the wooden floor, curling around the beam. Elizabeth backed toward the door. The flames no longer needed her to feed them.

They leaped to the wardrobe where Reuben had kept the belt he had used on her. The stand where he had inverted his boots to dry. The box where he had kept his liquor . . . all burning. All consumed by the fire that had started from the single flame of her match.

Elizabeth pushed against the door, making her way outside, and air rushed in. The inside of the cabin grew into a ball of flame. Elizabeth fled to her garden and stood, watching the fire. Flames licked the logs through the places where Aaron had pulled out the chinking. The orange and yellow fingers crawled up the dry logs to the roof, completely consuming the cabin. Soon it would be reduced to a pile of ashes.

Tears streamed down Elizabeth's cheeks as she watched the fire devour years of nightmarish memories . . . destroying them forever.

"*Look to Christ,*" Gideon had said, "*and he will set you free.*"

"Why don't I feel free?" Elizabeth sank to her knees. "Dear Lord, why don't I feel free?"

Aaron sat by the stream that ran through the corner of the Beilers' farm, plucking blades of grass and throwing them into the water. The place was pleasant in the shade with the sound of the water trickling through. The picnic lunch that Katie and Elise had brought was delicious, including the blackberry cobbler Katie had made for dessert. She had even brought a small jar of cream that she set in the running water until it was time to pour the cool rich liquid over the treat at the end of their meal. Aaron hadn't tasted anything that good since he was a young boy.

But now the sun was past the noon hour and the two couples had gone for a walk, Katie and Jonas in one direction and Levi and Elise in another.

"It's no problem," he told the chipmunk that peered at him around a tree trunk. "They want to be alone together, I understand that."

But . . .

He threw another blade of grass into the water and watched it float away. Katie had said Elizabeth might come. She had told her she might be late, but she would try to come.

Aaron yanked a dandelion from the grassy bank and threw the yellow flower into the stream after the grass.

She was with Solomon. Of course, she was with Solomon.

He plucked another dandelion blossom and spun the stem between his fingers.

Most likely making plans for their wedding.

The stem dissolved into a mess of pulp and he threw that flower into the water too.

He didn't blame the others for leaving him behind with the excuse that someone needed to be in the agreed-upon spot when Elizabeth showed up. He wasn't good company today.

A cloud passed over the sun and he looked up. It wasn't alone. Other clouds in the west were following on its tail on a gust of wind. It might rain tonight.

Then, on the next breeze, he smelled smoke. A brush fire? Aaron got to his feet and climbed to the top of the rise above the stream. Another whiff of smoke. Not grass or brush. This was a wood fire.

"Jonas!" He turned, looking for his friends. "Levi! Where are you?"

The smoke smell grew heavier.

The two couples came running toward him.

"Where is that smoke from?" Jonas said when he came closer.

Aaron pointed south, toward the Weaver's Creek valley. "In that direction. It's wood smoke. Could be a house or a barn. We should see if there's trouble."

"I knew I should have brought the wagon. It would be quicker." Jonas went to help Katie put the blanket in the picnic basket.

"You go on," Aaron said. "You can move faster without me. Leave the basket and we'll pick it up later. I'll come behind you."

Jonas and Levi left with the girls, running across the field to the road. Aaron followed, using his cane for balance on the rough surface. The others would arrive at the fire long before he did. They would find out if it was someone's house, or if it was just someone cooking dinner.

Smoke rolled toward him on the south wind, strong and deadly. It wasn't someone cooking dinner.

Step by step, Aaron made his way to the road. He couldn't move any faster, not in the long grass of the pasture, but the possibility of someone being in danger made him careless. He stepped wrong with his wooden leg and stumbled, falling headlong in the soft grass.

He felt the self-pity start closing in and shoved it away. He got back on his feet and started again. He might not get to the fire in time to help, but he would get there, and then all he could do was try his hardest.

No. The thought came to him with sudden surety. No, that wasn't all he could do. He could pray. Ma had taught him long ago, and he had listened to the ministers pray in church. Gideon had prayed for him, and Casper. He wasn't as powerless as he thought.

Each step that brought him closer to his goal was accompanied by a word of prayer. For the safety of his friends, for the well-being of the people whose house or barn was burning, for his own careful steps. He glanced up at the sky and prayed for rain.

By the time he reached the road, he could see the column of smoke above the trees and increased his speed. He had been afraid it might be at Gideon's farm, but now he could see it was at Elizabeth's old cabin. Had she been there? He hobbled faster. Had she been trapped inside? That cabin was old and dry as tinder. It wouldn't take much to destroy it.

When he reached the fire, he let out a breath he didn't know he was holding when he saw Elizabeth sitting away from the cabin, surrounded by Katie, Elise, and Ruby. She was safe. The others who had gathered from the neighboring farms were hauling buckets of water out of the old well and running with them to the cabin, trying to keep the fire from spreading. One cabin wall had collapsed, and the roof was gone, but the fire still burned in pulses of searing heat.

Aaron placed himself at the well and took the rope from Samuel Weaver.

"I'll do this part. I can't carry water back and forth, but I can haul it out of the well."

Hand over hand, he brought up the wet rope and poured the water from his bucket into a waiting pail. Again. And again. He lost count of how many times he hauled that bucket up. His hands bled from the rope burns and everyone's faces were dirty with smoke and soot. Finally, the wind died down and Gideon motioned for him to stop.

"I think we're all right for now."

At that moment, a light rain started, growing heavier, the drops hissing as they hit the still-burning logs of the cabin, now lying in a heap. The whole crowd, at least a dozen people who had been helping with the fire, raised their faces and hands up, welcoming the cool water from heaven.

Aaron dragged the cover over the well and lay on the ground next to it. He couldn't remember being so exhausted since he was in his last battle. He held his hands up. Blisters had formed, then popped, then the skin had turned raw across both palms. He sat up as folks started going home. Jonas found him.

"I'm going to walk Katie home. Levi and Elise have already left. Do you want to come with us?"

Aaron looked around for Elizabeth. She was still standing by Katie and shaking her head.

"I'll stay with Elizabeth, then walk home with her. It doesn't look like she's ready to leave yet."

Jonas gave him a hand to help him up, then walked over to Katie. As the couple walked toward the road, Elizabeth looked at Aaron, then back at the smoldering timbers. The rain had stopped, and the wind was still.

He made his way over to her. "Are you all right?"

Someone had thrown a blanket over her shoulders and she held the edges together in front of her. "I'm fine. How are you?"

He closed his hands, ignoring the pain of the broken blisters. "I'm all right. A little tired."

She gave him a small smile. "Ja, a little tired."

Everyone else had gone home, and the area around the smoking and steaming logs was empty, but from the road, Aaron heard a horse and buggy. Solomon drove into the yard, pulled his horse to a stop, and jumped down from the buggy.

He stared at the ruined cabin. "What happened here?"

Elizabeth lifted her head, her voice steady as she faced him. "I burned down Reuben's cabin."

Solomon turned on her, one hand half raised, until he saw Aaron standing near. He let his hand drop.

"What do you mean, you burned down the cabin? That was my cabin on my land. You had no right to do that."

Elizabeth's answer was calm. "It is not your land and not your cabin."

Solomon's gaze shifted from Elizabeth to Aaron and back again. He cleared his throat. "I meant, as soon as we marry, the land will be mine. You shouldn't have acted without consulting me first."

"I'm not going to marry you, Solomon." She walked toward the fire, her back to both of them.

Solomon shot a deadly look in Aaron's direction, but his eyes narrowed as he watched Elizabeth's back. He grunted as he seemed to come to some conclusion.

"You've proven to be more trouble than you're worth,

anyway." He turned to climb back into his buggy. "You'll be sorry you refused me, Elizabeth."

He turned the horse around and was gone, back up the road toward his house.

The sun had sunk toward the horizon as the rain clouds scudded east, and the evening star shone just above the trees. When Aaron looked back at Elizabeth standing huddled in her blanket next to the glowing coals, his mind went back to a thousand or more campfires glowing in the dusk, with the sound of taps being played softly on a distant bugle.

Someone else might shrug off Solomon's threat, but Aaron wouldn't. He walked up behind Elizabeth and put one hand on her shoulder. She leaned against him as if she had no strength left.

"Do you really think Solomon is dangerous, Aaron?"

"I do. But don't worry. I'll be watching both him and you."

She turned around in his arms and clung to him.

"I'll protect you, Elizabeth," he whispered into her hair. "I won't let anything happen to you."

⁓

Elise shivered as they left the scene of the fire, but Levi resisted putting his arm around her.

"Are you cold? I could let you wear my coat."

"Ne, not cold. I just can't get over how our peaceful afternoon almost turned to tragedy." She walked closer to his side. "The fire was so frightening. Didn't you think so? I'm thankful that no one was injured."

Levi stole a glance at the woman beside him. Not the first

time to enjoy her lovely profile this afternoon, with the walk they took after their picnic.

She ducked her head. "I hope you will come to our house sometime. My parents would like to learn to know you better."

"Do you want me to visit?"

"I would like that very much."

Continuing to walk, they passed Levi's house. Mother had lit the lamp in the living room, and he could see her sitting in her rocking chair. They were almost to Elise's house. The Zooks lived on the next farm past his own.

He ran a finger around the collar of his shirt. He should say something, but what could he say that would interest a girl like Elise?

"My brothers say you could be the next minister in the church." Elise stopped in the road and turned to him. "They said that even though you appear to be very shy, you are a scholar, and have read many books."

"Um . . ." What could he say to that? "I enjoy learning about theology." He glanced at her. "That's the study of God."

She nodded. "I know. My father, who passed away, was the bishop in our district. He also loved to study the Bible and read the writings of Menno Simons and other Mennonite and Amish leaders. He would often read aloud to us during winter evenings."

The tips of Levi's ears started to burn. She described a home life he could only imagine. "Did you enjoy that?"

She smiled at him. "I did. I know not many people enjoy learning as much as I do, but I can't get enough of reading."

"Which is your favorite writer?"

"Menno Simons. I particularly enjoyed his rules for the Christian life." She started walking again. "Do you think a Christian can follow those rules exactly, or are they guidelines for us to aim for?"

Levi caught up with her. By the time they reached her house, they had discussed five of the rules, plus debated whether the *Christenpflicht* was a collection of prayers that they should pray or examples of prayers. That led to a discussion of the Lord's Prayer as it was given in the book of Matthew. Levi was about to compare Matthew's version of the Lord's Prayer with Mark's when Casper opened the front door of their house. Suddenly, Levi realized they had been standing on the porch for at least an hour.

"Are you going to stand out here talking all night?" Casper asked, his eyebrows bristling.

Levi took a step backward. "I didn't realize it was so late. We got started talking . . ."

Elise slipped past Casper and into the house, but before she disappeared, she gave him a smile. "Denki, Levi. I enjoyed our talk."

"I did too."

Levi craned his neck to watch her as she continued into the house, but Casper stepped into his line of sight.

"I hear you're a fine young man," Casper said. "A scholar." He came out onto the porch and closed the door behind him. "Do you have something you want to ask me?"

Did he have . . . ? Levi swallowed. "Elise and I are just getting to know each other, but . . . I don't know how to say this." He looked at Casper. "I think she is the woman I'm going to marry."

Casper chuckled. "That wasn't a question, and it wasn't the question I had in mind. I thought you'd want to ask if you could spend time with our family some evening."

"Ja, for sure."

The older man squeezed his shoulder. "There is nothing like spending time together to know if two young people are right for each other."

Levi nodded.

"Why don't you come over tomorrow night after supper. Spend some time with Elise's brother Tobias and her mother. Let them get to know you."

Levi nodded again.

Casper opened the door and stepped halfway in. "Good night, Levi."

"Good night." He smiled, but his feet didn't move.

"Your house is that way, son." Casper pointed toward the road.

"Ja." Levi's mind started to work again. "Ja, for sure. I'll see you tomorrow, after supper."

"We'll see you then."

Levi walked down the farm lane, past the harness shop, and down the road toward home. The moon hung in the western sky, just past the last quarter and on its way to full. He went over every detail of his conversation with Elise.

"I should have told her," he said aloud, kicking at the step as he climbed the porch steps at home.

"Told her what?" Mother asked.

He hadn't seen her sitting on the porch in the dark. He sat on the chair next to hers and watched the moon.

"I walked Elise Beachy home."

Mother started tapping her toe on the wooden porch floor. "She seems like a nice girl."

"I'm going to marry her, Mother."

"Perhaps someday, after we have learned to know her parents better. The family has just recently moved into our district, and Casper Zook is only her stepfather. We must find out what her real father was like."

"No, Mother, we don't need to do anything. And I'm not going to marry her someday. I'm going to marry her soon."

The toe tapping increased. He had never contradicted Mother before.

"Please understand. I have been looking for the right girl to marry for a long time. Elise is the one."

"You thought Katie Stuckey was the one."

"I was young and foolish."

"And what are you now?" Mother's voice had taken on that waspish tone he hated.

"I am older and wiser now. And if I am making a foolish mistake, then it's mine to make. You need to trust my judgment."

The tapping stopped and Levi looked at her. The moonlight shone on her face as a tear traced its way down her cheek. He grasped her hand.

"What is wrong?"

"First Millie goes off and marries that boy. And now you want to leave me too."

"Millie lives in our district and has given you twin grandbabies. And I'm not leaving. I'll live somewhere close by. I don't know where yet, but I'll be in our district."

Mother's voice turned wheedling. "You could live here

with us. Married children often share a house with their parents."

Levi stood. "That is not going to happen." He bent down and kissed her forehead. "I love you, but I am not bringing my wife home to live with you."

Mother sighed.

"I'm going upstairs to bed. I'll see you in the morning."

Mother sighed again. "I suppose I could ask Elise if she would like to live here."

Levi stopped partway into the house. "No, Mother, you won't. You're not going to do anything to interfere in our lives or we will move to . . . to Indiana." He let the screen door slam closed behind him.

15

By Thursday, Elizabeth knew what she had to do.

Solomon had her marriage certificate, the only proof that she had been legally married to Reuben and was his heir. She had to get it back or she would never be free of Reuben or Solomon.

She tossed a forkful of soiled straw from Pie's stall out the door and thrust the fork into the bedding for another load. If only she could throw all men out of her life as easily as mucking out the barn.

Well, maybe not all men. Warring with the memory of Solomon's sneering face was the prickling warmth on her skin where Aaron had held her so lightly, so gently.

She shook her head and threw another forkful of straw out the door.

Why did she ever consider marrying Solomon? Tears gathered in her eyes as the answer echoed in her mind. To achieve her dream. Solomon's lies had led her to believe that he held the same dream, but his only goal was his own greedy lust for land. All he wanted was the farm.

And her dream of a home and family would never come true. She didn't deserve for it to happen. No Amishman would consider marrying her with the stain of her marriage to Reuben in her past. And without the certificate stating that it was a legal marriage? No one would marry her. Perhaps another Englischer might take the chance, but she would never make the mistake of marrying outside the church again.

The only thing she could do to keep her dream alive was to find that certificate.

She tossed another forkful of soiled straw.

To find that certificate, she would have to go to Solomon's house.

Trading the fork for the broom, she swept the last of the chaff and dirt out of the stall and onto the manure pile outside.

But if she confronted Solomon, she would lose. She would have to appeal to his better nature to hand it over to her, but after listening to him berate her on Sunday evening at the fire, she didn't think he had a better nature.

As she scattered fresh straw throughout Pie's stall, she remembered that Solomon often went to Millersburg on Thursdays. Perhaps he would be going today, also.

Changing her plans to spend the afternoon helping Margaret with her wedding quilt, she told Katie she would be going to visit Ruby, then hitched Pie to the pony cart. The drive to the burned-out cabin was quick, and she left Pie tied in the shade of the tree by the garden. She hauled a pail of water from the old well and made sure he could reach the grass. Elizabeth stopped at the end of the farm lane and glanced down the road toward Ruby's place. She would have to remember to stop for a quick visit on the way home.

Setting out on foot, she watched for any sign that Solomon was at home as she approached the house. His big black horse wasn't in the pasture. She kept walking until she could see into the open doors of the barn—no buggy.

Elizabeth stepped off the road and into the woods opposite Solomon's house and barn. Smoke trickled from the kitchen chimney. Dulcey came out the back door and hung some dish towels on the clothesline. Before she went back into the house, she stood by the clothesline, her arms crossed at her waist, looking toward the south, across the road and Reuben's woodlot. Would she indulge in those few minutes if Solomon was at home?

After Dulcey disappeared back into the house, Elizabeth took another look at the house and barn. No sign of Solomon anywhere. She crossed the road, hurried around the side of the house and up the back steps. Dulcey was at the stove, stirring something. Elizabeth rapped on the screen door.

"Is that you, Miss Elizabeth?" Dulcey moved the pot to the side of the stove and pushed the door open. "You shouldn't be here. Masta Solomon, he told me specially that you aren't to be here when he isn't."

Elizabeth closed her eyes and breathed a silent prayer of thanks. Solomon wasn't in the house.

"When do you expect him home?"

"He usually comes home on Thursday in time for supper, around six o'clock."

"Then we have plenty of time. I need to look in his study."

Dulcey shook her head. "If he catches you in there, you'd sure to be getting a whipping, and me too."

"He won't be home for several hours. I just need to find a paper that he stole from me. It has to be somewhere in his study."

"I don't want us to get in trouble." Dulcey turned back to the stove.

"If you're not going to help me, at least keep watch for me and let me know if he comes home early."

"That room is locked. Masta Solomon don't let anyone in there without him being there."

Elizabeth bit her lip to keep from screaming in frustration. Of course, Solomon would lock the door. But . . .

"You know where he keeps the key, don't you?"

Dulcey opened the oven door, letting a blast of heat into the already sweltering kitchen. "I know where he keeps the key." She poured gravy from the pan on the stove over a beef roast, then slid the roast back into the oven. "You got to promise me he won't find out I let you in there."

"He will never learn it from me, and I won't tell anyone else." Elizabeth's heart beat fast and she gulped for air as if she had been running for miles.

"All right, I trust you." Dulcey went to the kitchen door and beckoned for Elizabeth to follow her. "And I think Masta Solomon is the kind of man no woman should marry." She looked at her as she stretched as tall as she could to reach above the doorframe over the study door. "You've gotten that idea out of your head, I hope?"

"I was blinded by my dreams for a little while, but I know better than to marry a man like him."

"I need your help getting the key." Dulcey stopped in front of the study door. "Can you give me a boost?"

Elizabeth laced her fingers together and Dulcey stepped into her hands to reach the top of the doorframe. When she hopped back down, the key was in her hand.

Dulcey unlocked the door and peered into the dusky room. Elizabeth walked to the desk, then turned in a circle. A fireplace dominated one wall and a closed and curtained window was opposite the door. In the center of the room was the desk with a large leather-covered chair facing her. Papers were stacked in neat piles on the desk.

As she started looking through the piles of papers, Dulcey took a step into the room. "Careful you don't muss up them papers. He's particular about how they lay on his desk."

"I'll be careful." Elizabeth straightened the letters she had browsed through and went to another pile on the opposite side of the desk.

The top letter was from a bank in Charleston, Virginia. Underneath that was a familiar-looking envelope. It was from the same lawyer that had written to her, but the envelope was addressed to Solomon. She lifted the flap. The letter inside looked very similar to the one she had received, written in the fancy script she couldn't read. She put the letter back in the envelope. Then directly below that was another letter, this one from Solomon and addressed to Harlan Hoben, the lawyer in Vicksburg. She was about to put it aside with the others when she saw her name. Picking up the letter, she sank into the leather chair to read it.

"You find it?" Dulcey asked in a hoarse whisper.

"Not yet, but this is a copy of a letter that he sent to the lawyer in Vicksburg. It says that I am no longer considered to be Reuben's heir, so the land passes on to Reuben's next of kin, which is his son. It appears that Reuben's wife in Mississippi has passed away." Elizabeth read through the letter again. "Solomon has asked to be named the guardian of the child. He said the lawyer should bring the boy here as soon as he can."

She leaned back in the chair. What did it all mean? Why would Solomon want the child to come here?

A terrible idea passed through her mind. "Dulcey, you don't think he would hurt a child, would he?"

Dulcey sniffed as if an unpleasant odor had just entered the room. "If that boy has something he wants, and he could get it, ain't nothing would stop him."

"Then I have to find that marriage certificate. If I can prove I'm the owner of the land, then there will be no reason for Solomon to hurt the boy."

She riffled through that pile of letters and found nothing. Then she opened the center drawer of the desk, then the left-hand drawers, then the right-hand drawers. No certificate.

Dulcey looked into the fireplace. "You think he burned it?"

"I hope not."

Then Elizabeth remembered what she and Ruby used to do when they left notes for each other. They would stick the note under one of their dresser drawers. She pulled out the top right drawer and felt underneath. Pulling out the paper she found there, she unfolded it. It was the marriage certificate. Solomon had hidden it where he thought no one would ever find it.

She held it up for Dulcey to see. "Now Solomon doesn't have a chance to get that land."

"He won't be happy about that." Dulcey shook her head.

Elizabeth scanned the copy of Solomon's letter again, then noticed the date. "He has probably already mailed this letter, which means the lawyer could be on his way here with Reuben's son."

Dulcey motioned for her to hurry. Elizabeth straightened the piles of papers she had looked through and made sure the desk drawer was closed tightly. Then she followed Dulcey out of the room.

"Help me put the key away," Dulcey said.

Elizabeth laced her fingers together again and Dulcey slipped the key back onto the doorframe.

⁓

Gideon examined the harness Aaron had just delivered.

"What do you think? If there's something that isn't right, I can take it back to the harness shop and fix it right away."

His friend grinned. "This is good work. It should last for years with care."

Satisfaction in a job well done. Aaron could get used to this feeling. He grinned back at Gideon. "I'm happy you like it. I'll pass on the word to Casper."

Gideon hung the harness on the pegs set for it on the barn wall. The sound of a cart entering the barnyard drew their attention outside. Elizabeth pulled her pony to a stop and climbed out of the cart.

"Ruby will be glad of your company," Gideon said as he went to take the pony's lead rope. "I hope you'll be able to stay for a while."

Her face was flushed, her eyes bright as she glanced at Aaron.

"I can stay for an hour or so. Could you keep Pie in a shady place? It's a hot day again."

"For sure. I'll take good care of him."

"And can I talk to you before I go in, Gideon? I have something to tell you."

Aaron could take a hint. "I'll be getting back to the shop, then. Let me know if you run across anything you need done on that harness, Gideon, and I'll make it right."

"Don't go, Aaron." Elizabeth held out her hand to stop him. "I want you to hear this too." She took a breath, glancing at each of them. "I found out that Aaron was right to warn me about Solomon."

A cold, sinking feeling ran to Aaron's toes.

"Solomon Mast?" Gideon asked. "What about him?"

"Aaron told me that Solomon might not be who he was trying to appear to be. I know he is a liar and can be cruel. I think he might not be Amish, like he claims he is."

"This is a serious accusation. Do you know this for a fact? You didn't hear it from someone else?"

She pulled a paper out of her waistband. "Solomon told me he had never seen this paper, yet he lied to me. I found it at his house."

Gideon took the paper and unfolded it. "It's your marriage certificate from when you married Reuben." He folded the paper again and paced to the back of the barn, then returned. "I had heard that you were never legally married to Reuben. Was that just a rumor started by Solomon? Why would he do that?"

"I think I have figured it out." She glanced at Aaron and he nodded, hoping to reassure her. "Solomon asked me to marry him, although I couldn't understand why. But I think it's because he wants Reuben's farm for himself."

"He isn't happy with the Patterson place?" Gideon asked.

"He . . . he gets a look in his eye when he talks about land. A greedy look. I don't think he would stop at anything to get his hands on more land."

Gideon tapped the folded certificate against his pursed lips. Aaron's mind raced to an unsavory possibility.

"By marrying you, he would be part of the Weaver family. If things happened in the right way, he could eventually own all of Abraham's land."

"But to do that, he would have to swindle his way through legalities," Gideon said.

"Or position himself correctly and wait."

"For what?"

"For Datt to pass away," Elizabeth said, breaking into their speculations. "He could write a new will, forge Datt's signature, then just wait for the end."

"Or make sure the end happened sooner than anyone would expect." As soon as the words were out of his mouth, Aaron realized what he had said.

"You're talking about murder." Gideon's face grew hard.

Aaron pulled his hat from his head and ran a hand through his hair. "If Solomon is the man I think he is, that could be exactly what he has planned."

Gideon turned to Elizabeth. "But now that you've found your marriage certificate, he can't do that, can he?"

She shook her head. "I don't see how he could. But there's something else. Reuben had a son, a little boy who is now an orphan. I saw a copy of a letter Solomon wrote to a lawyer in Mississippi, requesting that he be made the boy's guardian. If he went to court, he could find a judge who would say that Reuben's son actually owns the land instead of me, couldn't he?"

"Do you think he would steal the land from you, using this child?" Gideon's eyebrows were raised.

"I do. I can't see how he could gain control of Datt's land after that, but he might have some scheme brewing."

Aaron stepped closer to Elizabeth. "He knows how much you love children. What would you do if he threatened the boy's life? Would you marry Solomon to save him?"

As Elizabeth nodded, her face crumpled, and a tear slid down her cheek. "I would do anything to save a child from Solomon's control."

"This is something I need to talk over with the other ministers," Gideon said. "Solomon has established himself in our community, and we need to decide how to handle this situation." He grasped Elizabeth's hand. "Denki. I'm glad you came to me. We'll do everything we can to protect you."

He gave Aaron's shoulder a pat and then left.

"I suppose you want to go in and talk to Ruby now," Aaron said.

He should follow Gideon and go back to the Zooks' harness shop, but Elizabeth's tears had multiplied. Her shoulders shook as she covered her face. Aaron put an arm around her shoulders and steered her toward the bench near the barn door. He sat next to her, his arm still around her shoulders. She sniffed, then took a deep breath and wiped her eyes on her sleeve.

"You must think I'm such a fool."

Aaron pulled her closer. "Not at all."

"I was taken in by Solomon's charm and his looks, but I should have listened to you. You tried to warn me about him."

"I wasn't certain it was the same man."

Another sob bubbled out. "I thought he was the one I had been waiting for. The one who could fulfill my dreams."

Aaron let her cry. He didn't know what to do when a woman cried. His mind went back to his last membership class with Gideon, when the minister was discussing *Gelassenheit*, surrendering to God's will and plan.

"Maybe you're dreaming the wrong dreams."

Her shoulders tensed and she pulled away from him. "The wrong dreams? My dreams . . . they're mine. Who is to say if they're wrong or not?"

Aaron stretched his good leg out, letting the muscles relax. "Gideon told me that one of the first things the Amish teach their children is to give up their own will and surrender to God's. He teaches them to put Jesus first, others second, and themselves last. Perhaps your dreams have turned that around."

Elizabeth didn't answer, but she didn't walk away, either. Finally, she leaned closer to him again, under the arm that was still stretched out along the back of the bench. "Don't you have dreams? What about going west?"

He fingered a lock of hair that had escaped from her kapp and rested on her shoulder. "I think I was wrong about those plans. If I went west, then I would only be living for myself."

"Isn't that what you wanted?"

Aaron rubbed his stump, the leg that was closest to Elizabeth. In fact, since they were sitting so close together, it rested against her skirt. She hadn't seemed to notice. "Not anymore. Since I've been here, things have changed."

She turned toward him and rested her hand on top of his, the hand that had been rubbing his leg. Her fingers brushed his trouser as she laid her hand on his leg, near the edge of his stump. She didn't cringe. Didn't shy away. Didn't give him a look full of pity. She only took his hand again, allowing him to curl his fingers around her small, soft one.

~～

As Aaron's hand grasped hers, Elizabeth relaxed into his gentle touch.

"I know things have changed a lot. With your new leg you're able to get around much better."

"I'm not talking about my leg." His soft voice tugged at her heart. "I've found my true dream right here in Weaver's Creek."

"Your family." She smiled. "I always knew you needed a family."

He nodded. "The Zooks are part of that. But it's much bigger than that. The one thing I missed since the beginning of the war was my home. I had seen it destroyed and Grandpop killed in front of my eyes." His gaze took on a faraway look, as if he were seeing the past recreated in Gideon's barn. "But what I've found is my true home."

"Do you mean Weaver's Creek?"

Aaron smiled. "This place is just the beginning. But now I understand that my dreams are nothing without the Lord. He's the one who gives us our heart's desire."

Elizabeth's eyes grew moist again. She would never have her heart's desire. God had already shown her that.

"Do you understand what I mean?"

"You mean that you've given up making your own dream come true and now you're waiting for God to give it to you."

Aaron sighed. "Not exactly. I stopped thinking about what I want. Now I'm watching while God gives me what he wants me to have. Once I set my sights on pleasing him and obeying him, then I could see how he is working to give me what I want most, after him."

"You're talking in circles."

Elizabeth started to draw her hand away. Ruby would make more sense than Aaron. But he grasped her hand harder until she looked into his eyes.

"Let me say it plain, then. And in Englisch." He ran his thumb along the back of her hand. "My dream is to have my own home. A place to belong. A family . . ." His gaze dropped to her hand. "And a wife. A woman like—" He stopped. "No, not a woman like you." He looked into her eyes again. "You. No one else. I want you to be part of my dream."

"But—"

He stopped her with a kiss, quick and gentle, on her lips. She pulled back to see his face turn scarlet, his blue eyes boring into hers. He let go of her hand and touched her lips with one finger.

"Don't say anything. Not yet." He took her hand again, as if by holding it she could never leave him. "I love you, Elizabeth, and it has been painful to watch you over the past few weeks as you've grown closer to Solomon. But at the same time, I've discovered that I had the wrong dream. I needed to put God first in my life and accept what he had planned for me."

Aaron lifted her hand and kissed it. Her thoughts swirled.

He continued. "I hope what he has planned for me is you, but only if you want me. I will do almost anything for you."

A bubble of hope turned inside her breast and she smiled. "Almost?"

He nodded, serious. "I won't turn away from God for you, but I would do anything else."

Elizabeth chewed the inside of her lip. His dream sounded so much like hers, except for one thing.

"You aren't Amish, though."

"Not yet."

She shot her gaze up to his eyes. He wasn't teasing, but he was smiling.

"What do you mean? Ever since you came here you said you weren't Amish."

"I went to the ministers and asked about joining the church. I want to become part of this community. To set down roots here. To embrace the Amish faith and life my grandfather ran away from."

"You can't just decide you're Amish and then you are."

"I know. I'm not Solomon. But I didn't just decide to become Amish. I thought about it for a long time." He chuckled. "All right. I didn't think about it as much as I argued with God. But nobody can argue with him and win."

How often did she spend her prayer time arguing with God? Bargaining with him? "So, you want to join the church?"

"Is that such a surprise?" His smile was sure. "Of course, I'll have to finish my classes with Gideon and Jonas—"

"Jonas?"

Aaron grinned. "Now I've really surprised you. Jonas and I are taking the class together."

Elizabeth slumped against the back of the bench. She had been wrapped up in her own problems . . . Katie probably even told her about Jonas taking the membership class, but she hadn't noticed.

When Aaron squeezed her hand again, she looked at him. "I've told you what I want, and I'm willing to accept whatever God provides for me. If that is for you and me to hitch our lives together, then that would make me very happy."

Elizabeth closed her eyes. It seemed that his dream danced with hers in a swirling whirlwind of leaves on a fall day. But she had been so wrong about Solomon, and so wrong about Reuben. She couldn't trust her feelings or her ears when it came to Aaron. She couldn't risk making another mistake.

"I can't give you an answer."

She opened her eyes, expecting to see a frown on his lean face, but instead he was grinning.

"I hope you won't until you're certain. If that takes a long time, then I can wait. It seems like I've waited my whole life, so why not wait a little longer?" He ducked his head. "I'm sorry I kissed you earlier. I couldn't help myself."

Elizabeth put her fingers over her lips. His kiss had been so gentle, demanding nothing from her. She had never been kissed like that before, but suddenly she longed for another one. If she did marry him, would Aaron always be so gentle and thoughtful with her?

"I enjoyed the kiss." He turned bright red again and she smiled. "I will think about what you've said, but I don't know if I'll ever marry again."

He leaned over and brushed a kiss on her cheek. "Think about it and pray about it."

"I will." A sunbeam of clarity pierced her cloudy thoughts. "I'm going in to see Ruby now."

"And I need to get back to work. Casper is probably wondering where I am."

They walked out of the barn together, then Aaron winked at her as he turned to go toward the road and back to the Zooks'. Elizabeth went to the kitchen door, knocked softly, then opened the door. Ruby called from the front room.

"Come on in, Elizabeth." Ruby sat in her chair, a needle in one hand and a pair of boy's trousers in the other. "I saw you drive in. Have you been out in the barn this whole time?"

Briefly, she told Ruby what she had found at Solomon's house. "Gideon left to talk to the other ministers about the situation."

"They'll spend all afternoon discussing it, I'm sure. But Gideon left quite a while ago. You've been alone with Aaron since then?"

"Aaron and I were talking." She sat on a chair opposite Ruby's. "Where are the children?"

"Roseanna and Sophia took the boys down to Mamm's house, and Lovinia is taking her nap."

"And how are you feeling?" Elizabeth remembered how sick she had been for those few months when a little one was growing inside her.

"The worst of the illness is over and I'm feeling good. I do get tired in the afternoon. Sometimes I lie down and nap with Lovinia. Roseanna is such a help at those times." Ruby cut off the end of her thread and folded the small trousers. "I think of you often, since you told us about the baby you lost. I can't imagine how you must still grieve at times."

Elizabeth picked at a piece of chaff sticking to her skirt. "I wonder about that child often, if it had been a boy or a girl. If its eyes were brown like mine, or green like Reuben's. But it has been a long time since then . . ."

"Only a few years."

Six. It had been six years and three months. She would never forget.

Ruby picked up another pair of trousers, frowning at the hole in the knee. "I don't know how these boys can be so rough on their clothes."

Elizabeth grinned, forcing the sad memory to the background. "They're boys. They're supposed to be active."

"But do they always need to crawl on their knees when they play?"

They both laughed, and Ruby looked at Elizabeth.

"It is good to hear you laugh. I was afraid with what you told me about Solomon that you would not be happy. So, tell me. What is going on with Aaron?"

"Aaron?"

"He's the one who put that smile on your face, isn't he?"

Elizabeth found another piece of dust on her skirt. "It is nice to know a man who is gentle and kind."

"You know a lot of men like that. There's Gideon, and Jonas, and Datt."

"But they're all related to me. That's different."

Ruby threaded her needle and took a stitch. "Aaron comes by here every Friday evening."

"For his membership class."

"He told you about that?"

Elizabeth nodded. "I think it's wonderful that he's thinking of joining the church, but it will be hard for him, won't it?"

"From what Gideon said, he has his heart set on it. He's very dedicated and shows up early every Friday. His enthusiasm is wearing off on Jonas too. I was afraid Jonas was only going through the motions of joining the church so he and Katie could be married."

A warm feeling started in Elizabeth's middle. "So, you think Aaron is serious?"

Ruby smiled at her. "Very serious. He wants to become Amish."

The warm feeling expanded. He was becoming Amish because he wanted to, not because he wanted to impress her. He didn't give her an ultimatum and he didn't try to wheedle his way into her affections. He didn't even try to threaten her by saying he wouldn't continue the classes if she didn't marry him.

Whether there was any future between them or not, Aaron would still be Amish by his own choice.

16

The town of Millersburg was festooned with banners, bunting, and flags even today, two days after Independence Day. Solomon hunched his shoulders as he drove through the crowded street to the livery, keeping his gaze down. With this many people around, he couldn't keep track of them all. It was best to lie low and get his business done.

The livery stable was full again.

"You could try at Wilson's around the corner," a thin man with one eye said, jerking his thumb in that direction. "He usually has room since so many folks around here won't do business with one of his kind."

"No, thank you. I've patronized that establishment once, but I won't go back."

The one-eyed man grinned, then spat a stream of tobacco juice toward the corner. "Then I can put your horse up in the corral. There's water for him in there. Two bits for the afternoon."

Solomon peered into the corral that was already crowded

with a dozen horses or more and shook his head. The horse would have to make do with whatever he could find on the street.

He guided the horse to a watering trough on the side of the courthouse, and when the beast was finished, he found a spot along the hitching rail near the post office to tie him.

As he stood in line inside the building, Solomon pulled out the letters he had ready to mail. The most important was the one requesting to take over guardianship of Kaufman's son. He smiled at the thought of owning Kaufman's property free and clear without having to deal with Elizabeth. She had proved more bothersome than she was worth. Although, if he needed to, he could still manipulate her. She was foolish to trust him with such important papers as the deed to the land and her marriage certificate.

"Good afternoon, Mr. Mast," the clerk said when he reached the window. "I think I have a telegram for you today."

He went to the boxes lining the wall behind them and retrieved a folded paper. When Solomon saw that it was from the lawyer, he shoved the letter he had written to Hoben in his coat pocket and mailed the rest of his missives. Walking out of the post office, he fingered the telegram. It could be good news that would make his letter to the man obsolete. He sought out an open bench and sat down.

The message was short.

Court in Vicksburg awarded custody to aunt Elizabeth Kaufman. Will accompany boy to Ohio on first train.

Solomon checked the date on the note, then crumpled the paper in his fist. He was too late. Much too late. The court had already given the boy to Elizabeth and he was on his way here. Might even be here as soon as Saturday. He should have straightened out that misunderstanding about her relationship to Reuben early on rather than waiting to see if he could use it to his advantage, but instead the opportunity had slipped through his fingers.

He barely noticed the bank draft contained in the other letter, more proceeds from his investments in the South. He deposited the draft in the bank, then gathered his horse and set out for home.

All the way to his farm, he sifted through the possibilities of how to use the changed situation to his advantage, then discarded them one by one. The only way he could see to maintain his control of the situation was to marry Elizabeth. While at one time he had looked forward to having her close to him, available to him any time he wanted her, now the thought was a bit distasteful. He liked his women compliant and naive, and Elizabeth had turned out to be neither of those things. But since she had been named the guardian of the boy, she held the key to Reuben's property. Once they were safely married, then he would decide when and how to dispose of both of them.

He noticed Dulcey's guilty expression as soon as he entered the house. He watched her as she took his hat from him and hung it on the hall tree, followed by his jacket.

"Has anyone been here, Dulcey?"

She kept her gaze down. "Miss Elizabeth stopped by, but I told her you weren't at home."

Solomon's eyes narrowed. "Elizabeth? What did she want?"

"I don't know. She didn't say."

Dulcey cringed, her left shoulder rising, giving her a crab-like appearance. She was lying, but Solomon let it slide for now. He had plans to make.

"When will my supper be ready?"

"I can have it on the table in ten minutes."

Solomon checked his watch. Nearly six o'clock.

"I'll be in my study. Call me when it's ready."

Dulcey scuttled toward the kitchen as he strode across the hall to the study and reached for the key he kept above the doorframe. His fingers touched nothing. He groped to the left, and then to the right until his fingers touched the key. As he took it down, he glanced toward the kitchen door just as it swung closed. Suspicion filled his mind. Dulcey wouldn't go into his study when he wasn't in there. He had trained her better than that. But Elizabeth might have convinced Dulcey to show her where the key was.

Turning the key in the lock, he swung the door open and strode in. Everything looked just as it should. The desk was orderly, the piles seemed untouched. Why would Elizabeth come in here? Shuffling through the papers, a thought came to him. He had told her that marriage certificate didn't exist, and she had believed him. But what if . . .

He pulled the right-hand drawer open and felt underneath. The certificate was gone.

Solomon burst out of his study and grabbed the buggy whip from its holder.

"Dulcey!" He let his voice carry all of his rage as he thrust the kitchen door open. "Dulcey!"

He found her in the pantry, cowering behind a barrel of

flour. Grabbing her hair, he pulled her out into the open and shook her.

"You traitor. You helped Elizabeth betray me. No one crosses me, Dulcey. No one."

He threw her to the floor and raised his whip. The beating only fed his rage rather than satisfy his appetite. He struck the woman at his feet until the whip broke, then resorted to kicking, but nothing gave him the release he needed. Not even her sobs as she curled on the floor, begging him to stop.

He finally turned away from her, exhausted but not sated. He staggered up the stairs and fell onto his bed, cradling his pillow to his stomach. If she survived, Dulcey would never cross him again. But she wouldn't have done so today if she hadn't been coerced by Elizabeth.

Gripping the pillow in his fingers, he imagined Elizabeth's slim arms in his hands. The pain in her eyes as he gripped harder, his fingers sinking deep into her flesh, then he ripped his hands down and out, tearing the pillow in two. He lay back on the bed as feathers drifted around him. Someday he would have Elizabeth in his hands, and she would know the power of his wrath.

$\sim$

Aaron finished his work at the harness shop just before supper. He declined Casper's invitation to stay for the meal and started the walk home.

Home? He chuckled as he got into the rhythm of his stride. The Weavers' farm had become home for now, with Lydia mothering him as well as Jonas, and Abraham willing to give fatherly advice. Aaron watched Abraham's interactions with Jonas carefully. His own father had lost touch with his family and with reality when Aaron's mother died in childbirth, disappearing into the woods for days and weeks at a time while Grandpop had raised Aaron. As wonderful as Grandpop had been, he wasn't Aaron's father. Witnessing Abraham and Jonas together gave him an idea of what he had lost, but also gave him hope that someday he could be that kind of father with his own children.

Supper was ready when he arrived at the Weavers', but Lydia wasn't there.

"She went to help Susanna Lehman with her lying in," Abraham said as he flipped hotcakes on the stove. "She'll likely be there all night, so the three of us will be bachelors for supper."

"Datt always makes hotcakes when Mamm is gone at suppertime," Jonas said as he took a bottle of maple syrup from one of the cupboards and put it on the table.

"That's right." Abraham moved six hotcakes from the griddle to a covered plate inside the oven. "Easy to fix and easy to clean up."

Abraham had made enough hotcakes to feed the entire church, Aaron thought, but somehow the three of them managed to eat half of them.

"Don't worry about the leftovers," Jonas said as Aaron patted his full stomach. "We'll have them for breakfast, warmed up and rolled around sausage links. There's nothing like it."

After they finished eating, Abraham asked, "You're working at the Zooks' every day now, aren't you?"

Aaron leaned back in his chair. "Casper has me doing

small jobs to help out, but I'm learning as I go. Every week there's something new to work on."

"Have you heard what Elizabeth is going to do now that that old cabin is destroyed?" Jonas asked.

"She hasn't said anything to me about it. I'm just glad we were able to keep the fire from spreading."

Abraham stood and started clearing the table. "I've worried about that old well, sitting so close to the house. Reuben never repaired the cover, but so far it has held up. Now that no one is living there, we'll need to either fill it in or make the cover safe before one of the children falls in."

"I hadn't thought of that," said Jonas. "I'll work on that tomorrow morning. We don't have any farm work pending, do we, Datt?"

"The oats are cut and shocked, and the hay is cut. It needs another day or two to cure, and then we'll be able to start hauling it to the barn. So, tomorrow would be a good day for that project. I'll help you with it."

Aaron hadn't thought about the dangers of that old well. As he had been hauling buckets of water up out of it, he hadn't been able to see the bottom. But he had to drop the bucket down at least twenty feet before it hit water, and he had no idea how far the bottom might be.

"Are there many wells like that one around the area?"

Abraham sat at the table again and ran his fingers through his beard as he thought. "The original landholders in the last century didn't always build homes on their land grants, so there are only a few. I think I remember there being an old log house on Abel Patterson's place, about the same age as the one on Reuben Kaufman's farm. Abel never lived in that old place though, so I don't know if it's still there. But there's always a possibility that a well existed there at one time. The other farm from that time is where Gideon and Ruby live now. The house was rebuilt, and they updated the place when they got married a few years ago. They still use that old well, although they've cleaned it out and built a new cover for it with a windlass. Old root cellars and springhouses hold the same dangers, though. No telling how many of those are around the old homesteads."

Jonas and Aaron washed the dishes and straightened the kitchen for the morning.

"I'm going over to see Katie before it gets dark," Jonas said.

"I'll walk with you as far as the road." Aaron grabbed his cane. "I haven't heard Elizabeth's pony cart go past yet."

"Didn't you say she was at Ruby's this afternoon? She probably stayed and had supper with them."

"You're right, but still, I'm uneasy about it. She should have gone home by now. The sun is going down."

Jonas grinned as they left the house and walked toward the stone bridge. "It sounds like you're putting your claim on her, worrying like that."

"Would you mind?" Aaron grinned back. "I don't think she would."

"I think it would be wonderful if you became part of the family. I'm looking forward to it."

"Don't give out congratulations yet," Aaron said. "She hasn't said she would marry me."

"She will." Jonas stopped on the bridge. "She wouldn't dare turn you down, or she would have to answer to me."

"I think the woman knows her own mind."

Aaron chuckled as his friend continued onto the road and turned toward Katie's house. But even with the bantering, his unease continued until he finally saw Elizabeth's pony cart coming down the road. She saw him and turned into the farm lane.

"You look like you're waiting for someone." Her smile was calm.

"Did you have a good time with Ruby?"

She nodded. "It's always good to spend time with her. Even if I'm feeling sad, she never fails to lift my spirits."

Aaron stepped to the side so he could see the road more clearly. Up the hill, someone was coming, staggering with an uneven gait. Elizabeth turned to see what he was watching.

"It's Dulcey." She moved over in her seat. "Get in the cart, Aaron. It looks like she needs help."

Elizabeth turned the cart around and urged her pony into a quick trot. By the time they reached Dulcey, she had fallen in the middle of the road. Elizabeth handed the reins to Aaron and ran to her.

"Dulcey! Are you all right? What happened?" Elizabeth, as small as she was, pulled the other woman up off the ground, cradling her shoulders in her arms.

Aaron drove the pony closer to the two women, then eased out of the cart. "Is she badly hurt?"

"I don't know. She has blood all over and she has lost consciousness. Can you help me get her into the cart? We need to take her to Mamm."

Aaron braced his legs and lifted the young woman's shoulders while Elizabeth carried her legs. They laid her carefully in the back of the pony cart. Elizabeth climbed in with her and held her head on her lap.

"Hurry, Aaron. We have to get her home."

"Lydia isn't there," he said as he climbed onto the seat of the cart. "She's gone to be with someone during their lying in."

"We'll still take Dulcey there. We can clean her up and help her the best we can until Mamm gets home."

Aaron drove slowly to keep the cart steady until they reached the hitching rail at the kitchen door of the Weavers' house. Abraham came out to meet them.

"What is wrong?"

"It's Dulcey. She's hurt, badly. We have to help her."

Abraham lifted the slight woman out of the back of the cart and carried her in while Aaron held the door open. Elizabeth went into the front room and lit the lamp.

"Aaron, if you bring a sheet to cover the couch, we can lay her there."

She hovered nearby while Aaron got a sheet from the cabinet under the stairs and spread it on the couch. Abraham laid Dulcey down.

"I'll fetch Lydia's clean nightdress," he said, then looked at Aaron. "We'll need hot water, a basin, and some clean cloths."

Aaron nodded and headed for the kitchen, but before he left the room, he looked back. Elizabeth bent over her friend, wiping her face with the edge of her skirt. Where he came from, white women didn't treat the black women like that, but he could see the love in Elizabeth's expression. Nothing would keep her from helping Dulcey the best she could.

He smiled as he went to the stove and lit the fire laid for the morning. Maybe that was one reason why his love for Elizabeth was growing stronger every day. She was always surprising him.

⌒

By the time Aaron brought a basin of hot water and Datt found Mamm's clean nightdress, Dulcey had woken up.

She groaned and tried to sit up.

"Shh," Elizabeth said, holding on to her friend's shoulders. "You stay right there. We need to get you cleaned up and bandaged."

Aaron and Datt left the house, leaving the two women alone.

"He knows." Dulcey grasped Elizabeth's arm. "Masta Solomon, he knows you was in the study."

Ice water froze Elizabeth's veins. "Did he do this to you?"

Dulcey nodded and took a washcloth from Elizabeth's hands. She tried washing her face with it, but Elizabeth took it back and carefully dabbed at the drying blood.

"He's a hard man. I tried to warn you," Dulcey said.

Elizabeth nodded, tears filling her eyes. "It's my fault, Dulcey. I talked you into helping me." She rinsed the cloth and started washing the cuts on Dulcey's legs.

Her friend shook her head. "There's no one to blame but Masta Solomon. You didn't hold no whip, did you? He did this himself."

"I need to wash your clothes, there is blood all over them. You can wear Mamm's nightdress until your clothes are clean and dry."

Dulcey's eyes widened. "I can't. Your mama's nightdress? I daren't. It ain't right."

"But Mamm would want you to. What else will you do while you wait? I don't have any clothes here for you to wear."

"I'll wrap myself up in this sheet. I can't wear no fine lady's nightdress."

Since Dulcey was adamant, Elizabeth gave up. She held the sheet ready while Dulcey undressed, biting back a gasp of horror when she saw layers of scars on her friend's shoulders and legs. Finally, Dulcey's outer clothes were in a pile on the floor and she held the sheet around her.

"Will you be all right while I take your clothes into the kitchen?"

"I'll be fine." Dulcey lifted the washcloth from the basin and tried to wring it out, but her hands were trembling.

Elizabeth took the cloth from her and helped her lie back on the couch. "You're hurt and you're exhausted. Let me take care of you for once."

Dulcey's eyes grew moist. "I ain't never known a white woman who would do for one like me."

Elizabeth smoothed Dulcey's curly hair. "I don't know about that. We're equal in the Lord's eyes."

She waited until Dulcey closed her eyes, then took the clothes into the kitchen to wash. She took a pail of cold water that sat on the side of the dry sink and plunged Dulcey's dress into it to soak. Then she went to the back porch where Datt and Aaron were talking. The moon was rising in the east, nearly full.

"How is she?" Datt asked.

"She is bruised and bloody, but other than that and being

tired, she seems to be fine." Elizabeth clasped her hands together to keep them from trembling. "This isn't the first time Dulcey has been beaten. She has a lot of scars on her back and legs, old scars, as if she has endured these beatings most of her life."

Datt moved over on the bench to give her a place to sit. "I've never seen her before, but you know her. Who is she?"

"She works for Solomon. She's his cook and housekeeper, but before he hired her, she had been a slave somewhere in the south until the war ended."

Aaron frowned. "Did she say who beat her so badly?"

"She claims it was Solomon. But even though I've seen that he has a cruel streak, it's so hard to believe he would beat her like that."

Datt leaned forward, his elbows propped on his knees. "That is a serious charge, but I was at the Beilers' house when Gideon called for a meeting of the ministers this afternoon. From what he said, Solomon is never going to be part of the community in spite of his assumption that he will be."

"What can we do about Dulcey?" Elizabeth asked.

"She shouldn't go back to Solomon, no matter what she says." Aaron held Elizabeth's gaze with his own. "We'll need to be firm about that."

"Why do you think she would want to go back?" Datt asked.

"Because she hasn't left before now, even though I'm sure he has treated her badly ever since she started working for him." Aaron turned his cane slowly between his fingers, the end resting on the porch floor. "Someone in Dulcey's situation might not be willing to hope that another place could be any better than where they are. I've seen it happen. I used to go hunting with a slave that lived on a farm near ours. In spite of the freedom his master gave him to wander the hills, hunting and whatnot, Sam would never consider running away. Even though he was a slave, he had a better life than Dulcey found working for Solomon. He was safe, fed, and had a job to do. He wasn't willing to exchange that for the unknown he might encounter if he tried to escape." He clenched the end of the cane in his fist. "I wonder what happened to him. The last I knew, his master was burned out by the same Yankee patrol that destroyed our place."

The three of them sat in silence for a few minutes. Elizabeth understood Dulcey better than either Aaron or Datt could imagine. She had had many opportunities to leave Reuben, but she hadn't. Shame had held her back. Shame and fear. If she had left Reuben, he might have come after her, and then her situation would have been much worse.

The moon rose higher and Elizabeth stood up. "I'm going to finish washing out Dulcey's dress, then sit up with her tonight."

"Do you want me to sit with you?" Aaron asked.

His offer was tempting, as Elizabeth imagined them talking quietly in the moonlit room while Dulcey slept, but she couldn't ask him to stay only to keep her company. "I'll be fine. I'll call you if I need you."

Datt and Aaron went to bed, Datt to his room on the main floor off the kitchen, and Aaron upstairs to one of the bedrooms there. Elizabeth lit the kitchen lamp and worked to remove the stains from Dulcey's dress. Once it was clean, she hung it on the clothesline. The night was fresh after the hot day, and nearly as bright as daytime with the moon so large. If Datt had pressing farm work to do, he could work by the light of this moon.

She walked back into the front room, taking the lamp. Dulcey woke up as she came in.

"I didn't mean to wake you. Did you have a good rest?"

"I slept hard, 'til a dream woke me up. An old alligator was chasing me across the swamp and briars clung to my legs. Jus' like Old Scratch grabbin' at me 'til blood ran like a river."

Elizabeth smiled. "No alligator will get you here, whatever that is."

Dulcey didn't return her smile. "But Masta Solomon, he might. He might guess where I went to when he wakes up. I need to get back there."

"You'll do no such thing."

"But if he wakes up and finds I'm gone—"

"You have to stay here where it's safe. If you go back, you know he'll beat you again." Elizabeth took Dulcey's hand. "You never have to go back there again. You'll stay with us. Make your home here. Or we'll help you go wherever you want."

Dulcey looked at their hands. Elizabeth grasped tighter, her light fingers entwined with Dulcey's dark ones as she waited for Dulcey's decision.

"I won't go back if you'll help me. I daren't go back to the saloon either. That was an evil place."

"We'll look for a place to live. A nice place where you only need to work for yourself. We can build a lovely little cabin for you, and you could have a garden and chickens."

A tear dropped onto their hands. "That sounds like

heaven, sure enough. But it's just a dream. Masta Solomon, he's gonna be lookin' for me, and for you. We got to run and live however we can."

"Don't worry about that right now. You need to get some sleep. Things will look better in the morning."

"Only with Jesus's help. No matter what men do, Jesus is more powerful."

Elizabeth didn't answer. Even though she had done everything she could to be free of the memories of Reuben, she had no freedom at all. And now Solomon . . . would she ever be free from him?

Dulcey squeezed her fingers. "Elizabeth, you reckon that's right, don't you?"

"I believe Jesus can save people, but I don't know if he'll save me. I try to pull myself out of Reuben's clutches, but I'm still there. I don't know how to get free. I don't think I deserve to be helped by Jesus."

"Oh, Elizabeth! Hush now. None of us deserves Jesus's love. None of us deserves his saving." Dulcey rose up on her elbow, still grasping her hand. "And you said you tried to pull yourself free of Reuben? Honey, we can't never save ourselves. Only Jesus can. Pray for him to give you the faith you need to look to him and him alone."

"Faith? Not help to be safe from men like Solomon?"

"God never done promised to keep us safe on this here earth. But he promised he would never leave us or forsake us, just like it says in the Good Book. Our bodies may be beaten, and we may even be killed. But our Jesus suffered worse an' he always promises to be right here by our side. And when the time comes, he done promised to take us safely to heaven.

He has a home there waiting for us." Dulcey settled back on the couch. "Think about that. Turn to Jesus."

Elizabeth was full of questions, but Dulcey's eyes were closing with exhaustion. "I will think about it."

Elizabeth blew out the light, then waited until Dulcey's hand relaxed in hers and her friend's deep breathing told her she slept.

Dulcey's dress might be dry by now, so she went out to the clothesline. In the gentle breeze, the dress had dried quickly. She reached up to pull the pins off the line, but then a hand clapped over her mouth and an arm grabbed her waist and pulled her against someone large and strong.

"You did just what I wanted you to, Elizabeth, my dear. I was waiting for you to come outside."

Solomon. Elizabeth struggled against his hold. She had to call for help, to warn Dulcey.

His grip over her mouth shifted to cover her nose. As gray clouds swirled, she fought to get free. To get one breath of air.

A chuckle sounded in her ear. "You'll do what I want, I guarantee it."

Her lungs demanded air, but the blackness overtook her.

17

Aaron woke suddenly with the morning light. The weather had changed during the night with the wind swinging to the north and banging the shutter on his open window, then he had heard Jonas come home sometime after midnight. His sleep after that had been fitful, full of dreams. Now, trying to come fully awake, he sat on the edge of the bed, rubbing his face and scratching his beard. He couldn't shake the feeling of his dreams. The feeling that something wasn't right.

He dressed and went downstairs, careful to keep his wooden leg quiet so he wouldn't wake the rest of the house. He peered into the front room. Elizabeth had said she would sit up all night, but she wasn't there. Dulcey slept on the couch, one hand curled on her stomach. Perhaps Elizabeth had gone home once Dulcey had gone to sleep, but that hadn't been her plan last night.

Starting a fire for breakfast was the first chore. He didn't know when Lydia would be home, so he went ahead with the morning kitchen chores. Abraham had laid the kindling last night, so he struck a match and started it burning. Then he took the coffeepot from the back of the stove and filled it with the last of the water in the pail on the dry sink. Measuring the coffee grounds, he set it on the stove, then fed the fire with larger sticks.

Next, he went out to the wood box on the porch to bring in more split firewood. He stopped. Something hung on the clothesline, dark against the light fog that covered the fields. He took a step closer to the edge of the porch. It turned, swinging from one pin, like a crow, dead and hanging by one foot. Now he recognized what it was. Dulcey's dress, hung by a clothespin on one side, the other shoulder sagging toward the ground.

Footsteps sounded behind him in the house and Jonas stepped out onto the porch. "What is that?" he asked as he walked up beside Aaron.

"I think it's Dulcey's dress hanging on the clothesline. It spooked me, too, when I first saw it."

"Who is Dulcey, and why is it there?"

Aaron described how he and Elizabeth had found Dulcey on the road the night before.

Jonas shook his head. "But Elizabeth wouldn't leave clothes out on the line in this damp weather. And why hang it with only one clothespin?"

The unsettled feeling he had woken with now pushed Aaron off the porch and toward the clothesline, Jonas right behind him. The dress was clean, but damp from hanging in the morning mist. The second clothespin was on the ground.

Aaron swallowed. "Have you seen Elizabeth?"

"She hadn't come home when I left Katie last night. I

figured she decided to spend the night at Ruby's." Jonas turned to him. "Elizabeth and her friend were both here when you went to bed last night?"

"She was going to wash out Dulcey's dress, then sit up all night in case Dulcey needed something."

"And she's not in the house?"

Aaron shook his head. "Not in anyplace I looked." The house was large, but there weren't many rooms.

"We have to look for her. We'll go to every house in the area and ask if they've seen her, and we'll recruit helpers at the same time."

Jonas went into the house to wake Abraham and tell him about Elizabeth's disappearance while Aaron fingered the dropped clothespin. He would take Jonas's spring wagon and retrace Elizabeth's steps from last night. Maybe she had gone back to Gideon and Ruby's place. Or perhaps Solomon's house. She wouldn't have gone to confront him, would she? She had to know that he'd want to hurt her the way he had hurt Dulcey. A chill ran through him at the thought.

He finished unpinning the dress and took it inside the house.

By the time Aaron had the horse hitched up, Dulcey was awake and dressed. She came out on the porch along with Jonas and Abraham.

"We'll go in different directions to cover more ground," Abraham said. "I'll go to the Stuckeys'. Jonas, you head toward the Lehmans' and stop at every house in that direction."

"I'll start with Solomon Mast." Aaron's insides squeezed together as he remembered the veiled threat Solomon had made after Reuben's cabin had burned. "Someone needs to go there first. If she isn't there, I'll go to Gideon's, then head north to the Beilers' and the Zooks'," Aaron said. "Dulcey should come with one of us. If Solomon is out looking for her, she shouldn't be alone."

"I'll ride with you," Dulcey said. "I got to help you find Elizabeth."

Aaron moved over on the wagon seat and Dulcey climbed up.

"Are you feeling better this morning?" he asked as he clucked to Rusty and they headed for the road.

"A mite stiff and sore, but I slept better than I had done for a long time." Dulcey didn't meet his eyes. "We got to find Elizabeth. Do you think Masta Solomon done taken her away?"

"I don't know, but I don't think she left by herself. She wouldn't have left you alone, for one thing."

She nodded. "I know that. We just need to pray for Jesus to watch over her."

Dulcey closed her eyes, her lips moving. Aaron tried to pray with her but couldn't think of what words to say. The prayer from the *Christenpflicht* he was memorizing for membership class didn't seem to express the panic that threatened to overtake him.

As they drew near the top of the hill, Dulcey laid a hand on his arm. "Don't take me when you talk to Solomon, please. Let me out somewhere and I'll meet you again when you're done."

"All right." He pulled the horse to a halt at the drive leading to the burned-out cabin. "This is where Elizabeth used to live."

"With her husband? The one called Reuben?"

"That's right. There's a possibility she might have come here, but it's also a good place to hide. I'll meet you here after I get done talking to Solomon."

After Dulcey climbed down from the wagon, Aaron drove Rusty up the hill and turned on the Millersburg Road, heading toward the red brick house on the rise. The place was quiet, but Solomon, or Miller, as Aaron now knew he was, must have seen him coming. He stepped out onto the porch in fancy clothes, the kind a businessman would wear in town. It appeared that Simon Miller was ready to show his true colors instead of pretending to be Amish.

"What can I do for you?"

"Elizabeth is missing. I was wondering if you had seen her last night or this morning."

"So, she has run off? I was afraid something like this might happen."

"Why?"

"She refused to marry. The woman has no sense of morality at all. I wouldn't be surprised if she has gone off where no one will ever find her. You know what women like that are like. She'll find a place with others like her."

Aaron's fists clenched around the reins. For once, he was glad for his wooden leg, otherwise he would have launched himself off the wagon seat to plant a fist in Miller's smug face. Instead, he lifted the reins to drive off, but the other man took a step closer.

"In fact, she was quite dismayed at the news I gave her." His smile broadened to show his white teeth. "I have found Reuben Kaufman's true heir, his son. I will be acting as guardian for the boy until he comes of age. When she found out she would be left penniless, she became quite unhinged, even though I offered to marry her. Perhaps she'll come to her senses eventually."

"When did you talk to her?"

A slight hesitation. "Why, it was yesterday afternoon, I think. Sometime in the late afternoon, if I remember right."

Aaron let a smile lift the corners of his mouth. "I caught you in another lie, Simon Miller. I know for a fact that Elizabeth was at her sister Ruby's house then. I saw here there."

The other man's eyes narrowed. "Simon Miller? I haven't heard that name since the war and no one will hear it again."

Before Aaron knew what was happening, a gun was in Miller's hand, pointed at his chest. A very familiar braided lanyard dangled from the pistol's handle, Simon Miller's trademark. Aaron ducked to the side, throwing himself off the wagon seat, just as a shot rang out and Rusty jumped, taking off running with the wagon behind him.

A burning sensation in his side told Aaron he had been hit, but before he could check to see how serious it was, Miller planted a black boot on his head. Aaron's eyes closed as his enemy lifted Aaron's cane and it descended toward his head.

———⌒———

The first thing Elizabeth noticed was the sickening odor. She opened her eyes, but the only light came from a few narrow sunbeams swirling with dust motes. She was lying on a cold floor with her hands tied behind her and a gag in her mouth.

Struggling, she pushed herself to a sitting position and

leaned against a wall behind her. The faint light showed walls built of stone and a rock floor. Somewhere to her left, water trickled in a dark expanse. To her right, the rock wall continued in a circle. The light came from cracks in a wooden door at least seven feet above her.

She drew her knees up and huddled against the wall, trying to remember what happened.

Solomon. Her mind cleared and it came back to her. She had woken up on the seat of his buggy after she lost consciousness when he seized her at the clothesline. He had been talking. Whether it was to her or to himself, she couldn't tell. But from his mutterings, she understood that he was focused on one thing, owning Reuben's farm. When he saw that she was awake, he laughed.

"You will marry me, my dear, because you are the key to more than just Kaufman's quarter section. After I marry you, your father's farm will be next. You are an important part of my plan."

"Why?" Elizabeth's throat was raw as she spoke. "Why does the land mean so much to you?"

"Land is wealth. You understand that, don't you? When I own enough land, everyone will know how important I am."

"I will never marry you. You can't make me marry you against my will."

The darkness hid his expression, but the moon was still bright, and his teeth flashed in its light.

"That's the beauty of my plan, Elizabeth. Kaufman's son will arrive on Saturday from Mississippi, and that lawyer Hoben has instructions to deliver him to me as your representative."

She tried to twist her arm out of his grip, but he only tightened his fingers.

"We will marry as soon as the ministers admit me into the church. We will be the perfect Amish family, and little Jefferson Davis Kaufman will be our son." He chuckled.

"I won't do it."

Then he turned her arm around so far that she was afraid he would break it.

"You will, because if you refuse, that little boy will meet with a terrible accident. And I know you wouldn't want to live with his death on your conscience. Your family will be devastated when they hear that you took your own life."

At that, she launched herself toward the side of the buggy and the safety of the dark woods, but Solomon pulled her back so forcefully that her head hit the edge of the buggy seat and everything had gone black.

She shivered in the damp chill and her head ached. She must get out of this pit and warn the community. Thanks to Gideon's warning, the ministers would be watchful, but Solomon had fooled all of them. All spring and summer they had welcomed him into their midst and worshiped with him. Even considered him for membership. Only Aaron had been suspicious of the man all along. She felt the burn of shame as she remembered how close she had been to agreeing to marry him.

And now she was trapped. Helpless. How was she going to escape? With her hands tied, she couldn't hope to climb out, and with the gag she couldn't call for help. She pushed herself to her feet and walked around her prison, looking for a way out. The passage where the trickling sound came from was also where the worst of the odor was. With no light coming from that direction, she couldn't see how she would be able to get out that way.

She sank down to the floor again and laid her forehead on her knees. Was there no way out? Was there no hope? Solomon was right. She would marry him and go along with his charade for the sake of Reuben's son. A little boy she had never met. She would spend the rest of her life protecting that boy . . . Solomon knew her so well.

But Aaron would never understand her change of heart. Her chance at happiness with a man she could trust was gone.

Dulcey's words from last night echoed in her head. *"Turn to Jesus,"* she had said.

Full of doubt, Elizabeth closed her eyes.

I don't deserve anything from you, Lord God. But have mercy on me. Save me from this pit I've gotten myself into.

Suddenly, noise came from above her and dirt sifted from the ceiling. The wooden door opened with a bang and light streamed in, blinding her.

"Here's some more company for you, my dear."

A body dropped down and landed in the center of the floor. Elizabeth squinted as Solomon leaned over the opening.

"No, he isn't dead yet, but he soon will be. Enjoy your last moments together."

The door slammed closed again and Elizabeth heard Solomon driving away. She crawled forward on her knees and saw that the body Solomon had tossed into the pit with her had red hair. She pushed with her elbow until she was able to roll him over on his back. Blood soaked his shirt.

"Aaron." His name echoed in her mind but was muffled from the gag in her mouth. Was he dying as Solomon had said?

His head moved to one side. "Elizabeth?" He raised a hand to his head. "Is Solomon gone?"

She shook her head to show him she couldn't speak, then he reached for her gag and untied it.

"Solomon isn't here." She coughed. "He said you were dying."

"I don't feel like I'm dying, but he shot me and then hit me over the head. I hoped he thought he had taken care of me for good." He sat up. "Turn around and I'll untie your hands."

"You've been shot? And the fall down here was enough to kill a man."

"I came to while Solomon was driving me here but pretended to be out. He was talking about you and I had to find out where you were." Aaron stopped and cupped her cheek in his hand. "His talk didn't make much sense, but I heard enough to know that his mind isn't right. Perhaps it never has been."

After he finished untying Elizabeth's hands, he tapped his wooden leg. It was in two pieces, broken in his fall.

"I'm glad this is the only leg that broke." He unstrapped the leg and pushed it to the side. "We will have to work together. I need your help to get out of here."

"But you're bleeding."

Aaron pressed a hand to his side. "It's just a crease. I've had much worse than this."

Elizabeth helped him stand.

"It sure smells bad down here." Aaron looked around.

"Have you been able to explore much?" He pointed toward the dark passageway. "What is that way?"

"That's where the odor is coming from. I didn't see any light down there, so I didn't try going in that direction."

Aaron looked up at the door in the wooden ceiling. "If I had two good legs, I could boost you up there, but we have to work with what we have." He nodded toward the darkness. "Let's see where this goes."

Leaning on Elizabeth, he used her for a crutch. They went three steps into the darkness, then four. The sound of the trickling water grew stronger and so did the stench.

"Let's stop here for a minute and let our eyes get used to the darkness."

Elizabeth's arm encircled his waist. She could feel the strong muscles under his shirt and his confidence as he peered into the darkness. A sense of wonder broke over her.

"I prayed, and you came."

"What do you mean?"

"I prayed for the Good Lord to save me from this pit, and he sent you."

Aaron laughed. "Solomon sent me down here."

Elizabeth had no doubts. "Then the Lord used Solomon. Just like in the Bible story about Joseph and his brothers. Solomon meant it for evil, but God meant it for good."

After a moment, she felt him nod. "You're right. I used to think God wasn't interested in me, but the more I learn, the more I realize how good he is."

Elizabeth peered into the dark space in front of them. "I can see a little. It looks like it isn't a passageway at all. It's just more of the same wall all the way around." She couldn't see the source of the water, but the faint light gleamed off wet walls. She looked down. "But what is that on the floor?"

Aaron looked down at the heap at his feet and stiffened. "That's what is causing the putrid odor. Turn around and we'll go back."

They made their way to the light again, and Aaron lowered himself to the floor.

Elizabeth looked back. "Do you know what that is?"

"I thought I recognized the smell. It's a body, and it's been here for a while."

"A while? How long do you think?"

"A couple months, at least."

"Who do you think it is?"

"Is there anyone from the area who is missing? Anyone who has disappeared?"

"No one from the community." Elizabeth thought about it. "The only one who has left is Abel Patterson, but Solomon told us he had gone back east to live with his son."

"And sold him his farm and everything with it." Aaron put an arm around Elizabeth's shoulders and drew her close. "I don't think Abel moved back east. I think he's been here the whole time."

The thought of Abel in this pit, unable to get out . . .

"Do you think Solomon killed him before throwing him in here?"

Aaron's voice was grim. "I hope so, for Abel's sake." Then he drew her closer to him. "Remember, Solomon intends to come back here for you. He needs you for his plans, so he won't leave you in here for more than a day or two."

Elizabeth leaned her head on his chest, closing her eyes. "But even if he comes back for me, he'll never let you out of here alive."

His heart beat faster under her ear. "We'll pray for someone to rescue us. Both of us."

As Elizabeth slept, Aaron watched the beams of sunlight move across the floor. By now, the folks searching for Elizabeth would realize that he was missing, too. Did Dulcey go to find the others when he didn't meet her like he had promised? Did she tell them where he had gone?

But even if she had, did anyone know about this place? It was on the Patterson farm, but part of the old homestead, not the new and modern buildings near the road.

The sunbeams were slanted toward the wall when he heard a wagon coming.

"Elizabeth." He kept his voice to a whisper as he jiggled her shoulder. "Someone is coming."

She raised her head, instantly alert. "Is it Solomon?"

"I don't know, but we should be ready. Help me over to the shadowed part there, where he won't see us right away when he opens the trapdoor. Maybe he'll come down here to look for you."

"How will he get down?"

"There's a ladder outside. That was probably how he got you down here earlier."

They waited in the shadows, watching the trapdoor. At the sound of voices, Aaron drew a hopeful breath. Miller would come alone.

The door opened, silhouetting a man's head against the afternoon sky.

"Aaron?" It was Gideon. "Are you down here?"

"Ja," Elizabeth said. "We're both here."

"Watch out. We're going to send the ladder down."

As the ladder descended, Aaron held Elizabeth against the wall, then let her go once it was in place. She grasped the ladder, looking up at the familiar faces, then turned back to him.

"I'll be able to climb up, but you'll need help. You go first and I'll help you balance."

He hopped over to the ladder, grabbing it to steady himself, then reached for her. "Climb up there. I want to see you safe before another minute goes by. Then Gideon can help me out."

By the time Aaron emerged from the pit, Elizabeth was in the arms of Lydia, Katie, and Dulcey. Abraham and Jonas were also there, along with Levi and the Zooks.

"Has anyone seen Miller? I mean Solomon?"

"We saw him driving toward Millersburg a couple hours ago," Abraham said.

Aaron met Elizabeth's gaze. "We need to go there too. We have something to report to the sheriff."

As the group listened, Aaron told them what had happened, with Elizabeth interrupting with her version as needed.

"I never met Abel Patterson," Aaron said, "but if someone wants to go down there with a light, we could identify him for the police."

Gideon volunteered, his face grim. He lit one of the candles they had brought for the search and went down the ladder. He was back up within minutes, shaking his head.

"It's tragic. Ja, it's Abel Patterson. I recognized his clothes. He must have ended up in here soon after I last spoke with him." He passed a hand over his eyes. "We don't have any evidence to show that Solomon is the one who murdered him, but I think the circumstances might be enough for the sheriff to arrest him."

"One question I have is, how did you find us?" Aaron asked, looking around. "Who knew where to look?"

"It was Dulcey," Jonas said. "She said she saw Solomon come this way often, and one time she followed him. She thought he hid money somewhere around here. And when Rusty came home pulling the wagon behind him, but without you or Dulcey, we knew something was wrong."

"Then Dulcey told us that you had gone to talk to Solomon, and we thought we knew where to start looking," Casper added.

Dan and Ephraim helped Aaron into the back of Abraham's wagon where he could sit with his foot hanging over the edge. Elizabeth and Dulcey joined him, and the group started for home.

The Zooks headed north to their homes when they reached the Berlin Road, Dan and Ephraim shaking Aaron's hand. Before Casper followed his sons, he grasped Aaron's hand.

"Thank the Good Lord we found you. If it hadn't been for Dulcey, we would never have known where to look."

"He was watching over us, I think."

"He knows how much we need you." Casper's eyes were wet as he turned and followed his sons home.

Gideon went to his own home while the rest of the silent

group rode to the Weavers' farm. When they arrived, Abraham climbed down from the wagon, his face grim.

"Everyone come in. We'll have a quick supper and make our plans," Abraham said.

Aaron hopped off the back of the wagon while Lydia went to get his crutches. He patted them like old friends. He would make another wooden leg, but until then he was thankful to be able to get around.

Lydia tended to Aaron's wound while Elizabeth and Dulcey fixed a light supper. Aaron couldn't shake his exhaustion and ate less than he thought he might. Elizabeth, sitting next to him, took only one slice of bread and buttered it, but didn't finish even that morsel.

He took her hand under the table and squeezed it. "Are you all right?"

She nodded. "But I feel like we aren't done yet. Solomon is still out there somewhere, and tomorrow morning a little boy will be arriving on the train from Mississippi. If we don't do something, he will be in Solomon's clutches and under his influence."

Abraham leaned forward. "We need to decide what we're going to do. First, we need to meet that train."

"Elizabeth and I will do that," Aaron said. "The lawyer thinks she is the boy's aunt and is intending to give him into her care."

"The lawyer's name is Harlan Hoben," Elizabeth said. "We have to tell him who I really am."

Abraham nodded. "He needs to know the truth of the matter. We also need to go to the sheriff and tell them what we suspect about Solomon."

"His name is Simon Miller." Aaron looked around the table. "At least, that was the name I knew him by in the Shenandoah Valley. I couldn't be sure I had the right man until today. When I saw his pistol, I knew it had to be him. He kept it on a red-and-gold-braided leather lanyard. I've never seen another one like it."

"I'll go to the sheriff." Jonas looked at Abraham. "Will you come with me?"

Abraham nodded. "Is there anything else?"

Lydia spoke up. "What about Dulcey and me? Do we just wait for word of what happened in Millersburg?"

Abraham smiled at his wife. "I think you should both come with us. The sheriff might need another witness, and Dulcey can tell them what she knows."

"The law won't listen to me," Dulcey said.

"You're not in the South anymore," Jonas said. "If you are willing to make an accusation, the sheriff will take your statement. It could make a difference in whether they decide to arrest him or not."

Abraham stood up. "It's going to be a hard day tomorrow, and we will have to leave early in the morning to get there in time." He glanced at Elizabeth and Dulcey. "Until then, I don't think either of you should leave the house. We aren't certain that Solomon, or Simon Miller, went into Millersburg. He could still be looking for Dulcey, thinking he has Elizabeth safely imprisoned."

As Aaron attempted to settle down to sleep that night on a pallet on the floor of Jonas's room, the day's events ran through his mind. He tried to relax, but he still felt the jitters of facing down the barrel of Miller's pistol. At least he had found Elizabeth, safe and alive. He turned his head toward the door. Beyond that piece of wood, across the landing at the top of the stairs, in the bedroom he had been using since he came to the Weavers' farm, Elizabeth was sleeping in the company of her friends, Katie and Dulcey.

He prayed that they would all be even more secure by this time tomorrow.

18

Elizabeth was up before dawn. Datt had already milked the cow and hitched the horses to the wagon for the trip to Millersburg. Mamm and Dulcey had worked together to make biscuits and bacon, food that would provide both breakfast and dinner for them and could be eaten while they traveled, while the rest of them inserted board seats into the wagon bed. Seven of them would be driving to town, and it would be a long ride.

They were off before the sun had cleared the horizon. The morning mist lay on the fields but would soon burn off in the sunshine.

"It would be a good day for raking hay," Datt said.

Jonas sat on the wagon seat beside him. "The weather should hold until Monday. We'll have time to do the work then."

Elizabeth sat with Dulcey in the front of the wagon bed, on a seat facing the rear so they could chat with Mamm and Katie as they rode. Aaron rode alone in the last seat, his gaze never resting in one spot for long. He was as nervous as she was. Every once in a while, he caught her watching him and gave her a reassuring smile.

The morning was still early when they drove into town, but people were moving about and the stores were open. Datt walked the horses down the street.

"We'll put the team up in a livery stable," he said over his shoulder. "I rushed them to get here in time, so they deserve a good rest before we head home."

As they drew close to the livery nearest the courthouse, Jonas said, "That black horse in the corral looks like Solomon's."

Datt drove by slowly. Elizabeth sucked in her breath when she saw Solomon's gelding.

The horses turned the corner a block past the courthouse, and Datt pulled up at Elijah Wilson's livery. The place was quiet, unlike the stable they had just passed.

"Is anyone here?" Datt called.

A black man came from the back of the stable, wiping his hands on a rag as he came toward them.

"What can I do for you?"

"We need to stable our horses for a few hours. They need a good rubdown and some good feed. They've worked hard already this morning."

The man smiled. "I can sure take care of that for you."

While they were talking, Jonas helped the rest of their group out of the wagon. Elizabeth's arm was locked with Dulcey's. Her friend had been shaking with nerves ever since they had reached town.

"I'm Elijah Wilson," the man said, nodding toward the group but with his gaze on Dulcey. "You folks in town just for the day?"

"That's right. We have some business to take care of, but we don't know how long we'll be."

Elijah chuckled. "Well, as you can see, I have plenty of room for the horses. You can bring your wagon inside, too, if you want to keep it off the street."

While Datt and Jonas helped Elijah with the horses, Aaron gathered Elizabeth and the other women around him.

"Elizabeth will come with me to the train station while Jonas and Abraham go to the sheriff's office." He looked from Mamm to Katie to Dulcey. "What will you three do while you wait for us?"

Mamm looked at Katie and Dulcey. "I think we would like to stay in one place rather than walk through town visiting the shops."

Aaron nodded his agreement. "There might be a hotel near the train station where you could wait. They often have separate waiting rooms for ladies."

Dulcey shook her head. "You go on. I can't go there."

"Why not?" Elizabeth said.

Aaron frowned. "Dulcey's right. She would have to wait outside, and that won't do."

"That isn't right." Elizabeth felt her cheeks grow hot. "Why couldn't she come in?"

Dulcey squeezed her arm. "They got a sign there. I can't read, but I know what it says."

Datt, Jonas, and Elijah walked up to them. Elijah's face was stormy. "I can read that sign. It says, 'No colored allowed.' The lady is right, she would have to wait outside."

"Then we'll have to find somewhere else," Mamm said. "We can't leave Dulcey alone with Solomon in town."

"Y'all are welcome to stay here," Elijah said. "I don't have fancy chairs like at the hotel, but there's a bench in the back room and I can offer you some cool, clean water."

Datt smiled for the first time all morning. "Thank you. I have been worried about Dulcey, knowing who she might run into here in town."

"Are y'all in danger from something?"

"A man named Solomon Mast."

Elijah snorted in disgust. "I know the man. I won't serve him here, but I know what he looks like. I'll protect these women for you."

A train whistle sounded in the distance.

"We need to get to the train station," Aaron said. "How far is it from here?"

"Just two blocks," Elijah said. "One down and one over."

"We'll meet you there with the sheriff," Datt said.

Aaron could go quickly on his crutches when he needed to. Elizabeth hurried to keep up with him until they got to the crowded platform outside the passenger station. The train hadn't arrived yet, but the whistle blew again, closer than before.

Turning to Elizabeth, Aaron said, "It's the train from the south, so it should be the one with the lawyer. We need to keep an eye out for Miller. He is probably on the platform somewhere, and we don't want him to know we're here until the sheriff arrives."

They moved to a spot along the wall of the station and waited. Elizabeth watched the people, trying to calm her nerves. Reuben's son was likely on that train. When she rescued him from Solomon, then what would happen? She would keep him safe, warm, and protected, but could she ever learn to love this boy? Or would he grow up to be just like his father? She shuddered, suddenly afraid of what the future might bring.

"Are you all right?" Aaron grabbed her hand and pulled her closer to him.

"I'm nervous, I suppose." She looked into his eyes. "What if . . . what if I don't like the child?"

He smiled. "The Good Lord will give you a love for him and calm your fears."

Elizabeth smiled back. He was right. She could feel the assurance radiating from Aaron.

Then the whistle blew again, and the train was in sight. The noise grew too loud for any more talking, so Elizabeth just watched. As the train pulled to a stop alongside the platform, the crowd surged forward. In the middle, Elizabeth spied a familiar tall figure.

"There he is," she said, leaning close to Aaron so he could hear her.

At the same time, the doors to the passenger car opened and people spilled out onto the platform. Which door would the lawyer come out of? Would she know who he was?

"Follow me and stay close," Aaron said.

They wormed their way through the throng, Solomon's hat always floating above the thinning crowd ahead of them. Some people coming out of the car moved away quickly while others gathered in groups, visiting with the family or friends who had come to meet them. Finally, they were right behind Solomon as he made his way toward the passenger car.

Elizabeth saw movement on her left. Datt and Jonas were coming their way along with a heavyset man wearing a badge.

Then an older gentleman appeared in the doorway to the train car in front of them. In his arms was a sleeping child, no more than two years old. Aaron and Solomon started toward the man simultaneously. Solomon reached the lawyer and stretched out his hand.

"Welcome to Millersburg, Mr. Hoben," he said.

Aaron came up on his right. "Not so fast, Miller."

Solomon turned to him, his face blanching when he saw Aaron with Elizabeth behind him.

"No. You're . . . you're dead." He looked at the lawyer, then at the sheriff who had come up on his left side.

"Simon Miller? I'd like you to come with me. I have a few questions to ask you."

Elizabeth cringed as Solomon turned toward her, his face full of terror that turned in an instant to hatred. But as the sheriff put a hand on Solomon's arm, he tore away and ran down the platform toward the caboose at the end of the train. The sheriff ran after him as the crowd watched. Solomon launched off the end of the platform, stumbling as he landed, then limped around the caboose and out of sight.

"Stop!" the sheriff shouted. He followed Solomon off the platform and around the caboose. "Stop!"

Elizabeth heard a gunshot, then the sheriff lifted his pistol and fired. The sheriff went out of sight behind the caboose. In a few minutes, he came back into view and looked toward the crowd. He shook his head, and Elizabeth pressed her fist to her mouth. Solomon was dead.

At the sheriff's signal that Miller hadn't survived, Aaron looked at Elizabeth, then back at the lawyer. Mr. Hoben held the sleeping boy as if he were a sack of potatoes and fished in his vest pocket for his watch. He snapped it open, then looked toward the sheriff with distaste.

"It looks like my trip has been for nothing."

Aaron stepped forward. "Mr. Hoben? Harlan Hoben? My name is Aaron Zook, and this is Elizabeth Kaufman."

As he motioned for Elizabeth to come up beside him, the look on Mr. Hoben's face turned to relief.

"Thank goodness," he said, his voice rich with a familiar honey-smoothness that Aaron had missed since he had been in the North. "I have been corresponding with Mr. Mast, and he led me to believe that you were indisposed in some way, Miss Kaufman."

Elizabeth shook her head. "I think we have a few things to clear up—"

"But we should find somewhere quiet where we can talk," Aaron said.

"Very good," Mr. Hoben said. He shifted the boy in his arms, then finally handed the sleepy toddler to Elizabeth. "Is there an office somewhere in town where we can discuss these matters?"

"We'll try at the hotel," Aaron said. "It's over here next to the station."

The hotel was happy to rent them a room for a fee, which Mr. Hoben paid. "Send in a lunch for us also, if you will be so kind." He pulled out his pocket watch again.

"And can you tell me when the next train leaves for Cincinnati?"

Once they had settled themselves in a large room on the ground floor of the hotel and their lunch was brought in, Harlan Hoben picked up his knife and fork and glanced at them.

"Don't worry about me. I can talk while we dine. I only have an hour before my train leaves." He took a bite, then gestured to their plates. "Eat, please."

Aaron glanced at Elizabeth, then took the boy from her and set him on his lap. He was a handsome boy who looked nothing like Reuben. As he came fully awake, he started to fuss, so Aaron cut a bite of ham and gave it to him.

"One thing that needs to be cleared up," said Elizabeth, "is that I am not Reuben's sister as you assumed. I am his widow."

Mr. Hoben stopped chewing, then swallowed. "His widow? According to Mrs. Kaufman, that is, the woman I had assumed to be Mrs. Kaufman, he had said he was never married. She found your name and location in a pocket after Mr. Kaufman's demise, and came to the conclusion that you must be his sister."

"I understand that." Elizabeth pulled a folded paper from the reticule hanging from her wrist. "This is the marriage certificate from when I married Reuben."

Wiping his mouth with a napkin, Mr. Hoben took the paper and held it at an angle to get the best light.

"Yes. Yes, everything seems to be in order." He looked at Elizabeth. "But had he abandoned you or dissolved the marriage in any way before he married the other Mrs. Kaufman?"

Elizabeth shook her head. "He left to go to war, but I always assumed he would return, until I got word about his marriage and his . . ." She glanced at the boy sitting in Aaron's lap. "His son."

Mr. Hoben gave the child a look that told Aaron he didn't like children, especially two-year-old boys.

"I suppose I'll have to take him back to Mississippi, then. Unless there is an orphan home here?" He looked from Aaron to Elizabeth with a hopeful expression. "Not that I want to leave the boy," he added quickly, "but he is an orphan. His mother's people don't want him, considering how she had shamed them when she . . . well, that is a story that has no bearing here. Except that now that Mr. Mast is no longer with us, and you are not directly related to the boy, there is no other place for him."

The boy. Aaron felt the weight of the child on his lap and saw the bright curiosity in his eyes as he tried to capture a pea from Aaron's plate. He knew what it was like to grow up alone, without a father and mother. He had had Grandpop, but an old man's gruff companionship was a poor substitute for a mother's love.

"We'll take him." The words sounded before he thought. He glanced at Elizabeth's surprised face. "I mean, I'll take him. You don't need to find another place for him. I'll provide for him and raise him like my own."

Mr. Hoben finished the food on his plate and pushed it off to the side. He picked up a case and took some papers from inside. He read through them while Aaron and Elizabeth waited.

"These papers say that I am authorized to give the boy,

Jefferson Davis Kaufman, to Elizabeth Kaufman, or her representative, Solomon Mast." He looked at Aaron. "Are you related to Elizabeth Kaufman?"

Aaron couldn't look at her. He had spoken too soon. "No, I'm not."

Elizabeth leaned forward. "The papers only have my name on them, correct? There is nothing that states the relationship I'm supposed to have to the boy?"

He looked through the papers again. "That is correct."

"Then you can give the boy to me after all."

Mr. Hoben smiled. "Young lady, if you were a man, you would make a fine lawyer. If you're willing to take him, I can give the boy to you."

Aaron put one hand on her arm. "Elizabeth, are you sure?"

"More than anything in my life." The smile she gave him was clear and open, without any fear.

"Then that is settled." Mr. Hoben slid the paper across the table to Elizabeth and handed her a pen. "If you will sign here, my work is done."

She dipped the pen in Mr. Hoben's inkwell and signed her name without hesitation.

Mr. Hoben took another paper from the case. "Here is the boy's birth certificate. I must warn you, though. Do not try to contact his grandparents. Other than financing this trip to bring the child here, they want nothing to do with him. They have already paid a retainer fee to my partners and myself to react quickly if that ever happens."

"You don't need to worry about that," Aaron said. "When we said we would take him, we meant it."

"That is that, then." Mr. Hoben snapped his case closed

and stood up. "Please, feel free to stay and finish your meals. I have to arrange for my passage home."

The lawyer walked out, leaving Aaron alone with Elizabeth and the boy. She reached for him and took him on her lap.

"I'm not sure Jefferson is a good name for a child this young."

"He was named after the president of the Confederacy." Aaron gave the boy another bite of ham. "So, what should we call him?"

"We?" Elizabeth smiled as she brushed the boy's fine blond curls out of his eyes. "You heard the lawyer. I'm the one who was just awarded custody of him."

Aaron leaned closer, ignoring the teasing tone in her voice. "I meant we. A boy needs parents, not only a mother. I've told you before that I wanted you to be my wife. Over the last few days I've become even more certain. I can't go through my life without you. Will you marry me, Elizabeth? Will you be my wife?"

She rested her cheek on the boy's head. "How do you feel about children?"

"I love children." He grinned at her. "And I pray that we will be blessed with many of them, starting with little JD here."

"JD? What kind of name is that?"

"Then you come up with a better one." He scooted his chair closer to hers. "But first, I want your answer. Will you?"

Elizabeth's eyes grew moist. "You once told me that perhaps my dreams were the wrong dreams. That if I gave my will over to the Lord, he would show me the right way. The right dreams." She held JD closer. "I think that you were part of my dream all along. I still don't feel like I deserve this, but I will take it as a gift from my Father's hand."

"Does that mean that you will marry me?"

She nodded. "As soon as you join the church. And build your house."

Aaron stood and leaned over JD to kiss her, and the boy squirmed when his beard brushed his face. Aaron pulled back, just enough to look into Elizabeth's eyes.

"Will we always have children coming between us when I want to kiss you?"

She laughed. "I hope so, Aaron. I do hope so."

Epilogue

"Now you take care of yourself," Elizabeth said, hugging Dulcey. "I'm going to miss you."

Dulcey hugged her back. "God did a good thing when he brought us together, didn't he?"

Elizabeth held on to her friend with a tight grip. Letting her go meant that she would be leaving for Michigan and Elizabeth might never see her again.

"Are you going to write to me?"

Dulcey smiled, pulling away so she could see Elizabeth's face. "Don't you worry. Now that you and your mama taught me to read and write, I will send you letters regular. Just you see. And you got to write to me too. I want to hear all about how that boy of yours does when he grows up. You've got to tell me all about any others that the Lord blesses you with."

"You, too." Elizabeth shared a secret smile with Dulcey.

She was the only one Dulcey had told that she was expecting a child in the autumn.

A deep voice growled from the wagon seat. "We won't get any letter writing done if we don't get going."

Elizabeth and Dulcey laughed.

"That man of mine, he can sure try a woman's patience."

Elizabeth looked over Dulcey's shoulder at Elijah. The two had gotten married in December and had made their home in the Weaver's Creek community after the businessmen in Millersburg had forced him to close his livery stable and move out of town. Elizabeth still didn't understand why a freedman wasn't welcome in Ohio. But then Elijah had heard about a job possibility up north.

"You won't stay?" Elizabeth knew when she asked what the answer would be.

"You know there ain't no place for us here. Elijah has got to have a job." She gave Elizabeth a final hug and climbed into the wagon seat next to her husband.

Elijah started the wagon down the road, waving goodbye to Aaron while Dulcey waved her handkerchief at Elizabeth until they turned the corner at the Berlin Road and were out of sight.

Elizabeth sighed. "I'm going to miss her so much."

Aaron put an arm around her shoulders. "I know you will. It's too bad they couldn't stay for the wedding, but Elijah has to get to Grand Rapids to get that job and he couldn't waste any time."

"Mamm, Mamm, look!"

As Elizabeth turned to walk back to the house with Aaron, JD came running out of the barn with Dan's son Cap close behind. The three-year-old held a ball of fluff in his hands.

"JD," Cap called. "Bring that kitten back here. You know it isn't big enough to leave its mother."

Her son stopped as Elizabeth walked up to him. He was always collecting something to bring to her. This time it was a little gray kitten, its eyes not even open.

"Listen to Cap, JD. The kitten needs its mamm."

"But look!"

"I see it. Now obey."

JD gave the kitten back to Cap, who took it into the barn.

"You know he'll bring home a bobcat next," Aaron said as he held out his hand for their son to hold.

"I hope not." Elizabeth took JD's other hand so he could walk between them.

"Are you ready to see your new house?" Aaron asked.

"Is it finished?"

"Nearly." Aaron opened the front door. "We've been working almost every day on it so it's ready in time for the wedding next week."

Elizabeth stepped into the spacious front room. The movable walls weren't installed yet, so the ground floor was open, large enough to seat the entire community when it was their turn to host the church meeting.

"The kitchen is done. The stove was delivered last Friday."

"It's beautiful." She ran her hand across the smooth top of the big table. Large enough for several children to sit around it.

JD tried to pull his hand out of hers. "I want to run."

"Not inside the house."

Elizabeth smiled. Aaron's response had been automatic. A father's response.

"I'm not sure I can wait a whole week," Elizabeth said.

Aaron's eyes crinkled as he grinned at her. "You're the one who decided on the date."

"I know. And I do want Katie to be able to attend. Her baby is still so young."

"Jonas won't let her leave the house, you know."

"I know. We'll wait."

"Come upstairs," Aaron said. "The bedrooms are finished."

They climbed the narrow stairway from the kitchen to the second floor. Casper had said they would appreciate having a full upstairs instead of just a loft and Elizabeth agreed. There were four bedrooms, one in each corner of the house, with two windows in each room to catch the summer breezes.

"Which one will be ours?"

"Ah, that's the surprise I've been saving for you. Let's go back downstairs."

Aaron led them to a room Elizabeth hadn't seen before, next to the kitchen and behind the stairway. He opened the door and Elizabeth walked in. It was already furnished with a bed and a wardrobe.

Aaron grinned at her. "This is our room. It's handy to the kitchen, and I won't have to climb the stairs so much."

Elizabeth gave Aaron a hug that quickly turned into a kiss that took her breath away. It would have lasted longer, but JD pulled on Elizabeth's skirts.

"Outside? I want to play."

"We'll go sit on the front porch."

JD led the way this time. The porch had a special swing just for him, and he knew right where it was. Elizabeth and

Aaron sat in the comfortable willow chair for two that Rosina and Casper had made for them and watched JD play.

Aaron grasped Elizabeth's hand. "I don't know about you, but I know my dream has come true."

She smiled at him. "A home."

"A family."

"And you." She squeezed his hand.

He pulled her closer and cupped her cheek in his hand. "And you."

Then he kissed her, sealing their promises to each other once more.

After the kiss, Elizabeth sighed as he held her in his arms. "Next week can't come soon enough."

Read on for an excerpt from
BOOK 1
in the Journey to Pleasant Prairie series.

"A compelling story of family and place. A great read."
—ANN H. GABHART, bestselling author of The Innocent

A NOVEL

HANNAH'S CHOICE

Jan Drexler

JOURNEY TO PLEASANT PRAIRIE

1

Conestoga Creek, Lancaster County
October 1842

Hannah Yoder stamped her feet against the October evening chill seeping through her shoes. Darkness already reigned under the towering trees along Conestoga Creek, although the evening sky had shone pale blue as she walked along the path at the edge of the oat field minutes ago. The north wind gusted, sweeping bare fingers of branches back and forth against scudding clouds.

Where was Adam? She had been surprised to see his signal after supper, when *Mamm* had asked her to check on the meat in the smokehouse. She had been surprised to see the bit of cloth hanging on the blackberry bushes so late in the day. They had used the signal since they were children, ever since Adam had discovered that they both liked spying birds' nests in the woods.

She shivered a little. The cloth on the brambles had been blue instead of the yellow Adam always used. It could be a mistake. Perhaps one of her brothers had caught his shirt on the brambles instead.

A breeze fluttered dry leaves still clinging to the underbrush around her. She would wait a few minutes more, and then go back into the house. When a branch cracked behind her at the edge of the grove, Hannah lifted the edge of her shawl over her head, tucking a loose tendril of hair under her *kapp*, and slipped behind a tree. Let him think she was late. It would serve him right to worry about her for a change. He had been so serious lately. What was it about turning twenty that made him forget the fun they had always had? Would she be the same in two years?

Like a hunting owl, a figure flitted through the trees to her right. Hannah stilled her shivering body, waiting for Adam's appearance, but the figure halted behind the clump of young swamp willows at the edge of the clearing. So, he was waiting to frighten her when she arrived. Hannah smiled. She'd circle around behind and surprise him instead.

As she gathered the edges of her cloak to pick her way through the underbrush, she heard a giggle from her left. Liesbet? Hannah waited. She didn't want her younger sister spying on her conversation with Adam.

The wind tore fitful clouds away from the harvest moon, illuminating the clearing as Liesbet stepped into the light.

"Where are you?" Liesbet peered into the dark underbrush. "Come now, I know you're here."

Hannah clenched her hands. Liesbet was like a pesky gnat at times, always following her when she wanted to be alone. She was ready to step out from behind the tree to confront her when Liesbet spoke again, in English instead of *Deitsch*.

"George, stop playing games with me. You're going to scare me."

Hannah froze. Who was George?

Suddenly a man leaped from the trees behind Liesbet and caught her around the waist. She turned with a little shriek and fell into his arms.

"George, you did it again. I know you're going to be the death of me one day."

Hannah covered her mouth to keep a gasp from escaping. The man who had been hiding among the willows wasn't Adam.

"Ah, lass, you're so much fun to scare, but you know 'tis only me, not some ghoulie prowling around the woods here."

Liesbet giggled and snuggled closer to George. As he turned into the moonlight, Hannah could see him clearly, from his blue corded trousers to the snug-fitting cap perched on top of his head. His cocky grin reminded her of a fox carrying off a chicken from the henhouse. Certainly not an Amish man, or even Mennonite or Dunkard. She had never seen him before, but Liesbet had, for sure. She ducked farther behind her tree before either one of them could spot her.

"Give us a kiss, lass. The boys and I are only here for the one night. We're heading on to Philadelphia tomorrow."

Hannah could hear the pout in Liesbet's voice. "You're going away again? You never spend any time with me."

"Aye, and my sweet Lizzie, whenever I ask you to come along, you always play the little girlie who stays at home."

"It wouldn't be proper for me to tag along with you and your friends."

George's low laugh sent chills through Hannah. "No, lass, not proper at all." Then his voice took on its teasing tone again. "Admit it, you're just too young."

"I'm nearly sixteen!"

"Aye, like I said, you're just too young."

They grew quiet, and then Hannah heard a groan from George. She risked a glimpse around the tree. Liesbet was pressed up to him, her hands clinging to his shoulders while she kissed him. As Hannah watched, the man pulled Liesbet closer, one hand reaching up to pull off her kapp and letting her blond curls tumble to her shoulders. He buried his fingers in her hair, continuing the kiss until she struggled to pull out of his grasp. She stepped just beyond his reach and gave him a coy look.

Liesbet, what are you doing?

"Do you still think I'm too young?"

"Lizzie, you're enough to drive a man to distraction."

Hannah heard a warning in George's voice, but Liesbet turned her back on him and walked to the edge of the clearing. She was playing games with the man, but the look on his face in the moonlight was hungry. Predatory. Hannah shivered again.

"When will you get back?"

"In a week or so, you can bet on that, and then I'll be around for another of your kisses."

Liesbet turned to look at him, her face a careful pout. "Why can't you stay here? I don't like it when you're gone so much."

"I have to go, Lizzie, but you know I can't stay away from you too long."

There was another pause as Liesbet turned her back on the man. Hannah would have smiled if Liesbet's game wasn't so dangerous. It wasn't often she didn't get her way.

George snaked out a hand to catch her elbow and pull her close. "Lizzie, lass, give me another kiss. The lads are waiting for me."

After another lingering kiss, George released Liesbet and turned her around, giving her a solid swat on the behind before he took off along the creek bank, whistling as he went.

Hannah watched Liesbet as she stood in the clearing, bouncing on her toes, humming the same tune George had been whistling, her pretend pout gone.

Stepping out from behind her tree, Hannah tugged her shawl off her head. "Liesbet, what are you doing?"

Liesbet jumped, and then turned on her sister. "You were spying on me?"

"It's a good thing I saw you. Who is that man and what are you doing with him?"

Liesbet hugged herself and smiled at Hannah. "He's my beau."

"Your beau? You mean he's courting you?"

"Of course he is. You were the one spying on us. Didn't you see him kiss me?"

"Just because a man takes a kiss doesn't mean he has courting on his mind."

Liesbet waved her hand in the air to brush Hannah's concerns away. "You're just jealous because you're not the only one with a secret beau. I know how you and Adam meet out here in the woods and your silly signal flag on the bushes." Her voice gloated.

Hannah felt the blood drain from her face. "Adam's not so secret, and he's not my beau. We've known each other all our lives."

"*Ne*, Adam's not secret, but *Daed* doesn't know he's asked you to marry him."

Hannah caught her lower lip between her teeth to keep herself from retorting to Liesbet's accusation. *Ja*, Adam had spoken of marriage, but it was just a game they played. He wasn't serious.

Liesbet's smile set Hannah's teeth on edge. "And I know I saw him kiss you the other day."

Hannah felt her face heat up. Adam had stolen a kiss, one that had made her heart pound, but one kiss didn't mean anything, did it?

"Surely you can't compare that to what I just saw between you and that . . ."

"His name is George McIvey, and I'm going to marry him."

"Liesbet, you can't!"

"I am, and you can't stop me. If you say anything to Daed, I'll tell him all about how you and Adam have been sneaking around." Liesbet lifted her chin as she faced Hannah. "I'll tell Mamm too."

"Liesbet, not Mamm. You'll set her off on one of her spells," Hannah protested, but Liesbet had won the argument. There was nothing she could do to stop her sister except give in to her demands, the way she had for the last nine years. Liesbet still played the delicate invalid, even though Hannah suspected she had outgrown the effects of the diphtheria long ago.

And she couldn't have Liesbet spreading tales about their neighbor. It didn't matter that Hannah was eighteen and well into courting age. Adam wasn't Amish.

"Then you keep my secret, and I'll keep yours," Liesbet said.

Hannah hesitated. Liesbet smiled the way she always did when she knew she was getting her way, and her eyes glinted in the moonlight.

"But what if that man is dangerous? Can he be trusted? How long have you known him?"

A frown crossed Liesbet's face, and then the moon disappeared behind another cloud and the clearing was shadowed once more. Hannah could barely see her sister's silhouette against the darker trees behind her.

When Liesbet spoke, her voice was unsure. "I've known him long enough, and he's never been anything but kind to me."

"He isn't one of us. He isn't Amish."

"He isn't a backward Dutchman, you mean." Liesbet's voice was bitter, her uncertainty vanishing as quickly as it came.

Hannah gasped. "You better not let Daed hear you talk like that."

"Don't worry, I won't. But you can bet I won't be marrying any stick-in-the-mud farmer, either."

Hannah took a step toward her sister. "But, Liesbet, you'll break Mamm's heart . . . Promise me you won't see him anymore."

Liesbet shrugged, the movement only a rustle in the dark. "Whatever you want." She turned and ran back toward the house, a shadow in the night.

Acknowledgments

It's always bittersweet to come to the end of a series of stories. With this book, we say goodbye to the Amish of Weaver's Creek, and their future lives are left to our imaginations. At the same time, the end of one story means I have the opportunity to invest my time in new projects!

I want to thank Vicki Crumpton, Barb Barnes, Michele Misiak, Karen Steele, and the other editors and staff at Revell and Baker Publishing Group for their tireless work to bring the best in Christian fiction to you, the readers.

I also thank you, my readers, for enjoying my stories and telling your friends about them. I love meeting you, and I hope we'll have the opportunity to meet in the future if we haven't already.

And as always, thank you to my dear husband who patiently listens to my story knots and often comes up with just the right way to untangle the thread at the right time.

Most of all, I thank my Lord and Savior, Jesus Christ, for his call on my life.

Jan Drexler brings a unique understanding of Amish traditions and beliefs to her writing. Her ancestors were among the first Amish, Mennonite, and Brethren immigrants to Pennsylvania in the 1700s, and their experiences are the inspiration for her stories. Jan lives in the Black Hills of South Dakota with her husband, where she enjoys hiking and spending time with her expanding family. She is the author of *The Sound of Distant Thunder*, *Hannah's Choice*, *Mattie's Pledge* (a 2017 Holt Medallion finalist), and *Naomi's Hope*, as well as several Love Inspired historical novels.

SEPARATE BEDS

A History of Indian Hospitals in Canada, 1920s–1980s

Separate Beds is the shocking story of Canada's system of segregated health care. Operated by the same bureaucracy that was expanding health care opportunities for most Canadians, the "Indian Hospitals" were underfunded, understaffed, overcrowded, and rife with coercion and medical experimentation. Established to keep the Aboriginal tuberculosis population isolated, they became a means of ensuring that other Canadians need not share access to modern hospitals with Aboriginal patients.

Tracing the history of the system from its fragmentary origins to its gradual collapse, Maureen K. Lux describes the arbitrary and contradictory policies that governed the "Indian Hospitals," the experiences of patients and staff, and the vital grass-roots activism that pressed the federal government to acknowledge its treaty obligations.

A disturbing look at the dark side of the liberal welfare state, *Separate Beds* reveals a history of racism and negligence in health care for Canada's First Nations that should never be forgotten.

MAUREEN K. LUX is an associate professor in the Department of History at Brock University.

Separate Beds

A History of Indian Hospitals in Canada, 1920s–1980s

MAUREEN K. LUX

UNIVERSITY OF TORONTO PRESS
Toronto Buffalo London

© University of Toronto Press 2016
Toronto Buffalo London
www.utppublishing.com
Printed in Canada

ISBN 978-1-4426-4557-8 (cloth)
ISBN 978-1-4426-1386-7 (paper)

Library and Archives Canada Cataloguing in Publication

Lux, Maureen K. (Maureen Katherine), 1956–, author
Separate beds : a history of Indian hospitals in Canada, 1920s–1980s
Maureen K. Lux.

Includes bibliographical references and index.
ISBN 978-1-4426-4557-8 (bound). – ISBN 978-1-4426-1386-7 (paperback)

1. Native peoples – Hospitals – Canada – History – 20th century. 2. Native peoples –
Hospital care – Canada – History – 20th century. 3. Native peoples – Health and
hygiene – Canada – History – 20th century. 4. Discrimination in medical care – Canada –
History – 20th century. 5. Medical policy – Canada – History – 20th century. I. Title.

RA450.4.I53L89   2016   362.1089'97071   C2015-907180-1

This book has been published with the help of a grant from the
Federation for the Humanities and Social Sciences, through the Awards
to Scholarly Publications Program, using funds provided by the Social
Sciences and Humanities Research Council of Canada.

University of Toronto Press acknowledges the financial assistance
to its publishing program of the Canada Council for the Arts and the
Ontario Arts Council, an agency of the Government of Ontario.

**Canada Council Conseil des Arts
for the Arts du Canada**

ONTARIO ARTS COUNCIL
CONSEIL DES ARTS DE L'ONTARIO
an Ontario government agency
un organisme du gouvernement de l'Ontario

Funded by the   Financé par le
Government   gouvernement
of Canada   du Canada

Canadä

For Mila Grace and Nora Katherine

Contents

Illustrations

Acknowledgments

As I write, Canada's historic Truth and Reconciliation Commission is presenting its final report documenting the dark history and the damaging legacy of residential schools. *Honouring the Truth, Reconciling for the Future* demands that all Canadians not only acknowledge that our privilege came at a terrible cost, but that we might also listen and learn how to build a respectful future. I hope that in a small measure this work heeds the Commission's call that we learn from the past to build that future.

Many people aided my research, though all errors and omissions are mine. At the Stó:lō Research and Resource Management Centre, Tia Halsted took the time to walk me through the history and the grounds of the former Coqualeetza Indian Hospital. Janice Kennedy at the Battlefords Tribal Council Indian Health Services provided invaluable insight into the past, present, and future importance of community-directed health services. Gail Boehme took time from her Director's role to explain how the All Nations Healing Hospital came to replace the Fort Qu'Appelle Indian Hospital. Carol Greyeyes introduced me to Matthew Joseph, who spent a day teaching me the "people's history" of Fort Qu'Appelle. Kathy Kinew at the Assembly of Manitoba Chiefs helped ease access to archival records. I would also like to thank Siksika Chief Fred Rabbit Carrier and Councillor Kendall Panther Bone for their guidance and advice. These busy people patiently fielded my requests for help; without their encouragement and support this research would not have been possible. Thank you all. Most importantly, they also introduced me to their communities' most valued Elders.

I had the honour to meet and learn from Elders Agnes Cyr at Fort Qu'Appelle and Hazel McArthur at Stoughton, who experienced the hospitals in different ways. They are both gone now. Frank Malloway Sr invited me into his home and shared his history at Sardis, BC. Over lunch and tea in Winnipeg, Grace Anderson taught me about work in an Indian hospital; her daughter Renata Meconse took the time to chauffeur me around. At Siksika, Dave Melting Tallow graciously shared his most painful experiences with a stranger. I hope that I have told their stories with the honour and respect with which they were given. Finally, I would like to thank Linda and Roy Little Chief. Roy never let me forget why this history needs to be told.

I could not have asked for a more supportive and collegial group of scholars than Brock's history department, especially Renée Lafferty-Salhany, Carmela Patrias, John Sainsbury, Danny Samson, Dave Schimmelpenninck, and Liz Vlossak. History of medicine colleagues Erika Dyck, Geoff Hudson, and Peter Twohig have helped more than they know. I had the benefit of able and cheerful research assistants Charity Blaine, Austin Brooks, Steven Lee, and Leslie Wiebe. I would particularly like to thank Alma Favel-King, who lived the struggle over the North Battleford Indian Hospital. I also thank Julie Grahame of the Yousuf Karsh estate for permission to reproduce Mr Karsh's compelling portraits.

A Canadian Institutes of Health Research/Associated Medical Services operating grant supported my research. Some of the material in Chapter One appeared as "Care for the 'Racially Careless': Indian Hospitals in the Canadian West, 1920–1950s," *Canadian Historical Review* 91, no. 3 (2010); sections of Chapter Five appeared as "We Demand 'Unconditional Surrender': Making and Unmaking the Blackfoot Hospital, 1890s to 1950s," *Social History of Medicine* 25, no. 3 (2011).

Finally, I thank my family for the constant love and support that sustains me; the babies carry the hope for our brighter future so it is to them that I dedicate this book.

St Catharines
December 2015

SEPARATE BEDS

A History of Indian Hospitals in Canada, 1920s–1980s

Introduction

On a cool August morning in 1946, war hero and Canadian governor general, Field Marshall Viscount Alexander of Tunis, with a wave of his hand, officially declared Edmonton's sprawling Charles Camsell Indian Hospital open. Among the guests were the hospital's namesake, Charles Camsell (recently retired deputy minister of mines and resources), Indian Affairs bureaucrats, Catholic clergy from the Edmonton Residential School, medical staff, and "several Indians." The local press reported that Lady Alexander alone toured the wards (while her husband waited outside), where "many dark heads" had "prettied up" to greet the viscountess.[1] On the children's ward eight-year-old patient Doreen Callihoo from nearby Villeneuve, Alberta, presented her with a bouquet of roses.[2] High drama intended to demonstrate the gift of modern medicine, the opening ceremony also alerted Canadians to the arrival of a progressive and benevolent state actively guarding the national health. The Indian Health Service (IHS), once the poor stepchild of Indian Affairs, came under the expert management of the newly created department of National Health and Welfare. The Edmonton institution, not the first "Indian hospital" to be opened (though the largest, with up to 500 beds), was part of an aggressive postwar expansion that by 1960 included twenty-two institutions with more than 2,200 beds for the treatment of Aboriginal people (First Nations and Inuit).[3]

Much in that opening ceremony informs this study of Indian hospitals in Canada. It signalled the state's changing relationship with Aboriginal people in the latter half of the twentieth century. The rise of expert and objective medical authority supplanted often-meddlesome Christian missionaries, and redefined what was commonly referred to as the "Indian problem," or the anxieties Canadians experienced by

Aboriginal people's continued legal and cultural differences. The long-standing policy of assimilation, or "integration to citizenship" as it came to be known, would be pursued by other means. Moreover, with both growing population and presence in towns and cities, Aboriginal people came under greater scrutiny for their perceived threats to the nation's hygiene and morality. Indian hospitals not only promised to contain disease, but also assured concerned Canadians that theirs was a humanitarian government that extended the benefits of modern health care and a "fair deal" to the long neglected. At a time when Canada was consciously defining and investing in the "national health" that would culminate in Medicare, racially segregated institutions reassured citizens that their access to modern hospitals need not be shared with Aboriginal patients. Doreen Callihoo represented the people's gratitude – docile, infantile, and muted – effectively obscuring other meanings of Indian hospitals.

Indian hospitals represented a very different promise to the "several Indians" and "many dark heads" at the opening ceremony. The impact of the colonizing practices of the state and settler society – repressive legislation and economic dispossession – had plunged First Nations communities into hunger and disease.[4] Neglect and parsimony characterized the government's response, though rudimentary care, particularly vaccination, attempted to limit the spread of disease from reserve to town. Epidemic disease often prompted intense medical attention that, together with the police, confined and quarantined, only to leave when the immediate threat abated. Though never consulted, many First Nations leaders who had long sought relief from the burdens of illness and the socio-economic conditions of its rise, welcomed Indian hospitals, particularly those established near reserves. While communities recognized and attempted to ameliorate the underfunded hospitals' many shortcomings – the coercion, the overcrowding, and the high-handed, paternalistic management – the qualifier "Indian" came to define them as community institutions. First Nations hospital employees who performed the poorly paid domestic chores, also provided comfort and advocated for children and elders in their own language. Their presence as cultural brokers and interpreters for patients blunted the hospitals' colonizing impulses, reminding us to look beyond acts of resistance as the sole manifestation of subordinate power.[5]

Scholars of colonial medicine have drawn attention to the inadequacies of a simple binary of colonizer and colonized to explain a complex relationship. Certainly in Canada the rhetoric situated Western medicine as evidence of the colonizer's superiority, most often in order to disparage or repress competing systems of indigenous healing. As historian Waltraud Ernst argues, our understanding of the other social dimensions of medicine are lost in an approach that "conceives of medicine as determined mainly by the agenda of colonialism." The putatively colonized may well use Western medicine and its institutions in ways and for reasons never intended by the colonizer. Ernst continues: "There is more to medicine within a colonial setting than the discourse of colonialism."[6] Many communities saw nothing necessarily incompatible in incorporating Western biomedicine into their indigenous healing practices. Indeed, medical plurality is the norm in much of the world. With its single biomedical system that points to organized medicine's influence – and its insecurities – in marking out its ground to the exclusion of all others, Canada is an anomaly. Nevertheless, indigenous healers and midwives survived the formal and informal efforts to suppress their work in the nineteenth and twentieth centuries, though much was lost.

As systems of knowledge (including scientific biomedicine), all medical traditions emerge from rational cultural understandings of the place of humans in the environment. Consequently, there are many Aboriginal healing complexes that reflect the diversity of indigenous cultures in Canada. At the risk of oversimplification, one can say they share a world view that positions humans as but one part of the Great Circle of Life that includes the spirits of both the animate and the inanimate; there are few distinctions between the natural and supernatural, between medicine and spirituality. Healers, those best able to communicate with the spirit world, view illness as a loss of balance between mind, body, and spirit. Their cures vary from herbal treatments for commonplace ailments to community-wide spiritual rites of healing and regeneration such as the Sun Dance and the Potlatch. The Midewiwin that originated among the Anishinaabe (Ojibwa) in the early nineteenth century in western Ontario and subsequently spread west and south to neighbouring groups, is a hierarchical medicine society that teaches healing and the maintenance of spiritual and social harmony.[7] Midwives, too, continued their practice; for example, in the early years of settlement on the prairies they often shared their skill and expert knowledge of botanicals with struggling settler families.[8]

Under the changing circumstances of colonialism Christian missionaries worked with Indian Affairs officials and police to undermine healers and ban their practices. Furthermore, restrictions on people's

movement off reserve limited access to healing medicine, while intensive cultivation and agricultural settlement destroyed medicinal
plants. Moreover, indigenous healers acknowledged that some of the
sicknesses brought by newcomers might best be treated by settler
medicine. At the three on-reserve hospitals established in the 1920s –
southern Alberta's Blood and Blackfoot Hospitals, and the Six Nations'
Lady Willingdon Hospital (the latter two institutions originally owned
by the First Nations) – communities developed a medical pluralism or
syncretism that assimilated biomedicine into their healing practices.
However, for others such as the Inuit, who were relocated to southern
institutions for years at a time, the emotional and cultural impact on
patients and families was especially devastating. Clearly, the meanings
of Indian hospitals differed widely among Aboriginal peoples, but the
proximity of elders and community created some social and cultural
space to integrate Indian hospitals into indigenous notions of good
health. Indeed, by the 1990s, as communities regained some limited
autonomy in health care, Aboriginal medicine would emerge from the
secrecy imposed by state assimilationist policies that sought to undermine cultures and the languages that bore it.

First Nations communities also interpreted the IHS hospitals as the
state's concrete, if belated, recognition of its legal and treaty responsibility for health care.[9] Signatories to the eleven so-called Numbered
Treaties in the west and north understood medicines and health care to
be included in the treaties' terms. Medicine and medical care were discussed during many of the treaty negotiations, although the promises
invariably failed to appear in the written text. The sole exception was
Treaty Six (1876), whose text promised a "medicine chest." Vaccinations
and other medical care at annual meetings where treaty annuities were
paid confirmed the clear link of health care to the treaty relationship. The
federal government certainly anticipated this interpretation of Indian
hospitals. In his 1946 announcement of an expanded IHS, the minister
of national health acknowledged the existence of the "medicine chest
clause" in Treaty Six. But he promptly denied it in his next sentence.
His explanation at the time, which remained policy, was that IHS was
motivated by "humanitarian reasons and as very necessary protection to the rest of the population of Canada."[10] The understanding of
Indian hospitals as fulfilling a treaty right, held by many treaty people
(and a wide swath of the Canadian public), would be most vigorously
contested in the 1960s as IHS attempted to offload its responsibilities
to provinces. That understanding remains contested. By rejecting a

treaty right to health care, the state claimed instead to be pursuing a humanitarian policy (leaving it free to make frequent changes) that also characterized Aboriginal people as the objects of charity. Moreover, the minister's statement alerted Canadians to the dangers to their health and welfare that lurked in Aboriginal communities.

Indian hospitals reflected the changing role of health care in an emerging welfare state, but they were also firmly rooted in persistent, century-long government policies that, regardless of political stripe, sought to protect, civilize, and assimilate Aboriginal people.[11] Such a remarkably consistent policy stemmed from the notion that Aboriginal people could not be considered true individuals in the classical liberal model that was hegemonic in Canada by the twentieth century.[12] The liberal view of the individual as one whose body and mind were theirs alone stood in sharp contrast to Aboriginal world views that saw human beings as but one part of the larger circle of life. Theirs was a universe where individual wellness required community support and collective rites for its restoration and where the value of goods was realized in their redistribution. The Aboriginal legal status as wards of the state presumed the absence of rational citizenship and the inability to acquire it without fundamental social, cultural, and political change. As theorist Uday S. Mehta argues, at liberalism's core rests the "thicker set of social credentials that constitute the real bases" of citizenship.[13] The social credentials – race, ethnicity, gender, and class – defined the individual and marked those to be excluded, above all Aboriginal people.[14] Critical race scholar David Goldenberg draws attention to the "liberal paradox" where states, as they commit themselves to the principles of liberty and equality, construct a "multiplication of racial identities and the sets of exclusions they prompt and rationalize, enable and sustain."[15] Indeed, as Adele Perry notes, in Canada the liberal order and the nation that defined it "would find its own unique ways of rendering some people outsiders and, in the process, making itself."[16] Canada's liberalism, simultaneously "a utopian project of individual liberation *and* one of colonialism and subordination," cultivated its core of normal healthy white citizenship by marginalizing and excluding Aboriginal bodies.[17] This "liberal order" of governance attempted to subordinate and contain Aboriginal conceptions of the world and society; beginning in the 1880s schooling would accomplish this goal.

Historian Ian McKay calls residential schools "Christian/liberal manufactories of individuals, pre-eminent laboratories of liberalism" where Aboriginal children were "forced to be free, in the very particular

liberal sense of 'free,' even at the cost of their lives."[18] Christian churches
owned and managed the schools while government subsidized missionary zeal on a per diem basis rather than face the unpredictable and
ongoing costs of managing the institutions. But subsidies based on student enrolment to cover all institutional costs – food, clothing, wages,
and building maintenance – prompted churches to maximize revenues
by enrolling more students and feeding them less. Children spent less
time in the classroom and more time toiling in the laundry, the kitchen,
the fields, and the barns to maintain the institutions. This approach
was rationalized as a practical education and useful training for life
on the reserve. Early deaths at the schools or shortly after discharge
were all too frequent. Far removed from reserves and the influence of
concerned parents, residential schools significantly damaged the health
of their charges, who often brought disease back to the reserve.[19] As
early as 1907 Dr Peter Bryce, the chief medical officer for the Department of Indian Affairs (DIA), reported on the appalling condition of
children in residential schools and found an "intimate relationship
between the health of the pupils while in the schools and that of their
early death subsequent to discharge."[20] Bryce's report was widely distributed and caused considerable public criticism of the DIA, though
little change. Two years later Bryce advocated that a number of schools
be converted into sanatoria in recognition of the extent of illness in the
schools.[21] Some limited measures were undertaken in subsequent years
to guard schoolchildren's health, such as isolation rooms for infectious
disease and increased per capita grants to the institutions. Nevertheless, as historian Brian Titley notes, the DIA was often more concerned
with controlling its image than with improving the children's health.[22]
The surviving "ex-pupils" and their families were effectively isolated
on reserves. The contradictions inherent in the project to assimilate
through isolation would be recalibrated in the formation of the welfare
state, with similarly damaging results.

Foucault's famous "carceral archipelago" made scholars aware of
the continuities among institutions of isolation where experts attend
to those requiring reform or cure.[23] This "collusion of knowledge and
power" created institutions that "consolidated administrative authority, bureaucratic regulation" and colonial control.[24] In the broader colonial project of racial exclusion and segregation, Western medicine, far
from benign and apolitical, occupies what David Arnold calls a central
place in the "ideological as well as the technological processes" of colonial rule.[25] With the rise of the welfare state, where governing agencies

assumed increasing responsibility for aspects of life previously the remit of families or charities, isolation was, as Carolyn Strange and Alison Bashford argue, not a departure from liberal governance "but central to its internal logic." Public funds flowed into projects that, under the guidance of experts in human sciences and medicine, sought to normalize the behaviour of those who could not be trusted with the freedoms that healthy citizens enjoyed.[26] In what Robert Menzies and Ted Palys call the "gravitational forces" exerted by the state, medicine, and society to confine and isolate Aboriginal people, the Indian hospitals have much in common with the asylum, the school, the reserve, and the penitentiary.[27]

The meanings of Indian hospitals are also found in an increasingly shrill medical and bureaucratic discourse about the threat of rampant "Indian tuberculosis."[28] By the 1930s, reserves, the prime sites of segregation and colonization, seemed no longer adequate to contain disease. As historian Mary-Ellen Kelm notes, North American medical literature that pathologized the "discursive Indian" shifted its focus in the 1930s. From the deleterious impact of settlement and civilization (and the inadequate response of Aboriginal bodies) that led to notions of the "dying race," medical discourse increasingly concentrated on the threat that Aboriginal contagion posed to society.[29] Dr David Stewart, superintendent of Manitoba's Ninette sanatorium, advised that reserves were not "disease-tight compartments." Tuberculosis, he warned, "leaked" into ordinary communities through berries and handicrafts peddled by Aboriginal people. More alarming, the "racial carelessness and ignorance" of First Nations "soaked with tuberculosis" were spreading as Aboriginal populations were actually growing and "mingling with the general population," despite grave predictions of their imminent demise.[30] What historian Warwick Anderson calls the image of "disease-dealers" emerged to occupy physicians and bureaucrats alike.[31] Despite steadily declining tuberculosis rates in Canada generally, the healthy and clean were now vulnerable to the threat of "Indian" tuberculosis, which only fuelled the rhetoric. Though the disease's retreat began in the 1890s, well before any medical interventions, sanatorium directors like Stewart, represented by the Canadian Tuberculosis Association (CTA), naturally took full credit.[32] As medical experts whose social and political authority rose as tuberculosis rates fell, the CTA (which also included provincial health bureaucrats) urged the federal government to take responsibility for its wards. In a bold use of state power, by 1945 the CTA effectively designed the system of federally owned and operated Indian hospitals. Initially rationalized as tuberculosis sanatoria,

Indian hospitals in fact admitted patients suffering from all conditions based on race, not disease. The institutions not only isolated the alarming public peril of tuberculosis but also ensured that the CTA's member institutions would continue to be reserved for white patients. To paraphrase Foucault, an ascendant bureaucracy with its focus on Indian hospitals represented an effort not to isolate less, but to isolate better.[33]

Race, Class, and the Sanatorium Cure

Sanatoria – enduring institutions that adapted to the changing understandings of the disease, from "consumption" to tuberculosis – were established in Canada in the late nineteenth and early twentieth centuries. Fashioned after European spas with chalet-style architecture in bucolic settings far removed from the city's dank air and crowds, they offered "open air" treatment, bed rest, and nourishing food. Prominent citizens and volunteer groups ("anti-tuberculosis leagues") established most provincial sanatoria before the First World War, but the institutions soon came to rely on public funds. As the most popular, indeed the only, approach to the disease, sanatorium treatment required extended stays that focused on improvement and regulation of the self, where the "soul of the citizen" came under scrutiny.[34] A physician and former patient at the first Canadian sanatorium, in Muskoka in central Ontario at the turn of the century, G.D. Stanley recalled (fifty-three years later) that the "cure" consisted of fresh air, six daily feedings of milk and raw eggs, and, for him, exercise. Patients were expected to help each other: "The intimate association of one man with the others around him in entertaining one another, in extending help to one another ... all combined to create a fellowship that was indispensable ... and one of the outstanding treasures of my life."[35] His recollections evoke the picture of young, homosocial health and vitality, not disease. Stanley no doubt suffered from "incipient consumption" at a time when it was possible to feel "a little bit consumptive."[36] As treatment at Muskoka made clear, however, only the white upper classes suffered from the disease that could be cured at such institutions. By the 1920s, interventions that artificially collapsed the diseased lung, to induce it to "rest," augmented but did not supplant the focus on improving citizens. The director of Saskatchewan's Fort Qu'Appelle Sanatorium explained that the cure was not medicine or surgery but "an idea: a way of life ... the development of faithful endeavour, helpfulness, earnestness, good humour, kindliness and forbearance."[37]

As wards of the state deemed insufficiently advanced to benefit from training in rational citizenship, Aboriginal people were not generally accepted for treatment in provincial sanatoria. Neither Tranquille Sanatorium in Kamloops, British Columbia, nor Ninette Sanatorium in Manitoba admitted Aboriginal patients, and the Central Alberta Sanatorium only accepted them "when space was available."[38] Saskatchewan, with three public sanatoria by 1930 and more than 700 beds, made segregated space for them in the northern Prince Albert Sanatorium, while in the south the Saskatoon and Fort Qu'Appelle sanatoria reserved their beds for "taxpayers," though for a time the latter maintained a forty-bed "Indian wing" in order to repay debts to the federal government. Deserving patients, those judged by Indian agents as worthy of care and advanced enough to benefit from treatment, might be admitted, but only on the authority of the director of Indian Affairs in Ottawa. Social, not necessarily medical, criteria determined who might receive care: young residential school students whose families demonstrated progress along the path to assimilation.

Historians continue to debate the role of sanatorium treatment in the decline of tuberculosis.[39] Most agree that isolation of the ill may have protected the larger community from infection. However, sanatorium directors preferred to admit those whose disease was not too far advanced, those who stood a chance of recovery, leaving the most ill, or what were called the "hopeless cases," in the community. Historian F.B. Smith argues that the emphasis on sanatorium treatment, likely the least efficient use of public funds, served to enhance the medical reputation of sanatorium directors.[40]

A resilient institution that successfully incorporated changing understandings of tuberculosis, from open-air treatment to chest surgery to chemotherapy, the sanatorium has been studied as a site of exclusion and isolation. Confinement created healthy, self-governing citizens who, as Alison Bashford argues, were "released back into the community, as part of this new cultivation of the hygienic self."[41] The disciplinary function of the sanatorium emerged more clearly as tuberculosis became associated with the working classes and the poor. Reflecting nostalgically on his days as medical superintendent of Manitoba's Ninette Sanatorium, Dr A.L. Paine believed the pre–drug therapy regime created patients with "moral strength, courage and perseverance in fighting their disease." Through their struggle, patients became "more mature, better adjusted and educated, and with a higher potential for giving and receiving than ever before."[42] But as one expert admitted, "one

can marvel at how many recovered, though, in the final analysis, failures outweighed successes."[43] Armed with these attributes of safe and
healthy citizenship, the cured – or at least the improved – citizen could
leave the institution as a self-governing individual knowing they no
longer posed a risk to their families or community.

Antimicrobials developed in the late 1940s made tuberculosis much
more manageable, but institutional treatment remained necessary for
those who could not be trusted to follow the long course of chemotherapy. As Dr Wherrett, executive secretary of the CTA advised in a Department of Labour radio series *Canada at Work*, the sanatorium experience
not only restored health, but also improved workers. "Rest is still the
basic core of treatment," he advised, "but its effects are fortified and
augmented by new drugs and daring surgery." Wherrett recommended
state support for the rational (male) citizen to relieve anxieties about
his dependents while taking the cure; mortgage payments and life
insurance premiums should be paid by the province to "preserve these
props to family security."[44] Confinement in the sanatorium preserved
classed and gendered notions of the healthy family and society: "It's a
smart secretary too who sees that she doesn't lose her shorthand or let
her typing slip. Should she happen to be weak on spelling she can use
the months in hospital to become a better speller – a joy to any boss."
While science provided "miraculous tools" to fight tuberculosis "from
us it has a right to expect the knowledge and understanding which will
hasten mankind's victory over tuberculosis."[45] The medical discourse
of improvement through confinement is obvious, and clearly directed
at those who either through ignorance or social standing had not yet
acquired the ability to be rational, healthy citizens. As antimicrobial
treatment made the sanatorium cure increasingly obsolete, sanatorium
directors and the IHS again collaborated, filling their wards with Aboriginal, particularly Inuit, patients.

In Indian hospitals the treatment for tuberculosis was not aimed at
the soul as much as at the chest. The expansion of IHS institutions coin-
cided with the increased use of what Wherrett termed "daring surgery."
Aboriginal people – seen as incapable of healthy citizenship, that is,
unable to return to their presumed inadequate reserve homes without
infecting others, or "reactivating" their tuberculosis – spent long years
in hospital. Surgeons removed ribs, collapsed lungs, and, emboldened
by effective antibiotics, surgically removed the last foci of infection
in Aboriginal bodies. Indian hospitals, particularly Charles Camsell
Indian Hospital with its close association with the University of Alberta

medical school, provided "interesting clinical material" for teaching and research. As Jordan Goodman, Anthony McElligott, and Lara Marks argue, the concept of "usefulness" brings together medical experimentation, knowledge, and the state where otherwise "use*less* bodies were rendered use*ful* by being made use*able*."[46] Eight-year-old Doreen Callihoo, after presenting roses to Lady Alexander in 1946, would spend eleven of the next twelve years in the Charles Camsell Indian Hospital. She recalled that as a child she received streptomycin injections and twice-weekly painful pneumothorax treatments (air injected into the chest to collapse the lung). As an adolescent, she had two separate thoracoplasties (removal of several ribs at a time to collapse the lung), disfiguring procedures performed under local anaesthetic. She left the hospital after a year of antimicrobial medications, but returned the following year to undergo a pneumonectomy (the surgical removal of her lung) because of bronchiectasis, a chronic lung infection. But she survived. In her recollections for an in-house history twenty-three years later, she thanked the staff for the care she received because, as she put it, after spending her entire childhood in the institution "they were my family."[47]

Isolation and Integration

Indian hospitals need also to be viewed in the context of politics and the practice of postwar Canada's articulation of modern hospitals and the national health. North American hospital history emphasizes the expansion and transformation of the hospital in the late nineteenth and early twentieth centuries from almshouse to medical marketplace. In Canada, before 1890, hospitals, financed by charity and government, housed the sick poor while their social betters convalesced in the comforts of home. By the 1920s hospitals began to attract patients who demanded, and would pay for, the benefits that medicine seemed to promise: relatively safe and effective surgery, professional nursing, and technological innovations such as X-rays.[48] The modernizing hospital, where the poor were kept separate from the paying patient, actively shaped class inequality within and beyond its walls.[49] But even the "patient of moderate means" found access to hospital care increasingly difficult, leading to demands for the state to take a greater role in protecting and enhancing the national health. One of the first acts of the new Department of National Health and Welfare, created in 1945 as the flagship of the welfare state, was to take control of IHS and its expanding number of hospitals. A separate arm of the bureaucracy also

invested public funds into National Health Grants that for nearly two
decades beginning in 1948 provided matching funds for provincial projects of hospital construction, medical training, and disease control.[50]
By 1953 Canada had added forty-six thousand new hospital beds.[51]
The same bureaucracy managed Indian hospitals on the presumption
and promise that they would operate at half the costs of provincial
hospitals; in several communities the Indian and local hospitals were
literally side by side. This ensured that IHS hospitals would never draw
qualified staff or other resources away from community hospitals, with
dire consequences for Aboriginal patients. Indian hospitals reflected
and constructed racial inequality by making it seem natural that modernizing hospitals would be white hospitals.

Finally, the meanings of Indian hospitals are found in rapidly shifting federal policies in the 1960s that sought ultimately to sever the legal
and treaty relationship. With national hospital insurance in 1957, IHS
planned to close its hospitals and divert its funds to community hospital
expansion to accommodate First Nations patients. Local organization
and grass-roots activism, particularly (but not exclusively) in Treaty Six
communities in central Saskatchewan and Alberta, coalesced to protect
Indian hospitals as the only concrete acknowledgment of the Crown's
treaty promise of health care represented by the "medicine chest."
More threatening, national health insurance in 1968 would absorb First
Nations into provincial programs and ultimately dissolve the links
between the economic and political roots of ill health on reserves and
the state's responsibility for health care. Using the same liberal (and
Liberal) language of equality and "non-discrimination," it was an ominous foreshadowing of the infamous White Paper the following year
that proposed to dismantle completely the treaty, customary, and legal
relationship with Aboriginal people. While the White Paper's proposals were withdrawn within the year in the face of concerted and organized opposition, health and health care policy continued as contested
terrain. Indian hospitals emerged as sites of resistance where communities sought a measure of self-determination to address the poverty,
overcrowded housing, contaminated water, and inadequate infrastructure that gave rise to much illness.

Constructing Disparity

This thematic study examines the rationales for segregation in Indian
hospitals and the particular focus on tuberculosis; staffing and hospital

operations; coercion and the hospital experience; IHS efforts to shift responsibility for health care to the provinces; and community resistance and the articulation of the treaty right to health care. But such a singular historical focus on Indian hospitals risks repeating and reinscribing the state's vertical approach to health care, which sought to treat ill health without acknowledging or mitigating its economic, environmental, and political circumstances. Bad water and crowded houses are as important to this story as hospital beds and bureaucrats; the links between them form the backdrop to this study. The colonization of lands and resources, and the socio-economic inequities that create and maintain ill health, continued through the twentieth century, particularly as governments encouraged industrial resource development. Lest the connections between ill health and material realities become obscured in the telling, a brief and unsettling sketch of one community's experience with dispossession and its consequences at mid-century illustrates this study's broader themes.

Fort Alexander, 132 kilometres northeast of Winnipeg, was a trading and provisioning post on the Winnipeg River in the eighteenth and nineteenth centuries. Signatories to Treaty One in 1871, the Anishinaabe of the Sagkeeng First Nation made their homes nearby on reserved lands that straddled the river's mouth where it spilled into Lake Winnipeg. In 1927 the Manitoba Paper Company built a pulp mill and the company town of Pine Falls, complete with a hospital, eight kilometres upriver from the Fort Alexander community. Indian Affairs contracted with the local physician to provide health care for Anishinaabe residents, but when townspeople objected to their presence in the hospital, the government built an adjacent annex that in 1937 became the Fort Alexander Indian Hospital. During the Second World War local Anishinaabe men found work at the mill, although at war's end most lost their jobs to non-Aboriginal workers; some found work cutting pulpwood in the bush.

The Fort Alexander community, which relied on the Winnipeg River for its water supply, also suffered the environmental impact of the upstream mill and town. Pine Falls pumped its raw sewage into the river, and the pulp mill discharged twenty thousand gallons of toxic sulphur, lime, and sulphur dioxide into the river four or five times per day. Most of the sulphur dioxide occurred as a gas, which was stored until the prevailing winds blew away from the town of Pine Falls. It was then discharged into the air, though whether the toxic gas blanketed the reserve was "not considered too important."[52] Those who could afford it purchased water at the "unheard of price" of $0.60 to $0.75 per 45-gallon drum; even so, tests confirmed this "town water" was dangerously contaminated as well.[53] Between 1949 and 1958, in a population of less than 1,300, 462 infants were admitted to the Fort Alexander Indian Hospital with gastro-enteritis, and 19 died. In July 1958 alone, 33 infants were admitted and one died.[54] The IHS field nurse reckoned that mothers were negligent for bottle-feeding instead of breastfeeding their infants, although she did allow that many were forced to do so in order to work.[55] Accordingly, she advised that children should be taken from their parents as soon as possible and enrolled in the Fort Alexander Residential School. [56] But the school's water supply, also contaminated by raw sewage, was suspected as the cause of an infectious hepatitis outbreak in 1954.[57] Tuberculosis was also a problem that sent thirteen residents, escorted by RCMP, to sanatoria for treatment in 1957; however, a report to IHS suggested that gastro-enteritis caused by the polluted water supply "certainly outranks tuberculosis as a killer."[58]

Those made destitute by economic circumstances could apply to Indian Affairs for monthly rations, and the hospital's medical superintendent could recommend rations for the ill or incapacitated. For a family of two adults and four children (children received half an adult ration), calculated on a diminishing scale, adults received 950 calories per day, and children 805 calories per day (which included 330 calories in the one-pint milk ration for children under twelve).[59] A decade earlier Indian Affairs had conducted nutrition experiments at other Manitoba First Nations communities; they made clear the links between disease and an average diet that provided only 1,470 calories per day. Historian Ian Mosby compared those studies to a postwar University of Minnesota experiment that induced starvation in thirty-six adult volunteers with a diet of 1,570 calories.[60] As an IHS report noted, at Fort Alexander "the people who are in need because the man of the house is ill will get sufficient food for the family if the Medical Superintendent of the Fort Alexander Hospital is so inclined and not as a basic right."[61]

The thirty-bed Pine Falls Hospital with two resident doctors served the town's 3,200 residents. In the five years from 1955 to 1959 the occupancy never exceeded 43 per cent. The adjacent Fort Alexander Indian Hospital that served 2,800 residents of the Clandeboye Indian agency, with a rated capacity of thirteen beds had twenty beds and five bassinets. In 1959 the occupancy averaged 128 per cent. A provincial Hospital Survey Board, after inspecting the Indian hospital in early 1960, was "impressed with its inadequacy." Not only was the facility "obsolete" and constantly overcrowded, there were no fire exits, and inadequate isolation facilities. The Survey Board recommended its closure and an addition to the Pine Falls Hospital to accommodate the increased patient load; it urged that the addition not be segregated for the use of "Indian" patients, though "it might be necessary to provide a few separate beds."[62] The stark Fort Alexander experience, not atypical for communities in the path of resource development, highlights the synergies between environmental degradation, racial inequality, and the creation of health disparities.[63] It serves to remind us that ultimately Indian hospitals isolated and treated the consequences of colonization, and operated to maintain if not widen health disparities.

This history of Indian hospitals from the 1920s to 1970s is situated at the intersection of race, medicine, and public policy in the wider context of twentieth-century Canadian health care. This does not presume to be a comprehensive history of all the hospitals, but a thematic approach to the commonalities in the institutions operated by the bureaucracy initially known as IHS.[64] Although it was a national bureaucracy, the IHS established no hospitals east of the Ottawa River, reflecting both the Aboriginal population's distribution, and the political and medical anxieties in the west.[65] There has been little sustained scholarly attention to the history of the Indian Health Service or its hospitals. Progressive accounts, written by those most closely involved with the IHS and the Canadian Tuberculosis Association, focus on the bureaucracy's humanitarianism and particularly their role in the "conquest" of tuberculosis.[66] More recently, scholars have examined gender and colonialism in the IHS nursing service.[67] T. Kue Young's critical examination of the Sioux Lookout Indian Hospital in the context of cultural and socio-political dimensions of health and health care among northern Ontario's Cree and Anishinaabe, argues that without political and economic autonomy, medical and technological interventions have a limited impact on health status.[68]

This book builds on the compelling narratives of the subjective experience of Inuit in southern hospitals, and on oral histories of life in Indian hospitals that give voice to individual experience as embodied resistance.[69] It contextualizes these threads of experience in the larger fabric of twentieth-century health policy. To do so is not to create victims, but to acknowledge the often perilous world constructed at the intersection of race, medicine, and the imperatives of the nation's health. Indian hospitals, created and operated in the interests of Euro-Canadians as a modern reiteration of an older practice of quarantine, worked to maintain difference. By resisting the state's attempts in the 1960s to shed its legal and treaty commitments, First Nations were also pointing to the damaging futility of treating those made ill by poverty and deprivation, only to return them to the same conditions. When communities argued that they might best know their own health needs, and pursued a measure of autonomy to improve health, they were met with a bureaucratic and political resolve, striking in its intensity, to undermine and frustrate those efforts. To view Indian hospitals, like "Aboriginal history" generally, as ancillary to grander themes, obscures the links between marginalization, poverty, and disease. It is a "powerful fiction," then as now, to treat as distinct and unrelated two enduring twentieth-century narratives: the progressive march towards improved health care for Canadians and the seemingly intractable ill health in Aboriginal communities.[70] How it became normal and natural to see those narratives as separate is the subject of this history of "separate beds."

Chapter One

Making Indian Hospitals

Indian hospitals emerged from deep anxieties about Aboriginal people and their perceived threat to the public's health. Initially begun in concert with mission schools to keep ill children within the Christian embrace, with uneven support from the state, mission hospitals provided limited care to a "dying race." Literally and figuratively, through disease, isolation on reserves, and particularly the assimilationist policies in schools, "Indians" were expected to disappear as Canada embraced modernity in the twentieth century. That they did not, and indeed increased their presence in towns and cities, created considerable concern. By the 1930s, medical discourse shifted from civilization's supposed deleterious influence on Aboriginal people to the threat Aboriginal illness posed to the nation's health. With an increasingly strident rhetoric of the threat of "Indian tuberculosis," sanatorium directors working with provincial physician bureaucrats, pushed the federal state to protect society by creating Indian hospitals. Formalizing an already well-entrenched system of racially segregated care, Indian hospitals also made it seemingly natural that the sanatorium and the modernizing hospital would be reserved for white patients.

In the 1920s the Department of Indian Affairs (DIA) took control of some mission hospitals and nursing stations, providing limited physician and nursing services while continuing to subsidize missionary efforts. Though sporadic and piecemeal, increasing DIA involvement in health care was motivated by the foremost need to economize while isolating illness on reserves to protect the health of white communities, foreshadowing the more significant post–Second World War expansion of Indian hospitals. The department relied on mission and community hospitals, providing funds for construction and maintenance.

Unwilling to interfere with missionary control of hospital care unless forced by to do so by public criticism, the department confined its meagre medical efforts to isolating epidemic disease on reserves and hiring five travelling public health nurses to cover all the western reserves and schools. Dr Peter Bryce, appointed chief medical officer in 1904 to control medical costs, by 1907 began advocating for increased spending to stem the appalling death and disease rates of children in the department's schools.[1] Bryce's recommendations, calling for non-denominational schools and increased government financial commitment, were not well received. The DIA's Duncan Campbell Scott, rising from copy clerk in 1880 to chief accountant in 1893 to superintendent of education by 1909, found Bryce's recommendations "scientific ... [but] quite inapplicable to the system under which these schools are conducted."[2] After 1913, when Scott became deputy superintendent general (deputy minister) of Indian Affairs, Bryce's services were no longer required and he was pensioned in 1921.[3] That the DIA operated without a chief medical officer for fourteen years until 1927, and that the newly created Department of Health in 1919 did not include responsibility for Indian health, indicate a distinct lack of interest in health matters. Yet, at the same time, Canadians of the middling classes, increasingly health conscious, insisted on purchasing medical care in modernizing hospitals.

The transformation of the hospital from repositories of the sick poor to institutions that attracted paying patients actively shaped class and racial inequality within and beyond its walls.[4] Segregated wards and hospitals for racialized minorities were the norm in the Canadian west, mirroring the racial segregation in society.[5] For example, Chinese and Japanese patients in the early twentieth century suffered in Vancouver General Hospital's basement "Ward H" alongside "dirty indigent cases," those with particularly loathsome terminal illnesses.[6] Chinese tuberculosis patients in the 1940s were relegated to Vancouver's St Joseph's Oriental Hospital. Patients complained about the constant traffic noise from the railway lines on one side of the hospital, and the stench from the cannery on the other; there was little nursing care; patients were expected to clean the toilets; the food was unpalatable; and the Catholic missionaries actively proselytized dying patients. Many in the Chinese community avoided X-ray clinics for fear of being confined at St Joseph's. As community advocates noted, "Some have declared emphatically that they would rather die than go to St Joseph's Hospital." Public health nurse J.B. Peters urged: "When the Chinese were given the same type of facilities for treatment as occidental races they would cooperate in the same way."[7] Patients and their supporters who resisted such hospital care were deemed "racially indifferent" to health care and a danger to the community, further recommending their incarceration and segregation.

Community hospitals throughout the west and north also maintained "Indian wards" and segregated annexes; even hospitals that relied for their financial survival on DIA funds maintained strict racial separation. The Bella Coola Hospital on British Columbia's west coast received funds from the department for construction and equipment, but its "Indian ward" consisted of one bed and a chair, with neither chimney nor fire; Bella Coola was not an exception in British Columbia.[8] Like the Indian annex next to the Pine Falls Hospital, the St Boniface Sanatorium, owned by the Grey Nuns at St Vital Manitoba, maintained a separate Indian building.[9] Segregation likewise defined territorial hospitals in the post–Second World War period, when the privately owned hospital at Mayo, Yukon, simply refused to admit Aboriginal patients until the government built an Indian ward. In a tuberculosis survey in 1947 Whitehorse residents refused to share hospital gowns with "diseased Indians."[10] From its opening in 1948 the Yellowknife hospital confined Aboriginal patients to its ten-bed Indian wing with a separate entrance and waiting room.[11] As late as 1965 the Royal Commission on Health Services (Hall Commission) was told "there has been a tendency to place Indians in wards which are not as attractive or desirable as those used for white patients. Too often they have been treated in white institutions as indigent patients rather than as Canadian citizens."[12] The Indian annexes, Indian wings, and basement wards, demanded by community prejudice and inadequately funded by the state, actively shaped inequality and constructed an image of Aboriginal people as less worthy of care.

Government fiscal policy also worked to maintain the colour line in community and voluntary hospitals, especially its practice of paying somewhat less than the "indigent rate," or the rate paid by municipalities for the care of the poor. Defending the practice, federal bureaucrats argued that hospitals padded each bill to cover delinquent accounts, but since the department paid its bills eventually, hospitals should discount the rates charged for government patients. Not surprisingly, hospital administrators disagreed. In Alberta in the late 1940s the issue became particularly acrimonious when the manager of the Calgary Hospitals Board asked why the government expected Alberta communities to subsidize Aboriginal care: "Each Indian patient admitted and paid for by the government on the basis of $3.00 flat rate per day prohibits, during the period of his or her hospitalization, the admission of some civilian patient who likely would pay the full rates charged." Accordingly, he recommended that the "Calgary Hospitals Board adopts a policy of refusing to admit Indian patients."[13] The 846-bed Calgary General Hospital had treated only about eight Aboriginal patients in the previous six months.[14] To press the point the Indian Health Service (IHS) threatened that since the city's Calgary Stampede profited by Aboriginal participation, it would pay no accounts "incurred by Indians due to injury when competing in stampede activities."[15] Smaller community hospitals in Alberta also benefited in their efforts to attract and maintain paying patients. By 1950 Alberta hospitals had practically "ceased to accept a sick Indian except in the most emergent circumstances, and for the shortest possible time." Moreover, the hospitals "are overcrowded by patients from their own municipalities and for whose care they can depend on full rates."[16] State policy clearly aided hospitals' efforts to devote bed space to the right patient, the paying patient. As Lindsay Granshaw argues in reference to British hospitals, the active intervention of the state in providing hospital accommodation for the least advantaged in society removed them from the voluntary hospitals, thus reducing the stigma attached to the latter.[17]

The DIA only reluctantly moved from Indian wings to Indian hospitals. Beginning in the 1920s it came under increasing public scrutiny and criticism from provincial and national tuberculosis associations that charged the department was ignoring the threat posed by reserve populations, undermining their efforts to "clean up" provincial populations.[18] But unless Aboriginal communities funded their own hospital care, either directly or by paying for care in local community hospitals, if they could be admitted, the DIA only grudgingly invested in health care ("hospital" would be an exaggeration in many cases) in order to answer public criticisms. The conditions at Anglican boarding school on the Sarcee (Tsuu T'ina) reserve near Calgary, the subject of repeated medical inspections early in the century, had continued to deteriorate by 1920. Inspector Dr Corbett drew attention to one particular child in what had become grotesquely familiar reports:

> She lies curled up in a bed that is filthy in a room that is untidy, dirty and dilapidated in the northwest corner of the building with no provision of balcony, sunshine or air. Both sides of her neck and chest are swollen and

five foul ulcers are discovered when we lift the bandages. This gives her pain and her tears from her fear of being touched intensifies the picture of her misery.[19]

The "dirty and dilapidated" room was the school's infirmary. The following year inspectors found dirty floors and windows, and bed linens "stained with blood and puss [sic] marks old and recent."[20] Finally, the long-neglected school was fitted out with new sleeping porches and deemed a "hospital" with Dr F.T. Murray in the dual role of physician and Indian agent. Meanwhile the whole reserve became a "hospital area," with movement off reserve restricted while Calgarians were warned of the nearby threat of contagion.[21] Elder Helen Megunis, who attended the school in the 1920s, recalled: "We have lived an isolated life, after I became a young girl in my teens we were still isolated, there was no TVs, phone, electricity, plumbing, newspapers. It was strange, visiting Calgary during the stampede was our only contact with alien people of Calgary [sic]."[22] While it seems clear that infection crossed reserve boundaries, the direction of that spread was never questioned. The continued isolation of the reserve that literally adjoined the burgeoning city of Calgary was made possible through the formal and informal restrictions on the people's movements, always enforced by the Royal Canadian Mounted Police. The justification for isolation had certainly shifted from ostensible efforts to protect the Aboriginal people from unscrupulous whites to efforts to contain disease on the reserve and thereby safeguard the public's health.

By 1932, with only a "practical nurse" and cook in attendance, it was judged "scarcely a hospital."[23] The reserve's poverty limited treatment to little more than custodial care. Even X-rays were impossible since the reserve remained without electricity until 1937, although the adjacent city of Calgary enjoyed its benefits since at least the 1890s.[24] But the conversion of the mission school to "hospital" was more than merely discursive; it indicated an increasing concern to monitor the racial boundaries of reserve and disease. It also marked a shift towards secularization (accelerated in the postwar period) that removed the sometimes interfering missionaries, who often acted as mediators and advocates for Aboriginal communities.[25] Creating the dual role of Indian agent/physician, while economical, also afforded closer state regulation and medical surveillance. The fate of the Tsuu T'ina seemed sealed when government anthropologist Diamond Jenness arrived to conduct "rescue anthropology" that documented the last gasp of a dying race.[26]

Despite predictions of their imminent demise, the Tsuu T'ina by the early 1950s improved their economic circumstances by developing the reserve's oil and gas resources, and given their experience with the reserve boarding school, they were anxious to access medical care. But IHS continued to pay somewhat less for care than Calgary hospitals charged, leaving the Tsuu T'ina to subsidize hospital costs if they wanted treatment. Meanwhile reserve living conditions, especially housing, deteriorated, and as the supervisor of Indian Agencies noted, there was little logic in using their funds to pay hospital bills when they required so many necessities "before we can conclude that the people are not experiencing a substandard existence."[27] Despite devoting precious funds to pay for their care, Tsuu T'ina patients found themselves in the indigent ward. The modernizing hospital with patients anxious to purchase its services saw no need to take up valuable beds and offend middle-class sensibilities by admitting Aboriginal patients. Moreover, the state's minimal commitment to Aboriginal health care actively cultivated an image of the people as a burden on the community.

The largest (and wealthiest) reserves in the country – the Siksika (Blackfoot) east of Calgary and the Six Nations reserve in Ontario – at the suggestion and insistence of the DIA, built reserve hospitals in the 1920s.[28] At the Siksika reserve, the Anglicans' Queen Victoria Jubilee Hospital, built in 1897 in conjunction with Old Sun's mission school, became increasingly irrelevant by 1912 when the school was moved closer to the only source of electrical power on the reserve at the village of Gleichen. In 1923 the Siksika band council agreed to contribute to the construction and maintenance of a new hospital using the funds from the surrender of nearly half their reserve. Pushed by poverty and the promise of a better standard of living, in 1910 the Siksika had surrendered for sale 50,586 hectares of their reserve; by 1920 their trust fund from land sales amounted to nearly $1 million. As DIA inspector J.A. Markle reported, the Siksika agreed to the surrender on the condition that $400,000 would be for their immediate use, while the interest on the remainder was to be expended for the benefit of the next generations. It seems unlikely that the Siksika agreed (if they were aware) that all DIA operations on the reserve as well as goods and services promised in the treaty were henceforth to be paid from the band's funds. As Markle put it, "[the band] will soon have a sufficient income of their own to meet all their wants and … they will be no longer any expense on the government outside of what was guaranteed to them by the treaty, i.e. a cash annual annuity of $5 per head."[29] In January 1924 the sixteen-bed

Blackfoot Indian Hospital opened with two general wards, two semi-private wards, an operating room, dispensary, and living quarters for the matron and her four staff. At the Siksika council's insistence the hospital was to remain non-denominational and local Aboriginal healers were not to be disturbed in their medical work.[30] At Six Nations in 1927, at the suggestion of the DIA, the two-storey, twenty-bed Lady Willingdon Hospital opened at Ohsweken, for which the band council paid half the costs while also contributing to physician salaries. The DIA assumed complete control of the institution, limiting local Six Nations participation, despite their investment. Reserve women offered to form a hospital auxiliary to provide knit goods and incidentals, but the physician's influential wife rejected the proposal.[31] Both the Blackfoot and the Six Nations' Lady Willingdon hospitals would eventually come under complete government control by the 1950s.

Citing increased public criticism of the government in 1923, the Indian agent at Battleford in central Saskatchewan suggested an Indian hospital: "Many that should have gone to hospital have been attended at their homes on account of expense and several have died in filth and misery because there was no possible place to care for them and local hospitals would not take them having no accomadition [sic] for this class of patient which you cannot blame them after seeing some of these cases as we do in the course of our duties."[32] The next year the department considered building an Indian wing at the local Notre Dame Hospital where the Sisters of Providence would charge the government $2.50 per day for care. But hospital superintendent Sister Justinian demanded a separate Indian building with its entrance at the rear of the property instead of an Indian wing.[33] In the meantime Anglican bishop George Lloyd objected to the DIA "handing all our Anglican Indians in the Battleford area over to the tender mercies of a Roman Catholic institution at the time of sickness … You must know as well as I do the unfair leverage this gives to the Roman Catholics."[34] Fearing that funding an Indian wing at the Catholic hospital might necessitate an Anglican institution as well, Indian Affairs' D.C. Scott let the matter rest. There would be no hospital care for Aboriginal people in the Battleford area until 1947.

Aboriginal communities also actively advocated for better care. Elders recall that a delegation from Pasqua reserve in southern Saskatchewan travelled to Ottawa in 1928 (covertly circumventing the travel and fund-raising restrictions of the Indian Act) to protest their exclusion from community hospitals. A 1923 petition from the British Columbia

Indian Anti-Tuberculosis League likewise demanded improved care.[35] Indian commissioner in the west, William Graham, also agitated for hospital care in the 1920s, arguing that a departmental hospital in the Regina area with fifty to sixty beds with minimal staff could be maintained for less than half the per diem cost they were currently paying to local institutions. How those savings might be accomplished was left to the imagination. In any event, Graham was sure that most costs could be paid from band funds; indeed, from 1922 to 1924 Aboriginal communities paid for half their hospital costs. If Aboriginal people could find hospitals that would admit them, and they funded their own care, D.C. Scott saw little reason to entertain the notion of an Indian hospital. In reply to Graham's plea that he was faced every week with people "actually suffering and some of them dying for want of care," Scott replied that the "present system is adequate."[36]

Provincial bureaucrats and sanatorium directors who made up the Canadian Tuberculosis Association (CTA) held no such illusions. Anxious to know the extent of disease on reserves, they joined with the DIA to undertake medical surveillance of a number of British Columbia communities in 1926. For two years the survey X-rayed, examined, and gave advice to Aboriginal communities, with no offer of treatment. Researchers found a clear link between tubercular bone and gland infection in residential schoolchildren and the raw milk used in the schools. They concluded that the infection could not have come from home since few reserve families used cow's milk.[37] The DIA prevented that report from becoming public, and its 1928 *Annual Report* noted only that tuberculosis was about "five times more common among Indians" than among the general population (this statistic would vary widely depending on the circumstances), and that the Aboriginal people were too ignorant to make use of food supplies that would produce "robust health."[38] This desire to create a detailed "colonizing archive" while refusing treatment caused considerable outrage in communities.[39] A decade later physician bureaucrats found that surveys on reserves with no chance of treatment "only irritate the tuberculosis and public health authorities and the Indians."[40] Nevertheless, it seems clear that D.C. Scott was allowed to suppress the report linking schools with bone and gland infection in children if he agreed to appoint a chief medical officer, a position vacant for fourteen years since Dr Peter Bryce's ouster.[41]

Dr E.L. Stone, a colonel in the Canadian Army Medical Corps during the Great War and, since 1922, physician and Indian agent at Norway

House in northern Manitoba, took up the work of chief medical officer in 1927.[42] Stone's appointment, like Bryce's before him, was prompted by the need to manage the work and the costs of physicians contracted by the DIA to provide part-time medical care, particularly the quarrels between the physicians and the DIA's accountant who discounted their fees.[43] Departmental physicians, under strict supervision by the Indian agent lest they provide too many services, could do little more than recommend hospital care for their patients; ultimately bureaucrats and bookkeepers determined who was admitted to hospital and for how long, with a keen eye to the bottom line.[44] While Aboriginal patients were relegated to indigent wards or Indian wings and subjected to community prejudice, the DIA accepted the situation since its financial commitment was predictable and easily controlled.

In 1932 the top bureaucratic position in the Department of Indian Affairs (deputy superintendent) passed from the accountant D.C. Scott, to the physician Dr Harold McGill. Four years later the department itself was dismantled and made a branch of the Department of Mines and Resources with a severely reduced budget. Immediately, Indian agents were instructed to remove patients from hospital; there would be no funds for tuberculosis surveys or treatment in hospital or sanatoria; expenditures for drugs were reduced by 50 per cent; and "quarantine ... [was] to be rigidly enforced, with guards if necessary."[45] The expedient of ignoring the ill or confining them to reserve schools or mission hospitals rather than admitting them to local hospitals was dictated by the department's uppermost concern for economy in all things. But there were other considerations that influenced the form and place of medical treatment for Aboriginal people in the Canadian west.

In May 1937 sixteen-year-old "Mary" (not her real name) was discharged from Onion Lake's St Barnabas Residential School in Saskatchewan with tuberculosis after suffering haemorrhages for more than a year. Overcrowded residential schools had earned an appalling reputation for breeding disease among underfed students; when children like Mary became too ill they were sent back to their parents, with disastrous consequences for their home communities. Mary's father demanded she receive sanatorium treatment at the Prince Albert Sanatorium, but Indian Affairs' Dr Norquay refused. Mary's older sister, who had also contracted tuberculosis at the school and was treated at the sanatorium, had subsequently become pregnant though she was unmarried. According to the physician, the sanatorium cure – bed rest and the development of the attributes of healthy citizenship – had clearly failed, and it was her father's fault. Mary was therefore refused treatment, though the doctor did approve a $5 ration voucher. But when Norquay discovered that Mary's father spent it all on fresh fruit "which would necessitate the rest of the family participating if the fruit was not allowed to spoil," he warned that "this sort of foolishness would result in the withdrawal of such favours."[46] To appeal to the doctor's superiors, Mary's father engaged a lawyer who argued, "The child was well when she went to the school and contracted the disease there ... They [parents] know that there is care for sick white children and believe the same care should be afforded to Indian children." Publicly funded provincial sanatoria provided free tuberculosis treatment for "taxpayers," while DIA might purchase treatment when beds were available. Not until public criticism of government policy by a Saskatoon newspaper was director Dr Harold McGill moved to authorize treatment for a "a limited number of tuberculous Indians."[47] Physicians' keen surveillance and authority to enforce middle-class notions of sexual propriety and acceptable gender roles exposed medicine's collusion in the colonizing project. Mary died at the sanatorium four years later.[48] As a rule, and while there were white citizens awaiting entry to their institutions, sanatorium directors felt no obligation to treat Aboriginal people. Instead, through their Canadian Tuberculosis Association, they joined with provincial bureaucrats to pressure the federal government to establish racially segregated institutions.

The extent of tuberculosis on reserves remained the subject of much speculation. Manitoba's Dr David Stewart boldly claimed that in the western provinces the "death rate among Indians [is] ten to twenty times as great as that among white people, and over 30 percent of the total deaths from tuberculosis occur among the Indians, who comprise less than three percent of the total population."[49] Moreover, the statistical picture of Indian tuberculosis also illustrated a satisfying decline in the white death rate. As Stewart explained in 1932, the official death rate in Manitoba per 100,000, "if Indian deaths were dropped ... would become 40, and if the half-breed deaths were dropped, a non-Indian rate of 34/100,000 would emerge." Stewart's statistics became considerably muddled when he conceded that "half-breed deaths" were only an estimate because they were counted in the census "according to the white racial mixture, as French, Scotch or English." In a more candid moment he allowed that since so few Aboriginal patients were attended by physicians, "there is some doubt about the accuracy of death causes of Indians ... and there is the strong tendency to put down an Indian as dying of tuberculosis. The poor fellow scarcely is allowed to die of anything else."[50] Moreover, white tuberculosis deaths were not always recorded as such. With the disease's social stigma and its associations with poor living conditions and low income, many physicians cloaked tuberculosis deaths in euphemisms, further obscuring the statistical picture.[51] In white communities, as Wherrett admitted in his history of tuberculosis in Canada, "doctors did not always report the disease. Doctors avoided disclosure on death certificates."[52] Furthermore, those presenting themselves at tuberculosis case-finding clinics in white communities did so voluntarily; when such clinics began on reserves residents were routinely denied their Treaty annuity payments until they submitted to X-ray and examination.[53] Thus, despite the seeming isolation of many Aboriginal communities, the medical surveillance would become far more complete.[54] There are good reasons to question the oft-cited statistic that the tuberculosis death rate in Aboriginal communities was ten times the white rate.

The practice of keeping separate statistics for Indian tuberculosis rates and "white" (provincial or national) rates became routine, highlighting the source of danger while simultaneously emphasizing the good work accomplished by the sanatoria. Much of the tuberculosis statistic making,[55] intended as it was to emphasize the threat of "Indian tuberculosis" and prod the federal government to assume greater responsibility for treatment, tended to over- rather than underestimate the threat. This is not to argue that tuberculosis was not a problem, but those creating the statistics had reasons to construct Aboriginal people as "tuberculosis-soaked," according to Stewart.[56] As John O'Neil argues, the practice also constructed knowledge that reinforced unequal power relations: "an image of sick, disorganized communities can be used to justify paternalism and dependency."[57] While the threat of Indian tuberculosis was made clear, limited access to reserve communities frustrated a more thorough knowledge of the "Indian problem," which would have to await the bureaucratic regulation that the Indian hospitals afforded. In the meantime, efforts increasingly focused on the much more accessible residential schoolchildren and Aboriginal infants.

In 1933 Dr Ferguson, director of Saskatchewan's Fort Qu'Appelle Sanatorium, began an experimental trial of the controversial tuberculosis vaccine BCG (bacillus-Calmette-Guerin) on Aboriginal infants. He lived at the sanatorium, which was literally surrounded by reserves and the threat of contagion. Funded by the CTA and the National Research

Council, Ferguson's trial – premised on the understanding that "primitive" peoples were more vulnerable to tuberculosis and that resistance could not be acquired except on a evolutionary time scale – hoped to prove that BCG could provide effective resistance in "less evolved races."[58] The BCG vaccine, developed at the Pasteur Institute in Lille, France, found greater acceptance in Europe and especially in French colonies than in North America, where its use before the 1930s was limited to Montreal's working classes. But Ferguson's BCG trial required newborns who had never been exposed to the disease, that is, born in hospital; his unvaccinated controls were born at home on reserves. The nearby File Hills Indian Hospital, built in 1914 as the centrepiece of File Hills Farm Colony, which was intended to illustrate to dignitaries and foreign visitors the government's successful management of residential school graduates, was a fire hazard and severely overcrowded, with space for seventeen patients, but with a daily census of twenty-eight. Taking advantage of the federal government's Depression-era public works program in 1934, Indian Affairs secured $100,000 to build the Fort Qu'Appelle Indian Hospital, across Echo Lake from the provincial sanatorium.[59] Ferguson had the hospital he needed. His twelve-year BCG study was an apparent success: only six of the 306 children in the vaccinated group developed tuberculosis and two died; while 29 of the 303 in the control group developed tuberculosis and nine died. But Ferguson's research also revealed that 77 of the 609 children in the trial, or more than 12 per cent, died before their first birthday, while only four of these were tuberculosis deaths (two in each of the vaccinated and control groups.) In all, nearly one-fifth of the children in the trial died from other diseases, mostly gastro-enteritis and pneumonia.[60] Overcrowded housing, poor nutrition, and unclean water posed the greatest threat to children, but, unlike tuberculosis, did not spread to white communities.

The new Fort Qu'Appelle Indian Hospital, opened in 1936, was a dour three-storey brick building that shared none of the sanatorium architectural style's sleeping porches and expansive grounds (illustration 1.1). And while general hospitals rarely admitted tuberculosis patients for fear of cross-infection, the Fort Qu'Appelle Indian Hospital had no such qualms, keeping tuberculosis patients on the third floor, with maternity, medical, and paediatric patients on the second floor. By early 1938, of the hospital's sixty-five patients, fifty-one were treated for tuberculosis. The practice of isolating tuberculosis patients from the community, yet institutionalising them with non-infected patients, suggests that

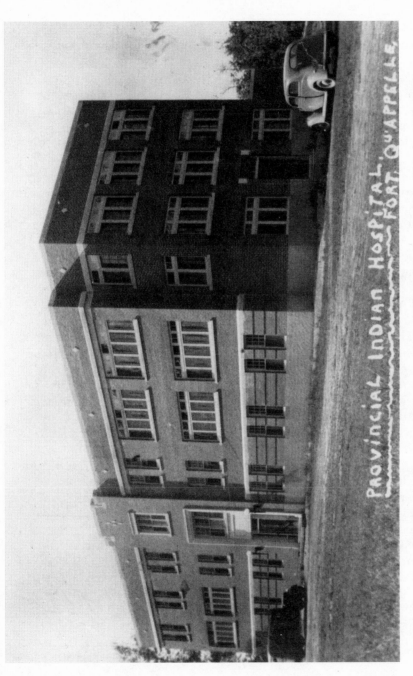

Illustration 1.1 Fort Qu'Appelle Indian Hospital. Built in 1936, the fifty-bed Fort Qu'Appelle Indian Hospital sat across Echo Lake from Saskatchewan's provincial sanatorium. It was the site of Dr R.G. Ferguson's BCG vaccine trial on Aboriginal infants in the 1930s and 1940s.

Source: Accession R96-472, Saskatchewan Archives Board.

their tuberculosis was seen as a threat only to the white community. As noted, the same year the hospital opened the Department of Indian Affairs became a branch of Mines and Resources, prompting director McGill's early 1937 directive mandating draconian cuts to all hospital treatment and explicitly ordering agents to remove patients from hospital. The bizarre logic of opening a new hospital while restricting hospital care cannot be explained without reference to the rationales for the hospital's creation: it emptied the forty-bed "Indian ward" that Ferguson's provincial sanatorium had been pressured by finances to maintain, while also providing facilities for his vaccine trial. BCG held great promise to control tuberculosis while leaving untouched the socio-economic conditions that led to its rise. The hospital was a success by the one standard that most mattered, as Indian Affairs branch director McGill enthused: "We have obviously a genuine sanatorium at this point which is taking care of these patients for almost exactly half what it costs to maintain a patient in a public institution." It is not clear how these savings were effected, but McGill added: "We have not had a single complaint of the treatment of patients."[61] The new Indian hospital, a tangible response to criticisms of state policies that left Indian tuberculosis untreated, came at the expense of medical care for Aboriginal people elsewhere, who, according to McGill's orders, were quietly removed from hospitals. Certainly Depression-era budget cuts adversely affected the chronically underfunded Indian Affairs, but endeavours like the Fort Qu'Appelle Indian Hospital suggest that expenditures were not necessarily or even primarily made in the Aboriginal people's interests.

In March 1936, the new Liberal minister of Indian Affairs, Thomas Crerar, agreed with the Catholic Archbishop of Winnipeg Alfred Sinnott that the department should contribute to a new hospital at Winnipegosis.[62] Despite Indian Health Service director Dr E.L. Stone's objection that it was not a suitable site since only 200 of the 1,200 residents were Aboriginal, Indian Affairs contributed nearly half of the $27,000 cost. The new Crerar Hospital, owned and operated by the Benedictine Sisters, opened in January 1937 with fourteen beds including a six-bed Indian ward. The hospital would be "freely open to sick Indians at such rates for maintenance as may be agreed upon from time to time," providing the Sisters with a small but steady income.[63] Though the Indian Affairs branch continued to contribute funds to finish the hospital, branch employees remained in the dark on many details since the minister and archbishop alone concluded the arrangements. In reporting on the newly opened building, Indian agent Waite and the departmental physician admitted their confusion: the Indian ward would treat tuberculosis, yet the new departmental policy prohibited the hospitalization of tuberculosis patients. The branch secretary replied: "I can give you no other answer in this connection than the instructions contained in the recent circulars on economy which have been sent to all Indian Agents."[64] It is not at all clear how many Aboriginal people were treated at the Crerar Hospital, despite the government's sizeable contributions in their name.

Reacting to the drastic cuts in Indian Affairs funding for tuberculosis treatment, the Canadian Tuberculosis Association warned that the "opinion has been expressed in some quarters that there is a higher incidence of the disease in communities adjacent to Indian reserves."[65] Physician and Liberal member of parliament Dr J.J. McCann cautioned the House of the threat of "Indian tuberculosis" during the 1937 debate on estimates of the Indian Affairs branch. Quoting from Dr Stewart's pamphlet, "The Red Man and the White Plague," McCann reminded MPs that falling white tuberculosis rates meant virtuous families – such as their own – with healthy, unexposed children were particularly vulnerable to "outside infection ... a spark in dry grass."[66] The CTA, representing sanatorium directors like Ferguson and Stewart, was the most powerful voice for racially segregated treatment. Established in 1901 by elites concerned with the economic impact of tuberculosis, the CTA exerted considerable influence on government policy. In a letter to the Manitoba premier, Stewart called the Aboriginal "dangerous neighbours," a "menace ... to the health of ordinary citizens," and an "uncontrolled nuisance."[67] At its 1935 annual meeting the CTA devoted a session to "Indian tuberculosis" and sent resolutions to the prime minister and minister of health, warning of the "menace of uncontrolled tuberculosis on Indian reserves to the surrounding white population" demanding more government action.

In June 1937 the CTA formed a joint committee of federal and provincial bureaucrats and sanatorium directors that met in Ottawa to consider how best to control the threat of Indian tuberculosis with the paltry $50,000 the Indian branch had at its disposal. IHS director Dr E.L. Stone opened the meeting by drawing a bold red line across the map of Canada from west to east that separated "those [Indians] to the south who are, generally speaking, in contact with and a menace to white populations, from those to the north, who ... are not."[68] Around 75,000 (of a total Aboriginal population of 115,000) lived in this "contact zone," representing just 0.6 per cent of the Canadian population of slightly more than eleven million. Despite their small number, Stone emphasized the threat: "Roughly two Indians out of three, are shown to be in contact with white people." Of the population in the "white contact areas" nine thousand were students living in sixty residential schools, but as Ferguson of Saskatchewan noted, the experience of the Tsuu T'ina reserve showed that schools were easily turned into sanatoria. Despite criticisms of residential schools, Ferguson claimed, "for the purpose of cleaning up tuberculosis among the children they are a wonderful institution." The irony that the schools, so clearly implicated in the spread of the disease, would now be the solution, seemed lost on Ferguson. But, as Dr Alexander, medical superintendent at Six Nations reserve near Brantford argued, adults were a greater threat: "I know of at least three families to whom an Indian maid has conveyed infection to the children." Though impossible to know, the source of infection seemed too obvious to be questioned. To stress the threat, the doctor lapsed into a telling military metaphor: Aboriginals were "an enemy in our midst, and while we have few guns trained on them there is no reason why we cannot attack them with such weapons as we have."[69]

The committee recommended dividing the $50,000 among the provinces based on a simple calculation of the number of "Indians in contact with white people (in the south) … and the probable amount of Tuberculosis among them."[70] Seventy per cent ($35,000) went to the four western provinces to establish "preventoria" in the schools that segregated children with "minimal lesions," and to pay the churches to provide sickly children with extra food and "one or two years better care than the rest."[71] Keeping infected and healthy children in the same institution likely only slowed the spread of disease within the schools. But, as Stone confided to his director, it might limit the spread from school to reserve, which posed a larger problem: "It would be hard to prove that the Residential Schools, as a group, are not agencies for the spread of tuberculosis."[72] Stone assured branch director McGill that he could keep ordinary annual medical costs to $10 per capita, or half the cost for white people, but more funds would be needed for medical officers and Indian tuberculosis sanatoria. Before it adjourned the conference also established an Indian Advisory Committee, essentially the management committee of the CTA, to keep the problem of Indian tuberculosis before the government and public.

The Indian Advisory Committee in 1937 recommended dramatically increased parliamentary appropriations for tuberculosis surveys in schools and reserves and an aggressive Indian hospital construction program. The CTA made clear that past efforts to ameliorate the predisposing causes of tuberculosis, diet and housing, only clouded the real problem that tuberculosis is a communicable disease, in the same way that "leprosy, typhoid fever, or smallpox are communicable diseases." Comparisons to historically frightening diseases emphasized the danger for those who remained complacent and implied the coercive measures that such diseases prompted. "Polluted with tuberculosis," Aboriginal people required a system of surveillance by medical personnel, as well as "training, supervision, treatment or segregation." Admitting that there was little understanding of the extent of disease on reserves, the CTA suggested that the elderly and "hopeless cases" should be segregated on reserves under the care of nurses, if any could be hired. But, the foundation of control efforts would be the confinement in special tuberculosis institutions of "young Indians ... [and] hopeful cases that can be cured, intelligent Indians whose education and sanitary habits will have some effect in raising the standards of the Indian generally." Such deserving hopeful cases might be trained to become healthy citizens.[73]

To satisfy curiosity about the extent of disease, in 1937 Drs Ross and Paine from Manitoba's Ninette Sanatorium surveyed reserves and residential schools in proximity to white population centres. They administered tuberculin injections that tested for exposure to tuberculosis (though not indicative of disease itself); they performed some physical examinations and attempted to take medical histories that were "usually meagre"; and, for good measure, took blood samples for the Wassermann test that indicated syphilitic infection. No treatment was offered. Their study, presented at the 1938 annual meeting of the CTA and subsequently published in the *Canadian Medical Association Journal*, proposed "to ascertain accurately the incidence of tuberculosis infection and disease ... there has been endless speculation but no statistical knowledge to temper the impression that the Indian was still overwhelmingly scourged by the disease." Hoping that their survey might be useful for a "future program" of treatment, the doctors found more than twice as much infection in reserve populations (11.6 per cent of 1,856 people) than in residential schools (4.2 per cent of 816 students), which is not surprising since it was common practice to remove ill schoolchildren for what was termed "observation at home." The house-to-house survey also provided ample opportunity to comment on living conditions – "uniformly poor, though in isolated cases quite good"; and on Indian character – "paradoxical" marked by stubborn superstitions, though "time and education" might correct these flaws. Surprised to find evidence of healed disease, given that it was generally conceded that the people had no natural resistance to tuberculosis, the physicians concluded: "If given the same opportunity as the white man, the Indian might respond to preventive and curative treatment measures almost as well." Marshalling more statistics for the cause, the Manitoba survey also provided a brighter side, diagnosing the Indian as "blessed with a natural indolence [that] should make him an ideal cure-chaser if he were not such an easy prey to periods of undisciplined activity."[74] The CTA needed little convincing of the threat to Canadians, and the solution would naturally be more institutional beds along the lines of the Fort Qu'Appelle Indian Hospital. For the government, the remarkable economy of that institution prompted McGill to advise his minister: "We have never wanted to go into building or operating of sanatoria, but if we can do so, as seems probable, on the standard of economy of the Qu'Appelle Indian Hospital, it is an open question whether we should not consider extension in the other provinces."[75] Unlike the purpose-built Fort Qu'Appelle Indian Hospital (and later the Moose Factory Hospital on James Bay), all subsequent Indian hospitals would be established in "borrowed buildings," slightly renovated military institutions and residential schools.

Naturally, the next Indian hospital to open was in Manitoba, home of minister responsible for Indian Affairs branch, Thomas Crerar. In 1939 the Anglican Church gladly sold its Dynevor Hospital, near Selkirk, to the government. The aging structure, built in the 1870s as a rectory for St Peter's parish and converted to an infirmary in the 1890s, became a fifty-bed Indian hospital managed for the government by the Sanatorium Board of Manitoba[76] (illustration 1.2). Friends of the government were no doubt pleased when the *New York Times* congratulated the government for its "steady progress" in the provision of hospitals for "sick Indians at a cost less than that of admitting them to public institutions."[77] The Dynevor Indian Hospital had its critics, however. Winnipeg's Catholic Archbishop Sinnott objected to its "Protestant" nature and demanded "a Catholic hospital for Catholic Indians." To that end he offered to sell the Catholic Crerar Hospital to the government; this time minister Crerar declined the archbishop's offer.[78] Dr J.D. Adamson of the Catholic St Boniface Sanatorium, which opened in 1931 in nearby St Vital and had recently added twenty beds to its Indian annex in anticipation of much-needed revenue from government patients,

Illustration 1.2 Dynevor Indian Hospital, Manitoba. Built in the 1870s,
the centre block was originally the rectory of St Peter's Parish, near Selkirk,
Manitoba. Converted to an infirmary in the 1890s, the building was sold to
the Indian branch in 1939 and opened as the Dynevor Indian Hospital
managed by the Manitoba Sanatorium board.

Source: Rupert's Land 150, Archives of Manitoba.

claimed that the Dynevor Indian Hospital would mean an "enormous
over-supply of beds."[79] But, explained Sanatorium Board's Dr E.L. Ross,
Dynevor was not intended to be a "fully equipped sanatorium," but an
inexpensive alternative providing rest and nursing care, well removed
from white populations. Indeed, Dynevor made do without an X-ray
machine when renovation costs exceeded the Indian branch budget.[80]

Because high death rates, the grim reality of tuberculosis treatment
in any sanatorium, threatened to tarnish Dynevor's image, the dead
were buried across the Red River at St Peter's Parish.[81] In its first year the
hospital admitted sixty-seven patients, nearly half of whom were children removed from schools. The most common treatment at Dynevor

was the painful pneumothorax "refills." Pneumothorax, or therapeutic lung collapse, was an extension of rest therapy surgically induced, but the lung naturally reinflated and a "refill" of gas injected into the pleural space maintained the lung collapse.[82] In its first year alone Dynevor performed more than 300 pneumothorax refills.[83] By its fifth year, 29 per cent of Dynevor's patients were dead, and another 12 per cent were "unimproved."[84] The efficacy of pneumothorax, the mainstay of surgical treatment in Canadian sanatoria in the 1930s and 1940s, is impossible to judge, but of the First World War veterans treated at the Central Alberta Sanatorium in Calgary, only half of the pneumothorax patients lived, and less than one-third improved.[85] Besides surgery, or often because of it, bed rest was strictly enforced. As in all sanatoria, some patients resisted the enforced idleness, strict routines, or the prospect of surgery, but Dynevor's physician suggested that "the philosophy of the Indian" made the problem more acute.[86] Police forcibly returned patients who "ran away" (left against medical advice) under the authority of the provincial Communicable Disease Control Act.[87] While all sanatoria faced recalcitrant patients, since much of the therapy was concerned with cultivating the proper attitudes of the hygienic self, patients were not held against their will. But Indian hospitals were different; as we shall see, the Indian Act was subsequently amended to compel medical examination, treatment, and hospitalization. Aside from the Indian hospitals operated by the Manitoba Sanatorium Board, IHS also operated its own Indian hospitals at Fort Alexander, Fisher River, and Norway House.

British Columbia had no sanatorium beds for Aboriginal people in the 1930s. Dr W.H. Hatfield, head of the province's tuberculosis program, warned their threat to health was more acute because they were not confined to reserves, but "free Indians" mixing with the white population and causing alarm.[88] In 1941 the Indian branch opened the Coqualeetza Indian Hospital near Chilliwack, British Columbia.[89] Founded as a Methodist mission school in 1889, it expanded in 1924 when the DIA built a larger 200-student residential school. A 1932 inspection found so much tuberculosis that the missionaries built a small preventorium for the most ill rather than send them home.[90] By 1938 the missionaries could no longer manage the school and turned it over to the government; three years later the 185-bed Coqualeetza Indian Hospital opened with six girls transferred from the preventorium. A 1948 fire destroyed much of the building; remarkably no one was killed, but conditions were far from ideal for the ninety-eight patients who remained in the undamaged wing, or for the twenty-two patients in "the converted hen house, known as the preventorium," which was rotting and in immediate danger of collapse.[91] Thus, the wartime increase in institutions of varying quality, a response to the CTA's campaign to expose the threat of Indian tuberculosis, also reflected Indian Affairs' constant search for economy.

At war's end attention turned to reconstruction, and, like Indian Affairs policy generally, the Indian Health Service undertook policy discussions in early 1945. Acting director Dr Percy Moore steered the policy deliberations. Moore got his start in Indian Affairs as a physician at the Fisher River Hospital in Manitoba after graduating from the University of Manitoba medical school in 1931. Appointed as assistant to director Dr E.L. Stone in Ottawa in 1937, Moore became acting director two years later while Stone served in the military. Moore subsequently became director in 1946 when the Indian Health Service was transferred to the newly created department of National Health and Welfare. He remained director for the next twenty years, until his retirement in 1965.[92]

An Order in Council established the Advisory Committee for the control and prevention of tuberculosis among the Indians, with a mandate to make recommendations to guide Indian Affairs' efforts. But the focus was entirely on the need for institutional care, repeating the recommendations of the 1937 Advisory Committee that advocated increased hospitalization and larger appropriations for tuberculosis control. The 1945 Advisory Committee, with its mandate that ten of the twelve members be nominated by the CTA, ensured that expert opinion – provincial health bureaucrats and sanatorium directors – would prevail over the federal bureaucracies that were limited to just two representatives, deputy minister and psychiatrist Dr Brock Chisholm from National Health and Welfare and Dr Percy Moore from Indian Affairs branch. Needless to say, no Aboriginal representatives were invited. Meeting for two days in May 1945, the committee concerned itself with establishing institutions for treatment of "Indian tuberculosis." While the extent of the disease was still unclear, committee chairman and executive secretary of the CTA, Dr G.J. Wherrett, made use of the available statistics to show a "satisfactory fall" in the white death rates and an increase in the death rate for the Aboriginal population, though he admitted that the Bureau of Statistics was "not quite satisfied" that the Aboriginal population figures were complete.[93] But the deliberations quickly widened from tuberculosis to a discussion of what was commonly referred to as the "Indian problem," or the place of Aboriginal people in society.

Moore stated the case bluntly: "Only a few years ago it was common, when one mentioned the Indians or the Indian problem, to have one shrugging his shoulders and say 'Oh, they are dying out, and the sooner the better.' Such is not the case. The Indians ... have the largest annual increase of any racial group." To which Brock Chisholm, deputy minister of Health and Welfare, replied, "That is one good reason why they should become citizens."[94] The term "citizenship" implied many things, but foremost was what an earlier generation called assimilation, or the removal of cultural, linguistic, political, and legal differences with other Canadians. Alarmed by the threat posed by an increasing, and apparently increasingly diseased, population, the committee approached their task with a certain sense of urgency. Manitoba's Dr J.D. Adamson noted that Aboriginal soldiers carried on as citizens, but upon return to their reserves "degenerate immediately ... we cannot do anything of a substantial nature until we endow them with the responsibility and dignity of full citizenship."[95] The discussion ranged widely from the need for Aboriginal people to embrace the values of Christian capitalist workers, to the value of education, indeed even higher education, to "raise up the Indian" to embrace the advantages and especially the responsibilities of citizenship. Only then might tuberculosis among them be defeated. An exasperated Moore successfully redirected the discussion back to the need for hospitals and a "direct attack" on tuberculosis, but the discourse made clear that until complete integration to citizenship there would be no solution of the "Indian problem." Ironically then, the deliberations focused almost exclusively on treatment in segregated institutions. For the committee, representing the interests of sanatorium directors and provincial bureaucrats, integration might be the desired goal, but it most certainly would not happen in their provincial institutions.

The Advisory Committee essentially mapped the program for post-war Indian Health Service. With representatives from all the provinces except Quebec, the committee agreed that it was an urgent national issue, though some provincial representatives feared threats from other racialized minorities. Nova Scotia's deputy minister of health Dr Peter Campbell admitted that he had no idea how much tuberculosis there was in the Aboriginal population, but the bigger problem was the province's "negroes." British Columbia's Dr Hatfield was more worried about the Chinese and Japanese, "and let me add that we hope we will not have the Japanese long."[96] Manitoba's contingent worried about "half-breeds." The acknowledged expert, Saskatchewan's

Dr R.G. Ferguson, whose twelve-year BCG vaccination experiment on Aboriginal infants was nearing completion, advocated a direct attack, including vaccination. And referring to the committee's earlier discussion about education and citizenship, "[it] made me wonder whether half the men in this room had ever seen an Indian." He thought the residential schools took fine care of the children and that the people on reserves were well nourished, if not overweight. The Indian agents were "loyal and hard-working men," and reserve houses were "pretty good for Indians." The problem, he continued, was not with living conditions, but with "genetics ... These Indians are born without any acquisitive instinct."[97] Reminding the committee that tuberculosis was an infectious disease, "something like typhoid or smallpox," Ferguson explained that the response should be to "vaccinate and segregate." As for higher education, Ferguson scoffed that they might be ready in "two hundred or possibly one hundred years." The young students who managed to get a high school education "go bad." Young women come home "in a pregnant condition, or a boy comes home as a useless smart Aleck." No, what was needed was a practical education along very simple lines "involving their learning to sweat and work."[98] At that, Brock Chisholm clarified his earlier comments regarding citizenship and education; he did not intend to suggest that Aboriginal people should be educated among whites, but their "method of living should be raised so that they would have their own schools, and train people in their own communities where they would provide their own education."[99] The rhetoric of integration aside, continued isolation clearly remained the prescription. As medical men they saw themselves as social experts, qualified to comment on all aspects of the "Indian problem," while demonstrating their understanding of race as a biological reality, if not a pathology requiring treatment. The ambiguity reflected in the committee's discussions – that integration to citizenship might be the goal, but segregation should remain the means – was ultimately incorporated into the emerging Indian hospital system.

The committee was clear that the strategy would be an expansion of institutional segregation and isolation in Indian hospitals. What was less clear was the extent of the disease. The most commonly cited figure, which fluctuated depending on the circumstances, was an Aboriginal death rate ten to twenty times the white rate. The statistics were badly flawed and extrapolated from very small surveys conducted in the 1920s and 1930s. But those surveys, to satisfy curiosity not to provide treatment, understandably outraged Aboriginal communities.

In Manitoba, an attempted repeat tuberculosis survey faced the ire of the community: "The chief and councilors nearly kicked us off the reserve. It took us three or four days to convince them to let us bring our x-ray machine ... because we had not done anything about it the first time."[100] As Saskatchewan's Ferguson told the committee: "If you survey a much greater area than you can treat, and just get the Indians on a waiting list, you discourage them. I think that is a rather serious thing."[101] Dr Barclay, DIA superintendent at Coqualeetza in British Columbia, admitted that there was little understanding of the extent of the disease, and to conduct surveys without offering treatment "they lose interest and you lose face."[102] Using a rough calculation of need – two treatment beds per tuberculosis death, three per death in areas near white populations – the committee recommended a focus on the western provinces, northern Ontario, and the Northwest Territories and Yukon. Brock Chisholm cautioned against modest proposals. Instead, the time was ripe for a rapid and substantial expansion of hospitals: "when reconstruction is on the map is the time to ask for what you want."[103] In addition to the hospitals already established, over the next few years two Indian hospitals were opened in British Columbia in redundant military facilities at Nanaimo and Miller Bay near Prince Rupert; two in Alberta, at Hobbema and in Edmonton, the largest institution, the Charles Camsell Indian Hospital in what had been the American military headquarters for its Northwest Command; one more in Saskatchewan at the Commonwealth air training camp at North Battleford airport; two more in Manitoba at the American military base at The Pas and the Brandon Military Hospital; the Moose Factory and Sioux Lookout Indian hospitals in Ontario; in Quebec City, tellingly, Inuit patients were held in the Parc Savard immigration and quarantine facility. But there were limits. In Halifax, the Rockhead quarantine and immigration hospital, a substantial building that had withstood the 1917 explosion and had recently been vacated by the Navy, was briefly considered for use as an Indian hospital. But, as the CTA's Dr Wherrett implied, it would be impossible to find white employees to work in such an environment, with the African-Canadian settlement, Africville, immediately in front of the hospital and the city jail to the rear. "Practically the only human activities to be seen from the hospital ... are those of colored people or jail inmates."[104] Nevertheless, by this expansion, in addition to the two band-owned hospitals – the Blackfoot Hospital in Alberta and the Lady Willingdon Hospital at Six Nations reserve – and other small cottage hospitals of one sort or another scattered across the country, there were twenty-two Indian hospitals by 1960.

The Advisory Committee meeting also considered what was, for the federal bureaucrats Moore and Chisholm, the principal reason for the meeting: sectarian hospitals. In what would be a fundamental shift in how health care for Aboriginal people had been delivered, Moore pressed for a recommendation that the Indian hospitals be strictly non-denominational. As he told the committee, the government was under considerable pressure from Christian churches to provide support for the expansion of religious hospitals connected to many residential schools, rather than establishing non-sectarian hospitals. While many committee members were loath to imply, for instance, that Catholic nuns were not competent to run a hospital, Brock Chisholm pressed for a resolution. It was not a question of religion or politics, Chisholm argued, but simply a medical matter; on that basis the committee was obliged to take a stand. "If this committee finds that the best medical care can be given by a sectarian hospital system, it should say so. If they believe ... that the best medical care can be produced by departmental control, and by the administration of non-sectarian hospitals, then it should say so."[105] Committee members bristled at being backed into a corner, arguing that it was not their remit to make the decision. Chisholm repeated the options. Calling the issue a "thorn in their side," Moore claimed that it had occupied more time and energy for ministers, deputy ministers, and everyone in the Indian Affairs branch "than has the consideration and treatment of tubercular Indians." After a prolonged discussion New Brunswick's Dr Charles MacMillan asked bluntly: "Would you like to run your own hospitals, Dr. Moore?" To which he answered, "Yes."[106] This was arguably one of the most important recommendations considered by the committee, marking the ascendancy of bureaucratic over missionary control of health care for Aboriginal people, while providing politicians with medical authority to face down the still powerful churches that resented interference in their work. It was a particularly vexing issue in the north, where government relied upon Christian denominations to provide all hospital care largely because the missionary societies themselves bore half the costs. As a result those northern hospitals were poorly equipped and understaffed. Committee chairman Wherrett's Arctic survey the previous year found deplorable health conditions among the Inuit, yet 150 of the Mackenzie Valley's 233 mission hospital beds were empty.[107] He urged the committee to recommend that Inuit patients be evacuated

to southern government hospitals, since in the Northwest Territories
they were "getting nothing more than board and room. You could not
say that they are getting bed rest, because they [missionaries] do not
keep them in bed."[108] To the argument that Inuit patients might be more
comfortable hospitalized in the north, Moore reckoned that once they
were removed from their communities it did not much matter if they
were 10 or 1,000 kilometres from home. Tuberculosis control, and ultimately hospital care in general, could no longer be left in the hands of
well-meaning but misguided missionaries.

Before the Advisory Committee adjourned, Moore wanted recommendations on two more issues that would come to define the institutions: staffing and the necessity of compulsory treatment. The Indian
Health Service employed twenty-four full-time physicians, but Moore
hoped to triple that number. The committee agreed that salaries would
need to be competitive with provincial medical incomes or else "there is
something peculiar" about anyone taking the job.[109] But physician salaries did not keep up with increasingly lucrative private practice after
the war; staff turnover was a constant problem. As for Aboriginal medical staff, there was no consideration of Aboriginal doctors, though the
committee agreed that young women might be trained as maids. With
the poor academic achievement in residential schools, nurse training
was impossible for most; Moore reckoned that throughout the country
there were maybe four or five "Indian girls" in training. In a revealing
comment that pointed to assumptions about the larger social purposes
of the hospitals, Moore recalled that in his travels he could spot the
"brighter" women right away. Surprised to find their homes well kept,
he learned that they had either been sanatorium patients for a number
of years or had worked as maids in the institutions.[110] Aside from their
medical value, Indian hospitals would also provide valuable training
in classed notions of respectability, as long as there was sufficient discipline and authority to keep patients institutionalized.

Finally, the committee was asked to recommend compulsory treatment. Moore stated frankly, "We certainly do not feel that our program
should be left to the whims of an Indian, as to whether or not he will
accept treatment."[111] The implication was that Aboriginal people would
not voluntarily accept hospitalization, though the sanatorium directors on the committee knew all too well that beds in their institutions
were reserved for provincial citizens. Nevertheless, Moore found the
existing "Regulations for Medical Services" (1934) did not provide sufficient authority; indeed, the regulations were principally concerned

with limiting medical officers' ability to incur expense by treating or hospitalizing Aboriginal people without departmental approval.[112] The regulations empowered an Indian agent to remove an individual with "acute communicable disease" for treatment, but there was nothing to compel the patient to stay in hospital. Moore explained: "We can ask the Mounted Police to pick up an Indian and take him to hospital, without taking him to court. Then if he refuses we can take him to court and sentence him to thirty days' imprisonment."[113] Provincial legislation was awkward and varied too much between jurisdictions. Compulsory treatment implied a detention cell or locked ward, and the committee's sanatorium directors were less supportive than Moore had hoped. Ferguson thought that detention wards in the hospital might sully the whole effort, unless it was carried out in a separate institution. Moore admitted that they had already built a detention ward in the hospital to be opened at The Pas. Manitoba's Dr Ross thought it easier to put a bed or two in a prison than to make a sanatorium into a jail. Moore persisted until the committee included a recommendation to Indian Affairs to revise the medical regulations to allow compulsory treatment and detention in Indian hospitals.[114] The next year he advised that the Indian Act be amended to include the authority to make regulations concerning compulsory treatment and hospitalization of venereal disease and tuberculosis, including detention in a sanatorium, and the compulsory return of patients who left against medical advice.[115] The 1951 revisions to the Indian Act's section 72 (1) that provided authority to make regulations was amended to include "compulsory hospitalization and treatment for infectious diseases," and, as we shall see, the subsequent Indian Health Regulations (1953) provided ample authority for coercion and compulsion. The Advisory Committee was allowed to adjourn having provided the state with the necessary medical expertise to manage the threat of Indian tuberculosis.

Overwhelmingly paternalistic, coercive in nature, and informed by the understanding of race as a biological reality that posed a threat to the nation's health, Indian hospitals were the mid-century answer to the failures of the past. Those who "graduated" from residential schools to Indian hospitals would no doubt recognize the institutional discipline and regulation. The lessons to be learned were individual self-control and the cultivation of healthy citizenship taught by the new medical experts. If they resisted they might well find themselves subject to the Indian Health Regulations and incarcerated in yet another state institution. The Indian Health Service also established nursing stations in remote areas, but its principal focus was Indian hospitals that would institutionalize and isolate not just tuberculosis but all Aboriginal patients.

Acknowledging the failure of past policies that left health care to poorly funded missionaries, the Indian Health Service was moved in 1945 from the Indian Affairs branch to the newly created Department of National Health and Welfare. A logical move in some respects, it obscured the links between poor health and its socio-economic causes while demonstrating faith in the power of biomedicine to cure the former while leaving the latter untouched. The move also alerted Canadians that a benevolent state, increasingly engaged in protecting and defining something called national health, would isolate the threat of Indian contagion while reserving community hospitals for citizens. The contradictions of the Indian hospitals' creation – isolating Aboriginal people while advocating for integration; segregating tuberculosis yet admitting all patients; coercing patients into hospital while characterizing the practice as humanitarian – point to the utility of the hospitals as economical institutions of confinement where surveillance, discipline, and surgery might cure the "Indian problem," or at least limit its spread.

Chapter Two

Neither Law nor Treaty

Neither law nor treaty impose an obligation on the Dominion government to establish a health service for the Indians and Eskimos, with the possible exception that in original treaties there is reference to the provision of "medicine chests." However, for humanitarian reasons and as very necessary protection to the rest of the population of Canada, it is essential to do everything possible to stamp out disease at its source where it may be within the confines of the country.[1]

      – Brooke Claxton, minister of National Health and Welfare, 1946

Postwar expansion of the Indian Health Service took place within a larger reformulation of government policy reflecting an unprecedented public interest in Aboriginal people's place in Canadian society. As minister Claxton assured Canadians recently troubled by the "Indian problem," the creation of Indian hospitals was motivated not by quaintly vague treaty promises, but by the highest humanitarian ideals. From this moral and ethical high ground enlightened self-interest came into sharper focus, as did the threats to the nation's health posed by Aboriginal people. Moving the Indian Health Service to the larger Department of National Health and Welfare, the state demonstrated its commitment to include Aboriginal people in the calculations of national health, if only to keep them sufficiently isolated. Two months after the minister's pronouncement, in August 1946 Canada's vice-regal couple officially opened the 500-bed Charles Camsell Indian Hospital in Edmonton. Though Aboriginal communities were never consulted or afforded any input, many welcomed the postwar expansion of Indian hospitals as a belated acknowledgment of the state's responsibility for

health care. The Charles Camsell Indian Hospital, the showcase of the
expanding Indian Health Service, also demonstrated the fundamental
contradictions at the core of racially segregated hospital care. Intended
to check the spread of tuberculosis in particular, the hospitals removed
and isolated sufferers from their own communities; at the same time,
as inexpensive alternatives to community hospital care that would also
protect the sensibilities of paying patients, Indian hospitals functioned
as general hospitals, admitting all Aboriginal patients tubercular and
otherwise. The costs of such contradictions were borne by patients
whose care and safety became seriously compromised. Moreover, postwar changes in tuberculosis treatment, from lung collapse therapy and
bed rest, to chemotherapy and aggressive chest surgery in the 1950s –
innovations that led to the "miracle of the empty beds" in Canadian
sanatoria – ensured, paradoxically that those beds would increasingly
become occupied by Aboriginal patients.[2]

The abject failures of the state's policy of assimilation through residential schools and isolation on dwindling reserves, policies developed for a "dying race," had become glaringly obvious by the 1930s;
and with Aboriginal populations growing, these were increasingly
expensive failures. According to historian John Tobias, "aimlessness"
marked Indian Affairs policy from the 1930s to war's end.[3] A less generous assessment of the Indian Affairs branch under the leadership of
"Colonel" H.M. Jones (where civil servants were expected to stand
when he entered the room) termed it "Colonel Jones' lost battalion."[4]
And after 1945 the place of Aboriginal people in society troubled many
Canadians. Prompted in part by their considerable contributions to
the war effort, Aboriginal people came to the attention of concerned
Canadians who wondered how, after fighting intolerance and racism
abroad, Native people were still denied basic citizenship rights at home.
An enthusiastic editorial in *Saturday Night* magazine, reflecting the
biases of urban Torontonians whose experience with Aboriginal people
was limited to summer vacations in cottage country, advocated for
"the Indian." Their admirable record of wartime service proved "that
they can work as well and endure discipline to as great an extent as
their white brothers." Women worked in summer hotels "as chamber-
maids, kitchen girls, laundresses – jobs which entail hard work and an
instinct for cleanliness. While they are doing these things, their men
serve as guides, boatmen, and handymen ... these jobs they do well."[5]
Canadians demanded a "new deal" for Aboriginal people so that
they might integrate into society, albeit at the bottom rung, as normal

working citizens. The government received petitions and resolutions from concerned citizens across the country: the Sudbury city council, the Army, Navy and Air Force Veterans' Association, the Sault Ste Marie city council, the Dock and Shipyard Workers' Union, the Alberta Teachers' Association, the Alberta Conference of the United Church, the Social Security Council of Canada, and "interested representative Canadian citizens" – a sociologist, an anthropologist, a police magistrate, and the director of Vancouver Folk Festivals.[6] The latter group, calling for a solution to the country's "vital question" through improved education and administration, also advocated for Indian hospitals on reserves. Though not the royal commission many called for, a special joint committee of the House of Commons and the Senate was struck in 1946 to enquire into the administration of Indian Affairs and to recommend revisions to the Indian Act.

For two years the Joint Committee heard from citizen, church, and professional groups and its deliberations were regularly reported in the press. But, as historian Hugh Shewell argues, the committee was a "tool of state propaganda" meant to elicit public consent to an agenda the state had already adopted.[7] Heavily influenced by the emerging social sciences, the committee's recommendations proposed that the "Indian problem" would only be solved when Aboriginal people became equal, normal citizens in a liberal view of the modern individual. In particular, they would receive services through their provincial governments, leading to reductions in the federal fiscal and legal responsibility for Aboriginal people. This certainly was not the message of the various Aboriginal organizations that submitted briefs to the Joint Committee in which they stressed the obligations that stemmed from their special relationship with the federal government. Nevertheless, the revised Indian Act (1951) removed some of its most repressive features while maintaining the earlier assimilation policy, which came to be termed integration for "citizenship."[8] To that end, the Indian Affairs branch was again moved in 1949, from the Department of Mines and Resources to the Department of Citizenship and Immigration, where, ironically, alongside immigrants, Aboriginal people could eventually become Canadian citizens.

Popular support for Aboriginal citizenship emerged within a broader climate of rising expectations for an activist and reformist state. In 1945 the Indian Health Service was transferred from Indian Affairs to the newly created Department of National Health and Welfare, the heart of the welfare state. Though severing the treatment of disease from its social and economic causes on reserves, medical men (the IHS bureaucracy was exclusively male) would direct health care. But the Liberal government's Green Book proposals for a comprehensive postwar welfare state, including universal health insurance, met concerted opposition, and by May 1946 Prime Minister Mackenzie King had lost the political will to carry out the reformist program.[9] One month later health minister Brooke Claxton addressed the Special Joint Committee. His submission, as we have seen, acknowledged federal responsibility for Aboriginal health care, though stressing a moral rather than legal obligation, a position successive governments maintained. While failing to deliver on the promise of universal health insurance, Claxton nevertheless reassured Canadians that an expanded IHS would protect the national health by doing "everything possible to stamp out disease at its source."[10] The new IHS, evidence of a vigilant yet generous state caring for the poorest of the poor, also marked Aboriginal people as a looming health threat. As one of its first acts the new bureaucracy took possession of the army's sprawling military complex in Edmonton that would become the Charles Camsell Indian Hospital, its showpiece institution.

Built in 1913 as a Jesuit college for boys, in 1942 the three-storey brick building became the headquarters of the American military's Northwest Command, when they added large California redwood frame buildings eventually covering three city blocks[11] (illustration 2.1). With the American withdrawal in 1944 the Canadian army purchased the facility but by 1945 deemed it redundant and eventually turned it over to IHS for use as an Indian hospital.[12] Local protests erupted as soon as residents learned that the "Jesuit College" would become an Indian hospital. Petitions from veterans groups, the mayor, local politicians, and the hospital's neighbours demanded the redwood buildings be used to relieve the local housing shortage, while the hospital itself should be reserved for veterans. According to the city's mayor, "tubercular Indians" posed a particularly dangerous threat.[13] A mass public meeting in late November attracted more than 300 angry citizens, along with at least one RCMP confidential informant sent to keep an eye on the supposed volatile combination of disgruntled veterans and leftist political activists.[14]

To reassure Edmontonians, the government clarified its rationales for segregation and isolation: the hospital would treat all conditions, not just tuberculosis, "and thus relieve the public wards of the Edmonton hospitals from treating Indians in these institutions." Moreover the

Illustration 2.1 Charles Camsell Indian Hospital Complex. The brick central
building, originally a Jesuit college for boys, became the headquarters of the
American military's Northwest Command in 1942, eventually covering three city
blocks. Deemed redundant by the Canadian military at war's end, the warren
of wooden buildings became the Indian hospital wards.

Source: PA-139304, LAC.

hospital's grounds would be fenced and patients completely confined
in the institution, noting that it was better to have "these people under
treatment than to have tuberculous Indians wandering about the streets
of Edmonton … spreading the disease."[15] Minister Brooke Claxton also
reminded citizens of the hundreds of jobs the hospital would bring,
and that "tuberculous Indians who are not in hospital are a danger
to the community." Appealing to veterans, he noted that nearly 3,000
Indians (124 from Alberta) served in Canada's armed services during
the war, and 167 made the ultimate sacrifice.[16] To appease the critics,
100 of the hospital's 500 beds were reserved for veterans until a new
sanatorium for their use could be built. IHS, anxious to take control of

the institution, quickly transferred fourteen Aboriginal patients from local Edmonton hospitals to the newly named Charles Camsell Indian Hospital.

The discursive practice of naming the pre-eminent IHS institution reflected the Canadian state's new interest in the resource-rich north, and thus honoured one of its sons. Charles Camsell (1876–1958), a geologist and deputy minister of Mines and Resources (at the time the bureaucratic home of Indian Affairs), was not the first name to be considered for the hospital, nor the second. Bureaucrats rejected some of the usual sources: "The Tweedsmuir Indian Hospital" for the late governor general, Sir John Buchan, 1st Baron Tweedsmuir of Elsfield, and "The Royal Tunis Hospital" for the current governor general's proud military career in the late war. "The Alexander Indian Hospital" would only cause confusion since Edmonton already had a Royal Alexandra Hospital. *Kapasowin*, Cree for "place of rest," was briefly considered, but Percy Moore warned that neither Cree nor Blackfoot names should be used for fear of provoking the supposed "great rivalry" between them, and besides, a Blackfoot name would be "difficult to spell and pronounce."[17]

Camsell was born at Fort Liard in the Northwest Territories, where his father was the Hudson's Bay Company's chief factor of the Mackenzie River District. As his autobiography claimed, he was a true *Son of the North*.[18] In 1884 the eight-year-old Camsell travelled to Winnipeg to begin his education. The trip by York boat, ox cart, river steamboat, wagon, and train, took three months, including a detour around the Saskatchewan Metis settlements that would descend into violence the following year.[19] Years later he noted approvingly that he flew from Winnipeg to his birthplace in less than three hours. His life spanned the era of technological and economic change captured by the term "opening the north." That Camsell was instrumental in those changes is not lost on the reader. His autobiography makes rare, yet harshly critical, mention of Aboriginal people: "The Indians were a miserable, dirty lot, always in a state of semi-starvation ... Like most of their race they were improvident, gorging themselves when food was plentiful and starving quite cheerfully when it was scarce."[20] Camsell's own experience of nearly starving in an unsuccessful attempt to reach the Klondike goldfields in 1897 was put down to bad luck, not improvidence. Indeed, as a commemorative history of the hospital explained, as a consequence of his experience Camsell "developed a strong, cheerful disposition, an even temperament, a splendid physique, as well as coordination and stamina."[21] As deputy minister of Mines and Resources he was also commissioner of the Northwest Territories, thus responsible for both the administrative and legislative functions of northern government, directly influencing Canadian policy. Camsell resisted territorial self-government and saw nothing inconsistent with administering the north from an office in Ottawa.[22] Camsell and his wife, along with other senior government officials, demonstrated their support for Indian Affairs' integration policy by employing young Aboriginal women as domestics in their tony Ottawa homes.[23] Interestingly, his autobiography does not mention that his mother was in fact Metis, which would not have been unusual given his family's involvement in the fur trade.[24] Camsell thoroughly embraced capitalist and Christian Euro-Canadian society, while deriding the backwardness of the north's Aboriginal people. A stint in the Charles Camsell Indian Hospital might inspire the Aboriginal sons and daughters of the north and west to admire, if not emulate, Camsell's life. Perhaps ultimately, this successful assimilation explained why he was honoured by the state. Camsell agreed to lend his name on the condition that it always be referred to as the *Charles* Camsell Indian Hospital. He was present at the opening ceremonies, which "pleased him greatly."[25]

The largest of the IHS institutions, the Charles Camsell Indian Hospital provided tuberculosis treatment for Aboriginal people from Alberta, northeast British Columbia, and the Territories as well as admitting patients for general hospital care in its obstetric, medical, surgical, and paediatric wards. The solid brick main building, the former Jesuit college, hid from view the maze of tinder-dry wooden buildings that became the hospital's wards and the covered wooden walkways that connected them. Deputy minister of health Brock Chisholm declared that the Indian hospitals would operate on two "cardinal policies." First, that "no effort or reasonable cost should be spared to give the patients the best hospital care attainable"; and second, that "Indian wards of the Government of Canada should have the highest priority in employment and that in particular the [Charles Camsell] hospital should become a training centre for Indian health workers."[26] Ultimately, the seeming generosity of his cardinal policies was quietly ignored, as patients were crowded into shoddy borrowed buildings. The second cardinal policy will be examined in detail in the next chapter, but suffice it to say that, but for a short-lived program to prepare young women to train elsewhere as ward aids, IHS undertook no formal health care training. Aside from a few graduate nurses who struggled to find schools to accept them, Aboriginal workers filled the least-skilled and lowest-paid positions in IHS hospitals.

The Charles Camsell Hospital's shortcomings were obvious when IHS took over the institution, and the centralized bureaucracy made resolution of seemingly simple maintenance problems time consuming and at times impossible. As Dr E.L. Stone, former IHS director and by 1945 Alberta regional superintendent, admitted on first inspecting the complex, "My worst misgiving is about the buildings. That the fire hazard is very serious goes without saying ... Sooner or later their settling will break gas mains to the heating units and they will burn."[27] The natural gas lines were so badly corroded that an inspector warned, "many gas leaks are almost certain to develop with the resultant hazard and danger of explosion."[28] The electrical wiring was defective and "a major fire hazard."[29] Worse yet, in case of fire, the water supply was not dependable because of badly damaged water lines throughout the institution. A ruptured sewer line under the main kitchen floor, first brought to the department's attention in January 1949, that smelled like "long-dead rats" was still festering eleven months later.[30] Without its own laundry the hospital relied on local commercial services, which refused to handle some of the most soiled hospital linens. In May 1946 surgeries were cancelled for a lack of clean sheets and surgical drapes; linens were instead sterilized and resterilized rather than washed. Patients' pyjamas and bedding went unchanged for weeks. A decade later the hospital finally got its own laundry.[31] The building's shortcomings certainly compromised the comfort and safety of both patients and staff, but there were no efforts to upgrade the facility for more than twenty years until it was rebuilt in 1967. As the IHS flagship, the Charles Camsell Indian Hospital was in better repair than other less visible Indian hospitals located in remote and isolated locations. But just as the pomp of its opening ceremony obscured the hospital's segregating and isolating impulse, the building's facade hid its many shortcomings. Passing by the Charles Camsell Indian Hospital though, citizens might be reminded of the threat lurking within while being reassured that theirs was a most economical humanitarianism.

The Camsell Hospital's first medical superintendent, thoracic surgeon Dr Herbert Meltzer, was appointed in 1945. Circumstance more than anything made Meltzer an ideal – indeed the only – candidate for the position. A thorough national search conducted by the Canadian Tuberculosis Association's George Wherrett found that Meltzer was the only chest surgeon with tuberculosis experience who would take the work at "anywhere near the [civil service] salary."[32] But a 1929 University of Manitoba graduate like Meltzer had few choices. Joining the staff of Manitoba's Ninette Sanatorium upon graduation, Meltzer left two years later in 1931 to open a private practice. However, like many physicians of his generation who subsequently landed in the IHS, he found private practice impossible during the Depression. After a year of postgraduate training in New York he returned to Ninette in 1935 as resident surgeon, and again resigned in 1941 to join the Army Medical Corps.[33] After his discharge in 1945, Meltzer accepted the offer as medical superintendent of the fledgling Camsell Indian Hospital, while also serving as chief of staff, radiologist, and thoracic surgeon. The new superintendent brought along his friend Dr Matthew Matas, also discharged from the medical corps, though there was concern that with these two the IHS might be criticized for having "too many Jewish people on staff."[34] Drs Margaret and William Barclay as well as much of the nursing staff were also recruited from the army, giving the hospital a distinctly military character.

William Barclay recalled that Meltzer administered the Camsell Hospital with the "discipline and chain of command" of an army hospital. Strict discipline for Aboriginal patients, deemed necessary if not beneficial in its own right, did little to inspire trust.[35] Meltzer, more comfortable giving orders than taking them, was an uneasy fit with the civil service. Demanding, tempestuous, and given to histrionics to get his way, he threatened resignation at least four times between February and March 1946 alone.[36] But more fundamentally, Meltzer disagreed with the unorthodox practice of combining tuberculosis and general hospital treatment in the same institution: "To me that is a very serious matter, and one that I cannot fit in with my conscience. As the Department insists that we look after these non-tuberculous cases, we must do something to increase the protection of these individuals from tuberculosis."[37] A month later Meltzer threatened to stop admitting non-tuberculous patients, instead referring them to the city's general hospitals, thereby undercutting the promise of Indian hospitals.[38] As Meltzer's direct superior Dr E.L. Stone put it, "The feeling in the city is that now we have an Indian hospital, why do we ask downtown hospitals to take Indians."[39]

Given that the hospitals were intended as alternatives to care in expensive community hospitals, economy and efficiency guided IHS efforts, from repurposing military barracks and residential schools, to keeping operating costs to a bare minimum. The logic of hospital efficiency, calculated as per diem cost per patient, meant that hospitals could maintain a low per diem rate by cutting costs or admitting more patients, or both. Since operating costs such as building maintenance and wages remained relatively constant regardless of occupancy levels, by definition a full – or overfull – hospital was an efficient hospital. Like the pre-war Fort Qu'Appelle Indian Hospital that operated at half the cost of admitting patients to local institutions, the Camsell Indian Hospital established maternity, paediatric, and medical wards alongside tuberculosis wards. But the former army hospital's large dormitory wards were completely inappropriate for a combined tuberculosis/ general hospital treating men, women, and children, creating dangerous conditions. In a frank explanation for overcrowding Percy Moore rationalized the practice:

> I know the larger units of the hospital adapt themselves poorly to what would be an ideal for treatment, but sometimes we have to make a compromise. We have never had sufficient funds for a fully adequate program and I am anxious to do the maximum good with this institution to the maximum number of people possible ... The sooner we are operating to capacity, the sooner our high per diem rate will be reduced.[40]

Meltzer rightly questioned how the "maximum good" could be served by placing tuberculous patients in the same ward as the uninfected: "We already have one case of a little girl from Edmonton School who was investigated for diabetes. Exactly one month after her discharge, she was re-admitted with a Highly Positive Tuberculin [indicating exposure to tuberculosis], Erythema Nodosum [inflammation of the skin] and Pulmonary Lesion [tuberculosis]."[41] By 1950 Meltzer's services as the hospital's superintendent were no longer required. The bureaucracy was faced with the necessity of either discharging him or "making things so uncomfortable that he would [finally] resign."[42] They ultimately negotiated an agreement where Meltzer left the civil service for private practice, but continued as a consultant and the hospital's chief of surgery. Dr Lynn Falconer, another Manitoba medical school graduate who joined the IHS in 1938 and was Percy Moore's assistant by 1940, took over as superintendent, creating a clearer chain of command from Ottawa to Edmonton. Shuffling personnel eased some tensions at the hospital, but the abysmal infrastructure remained. Moreover, patient care and safety became seriously undermined in all the Indian hospitals by the self-serving and contradictory policies of their creation – segregating Aboriginal patients from expensive community hospitals while isolating tuberculosis patients from society to protect the national health. The central premise, indeed the promise of Indian hospitals, was that they would always be less expensive than provincial institutions.

More Indian hospitals opened in the late 1940s. Anxious to demonstrate their efficiency, Moore estimated that it cost between $8 and $10 per day to treat patients in general hospitals, while the per patient rates in the four largest Indian hospitals were half that: Camsell Hospital at $4.18, Miller Bay $4.66, Coqualeetza $3.91, and Brandon $3.99; at Nanaimo Indian Hospital on Vancouver Island, another former military institution, the $8.10 rate was temporarily anomalous because the institution was not yet full. As Moore's assistant made clear, "these figures are appreciably lower than the rates that can be obtained at even the smaller hospitals operated by communities or even religious orders and that we should be able to keep our institutions at full occupancy is a very appreciable saving of public funds."[43] But the repercussions of "full occupancy" did not go unnoticed by the Indian hospitals' constituency. The Indian Association of Alberta, though never asked for its input, regularly sent copies of its minutes to IHS. In 1949, after passing several resolutions praising the Camsell Indian Hospital's work, the Association voiced some concern: "We see old people in the same wards as TB patients and children playing in the same rooms where old people are lying sick. We fear there is great danger of infection spreading under such conditions."[44] Dr Falconer, as IHS regional superintendent, attended the Indian Association's annual meetings for a time, but as criticisms of policy and practice increased he charged the Association with encouraging "the malcontents on the various reserves ... a good sound sane well-meaning Indian does not take too much interest in it."[45] Many IHS physicians, not unaware of their peers' increasingly lucrative incomes in private practice, accepted that theirs was a higher calling as the embodiment of the institutions' humanitarianism. They would brook no criticism of their efforts, especially not from the recipients of the IHS largesse.

In the early 1950s the Camsell Hospital became seriously overcrowded with 560 patients in an institution with a capacity for 475.[46] Despite the strident rhetoric of "tuberculosis-soaked" reserves, in the Camsell Hospital's first full year of operation, 69 per cent of admissions were for some form of tuberculosis; in 1947 tuberculosis admissions dropped to 40 per cent, and the following year tuberculosis accounted for

36 per cent of admissions.[47] This is not to argue that tuberculosis was not a burden on Aboriginal communities, but it does suggest that it was neither the most burdensome nor the most likely reason for Aboriginal people to seek treatment. By the end of 1957, with all tuberculosis patients in Alberta and the Northwest Territories under care,[48] tuberculosis accounted for only 13 per cent of admissions to the hospital. A near equal number of admissions were of parturient women and their newborns (12 per cent). More than 60 per cent of patients admitted were children, and the single greatest cause was pneumonia or bronchopneumonia (30 per cent of all non-tuberculosis admissions).[49] Poor and overcrowded living conditions likely accounted for these admissions.

The overcrowded hospital quickly became a hazard. Initially, "Unit 3" served as a general and isolation ward, but it soon developed into "a conglomerate mass of women and children with every disease you would think of. It became more or less a pest house."[50] Nevertheless, Dr Falconer judged the "patients themselves were better off than in their primitive conditions at home and statistics would tend to substantiate this."[51] It is not clear to which statistics he referred, but patient care tended to be judged not against accepted hospital standards, but against perceived inadequate home conditions. On that basis, institutionalization itself, even in a "pest house," was seen as both necessary and therapeutic, regardless of the outcomes. But patients continued to be made more ill by their time in hospital. As Dr Matas admitted, "It is unusual for a child to be admitted with one condition and be discharged without having had some other infection or communicable disease. Isolation is carried out as far as possible and more so in surgical cases, but this does not seem to insure freedom from intercurrent diseases." For instance, an Inuit boy was admitted on 17 September 1957 for repair of an umbilical hernia, but "purulent otitis media" (acute inflammation of the middle ear with discharge) prevented surgery; shortly after the infection subsided, he developed, in turn chickenpox, measles, bronchopneumonia, rubella, and a recurrence of otitis media. He was finally discharged four and a half months later.[52]

According to Falconer the problem was not overcrowding as such, but the building, the staff, and, ultimately, the patients themselves. In a rather cryptic passage that pointed to the perceived need for strict patient discipline, he explained that the hospital needed first "proper facilities to control the patients with a firm hand and secondly better control of and more staff ... to properly run an isolation ward."[53] One staff member, Kathleen Steinhauer-Anderson, one of the very few Aboriginal nurses employed at the Camsell Hospital, recalled for historian rie Meijer Drees: "The conditions there [pediatric ward at the Camsⅽ Hospital] were pretty bad. The babies were all dried with the same towel! I had to petition hard to get separate towels and towel racks for each baby patient. Some things were just improper."[54] Not surprisingly, "infectious hepatitis" (hepatitis A), a liver infection transmitted in food and water contaminated with infected fecal matter, frequently spread among staff and patients. From four cases in 1951, to thirty cases in late 1954, and ten more in the first three months of 1955, it was deemed an "epidemic," though it might have been more properly termed an endemic condition in the hospital.[55]

More troubling, discharged patients became vectors of disease transmission to their home communities. An Inuit woman, discharged from the Camsell Hospital to her home at Bathurst Inlet in the high Arctic, developed measles and pneumonia a week later. She was flown to Yellowknife, but not before spreading measles to others, resulting in three or four deaths. Making a virtue out of necessity, Falconer advised: "It is felt particularly with natives that we should not isolate them from measles but rather let them have the infection while in the hospital where they can be looked after with a better chance of survival."[56] Certainly the hospital attempted to protect the most vulnerable patients, especially children. With a particularly dangerous measles epidemic raging in the hospital, an infant from the Arctic with cleft palate spent three and a half months in the community hospital at nearby Cold Lake before he could be transferred to Camsell Hospital for surgery. Yet director Moore considered this a "virtual waste of money."[57] As the costs of community hospital care continued to climb throughout the 1950s Moore hoped to further increase the bed capacity at Charles Camsell Indian Hospital: "It is becoming more and more necessary to avoid prolonged hospitalizations in non-departmental institutions whenever possible."[58] But institutionalization had its limits. Filled to capacity and beyond, the hospital found it necessary to transfer some of the chronically ill and severely handicapped to Indian hospitals in other provinces, or, ironically, to northern mission hospitals that would take a "boarder" rate of as little as $2.50 day. This, according to Moore, "would appear to be a very good chance to unload a few bodies from our hospitals." Patients' families, however, were rarely informed about where their loved ones might be sent.[59]

Aside from concerns for efficiency, IHS motivations for moving chronically ill patients from the Camsell Indian Hospital was to make room for "problem cases" or patients with medically interesting conditions. As Moore explained to the hospital's superintendent, "Charles Camsell is a very large hospital and with outstanding diagnostic and consultant facilities and should be used as such rather than as a boarding home ... Vigorous action must be taken to make it possible to use Camsell as a consultant hospital."[60] From the outset IHS had intended that the Camsell Hospital would be associated with the University of Alberta's medical school. A close relationship certainly made the hospital a good medical neighbour in Edmonton, offering up interesting cases for medical students and researchers, while taking advantage of specialists' services. And despite its otherwise overwhelming concern for economy, IHS directed the superintendent at the hospital's opening: "Regardless of the extra costs involved and in order to become affiliated with the medical school university professors are to be consulted in genitourinary, orthopaedics, ear, eye, nose and throat, obstetrics and gynecology, to give them direct access to the hospital's interesting material."[61] Many of these patients, the "interesting material," were subjected to intense medical scrutiny and photographed before their deaths, adding to the hospital's macabre image archive of patients suffering from gross deformities and far advanced diseases. The hospital also kept a museum of pathological specimens of various organs of the body infected with tuberculosis.[62] But in order to become a teaching hospital for intern and graduate training the Camsell Hospital needed accreditation, a voluntary process of peer review to maintain minimum standards. IHS hoped too that accreditation would "add prestige" to the Camsell Hospital and "ease some of our difficulties in the recruitment of top drawer staff."[63]

Never a terribly rigorous process, hospital accreditation emerged from the realization that "if the health professionals don't police themselves, somebody else will."[64] More self-study than critical evaluation, accreditation required hospitals to complete a questionnaire and (with ample advanced notice) undergo an inspection. The American College of Surgeons conducted hospital accreditation in Canada until 1951, when a joint Canadian and American commission took over inspections. Not until 1959 did organized medicine (Canadian Medical Association, Royal College of Physicians and Surgeons, Association des médecins de langue française du Canada) and the Canadian Hospital Association establish the Canadian Council on Hospital Accreditation. Described as a "low-key enterprise" with only seven staff by the 1970s, the Council had no mechanism for enforcement. As the executive director noted, "We can say 'there's your trouble boys' – and they'll do everything they can to put it right."[65] But accreditation also required hospitals to keep extensive medical records; draft by-laws and regulations for medical staff; hold monthly staff conferences attended by at least 75 per cent of the medical staff; conduct regular nursing staff conferences; and employ registered X-ray and laboratory technicians.[66] But, as Moore well knew, most IHS hospitals fell far short of having enough trained staff for minimal patient care, much less for attending to increased administrative duties.[67] Presumably, though, it was the very absence of administrative and technical departments and employees that allowed the Indian hospitals to operate at half the per diem rates of other hospitals. Acknowledging the futility of attempting to receive accreditation in the other Indian hospitals, IHS agreed that the Camsell Hospital alone would apply for accreditation as a "pilot project."[68] In 1956 Camsell Hospital received a one-year provisional accreditation, and subsequently a three-year accreditation, principally because of its affiliation with the university's medical school, but the Joint Commission warned that it would not again accredit the hospital "unless radical renovations are made eliminating the present fire hazards or a new hospital constructed."[69] By 1958 the Canadian Medical Association recognized it as an approved hospital for postgraduate training in thoracic surgery.[70]

Interns and residents at the Camsell Hospital studied under former superintendent and, after 1950, surgical consultant Dr Herbert Meltzer. As noted, the doctor's stormy relationship with IHS bureaucrats stemmed in part from his concerns over hospital policy. And as a surgeon, Meltzer also clashed with his peers over therapy at a time of profound shifts in how tuberculosis was understood and treated. The "conquest" of tuberculosis is often told as a linear and progressive story, from the early days of long sanatorium stays focused on bed rest, to surgical collapse therapy, and finally to ultimate victory in the advent of effective chemotherapy, but there were no such certainties in Canada in the 1940s and 1950s.[71] From the hospital's opening in 1946, Meltzer as a thoracic surgeon wanted "selective cases": otherwise strong, young, and minimally infected patients who stood a good chance of surviving chest surgery. His immediate superior, Dr E.L. Stone, thought otherwise:

I would do away with most of the tuberculosis surgery and emphasize the function of the hospital as a place of isolation, that is use it as a means of controlling infection rather than as a place where a few

selected patients get highly specialized treatment. I am not sure whether
the chief result of chest surgery for Indians isn't to produce surgical
cripples and eternal dependents ... cut down the cost on everything but
nursing and feeding.[72]

William Barclay, who performed all the autopsies, "of which there
were many," recalled that other doctors on staff were equally troubled
by the surgical treatments undertaken "with little or no evidence as to
their effectiveness."[73] Nevertheless, chest surgery became fundamental
to tuberculosis treatment at the Camsell Hospital. But Meltzer's careful
approach, keeping patients in hospital for at least a year after surgery,
put him at odds with the hospital superintendent, who pressed Meltzer to
perform more surgeries and perform them more quickly once patients
were admitted to hospital. Falconer complained that patients were
spending too much time in hospital: "This, at present rates, indirectly
costs thousands of dollars a year and of course keeps the individual
patient occupying a bed longer than can be justified ... I do feel that if
the surgery service were stepped up, in a year or more we would have
more beds available for patients."[74] For his part Meltzer criticized the
practice of admitting "chronic bone cases and older-age-group cases"
(not suitable for surgery) and filling half the beds with "a permanent
population ... I maintain, that to use the Camsell as a surgical hospital, it cannot be crowded – let alone overcrowded."[75] But overcrowding
was not the only threat to the surgical program.

In 1953 the source of "serious" infections in surgical patients was
traced to the practice of keeping the doors open between the hospital's
laboratory and the adjacent operating room. Cultures obtained from
the air during an operation showed "staphylococci in rather profuse
growth."[76] Increasingly frustrated, in 1954 Falconer withdrew from
the hospital's administration and replaced Stone, who had retired as
IHS superintendent of the Foothills region (Alberta and Northwest
Territories). Meltzer's friend and Camsell physician, Dr Matthew
Matas, succeeded Falconer as hospital superintendent. With the mild-
mannered Matas as hospital superintendent Meltzer declared himself "much happier" and continued to direct the hospital's focus on
surgery, though he complained that his meagre consultant's salary
was "ridiculous in comparison with the volume of surgery I do."[77] By
early 1960 Meltzer, despite his resentment at being overworked and
underpaid, would not relinquish his position as chief of surgery at
the hospital.[78]

In 1953 Meltzer undertook major chest surgery on 105 of the 350 patients with pulmonary tuberculosis, 68 per cent of all surgeries in the hospital.[79] The most common chest surgery, performed on eighty-seven patients that year, was thoracoplasty, a surgically induced "rest cure" where several ribs were removed to collapse the diseased lung and paraffin wax (plombage) inserted to maintain the collapse and prop up the chest wall. The procedure usually required the removal of seven or eight ribs, but surgeons were reluctant to remove more than two or three at a time, so patients endured several excruciating procedures. By 1953 Meltzer reported that he changed his technique from a two- or three-stage thoracoplasty to a single operation: "As a result, with some increase in our tempo of surgery, we are completing surgery on exactly twice as many patients."[80] Performed under local anaesthesia, the operation was "painful and deforming" according to Dr Barclay.[81] Local rather than general anaesthesia was deemed necessary to maintain the patient's cough reflex to prevent aspiration and the possibility of infecting the other lung. As for the terrified patient, awake and aware of the saw cutting into their ribs, Meltzer claimed, "the argument that patients suffer mental torture under local anesthesia cannot be entertained. Mild hypnosis counteracts mental strain almost completely."[82]

In the five years from July 1949 to August 1954 Meltzer performed thoracoplasty with plombage on 324 patients, reporting "good results after a short follow up" in 314 patients (96.9 per cent); 9 patients were deemed "improved"; 4 patients "relapsed after discharge"; 70 were still in hospital, and 253 were "at home." There were no "early" deaths (as a direct result of the surgery) and only five "late mortalities." As the surgeon explained, "The proof of the pudding is in the eating, and the proof of good results similarly depends on how they are maintained after discharge and under adverse home conditions … I feel these results justify continuing our present principles of therapy."[83] But with collapse therapy, as Dr E.L. Ross, the longtime medical superintendent of the Sanatorium Board of Manitoba noted in 1953, "about one-third of our patients died, about one-third *half recovered*, and about one-third became cured."[84] Surgery left long, disfiguring scars, the plombage often migrated from its original site creating infection, and patients were left with limited lung function and lifelong deformity – "surgical cripples" as Dr Stone put it.

Admitted to Camsell Hospital as a sixteen-year-old in 1956, Dave Melting Tallow from Siksika (Blackfoot) reserve east of Calgary spent three years on bed rest and antimicrobial medication and, in 1959, underwent lung resection, or the surgical removal of a part of his lung:

> They removed three ribs, and scraped three. And they removed part of my lung. I think that was to access my lung, I'm not sure. But for some reason they took three ribs. Now I've got these stumps in my back on my left side and no ribs there. And the rest of them were scraped. They cut a part of my lung out and I think they put wax in there to hold it together until it healed shut.
>
> They used a saw. I was awake and I could hear the saw. They got part way and then they told me, now we're breaking the ribs off. They said, get ready, then they broke the ribs off. When they did that it felt like somebody hit you inside the chest. And they did that three times. When they broke it off that's when it hurt. Felt like somebody hit me with a fist inside my chest. I just heard the saw buzzing away and cutting stuff. I could hear it inside me, but there was no pain really until they broke them off. And I didn't even really feel them taking a part of my lung off. That's what they said they did. I didn't feel any of that.[85]

He recovered from his surgery, and at seventy years of age in 2010 reported only occasional shortness of breath, but he was particularly bothered by the suggestion made by a physician who examined him years later that perhaps he had been the subject of medical experimentation, a disturbingly frequent charge made by former Aboriginal patients that will be examined in greater detail later. As a thoracic surgeon, Meltzer continued to cut into chests to treat pulmonary tuberculosis precisely because effective antibiotics ensured greater success in surgically excising even the smallest area of infection.[86]

Another elder – Roy Little Chief, also from Siksika – after twelve years at residential school suffered a haemorrhage in 1956 and was admitted to Charles Camsell Hospital. He spent nearly a year in hospital and understood that the only way out of the hospital was to have surgery: "So this was my life in there for eleven and half months. And what we were told there by the other patients was, the only way you'd get out of the hospital is for you to have surgery." His surgery was performed under local anaesthetic "I got on the operating table and then they started putting needles in me. Probably to freeze my back and I remember coming to, I was facing down and I felt … when they were cutting it open and then I felt hot water on my back. It must have been the blood coming out. And I heard the doctors say, there's blood."[87]

For IHS physicians, surgery seemed to offer certainty in the uncertain world outside the hospital: patients could be returned to their still-impoverished homes with less chance of relapse; or they might be encouraged to integrate into society as cured (with the scars to prove it), posing little threat to the public. Dave Melting Tallow chose neither. After a brief rehabilitation attending school in Edmonton, he left for the United States, travelling, working, and enjoying freedom from the surveillance of Indian agents, police, teachers, and physicians in a society that chose instead to isolate and segregate African Americans.

Thoracic surgery, made more daring and heroic with effective antibiotics in the 1940s and 1950s, did not easily give way to the new chemotherapy regime, particularly for Aboriginal patients. In Manitoba IHS contracted with the private corporation Sanatorium Board of Manitoba to provide tuberculosis treatment for Aboriginal patients in three segregated institutions: Dynevor Indian Hospital near Winnipeg, the former American military hospital at Clearwater Lake at The Pas in northern Manitoba, and the redundant Brandon Military Hospital.[88] The arrangement relieved IHS of providing tuberculosis treatment while providing the Sanatorium Board with a steady income of more than $800,000 annually.[89] Treatment at Dynevor and Clearwater Lake Indian hospitals consisted of bed rest, while patients requiring surgery were transferred to what became known as the Brandon Indian Hospital. Dr Arthur Povah, a 1945 medical graduate who contracted tuberculosis and spent a year in Ninette Sanatorium as a patient, continued his association with tuberculosis as chest surgeon at Brandon.[90] The 260-bed hospital, owned by the Department of Health and Welfare, but operated by the Sanatorium Board, treated Manitoba Aboriginal people and, increasingly after 1950, Inuit patients. By 1953 Povah noted that in his practice "pulmonary resection [surgical removal of a section of lung or the complete organ] has pretty well replaced other surgical procedures for the treatment of tuberculosis and arrangements have been made to do three of these operations every two weeks."[91] And though antibiotic treatment at Brandon increased by 1956, the rate of chest surgery increased nearly threefold, from six surgeries per month in 1953 to sixteen pulmonary resections per month three years later.[92] By 1959 Brandon Indian Hospital's patients were transferred to the once exclusively white Manitoba Sanatorium (Ninette) for surgery, and the former Indian hospital, renamed the Assiniboine Hospital, was renovated for the chronic care of white patients "of slightly more refined tastes" by adding new beds, dressers, night tables, and curtains.[93]

Canada only slowly followed the trend in other jurisdictions away from surgery towards a greater reliance on chemotherapy alone. The "tuberculosis trade" was reluctant to change. As Sanatorium Board of Manitoba's Dr E.L. Ross put it, "tuberculosis is an aggressive disease and demands aggressive and bold measures to combat it. Antimicrobial therapy has opened the door for definitive (excisional) therapy [surgery] and in a few years we will, no doubt, have a much better understanding of what should be excised and what can be safely left."[94] By 1956, American sanatoria, or at least those represented at Wisconsin's Pembine Conference, embraced chemotherapy to a much greater extent than Manitoba practice, which continued to rely on surgery. Ross admitted that the Sanatorium Board was not continuing drug treatment long enough: "We need to accept the fact that post-sanatorium chemotherapy is a phase of the overall treatment program, but, of course, not a substitute for sanatorium ... our indications for resection are fairly aggressive [compared to American practice]."[95] In 1959, British specialist Dr P.E. Baldry from Middlesex toured Canadian sanatoria, where he found a disturbing number of surgeries because, he said, there was not the "same confidence placed in long term chemotherapy" in Canada. He expressed surprise at the continued practice of lung resections for small foci of infection, while noting with approval that most sanatoria undertook far less surgery than in previous years. Baldry also noted that Canadian sanatorium doctors have "little faith in their patients and by British standards separate them from their homes for rather long periods."[96] And an increasing number of patients in sanatoria were Aboriginal.

For instance, in Saskatchewan in 1953 the superintendent of nurses at the Prince Albert Sanatorium noted the institution was filled to capacity with 270 to 280 patients daily, "a little less than one quarter of these being white people, which is further proof that we are winning our battle against tuberculosis among the whites." The other patients were Aboriginal.[97] The Mountain Sanatorium in Hamilton, Ontario, with 753 beds (126 vacant) in 1956 was home to 332 Inuit patients; a year later there were only Aboriginal patients in the institution.[98] As the unfortunately named Dr A.L. Paine, medical superintendent at Manitoba Sanatorium, explained, "More white patients with residual minimal lesions are being treated conservatively, though resection is still favoured to prevent relapse in those of Indian blood."[99] Paine undertook what he called "salvage surgery," or lung resections to reduce the perceived risk of relapse once Aboriginal patients returned home.[100] In Canada generally, surgical treatment for tuberculosis outpaced both American and British practice, while Aboriginal patients underwent chest surgery to a greater extent than other Canadians. As patients who continued to be viewed as careless in their own health, posing an ongoing threat to the national health, and subject to relapse in their "adverse home conditions," Aboriginal patients underwent more aggressive treatment.

Long-term hospitalization in sanatoria continued even after Aboriginal patients received the benefits of chemotherapy treatment. For most non-Aboriginal patients outpatient chemotherapy treatment was increasingly the norm in the 1950s, leading to what the Canadian Tuberculosis Association called the "miracle of the empty beds." As inpatient populations fell, costs per patient rose, prompting many sanatoria to close and transfer patients to centralized institutions. In Manitoba the Sanatorium Board closed the segregated Indian hospitals at Dynevor in 1957, Brandon in 1959, and Clearwater Lake in 1965, transferring all patients to the Manitoba Sanatorium. In 1956 the medical superintendent at Ontario's Fort William Sanatorium, facing falling patient populations and rising costs, wondered if some Aboriginal patients from Manitoba could be transferred to his institution, but with more than 500 available beds, Manitoba refused.[101] At the same time, IHS policy was "not to treat Indian tuberculous patients on an out-patient basis in view of the fact that we cannot supervise their activities very closely while they are at home and in the majority of cases their medication would not be taken regularly. The Indian people, at the present time, do not have the educational background for home therapy of active tuberculosis."[102] In Saskatchewan, after 1965 the Anti-TB League that operated the provincial sanatoria assumed treatment for Aboriginal patients. As the League's general superintendent reported in that year, the average length of treatment for non-Aboriginal patients decreased from the previous year, from 10.11 months to 8.63 months; for Indian patients the average length of treatment increased from 14.41 months in 1964 to 17.93 months in 1965. "As the proportion of Indian patients increase the average length of treatment in Sanatorium will increase, as we normally treat Indian patients longer in Sanatorium in order to ensure that they receive adequate chemotherapy."[103]

Manitoba maintained a similar policy. The Sanatorium Board's Dr Paine explained in 1967: "Until recently patients of native extraction were kept in sanatorium for the entire period of drug taking [one to two years]."[104] At the same time, with the advent of national hospital insurance in the late 1950s, IHS was attempting to close many of its Indian hospitals and "get out of the hospital business."[105] With empty beds to fill, and patients with little power to influence their own treatment, sanatoria continued to institutionalize Aboriginal patients far from their homes and families. Moreover, the practice aided considerably the Sanatorium Board's financial health. In 1965 it received $680,730 from IHS for the treatment of Aboriginal patients.[106] Interestingly, Paine reckoned that treatment policy changed because of an altered "native psychology" and a "more responsible attitude" from a "fatalistic acquiescence of this situation to active demand for earlier discharge to drugs at home as is commonly practiced in white patients."[107] While Aboriginal demands for a voice in treatment predate the late 1960s, home treatment was certainly prompted by the desire to close the increasingly dilapidated and expensive institutions. Sanatoria across the country closed in the late 1960s; the province closed the Manitoba Sanatorium in 1972 and put it up for sale the next year.[108]

Treatment for Aboriginal people was determined by medical perceptions of an essentialized "Indian" patient as irresponsible and reckless, requiring the surveillance and discipline that institutions provided. Meanwhile, the appalling conditions on many reserves – overcrowded homes and inadequate infrastructure that bred much disease – were allowed to remain essentially unchanged (though ex-patients were sometimes provided with extra food rations for six months after discharge.) Indeed, these "adverse home conditions" justified institutionalization in dangerously crowded wards while surgeons, emboldened by antibiotics, continued to open Aboriginal chests as the price to be paid in order to leave the institutions and no longer pose a threat to the national health. As a humanitarian effort to extend the benefits of modern medical care, there could be little room for criticism or complaint. There were clear parallels to residential schools, where, despite the acknowledged poor conditions and worse treatment, children were presumed to be better off than under the care of their purportedly unfit parents in unfit homes. Many students in residential schools, "agencies for the spread of tuberculosis," graduated to Indian hospitals.[109] Institutions of confinement, increasingly seen as necessary and a normal environment for Aboriginal people, continued to damage families and communities. But Indian hospitals also promised to become "training centres for Indian health workers," according to the deputy minister, and while Aboriginal employees became integral to the operation of the institutions, they rarely rose above the least-skilled and most poorly paid positions.

Chapter Three

Everyone in Their Place: Labour in the Indian Hospitals

It is proposed to make every effort to train Indians as doctors, nurses and sick attendants wherever possible. It is felt that the true interests of the Indian will best be served when they are taking an active part in looking after their own people. This may be taken as a necessary part of the development, which is essential to the well being of the Indians. What must be done is to encourage their natural pride in their own race and customs while at the same time learning the ways of life, which will enable them to live in association with the white man.[1]

– Brooke Claxton, minister of National Health and Welfare, 1946

The Indian hospitals' first "cardinal policy" – that no effort or reasonable cost should be spared to give patients the best hospital care – was, as we have seen, rather loosely interpreted. The second cardinal policy, that the hospitals should function as a training ground for Aboriginal health workers, was never seriously pursued. Minister Claxton's qualified promise in 1946 to make "every effort" to train Aboriginal health workers rang hollow from the outset. While some Aboriginal registered nurses and aides who trained elsewhere found employment in the hospitals, most workers, without formal training, struggled to advance beyond the least-skilled and lowest-paid positions, yet this Aboriginal staff made up a significant segment of IHS support personnel. The professional ranks were initially dominated by an enthusiastic group of Canadian-born male physicians and female nurses whose careers had been interrupted by Depression and war, and managed by a small bureaucracy of their physician peers. But soon enough, doctors found few opportunities for career advancement outside of the quickly growing IHS bureaucracy itself. Moreover, as state investment in national hospital infrastructure and health care increased exponentially in the postwar years, nurses and other staff were drawn to better positions elsewhere. However, state investment in IHS failed to keep pace, creating constant turmoil in staffing the Indian hospitals. Some European refugee physicians, so-called "DP doctors" (displaced persons) found temporary work, but IHS professional staff was overrepresented by those either at the beginning or near the end of their careers. Patient care was seriously compromised by often dedicated, but poorly trained, underpaid, and overworked staff.

In 1946, Dr Stone, regional IHS superintendent, advised the medical director at Charles Camsell Hospital that support staff recruiting should begin with recovered patients, specifically, "a reliable middle aged Indian woman" who might form the nucleus of the Indian staff, but, he warned, "do *not* try to use recent graduates of Indian Residential schools. They are too young." He might well have mentioned that female residential school graduates rarely had more than a grade eight education, and of course no medical training. Though Stone thought the Camsell Hospital might eventually establish a graduate nurse-training program, it never materialized.[2] The few Aboriginal registered nurses (RN) who worked in the Indian hospitals took their training in accredited programs at provincial institutions, despite very limited support from Indian Affairs and discrimination in the educational system and society generally.[3] Many Aboriginal nursing students entered training specifically to work in their own communities but were often passed over for the positions since Indian agents fretted that by returning women to reserves they would undergo a cultural regression when faced with supposedly perilous social influences. After all, the state policy of integration presumed that Aboriginal RNs would take their skills and fade into the urban Canadian landscape, not return to reserves. As historian Mary Jane McCallum argues, "It was assumed that medical services for Aboriginal people would be delivered by those same agents who also provided the army, the police, the education system, the missions and in many ways regulated the lives of Aboriginal people – the State and the Church."[4] IHS preferred instead to hire non-Aboriginal registered nurses, and when few applied, they recruited overseas. Historian Laurie Meijer Drees argues that IHS "did little to encourage or recruit" Aboriginal people into formal health care roles providing instead sporadic on the job training for service positions.[5] Though the Indian hospitals failed to offer training, many Aboriginal women enrolled in provincial Registered Nurse Assistant and Licensed Practical Nurse programs and found work with IHS. These programs, requiring a grade eight education, appealed to Indian Affairs policies of low academic standards with a focus on manual or vocational training for Aboriginal people. Two programs in the west provided courses specifically for Aboriginal women that required candidates to take a preliminary two-month training period in IHS hospitals to determine their "fitness and aptitude" for the course.[6] Training Aboriginal workers for semi-skilled and low-paying positions rather than for professional or para-professional careers resulted in part from the state's limited commitment to health care, which it characterized as a moral rather than a legal obligation. Despite pledges to do so, the IHS would not commit to the long-term investment that formal career training required.[7] It is also clear, however, that the hierarchical, paternalistic, and physician-dominated IHS bureaucracy perceived Aboriginal participation as limited to the role of patient or ex-patient, such as Stone's "reliable middle aged Indian woman." It is safe to say that those who rose above service roles in the hospitals did so in spite of, not because of, IHS policies.

Scholars of colonialism and medicine, examining local participation, especially the role of "subordinates and intermediaries" in the health work of empire, draw attention to their significance in translating across language and cultural barriers.[8] Working as aides, maids, domestics, kitchen help, orderlies, drivers, and janitors, Aboriginal employees acted as unpaid translators and cultural brokers, providing comfort and support for patients.[9] But hospital employees, women trained to wash and scrub, were also assumed to carry the benefits of Western medicine back to their communities, which were still supposedly mired in "backward" and "superstitious" notions of health care. Percy Moore observed that in his travels he found that women who had been patients or maids in hospitals lived in the best-kept reserve homes.[10] Moreover, IHS deemed the labour itself as valuable instruction in self-discipline and self-improvement. Vocational training as X-ray and laboratory assistants was also most often provided in terms of rehabilitation.[11] Indeed, as IHS claimed, "as soon as our patients are able, they engage in rehabilitation employment around the hospital."[12] The discourse of employment as improvement and rehabilitation also served to justify low wages.[13]

Minnie Aodla Freeman, born in 1936 in an Inuit community on Cape Hope Island in James Bay, worked for a time in a hospital in Fort George. After she became ill herself, she was sent to Moose Factory

Indian hospital on the James Bay shore, then to Hamilton's Mountain Sanatorium. "No preparation, no warning, no choice, and no reason given why [we] had to go so far away to be cured. One afternoon we boarded the train to Hamilton."[14] Though she was on strict bed rest for a "spot" on her left lung, with her knowledge of English she was quickly recruited as a translator for the staff. She resented being "shipped like cargo and meant to behave like cargo."[15] In 1952, after a year in hospital sixteen-year-old Freeman expected to be released, but instead she was offered work at the Mountain Sanatorium as a translator. Living in the nurses' residence, she was put to work on the children's ward and once a week read anatomy texts with a nurse, but she was expected to drop everything when she was needed as a translator. "The nurses and doctors spoke to me only when they needed a translator. Otherwise I was different and strange to them ... I saw and I heard. I never made known my feelings or frustrations."[16] She left after two years. Back in Moose Factory, Freeman hoped to find a job, and since the Hudson's Bay Company did not hire Aboriginal people, she applied at the Indian hospital. "I went to see the administrator, who had no manners whatever and not one polite word. I could see that he felt very important with himself and was eager to impress the natives with his high and mighty job. He hated his job because there was no one there who understood his importance. He was not listening when I introduced myself."[17] Freeman explained she could type forty words a minute and was also interested in nursing at the hospital. Instead she was offered a position as a live-in domestic for one of the hospital's secretaries. Freeman eventually accepted a position with Indian Affairs as a translator, and in 1957 she was sent to Edmonton to visit and translate for Inuit patients at Charles Camsell Indian Hospital, though no one thought to enquire if she spoke the same dialect. "It was very sad to see all these Inuit. Some had children in the North from whom they had not heard since they arrived. So many worries ... I had never heard the Inuit language of the western Arctic. I tried to speak with some but could not understand. They didn't understand when I spoke to them and yet they seemed so happy to see me. All I could do was return my Inuk smile to let them know that I felt for them."[18] Freeman found herself in the "middle," expected to explain qallunaat (non-Inuit) culture to the Inuit, and Inuit culture to the qallunaat.[19]

Women from Carry the Kettle First Nation east of Regina recall working as aides in the Fort Qu'Appelle Indian Hospital, where they helped patients navigate the rigid hospital routine: bringing food trays to hungry patients between meal times; visiting with lonely patients despite hospital policy; accepting an elder's choice not to take their medications.[20] Grace Anderson from Fairford Reserve (Pinaymootang) worked as a nurse's aide at Clearwater Lake Indian Hospital at The Pas, Manitoba, in the early 1960s. Anderson, struck by the rigid social and professional hierarchies among the staff, recollected that the British doctor and head nurse remained completely aloof from the Aboriginal aides. "These people [non-Aboriginal staff] were just functioning from day to day, same thing day in and day out. There were no pictures on the wall, there were no plants anywhere, nothing to give you a feeling of anything pleasant. It was, as they use the word, sterile and foreign, uncaring to put it plainly."[21] The strict racial divisions among staff had not changed much from the hospital's early postwar years when "white girls" employed as aides refused to room with young Aboriginal staff. The hospital built cubicles in the army barracks for the "Indian girls," reserving the maids' quarters for white staff.[22] The patients, by the 1960s almost exclusively Inuit, struggled to communicate with anyone in the hospital, though a Cree nurse's aide managed to interpret to a limited extent. Anderson worked in the seventy-two-bed women's ward where patients kept busy sewing mukluks from duffel, no doubt destined for federal employees in the north. Never allowed outside, the mostly Catholic Inuit patients' grim existence was relieved by Sunday prayers. An old accordion provided some entertainment, Anderson recalled, "But the other nurses wouldn't allow them, but when I was in charge working evenings I allowed them to dance ... And they did square dancing and that was the high, very great thing. They would come and hug me."[23] The women arrived at the hospital with nothing beyond the clothes on their backs, Anderson recalled, without toiletries and only a few combs for the whole ward to share, yet each patient was provided with a clock, so they might learn the value of time. Aboriginal employees, like Anderson, aided and also resisted IHS plans while creating a healthy space in the institutions that eased anxious and vulnerable patients. A significant if rarely acknowledged fact in the Indian hospitals was that Aboriginal workers accounted for up to 15 per cent of the IHS workforce by the 1960s.[24] Racialized and professional hierarchies rendered them all but invisible in the documentary record.[25] Despite the limitations and low expectations placed on Aboriginal workers, they were fundamental to the hospitals' operations while rendering Indian hospitals less foreign for patients.

The hospitals also provided workers with a relatively stable though meagre income. As a teenager Frank Malloway spent nearly three years at Coqualeetza Indian Hospital at Sardis, British Columbia, with pleurisy, misdiagnosed as tuberculosis. He returned to the hospital in 1954 and trained to be a nursing orderly; he worked for four years on shiftwork and six more years on permanent night shift. He recalled that it was "a good place to work. There was a lot of Natives working there ... All the medical staff that I remember were white people. There was no Indian nurses. They had Indian ward aides, there was no Indian nurses." He met his wife, who also worked at the hospital, and when they started a family he worked the night shift, which allowed him to spend time with his children during the day.[26] In 1964 Frank left hospital work for better wages as a logger.

At the Fort Qu'Appelle Indian Hospital, Agnes Cyr worked in the laundry and the sewing room for more than twenty-five years until her retirement in 1977. Born in 1912, she had attended Lebret School for only two and a half years when she was sent home to the Pasqua reserve to care for her blind mother and younger siblings. Her early life spent managing a household and farm during the Depression taught her hard work and disappointment, as she planted gardens only to watch them blow away in the dustbowl. As a parent she made "darned sure" that her children got an education. Her daughter trained as a registered nurse in Saskatoon and worked in Toronto; her son trained as an X-ray and laboratory technician. At the hospital Cyr worked in the laundry and as a seamstress turning huge bolts of flannelette into baby clothes, diapers, "little dresses, lots of things, little vests for newborns." It was clean and quiet work, "the best part of my life when I was there. We always enjoyed each other's company. And the staff – the nursing staff – well in fact everybody was really good. We all got along." She admitted that the wages were never very good and that much of her income was spent on car payments "so I could get to work. I made sure it [the car] was brand new. I enjoyed them. If I wanted to go somewhere I'd just get in the car and go" (she gave up driving at the age of 93). In the evening her husband then drove to Regina for his night shift as a heavy-duty mechanic.[27] Their long service suggests that, for these workers, caring for community members even in a restricted capacity was meaningful and rewarding work. Though a valuable source of waged work, the hospitals might have been the means to develop Aboriginal professionals and administrators to interpret and control the delivery of health care. But, despite the minister's qualified 1946 promise to provide training "wherever possible," it was obvious to IHS medical bureaucrats that only they could know what was "essential to the well-being of the Indians."

All the Indian hospitals struggled to maintain even the most basic nursing service in the 1950s. A rapidly increasing national demand for health care, and specifically hospital services, and a 40 per cent increase in patient loads from 1950 to 1955 alone, resulted in serious nursing shortages across the country. The strong demand for their services allowed registered nurses and their provincial associations to press for improved wages and working conditions. In 1947, for instance, the Manitoba Association of Registered Nurses advised that nursing short-ages in hospitals resulted from "instability" in nurses' employment, or staff turnover. Hospitals, it recommended, should improve nurses' living quarters, which were often just small bedrooms in the hospital building itself; reduce hours of work from the common 48 hours to 44 hours per week; provide regular, scheduled time off; and increase salaries. "A satisfied staff is a stable staff." The Manitoba association reported that hospital nurses were often underpaid and that salaries should be adequate to provide security and "commensurate with the value of her service to the community."[28] It was a competitive market for nurses' services and the IHS, in the interests of efficiency, hired fewer registered nurses and relied increasingly on the cheaper labour of ward aides and inexperienced "Indian maids" to staff the hospitals. Faced with persistent staff turnover, hospital superintendents – civil servants with limited autonomy in a highly centralized bureaucracy – could do little but plead for improvements in salaries and working conditions. All Indian hospitals struggled with "instability" in their professional staff, but some were worse than others.

Miller Bay Indian Hospital, an air force hospital on British Colum-bia's north coast thirteen kilometres from Prince Rupert, was hastily built in anticipation of a long Pacific war but was never used, and became redundant before war's end. Certainly the influx of wartime American and Canadian military personnel disrupted Aboriginal com-munities throughout the northwest through the severe epidemics of infectious disease that followed the building of the Alaska Highway and the Canol pipeline.[29] But the urgent necessity for an Indian hos-pital in the Prince Rupert area stemmed from the apparent threat that local Aboriginal people posed to citizens and the troops. A 1944 petition from the Prince Rupert board of health and concerned citizens, calling themselves the Community Council Association, demanded protection from "infected natives [that] act as a reservoir of infection for other people."[30] Local hospitals refused to admit active cases of tuberculosis or venereal disease, and were already full. Claiming that tuberculosis went untreated, and that "80 per cent of alleged sources of venereal disease reported to local health authorities in 1943 were native women," the petitioners urged the federal government to open an Indian hospital at Miller Bay. Citing the petition, the minister responsible for Indian Affairs, Thomas Crerar, explained to minister of National Defence J.L. Ralston the danger of untreated tuberculosis: "More urgent still, there are some 28 Indian women who have been reported as sources of venereal disease. This is a distinct hazard to troops in the area."[31] Crerar had in mind the vacant and fully equipped seventy-five-bed army hospital across the street from the Prince Rupert General Hospital. Instead, the more remote and unequipped Miller Bay Hospital became available.

At the hospital's official opening in September 1946, local dignitaries, politicians, and the press toured the institution, hailing it as the "most modern tubercular unit in the Dominion." Aboriginal leaders such as Mr and Mrs Henry McKay of Greenville (Laxgalts'sp), Leonard Leighton of Metlakatla, and Henry Kelly, councillor for the Tsimshian at Port Simpson (Lax Kw'alaams), attended the opening. Kelly spoke of the hospital as a "milestone along the road of progress in the new deal promised by the government of Canada for my people."[32] Long excluded from local hospitals and left without treatment, Aboriginal communities welcomed the prospect of improved health care. But the government's extension of medical services cannot be separated from its larger colonializing project to isolate Native people in the interests of settler society. Dr W.S. Barclay, inspecting local conditions for IHS, recommended the Miller Bay institution, noting that it would "go a long way to quieting any criticism and of course would provide a certain amount of supervision and actual hospital care."[33] This neat summary of the institution's usefulness, in order of importance, reflected the broader IHS raison d'être, where community and national safety required the close surveillance and "actual care" of Aboriginal bodies. The bureaucracy's wildly uncharacteristic alacrity in establishing the hospital signalled the intensity of danger that Aboriginal illness suddenly posed to national health and military vigour; the enemy was already among them. Regardless, with its promise of renewed health for Aboriginal communities and a tangible recognition of government responsibility for health care, the hospital was welcomed, as Kelly put it, as "the new deal promised."

A one-storey flat-roofed olive green building, the hospital was perched on rocky terrain surrounded by muskeg soil. Staff residences in adjacent buildings contained small bedrooms for nurses and larger dormitories for Aboriginal maids. With its brown battleship linoleum and light green walls, the institution retained a distinctly drab military appearance (illustration 3.1). For patients, whose families and friends found it difficult to visit, it was dreary if not a dangerous place. Most of the hospital's beds were in two large dormitory wards, each with one nurse to care for seventy-five patients, ranging from children to adults. Not unexpectedly, it became difficult to find nurses to work in such conditions for the same wages that they could demand in city hospitals, a situation predicted during the hospital's hurried planning stages. As Barclay had warned, the hospital would require trained nurses to carry out the separate technique for hospitalized venereal disease, as "this could not be delegated even to ward aides."[34] By 1949 the hospital superintendent complained that poor IHS salaries resulted in "a large proportion of inferior nurses who for lack of provincial registration are unable to secure positions elsewhere." Better wages and working conditions might attract "a better type of nurse."[35] The alternatives seemed clear enough: either reduce patient admissions or increase nurses' salaries to attract qualified candidates. But Miller Bay, already one of the least efficient of the larger Indian hospitals, judging by its $4.88 per patient per day costs, could ill afford to close beds. It was clear to director Percy Moore and to all Indian hospital medical superintendents that "considerable use will have to be made of "Practical Nurses" if patient strength is to be kept high."[36] Indeed, the next year the hospital increased its capacity from 158 to 172 beds, further reducing its per diem costs.[37]

The staffing problems only increased. Advocating in 1951 for a special living allowance to attract nurses, Miller Bay's medical superintendent Dr J.D. Galbraith suggested that few nurses were interested in tuberculosis nursing, fewer still in nursing Indians, though he allowed that Nanaimo Indian Hospital on Vancouver Island did not suffer the same shortages as Miller Bay. Increasingly frustrated, he pleaded with Ottawa: "We simply have to get some more graduate nurses immediately." Later that year, after two more nurses resigned, the situation was described as "desperate."[38] Of twenty registered nurse positions, eight were filled by RNs, five by ward aides, and seven remained vacant. Moreover, labour shortages in service positions, principally Aboriginal maids and janitors, occurred regularly as the local canneries'

Illustration 3.1 Miller Bay Indian Hospital, near Prince Rupert, BC, 1947.
Carved out of the bush thirteen kilometres from Prince Rupert, Miller Bay
Indian Hospital's isolation made life difficult for patients and staff.

Source: Prince Rupert City & Regional Archives & Museum of Northern B.C.; Wrathall
collection, JRW1267 acc WP1998-071-17552.

better wages drew workers from the hospital. Low salaries and grim
living conditions in the hospital's staff residences, thirteen kilometres
from town and without regular transportation, did nothing to encourage staff to remain. Recreation was limited to drinking parties in staff
residences. Galbraith worried about the influence such parties would
have on the maids "Indian and white," but the hospital's matron
(and ex-army nurse) defended the practice, pointing out that the residences were in fact their homes, and "we did it in the army." More
worrying was the use of liquor by male staff who lived in one wing
of the hospital.[39] When the superintendent prohibited liquor in junior
staff residences, they travelled to Prince Rupert's "beer parlours and
other questionable spots in the red light district." This was a problem

"especially for our Indian maids ... almost every week some of them are jailed." Their crime – drinking in a bar – applied only to Aboriginal workers. As the superintendent complained, the situation not only gave the hospital a bad name, "but leaves us short of staff."[40] A standard RCAF-issue recreation hall was quickly moved to the Miller Bay Hospital grounds and minister of Health and Welfare Paul Martin sent his congratulations on the new facility's opening as a "tangible expression" of the department's sincere appreciation for the staff's "devoted service."[41] Staff might have appreciated higher wages and better working conditions as a more tangible expression of IHS gratitude. Nevertheless, medical superintendent J.D. Galbraith, who left Miller Bay for Coqualeetza Indian Hospital shortly thereafter, suggested that staff discontent seriously impeded hospital operations, translating into a "lack of discipline among the patients."[42]

Discipline, self-imposed or administered by staff when deemed necessary, was considered essential to tuberculosis treatment. Though they were in fact hybrid institutions that included tuberculosis care, Indian hospitals nevertheless operated very much as sanatoria. Graduated degrees of enforced idleness, called "routines" or "classes," from absolute bed rest to limited activity such as walking to the bathroom, to increased movement about the wards, defined classic sanatorium treatment. Patients participated in their own cure, learning self-control, by following the strict rules. Closely regulated, patients followed rigid schedules for bathing, sleeping, and eating; they were told when to cough and how to spit. One sanatorium director put it succinctly: "Everything which is not expressly allowed is forbidden."[43] As historian Alison Bashford argues, the sanatorium was a disciplinary institution, but also instructional – "highly policed but aiming to produce self-policing subjects."[44] In Indian hospitals the disciplinary function predominated since Aboriginal people were deemed to lack the capacity for self-discipline, independence, prudence, and foresight – the attributes of healthy citizenship. Indeed, Indian hospitals as segregated institutions were seen as necessary precisely because Native people were not deemed sufficiently "advanced" to benefit from the sanatorium cure among whites. Prolonged hospitalization and bed rest, even when treatment also included surgery and antibiotics, continued to define the Indian hospitals, where the attributes of self-discipline might be learned. In the highly patriarchal, gendered, and racialized structure of Indian hospitals, the medical superintendent as the authority figure was aided by the nurse matron, who managed the graded ranks of mostly female staff, who in turn tended to patient care and domestic duties. Smooth operation of what historian Kathryn McPherson termed the "hospital household" depended on the firm authority of the medical superintendent.[45] Lack of "patient discipline," engendered by staff turnover, was thus a central preoccupation of Miller Bay's superintendents.

Dr G.R. Howell, himself a former sanatorium patient, replaced Galbraith and in 1954 undertook an investigation into the apparent breakdown in patient discipline, particularly in the women's ward, which, he said, was characterized by "sullenness, lack of co-operation with staff, rule breaking, rudeness," leading to further staff discontent. Wards were overcrowded, with the women's thirty-three-bed Ward B adjoined to the large children's Ward C. Unlike male patients, women were not allowed outside for walks; windows did not operate properly so they were kept shut; there were no privacy screens around beds for patients having bed baths or using bedpans; the whole ward was disciplined if one patient broke the rules; and patients required a note from the medical superintendent to visit one another if they were not close relatives.[46] For the twenty-six boys in Ward A there was one toilet in a bathroom with no window, and, without bedpan sterilizers in the children's wards, infectious hepatitis became a problem.[47] Some minor improvements resulted from Howell's investigation: Wards B and C were divided into two administrative units; privacy curtains were installed in the large adult wards; women were allowed supervised walks on fine days; new patients were to be instructed in hospital rules, especially the use of Kleenex and the importance of bed rest; four nurses were transferred from the women's ward and one resigned. Howell imagined the enquiry itself was cathartic and improved morale.[48] But the superficial reforms did little to improve care for the hospital's 175 patients or the living and working conditions for its 147 employees. One nurse at Miller Bay called the working conditions "extremely primitive."[49]

Continued operational problems prompted another inspection in 1956 that found serious shortages of medical and service staff. On a seasonal basis, local canneries and the fishery continued to attract workers with consistently better wages. The hospital's matron attempted to operate the pharmacy, supervise the kitchen staff, arrange schedules, recruit personnel, and file the endless paperwork required by the centralized IHS bureaucracy, all of which left her with little time to manage the staff. Moreover, with too few trained RNs, ward aides performed nursing duties, and untrained maids acted as ward aides. Howell's deteriorating health meant he was often at home in Prince Rupert while three staff medical officers provided care for 175 patients. One of the officers handled the laboratory work as well as ward duties, though, as the inspector noted, he was "not licensed to practice medicine and probably will not be able to obtain a license."[50] Low staff morale, seen as both cause and consequence of high turnover especially among RNs, made the mood at Miller Bay as gloomy as the wet, grey weather. But, as much as IHS bureaucrats portrayed Miller Bay's problems as a combination of poor patient discipline and even worse management, it is clear that in order to keep patient day costs as low as possible, capable employees were pushed to take on work that was often well beyond the scope of their training. Moreover, patient care would certainly have suffered at the hands of overworked and disgruntled staff. And while IHS accepted the situation as inevitable, the provincial nurses associations did not.

Among the workers at Miller Bay (and in all Indian hospitals) were a number of nurses who could not or would not write the necessary examinations to become registered with the provincial nursing associations. Some had trained at small non-accredited hospitals; others trained at European centres, while others trained at mental hospitals. None were considered qualified for registration. They did the work of hospital RNs, administering medications, inserting catheters, assisting doctors with procedures, and supervising other nurses, while being paid as ward aides or "practical nurses" whose normal duties, while similar to RNs, excluded assisting doctors and inserting anything into patients' bodies.[51] According to the Canadian Nurses Association a ward aide was to be at least eighteen years of age with a grade eight education and have a training course of six to nine months.[52] IHS drew censure from the Canadian Nurses Association for employing ward aides to do the work of RNs, for hiring nurses who could not register in Canada, and, particularly at Miller Bay, for putting ward aides in supervisory positions.[53] The British Columbia Nurses Association stressed its recommendation that "at no time shall a non-registered nurse be placed in the position of supervision or authority over registered nurses."

Throughout the west the IHS was heavily criticized for its employment practices, and in British Columbia, the Nurses Association advised its members against taking positions in IHS hospitals.[54] By 1958, in an effort to appease the nurses associations, IHS in British Columbia deducted $20 from nurses' salaries if they did not maintain their registration. Regional superintendent Dr W.S. Barclay judged that IHS's "reputation as an employing agency has gradually improved" by respecting the provincial nursing standards, but director Percy Moore would not commit to a policy requiring registration in the nursing service: "As far as actual standards of nursing service are concerned it is believed that it can be demonstrated that our sights are high. Also it is believed that comparison with organizations doing similar work is favourable … within reason, we must and shall do our best to comply with local association requirements."[55] Nevertheless, the following spring the hospital advertised for ten ward aides, "senior high school students and/or other suitable female personnel," to cover registered nurses and ward aide positions vacant because of shortages and summer vacations.[56] Not until the 1960s did the Miller Bay Indian Hospital attempt to provide a training program for Aboriginal women. The six-week course for "Indian girls" who lacked the grade eight education required by schools for ward aide training, aimed to improve the "quality of work done by such applicants, and gives them a valuable insight into hospital ethics and nursing staff procedures."[57]

Saskatchewan fared little better in its attempts to recruit and retain qualified employees at IHS wages. Fort Qu'Appelle Indian Hospital in southern Saskatchewan, further restricted by an unwritten agreement with the bishop that its hospital matron (nurse supervisor) must always be Roman Catholic, did without a supervisor when no acceptable candidates could be found.[58] By July 1952, and without a matron for some time, the hospital hired an experienced (though Protestant) candidate. As the past vice-president of the Saskatchewan Registered Nurses Association, she was seen as "invaluable" in rehabilitating somewhat the IHS's reputation as an employer.[59] Percy Moore conceded that the other federal agency operating hospitals, the Department of Veterans Affairs, required nurses to maintain registration, calling it a "good policy," yet "we are not prepared to say that any nurse entering Indian Health Services must have registration."[60] Moreover, IHS required its staff to work forty-eight hours a week while the norm by 1949 was a forty-four-hour week.[61] Refusing to work under such conditions, Fort Qu'Appelle Indian Hospital's matron resigned after just three months, prompting the medical superintendent to plead, "As she is the only registered nurse on the staff, the matter of obtaining an acting matron of any grade is quite urgent."[62] Three months later the medical superintendent also resigned, leaving the sixty-bed institution without a matron, any RNs, or even a physician. Instead, the provincial sanatorium across Echo

Lake sent a doctor to the Indian hospital "for an hour or two occasionally."[63] IHS hospitals earned a reputation as an employer that ignored professional nursing standards and ethics, and where low wages and long hours taxed a poorly trained and ever-changing staff.

Indian hospitals were not immune to the dramatic increases in health care costs in the postwar decades. Across the country hospital expenditures soared, increasing an astonishing 275 per cent between 1945 and 1954.[64] Indeed, Canadians continued to demand modern hospital care though fewer and fewer could afford the ballooning costs, prompting the Department of National Health and Welfare to establish the 1948 National Health Grants program that matched provincial investments, subsidizing health care for "patients of moderate means." But the same bureaucracy continued to limit the funds available to IHS and Indian hospitals, which simply could not meet the increased costs for labour and services. Patient care, indeed patient safety, in Indian hospitals suffered in the interests of the national health.

The North Battleford Indian Hospital in central Saskatchewan, opened in redundant RCAF barracks at the airport in 1949 with sixty beds, had by 1955 an average daily occupancy of sixty-five patients. In that year IHS director Dr Percy Moore cut hospital staff. According to the Saskatchewan Registered Nurses Association's recommendations, adult patients required 3.2 nursing hours per twenty-four-hour period, while the ratio of registered nurses to non-professional employees (ward aides, nurse's aides, and orderlies) should be 67 per cent to 33 per cent. By those standards the North Battleford Indian Hospital needed thirty-seven staff (twenty-five RNs and twelve non-professionals), yet its already inadequate staff of twenty-four was to be reduced to twenty, including just seven RNs. Matron Jessie Morton advised that the forty pre-school children in the hospital required specialized nursing care that ward aides simply could not perform.[65] Medical superintendent Dr P.W. Head did not see how the hospital could manage its surgical, medical, obstetrical, paediatric, and tuberculosis patients with fewer than eleven RNs.[66] Tragically, but perhaps inevitably, a four-month old baby, admitted with "severe bronchopneumonia," but whose condition according to the physician "could be described as fairly good," was found dead in his crib the next day. With one RN and one aide on the ward of fourteen seriously ill infants, there was neither the time nor the hands to care adequately for the patients. The attending physician reported, "No reasonable explanation could be obtained as to why this baby should die unnoticed." Though he decided there was "a certain

amount of negligence on the part of the nurses evidently," he advised
that "since most of the babies are very ill the staff in the nurseries is
totally inadequate."[67] He recommended two more ward aide positions
for the hospital. The matron reported that with a patient increase to
seventy, including forty to forty-five infants, "the nursing services are
very inadequate" since seriously ill infants required at least five hours
of nursing yet with the current staff they were only able to provide two
hours each.[68] There is no evidence in the documentary record of any
repercussions in the wake of this infant's death. Further, it would be
naive to think that this was the only victim of the ruthless economizing at IHS. But aside from replacing the medical superintendent at the
hospital, little changed.

Dr Thomas Orford, the new superintendent and a long-serving
employee who began his career with IHS during the Depression, bluntly
stated that with the staff allotted to the institution, "it is impossible to
provide nursing care approaching requirements considered adequate
by the American Hospital Association." The minimum standard for
all paediatric care was 4.6 hours, while the North Battleford Hospital
could barely provide 2.5 hours. Nurses and aides, Orford continued,
"are overworked, tired, hurried and tend to become careless. Cross
infection is a problem and some of the staff themselves are picking up
staphylococcal lesions." To provide a minimum standard of care, the
hospital needed at least two more nurses and four more aides, though
Orford recognized that nothing would be done in the current year, and
"to ask for four more Aide positions would be barking at the moon."[69]
Director Moore, using his own formula that he acknowledged was
"much more moderate than those generally accepted," calculated that
Indian hospitals need only provide 3.2 hours of nursing care; that the
ratio of RNs to non-professional staff should be 52 to 48 per cent; and
that North Battleford had only sixty beds when in reality there were
seventy. And though IHS had acceded to the forty-four-hour work-
week, the industry standard was by this time a forty-hour week. On
that basis Moore reckoned that North Battleford should have eighteen
RNs and seventeen ward aides, or seven new nursing positions and
two more aides. But, as he put it, "it is appreciated that it is not possible to obtain all of the positions," and that an attempt should be made
to "move toward" filling the vacancies.[70] IHS, however, was allotted a
limited number of civil service posts, and any expansion required time-
consuming and often fruitless applications to Treasury Board while
the civil service commission did the actual hiring. Instead, increasing

staff strength in one Indian hospital came at the expense of other hospitals. Staff positions were "borrowed" from one hospital and "lent" to another. Seven years later, by 1965, North Battleford Indian Hospital continued to operate without adequate staff. Borrowing positions from Charles Camsell Hospital in Edmonton and diverting nurses from public health work to the hospital's wards temporarily papered over the problem, but the nursing shortages were chronic and it was obvious to all that poor wages and working conditions continued to hamper recruitment.[71] But by this time IHS, actively working to exit the hospital field altogether by inducing local hospitals to accept Aboriginal patients, began closing wards at North Battleford in response to the labour shortage. That the local community refused to allow the closure, recognizing it as an attempt to abrogate the treaty right to health care, came as unexpected and unwelcome interference in IHS plans, but that story will be treated later.

The same factors that drew nurses away from Indian hospitals – the soaring patient demand for hospital care and the substantial and growing federal interest and investment in national health – created even greater opportunities for physicians in postwar Canada. In 1945 Indian Affairs employed twenty-four full time physicians who became the core group as IHS moved to the Department of National Health and Welfare. It was obvious, however, that in the past Indian Affairs had struggled to attract a full complement of capable physicians; further compounding the problem, it refused to consider women physicians in the service. "Lady doctors are unsuited for dealing with Indian patients and it has never proved satisfactory where we have employed one."[72] Moreover, the 1930s budget cuts had completely discouraged some incumbents. The Edmonton-area reserve physician, described as "wholly useless," diagnosed patients from his car "without as much as going into the house to see the sick person."[73] Though Dr Stone recommended a "clean sweep" to remove some of the worst offenders, the market for ambitious young physicians did not favour IHS. With war's end veterans of the military's medical corps offered better prospects for IHS recruitment, especially with the so-called veteran's preference in civil service employment. But IHS was not the first choice for medical officers and nurses who also had preference for positions at Veterans Affairs and the newly created Department of National Health and Welfare itself. Stone advised that IHS concentrate its efforts on attracting veterans who had never established a private practice and therefore had "nothing to lose" by working in the civil service.[74] As a

result, Indian hospitals took on a decidedly military cast, both in personnel and the actual buildings. This cadre of IHS physicians – male,
white, and Canadian born; some former Indian Affairs employees and
others from the military – rose through the ranks of the new bureaucracy. Creating positions for themselves as they went, the administrative side of the IHS inevitably grew from a string of Indian hospitals
with a limited central office to an extensive system of zones and regions
that all needed superintendents. But the medical bureaucrats found it
increasingly difficult to recruit their own replacements for actual clinical work. Young graduates took positions in IHS hospitals for a year or
two, just until they could establish themselves in the booming postwar
marketplace for physicians in private practice and modern hospitals.
The regional superintendent in British Columbia stated bluntly, "There
appears to be little change in the situation here as to the supply of medical men. Experienced doctors are not interested in salaried positions."[75]
In his study of the Sioux Lookout Hospital, T. Kue Young observed that
there were two kinds of people who worked in Indian hospitals, those
looking for a new experience, often with a missionary zeal, and those
who could not find employment elsewhere.[76]

Of the latter group, Central European refugee physicians, so-called
"DP doctors," could not work in Canada after the Canadian Medical
Association refused to recognize their foreign medical credentials.
But IHS, increasingly desperate for physicians, took advantage of the
opportunity to hire a number of the émigré physicians. At Charles Camsell Hospital, Dr Meltzer proposed that the men be paid as orderlies
and the women as ward aides at $150 and $100 per month respectively,
though they performed the duties of medical officers.[77] Interestingly,
the concerns that occupied IHS administrators were that by having the
"DPs occupying positions as orderlies and ward aides, the rights
and privileges of Canadian workers might be infringed."[78] However,
deputy minister of National Health and Welfare Dr G.D.W. Cameron
thought it important to make a distinction between "allowing medically trained persons to use their position of orderly to brush up their
medicine and prepare to take qualifying examinations, and employing
them as orderlys [sic] and using this as a device to get cheap doctors."
How such a distinction might be made was not at all clear. Cameron
did not think his department could be criticized for doing the former,
but "I certainly think we would be putting ourselves in a bad position
if we use them to do medical work ordinarily done by a doctor unless
it is impossible for us to secure the services of a Canadian doctor."[79]

A year later eight émigrés (along with a woman doctor and a Korean) remained employed at Charles Camsell Hospital; though now deemed medical officers, they were all paid on a "voucher" or casual basis at rates well below the lowest pay grade. Administrators continued to worry that organized medicine might censure the practice of hiring "displaced persons who probably sought entry to Canada on grounds other than their medical qualifications," but recognized that "we get good value for our money in such cases." So long as the positions with IHS remained casual and carried no security of employment for the doctors, the Canadian Medical Association looked the other way.[80]

Unlicensed doctors shouldered much of the medical work in IHS hospitals. At Miller Bay Indian Hospital in 1951 medical superintendent JD Galbraith struggled to provide care to 175 patients. With "two displaced doctors and myself, the matter of medical coverage is spread as thin as it can possibly go." Admitting that considerable medical work was not done at all, Galbraith also pointed out that with "two DP medical doctors, a DP dentist, and a DP eye specialist here at the present moment, it is pretty evident that professional staff simply can't be attracted to this hospital at present salary rates." But aside from low salaries, tuberculosis work did not attract many professionals after the war. "They [interns] consider it to be a very limited specialty which most people seem to want to avoid."[81] Galbraith continued to press for "a fully qualified Canadian doctor" at Miller Bay, complaining, "We have just about reached the saturation point with DP's; they are so very helpless when it comes to dealing with behaviour and discipline problems on the wards."[82] Recall how Miller Bay, also beset by staff problems for placing ward aides in supervisory nursing positions, identified patient discipline problems as both cause and consequence of its seemingly chronic "low morale." Not surprisingly, most of the émigré professionals left the service as soon as they qualified for Canadian licences. By 1953, and with only one physician to help him, Galbraith admitted that medical work had all but stopped; even the laboratory closed when the "DP doctor," paid as a "lab boy," left.[83] And yet, even given the serious shortages of medical help, fully qualified women doctors were still denied consideration.

As Moore explained regarding an application to Miller Bay in 1955, "We are not anxious to take female doctors on for continuous employment but if [a female physician] were to be available for two or three months she might be useful."[84] IHS also employed unlicensed doctors to provide care on reserves and small communities. One physician, though "not qualified," was a "very able man and is willing to go on any special duties required of him."[85] Despite the impact on patient care, the arrangement was mutually beneficial: IHS exploited the labour of unlicensed doctors for much less than the market demanded, while at least some of the unqualified physicians earned a modest income while learning English and preparing for licensing examinations. But displaced persons were not the only unqualified medical men working for IHS. Well into the 1960s, an unqualified anaesthetist working at Charles Camsell Hospital "demonstrated an incompetence in administering the modern type of controlled anaesthesia." Dr Meltzer attributed at least two anaesthetic deaths at the Camsell Hospital to the unqualified doctor, calling him a "very great and unnecessary hazard."[86]

When the superintendent of Charles Camsell Indian Hospital described the staffing situation as "not healthy" he referred not to patient care, but to the impact of surging private practice incomes on IHS physicians. Dr Falconer judged that senior medical officers, not willing to lose the benefits of superannuation, "see and hear of medical officers younger than themselves making two and three times their salary in private practice ... so in all it is not a healthy situation [and] ... leads to a feeling of frustration and results in the classic picture of a Civil Servant who watches the clock and looks forward to his holidays."[87] Moreover, given the great opportunities in private medical practice, IHS bureaucrats viewed with deep suspicion the motivations of any well-qualified applicants to its service. Falconer wondered about one young surgical intern recommended to him. "From bitter past experience we are a bit skeptical of referred medical officers with high qualifications who are recommended to this region. We would like to question why, if he has a Fellowship, is he seeking employment in government service when it is understood they can do so much better in private practice, particularly when he is apparently presently in private practice."[88]

At a time when most non-Aboriginal patients with pulmonary tuberculosis underwent chemotherapy treatment alone, Charles Camsell Hospital's continued program of chest surgery seemed to offer opportunities for surgical interns not available elsewhere. While he received a number of letters of enquiry from candidates, Falconer complained that most were only interested in surgical work. He reluctantly recommended applications from non-citizens, in particular, "a Chinese boy ... I think we must make the best of a bad situation and try and employ people who are available."[89] Though patient care was surely compromised, only rare references to negligence, or worse, exist in the documentary record.

At the Lady Willingdon Hospital on the Six Nations reserve unlicensed physicians created dangerous situations for patients. The two-storey, twenty-bed institution built with band funds in 1927, was expanded to fifty-four beds in 1954. Six Nations continued to pay the doctor's salary until this mid-century expansion when IHS took over all costs and medical direction. The long-serving superintendent, Dr Walter Davis, graduated from University of Toronto medical school, and in 1914 began work at the Six Nations reserve, staying thirty-five years until his retirement in 1950. Not Aboriginal, but raised on the reserve after his parents abandoned him as an infant on the doorstep of a Six Nations family, Davis was a popular, respected, and active community member. Describing Davis in 1966, reserve residents told anthropologist Sally Weaver: "People didn't consider him a white man. He was one of us."[90] His reputation as an esteemed community resident arose from his respect for the traditional medical and cultural beliefs of the Longhouse people. Encouraging a medical syncretism, the doctor often advised patients to combine Indigenous and Western medicine.[91] With Davis's retirement in 1950, hospital expansion, and closer IHS control of medical operations, the community became increasingly critical of the quality of IHS physicians and the medicine they practised. The stability of Davis's tenure ended abruptly as no less than twenty-nine different physicians served the reserve in the next sixteen years, nineteen of whom were born and trained outside of Canada. Reserve residents, aware that some of the doctors were unlicensed, understood that the physicians were "second rate" and would not be allowed to work in white hospitals. Weaver found "the not infrequently expressed belief that the physicians are using the Indian people as 'guinea pigs.'"[92] Writing in 1967, the anthropologist accepted uncritically the IHS position that community criticisms of the quality of care stemmed not from inadequately trained personnel, but from the people's inability to adapt to, or understand, changed medical practices. However, Dr Davis's replacement as medical superintendent, Dr J.H. Wiebe, also expressed, in confidence, deep concerns about the quality of the hospital's medical officers well before a 1954 incident of negligence causing death.

In June 1953 Wiebe called the need for "fully qualified" medical officers "urgent." He complained that his current staff needed supervision at every step, and their difficulty with the (English) language caused "undesirable repercussions" among the reserve residents. Wiebe

recommended to director Moore the need for young medical officers rather than older men who had failed at private practice, a necessary sacrifice of experience for enthusiasm. Under no circumstances,
he explained, should the "burned out man, regardless of age, who has
shifted from position to position over the years and is looking for a
soft 'berth' be considered."[93] Wiebe needed help with surgery, someone
interested in administering anaesthesia, and a radiologist. Of the new
graduates who applied, two men would consider moving to the Lady
Willingdon Hospital only if they could work together. Also expressing
concern about another candidate's "handicap," Wiebe noted that "our
experience has been uniformly unpleasant and unsatisfactory with people of this type." While never naming the particular handicap, Wiebe
suggested it "is closely associated with inadequacies which reflect
adversely on the work of the individual and the welfare of our institution." He did agree that "these people do have a right to an opportunity
to rehabilitate themselves," and, if necessary, he would welcome the
particular physician at Lady Willingdon Indian Hospital.[94]

Tragically, the following May 1954 Wiebe reported a woman's death
by cardiac arrest on the operating table as she underwent a hernia
repair: "This unfortunate episode again points out very specifically
the urgent need for well-qualified medical staff. We were fortunate in
having a coroner with an *unbiased mind*, otherwise an inquest might
have resulted in undesirable publicity concerning an unqualified anes-
thetist. An autopsy was performed and no cause could be determined
to which the cardiac arrest could be attributed."[95] The people's concerns
about the quality of care seemed more than justified, but with collusion
between IHS officials and an "unbiased" coroner, the appalling affair
never came to light. Wiebe's frank report, blaming the unqualified
anaesthetist, drew attention to the consequences of IHS hiring policy.
But as hospital superintendent and the surgeon responsible, he might
well have been motivated by self-preservation.

Wiebe went on to "strongly recommend" that IHS hire fully qualified medical officers. "It is clear that we are attracting medical officers,
many of whom have been failures elsewhere, or who have handicaps
which militate against a successful ordinary practice."[96] Nevertheless,
given the widespread use of unqualified physicians, it is doubtful that
this "unfortunate episode" was a rare occurrence. While death in hospital was, and is, hardly unusual, death by negligent treatment documented by autopsy should have been cause for fundamental changes in
the IHS system. That it was not suggests a deep bureaucratic cynicism,

one shared by Six Nations, who understood that the care at the hospital was "good enough for Indians."[97]

One year later, Wiebe still did not have the help he needed at Lady Willingdon Hospital. With one unqualified medical assistant for all the outpatient work in a community of more than five thousand residents, and the often overcrowded fifty-four-bed hospital, the medical superintendent outlined some of the disadvantages of unlicensed doctors, "aside from the very precarious legal and ethical situations in which we find ourselves so frequently involved." His medical assistant could not work alone without "constantly having to be bailed out of awkward, embarrassing, and dangerous situations," not to mention the "frequently prodigious amount of mental and physical effort which this type of assistant exerts in order to achieve inadequacy."[98] By 1957 Wiebe left the hospital to take up a promotion to regional superintendent. The unlicensed anaesthetist remained at Lady Willingdon Hospital, however.

In June 1960 Six Nations Council passed a resolution requesting the removal of this particular physician for his "negligent medical attention to out-patients." It is clear, however, that the community remained unaware of the anaesthetist's role in the 1954 death. The Council resolution also threatened the hospital's other doctors with removal if they were found to be neglecting their duty to "give attentive and proper medical attention to patients."[99] The medical superintendent, Dr Hayward, clarified for his superior (Dr Wiebe) that the resolution did not actually accuse the physician of negligence, but Council complained that the doctor was inaccessible when he was most needed. Wiebe then interpreted the resolution for his superiors, calling the Six Nations people "somewhat unreasonable." Suggesting that the Council itself be censured for not fostering more responsibility, Wiebe did not think it "to the advantage of the Indians or the [Indian Health] Service if they are allowed to hold our medical and hospital staff under threat."[100] Six Nations Council, however, considered it "their" hospital and its physicians should answer to the people. Beyond the specific grievances over care and accessibility, Six Nations residents were anxious about IHS continued efforts to have individuals pay for medical services directly or indirectly through a group health insurance plan, despite repeated Council rejections of all such schemes.[101] At the same time, after 1961, IHS began redirecting medical care away from the reserve hospital to surrounding communities in keeping with its plans to shut the hospital and retreat from health services generally.

Not coincidentally, complaints of medical negligence, if not malpractice, increased steadily until Six Nations Council demanded a meeting with hospital personnel and regional superintendent Wiebe. When
the meeting was not forthcoming Council took their concerns to the
local press, which drew the immediate attention of bureaucrats, and a
conference was quickly arranged.[102] In a confidential report to Director
Moore, Wiebe described the specific complaints raised by Council. He
found in one case that "the patient would have benefitted by hospitalization and a more vigorous form of therapy"; in the next case, the physician's treatment was judged "entirely adequate"; in another he found
"an error in judgment re the gravity of the situation and the method of
treatment"; in yet another, "the method of treatment would find general
acceptance by the medical profession." In sum, Wiebe found "errors
in judgment," but "no evidence suggesting gross neglect."[103] Finding
little fault with the quality of care, Wiebe suggested the complaints
arose from "the lack of rapport" between doctor and patient, and from
the lack of free choice of physician. However, director Moore, in a letter
to his minister, instead reported that the Six Nations Council regretted the publicity, and stated that "many of the complaints were indeed
irresponsible."[104] That IHS medical bureaucrats investigated their own
colleagues was not lost on Council, and according to anthropologist
Weaver's informants in 1966, Wiebe's conclusion that there was no evidence of malpractice "did not rest easily with the Council, nor does
it still among some Council members."[105] While their criticisms of the
quality of care were dismissed as unreasonable and irresponsible, they
were soon shared by a most unlikely source.

A 1962 Royal Commission enquiring into government services,
headed by the accountant and prominent businessman Grant Glassco,
found the quality of care in Indian hospitals "not comparable" with
community hospitals. The facilities were old, ill equipped, and inadequately staffed. Of the 117 physicians who joined the department of
national health since the mid 1950s, 47 per cent were graduates of foreign medical schools. "Many of them have not passed their Canadian
licensing examinations and are therefore not qualified for private practice." Of the Canadian physicians who joined the service in the same
period, their average age was forty. "The great majority of these have
left private practice." The Commission also noted that the department
found it difficult to attract suitable personnel at all ranks, while medical graduates avoided the IHS "because of the remoteness of places of
employment, the ill equipped hospitals, and limited opportunities for

career development." The Commission report recommended, among other things, "the rapid transfer of Indian health care to normal community facilities." The Commission supposed that with the introduction of national hospital insurance, and available insurance plans for physician services, medical care should be relatively simple to arrange.[106] Of course, the accountant-led Commission overlooked several critical realities: the reluctance of provincial hospitals to accept Aboriginal patients and the increasingly vocal Aboriginal communities' demands that the federal government increase its commitment to health care and improve, not abandon, its facilities. In any case, the Glassco Commission's findings did not come as any surprise to IHS bureaucrats, who were well aware of the deficiencies.

Indian hospitals, as the minister pledged in 1946, might have served a most beneficial function as a training ground for Aboriginal health workers – nurses, doctors, and administrators – as was accomplished in similar circumstances elsewhere.[107] Yet, IHS provided only the most basic instruction for Aboriginal workers to fill the lowest ranks as support personnel. Indeed, it was difficult for Aboriginal RNs, for instance, to find work in their own communities. More than representing a benign "opportunity lost," the refusal to use the hospitals as training centres exposes the work of the disciplines, medical and social, in maintaining hierarchies and colour lines in the health care professions and Canadian society generally. That patients suffered and died at the hands of the overworked, the unqualified, and the negligent suggests a deep cynicism most clearly articulated by IHS director Moore himself in 1962 in reference to the inadequacies of professional staff: "Today we are stuck with what we have allowed ourselves to be satisfied with."[108] Indian hospitals, continuing the colonizing work of reserves and residential schools, kept people in their places: some as patients and poorly paid labourers; others as physician bureaucrats managing doctors who could not find work elsewhere. Yet, the presence of the intermediaries and cultural brokers – the Aboriginal RNs, nurse's aides, and orderlies – eased somewhat the hospitals' harsh conditions.

Chapter Four

Life and Death in an Indian Hospital

"Never were there photographs that showed the truth about my people's lives."[1]
– Minnie Aodla Freeman

Patient experiences – life and death – in Indian Hospitals varied tremendously, making any description partial and incomplete. Hospitalization,
anytime and anyplace, would be nothing less than traumatic – endured
certainly not enjoyed. And many patients, if not most, became well in
the institutions, where, by the early 1950s, effective antibiotics saved
lives. But patient narratives, some as remembered childhood experiences and others gleaned from the archival record, rarely refer posi-
tively to the institutions, the caregivers, or medicine itself. Working at
the Camsell Indian Hospital, Aboriginal RN from Saddle Lake, Kathleen
Steinhauer-Anderson observed: "Most of the patients demonstrated
that sense of despairing resignation so evident at a residential school ...
Gaols seem to elicit somewhat the same response from native people
familiar with such institutions."[2] Linking these sites of isolation and
discipline, she points to a persistent reality in the lives of many Aboriginal people. Though individuals experienced hospitalization differently,
given Indian Health Service's centralized bureaucracy and its hierarchical and paternalistic structure, patients faced common circumstances.
The most common of all was coercion, which was in keeping with the
state's broader colonizing agenda to control, regulate, and assimilate
Aboriginal people. Compulsion informed most interactions with IHS
even though individuals and communities had pleaded for medical
attention. They welcomed Indian hospitals, sought employment with
IHS, and took an active interest in negotiating for better facilities and

improved treatment. Despite evidence to the contrary, for IHS the existence of coercive policies was made to imply their necessity. In a 1945 warning of things to come, Percy Moore boldly stated, "We certainly do not feel that our program should be left to the whims of an Indian, as to whether or not he will accept treatment."[3] From mass annual X-rays to mass BCG vaccination, from forced relocation to forced institutionalization, from lost patients to lost graves, patients felt the objectifying reality of Indian hospitals.

In the decade before 1945, with limited budgets and few beds, admission to an Indian hospital was highly selective. The best candidates were those most likely to be "cured," a pragmatism not unknown to hospital and sanatorium directors everywhere who were concerned to create public confidence in their institutions, but a practice that left the most ill with tuberculosis in the community.[4] Indian hospitals initially preferred two groups in particular: tuberculous schoolchildren, easily controlled and an acknowledged threat to the larger civilizing mission of the schools, and pregnant women. The physician at Manitoba's Fisher River Indian Hospital, where Moore got his start in the 1930s, called it an "unholy combination."[5] The putative social value of the hospital, to teach the superiority of Western medicine, clearly trumped the medical, but pregnant women may well have chosen a hospital birth for its more prosaic appeal – running water and a warm building in winter. Nevertheless, the postwar expansion of institutions and treatment beds allowed for more extensive and aggressive medical surveillance of communities that often began with a chest X-ray. At times partnered with provincial tuberculosis associations, at other times with their own X-ray equipment, IHS undertook annual surveys of schools and reserve communities.

Mass X-ray surveys, a significant aspect of tuberculosis campaigns in non-Aboriginal communities in the 1940s and early 1950s, were made possible by the military's development of the portable X-ray machine. The new technology, actually a fluoroscope fitted with a camera to capture the image, was easily transported by truck or airplane and made it possible, and economically feasible, to X-ray whole communities, indeed whole provinces.[6] These "travelling clinics," preceded by much media fanfare, relied on enthusiastic service club volunteers to encourage neighbours to be "tuberculosis conscious" and line up for their chest X-ray, creating an opportunity to demonstrate responsible, healthy citizenship to friends and strangers. Organizers understood, however, that the "improvident and careless" would never present themselves for X-ray; neither would older elite men and ex-servicemen, those whose credentials as responsible citizens could not be questioned.[7] Portable fluoroscope machines made province-wide campaigns (of mostly healthy people) feasible, but they also involved a significantly higher radiation dose than radiographs using a full-size film.[8] As fewer and fewer cases of tuberculosis were discovered in the surveys, and especially once the dangers of exposure to ionizing radiation became widely understood by the mid-1950s, the enthusiasm for mass surveys quickly faded. By 1957 tuberculosis authorities in British Columbia, concerned about the hazards to children in particular, instructed that *"no person 15 years or under should have a routine or admission chest x-ray unless he has shown a positive tuberculin reaction."*[9] But, while citizens might line up for a chest X-ray, would they submit to a much more invasive tuberculin test? A 1957 survey of the white and Aboriginal population of Manitoulin Island in Ontario studied the participation rate in a community survey that added tuberculin testing to its usual X-ray examinations. It concluded that there was no reason to expose to X-ray those not infected with tubercle bacilli. Tuberculin testing could easily identify positive reactors, and only they needed an X-ray.[10] The study also emphasized the marginally higher infection rates among whites living in close proximity to Aboriginal communities, highlighting the presumed source of infection. But, at the outset the researchers eliminated from their study 348 people (presumably Aboriginal) who, having been previously vaccinated with BCG, would show a positive tuberculin reaction. Beginning in 1946 the widespread use of the BCG vaccine in Aboriginal communities, while conferring some protection against tuberculosis, also rendered the tuberculin test useless, making frequent X-rays necessary despite the recognized dangers.

Most provincial health authorities, except Quebec, rejected systematic BCG vaccination because of persistent concerns about its efficacy and potential risks, particularly because it interfered with the tuberculin test. Alberta and British Columbia refused to consider its use, while other provinces employed it selectively for nurses and others routinely exposed to tuberculosis.[11] Yet R.G. Ferguson's Qu'Appelle BCG trial on infants, completed in 1945, convinced IHS of the utility and economy of the vaccine for Aboriginal communities. In Manitoba, IHS initiated BCG vaccination in 1948 in southern reserves and schools, and four years later in the north. In an admittedly "unscientific" study from 1948 to 1954, morbidity and mortality dropped steadily, though the role of BCG could not be determined with any accuracy. Nevertheless, fewer vaccinated children developed active disease, prompting the conclusion: "We know it [BCG] is safe ... We will continue to use it as extensively as possible."[12]

But it was not always safe. The protection offered by BCG diminished after two years, making revaccination necessary. Armand Frappier, director of Montreal's Institute of Microbiology and Hygiene and the driving force behind BCG production and distribution in Canada, advised that only newborns or those never exposed to the disease (verified by a negative tuberculin test) should receive BCG.[13] The tuberculin skin test, however, took one to three days to develop a reaction, a waste of time for hurried survey crews that spent as little time in Aboriginal communities as possible. Frappier instead devised a simpler scratch test to gauge sensitivity using a diluted dose of BCG that produced an immediate reaction. The Manitoba study's recommendation of mass testing of "all Indians under 16" by the BCG skin test at least every two years and an X-ray every year, appears to have been taken up by IHS nationwide.[14] But when two schoolgirls were admitted to Sioux Lookout Indian Hospital with tuberculous lymphadenitis (tuberculosis of the lymph nodes) after revaccination with BCG, there was considerable consternation. While director Moore thought it an interesting case report that might be published in the medical press, his superior, deputy minister of health Dr G.D.W. Cameron, found it "disturbing ... The clear inference is that our people are being careless about their sensitivity testing whether it is the standard mantoux or Frappier's own test using diluted BCG." In order to keep the "confidence and goodwill of the Indians," he advised against publishing anything that would lead to questions of what went wrong, "was it the BCG or was the job improperly done?"[15] Despite Cameron's personal concerns about the safety of the BCG skin test, its use continued in Aboriginal communities in conjunction with annual X-ray examinations.[16]

As late as 1966, IHS continued to vaccinate with BCG without first determining a negative reaction through tuberculin testing. Dr Matthew Matas, then regional superintendent for Alberta and the Northwest Territories, assured the joint meeting of the Department of National Health and Welfare and the CTA that IHS continued to encourage BCG vaccination "without being too concerned about tuberculin sensitivity, fully realizing that some severe local reactions may occur ... The risk of an Indian or Eskimo contracting tuberculosis is infinitely greater than any risk of his developing a serious reaction to BCG vaccination."[17] Another risk IHS was willing to take was annual X-ray examinations.

Conceding that a biennial X-ray survey would likely suffice, Matas explained that communities were conditioned, "brainwashed," to the yearly visit of the X-ray team. "If the survey were conducted less frequently, less cooperation might be received as fewer visits might be interpreted as indicating that there was no problem."[18] In areas where tuberculosis infection remained high, X-ray surveys were undertaken two or three times a year.[19] The damage caused by "serious BCG reactions" and the long-term impact of thirty to forty or more years of (at least) annual X-rays beginning in early childhood may never be known, though the risks to white Canadians were deemed too great.[20] Indeed, by IHS calculations, iatrogenic injury to Aboriginal bodies was the price to be paid to contain tuberculosis infection in Aboriginal communities and, ultimately, to protect an increasingly tuberculin-negative Canadian public.

Mass X-ray surveys of Aboriginal communities usually accompanied the treaty party: Indian agent, police, and doctor. Treaty time in summer was an occasion for often widely scattered hunting and trapping bands to reunite for wedding celebrations, to renew friendships, and to discuss issues and concerns with each other and the Indian agent. While tuberculosis surveys in towns and cities relied on citizens to voluntarily present themselves for examination, reserve communities were not allowed the same autonomy. A convenient, if disreputable, practice of withholding treaty annuity payments until every family member consented to X-ray examination allowed for far more thorough surveillance than was possible in white communities.[21] As CTA's Dr Wherrett put it, "The Indians and Eskimos were easy to screen because they were congregated on reserves and in small communities."[22] In the summer of 1949 the treaty party and X-ray crew flew into remote Manitoba communities. At Shamatawa, 176 people were X-rayed; Dr Yule pulled teeth, while the RCMP constable and Indian agent (as magistrate) dispensed justice. They fined a trapper for taking a beaver out of season, though the treaty party, including the constable, later dined on illegally caught sturgeon. In the evening's soccer match, "natives against whites," the X-ray technologist recalled that Chief Beardy called out to his players in Cree "telling his boys to go easy on us. Thank goodness, for they still nearly ran us to death!"[23] It was a very public demonstration of a healthy and vital community. Likewise when the survey crew arrived at Nelson House reserve (Nisichawayasihk Cree Nation) treaty day celebrations were underway with ball games, contests of strength and stamina, canoe races, and a dance in the evening. These were not the diseased and decaying communities they expected to find. The survey party took 7,038 X-rays that summer, though many were never interpreted since the 158-bed Clearwater Lake Indian Hospital at The Pas was full.[24] The surveillance of Aboriginal communities continued apace with schoolchildren and whole communities X-rayed at least annually from the early 1940s until the late 1960s, creating a detailed archive of personal information on thousands of people.[25]

Much depended on the X-ray findings, but the gains in machine portability and economy were often lost in accuracy. Detail was less clear than on a full-sized chest X-ray, and any slight movement caused a blurred image. Ten per cent of abnormalities were not recognizable on the miniature films, though more advanced tuberculosis could be detected.[26] In the rough conditions of field surveys, and especially the hurried shipboard examinations that brought many Inuit from the eastern Arctic to southern hospitals, the opportunities for misdiagnosis were manifest. A skill learned through long practice, X-ray interpretation was an inexact science at the best of times. As visiting British physician P.E. Baldry reminded Canadian colleagues, "large numbers of Eskimos are radiographed and in each case a decision has to be made on a single film whether or not there is an abnormality which requires the individual to be brought out for treatment. It is obviously not always easy to be certain on a single radiograph whether a shadow is due to active tuberculosis. Nevertheless in view of the fact that once patients have been evacuated some of them cannot be returned home until the ship makes another journey the next year it is obviously important to make the correct interpretation."[27] Baldry's caution, while recognizing the significant disruption in patients' lives by an incorrect diagnosis, also points to the acknowledged subjectivity in X-ray interpretation: survey crews expected to find tuberculosis. In her study of the changing cultural meanings of tuberculosis and its treatments, historian Katherine Ott notes how subjectivity influenced physicians' judgments. A 1951 study found that physicians' and radiologists' interpretation of 150 X-ray exams differed one-third of the time, and when shown the same X-ray twice (without their knowledge) their own readings differed one-fifth of the time.[28]

Though tuberculosis was the principal focus of the surveys, potential patients were screened for any signs of disease. Inuit, identified by their disk number and sometimes their name, were boarded on the annual patrol ship, which they termed "*Matavik*" or "where you strip" in Inuktitut.[29] They were moved through the shipboard medical examination

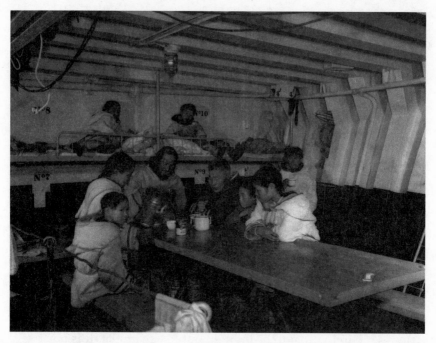

Illustration 4.1 Inuit on-board ship heading south. This carefully constructed image did not reflect reality for many Inuit relocated to southern hospitals. It would have been unusual for families to travel together as this image implies. Children were often sent alone and unaccompanied by family members.

Source: PA-176873, LAC.

process with a serial number written on their left hand: "X-P-D-I" denoting X-ray, physician, dentist, and immunization. An arrow drawn under the letters meant they were free of disease and could go home, but "TB" written on the hand meant evacuation to a southern hospital. They were kept on-board until the ship sailed with no chance to bid goodbye to family and friends.[30] Without proper interpreters and treated as so much cargo, Inuit patients were numbered and stowed aboard, with no opportunity to question their diagnosis or their fate. Their bodies literally inscribed with the colonizers' diagnosis and marked for relocation, patients felt the disciplining power of Western medicine[31] (illustration 4.1).

It is not possible to generalize about the experience of life in an Indian hospital. The *Camsell Mosaic*, a 1985 celebratory history edited and published by former Camsell Indian Hospital employees, includes a triumphantly alliterative chapter "Moccasins, Mukluks and Miracles" in which grateful ex-patients recall the kind and caring ministrations of nurses and physicians. Patient narratives could hardly be otherwise in a progressive history, "a tale worth preserving," told by those who placed themselves at the centre of nothing less than "one of the more notable successes in recent medical history – the conquering of a killer disease."[32] Nevertheless, individual encounters with the hospitals varied tremendously. Some patients spent years in the institutions, and some a short time; some were treated with kindness and compassion, and some with indifference and disdain; some were young and quickly adapted, while older patients worried constantly about families at home; some lived to tell about it, and some did not. George Manuel, born in 1921 in the Secwepemc territory of the Shuswap people in British Columbia, and by 1970 the chief of the fledgling National Indian Brotherhood, recalled his teenage years in the Coqualeetza Indian Hospital in the 1940s. Diagnosed with tuberculosis of the hipbone, he entered hospital from the Kamloops Residential School, where the children were made to carry fifty-pound packs of cordwood a mile and a half up the riverbank to the school under the watchful eye of adult overseers who berated them. "Hunger is both the first and the last thing I can remember about that school. I was hungry from the day I went into that school until they took me to the hospital two and a half years later. Not just me. Every Indian student smelled of hunger." But in the hospital, he recalled, the nurses brought him the books and games he never saw at school. They taught him to read and to make the best use of his years of enforced quiet. He remembered "the baths and towels, meals, and beds, which were all warm and plentiful." He honoured the nurses for "rekindling the imagination of my childhood" and for keeping him alive "as though they were grandmothers of our own nation."[33] Manuel's sharply juxtaposed residential school and hospital experiences highlight the abusive treatment in the former institution and, despite his illness, the relatively positive experience in the latter.

In her collection of former patients' experiences, historian Laurie Meijer Drees found some common themes: tedium, boredom, loneliness, and emotional and physical harm. But patients also stressed more positive experiences, often recounted with a good deal of humour: a determination to get well, close friendships forged with other patients, and opportunities for growth through education and rehabilitation. Significantly, few patients recounted positive relationships with medical staff.[34] These and other narratives transcribed in the last decade are predominantly the stories of childhood or adolescence that reflect the vulnerability of youth but also acknowledge their hospital experience as an episode in the continuum of lived reality. Dave Melting Tallow, when asked about his hospital experience, replied: "It wouldn't be sad, and it wouldn't be a happy story. It would be just a story but it wasn't sad; it wasn't a good time. But then I had the operation [chest surgery]. Except for that time, the only really bad time I had was when I think they experimented on me. I don't know if they did or not."[35] Far different in tone and emphasis from the *Camsell Mosaic* narratives, these accounts also highlight another essential reality – survival – in spite or because of treatment. William Tagoona, a five-year-old in the mid-1950s, spent eighteen months in the Clearwater Lake Indian Hospital in Manitoba. He recalled that when nurses read them bedtime stories the children were told to keep their eyes on the nurse's face. If they looked away and were caught, "she'd take her belt off and hit you with it." The goodnight kiss was another strictly enforced duty. "If a child turned his head away from the nurse, then you'd get it again." Tagoona recalled vomiting in his plate of macaroni, "The nurse got really angry and mixed up the macaroni and vomit and force fed it to me."[36] Survivors' stories anchor bureaucratic policy and shifting medical discourse to the embodied experience of the Indian hospitals. Vulnerable but never completely victimized, patients, with the help of families and communities, resisted where they could and attempted to shape the institutions for their own purposes.

Access to hospital care, which in the past had been carefully mediated by Indian agents and departmental physicians, was understood in many communities as a long-promised government obligation that was finally fulfilled with the advent of Indian hospitals. The close association of medical care and treaty payments served to reaffirm the understanding that health care was a treaty right, a claim that IHS continued to deny, despite its practice. At the grand opening of Miller Bay Indian Hospital, as noted earlier, Henry Kelly, councillor for the Tsimshian, characterized it as fundamental to the "new deal promised" by the government of Canada.[37] The leadership of the Hobbema agency reserves toured the newly opened Charles Camsell Indian Hospital and presented the administration with a cash donation to demonstrate their support.[38] In the early 1950s the elderly Sweetgrass Chief Sam Swimmer spent his final years at Saskatchewan's North Battleford Indian Hospital and rarely missed an opportunity to link the hospital to the treaty right to health care. As he put it, "The Fort Carlton Treaty was made between God, the Queen, the White Man and the Indians. God remains with us. We have a Queen on the throne. The Treaty must never be broken."[39] Elders today agree with Chief Swimmer that, aside from a treaty entitlement, "their" hospital was a valuable community institution. Gordon Albert remarked: "I feel it was a very important part in the lives of Indian people that utilized the facility – not only because it was called an Indian hospital but they could identify with their own people who were in there and utilized that facility. They felt at home ... A lot of old people utilized that facility and it was to their liking."[40] Rose Atimoyoo recalled, "I was really impressed when I had my baby there because I felt right at home. The cleaning ladies were all native and I heard that language a lot there too. It was home to me and that is how I think mostly everybody felt, especially the old people."[41] Indian hospitals, particularly those situated close to reserves and increasingly staffed by Aboriginal workers, became tangible manifestations of a treaty or legal right, and community leaders took a proprietary interest in their operations.

Shortly after the Clearwater Lake Indian Hospital opened in northern Manitoba in 1947, Chief Cornelius Bignell and councillors of the local Pas Band (Opaskwayak Cree Nation) felt compelled to advise that "steps be taken to improve the conditions in the San so that people will gladly go there." Patients needed fresh air and requested permission to walk outside on warm days. There was not enough staff to comfort dying patients, who called out for water "until death claims them." Injections were administered too roughly and patients had severe reactions to the medications. A man working at the cemetery found out only later that he had buried his own wife. The chief and council questioned superintendent Dr Ridge's management: "Too many persons have died, and are dying too fast in such a short time. Very few leave the San cured." High death rates and few cures, a disturbing reality in the early years of IHS hospitals, reflected not only the limitations of tuberculosis treatment in the pre-antibiotic era, but also the practice of admitting the very ill in order to limit the spread of disease. It was a sharp departure from an earlier protocol that left the terminally ill, especially the elderly, in the community to spare hospital reputations. As Chief Bignell put it, "Now we wish to ask the Department to do its utmost to make the poor people feel happy and proud to go to this Sanatorium."[42] The implication was that if the hospital was met with non-cooperation, it was for good reason.

In response to the complaints, Dr E.L. Ross, medical superintendent of the Manitoba Sanatorium Board that operated the Clearwater Hospital for IHS, inspected the institution and, not surprisingly, found himself "very satisfied" with the medical treatment and the cleanliness of the wards. Ross admitted, however, that staff shortages were a serious problem, with Dr Ridge and only the assistance of a "DP doctor," just two graduate nurses, five practical nurses, and eight ward aides to care for 158 patients. Dr Ridge and Indian Agent Low agreed that the chief's statements "were grossly exaggerated and almost entirely unjustified."[43] While community concerns were not entirely ignored, the Indian agent assured IHS that the chief later "regretted" his complaint. IHS, explicitly rejecting claims that the hospitals represented any obligation more than humanitarian concern, dismissed community criticism as unwarranted and ungrateful grousing. Community involvement and activism only increased, particularly after government attempts in the mid-1960s to close the hospitals, which was interpreted as an abrogation of treaty responsibilities (a phase of the Indian hospitals that will be examined in depth in the next chapter). Reserve leaders were limited in their ability to act as patient advocates by the vastly uneven power relations, especially since IHS bureaucrats investigated community concerns and complaints about their own colleagues.

Patients also attempted to influence their own experience, often with limited success. The nature of tuberculosis care, premised on the rest cure to allow the body to heal, involved elaborate "routines" from complete bed rest to graduated degrees of activity that often took years to accomplish. This medical paradigm readily incorporated surgical lung collapse and only slowly shifted with the advent of antibiotic drug treatment. Patients quickly learned that discipline, self-imposed or administered, defined their lives in hospital while they underwent monthly chest X-rays and had their sputum regularly tested to gauge their progress. Minnie Aodla Freeman, from the Inuit community on Cape Hope Island in James Bay, recalling her treatment in the Moose Factory Indian Hospital, illustrates the essential helplessness of patients:

> Every week we had different faces catering to us. The doctors and nurses were all imported from the south. The ward I was in became very fond of one particular nurse and so did I. She had such a gentle face and nature ... When she was on duty, we behaved for her, her pleasantness kept us pleasant. When she was off duty, we were just the opposite. We wore long faces like the ones that were on duty. We sneaked around behind their backs.

We ran to the windows to look out. They treated us like children, so we acted like children.[44]

After her transfer to Mountain Sanatorium in Hamilton in 1951, the fifteen-year-old Freeman, who had learned English in school, was quickly put to work translating for staff and Inuit patients. Suspecting that her language skills were the sole reason for her hospitalization, she inquired about her treatment and shortly thereafter began to get injections (likely streptomycin). "I dreaded them. Some nurses did not hurt, but others gave needles that sent pain all the way down my leg. We began to recognize which ones were not painful and which ones were."[45]

Children were often physically restrained to teach the discipline of bed rest. At Miller Bay Hospital younger children, tied in their beds, soon learned to untie their restraints.[46] The staff at Charles Camsell Hospital jokingly referred to a condition they called "cantstayinbedi-tis," which was followed by "castitis," in which patients were immobilized by plaster casts on both legs with a bar connecting the casts. Patients who struggled free of the leg casts were fitted with body casts extending up to the chest. The "condition" resolved itself when the "victim is convinced of the necessity for cooperation in the cure of his disease."[47] Agnes Bruno recalled how as a child in the Camsell Hospital all the girls on her ward were put in casts as punishment for misbehaving.[48] At Fort Qu'Appelle Indian Hospital disobedient children were restrained in straitjackets.[49] A former non-Aboriginal RN recalled her less restrictive, but perhaps more insidiously coercive, method of controlling young children at Camsell Hospital. "They [young boys] liked to call me 'Momma' and most days before afternoon rest period, as a special treat, I would carry each one to look out the window. Punishment for misbehaviour was withdrawal of these privileges."[50] Adult male patients had their pajama bottoms taken away to keep them in bed, or isolated within the hospital. Dave Melting Tallow recalled, as punishment for getting out of bed, being moved onto a ward with Inuit patients with whom he could not communicate.[51] The therapeutic value of highly regimented "routines" was extended to include patients who were hospitalized for conditions other than tuberculosis; all were seen to require the strict institutional discipline that for many began in residential school. "Up patients" at Camsell Hospital, identified by red armbands on their dressing gowns, were allowed to attend Friday evening movies in the recreation hall. However, if anyone took liberties to go elsewhere the privilege was withdrawn for all patients.[52]

Adult patients worried about families and children at home. "George," a twenty-eight-year-old father of four sons who spent a year in the Fort Qu'Appelle Indian Hospital in the 1950s, recalled his frustration at lying around idle, unable to help his young family who were struggling to put food on the table.[53] Minnie Freeman, who was hospitalized with older female relatives, recalled their anxieties: "My aunts talked about the cold weather at home, wondering how their families were, and how they were coping with their clothes for the winter."[54] After her discharge from hospital Freeman worked as a translator for Indian Affairs, and recalled meeting a group of adult Inuit patients at Brandon:

> Most of these patients were mothers and fathers. How were their homes managed with all the work that had to be done, especially the provision of food and clothing? Some of them had been in hospital for two years, some for one year and others for six months. Some had heard nothing of their relatives for a long time. Some did, and had had bad news about loved ones who had died.
>
> Our next visit was to a hostel. There we met people who were waiting to go home. The house ... had the smell of a human who has not washed for years. The Inuit looked as if they had not been out for months. They were so pale, not like the skin I am used to seeing on Inuit – wind-burned and sun-tanned. Their lavatory was horribly messy, dirty and smelly. And these were the people who were waiting to go home after hospital care. It would be no wonder if they went right back to the hospital.[55]

By the early 1960s Inuit patients began writing letters in syllabics to translators in the northern administration's welfare division ("Eskimology section") hoping to make contact with family at home, and to ask for help with their hospital experience. Anna wrote to ask when she would be released. She reassured "Bobby" (likely Robert Williamson, welfare section anthropologist and translator) that "we are fine, we Eskimos," though she expressed concerns that all the doctors in the hospital were "bearded ones ... when they talk they are not understandable. I really want to go home." The letters usually included expressions of gratitude for their treatment, which may have been a formality since patients understood they were writing to a government agency. One patient was thankful for his treatment and being "fed every day" though it was white man's food. Tommy, frustrated that there was no interpreter at the hospital, and worried about his wife and blind mother at home, wanted to leave even though he was not completely cured: "Even if I am made to stay here a long time yet I'm not likely to be made immortal." He closed with: "Go ahead and translate my words. Write them in English. The hospital is disgusting – awful." Lucy thought the nurses were rough: "being pushed by them is very miserable … please tell the doctors that we are being treated badly … I'm telling the truth." Leah expressed her gratitude, but she was lonesome: "Sometimes happiness can't reach me."[56] In larger hospitals with many long-stay patients, Indian Affairs provided funds for rudimentary education and occupational therapy programs where patients relieved their boredom and anxiety by producing crafts, clothing, and sculpture.[57] However, the programs were the exception rather than the rule.

Miller Bay Indian Hospital's isolated location, drab buildings, and poor management made patients' lives even more dismal. The perennial problems of staff shortages and high turnover (see chapter 3) were deemed by administration to stem from patients themselves. "Poor patient discipline," or discord with nursing staff and sullenness, was a particular concern on the women's Ward B. In a highly unusual step the hospital asked the patients for their feedback in a written questionnaire (which may have left out many patients): "I just haven't talked to [nurse] since she told me to shut up and mind my own business, when I told her not to force [a patient] to eat. I just told her in a polite way. Just not talking in case she makes me feel bad again." Another patient noted: "If we are good patients they are good to us but if we don't do as they tell us, sure mean." Patients complained about the food, asking for something other than jam sandwiches and cake. "Can't we afford a dietician?" one patient asked. Aside from concerns about hospital operations, patients also expressed their loneliness and frustration with their long-term hospitalization: "I am getting so tired of this hospital life and I am getting so lonely too." Feeling well yet not released from hospital, another patient wrote, "I am complaining of not being sick and you doctors had to keep me here for nothing. You doctors left me laying in my bed worried about my little girl at home."[58]

A newly hired social worker in 1955 suggested that an organized body to represent patient interests might improve hospital discipline and morale. A fairly common device in sanatoria where "self-policing" was the goal, patient committees were rare in Indian hospitals. Charles Camsell Hospital established a health committee in 1958, but, dominated by medical staff, it focused on teaching the five patient representatives about tuberculosis, general health rules, and parliamentary procedure for conducting meetings.[59] With slightly more autonomy, the Miller Bay Hospital's patient committee elected representatives for president, secretary and two councillors from each of the men's and women's wards. Informed that it was to concern itself solely with patient recreation, the committee, however, quickly extended its authority by issuing directives and recommending staff changes. To superintendent Howell's dismay, "they desired, indeed, to participate in the operation of the hospital." Within the year the committee pursued its interests more directly. Changing its name from "The Patients' Recreation Committee" to the "Miller Bay Indian Hospital Native Council," it shifted identity and focus from patient recreation to advocacy and expanded its mandate to include grievance and food committees. The superintendent viewed the Native Council as having some value "in the process of integration with the rest of the population," but warned again, "they should never be permitted to pass from an advisory stage to a stage in which they participate in the actual operation of the hospital."[60] Howell's concern that an organized patient voice might presume to adjust the hospital's power relationships points to deeper anxieties that patients and their supporters might indeed know and articulate their own health care interests that challenged IHS.

Patients in the men's ward at Fort Qu'Appelle Indian Hospital in 1962 bypassed the bureaucrats and appealed directly to the prime minister. The frustrated petitioners reminded John Diefenbaker of their special relationship, quoting the treaty promise that "the ears of the Queen's government will forever be opened to our complaints and wishes." They also appealed to the government that had not only recently granted Indians a measure of legal equality with the vote, but was also preparing the first Canadian bill of rights. Yet, they said, they were still treated as "children or a flock of sheep." They wanted the same respect and to be granted the same privileges – longer visiting hours and hospital leaves – accorded to white tuberculosis patients in the provincial sanatorium on the other side of Echo Lake. They appealed to the prime minister to stop the staff from opening and searching parcels that were sent to them in the hospital; they wanted to wear their clothes, not pyjamas, outside for their one hour of exercise in the small yard behind the hospital; visiting hours were too short and staff turned away their relatives who had travelled long distances. The petition might be read as reflecting little more than an understandable impatience with the banality of institutional life and its everyday indignities, if not for their final plea to the prime minister to protect them from retaliation.[61] That the petition was found in IHS files suggests that it missed its intended recipient, though the hospital was no doubt informed of the petitioners' identities and complaints.

Many patients recognized the strict discipline and rigid routine in hospital as a continuation of their residential school experiences. Indeed, many became ill in school and were moved from one institution to the other and back again, as students, patients, and, for some, workers.[62] A teenaged patient at Camsell Hospital in the 1950s, Roy Little Chief from Siksika recalled, "Well, I guess at that time we were well trained in the residential school, we followed authority. In the Camsell we could have been rebellious, but we learned to sneak around; run around during rest period."[63] Kathleen Steinhauer, from Saddle Lake reserve in Alberta, a nurse's aide and later an RN at Camsell Hospital in the 1950s, likened patients' "despairing resignation" with the residential school experience.[64] For some, though, the comparison was not apt. Dave Melting Tallow, who attended Crowfoot School at the Blackfoot reserve and was later hospitalized at the Camsell Hospital, recalled: "It wasn't like school at all. In school you were getting hit all the time, getting beat up, and hit all the time by the nuns. They punched like a priest. Those things happened in school. School was bad. Over there [Camsell Hospital] you could get visitors any time you wanted a visitor. They'd come and visit you and they didn't beat you up."[65] Frank Malloway from Sto:lo Nation at Sardis, British Columbia, a child patient in the Coqualeetza Indian Hospital in the late 1940s, witnessed what he only later understood to be the sexual abuse of another child in the hospital.[66] Patient narratives linking the experiences of residential schools and Indian hospitals point to the continuities of institutionalization as government policy. The terrible legacy of removing children from the supposed deleterious influences of families and communities, putting them in the hands of teachers, nurses, doctors and social workers who were deemed to know the children's best interests continues to damage individuals, their families, and indeed the nation itself.[67]

Another disturbingly common theme in patient narratives was the suspicion that they were subjected to medical experimentation; such mistrust of the motives of medical personnel was not without foundation. In the 1940s and 1950s Percy Moore, using IHS hospitals and in cooperation with Indian Affairs and leading national and international scientists, conducted a series of experiments in the then cutting-edge research into vitamins and malnutrition. They found ideal subjects in hungry, if not starving, Cree communities in northern Manitoba and James Bay, as well as in a number of residential schools. In the initial reporting of the Manitoba research the investigators noted:

> It is not unlikely that many characteristics such as shiftlessness, indolence, improvidence and inertia, so long regarded as inherent or hereditary traits in the Indian race, may, at the root, be really the manifestations of malnutrition. Furthermore, it is probable that the Indians' great susceptibility to many diseases, paramount amongst which is tuberculosis, may be attributable among other causes, to their high degree of malnutrition arising from lack of proper foods.[68]

"Shiftlessness and indolence," or the "Indian problem" needed the expert management of Indian hospitals and scientific study. The study, widely quoted in the press, was submitted as evidence to the 1946 Special Joint Committee of the House of Commons, and the Senate struck to recommend revisions to the Indian Act.[69] Historian Ian Mosby argues that the research resulted in little amelioration of the conditions in communities or schools that led to the people's hunger and malnourishment. While the bureaucrats and scientists recognized the connections between disease and malnutrition, they also "came to view Aboriginal bodies as 'experimental materials' and residential schools and Aboriginal communities as kinds of 'laboratories' that they could use to pursue a number of different political and professional interests."[70]

Indian hospitals also provided ample experimental material. As Aboriginal RN Kathleen Steinhauer told historian Laurie Meijer Drees in 2004:

> There is the thought that the hospitals were used for medical experiments. Occasionally new treatments for tuberculosis emerged and it seemed to many people, including patients and staff, that these treatments were pioneered on patients in the Indian Hospital system. When patients consented to treatment, I believe they often did not fully understand what was being asked of them.[71]

Several of Meijer Drees's other informants raised similar concerns, as did Frank Malloway and Dave Melting Tallow.[72] Elders from Piikuni (Peigan) and Kainai (Blood) First Nations in Alberta, and Carry the Kettle First Nation in southern Saskatchewan likewise expressed apprehensions about the medical care in Indian hospitals, suggesting patients were used as "guinea pigs."[73] Certainly, R.G. Ferguson's BCG vaccine trial in the 1930s and 1940s conducted on Cree and Assiniboine (Nakoda Oyadebi) infants in the Fort Qu'Appelle Indian Hospital was experimental (not unlike the 1950s trial of isoniazid [INH] on the Navajo at Many Farms, Arizona).[74] Residential school principals, not parents, consented to BCG, smallpox, and diphtheria vaccinations for schoolchildren, though as early as 1921 Ferguson sought parental consent to tuberculin test non-Aboriginal children.[75] In Indian hospitals tuberculin-negative patients under twenty-one years of age were routinely given BCG vaccination since signed hospital admission forms were deemed to cover all hospital treatments. As late as 1966 the Saskatchewan Anti-TB League vaccinated children with BCG without parental consent because the consent forms were awkward and time consuming, and besides, "it was good for them."[76] While white hospital employees were asked to sign a voluntary consent form for BCG vaccination, Aboriginal employees' consent was simply assumed. The assistant director advised hospital superintendents "not to stress this point [BCG vaccination] and suggest that you carry on as if it were a normal routine procedure and take it for granted that they do consent to vaccination." While admitting that there was no way to enforce vaccination if an employee refused, Moore's assistant did suggest that an Aboriginal employee should willingly cooperate "if he wishes to retain his job in the hospital."[77] IHS Indian hospitals' paternalistic and authoritarian structure, where medical personnel presumed to know what was best for them, left little room for patients, or Aboriginal employees, to question or indeed consent to treatment.

Moreover, patients with little experience of the frightening world of hospitals would find the cultural and language differences intimidating at the very least. The use of untrained interpreters who were often young domestic workers or patients with little understanding of medical terms and procedures created further confusion. Even patients who understood English found themselves distressingly vulnerable. Minnie Freeman, who was left for weeks to wonder what treatment she might receive, recalled: "My culture told me not to ask, that in this situation I might cause the people who were taking care of me to alter their behaviour completely, that I should accept what was happening and not force the hands that held my destiny. I figured they would tell me when they were ready."[78] Medical staff interpreted such culturally appropriate behaviour as an inherent Inuit stoicism, and as consent.

At Camsell Hospital, for instance, staff presumed that Aboriginal people had a "high pain threshold" and required minimal sedation, but, remarked a former nurse in retrospect, "they do have the same pain as other people."[79] Inuit patient Joanasie Salomanie suspected that he was part of "a medicine experiment using different things on us. I'm sure they were practicing on us because there were so many patients there." But author Pat Sandiford Grygier disregarded his informant's concerns, suggesting instead that medical personnel were "not sure of the correct dosages or applications of the new drugs just coming in, but were probably eager to use anything that offered an improvement."[80] Indeed, the treatment for tuberculosis shifted quickly in the 1950s, but patients' suspicions stemmed not just from an imperfect understanding of medical culture.

The difference between medical research's clinical trials and human experimentation is patient consent.[81] Given the very unequal power relationships between medical staff and patients, coupled with often perplexing language barriers, and the widespread perception that many Aboriginal people would not willingly accept treatment, patient consent for treatment was often simply taken for granted. Camsell Hospital, from its founding, developed a close relationship with the University of Alberta medical school, which offered specialist consultants to the hospital, while the hospital's patients provided interesting teaching and research "material" for the medical school.[82] In a statement intended to demonstrate the Camsell Hospital's successes, IHS claimed that in the late 1940s it was "one of the first hospitals to experiment with the use of streptomycin and to achieve a breakthrough in tuberculosis treatment."[83] The Camsell Hospital also undertook a 1956 trial of various different preparations of the common anti-tuberculosis drug para-aminosalicylic acid (PAS) on "Indian and Eskimo" patients. The experiment, which involved forty-eight patients, required five daily blood samples to be taken by vein puncture.[84] The blood of Inuit patients was of particular interest to researchers conducting metabolic tests for the Defence Research Board.[85] Blood samples were taken from "nearly two dozen hospitalized Eskimo patients" for an American researcher studying "widely separated ethnic and geographic racial groups." Consultant Allan Edwards conducted clinical trials of TSH (thyroid-stimulating hormone) from drug maker Nordic Pharmaceuticals for his study of hypothyroidism in "Native races."[86] He proposed to bring in another university consultant and, with grants from pharmaceutical companies Bristol Laboratories or Ayerst McKenna

Harrison, run trials of new antibiotics for treatment of pneumonia and renal infections. As he noted, the hospital had "adequate clinical material" and it had long been recognized that "patient treatment is very likely to benefit when a clinical study is being conducted." But IHS director Moore did not think it would be "politic" to accept grants from drug companies. Instead the studies could be performed by hospital staff using the hospital laboratory and would be a legitimate expense of public funds. But, he continued, if the drug companies wanted to "give us some 'samples' to use in the study, or if, because of our interest and theirs, they wished to offer us a special price on a batch of drugs to be used in the study, that is quite a different matter."[87] By the 1970s the department became more diligent in securing consent, especially for sexual sterilization, but not without controversy.[88] The ubiquity in patient narratives of distrust of medical personnel not only reflects the reality of life in an Indian hospital, it also points to a wider suspicion of the intentions of the colonizing state's myriad policies and its institutions intended to eliminate their languages and cultures.

Patient narratives also highlight resistance. Challenging their incarceration, and rejecting the treatment regime of the strictly controlled environment, some patients left hospital. The recalcitrant patient was a common problem in sanatoria, but in the pre-antibiotic era when treatment relied on bed rest and the cultivation of self-discipline, where cures were rare and wards were full, patients were not kept against their will. But Indian hospitals were not sanatoria. Certainly patient narratives of resistance that emphasize survival and the strength of the people, individually and collectively, are an important counterweight to persistent images of dependence and victimization.[89] But it is important that historical interpretations that stress the people's agency through narratives also provide the historical context of the coercive nature of IHS policies and its close collaborations with police and courts lest they imply that resistance and resiliency somehow mitigated the damage done to communities and individuals.[90] For example, in Manitoba, in a most single-minded search for the contagious, medical superintendents made liberal use of the provincial public health act, sending the police to return patients to hospital. In 1946 "George Hamilton" from a northern reserve presented himself at the Dynevor Indian Hospital for treatment, and after two months he was allowed to go home to tend to family matters. When he did not return to hospital the medical superintendent, Dr Campbell, swore out a warrant and the local RCMP arrested Hamilton and escorted him back to Dynevor Hospital. Dr Campbell hoped to operate and remove some of his ribs, and though Hamilton refused that treatment, he remained in hospital. In his absence, Hamilton's family had no means of support, but only after two of his young children died did Indian Affairs finally arrange for a $10 monthly ration and a wood supply to keep the rest of the family alive. Hamilton was kept in hospital. When community members complained to Indian Agent McPherson about Hamilton's plight, he "informed the Indians that any person with T.B. could be arrested." McPherson reported the appalling case to his superiors only because, as he warned, "these Indians have a habit of going to some outside white people preferably Lawyers and Politicians in whose hands they will put this matter."[91] The details of Hamilton's experience are exceptional in the archival record, but the files are replete with RCMP reports documenting the arrest of "Indians" and their usual one-year sentence to hospital.[92] Historical interpretations that foreground resistance as survival, without inquiring into its wider social, political, and economic contexts, relieve us from confronting the conditions that made resistance necessary. While Manitoba was especially vigilant in bringing the ill to justice, it is clear that white Manitobans were not likewise subject to arrest.

One can only imagine the distress of patients such as the two Inuk women who walked out of Parc Savard Hospital in Quebec City in February 1952. Dressed only in bathrobes and slippers, the women walked a considerable distance before they were brought back to hospital. They had been in Parc Savard for four years, and with no one on staff who could speak their language they likely assumed they would remain there, forgotten indefinitely. Leo Manning, former Hudson's Bay Company manager and by the early 1950s one of a very few Inuktitut speakers working for the northern administration, acted as interpreter and visited the hospital in 1952. At the time there were ninety Inuit patients (fifty-five adults and thirty-five children) as well as immigrants requiring medical care, ill mariners, and a few veterans in the hospital. Some Inuit men kept busy with wood carving, while women knitted socks and sweaters and produced beadwork for slippers for a local firm that paid them $2 per dozen. Manning found Inuit patients' morale "very low" and in his three-day visit recorded patient messages to be broadcast by CBC Northern Message Service out of Winnipeg.[93]

Parc Savard (see illustration 4.2), originally built at the turn of the century as a quarantine hospital for immigrants, began accepting Inuit patients in the late 1940s and by 1956 operated as a general hospital with surgery, obstetrics, gynaecology, paediatrics, orthopaedics, cardiology,

Illustration 4.2 Parc Savard Immigration Hospital, later Parc Savard Indian Hospital. A quarantine hospital for immigrants, Parc Savard at Quebec City also accepted Inuit patients by the 1940s. The insect- and rodent-infested building had 198 general hospital beds.

Source: PA-117288, LAC.

and diagnostic radiology with a daily average of 198 patients. Hospital superintendent J.E. Labrecque complained that he had only three physicians on staff; the buildings were literally crumbling; the heating and lighting were inadequate; in Ward D, which had twenty-eight beds, there were only three toilets and one bathtub; and the hospital was infested with cockroaches, fleas, bedbugs, mice, and rats. Worse yet, the slum adjacent to the hospital property was home to a factory that repaired old mattresses. "Needless to say that it is a nest for rats which are causing us great inconvenience."[94] It is not clear where the two Inuk women hoped to go when they left the hospital in bedclothes in February, but they could be forgiven for thinking they would be better off elsewhere.

Generally, provincial sanatoria did not keep patients against their will. Certainly public health legislation provided the authority to remove the infectious to sanatorium but rarely the power to keep them there. Sanatorium directors worried that to treat patients as criminals risked losing public confidence in the institutions. The ill might avoid medical treatment for fear they would be incarcerated.[95] In most jurisdictions citizens' civil liberties were not sacrificed for the public good. Public health bureaucrats in Saskatchewan contemplated compulsory detention for the "incorrigible open case of tuberculosis," but when the Anti-TB League that operated the provincial sanatoria refused to provide a locked ward, the matter rested.[96] The exception, however, was Nova Scotia, where amendments to the provincial public health act in 1948 provided the authority for detention and compulsory treatment of patients with "open" pulmonary tuberculosis who would not conduct themselves responsibly, though the "intelligent and co-operative" could carry on safely at home. Class and race most often marked the difference between the "irresponsible" and the "co-operative." By 1954, as J.E. Hiltz, medical superintendent of the Nova Scotia Sanatorium in Kentville, told the readers of the *Canadian Medical Association Journal*, fifty-two patients (including five "Indians") were convicted and sent to the detention unit, 200 kilometres away on the grounds of the Roseway Hospital in Shelburne. The locked ward was a "fireproof and escape-proof" concrete bunker situated far from hospital buildings so "the noise" did not disturb others.[97] But not all provincial jurisdictions were as accommodating.

The 1953 Indian Health Regulations filled the void by providing the necessary authority for detention "when a province is unable or unwilling to take the appropriate action in connection with some communicable disease among Indians."[98] On director Moore's recommendation, the 1951 amendments to the Indian Act (section 72) included the authority to make regulations to provide "compulsory hospitalization and treatment for infectious diseases among Indians."[99] The Indian Health Regulations that soon followed made possible the detention and incarceration of the dangerous. Exposing the limits of Canada's liberalism, the Regulations' expressed intent was to "eliminat[e] any discrimination between those Canadian citizens of Indian status and other citizens of Canada" by applying all provincial public health laws to status Indians. But in order "to protect and promote the health of the Indians" the regulations contained compulsory provisions.[100] The Regulations applied to all Indians who lived on reserve and "every Indian who follows the Indian mode of life" (to cover those in the north where reserves were not set aside), as well as those who lived in non-Aboriginal communities. Thus, "an Indian who suspects himself to be infected with an infectious disease" must be treated by a doctor. Violators faced a $100 fine, or three months' imprisonment, or both. Patients could appeal their detention by petition served on the superintendent (Indian agent) before a magistrate or two justices of the peace, with the physician present, though one wonders if patients were informed of their rights, or indeed of the Regulations themselves. Included in the Regulations were IHS Forms 7018 parts a, b, and c authorizing (respectively) compulsory medical examination and treatment; apprehension and detention; and the forced return of patients to hospital. The new Regulations recognized that "some Indians object strongly to having the police called in to force them to undergo examination and treatment … [but] it is necessary to take compulsory action."[101] Not unlike the efforts to identify Inuit patients through fingerprinting by the RCMP in the 1930s, the Indian Health Regulations made clear the association of Aboriginal illness with criminality and subsequent incarceration.[102]

Dave Melting Tallow recalled how he left Camsell Indian Hospital against medical advice to attend the Calgary Stampede. His cousin brought him clothes and he climbed out a window, though the police eventually caught up with him. On another occasion he did not get as far:

> See what they used to do was they could put you in jail. They'd put you in jail in a cell. You had to go to court. I did one time. I had to go to court. I was running away from the hospital, they took me up there. I don't know what I was charged with, but they charged me with something. I just had pajamas on – in jail with pajamas on. The judge said that I had a choice – if I didn't want to go back to the hospital, he'd put me in jail and I'd have to stay there in jail until I was cured or something. Or I could go back to the hospital. Naturally I chose to go back to the hospital. They told me that I was giving TB to everybody.[103]

After three years in hospital Melting Tallow was finally released after undergoing a lobectomy and the removal of several ribs (see chapter 3). Not surprisingly, Indian hospitals maintained locked detention wards, usually constructed during renovations before the hospitals opened, and well before the Indian Health Regulations were enacted.[104]

A former nurse recalled hearing about, though never seeing, the "jail," a small room on the roof of the Charles Camsell Hospital where patients were kept under guard.[105] The RCMP delivered a man in leg irons to the ward in 1958. The superintendent warned, "Any patient who has tuberculosis and who runs away from the hospital will be locked in a private room when brought back to the hospital and all privileges suspended for one week, e.g. radio, visitors, etc."[106] Most provincial jurisdictions did not infringe on civil liberties of the tuberculous through compulsory detention, but the sweeping powers of the Indian Health Regulations were another reminder that Aboriginal people remained wards of the state without the liberties of citizens.[107]

Indian Health Service, a centralized bureaucracy with a network of interrelated institutions and a wide legal mandate, used its authority to move patients into and within its system, and, later, to provincial sanatoria. By the mid- to late-1950s the trends in tuberculosis treatment were mirrored in Indian hospitals: the success of antibiotic treatment further slashed already falling tuberculosis rates. But, Indian hospitals, unlike sanatoria, did not quickly empty because the institutions admitted patients with all medical conditions, determined by race not disease. What were once "tuberculosis" beds became general treatment beds since only a full hospital kept per diem rates from rising. Perhaps not surprisingly then, Indian hospitals continued to rely on compulsion. For example, asked to explain the cause for vacant beds at Miller Bay Indian Hospital in 1956, medical superintendent G.R. Howell suggested that tuberculosis in the region was coming under control. To fill the beds in his hospital would involve "scraping the bottom of the tuberculosis barrel" through more intensive surveillance and "the persistent use of persuasion and I.H.S. 7018a [Indian Health Regulations] to bring unwilling patients to hospital."[108] In 1957 Alberta's zone superintendent, Dr Falconer, informed Moore: "practically all the T.B. patients found in the province are under treatment and there is no waiting list. All the patients in the N.W.T. recommended for surgery have been admitted."[109] Saskatchewan, with its three provincial sanatoria, began accepting more Aboriginal patients in the 1950s, but patients who left against medical advice often found themselves admitted to the more "secure" Fort Qu'Appelle Indian Hospital.[110] Nevertheless, some patients chose to resist by isolating themselves from family and community in the bush rather than in hospital. Nevertheless, arrest warrants were issued. In Saskatchewan in 1961, IHS bureaucrats complained that patients who should be institutionalized "are hiding in the bush, even though a warrant has been issued for their apprehension ... Right now there is an old lady 77 years old who is hiding herself somewhere in the bush to avoid the RCMP."[111] As late as 1966 Dr Matas assured tuberculosis professionals that recalcitrant Aboriginal patients were not a problem. But, he continued, since provincial public health regulations "are much less severe than are the Indian Health Regulations," if the latter were ever abolished he hoped that "with patience and persistence" the provinces could be convinced to make full use of their regulations when required.[112]

Patients, first relocated to distant hospitals, were then shifted between institutions for medical reasons, to undergo surgery for example, or for bureaucratic convenience – to make use of bed space. Parallels can be drawn with the colonizing state's disturbingly frequent relocations of individuals and communities in the interests of resource development, bureaucratic convenience, and national security, while the "removed" were assured it was "for their own good."[113] Inuit, the most dramatic example, were transported thousands of kilometres to southern hospitals with minimal consultation and few opportunities to question their fate.[114] In October 1945 the Clearwater Lake Indian Hospital at The Pas in northern Manitoba received thirty-nine patients from Norway House Hospital without names, treaty numbers, histories, or records, including an infant of seven months – "nameless, numberless with no instructions for treatment. It has recovered at the Pas, on Penicillin, but no one knows who it is."[115] Children were especially vulnerable. Harry Kegiuna spent seven years in hospital as a child. Sent from the north by ship, where he sat in the corner by himself, then by airplane, he eventually reached Charles Camsell Indian Hospital. No one knew his name so he was simply called "Harry Hospital." After spending years in the hospital he was woken one night, told to put on some clothes, and sent across the country to Ottawa by train, with no chance to say goodbye to anyone: "They never told you what was going to happen."[116] Working as a government translator, Minnie Aodla Freeman visited Inuit patients at the St Boniface Hospital in Manitoba in 1957: "We saw a child there who had forgotten his language completely. This was as sad as any illness. How will he communicate with his parents when he goes home?"[117] Author Grygier notes that Inuit infants and children whose mothers were in treatment were fostered out on southern reserves, or more usually placed in Indian hospital wards, while others were informally adopted by white staff.[118] The medical superintendent at Dynevor Indian Hospital hoped to keep one of his "cute" Inuit patients. "In fact,

I told him [Louie] if he wanted to stay I would take him over myself for adoption. But he wanted to go back to his family and no doubt, it was the better plan."[119] Patients also found themselves moved about (and it is fair to assume they were never consulted) for reasons that had less to do with medical treatment.

The rapid change brought about by antimicrobial treatment for tuberculosis in the 1950s was celebrated as the "miracle" of the empty beds only in retrospect. At the time, sanatorium boards and their business managers faced rising per diem costs and growing deficits. In a particularly pathetic irony, not lost on IHS director Moore, sanatoria competed with each other and with Indian hospitals for Aboriginal bodies that had been for so long denied admission to their institutions.[120] In 1954, for instance, seven patients from Athabaska reserve in northern Alberta, and twelve from Yukon were taken south to the Charles Camsell Hospital and subsequently found themselves on the prairies in the Fort Qu'Appelle Sanatorium in southern Saskatchewan.[121] In 1955, C.B. Ross, superintendent of the venerable Muskoka Hospital in Ontario (established in 1896 as the first sanatorium in the country), thanked Moore for "another shipment of eleven Indians." With forty empty beds Ross wondered if Moore might direct more patients his way: "Anything which you might be able to do along this line would be greatly appreciated."[122] In an arrangement with IHS, Moose Factory Indian Hospital on James Bay sent Inuit patients to Mountain Sanatorium in Hamilton and Indian patients to Muskoka. But confusion set in when some Indians were sent to Hamilton; they were to be sent back to Moose Factory, like so much freight, as soon as beds were made available by shipping "new Indians" to Muskoka. The IHS regional superintendent reminded Moose Factory to advise the office when moving "Eskimos ... giving name, number, age and diagnosis and name of place he came from or to which he was sent."[123] Patients who did not understand English were at times "misplaced" in the system, and without communication with home, families were left to wonder what had become of their loved ones.

Clearwater Lake Indian Hospital in Manitoba, operated by the Manitoba Sanatorium Board on behalf of IHS, likewise felt the financial impact of increasingly effective treatments. In 1952, 195 patients were in residence; although this number eventually rose to 207, occupancy dropped sharply after 1959. By October 1961, the hospital reported a financial loss of $18,377, and the year was not yet over. But arrangements were soon made to improve the bottom line. As the hospital reported to the Sanatorium Board, "It was extremely difficult to see how these liabilities could be met, but as a result of discussions with Dr Moore, arrangements were made to transfer 58 tuberculosis patients to Clearwater Lake from Hamilton. As a result of this, and other increases in our tuberculosis occupancy, we are now in a satisfactory financial position."[124] The hospital committee minutes in October 1962, however, reported that the Inuit patients were transferred from Hamilton because of "disciplinary problems."[125] The trip from southern Ontario to northern Manitoba would have been particularly exhausting for the ill and increasingly perplexed patients. As noted in chapter 2, Aboriginal patients were kept in the institutions for one to two years in spite of the effectiveness of chemotherapy. Patients who survived were eventually relocated home (although some Inuit patients chose to remain in the south), but that process too was made more difficult by shoddy record keeping and at times callous disregard for patients' needs.[126] Many patients died at hospital and were never returned home, their families left to worry and wonder where they might be.

From the outset, IHS did its utmost to avoid responsibility for an issue it hoped to ignore: what to do with patients who died at its hospitals. Indian Affairs, for its part, was steadfast that it would pay no more than "absolutely necessary for the burial of indigent Indians." If the family wanted to transport and bury their loved one at home, it would be at their own expense.[127] When Dynevor Indian Hospital opened in 1939 the dead were buried across the Red River at the local parish, though the Sanatorium Board's George Northwood decried Indian Affairs' policy of limiting costs to $25 when the government allowed $100 for military burials.[128] At the Charles Camsell Hospital the issue emerged as soon as the institution opened. Regional superintendent E.L. Stone suggested that in the interests of good relations with local reserves IHS should show a "reasonable appearance of generosity" by notifying the undertaker and paying for embalming and a rough box to prepare the body for shipment to reserve, about $45.[129] But IHS refused to assume any responsibility for the burial of Aboriginal patients. Moore's assistant did acknowledge that families might be reluctant to send their sick to distant hospitals if they were not assured that in the event of death they would be buried at home.[130] Indian Affairs, rather unhelpfully, proposed that IHS develop a form to be completed by hospitalized patients outlining their financial resources and also indicating whether, in case of death, the patient's family wanted the body returned to the reserve. Failing that, Indian Affairs agreed to pay the costs of a burial in a cemetery closest to the Indian hospital if the family lacked the funds to return the body to their home community for burial.[131] By August 1947, with "considerable" mortality at the Camsell Hospital, Protestant patients were interred on the grounds of the Edmonton Residential School (where students were paid to dig the graves), and Catholics were buried at Enoch's on the Stony Plain reserve.[132] When they could, the hospital carpentry shop made small coffins for parents who wanted to take their deceased infants home with them.[133]

This policy, maintained across the country, was particularly harsh for northern communities, who could rarely afford the costly flights to return their family members. Yet into the 1960s Indian Affairs continued to refuse to provide transportation for deceased patients "if this will exceed the cost of burial at the place he died."[134] The policy also provided IHS with access to bodies for autopsy without having to secure the family's consent. In 1964, the IHS regional superintendent for Saskatchewan, Dr Orford, blithely stated: "Disposal of the body of an Indian after death is a matter which concerns Indian Affairs Branch. Indian Health Services is concerned only with the living."[135] Given the frequent and arbitrary shifting of patients throughout the IHS hospital system, the incomplete record keeping, and unmarked graves in back corners of cemeteries scattered across the country, it is little wonder that families lost forever their sons and daughters, mothers and fathers. It is only in the last decades that communities have begun to locate and honour some of the lost patients who lived and died in Indian hospitals.[136]

A far more pervasive and progressive narrative of life in Indian hospitals, constructed by and for IHS, demonstrated the state's noble intentions and its heroic efforts to cure the Aboriginal condition. From its founding the Charles Camsell Indian Hospital was to be the showcase of IHS efforts to provide care and, as importantly, to be seen to provide care. In February 1946 the hospital superintendent proposed having the National Film Board feature the hospital: "This film would be useful for showing to groups from various agencies and would be excellent propaganda."[137] It would be a decade before the film appeared, but in the meantime IHS and hospital staff went to considerable effort to educate and inform its Aboriginal constituency and the public generally about the hospital's good work. Staff produced the *Camsell Arrow*, an in-house newsletter, not uncommon in sanatoria, intended to help with patient morale and develop literacy skills (though it is unclear how much patients contributed). The *Arrow* featured short, gossipy "ward news" (including the apparently obligatory expressions of gratitude to nurses and doctors), and longer articles, such as travelogues submitted by vacationing staff. The *Arrow*, like newsletters in other large Indian hospitals (for example, the *Coqualeetza Courier* and Miller Bay's *Totem Tattler*) was also a convenient vehicle to discipline patients in correct attitudes and behaviour. However, the Miller Bay patients' committee had to ask when the *Totem Tattler* was produced and whether patients would be allowed to participate.[138] In the interests of public relations, the *Camsell Arrow* was combined with an annual *Pictorial Review* and distributed to Indian agencies and visiting dignitaries.[139] IHS and the National Film Board created hundreds of images of smiling and, oddly, healthy-looking patients (illustration 4.3). Indian hospitals also welcomed curious local citizens to tour their wards to view the curiosities. At the Camsell Hospital a heavily tattooed Inuit woman gave the gawking onlookers something to remember by lifting her top to show her tattooed chest. Dynevor Hospital invited visitors to see "our two very cute Eskimos."[140] In 1952 the gifted portrait photographer Yousuf Karsh, already famous for his 1941 portrait of a scowling Winston Churchill that graced the cover of *Time* magazine, visited Edmonton and the Charles Camsell Indian Hospital for *Maclean's* magazine. His compelling portraits of patients Mrs Susan Philippe, Daniel Makokis from Saddle Lake Cree Nation, Lucy Michel from Fort Nelson, BC, and young boys, Joe Koaha and Peter Naitit, from Cambridge Bay, and a "Metis lad" from Whitehorse, capture their loneliness and frustration (see illustrations 4.4 to 4.7).

In 1956 the National Film Board, with the cooperation of Indian Affairs, Indian Health Service, and the Camsell Hospital, produced the short film *The Longer Trail*.[141] Although the film is a fictionalized narrative ostensibly about "Joe Lonecloud" and his successful struggle with tuberculosis in the Camsell Indian Hospital, the film's real hero is Mr Mosley, the intrepid Indian Affairs rehabilitation officer who fights to win Joe's trust and battles the prejudices of Edmonton's employers and boarding-house owners. Like the National Film Board's other short film on the subject, *No Longer Vanishing* (1955), it is a narrative about Indian struggles with modernity. Protected and sheltered on reserves, they must inevitably relocate and integrate into Canadian society as useful manual labourers.[142] *The Longer Trail* opens with Joe happily riding his horse on the prairie when a nurse approaches with the unfortunate news that his chest X-ray is positive. He is delivered to Charles Camsell Hospital, where doctors give him a 95 per cent chance of recovery through "drugs and sometimes surgery." Joe, however, can never

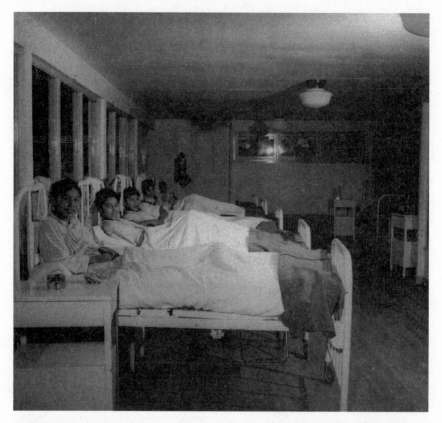

Illustration 4.3 Charles Camsell Indian Hospital. Indian Health Service enlisted the National Film Board to create hundreds of images of Aboriginal patients who are invariably portrayed as smiling and happy. The NFB also produced films depicting the hospitals as fundamental in the process of integration and assimilation.

Source: PA-139319, LAC.

return to his strenuous work on the "ranch." Joe, mute throughout the film except for his interior dialogue, admits to being afraid, misses his family and his horse, and muses, "I wonder if horses cry at night?" He escapes from hospital, but soon realizes his error and returns. Mr Mosley finally reaches Joe with an impassioned speech telling the young man that he is not the first to get TB. He can stay in hospital for five years, ten

Illustration 4.4 Daniel Makokis, Saddle Lake, Alberta, at Charles Camsell Indian Hospital. Yousuf Karsh 1952.

Source: PA-165895, LAC.

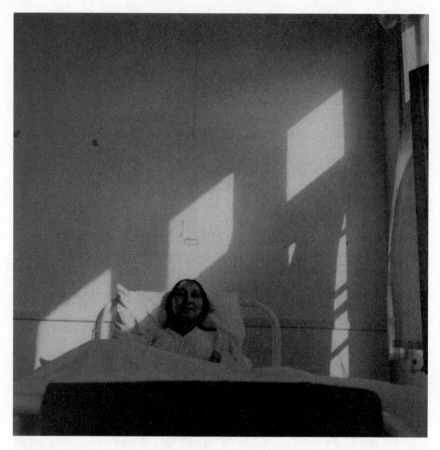

Illustration 4.5 Mrs Susan Philippe, Charles Camsell Indian Hospital.
Yousuf Karsh 1952.

Source: e011083918, LAC.

years, or he may never leave, because with TB "you have to want to get
well and right now you don't want to." Joe must change. Mosley promises to help him get an education in hospital and a job upon discharge.
When Joe asks what job an Indian can get, Mosley has no answer, except
to point out that there are no opportunities on the reserve. Joe subsequently embraces leatherwork, demonstrating that he is "good with his
hands." And so, after two years, he is finally released. With a job in a
carpentry shop and a quiet room, he does not think too much about his

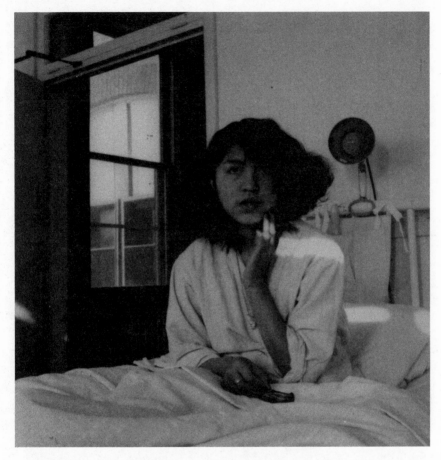

Illustration 4.6 Lucy Michel, Fort Nelson, BC, at Charles Camsell Indian Hospital. Yousuf Karsh 1952.

Source: e011083919 LAC.

horse or his home anymore. In the final scene Joe walks alone through a suburban Edmonton neighbourhood dreaming about someday fitting in on a quiet street with good neighbours, a wife, and kids. "I dream. I think, who knows?" *The Longer Trail* articulates a mid-century view that equates reserves with disease and dependency and professes faith in medicine and its institutions to solve the "Indian problem" through urban relocation and assimilation. Joe's trail to healthy citizenship,

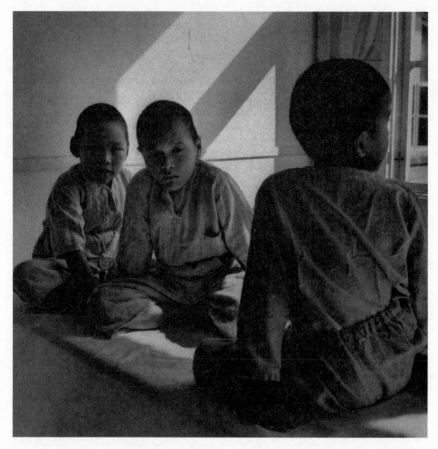

Illustration 4.7 Joe Koaha and Peter Naitit, Cambridge Bay; "Metis lad,"
Whitehorse at Charles Camsell Indian Hospital. Yousuf Karsh 1952.

Source: PA-165896, LAC.

made longer by his own ignorance and society's bigotry, was finally
successful when he accepted his place in the economic order and left
the reserve behind.

It is not clear what the Aboriginal participants in these carefully
constructed narratives made of their experience, but Minnie Freeman, working in Ottawa was outraged and sickened to find herself
being used as a token Inuk for state propaganda. Told to report to

an unfamiliar bureaucracy, she was directed to smile and hold up a Canada Savings Bond while gazing at an Inuit carving; a photographer took her picture. Upset to find her image in the local newspaper the next day, she recalled: "The story read: 'Eskimos buying bonds, keeping up with progress,' some remark like that. I felt sick. I had no idea what bonds were ... I felt sick because I was being used to show the *qallunaat* in the South how well the Inuit are treated in the North ... I became very apprehensive after that when someone phoned, asking to interview me. I felt I could not be a part of something which was not really happening. Never were there photographs that showed the truth about my people's lives."[143]

Positive images of life and death in Indian hospitals, "excellent propaganda" in the construction of the welfare state, reassured Canadians that even the most recalcitrant and irresponsible received care, by force if necessary. In the hands of harried, if not unqualified staff, in crowded and dismal institutions, patients endured medicine's supposed great benefits. Their narratives of abuse, compulsion, and incarceration demonstrate a grim determination to survive at times despite, rather than because of, their institutionalization. Medicalizing inequality and pathologizing Aboriginality in the interests of the wider Canadian community, IHS carried out the colonizing state's contradictory policies: to segregate in order to assimilate and to isolate in order to integrate. But despite the Indian hospitals' obvious shortcomings, they remained a tangible state commitment to the people's health care, if not an acknowledgment of the treaty right to health care that communities would not easily forfeit.

Chapter Five

Getting Out of the Hospital Business

In early 1961 Indian Health Service bureaucrats mused that their objective should be to "get out of the hospital business wherever we can. The key word is *quiet*. There is no need to make a big to-do."[1] In particular, they had in mind the on-reserve hospitals in southern Alberta. That IHS policy makers presumed such a fundamental shift in health care delivery would escape notice highlights their continued insularity and paternalism, but it was also a tacit admission of the hospitals' serious deficiencies. By the 1960s there were more than enough empty sanatorium beds to meet the steadily declining need for in-patient tuberculosis treatment. Heavy investment in hospital and health care infrastructure under the continuing National Health Grants program meant that Canadians who could afford it had access to care in modern, well-staffed acute care hospitals. And by 1957, with the introduction of national hospital insurance, federal and provincial funds helped pay the spiralling hospitalization costs for all Canadians. New definitions of the "national health" meant that Indian hospitals would be quietly closed and community hospitals would be prevailed upon to expand (using IHS funds) to accept Aboriginal patients. Part of the broader postwar push for integration and "equality," Indians would disappear finally into the larger fabric of society and with them would go their "special status," treaties, and reserves.[2] Warning that the move to close hospitals would be "resisted by the Indians," bureaucrats assured their minister that they only needed to point out that community hospitals would provide better care.[3] Indeed, resistance emerged from all sides as the national projects of integration and Medicare became snarled in nasty federal–provincial jurisdictional disputes. Aboriginal communities argued that funds intended for their health care should be spent on much-needed improvements in Indian hospitals, and not invested in non-Aboriginal community institutions. For their part, some community hospital boards and provincial health departments also resisted Indian hospital closures, deeming Aboriginal patients a burden best cared for by the federal government. Aboriginal communities had good reason to fear a return to restricted access and basement wards in community hospitals. A focus on the experience in Alberta provides an opportunity to untangle the threads of these broad programs to assess their impact on Aboriginal health and health care. "Getting out of the hospital business" by starving the Blackfoot Indian Hospital while rebuilding the Charles Camsell Hospital suggests that integration in hospital care had as much to do with asserting medical authority and bureaucratic control as improving health. Likewise, the march to Medicare – hospital insurance and health care insurance – widely considered a great national success, was particularly damaging to Aboriginal people, who, caught between jurisdictions, came to be seen as unwanted patients in community hospitals and less deserving of care.

Particular targets for closure were the Blackfoot and Blood Indian hospitals in southern Alberta. Both hospitals, substantial three-storey brick structures built in the 1920s on their respective reserve lands, pre-dated IHS postwar expansion. Serving their reserve communities exclusively, the hospitals developed to meet local needs. The Blood Hospital, a Catholic missionary institution operated by the Sisters of Charity and built in 1928 on the southern edge of the reserve, sat on the main street of the Mormon settlement at Cardston, across from the community hospital. The Blackfoot Hospital further north replaced Anglican missionary care on the reserve in 1924. Owned by the Siksika (Blackfoot) and built with funds realized by the sale of nearly half their reserve lands, the hospital was unique as the only band-owned "Indian" hospital in the west and one of only two in the country.[4] The Siksika agreed to fund the hospital on the condition that their indigenous healers and midwives be allowed to continue their practice.[5] Over the next thirty years or so both reserve communities developed a medical syncretism or pluralism combining Western medicine with indigenous healers, a pragmatic accommodation to the changed circumstances of colonization.[6] With the independence that ownership conferred, the Siksika cultivated a measure of local control that became increasingly unpalatable to IHS. To understand why IHS planned to close the Blood and particularly the Blackfoot Hospital, it is necessary to examine the tensions between local pluralism in health care and the ascendant authority of medical bureaucrats to define and direct care in Indian hospitals.

While the Blood and Blackfoot hospitals replaced the rudimentary missionary hospitals that had been established in the nineteenth century in conjunction with denominational boarding schools, the majority of patients continued to be schoolchildren. As historian John Milloy notes, contagious disease spread easily among the weakened and poorly clothed children in badly constructed school buildings.[7] At the new Blackfoot Hospital, the resident Indian Agent George Gooderham reported in 1926 "children from the schools are admitted without asking the consent of the parents except when it is an operation case of a serious nature. It is among the children of 8 to 16 years of age that very good results have been obtained … The doctor does minor operations when necessary; tonsils, adenoids, light tracoma cases and curettating tubercular affections [sic] make up the large proportion of these operations." Convalescing patients, especially older schoolgirls, were put to work washing and scrubbing at the hospital.[8] While children were forced into the hospital and kept there, their parents remained sceptical, preferring the services of their own healers and midwives.

Male physicians, in particular, had little to offer Siksika women. But the appointment in 1928 of Dr Frances Evelyn Windsor as medical superintendent of the Blackfoot Hospital may have attracted women to the hospital. Windsor, single and with a young child to care for, gladly accepted the appointment as medical superintendent, which came with regular rations and a house. Few other physicians wanted the small salary on an isolated reserve, though, as the 1920s slid into the Depression and private practices dried up, male physicians jealously eyed her appointment. As a friend of Calgary's member of parliament and prime minister, R.B. Bennett, Windsor was secure in her position.[9] She may have encouraged women into the hospital by acknowledging the Siksika's great reluctance to leave sick family members in the care of strangers. Though the Blackfoot Hospital's records are not extant, admissions at the Blood Hospital, especially among women, increased in the 1920s and 1930s. That hospital's records may point to a cultural explanation for increased use. Owned by the Department of Indian Affairs, but managed by the Catholic Sisters of Charity, the Blood Hospital allowed ill women to keep their young children with them in hospital, and permitted mothers to stay with their sick children, often bringing along healthy siblings as well. Moreover, government doctors did not attend the hospital unless called for. In October 1923, for example, the hospital admitted fourteen women, thirty-six children, and two men. Nine of the women were not ill, but accompanied their sick children; thirteen of the children were healthy and staying with sick mothers or siblings. Nearly half the hospital's residents (42 per cent) were not sick, which suggests the hospital was made to fit larger Kainai (Blood) cultural and social perceptions of health care.[10] However, the reserve's DIA physician Dr Alan Kennedy disapproved, urging "discipline" to make the institution a "true hospital ... not a comfortable place to stay, as some of the Indians seem to consider it now."[11] It seems likely that the Siksika made their hospital a "comfortable place" since they owned the institution.

Young women on the reserves, particularly residential school _____ _____ under Christian influence, chose to attend _____ hey also learned to sew a com- _____ 926 photograph Siksika women _____ at the hospital's baby clinic[12] _____ agent believed the maternity _____ cial results to the general health _____ had more practical advantages, _____ t in winter, services that reserve _____ for an additional bathroom in the _____, could secure a bath. At present _____ ugh we want to encourage clean- _____ ion."[14] Nurse Pesquot, a hospital _____ that women used the maternity _____ wn midwives in summer. As she _____ Hanks, "Women seldom come in _____ omen come in with their children _____ ng with them. It is in order to get _____ d the peoples' pragmatic hospital _____. [T]hey always want something." _____ id not feel pain. "At childbirth we _____ y groan a little." When the anthro- _____ n felt pain but did not express it, _____ nimals." Her invective, prompted _____ eoples' continued autonomy, was _____ ordinate position in relation to the Siksika, whom she saw as inferior.[15] Nevertheless, the Siksika used the hospital according to their social and cultural notions of care. But that autonomy would soon be undermined by rising costs and the continued poor health of the residential school students.

Illustration 5.1 Contestants in the first baby show held at the Blackfoot Hospital, 1926. Front row, L–R: Mrs Charles Joe Royal (1st prize winner); Mrs Harry Red Gun (2nd prize); Mrs A. Youngman (3rd prize). Mrs Jack McHugh is in the back row, right, in the cloche hat. Earl Calf Child, on the extreme right, the Indian agent's interpreter, is holding the baby of Mrs Spring Calf, who died in childbirth. The child was raised in the hospital.

Source: PA-32–1, Glenbow Archives.

A 1934 X-ray clinic at the Siksika's residential schools found a number of children requiring observation and eleven pupils who required immediate hospitalization. Students filled the enlarged forty-six-bed hospital, leaving little room for "ordinary cases."[16] It was clear to the agent that ill children could not be left in school under missionary care. While the Anglican Old Sun's School had plenty of dormitory space, it had no nurse, and the Catholic Crowfoot School had a nurse but was so overcrowded that staff slept in the infirmary. "Beds in the dormitories are so close together, one can barely move about. This school cannot keep a diseased child at present."[17] But despite children's poor health, missionaries resisted the loss of their students to the hospital, and the per capita grant that went with them. Crowfoot School's Father Jacques Riou insisted that the school, with its "home atmosphere," actually provided better care than the hospital.[18] Missionaries opposed what they considered unwarranted interference in their schools, while Gooderham pressed for hospital expansion.

Dr Windsor, in keeping with accepted tuberculosis treatment at the time, suggested a two-storey addition with balconies, where patients could enjoy complete bed rest with access to sunshine and the open air.[19] Instead, the agent thought it better to build a new residence for staff, while tuberculosis patients could be isolated in the old staff wing. While he was sure Siksika Council would approve the estimated $8,000 for a staff residence, he cautioned his superiors: "The Indians do not want to spend one more cent for medicalization than is necessary but they realize the need of more ward space and also the desirability of segregating the tbs [sic]. They will agree to this suggestion, I am sure."[20] The following day, in a more candid letter to the DIA's medical director, Dr EL Stone, the agent admitted they were spending Siksika funds like a "bloated Millionaire." As the Depression worsened the Siksika Council became increasingly concerned about DIA management of their funds. And while they paid for all medical services, Siksika Council worried that their hospital was no longer able to provide needed care for tuberculosis patients. As Gooderham put it, "Our young Indians know the situation in this regard and are, even now, complaining that the Department makes the Blackfoot pay the bill when other Bands receive equal or better hospitalization from Consolidated Revenue [DIA]."[21] Moreover, by 1940 the Siksika also paid for the treatment of up to six patients in the Central Alberta (Keith) Sanatorium. Aboriginal people were not usually admitted to provincial sanatoria because of community prejudice and the DIA's reluctance to pay for treatment, but the Siksika paid $5,875 annually to the sanatorium, even though other Albertans received free treatment under the 1936 Tuberculosis Act.[22]

The Siksika's large trust fund was an anomaly in Canada, and the DIA used it to pay for all its reserve operations, including items promised in the treaty such as aid for agriculture, equipment, and wages for white employees. By the terms of the original 1910 land surrender agreement the Siksika insisted that everyone receive annual cash payments, rations, and extra assistance for the elderly from the interest payments on invested capital, a reasonable reaction to years of poverty. As the Depression continued and interest rates fell, so too did their annual income. Agent Gooderham worried that they might cut funding for the DIA operations: "The minute the Interest Rate is reduced and the income lowered to a point when the major services such as Medicalization Staff salaries, take so much of the income that the Indian cannot get that direct assistance or payment which he had been receiving, there will be a wild cry to get rid of hospitals, Doctor [sic], farming Instructors, Stockmen etc. This time may not be far distant."[23] Nevertheless, by 1940 the Council's annual expenditure was $115,000, which included $30,000 for medical care, $10,000 for equipment, $7,000 for livestock, $6,000 for maintenance, and $9,000 for wages for white employees; the remainder went for the mandated distribution of cash, food, and clothing. As was the DIA design in 1910, all expenses besides wages for the agent and his clerk and the five-dollar annuity promised in the 1877 treaty were paid from Siksika funds, which meant a considerable saving for the DIA.[24]

When, in 1942, the Central Alberta (Keith) Sanatorium warned that the beds occupied by Siksika patients would be required by the military, the DIA's assistant medical superintendent, Dr W.L. Falconer, urged the Blackfoot Hospital to treat more tuberculosis patients. The Siksika were uncooperative, according to the doctor, with their "'millionaire' complex ... [they] do not object to being admitted to Keith Sanatorium [but] they are more difficult to handle in their own hospital. They consider this hospital as their own." The Siksika needed to be disciplined to use their hospital properly, as Falconer put it; with "control and supervision ... persuasion and instruction" the Blackfoot Hospital could be made to treat more patients. Moreover, he disapproved of Dr Windsor's management and urged her to show "more enthusiasm" for the work by undertaking surgery on her patients. Ultimately, he advocated complete bureaucratic control of the hospital in order to impose compulsory hospitalization.[25] As it happened, veterans did not need the sanatorium beds due to thorough X-ray screening of recruits and the steady decline of tuberculosis generally. Nevertheless, the tendency to compulsion, while a long-standing DIA policy, gained new vigour after 1945, when IHS was incorporated into the Department of National Health and Welfare.

The Blackfoot Hospital came under IHS management while the Siksika continued to finance its operation and maintenance. Immediately, Dr E.L. Stone, now the IHS regional supervisor in Alberta, advised complete bureaucratic control of the Blackfoot Hospital; the Siksika trust fund should be relieved of all operational costs. As he explained to IHS director Moore, "If they contribute to annual operations they will naturally want to exercise about as much control as they now do."[26] Stone, like Falconer, considered the Siksika's continued medical pluralism a direct challenge to their authority. Likewise, further north at Hobbema, where local reserves wished to help finance a new hospital, Stone actively prevented it: "A money interest implies a share of control. It does not work well."[27] Meantime, reacting to minister of national health Brooke Claxton's 1946 statement that IHS would pursue a hospitalization program, Siksika Council announced that it would no longer fund the hospital operations. Council reasoned that since it was "tacitly accepted throughout the Dominion that hospitalization of Indians is a Government obligation ... the Department [should] pay all costs of operation of the Blackfoot Hospital as they are doing in every other Indian hospital."[28] Stone, of course, fully supported their decision, explaining that as long as the Siksika paid the expenses, the department would have little control over the people or the hospital. While director Moore considered the issue a matter of "high policy" to be decided at the ministerial level, he dismissed Stone's concerns, arguing that the Siksika should be made to pay for their own health care. He heartily endorsed state policy that Aboriginal people, unless absolutely indigent, should pay for their own medical care, agreeing with many of his contemporaries that medicine was most effective when paid for. Moore considered Stone's suggestion to finance the Blackfoot Hospital a "retrograde step." Instead, he urged the Indian agent to exert "some persuasion" on the Siksika Council to reverse their decision.[29]

The new minister of national health in 1947, Paul Martin, agreed with Moore that the Siksika should be forced to pay for medical care by the terms of their 1910 land surrender agreement. Moreover, he warned, if the Council continued to object he would have the Indian Act amended to override its wishes.[30] Moore meanwhile assured his minister that the Siksika were indeed millionaires with $1,147,304.40 in their capital fund. But Moore failed to also note that the seemingly impressive fund amounted to slightly more than $1,000 per person; moreover, it could only be used for capital expenses and to generate interest, which, at 5 per cent, netted $57,365 annually, with hospital expenses taking 60 per cent. Just days later Siksika Council reversed its position and authorized an expenditure of $35,000 (a 28 per cent increase over the previous year) for the Blackfoot Hospital for 1947–8.[31] It is not clear what prompted Council to reconsider, but the influence of both the minister of health and the minister responsible for Indian Affairs Branch was not inconsiderable. For Moore and minister Martin, their policy to make the Siksika pay was doubly virtuous: it would teach them to value medical care while relieving the beleaguered white taxpayers of the cost. But, as the 28 per cent increase in the Blackfoot Hospital accounts revealed, the costs of hospital care in Canada soared in the postwar period, prompting the federal government to embark on its National Health Grants program of generous aid for health care.

By 1946 the federal Liberal government had retreated from its expansive and expensive postwar promises of social security including universal health insurance.[32] Canadians nevertheless continued to demand and were willing to pay for modern hospital care though fewer and fewer could afford the postwar ballooning costs.[33] Instead, in 1948 Mackenzie King's government established annual matching federal grants to provinces, targeting, among other things, public health, tuberculosis control, mental health, and $13 million annually for hospital construction. Minister Paul Martin publicly announced each of the thousands of hospital project grants, prompting journalists to dub the program "milking Martin's millions."[34] National Health Grants funded Canada's hospitals to expand and modernize, aiding their efforts to attract the paying patient, while the burgeoning system of IHS Indian hospitals relieved them from treating Aboriginal patients. But the Blackfoot Hospital, not considered a normal hospital, was deemed ineligible for any grants. By 1954 the hospital seriously depleted the Siksika trust fund, prompting the new agent, J.E. Pugh, to plead with the IHS to relieve some costs, if only staff salaries.[35] But Moore refused: "I do not believe that it would be in the public interest to relieve the Blackfoot Band from the costs they are carrying in connection with the hospital and the doctor providing medical care to the Band at present. It is our objective to make more and more Bands who are in a position to meet all, or a share of, their medical costs, assume this responsibility."[36] Neither minister

Martin nor Moore acknowledged the stark irony that the wealthiest provincial hospitals received considerable support from public funds through the National Health Grants, yet the Siksika were made to bear all hospital costs. Moore, characteristically overbearing, demanded that the Siksika "millionaires" pay. An unsigned note in his own office questioned Moore's policy: "We are rather hard on the Blackfoot. No one else can support a hospital these days."[37]

By July 1954 Moore relented. He subsequently retreated to a familiar discourse that characterized Aboriginal people as diseased and careless about their own health, and posing a threat to the nation; they required the control and regulation that only IHS could provide. He declared that Siksika control of the hospital was not in the best interests of the "Indians, the hospital, or the staff employed." In particular, he objected to the Siksika's continued autonomy in presuming to dictate hospital policy that threatened medical authority: visiting hours were too lax, patients left hospital when they felt better, and young children and the elderly were admitted to hospital when their caregivers needed to travel. Moreover, he noted, the building was deteriorating because the Siksika could no longer afford to replace equipment and furnishings. He proposed that the IHS assume responsibility for all operating costs, while the Siksika would still pay $6 per day for adults admitted to the hospital and $1.50 for newborns.[38] Council accepted the offer for a fifteen-month trial beginning January 1955, but argued that maternity care should be free, as was the accepted practice in all Alberta hospitals.[39] Sharing hospital costs might also address Council's anxiety for patient safety in the deteriorating building. Fire, caused by bare wiring and overloaded fuse boxes, was a constant concern, while the already inadequate water supply and leaking pipes would be completely overwhelmed in the event of a fire. The building needed paint, and a ruptured sewer line contaminated the soil and rotted the floor.[40]

When the cost-sharing agreement expired in April 1956, Siksika Council again refused to vote any more funds for hospitalization, arguing that hospital costs had nearly depleted their trust fund. Council was unmoved by rumours that Moore would shut down the hospital unless they paid.[41] Moore then threatened that necessary hospital renovations, especially rewiring, would not proceed, and he ordered individual Siksika patients to pay in advance for their care or they would not be admitted to the hospital. "I feel the Blackfoot have long abused their privileges in this institution and that it might be best for all concerned if we could abandon it." Moore was determined to refuse treatment rather than fund the hospital even while DIA officials assured him that Siksika finances could no longer meet essential community needs such as housing, water supplies, and roads. In late 1957, Moore, at his most autocratic, demanded complete control of the hospital buildings and all equipment. As he put it, he would accept nothing less than "unconditional surrender" from the Siksika.[42]

The shift in position, from insisting the Siksika pay all hospital costs to demanding they cede complete control, reflected increasingly coercive IHS policies. As more institutions came under its control IHS stepped up compulsion through, among other things, the 1953 Indian Health Regulations. Marking Aboriginal bodies as particularly dangerous justified legalized state coercion. Facing the intransigence of a coercive bureaucracy intent on regulating and disciplining bodies "for their own good" and in the interests of national health, the Siksika saw their trust fund diminish. Not coincidentally, in 1957 at the same time as Moore demanded unconditional surrender, the national health benefited by the federal Hospital Insurance and Diagnostic Services Act, which provided non-Aboriginal Canadians free care in the hospital of their choice.

In May 1958 Siksika Chief Clarence McHugh and councillor Matthew Melting Tallow travelled to Ottawa to meet with IHS officials and request a complete refund of all money expended on medical care and staff salaries. They also wanted the DIA to refund their expenditures on wages, vehicles, and housing provided for agency employees, $6 million by their count.[43] Moore, flanked by the department solicitor and four bureaucrats representing Indian Affairs and IHS, made it clear that he would not spend one cent on renovations until the hospital was turned over to IHS; moreover, the Siksika would continue to pay for hospital care. The chief countered, suggesting they would rent their hospital to IHS for $400 a month, since it was government policy to build and maintain hospitals for Aboriginal people. Moore acknowledged that the hospital building was increasingly dilapidated and threatened that Siksika patients would soon be hospitalized elsewhere. Nevertheless, for the previous year, the thirty-seven-bed hospital had only half the necessary staff with an average occupancy of only fifteen patients.[44] The IHS continued to refuse more than minimal care in a rapidly decaying building, forcing Siksika patients into state-run Indian hospitals. Patients, like Siksika Elder Roy Little Chief, were sent to the Charles Camsell Indian Hospital in Edmonton. Still resentful and suspicious fifty years later, he recalled the pain and loneliness of a year of bed rest and then chest surgery, and the anger and heartbreak upon his return to be told that his father had died.[45] The Siksika trust fund, created by the surrender of precious territory and intended to temper the impact of colonization for future generations, was all but gone by the late 1950s. When a reporter, in a 1958 interview about the Siksika's dire economic situation, asked Chief McHugh why they did not just sell the hospital to the government, he replied with not a little irony, "I suggested this to them and they told me we should give it to them as a grant!"[46] The Blackfoot Hospital – where resistance to assimilation emerged in the people's medical pluralism, and ownership created space for culturally appropriate care – was a direct challenge to medical authority. As a community the Siksika paid dearly for that autonomy as their trust fund dwindled and their health care deteriorated. But by the time of his retirement seven years later in 1965, Moore had yet to receive their "unconditional surrender."

In the meantime, in the late 1950s Moore was busy planning to rebuild the aging Charles Camsell Indian Hospital farther north in Edmonton. The hospital represented the best the IHS had to offer. With its close affiliation with the University of Alberta medical school's consulting faculty, its accreditation for postgraduate training that supplied much of its medical staff, and its urban location, it was quite unlike other Indian hospitals. It was the base for the IHS northern service in the western Arctic that sent often very enthusiastic physicians and nurses to northern nursing stations to remove patients to the hospital. Accounts of intrepid staff and pilots rescuing grateful "Eskimos" were a regular feature in the *Edmonton Journal*.[47] The Camsell Hospital was the public face of its bold humanitarian efforts, as well as the heart of the IHS system where medical bureaucrats got their training.[48] The hospital's senior nursing and administrative staff were remarkably loyal, most having worked at the hospital since it opened. Its on-campus residences for married and single employees created a healthy esprit de corps among non-Aboriginal staff that was maintained through regular rounds of parties and social activities. As one nurse recalled, "What impressed us the most at the Camsell was the friendly, 'happy family' atmosphere. Everyone, no matter what position, got along with everyone else."[49] In short, for IHS bureaucrats and staff, the Charles Camsell Indian Hospital was a source of both personal and professional pride. But physically, the institution showed its age. An ad hoc maze of wooden buildings connected by covered walkways, linked to a sagging fifty-year-old brick building, the hospital's dilapidated buildings caused great concern, not least for the Canadian Council on Hospital Accreditation. In

1957 the hospital received a three-year accreditation but was warned
that it would not again receive accreditation (and access to trained
postgraduate staff) unless it undertook radical renovations or rebuilt
the hospital.[50] The hospital's tight-knit cadre of professional staff and
IHS bureaucrats worked tirelessly to plan the new modern six-storey
facility in which to continue their work.

But before construction of the new hospital could begin, the Diefenbaker Conservative government announced severe spending freezes
and in September 1960 established a royal commission to rationalize its
growing bureaucracy along a private-sector model in order to control
government spending. Chaired by accountant and business executive
Grant Glassco, the commission tabled its five voluminous reports in
1962. Its brief examination of the Indian Health Service, written by a
group led by Dr John McCreary, dean of University of British Columbia's faculty of medicine, was highly critical of the Camsell Hospital
facilities and staff.[51] It began by stating that the "extent and nature of the
responsibility of the federal government to provide free health services
for Indians in populated areas of the country is not clearly defined."
It recommended scrapping entirely the planned $7 million Camsell
Hospital construction project. Noting that tuberculosis patients con-
stituted two-thirds of the patients in the Camsell Hospital, the commission recommended they be treated in empty provincial sanatorium
beds, while the remaining 120 patients could be accommodated in local
Edmonton hospitals. In general, the commission endorsed the larger
program of integration actively pursued by the government. It therefore recommended the rapid transfer of Indian health care to "normal
community facilities"; medical and dental care should be provided by
privately practising physicians and dentists with the federal government covering prepaid medical plans where necessary.[52] The Glassco
Commission's decision that a new Camsell Hospital was neither necessary nor desirable caused the bureaucracy to mount a vigorous defence
of its plans, while the other recommendations aroused considerably
less comment.

Before the commission's findings were made public, a draft report
was forwarded to National Health and Welfare for comment. In mar-
shaling arguments in defence of a rebuilt hospital, IHS director Moore
provided the Treasury Board and his deputy minister, G.D.W. Cameron,
with a list of "points to stress." It is hardly surprising that Moore would
vigorously defend the institution that he viewed as his crowning professional achievement. He stressed the Camsell Hospital's efficient

and economical operation, its importance as a base for its northern programs, and its role in medical education, with its "excellent teaching material," and as a training ground for new recruits, including a two-month appraisal program for "Indian girls" hoping to enrol in the provincial nurse's aide school.[53] Essentially, the Charles Camsell Indian Hospital was good for the IHS. Moore went on to argue that Aboriginal patients could not be treated successfully in provincial institutions such as the Aberhart Sanatorium in Edmonton. Geared to the "total needs of the patient," tuberculosis treatment at the Camsell Hospital recognized differences in social custom and language in a way that community institutions could not. Moreover, he argued, the "freedom and liberties provided [Aberhart] patients would be the ruin of a [IHS] treatment regime."[54] Moore refused to even consider admitting tuberculosis patients to the older Baker Sanatorium near Calgary because the buildings were in a worse state than the Camsell Hospital. He noted that, though there was a time when public opinion would tolerate care in ramshackle buildings, "that era is gone and conditions cannot excuse congregating Indians in a second-rate facility." It was also noted that Aboriginal people might also object to the hospital's closing, a "distinct shock ... and a thoroughly unpopular move." Though Moore did not mention that most patients had no choice of hospital, he claimed that many Aboriginal people "have shown a marked propensity for admission to this hospital. It enjoys a most favourable reputation despite a more disciplined regime than is imposed on natives in many other institutions."[55] As for the director's recent pronouncement that IHS wanted to "get out of the hospital business," Moore claimed that the policy "derived from my own personal conviction." As he continued, "There is ample evidence that we are pursuing it vigorously on many fronts and to an extent perhaps not generally known. I hope this will not now be pushed down our throats and our long-term objective thereby sacrificed or imperiled by what might seem expediency at the moment."[56] In other words, Moore wanted a new hospital at Edmonton while being free to close hospitals elsewhere. Nevertheless, while many of the rationales for rebuilding the Camsell Hospital served bureaucratic and professional needs, they also touched on the very arguments that Aboriginal leaders were urging on IHS to maintain hospitals close to their communities – without success. Though hardly sharing Moore's insistence on the need for rigid discipline, Aboriginal leaders did agree on the need for hospitals with Aboriginal employees who could mediate between medical staff and elders and children who did not speak

English. They also wanted their hospitals to stay open because of the continued discrimination Aboriginal patients faced in provincial institutions, and, Aboriginal communities argued, funds that were intended for their health care should be used to improve existing hospitals rather than being invested in non-Aboriginal institutions. Of course, they also argued that Indian hospitals represented the state's acknowledgment of their treaty right to health care, a position that would be emphatically denied by the government.

Whatever else the Glassco Commission meant for government organization, it had little impact on IHS operations; the defeat of the Conservative government in early 1963 allowed the Department of National Health and Welfare to ignore its recommendations. By December the minority Liberal government approved plans to replace the Charles Camsell Hospital (notably dropping "Indian" from the name), citing the ongoing need for a hospital to serve the Arctic and the provincial north, while blaming the Alberta government for rejecting further hospital integration.[57] Director Moore officiated at the formal sod-turning ceremony in October 1964, declaring it "one of the happiest days of my life."[58] The new Charles Camsell Hospital opened in 1967, dubbed a "centennial gift from southern Canada to our northern people."[59] At the official opening, Minister of Health Allan MacEachen's address praised the doctors and nurses for their "love of humanity ... courage, curiosity and spirit of adventure." The new hospital marked a milestone for his department, he noted, and "indicates the ever expanding services" provided for the north and the Indians of Alberta.[60] Of course, services were contracting, not expanding, as IHS actively worked to close other hospitals.[61]

While IHS bureaucrats defended their decision to rebuild the Camsell Hospital, they were continuing their efforts to quietly close the other Alberta institutions – the Blackfoot, Blood, and Hobbema Indian hospitals. Unlike the Charles Camsell, these were all small hospitals situated on reserves, and without influential supporters. Apparently aiding IHS efforts was Alberta's hospital insurance scheme, which refused to include the small, inefficient Indian hospitals in their plan, insisting that patients be directed to community hospitals. Provincial health minister Dr J. Donovan Ross, at least publicly, assured federal officials that his government was committed to integrating community hospitals by accepting Aboriginal Albertans. In June 1961 the Bassano Municipal Hospital complained to the minister that it was unfair that it should be required to treat Blackfoot patients once their hospital closed.

Dr Ross advised the hospital that such attitudes were contrary to the larger "desegregation" policy. The federal government would contribute financially to hospital expansion, but the province would not approve separate wings for Indian patients. In July he informed the forty-bed Cardston Municipal Hospital that it should prepare to accept patients once the thirty-nine-bed Blood Hospital (that sat across the street) closed. Further, he advised the Cardston Hospital that he approved plans to develop a basement ward, but that it must render "service to Indians on the same basis as other residents without attempting to designate certain areas of the hospital for use by the Indians."[62] However, despite forwarding these letters to IHS to demonstrate his commitment to integration, privately Ross informed IHS assistant director Dr Harry Proctor that "integration" was a poor term and unattainable in the foreseeable future, preferring the term "simultaneous development in association." Even with its planned basement ward expansion Cardston Municipal Hospital remained too small to accommodate patients from the Blood reserve. In any case it remained adamant about not accepting Aboriginal patients. Ross announced he was "not anxious or in a position to force them." Proctor informed his director Moore that Alberta would insist that all hospital construction costs be met by the federal government: "Dr. Ross has a very strong opinion of what the federal govt [sic] should pay for its *past* neglect of Indians."[63]

Alberta, increasingly at odds with the federal government over the national hospital insurance program's imposed conditions and annual audit, resented federal intrusions on provincial autonomy.[64] Therefore, health minister Ross did not look kindly on any IHS initiatives that required provincial cooperation. At the same time he was determined to control how hospitals in the province were used. When, in 1961, the city of Wetaskiwin in west-central Alberta proceeded to build a new sixty-bed hospital, provincial health officials suggested that a new federally funded "Indian wing" for patients from the Hobbema reserves might be added to the hospital. They wondered if the federal intention was to absorb the "Indian patients into the general services of a hospital" or if there would be a separate wing, which was the local wish.[65] The new hospital project was expanded to ninety beds to accommodate the two thousand people of the nearby Hobbema reserves.[66] According to IHS officials, the people of Wetaskiwin were not happy to "provide for Indians but have been prevailed upon." A handwritten note on the file added "And How!"[67] Ross issued a press release to announce a third-floor addition to the Wetaskiwin Municipal Hospital to include patients from the soon-to-be-shuttered Hobbema Indian Hospital, frustrating IHS plans for a "quiet" closing.[68] IHS bureaucrats understood that their integration policy would require negotiations with provincial and municipal officials, but they refused to acknowledge that Aboriginal communities had any interest or, indeed, should be allowed any input in negotiations. The Hobbema communities were therefore shocked to hear that their hospital that had opened only ten years earlier was to be closed.

The Treaty Six communities at Hobbema had advocated for a hospital in the late 1940s. While their leadership welcomed and supported tuberculosis treatment at the Charles Camsell Hospital in Edmonton, ninety kilometres to the north, there was a very real need for more accessible maternity and paediatric care for the then more than 1,500 residents. The local Wetaskiwin hospital twenty kilometres away admitted some Aboriginal patients, but as regional superintendent Dr E.L .Stone put it, the hospital situation was urgent: "Indian heads are sticking out of both ends of the cribs at the Wetaskiwin hospital."[69] When the Hobbema leadership offered to help finance a new hospital from their capital account, Stone actively discouraged them, fearing that, as at the Blackfoot Hospital, a financial interest might imply a voice in the hospital's management.[70] On the eve of its opening in early 1951, Stone, having in mind the Blackfoot Hospital's challenge to IHS authority, set out the conditions and rules by which the people could access the new twenty-three-bed Hobbema Indian Hospital. He began by noting that the hospital was the property of National Health and Welfare and that no band funds were used for the construction or operation. Only the doctor or, in his absence, the charge nurse could admit or discharge patients. There would be no ambulance and the people would be expected to bring their sick to the hospital and take them home. Visiting hours would be strictly enforced. Local people would be employed "for any work which they can do well," as ward aides or janitorial help. And finally, "No sick Indian will be required to pay for his care in the hospital unless his sickness or accident is the result of drinking alcoholic liquor."[71]

Nevertheless, five years later, in July 1956 (and two years before national hospital insurance), IHS approached the Hobbema area leadership to announce that according to new policies, they were to "stand on their own feet and to become independent in matters relating to medical and hospital costs."[72] Though regional bureaucrat Dr T.J. Orford explained that it was a general policy change and not directed at Hobbema specifically, it was clear that their oil and gas income attracted IHS attention. They were now to pay $6.00 per patient day at Hobbema, Charles Camsell, or any other hospital and $1.50 per day for newborns for ten days and $6.00 per day thereafter. Accordingly, the area chiefs were presented with the Hobbema Hospital accounts for April and May: $2,443.50 and $2,137.50 respectively. At the same time, Indian Affairs and IHS worked to interest Blue Cross in providing hospitalization insurance with the premiums automatically deducted from the reserves' oil revenues.[73] Two months later the chiefs rejected the IHS ultimatum, refusing the principle of payment for hospital or private insurance costs. Citing Treaty Six, the chiefs argued that they had surrendered all their lands for $5.00 per year and other treaty promises including medical care; their hospital was the belated fulfilment of that promise. They were especially disturbed at not being consulted or given a voice in the policy changes. Despite increased income in recent years, the standard of living remained far from adequate and their funds were required for housing and other essentials. The chiefs explained that they already contributed plenty since the hospital and all houses occupied by Indian Affairs and IHS employees were built on reserve lands and given free rental by Council. Moreover, the treaty promised one quarter section (160 acres or 65 hectares) of land for each family of five, but with an increasing population there was not enough land available and no way to access more. The chiefs saw clearly that the IHS demands were the thin edge of the wedge towards making them pay taxes, removing all their treaty rights, and "integrating" them into the general population. Dismissing their concerns, Orford viewed their treaty right argument as a "lack of desire to understand plus the ingrained acceptance of everything for nothing – the perpetual welfare attitude."[74]

So, in early 1962 local IHS officials finally met with the Hobbema leadership to announce that their hospital would become an outpatient clinic, and they would be hospitalized at Wetaskiwin. Bureaucrats explained that the change would mean improved medical services. The Cree chiefs wondered how people would get to Wetaskiwin for treatment since few owned cars and IHS would not provide transportation. They also wanted to know if any hospital staff could speak Cree since many of the elderly could not speak English. They were met with vague promises that the matter would be considered. Perhaps to make their point, Chief Sam Curry of the Montana Band and Chief Jim Bull of the Louis Bull Band spoke in Cree to IHS officials. The chiefs argued that the Hobbema Hospital represented the treaty right to health care, and that IHS had no authority to break the treaty: "When the Queen and the Indian Chiefs signed treaty, it was understood that hospital and medicines would be given and there would be freedom from taxes." IHS bureaucrats replied that they were just following orders from their superiors in government.[75] The Wetaskiwin Hospital Board, in receipt of a letter from the Indian Association of Alberta, fully supported a resolution protesting conversion of the Hobbema Hospital to an outpatient clinic. Local newspapers reported the board's resolution that "the Indians should use every effort to maintain their present hospital ... and the new Wetaskiwin hospital will be filled as soon as it is opened."[76] When Harry Moore, local Conservative member of Parliament, also protested his own government's plans to close Hobbema and integrate the community hospital, minister of health Monteith explained that it was a common misconception that Indians were entitled to any special benefits. "The other point sometimes raised by Indians is the mention in Treaty Six, one of the 12 treaties [sic] ... of the provision of a 'medical chest' [sic] at the home of the agent." Though the provision of simple medicines has been "scrupulously observed," the minister informed his backbencher that Parliament only acknowledged a moral obligation to assist Indians until they could be integrated into the community.[77] The deliberate plan to exclude the most affected Aboriginal communities from any negotiations – to "quietly" close Indian hospitals – stemmed from the state's contention that health care was a humanitarian, not statutory, commitment. IHS alone would determine the Aboriginal people's best interests while dismissing any claims to a treaty right to care.

While provincial and federal bureaucrats insisted that hospitalization at Wetaskiwin and the conversion of the Hobbema Hospital to a clinic would improve health care, the reality was far different. In early 1963 the Hobbema chiefs and councillors met with the provincial minister of health Dr Donovan Ross to plead for their hospital to be reopened. Many people had no means to travel twenty kilometres to Wetaskiwin, or ninety kilometres to Charles Camsell Hospital in Edmonton. In any case, the reserves only had wagon roads, all but impassable in winter. The people were required to first see an IHS physician at Hobbema before referral to the community hospital, which was a particular hardship for the seriously ill and maternity patients. People felt considerable discrimination in the Wetaskiwin Hospital. As the chiefs put it, "White people in Wetaskiwin feel that they are being displaced by the

Indians due to the tight bed situation in their hospital and therefore feel resentful towards the Indians."[78] Ross lectured the chiefs that though integration would take many years, the Indians should become more self-sufficient. He told the delegation that his department would not approve the Hobbema Hospital under the hospital insurance plan. If it were reopened Ottawa would need to pay the full costs. Community hospitals "with their excellent facilities and larger medical staffs, were to the advantage of the Indians." He said he looked forward to the day "when Indians in this Province would consider themselves as Albertans."[79]

But the now more than 2,500 Hobbema-area people were left with singularly poor care. The Hobbema clinic was without a physician after April 1963, yet IHS, always reluctant to pay non-departmental physicians on a fee-for-service basis, left it to clinic nurses to provide treatment or refer patients to community hospitals. At the same time, the staff was "quietly cut down" to four nurses, but only two worked full time. Rather than pay for prescriptions in town, IHS required non-departmental physicians to send them to Hobbema to be filled. Patients then had to travel back to Hobbema to collect their medications, but with minimal staff and restricted hours at the clinic, as well as an average of 600 patient visits per month, they were made to wait for care. Recommended renovations to the clinic included more than $2,000 for the installation of more benches![80] In an understatement, IHS director Moore remarked: "The Indians are up in arms about this and much resistance is being encountered in getting our patients admitted to the general hospital at Wetaskiwin."[81]

Jurisdictional disputes over cost sharing and administrative control that accompanied provincial insurance programs highlighted the increasing vulnerability of Aboriginal people as the policy of integration played out. In Alberta, ideological differences between the premier Ernest Manning and the Liberal government in Ottawa over national health insurance did nothing to improve health care for Aboriginal residents. By 1963 the province established its own health care insurance plan, the Alberta Medical Plan. Fully endorsed by the Canadian Medical Association and health insurance companies, it required residents to pay health care premiums and offered government subsidies for those who were too sick or too poor to purchase private insurance. Intended to influence the sitting Royal Commission on Health Services (Hall Commission 1961–4) with an alternative to the 1962 Saskatchewan health insurance model that was funded through taxation, "Manningcare" as journalists dubbed it, rejected what health minister Donovan Ross called Saskatchewan's "socialistic type of program."[82] But more than half of those who were eligible for subsidies under the Alberta plan were not protected because they could not afford to pay the high premiums ($140 per family, $69 for individuals).[83] Likewise, under the tax-funded Saskatchewan plan things were little better. Aboriginal people were excluded because the province deemed they were not taxpayers.[84] When IHS offered to pay the modest medical insurance plan premiums ($24 per family, $12 for individuals) on their behalf, Saskatchewan countered that it would pay all the bills for their care, with the federal government refunding the total costs involved, ignoring the fact that Aboriginal people paid provincial taxes.[85] In British Columbia, the province included Indian hospitals in its 1949 insurance plan but by 1960 insisted that its plan would only pay for hospitalization in federal hospitals after denial of treatment in a provincial hospital. So, for example, Aboriginal patients were forced to provide proof of denial of treatment at Prince Rupert Public Hospital before they could be admitted to Miller Bay Indian Hospital. Again, when British Columbia established its health insurance plan, Aboriginal people were excluded on the basis that the federal government was responsible for their care.[86] The policy of integration and the quiet closing of hospitals, measures intended to shift hospitalization and its costs to provincial plans, ran up against considerable opposition, not least from Aboriginal people, who found their health care compromised by jurisdictional squabbles.

With the provincial health insurance plans denying access to Aboriginal people, IHS continued its long-standing policy of contracting with particular local physicians, or physician groups, to provide care for all Aboriginal patients. Intended to keep costs predictable, and to direct patients to particular hospitals, the practice also compromised care. Aboriginal patients could expect not only long waits until the physician treated the full-fee patients, but also hurried consultations. As George Manuel recalled, "If you sat in most doctor's waiting rooms … you did not need to look at the patient's faces to see who were the Indians. You just had to time the length of each patient's visit in the examining room. Half a fee, half a visit."[87] It was a practice also widely resented by the medical community, with the Alberta Medical Association condemning the prorated fee schedule as "penalizing" physicians who were unfortunate enough to practise near reserves.[88] Moreover, as physicians and provincial governments maintained, the federal government's responsibility for the abysmal housing conditions, lack of rudimentary sanitation, and widespread poverty on reserves in turn created a federal responsibility for much of the ill health that was the consequence. The attempted integration of health services under the various western provincial plans left Aboriginal people as pawns in the negotiations between jurisdictions, but they fared worse under national health insurance or "medicare."[89]

In Alberta, Premier Manning's overheated rhetoric only increased when the Pearson government announced in 1965 its decision to fashion its medical care plan after the Saskatchewan model.[90] Manning derided the comprehensive and universal features of the national program as state compulsion that violated the fundamental right of every citizen to exercise freedom of choice; a state-run monopoly on health insurance violated the principles of a free enterprise society.[91] Indeed, so ideologically opposed was he to the federal plan, health minister Donovan Ross resigned the position he held for twelve years after Alberta decided to participate.[92] Needless to say, as federal bureaucrats working in Alberta, IHS officials did not expect a lot of cooperation with their provincial counterparts, nor did they offer much. Aboriginal people generally, and the Hobbema Cree specifically, bore the brunt of this tension. While the provinces, municipalities, and Aboriginal people themselves viewed their hospital care as a federal responsibility, IHS insisted that all health care was a provincial responsibility. When the Wetaskiwin Hospital became crowded in the mid-1960s citizens resented Hobbema residents taking up beds they considered rightfully theirs. A 1966 petition from the Alberta Local Council of Women requested that the Hobbema Hospital be reopened because the community hospital was overcrowded: "Often a bed is unavailable because of the large number of patients from the Hobbema reservation. We feel that this matter requires urgent attention."[93] After a further expansion in the late 1960s the Wetaskiwin Hospital fell into serious deficit, which the Hospital Board blamed on Hobbema residents, who accounted for about 30 per cent of admissions. Why should local taxpayers be expected to fund a federal responsibility? they asked. Appeals by the board to both levels of government were met with denials of responsibility.

IHS argued that the Wetaskiwin Hospital was a creation of the Alberta Hospital Commission and if it wanted to receive a federal contribution beyond what was already paid under the Hospital Insurance and Diagnostic Services Act then the province had to pay the "so-called deficit" and recover half of it under the terms of the Act.[94] But the per diem rate the province's hospital commission paid the hospital was so low that it continued to incur operating deficits of $75,000 per year.[95] The Hospital Board declared that its only alternative was to refuse service to Hobbema residents. The dispute only soured relations between the two communities, with the Hobbema residents cast as intruders and a burden on local ratepayers. Locally the hospital and the chiefs attempted to ease tensions by appointing a Hobbema representative to the Hospital Board, albeit in an "advisory" or non-voting position, but the province rejected the proposal since it interfered in what it claimed was an exclusively federal jurisdiction.[96] The national minister of health, John Munro, explained to the Hospital Board that he could not interfere. His department, he argued, already shared with the province half of hospital costs for all residents – including Aboriginal people. Moreover, he explained, IHS paid the Alberta hospital insurance premiums on behalf of most Aboriginal people as well as the hospitalization plan's deterrent fees ($5 for the first day and $2.50 thereafter). In reply to a request for financial help from Chief Simon Threefingers of the Louis Bull Band at Hobbema, Munro noted that he could do nothing since deficits were a problem between the hospital and provincial authorities, saying, "this is a matter in which unilateral federal action would be most inappropriate."[97] As Canada achieved its long-awaited program of universal health care, the Hobbema Cree found themselves without their own hospital and increasingly resented as a financial burden on their neighbours. One can imagine that the ever more strained relationship in town caused Hobbema patients to think twice about travelling to Wetaskiwin only to be turned away. What kind of reception might children and elders expect? The local impact of hospital integration was largely damaging to those in most need of care, and caught between jurisdictions, the Hobbema Cree had no voice in the negotiations. What they understood to be a treaty right to health care was sacrificed to the imperatives of health insurance plans that entitled other Canadians greater access to care but left them begging. The sad irony of the Wetaskiwin situation was not lost on other communities that still had hospitals, particularly the Siksika and the Kainai in Alberta. It served as a vivid demonstration of what to expect if their care passed into municipal and provincial hands.

The Siksika refused to surrender their Blackfoot Hospital as director Moore had demanded in 1957, but as a result the building was allowed to continue to deteriorate. By the mid-1960s the hospital had been "obsolete for many years." Its fourteen beds, maternity, pediatrics, and medicine, were all on the same floor since there were not enough nurses to cover two floors. As a result, it could not accept adult men, who were sent to other hospitals for treatment. Physicians from a group medical practice at Bassano visited once or twice a week, an arrangement IHS officials agreed was unsatisfactory.[98] Further south at the Blood Indian Hospital, IHS bureaucrats agreed "nothing could make it into a good hospital." Though there was medical attendance available locally, physicians only reluctantly treated patients in the aging hospital.[99] Alberta's hospital commission refused to insure the small Indian hospitals, forcing IHS to continue funding operations, though it did so by restricting admissions. At the same time, as was made glaringly obvious at Wetaskiwin, municipal taxpayers were responsible for any hospital deficits. Unless Indian reserve lands were included (and taxed) as part of the municipal district, community hospital boards were not inclined to open their doors to reserve residents without firm assurances of support from the federal government. Other integration policies such as education, where Indian Affairs devolved its responsibility to the provinces through cost-sharing in lieu of property taxes on reserve lands, were effective with nearly 60 per cent of Aboriginal children attending provincial schools by 1969.[100] IHS likewise had a long-standing practice to make special grants to community hospital construction or expansion costs in proportion to the local Aboriginal population to be served, but under provincial hospital insurance plans, IHS refused to recognize any responsibility for operating deficits regardless of the cause.[101] Neither the community hospital at Bassano, near the Siksika reserve, nor the community hospital at Cardston had any plans to expand their institutions to accommodate reserve residents. As bureaucrats noted, there was "a certain amount of racial discrimination in Cardston against the Indians and 'incidents' occur from time to time in this connection."[102] By the same token, the Siksika and the Kainai viewed with growing suspicion federal plans to shut their hospitals, though the reality was such that care was deteriorating as quickly as the buildings themselves.

In early 1968, on the eve of Medicare, IHS announced its "Health Plan for Indians." An effort by National Health and Welfare to cut budgets in anticipation of the costly national health insurance to begin in mid-1968, it was couched in the same language of "equality" and "non-discrimination" for Aboriginal people that would inform the disastrous White Paper on Indian Policy the next year. Like the White Paper, it was a move to force Aboriginal people to receive services from provincial agencies, but unlike the White Paper, the Health Plan did not bother with even the pretence of consultation with Aboriginal communities. Letters were simply sent to band councils announcing that IHS would no longer subsidize their health care. It was a mean-spirited and draconian measure that required individuals to provide evidence to hospitals, doctors, druggists, transportation companies, and IHS that they were indigent and that they had applied and been refused assistance from their band funds. They had to prove that they could not obtain assistance from the provincial health or welfare departments, and only then would IHS provide assistance for any or part of their costs. IHS contemplated that a "health assistance card" as proof of indigency might ease the plan's administration but advised that "there should be nothing on the card to indicate Medical Service's Branch [IHS] responsibility, either directly or indirectly, now or in the future."[103] As provinces adopted Medicare plans Aboriginal people would be responsible for payment of all premiums and co-insurance charges, and if indigent they would need to apply to the province for assistance. Only after provincial assistance was denied would IHS "consider" making the payments, and only with proof of indigency. But access to all health services was also limited under the Health Plan, with IHS staff, dentists, and medical officers ordered to "give priority to diagnostic and preventive care." Where IHS did provide health care services or medications, patients were to be charged in the absence of proof of indigency. Admissions to hospitals were to be "controlled to prevent over-utilization" and outpatient care emphasized. Active case finding for mental illness would cease, and IHS would not be responsible for any hospitalization accounts. Limits were placed on all physicians', dentists', and optometrists' accounts, and available funds would be distributed on a proportionate basis. Health professionals were warned that current rates would not increase and would likely decrease. Dental care, glasses, and prosthetics would only be provided with proof of indigency, and IHS dental officers were only to provide "preventive dental care" for schoolchildren. Only "necessary" personal health care costs were to be paid by IHS and only with proof of indigency, though IHS would determine "necessity." Indian Affairs undertook a survey of all reserves to create an "indigent list," and band councils were told to determine who was eligible for care and who was not. Aboriginal people would become equal to other provincial citizens through a policy that severely limited access to medical services for all and in effect required the ill to exhaust all their resources before they would be helped, the very situation that Medicare presumably sought to remedy for other Canadians.

Not surprisingly, the Health Plan was met with considerable alarm in Aboriginal communities, and, coming in an election year, it received some comment in the press. In April 1968 IHS regional director O.J. Rath addressed the Alberta Chiefs' Conference with a brief statement explaining that there was really no change in policy after all. He quoted health minister Allan MacEachen's statement in the House of Commons that "Indians and Eskimos will receive the same consideration and treatment by this Department with regard to health as they received last year."[104] This was disingenuous, if not duplicitous, and referred to past unenforced IHS policy (more of a desideratum, in fact) that required payment for services by those who had the means, and by those who had not lived on their reserve for twelve months. Only the indigent were eligible for IHS medical services. It was not enforced because it was unenforceable without a means test, while the very aggressive protocols of the 1940s and 1950s, in the interests of protecting the national health, meant that IHS physicians, not patients, made decisions about hospitalization and treatment. As a result, it came as a distinct surprise to physicians, provincial officials, and Aboriginal people to learn that such a policy existed. Dr Rath reiterated the minister's claim that nothing had changed, and the only problem was a lack of communication of the true policy. He then told the increasingly hostile Chiefs' Conference that IHS wanted them to become involved in the "administration of health care programs"; essentially, band councils would be asked to decide which of their friends and relatives earned enough to pay for care so that assistance "may be directed to those of your people in greatest need." On larger policy direction, Rath quoted the minister directly:

I believe it ought to be borne in mind that Indians are residents of the provinces. One of the objectives for progress of the Indian population is certainly to integrate them within the general population of a province. If they are to be regarded as separate citizens to be treated on a different basis in respect of education, health and welfare then the process of integration within the total community will be impeded and will never become equal citizens as we all want them to be.[105]

One had only to look to the experience of the Hobbema Cree to see how integration as "equal citizens" played itself out.

Cast in the language of equality and freedom, and part of the new Liberal Party leader Pierre Trudeau's broader liberal ideology that focused on political rights of the individual, the Health Plan would dispense with "special status" such as the treaty right to care.[106] The *Calgary Herald* reported that Dr Rath had a "rough afternoon" explaining the policy to an angry crowd. "Even when their protests came in Cree," the *Herald* reported, "the tones of bitterness and sense of betrayal needed no translation."[107] The chiefs wondered how this "middle-man" could simply announce their treaty rights no longer existed. Provincial governments were also alarmed. Alberta claimed that the plan to "slough off its responsibilities for the health care of Indians" made a mockery of the Constitution and the treaty agreements.[108] By the fall and with the election over, the new health minister John Munro repeated his predecessor's insincere claim that policies had not changed. Furthermore, he argued that IHS assistance for registered Indians who were living on reserves and were medically indigent was actually unfair: "While it appears to discriminate in their favour, it may not be to their ultimate advantage since it tends to differentiate Indians from other Canadians. Our hope is that Indians will become integrated in the main stream of Canadian life."[109] Nevertheless, bureaucrats continued to insist that limited medical assistance was provided because the people were poor, not because of any treaty right. Resistance to that claim emerged immediately.

Harold Cardinal, the youthful president of the Indian Association of Alberta, charged that the department's Health Plan was a clear abrogation of treaty rights. He advised that to pay health care premiums would be to lose the treaty right to health care; that once their care passed to provincial jurisdiction they would lose any claims to federal responsibility; and that to lose one treaty right would jeopardize them all.[110] In reply to Cardinal's concerns over the treaty right to health care, minister of health Munro informed him that Indian Affairs, not Health and Welfare, dealt with treaty rights. Moreover, he claimed that the provision of health care in the past, as in the present, was based solely on need, and stated: "Our efforts have never been related in any way to Indian treaties."[111] The following month, the government outlined its intentions and the logical conclusion to its integration policy in the *Statement of the Government of Canada on Indian Policy 1969*, or the "White Paper": to terminate completely the treaty relationship, dismantle the bureaucracy, repeal the Indian Act, and replace it with "Indian control" of reserve land that would eventually open them to provincial taxation. There can be little doubt that the Health Plan was developed to ease the process and prepare the ground for the White Paper. Aboriginal groups across the country responded with a clear rejection of the badly flawed policy that had been developed without consultation with the affected groups, articulating a defence of treaty and Aboriginal rights and demands for greater economic and educational development. The Alberta chiefs' response, its "Red Paper," or *Citizens Plus*, took its name from a phrase coined in the *Hawthorn Report* (1966), a survey of the conditions of Indians in Canada commissioned by the Indian Affairs branch itself. It recommended special status for Indian people as "citizens plus": "Indians can and should retain the special privileges of their status while enjoying full participation as provincial and federal citizens."[112] As *Citizens Plus* put it, the benefits outlined in treaty promises were not "handouts" as the White Paper implied, but the fair exchange for settler access to the Aboriginal peoples' lands and resources. One of those rights was health care: "the provision of health services to the Indian people on the reserve or off the reserve at the expense of the Federal government anywhere in Canada."[113] The widespread denunciation of the White Paper, supported by the press, led to its withdrawal by early 1971. But the White Paper's legacy, aside from being the impetus for regional groups to organize into a national Aboriginal voice, was the deepening distrust of government and a lingering suspicion that termination remained a "hidden agenda" in policy making.[114]

It was in this climate of cynicism arising from the Health Plan for Indians and the White Paper that greeted the continuing efforts to shut down southern Alberta Indian hospitals. Moreover, the Siksika and Kainai, closely watching the ongoing difficulties experienced by the Hobbema Cree, were increasingly wary of any further federal initiatives towards hospital integration. The White Paper may have been withdrawn, but the Health Plan remained the basis for National Health and Welfare's policy decisions. The Indian Association of Alberta advised its membership that they should present their treaty cards not Medicare numbers when receiving medical services, while IHS agreed to pay their premiums on a temporary basis.[115] Nevertheless, by 1972 IHS continued to insist that regardless of the legal responsibilities that Indian Affairs might have for education or social welfare, there was no legal responsibility for health services. The only guideline that IHS recognized was "those Indians who can pay for the health services, do pay."[116] As for reserve hospitals, IHS continued to negotiate with the provincial government for their closure, yet band councils saw their hospitals as the (now crumbling) bricks and mortar acknowledgment

of their treaty right to health care. If there were funds for hospital construction, they argued, then it ought to be put towards improved Indian
hospitals.[117]

Nevertheless, both the Blood and Blackfoot hospitals were closed by
degrees. At the Blood Indian Hospital, serving nearly five thousand
residents, IHS reduced the number of adult beds and limited the allo-
cation of beds to physicians so that most adult patients were admitted
elsewhere. The beds per room were gradually reduced and physically
removed from the building so they could not be pressed into service.[118]
The Siksika and the Kainai could keep their hospitals, but they certainly
would not be good hospitals. Protracted and circular negotiations in an
increasingly poisoned atmosphere continued throughout the decade.
For example, the Blackfoot band council refused to sign any agreement
to shut their hospital and open a health centre until the federal government agreed that this would not diminish their treaty rights, and
until the Bassano Hospital began construction of an expansion to serve
the Siksika; the provincial hospital commission refused to approve
an expansion of the community hospital at Bassano to accommodate
Blackfoot patients until IHS closed the Blackfoot Hospital; IHS maintained that treaty rights were an issue for Indian Affairs, not Health and
Welfare.[119] At the local level, the impasse did nothing to improve relations between reserve and town. According to federal officials attending a Blood Band Council meeting to discuss the closure, "One of the
main reasons the people of the Blood Band do not want to close the Blood
Indian Hospital is the fact that they are afraid they will not get adequate services at the Cardston Municipal Hospital in view of the 'discrimination' against the Indian people by the people of Cardston."[120]
Finally, with written assurance that treaty rights would not be affected,
the aging hospitals were replaced by band-managed, but federally
financed, reserve health centres, or outpatient clinics, though the Blood
Indian Hospital, designated as a "Heritage Building" in 1991, continued
as a seniors' long-term care facility until 1999.[121]

The Charles Camsell Hospital came to a more ignominious end.
Shortly after the new hospital opened in 1967 it became something of
a white elephant. With steadily falling tuberculosis rates, an increased
emphasis on outpatient care, expansion of acute care facilities in the
north, and its Aboriginal clientele directed by their physicians to other
institutions, the hospital became seriously underused. To keep beds
full, private local practitioners were accorded admitting privileges to
the hospital, which subsequently developed into a community acute

care hospital with only 23 per cent Aboriginal patients.[122] But, for its own reasons, the Alberta Hospital Services Commission would only approve a $78 per diem rate for the Camsell Hospital, compared to $125 for other city hospitals, forcing National Health and Welfare to subsidize what had become a general city hospital to the tune of $3 million annually.[123] No fewer than four different audits, reports, and studies between 1972 and 1976 attempted to find a future for the hospital, which senior IHS officials concluded was a "relic of an age that has already passed."[124] Yet in the hope of eventually transferring the hospital to the province, IHS sought to maintain it as a viable institution. However, in the politically turbulent post–White Paper years of unprecedented Aboriginal activism, the Alberta government wanted nothing to do with an "Indian" hospital. In 1972 IHS was prepared to transfer the hospital to Alberta for a nominal fee of $1, as well as a $3 million "transitional grant" (or the equivalent of one year's operating deficit) to the province to take it off their hands. The provincial hospital commission chair refused the offer, bluntly stating the provincial position: "We would prefer an empty hospital and no Indian involvement." Four years later and with negotiations ongoing, the hospital's annual operating deficit ballooned to $4 million.[125] Both levels of government agreed to leave the Indian Association of Alberta and other interested Aboriginal organizations out of the negotiations. Ultimately, the 1978 transfer agreement was reached only after the federal government agreed to two provincial demands: that it provide written assurances to "honour its existing obligations for the provision of health services" to the province's Treaty Indians; and that the federal government commit the substantial savings accrued from the transfer to enrich health services on reserves.[126] The formal transfer in 1980 was accompanied by national health minister Monique Bégin's announcement of a $2.5 million commitment to an Indian Health Care Commission to "promote and encourage native self determination" in the delivery of health services.[127] By 1996 the province closed and abandoned the Charles Camsell Hospital, in part due to asbestos contamination. The derelict building and its 4.7 hectare (11.5 acre) site, a frightening place patrolled by dogs, sits fenced, boarded, and scrawled with graffiti, "a nasty, nagging, neighbourhood eyesore."[128] It is a shameful and sorry end for a place that had such a profound impact, for good or ill, on so many lives.

Canadians are particularly pleased with Medicare, telling the latest Royal Commission that it defined their notions of citizenship.[129] Yet that healthy national citizenship excluded Aboriginal people, as the

"Health Plan for Indians" made clear. Limited health care would be withheld until and unless Aboriginal people remained destitute and on their reserves, while the "integration" policy constructed them as beggars at the doors of community hospitals. As Alfred Blood of the Blood Indian Hospital committee put it, "Since Medicare was introduced the Indian has been at a loss."[130] The slow demise of the Charles Camsell Hospital in the 1970s was only the most glaring example of how the integrationist agenda and the dark politics of Medicare came to damage those most in need of care. As the only new and modern Indian hospital, the Charles Camsell primarily benefited the non-Aboriginal population of Edmonton who made up the majority of its patients. The costs of that care, and especially the decade's operating deficits, conservatively estimated at $25 million ($3 million per year to 1975, and $4 million per year to 1980), funds earmarked for health care for Aboriginal people, instead went into the coffers of the nation's wealthiest province, while the small local institutions such as the Blood and Blackfoot hospitals were deemed too expensive to operate. One could be forgiven for viewing with cynicism the health minister's 1980 "gift" of $2.5 million for an Indian Health Care Commission to encourage "native self determination" in health care. Nevertheless, Aboriginal communities refused to accept a contingent citizenship and continued to press for better care based on their treaty rights.

Chapter Six

"The Government's eyes were opened":
The Treaty Right to Health Care

When the treaty was first made with the Queen the Indians were told the government that was to look after them was pretty nearly as strong as God. But the government was blind in both eyes, and the Indians suffered. As the years passed by, the government's eyes were opened, just enough to give us our own doctors and hospital.

– Sweetgrass Chief Sam Swimmer, North Battleford Indian Hospital, 1953

The treaty right to health care remains contested. The basis for the claim is the "medicine chest" clause in Treaty Six (1876) that included Cree communities in a wide swath of prairie and parkland in what became central Alberta and Saskatchewan. Over the course of the late nineteenth and twentieth centuries, the state's provision of medical care, at first sporadic and grudging, became increasingly comprehensive, including vaccinations, X-ray examinations, physician services, and Indian hospitals. As a result, Aboriginal communities, and Canadians generally, came to the not unreasonable understanding that health care was a federal responsibility, if not a treaty right. In government circles, however, the point was moot. Overwhelmingly paternalistic, IHS physician-bureaucrats dismissed treaties as dusty relics, and treaty claims as symptomatic of a stubborn backwardness that was surely as dangerous as disease itself. As tuberculosis receded as the primary threat to the national health, Indian hospitals came to be seen as costly obstacles to wider state efforts to "integrate" Aboriginal people to normal, healthy citizenship. Medicare, not medicine chests, would define access to hospital and health care. But, as we have seen, resistance to hospital closures emerged immediately. Though historians peg the resurgence of Aboriginal political organization to the White Paper and its aftermath, the process began earlier and emerged in many cases from grass-roots efforts that coalesced around issues of health care and Indian hospitals. For nearly two decades, Treaty Six community activists at the North Battleford Indian Hospital in central Saskatchewan struggled with countless bureaucrats and seven successive health ministers in an attempt to improve their health by holding government to its treaty promise of health care. A focus on one particular community's well-documented activism illustrates how bureaucratic surveillance and control maintained relations of power based on race that worked to undermine health.

The treaty right to health care emerged from the 1876 Treaty Six negotiations at Fort Carlton on the North Saskatchewan River between the Cree and the government's treaty commissioner Alexander Morris. While the nascent Canadian state understood the treaties as ultimately land cessions to facilitate agricultural settlement, Aboriginal negotiators saw the treaties as a mutually beneficial relationship whereby they agreed to share their land with newcomers in exchange for assurances of future livelihood secured by specific promises, such as aid to agriculture, schools, and annual cash payments.[1] Thus, at Fort Carlton senior chiefs Mistawasis and Ahtahkakoop, recalling the recent 1870 smallpox epidemic and alarmed by the rapidly dwindling bison herds, negotiated for, among other things, a promise of government assistance in the event of famine or pestilence, and a promise of a medicine chest. The written text of the treaty however does not reflect the actual treaty discussions, a point consistently made by Aboriginal people and only recently recognized by scholars and the courts.[2] During negotiations the Cree leaders presented treaty commissioner Morris with a request for additional terms. One witness to the proceedings, Metis trader Peter Erasmus engaged by the chiefs as their interpreter, noted that they asked for a medicine chest to be "placed in the house of every agent for the free use of the band." A.G. Jackes, secretary to the Treaty Commission, recorded the request slightly differently – "That we be supplied with medicines free of cost" – and the commissioner's reply – "A medicine chest will be kept at the house of each Indian agent in case of sickness amongst you."[3] The text of Treaty Six states "a medicine chest shall be kept at the house of each Indian Agent for the use and benefit of the Indians, at the direction of such Agent."[4] Slight differences perhaps, but the "direction" of the Indian agent was inserted in the treaty document. The "medicine chest clause" was exclusive to Treaty Six, though there is considerable evidence that requests and promises of medical care were negotiated at Treaties Seven (1877), Eight (1899), Ten (1906–7) and Eleven (1921), but no mention appears in those treaty documents.[5] For treaty Aboriginal groups across the west and north, the provision of medical care at subsequent annual treaty ceremonies no doubt confirmed the link between the two.

The first judicial test of the medicine chest clause came in 1935 when George Dreaver, chief of the Mistawasis Band in central Saskatchewan, sued the federal government to recover band funds that were spent on, among other things, drugs and medical supplies. The Exchequer Court found that from 1876 to 1919 the Department of Indian Affairs (DIA) provided medicine and supplies at Mistawasis, but after a land sale in 1919 medical supplies were charged to the band's funds. Chief Dreaver was witness to the Treaty Six negotiations and related for the court his recollection of the commissioner's promise. Justice Angers ruled that the medicine chest clause indeed meant that all medicines and medical supplies should be supplied free of charge: "I do not think that the Department [Indian Affairs] had, under the treaty, the privilege of deciding which medicines, drugs and medical supplies were to be furnished to the Indians gratuitously and which were to be a charge to the funds of the band." Angers continued: "The clause might unquestionably be more explicit but, as I have said, I take it to mean that all medicines, drugs or medical supplies which might be required by the Indians of the Mistawasis Band were to be supplied to them free of charge." He ordered the DIA to reimburse the Mistawasis Band $4,500.[6] Aside from supplies of medicines on reserves, often dispensed by the agent's wife or local schoolteacher, and occasional visits by government physicians, Aboriginal people were expected to pay for their medical care, while the state only sporadically and reluctantly provided care for the indigent. As part of a larger project of assimilation, the policy maintained the close collaboration between medicine and the colonizing state. To seek out Western medicine, and pay for its benefits, was long seen as a marker of progress towards "civilization," which necessarily trumped any quaint treaty promises.

Hospital care for Aboriginal people in the Treaty Six communities in central Saskatchewan's North Battleford area was severely limited.[7] An effort in the 1920s to build an "Indian annex" at the local Notre Dame Hospital was frustrated by denominational rivalry when the Anglican bishop objected to Catholic influence at the hospital (see chapter 1). By 1945 the Indian Affairs physician advocated for improved care for the area's 4,200 Aboriginal people, noting that beds were rarely available at the local Notre Dame Hospital, where "other patients rather object to Indians being placed in the same ward with them, and there are no wards that can be set aside for Indians only."[8] He had in mind the military's thirty-five-bed hospital in the redundant Commonwealth Air Training Camp at the airport. IHS director Percy Moore emphasized the economy in taking over the facility, including kitchen equipment, beds, and a complete supply of surgical instruments, that could be "turned over lock, stock and barrel" by the military. He also noted "hospital costs for the Battleford Agency for the past year were $38,662.50, of which $33,000.00 was for the care of sanatorium patients in the Prince Albert sanatorium."[9] The source of those funds (whether band funds or parliamentary appropriations) is not clear from Moore's statement, but it is clear that sanatorium treatment had become the overwhelming priority, highlighting the limited number of admissions to the local hospital.

In 1949 the IHS opened the North Battleford Indian Hospital with sixty beds under Dr P.W. Head, known locally as "Chief Medicine Knife," for the many surgeries he performed. Like other Indian hospitals opened in what were intended to be temporary military facilities, it was makeshift and drafty, pipes froze in winter and patients sweltered in summer, and fire was a constant threat. Cross-infection was a particular hazard in the military-style open dormitories. As noted previously, by the mid-1950s staff shortages had created a dangerous situation, especially in the two large wards for infants and children, where nursing staff moved from patient to patient without changing gowns or washing their hands. Children and infants were bathed in a common tub; infant formula was improperly prepared; bottles were propped for feeding and then left in cribs; soiled diapers were left in the ward and then laundered with other linens. The hospital's superintendent was advised to move adults into the large wards and keep children in smaller wards, and windows were to be opened whenever possible. Visiting hours were to be restricted to one hour a day and limited to close relatives.[10] But, despite its deficiencies, the hospital was much needed and became a valuable source of wage labour, as we have seen, though always in the least skilled positions. Nevertheless, patients felt comforted by Aboriginal staff who spoke their language and understood their culture, unlike many peoples' experiences in the community's Notre Dame Hospital.

The Treaty Six communities at North Battleford also viewed the Indian hospital as the government's acknowledgment of the treaty right to medical care. Sam Swimmer, the elderly chief of Sweetgrass, spent the last years of his life in the early 1950s in the hospital. He cultivated a close relationship with Dr Head and Mrs Wetton, a newspaper correspondent and local historian who referred to herself as an honorary member of the Sweetgrass band. Her columns focused on the hospital staff's quiet sacrifice and their life-saving efforts, while she characterized Chief Swimmer as enlightened by his hospital experience: "He cherishes no longings for the olden days of the medicine man and their crude tents and magic, but looks forward to the time when all his people will turn to real doctors to cure them of their ills." Chief Swimmer, for his part, used the media attention to praise the hospital as the state's commitment to the treaty right to health care. In his metaphorical style he stated: "When the treaty was first made with the Queen the Indians were told the government that was to look after them was pretty nearly as strong as God. But the government was blind in both eyes, and the Indians suffered. As the years passed by, the government's eyes were opened, just enough to give us our own doctors and hospital."[11]

The hospital was also a vast improvement over the public health facilities on the North Battleford area reserves, "fire traps" according to medical superintendent Cameron Corrigan, who visited them in 1956. At Onion Lake, 200 kilometres northeast of North Battleford, and at Mistawasis reserve, 130 kilometres west, the reserve nursing stations were fifty-year-old abandoned Indian agency houses taken over by IHS. Both were two-storey buildings with holes in the roof and cracked and leaking basements. At Mistawasis a woman with a cerebral haemorrhage was carried up the winding stairs on a blanket. She died immediately, as Corrigan noted: "I imagine the handling she got being taken up stairs would not have helped her cerebral haemorrhage."[12] No nurse had stayed in the house longer than six months. The water pump frequently quit, and in February when Corrigan visited, the attic was frozen. He sat with his feet on the table to keep warm, yet the kitchen wall was too hot to touch because of a cracked chimney. Corrigan suggested abandoning the cottages completely in favour of more beds at the North Battleford Indian Hospital. Instead, four years later IHS embarked on plans to "quietly" close the Indian hospital.

In early 1962 IHS actively negotiated with the province and the Notre Dame Hospital to close the Indian hospital, leaving the Cree communities out of the discussions. But in a small town nothing stays quiet for long. In March the chiefs and councillors from Sweetgrass, Poundmaker, Onion Lake, and Little Pine petitioned IHS to protest the hospital closure plans and the proposal for a new thirty-bed wing for Notre Dame Hospital. As the petition made clear, "If funds are available, we request that a new larger Indian hospital be erected." Besides, the petition asked, what would become of the Indian hospital's Aboriginal employees who cared for children and elders in their own language? Noting that the sixty-bed Indian hospital was overcrowded and the reserve populations increasing, how could a thirty-bed replacement suffice?[13] A week later regional bureaucrat and former hospital superintendent at both Hobbema and North Battleford, Dr Thomas Orford, surprised to be contacted at his Regina office by provincial media about the hospital's fate, told reporters that no decision had been made. Putting the best face on the government's self-serving policy, however, Orford told the press that closing the Indian hospital and adding beds to the general hospital would aid the "Indians towards becoming members of the community."[14]

IHS bureaucrats, facing similar resistance to their closures in Alberta and Saskatchewan, characterized Aboriginal opposition as illogical and disruptive, and as evidence of unredeemed backwardness of their leadership. According to Orford, Saskatchewan Indians were split into two factions, a "fairly large element who vaguely grasp at integration ... but who frighten easily when faced with reality" and a "more vociferous element who are not ready for anything different than reserve life and 'Treaty' agreements." The first group will "in time dig themselves out of apathy and indecision, while the other group will in ten, twenty, fifty years from now will [sic] still be clamouring for treaty rights." Orford maintained that the future of the hospital would rest on whether "we cater to the old guard or enhance the trend of swinging Indian thought towards full Canadian citizenship."[15] The dichotomy was seemingly evident and linked the hospital's closure and integration in the community hospital with progress and citizenship. However, IHS plans would have to wait as Saskatchewan's program for health insurance faced stiff opposition that summer with a bitter doctors' strike. Medical bureaucrats were advised to "temporise" in the meantime.[16] But the Indian hospital continued to deteriorate, requiring more than $50,000 in repairs to bring it to a "reasonable" standard according to the department's building inspector.[17] Instead, inpatient services would shrink, forcing admissions to the community hospital, if beds could be had, while maintaining a very limited outpatient service.

Complaints about the hospital increased as services deteriorated. Letters to the minister of health and to the local press charging discrimination, restricted access, and negligence causing death caught the attention of Ottawa bureaucrats. While Orford, as senior Saskatchewan bureaucrat, attempted to explain away the incidents as miscommunication between doctors and patients, it was clear that staff shortages and economizing had created a dangerous situation. But his reaction to charges of discrimination, calling them "unjust" and "unkind," was especially revealing of bureaucratic attitudes that stemmed from the state's insistence that its medical service was ultimately humanitarian. "I'm sure that if ... all the other Indians would reflect on the years of hard work and sacrifice undertaken by doctors and nurses in an effort to treat and improve health conditions for them, the suggestion of discrimination would be difficult to substantiate."[18] Orford's reaction was shared by many in the IHS who saw themselves as motivated by equal measures of service and science. Patient grumbling about treatment and conditions was further evidence of the ingratitude and fecklessness they were trying to uproot.

Nevertheless, the charges were serious enough for a delegation of senior administrators to visit the hospital in the spring of 1965. They found considerable cause for concern. Topping the list of their recommendations was a directive to stop talking about closing the hospital since staff were becoming demoralized; other problems stemmed from serious understaffing, resentment against senior staff, and an absence of privacy and security. They found that medical staff showed little respect for patients, in particular, refusing to discuss with patients their medical diagnosis or their course of treatment. For their part medical staff complained about the "rebellion of the Indian patients."[19] As a result of the visit by the Ottawa inspectors, the hospital's senior staff – medical superintendent, matron, and administrator – was all transferred elsewhere.[20] Moreover, as suggested by the community, an advisory board was established to deal with complaints.

Bureaucratic hopes that the "Lay Advisory Board" would smooth the choppy waters were quickly dashed. Chaired by Sidney Fineday from Sweetgrass, the Advisory Board saw itself as a liaison between the community, government, and hospital staff to protect patient interests while participating in major administrative decisions.[21] The election of two non-Aboriginal members, Zenon Pohorecky, newly appointed professor of anthropology at the University of Saskatchewan, and Reverend James Williams, minister of the Pentecostal Church of Christ, both outspoken critics of the hospital, worried medical bureaucrats. Dr Orford, in particular, suspected that the non-Aboriginal members had hijacked the Board. Displaying a newfound appreciation for the people's judgment, he recommended an all-Aboriginal Board: "I am confident that left to themselves, the Indians will amicably and satisfactorily resolve past difficulties and carry on a good partnership with hospital personnel."[22]

In August Orford and the new hospital superintendent, Dr M.L. Webb, attended the Advisory Board's first meeting and were dismayed to find Metis political activist Malcolm Norris speaking out against the "mediocrity of civil servants." Orford objected to the presence of non-Aboriginal people who "disrupted" the proceedings and a newspaper reporter who stirred up mistrust, undercutting the purpose of the board, which according to Orford was to "restore good will and respect between the Indians and the hospital." Speaking for Aboriginal communities, Orford contended they were "extremely capable of speaking for themselves when given the opportunity and I believe this is the way they would prefer."[23] The Advisory Board meeting revisited the previous year's incidents of discrimination and negligence at the hospital and the refusal of local Notre Dame Hospital to accept Aboriginal patients, which made front-page headlines in the *Saskatoon Star Phoenix* and the *Toronto Telegram*.[24] Worse yet, a CBC television program aired in October further publicizing for a national audience the problems at North Battleford Indian Hospital, and bringing the issue into the living rooms of Ottawa bureaucrats. Sidney Fineday told the CBC about charges of malpractice at the hospital, which the IHS director saw as "vague complaints which would not much impress any reasonably intelligent viewer." Anthropologist Pohorecky also appeared on screen, recounting charges of neglect that prompted the headquarters visit in April, while Dr Webb countered that major changes in the hospital's administration had resolved the problems. New IHS director Dr H.A. Proctor reassured himself that Webb's explanation left viewers with the impression that whatever grounds for complaint had existed, they were resolved.[25]

Back of the tensions and hostility at the Indian hospital were the ongoing negotiations with provincial authorities and Notre Dame Hospital for an expansion for which IHS offered $325,000 to accommodate Aboriginal patients. But in the middle of negotiations in April 1965 the hospital's owners, the Sisters of Providence, retired from the hospital field, forcing the city and surrounding municipalities to scramble to form a Union Hospital district to take over the hospital. With no hospital construction in the near future, IHS was forced to maintain and perhaps expand the Indian hospital to service the more than 8,000 people on twenty-one reserves in the Battleford and Meadow Lake agencies, especially since the surrounding small-town hospitals showed a marked preference for non-Aboriginal patients.[26] With the realization that the Indian hospital would not be closing for at least another five years, IHS took the Advisory Board's concerns more seriously, if only to avoid more damaging publicity.

Medical bureaucrats saw the Advisory Board as an exercise in educating and disciplining Aboriginal people to accept "integration" into the Union Hospital, and provincial society generally. Proctor and Orford, from their offices in Ottawa and Regina respectively, believed that much of the opposition to integration by the area chiefs was a gesture to "their so-called [treaty] rights," not sincerely held. But the chiefs, concerned especially about the treatment that elders would receive if none of the staff spoke their language, also asked the pressing question: was the Union Hospital prepared to receive Aboriginal patients? Dr Webb admitted that while the hospital management was ready to accept patients, it might take some time to convince other hospital patrons.[27] Burton Baptiste, councillor from Little Pine, raised the critical question at the Advisory Board meeting in early 1967: what would IHS do if the Aboriginal communities refused to accept an integrated hospital? Webb's reply was "rather unspecific." IHS would take this into consideration, but, as he put it, "I did not intimate ... that we would comply with such a request."[28] Despite medical bureaucrats' dismissal of treaty rights, the issue was especially pressing in the mid-1960s.

In 1965 provincial authorities charged North Battleford Indian Hospital employees Walter Johnston, Harry Wuttunee, and Andrew Swimmer with failure to pay the 1963 hospital insurance premiums under the Saskatchewan Hospitalization Act, a move apparently instigated by the hospital's administrator.[29] The charges stemmed from the IHS policy that it would only pay the provincial hospitalization insurance premiums, or tax, for indigent Aboriginal people living on reserves, and those who had lived off the reserve for less than a year. As hospital employees, none of the charged were indigent. Since all defendants intended to raise the same defence – that the treaty right to health care exempted them from the tax – Saskatchewan's attorney general proceeded against Johnston alone. At the time, IHS director claimed "it is not considered that Indian Canadians have any special entitlement to free medical care, hospitalization and similar services ... None of the various Treaties between the Crown and the Indians has been judicially interpreted as conferring this right."[30] This was narrowly correct, since the 1935 *Dreaver v The King* judgment dealt only with medicines, not medical care. Just days before Johnston went to trial, deputy minister of health Donald Cameron provided a strange, and vaguely threatening, interpretation that the medicine chest clause might well limit medical care to nineteenth-century standards. In response to an inquiry about the treaty right, Cameron said that when Treaty Six was drawn up in 1876 the contents of a medicine chest would have been rudimentary "since most of the medicines of greatest use today have been developed in the past few years. This development of new and presumably better medicines is going on all the time. If we were to interpret what is to be meant by a 'Medicine Chest' it might restrict the use of some of the latest proven materials as they become available. I believe that Indian Health Services tries to use good up-to-date medicines and other medical materials."[31] The government did not pursue this bizarre line of reasoning, but it reflects IHS thinking that, whatever else the treaty might mean, the benefits of modern medicine had long ago surpassed its outdated promises.

In March 1965 Walter Johnston alone went to trial and pleaded not guilty, arguing that the medicine chest provision of Treaty Six conferred a right to free health care and hospitalization. Interestingly, Johnston provided the court with the original Treaty Six document that had been carefully preserved in the community for nearly a century. The government's copy was compared closely for accuracy. Judge J.M. Policha, referring to the 1876 treaty negotiations in his ruling, said he was "greatly impressed by the representations and submissions made by various Indian Chiefs and the concern they felt with the welfare of their people." In acquitting Johnston, he ruled that the medicine chest clause of the treaty should be interpreted to mean that Johnston was entitled to receive all medical services and hospital care free of charge. Further, he stated, the "entitlement would embrace all Indians within the meaning of the Indian Act, without exception."[32] Shocked at this unexpected outcome, IHS director Proctor immediately advised that it would be "judicious" to suspend any further "Loss of Benefit" notices while the courts studied the Johnston ruling, and most especially since they were still in "negotiations to placate the Indians in the North Battleford area." He further directed IHS bureaucrats to say the "least possible" about the Johnston case. As far as IHS was concerned, treaty interpretation was an issue for Indian Affairs and the Department of Justice: "We will keep out as far as possible until the smoke clears."[33] An appeal of the ruling seemed inevitable, but only Saskatchewan's attorney general could launch it.

Though the ruling's impact would be more keenly felt in Ottawa than in Saskatchewan, both bureaucracies recognized that the Johnston ruling represented a major shift in how Aboriginal people and their rights would be understood. Orford summed it up succinctly, descending to a tactless stereotype to make his point: "He [Judge Policha] seems to think that in perpetuity the Federal government is stuck with supply [sic] of full and total medical care for Indians regardless of their place of residence or financial status. I imagine the Indians in Battleford and other areas of Treaty 6 are jumping with joy right now. Fortunately, I'm nearly bald so my scalp would be of little value."[34] His statement highlighted an increasingly acrimonious relationship with the local community, while betraying considerable anxiety that medical and bureaucratic control might be eroded. With Liberal administrations in both jurisdictions, the provincial health department's solicitor informally advised Orford in Regina that there were just ten days in which to launch an appeal, and that the federal government should make representations to the province's attorney general to do so. But neither Health and Welfare's IHS nor the Indian Affairs branch, both putatively representing Aboriginal interests, wanted to be seen to be supporting the appeal. Minister of health Judy LaMarsh, advised by her deputy Donald Cameron, declined to take any action "that could easily be interpreted by the Indians as opposition to their interests and legal rights."[35] She promptly advised her cabinet colleague John Nicholson at Citizenship and Immigration, the bureaucratic home of Indian Affairs, to contact the provincial attorney general regarding an appeal.[36] But Indian Affairs returned the volley, arguing that Health and Welfare should ask for an appeal since the matter concerned medical insurance paid from that bureaucracy's parliamentary appropriation. Advising his minister, assistant deputy R.F. Battle stated the obvious: "At the moment, the decision is in favour of the Indians. If the Department of Citizenship and Immigration takes action to appeal, then it will appear in the eyes of the Indians that we are not favourably disposed towards the decision." In case the minister had forgotten, Battle continued, "our role should be to defend the Indians' interests. If we initiate action to appeal then I am afraid it will have a damaging effect on our position with the Indians concerned." To be clear, Battle pointed out, "our relationship, which might be stated publicly, is to provide assistance to insure that in the event of an appeal the Indians' case is properly presented."[37] Bureaucratic manoeuvring

aside, claims that either ministry was working in the "Indians'" interest were strictly for public consumption. For Aboriginal people, that
mask had slipped years ago as the government continued its policy of
restricting their economic, social, and political self-determination in the
interests of assimilation to a Euro-Canadian norm. Indeed, in the wake
of his apparent victory, Walter Johnston and his original co-accused,
Andrew Swimmer, applied for necessary glasses and dentures at the
North Battleford Indian Hospital. They were promptly denied. Orford
advised IHS employees in Saskatchewan that policies had not changed,
warning them not to speak to the press or to otherwise embarrass the
government.[38]

Saskatchewan's minister of public health, Davey Steuart, pressed
both ministers for an answer: "If you would like our Government
to proceed with an appeal ... it would be appreciated if you would
advise me in this regard at an early date."[39] The province subsequently
launched its appeal in late October 1965 with covert support from
Justice Department's lawyer R.E. Williams. Meeting with R.L. Barclay
of Saskatchewan's attorney general's office, Williams proposed an
argument: the medicine chest provision in the treaty was an ad hoc
attempt to meet a specific problem before there was a provincial government, but with the advent of modern provincial medical services,
the provision had become a "historical appendage." The costs for care,
the argument went, were borne by Canada for some Aboriginal people, but Walter Johnston, integrated into the white community and a
"normal citizen" of the province, was required to bear the same responsibilities as other citizens, including paying the hospitalization tax.[40]
This argument, neatly reinforcing government policy, was particularly
appealing to Indian Affairs, and, it was hoped, it might also appeal to
the good sense of the Appeals Court justices. Williams also provided
Barclay with copies of Treaty Six and other documents from Indian
Affairs archives.[41]

In March 1966 Saskatchewan's chief justice, E.M. (Ted) Culliton, a
faithful Liberal, delivered the court's judgment.[42] He began with the
question of historical evidence, arguing that the words in the treaty
should be interpreted literally. He referred to treaty commissioner Alexander Morris's 1880 account of the treaty negotiations as "authorita-
tive."[43] But, as noted, in Morris's account the people asked for a "a free
supply of medicines," and later, that they be "supplied with medicines
free of cost," though the written treaty states that the medicine chest
will be kept at the agent's house and used at his direction.[44] There is

no evidence that Culliton looked further than Morris, but if he had, he might have consulted the acknowledged expert and government anthropologist Diamond Jenness's *The Indians of Canada*, first published in 1932 and in its sixth edition by the 1960s.[45] A durable anthropological survey of Aboriginal contributions to Canada's evolution, *Indians of Canada* placed their usefulness in the far distant past: "Doubtless all the tribes will disappear ... Some will merge steadily with the white race, others will bequeath to future generations only an infinitesimal fraction of their blood. Culturally they have already contributed everything that was valuable for our own civilization."[46] The discourse was pervasive in postwar Canada. Aboriginal people needed to be "Canadianized"; to that end Indian Affairs was made a branch of the Department of Citizenship and Immigration where, like European immigrants, they might take their place on the bottom rungs of Canadian society as reformed citizens.[47] In government policy and expert opinion, modernity demanded that Aboriginal people forget their past, shed their "Indianness," in order to become Canadians. Clinging to the "historical appendages" of treaties was symptomatic of their refusal to become normal citizens. Culliton's ruling, referring to the *Dreaver* case, found no reason to support a wider interpretation than had Justice Angers in 1935. Yet Angers's ruling did not consider medical services or hospitalization since only medicines were under consideration. Furthermore, in 1935 Angers had interpreted the "medicine chest" in a contemporary manner to mean all "medicines, drugs and medical supplies," as had the magistrate in Johnston's lower-court ruling. Culliton, however, ruled on the "plain reading" of the clause to mean "no more than the words clearly convey" – a first-aid kit.[48] Walter Johnston was ordered to pay the $72.00 hospital insurance tax.

The Johnston ruling did nothing to ease tensions at the North Battleford Indian Hospital. IHS bureaucrats naturally saw the decision as a vindication of their authority to make and change policy. Negotiations with the province and the Battlefords Union Hospital (the new entity operating the former Notre Dame Hospital) for a funding agreement continued, while local IHS employees were directed to "discreetly elicit" community and "Saskatchewan Indian Federation [*sic*]" support for their plan to withdraw from the hospital field.[49] The new IHS regional director felt sure that "deep down they appear to accept this closure as inevitable and will, I'm sure, agree with time and further discussion."[50] This was an increasingly common response from IHS officials in their correspondence with headquarters in Ottawa. As local bureaucrats, their role was to implement policy, and despite strong indications to the contrary, they assured their superiors that community opinion was swinging their way. But the 1968 "Health Plan for Indians" that required proof of indigency in order to access medical care from IHS, and the 1969 White Paper alarmed the Advisory Board. It refused to enter into any agreements. Besides, the treaty right to health care was again before the courts.[51]

In 1968 Andrew Swimmer, Chief Sam Swimmer's son, continued his father's struggle to protect treaty rights. He was charged with failing to pay the joint Saskatchewan hospitalization and medical care insurance tax. As in the Johnston case, the lower court ruled that the medicine chest clause in Treaty Six entitled Swimmer to free medical and hospital care, and thus he was exempt from paying the tax. The province was again preparing an appeal. Of more immediate concern to the Advisory Board were the deteriorating living conditions on the reserves, particularly the overcrowded and dilapidated housing that contributed to the high rates of hospitalization, especially among children. But IHS continued to deflect responsibility, directing the Advisory Board to take their concerns about housing, water, and sanitation to Indian Affairs bureaucrats. But by mid-1970 the climate had changed. In June, after a year of concerted and scathing criticism of government policy by an increasingly politicized national and local Aboriginal leadership, the Trudeau Liberals backed away from the disastrous White Paper proposals.[52] Echoing Trudeau's 1970 comments to the National Indian Brotherhood that the government "won't force any solution on you," a slightly chastised bureaucracy at Battleford promised that unless the community desired integration with the Union Hospital no one on the federal side would try to pressure them.[53]

Health minister John Munro assured the Advisory Board that he would make a substantial construction contribution to the Union Hospital on behalf of Aboriginal people, the generosity of which depended on the willingness of the hospital and the province to allow Aboriginal representatives on the Union Hospital board, and the assurance of Aboriginal employment in the new hospital. The total cost for the proposed 160-bed hospital was now estimated at $3.5 million. The province would pay half, the federal contribution on behalf of Aboriginal people would be $1.2 million, leaving $500,000 to be raised by the community. Regardless, over the previous decade the Indian hospital had been closing by inches. The maternity ward was closed in the mid-1960s and the outpatient clinic closed in early 1970. Aboriginal patients, mostly children, admitted to the Union Hospital increased from 8 in 1968 to 260 the following year.[54] Hospital integration, an increasingly difficult political position, was accomplished by other means.

Despite the government's more conciliatory tone, a pall of suspicion hung over discussions. The Advisory Board's chairman, Ernie Tootoosis, insisted that "integration" was an unacceptable term; amalgamation might be more suitable. They would not negotiate with provincial officials, since they had no treaty with the province. Furthermore, the Advisory Board could do nothing until all the band councils had consulted with their people about amalgamation. They invited the ministers of Indian Affairs, Jean Chrétien, and Health and Welfare, John Munro, to visit North Battleford to discuss how the proposed amalgamation would affect treaty rights.[55] Six months later band resolutions from five reserves rejected amalgamation. The leading negotiators on the Advisory Board, George Nicotine, Burton Baptiste, and the new chairman Joseph Weenie, argued that since the federal government was willing to spend $1.2 million for their health care, those funds should be used to build a new Indian hospital instead of investing in the community hospital. They also wanted all other hospitals to open their doors to Aboriginal people.[56] But an increasingly frustrated Advisory Board could only watch as IHS effectively abandoned the Indian hospital. The medical superintendent position remained vacant, and the steady succession of bureaucrats at the local and regional level did little to maintain a level of understanding of the Aboriginal position. Dr Hicks, the acting regional director at Regina, assured his superiors that the Advisory Board's concerns that their treaty rights be addressed before the hospital closed were not sincere: "finally they will allow themselves to be 'conned' into it, after making sure that still 'the rivers flow, the grass grows and the sun shines.'"[57] Besides, as the bureaucrats repeatedly intoned, only Indian Affairs, not IHS, could discuss treaty rights.

The increasingly acrimonious atmosphere did nothing to improve the racial discord in the town and at the Union Hospital. Some Aboriginal people were turned away without treatment, while other patients were left in the hallway. Union Hospital administrators cited overcrowding as the problem and stated that an expanded hospital would resolve the issue. But hospital patients, the community's most vulnerable elders and children, would also have been subject to the more fleeting and subtle sneers from admitting clerks and scowls from hospital personnel, subjectively felt and impossible to quantify. A bureaucrat familiar with the town later admitted that "there is indeed a great deal of discrimination in North Battleford," though he felt sure it did not affect hospital patients.[58] Furthermore, integration with community schools was proving disastrous for many Aboriginal children, especially since their parents had no representation on local school boards. Dr Webb, once the hospital's superintendent and now at headquarters, led a delegation from Ottawa to convince the Advisory Board to approve their integration plans. He suggested the only way to overcome discrimination in the community was to amalgamate. Sharing a hospital would be a great opportunity for Native and white people to get to know each other.[59] An exasperated Joseph Weenie insisted that the discrimination began in the hospital! But the colour line in North Battleford was clearly drawn. Police regularly rounded up Aboriginal patrons in public spaces and beer parlours and sent them on their way back to the reserve. The newspaper *Saskatchewan Indian* noted in 1972 that North Battleford "remains one of the most racist and anti-Indian towns in Saskatchewan."[60]

Impatient with the seemingly endless discussions, the Union Hospital threatened that it would proceed with a smaller expansion that excluded Aboriginal people unless it had a decision on the government's $1.2 million contribution by the end of November 1971. Adding urgency was the realization that, regardless of Aboriginal support, IHS would be forced to make a substantial contribution since every year more Aboriginal patients were treated in the Union Hospital. Health minister John Munro, in order to "sell" integration, invited Advisory Board chairman Joseph Weenie and six area chiefs to meet him in Ottawa on 22 November 1971. He promised to "sweeten" his offer with expanded public health facilities on reserves and improved transportation, which he calculated would cost less than $200,000 per year – the equivalent of the current deficit at the Indian hospital. Further, Munro attempted to convince the delegation that IHS was sincere in wanting to improve health services without compromising the long-term solution of the treaty rights question.[61] The minister's offer: to contribute $1.2 million towards expansion of the Union Hospital and the Indian hospital would close. He made a vague promise to convert the old hospital into a senior's home, and IHS would station a physician at the new hospital. The minister also promised to ensure adequate Aboriginal representation on the Union Hospital board, though provincial legislation made this impossible. Finally, Munro assured the delegation that discrimination would not be tolerated. The North Battleford delegation, for their part, explained that amalgamation would jeopardize their treaty rights, and they wanted to discuss Andrew Swimmer's case and the treaty right to health care. They explained that through the treaties Aboriginal people had already contributed plenty, in return for promises such as health care. The amalgamation of the schools was not working, and they wanted a new Indian hospital.[62] But Munro deflected the treaty issue since the Swimmer appeal was before the courts. The province had appealed Swimmer's acquittal and in December 1970 Chief Justice Culliton, referring to his judgment in the *Johnston* appeal ruled "the terms of Treaty No. 6 do not impose upon the Government of Canada the obligation of providing, without cost, medical and hospital services to all Indians."[63] Swimmer was ordered to pay the hospitalization and Medicare Insurance taxes. An appeal to the Supreme Court was filed, but it remained dormant.[64] In the meantime the Federation of Saskatchewan Indians negotiated a compromise with the provincial government to cease requiring individuals to pay insurance premiums, forcing the federal government to do so.[65] In short, since Munro would not discuss the treaty issue, positions became hardened with Poundmaker's David Tootoosis declaring at one point that they were in deadlock. The delegation left Ottawa, agreeing only to take the minister's proposal to their people. But, well before the meeting had begun, the minister had already determined that regardless of an agreement, the government would contribute the promised $1.2 million to the Union Hospital, and the Indian hospital would finally close.[66]

In anticipation of the minister's announcement to that effect, IHS bureaucrats attempted to reassure the Advisory Board that amalgamation was in the best interests of the whole community. At increasingly stormy joint Union Hospital–Advisory Board meetings, it became clear that amalgamation would proceed regardless of Aboriginal opposition. IHS officials and Union board members were particularly insulted when the discussion was held in Cree.[67] A frustrated George Nicotine feared that Aboriginal representation on the Union Hospital board could not counter the everyday discrimination felt in the community. "In North Battleford" he said, "there is so much discrimination ... Let's trade hospitals."[68] Dr Webb assured his deputy minister that with the decision made, "the Indians will probably cooperate in arranging and effecting an orderly transition."[69] But beyond the concerns about discrimination in the community and at the Union Hospital, the Cree leadership remained adamant that until the minister assured them in writing that their treaty rights would not be affected, they would not consent to their hospital's closure. Despite the Indian hospital's many shortcomings, and the fact that IHS effectively abandoned it by admitting most patients elsewhere, it remained the community's touchstone in the continuing effort to assert the treaty right to health care. Like the efforts by the Kainai and Siksika in the 1970s, the leadership had little recourse but to defend what their hospitals represented. With the *Swimmer* appeal to the Supreme Court in abeyance, the issue also remained very much alive for IHS.

In early 1973 IHS asked its legal services for an interpretation of the medicine chest clause. Dr Webb, now assistant deputy minister, wished to know if there were any federal legal obligations to provide health care to Indians, especially in relation to Treaty Six. Regardless of the court rulings in *Johnston* and *Swimmer*, and despite bureaucratic efforts to deride, dismiss, and ignore the treaty right to health care as a fantasy not sincerely held, significant concerns remained. The arrival in late 1972 of the new minister of Health and Welfare, Marc Lalonde, likely prompted Webb's inquiry. In reply, legal services outlined that for many years Parliament had voted funds to provide health care services, including paying health care premiums for the indigent to provincial hospital and medical care plans, but that such voluntary payments did not endow Indians with an enforceable right to demand payment. However, the brief continued, "tradition, custom and usage (and dependency) may ultimately produce a strong moral right." After describing the case law including the judgments in *Dreaver*, *Johnston*, and *Swimmer* regarding the treaty right to health care, the legal brief noted that the provision of such medical care services over the years "will undoubtedly have made the Indians believe that they are entitled, as of right, to such services. It is a truism to state that, for governments, a benefit once given is very difficult to take away. There are undoubtedly many Indians today – particularly those who are politically active – who believe that the Federal Government has a legal obligation to provide such care." Legal services then cited a 1950 Supreme Court decision, *St Ann's Island Shooting and Fishing Club Ltd. v the King* (dealing with Crown leasing of Indian reserve lands, not health care), which nevertheless stated that Aboriginal people were in effect wards of the state "whose care and welfare are a political trust of the highest obligation." This Supreme Court statement, warned the legal services' brief, conveyed a "judicial attitude which cannot be ignored." Legal services advised that, in transferring health services to territorial and provincial jurisdictions, IHS should negotiate with affected Aboriginal groups to solicit their agreement.[70] Thus, despite the Saskatchewan appeal court's ruling, the federal state acknowledged a political imperative to consult, if only to avoid controversy.

The following July 1973 the Indian hospital's Advisory Board met with health minister Lalonde in Ottawa, where they pressed him to reconsider his predecessor's decision to contribute funds to the Union Hospital and close the Indian hospital. Unsuccessful on that front, the Advisory Board did persuade the minister to provide assurances, in writing, that membership on the Union Hospital board (made possible by amended provincial legislation) and cooperation in "amalgamation" of hospital services in the Union Hospital "will not in any way prejudice your legal rights under Treaty Six."[71] Wording his statement carefully so as to neither admit nor deny a treaty right to health care, the minister pledged to continue to pay health care premiums and other health services costs as a matter of government policy. Lalonde also made a vague promise to endeavour to have Aboriginal employees at the Indian hospital transferred to the Union Hospital or otherwise deployed in departmental activities in the area. But North Battleford ratepayers took some time to approve the hospital expansion plan, and coupled with construction delays, by late 1973 the original federal contribution would need to double to $2.2 million. The Indian hospital continued its limited operations, but was slated to close in April 1977.

As the 1977 deadline approached, Sweetgrass Chief Steve Pooyak and Gordon Albert, representing the Federation of Saskatchewan Indians, met with the deputy minister in late November 1976 to postpone closure of the Indian hospital until the situation could be studied. They argued that for the previous fourteen years since 1962 when the hospital's closure was first considered, there had never been meaningful input by the Aboriginal people; meetings with the Advisory Board were little more than gestures on the part of IHS and the white community. In particular, they argued that the hospital expansion plan was unworkable. It called for the closure of the Indian hospital's 39 beds and the Union Hospital's expansion from 167 beds to 168, or a net increase of just one bed. Though forty of the Union Hospital's chronic care beds were to be converted to acute care, there was no facility that could accommodate those patients. More pressing was the perennial concern about discrimination in North Battleford. The delegates termed it "rampant," and said that white people were "proud" of their low regard for Native people. Though the deputy minister dismissed their concerns, he told the delegation that if they had a counter-proposal he would convey it to minister.[72] They then produced a proposal by the North Battleford District Chiefs to study their concerns about hospital care.

The chiefs' proposal began with an articulation of the Treaty's promised right to health care and how their people's social and economic position had since deteriorated, creating many of the existing health problems. They claimed the right to "regulate and control" the treaty right to adequate medical services in the people's interests. Their concerns echoed those voiced since the Indian hospital's closure was first proposed. The elderly would be disadvantaged, and "non-Indian patients have in certain instances refused to share hospital rooms with Indians."[73] The proposal asked for one year and $60,000 to study the Aboriginal and white communities' attitudes to the Indian hospital's closure, and the experience in other integrated hospitals. Not surprisingly, deputy minister Bruce Rawson refused to consider the proposal, maintaining that there had been adequate consultation, though he recognized that there was no agreement between Aboriginal people and IHS on the right to care under Treaty Six.[74]

The Battleford chiefs took it upon themselves to study hospital services and the impact of the Indian hospital's closure on local health and health care. In March 1977, with the Indian hospital's closure imminent, they presented ministers Marc Lalonde of Health and Welfare, and Warren Allmand of Indian Affairs with evidence that the $2.2 million investment in the Union Hospital "will be of far greater benefit to non-Indians than it will be to Indians." They charged that negotiations with the Advisory Board over the years were "simply a public relations effort to convince the Indians this would be good for them." Their position – except for minor concessions such as a minority position on the Union Hospital board and vague promises to reduce discrimination – "has never seriously been considered."[75] These claims, as we have seen, are borne out by the documentary record, where a succession of bureaucrats consistently dismissed the Advisory Board's concerns. The direction of government policy, the chiefs contended, remained to unload its constitutional and treaty responsibilities. It continued to upgrade non-Aboriginal schools and hospitals, while facilities serving Aboriginal people deteriorated. The chiefs also charged that when they requested documents in 1976 relating to the ongoing negotiations, Health and Welfare claimed they only retained files for five years before being destroyed. Again, as we have seen, the documentary record still exists.

The chiefs' brief used hospital utilization rates and a 1975 Indian Affairs housing survey to calculate that the planned Union Hospital expansion would provide forty-nine fewer beds than required; moreover, the area reserves' appalling housing and infrastructure contributed to their misery.[76] They determined that from 1971 through 1975 infant mortality was ten times the national rate, and the average age at death was just forty-one years. Moreover, 37 per cent, or 422 families, had no home; 98 per cent of houses had no sewer or water, and no telephone to summon help in emergencies. There were just nine wells for 5,480 people. "This is the heritage," the chiefs stated, "of a people whose ancestors surrendered the land and resources, which produces all the wealth of Canada, in exchange for a guarantee of certain rights and services for as long as the sun shines, the grass grows, and the rivers flow. One of those services promised was health care."[77] The brief recommended that the on-reserve nursing stations "should be condemned," and that government fund training for personnel to operate proper clinics. They urged the government to undertake an extensive housing and infrastructure construction program. Finally, they recommended that the Indian hospital remain open until a task force of representatives from government and the community could investigate hospital care facilities.

The chiefs' brief was sufficiently alarming, and potentially damaging, for the ministers to agree to establish a task force inquiry. It was also the least costly of the chiefs' recommendations. The five-member task force – David Ahenakew, president of the Federation of Saskatchewan Indians; Steve Pooyak representing the Battleford area Chiefs; Alex Taylor, for the Saskatchewan government; Alex Pinter from Indian Affairs; with Luc Laroche, from University of Ottawa as chairman and representing Health and Welfare – was formed in mid-May 1977 and directed to report in just six weeks. It would receive no funding, the members were to pay their own way, and there would be no new research. Essentially, the task force was to investigate the chiefs' brief and to review existing health programs, hospital utilization, and problems relating to housing and sanitation. The task force operated under one further constraint: "In any event, it is important that the task force come up with a recommendation relating to a unified, integrated system. The minister is not prepared to consider any dichotomy in the health service, eg a special service for Indian people outside the existing health services."[78] But it was also made clear to all that the task force was to be the "court of last appeal." The minister would use its recommendations to finally decide on the dilemma of the Indian hospital.[79]

To appear impartial, Health and Welfare appointed an outsider, Luc Laroche from University of Ottawa's medical school, to chair the task

force and represent the department. Alas, the appearance of impartial-
ity was deceiving. After a hurried investigation, the task force chair
submitted his report on 30 June 1977, and immediately health minister
Lalonde announced the Indian hospital's closure. Of particular significance to the minister was the report's Recommendation #1: "The present physical entity known as the Indian hospital to cease existing as
an active treatment facility and that the Minister consider the feasibil-
ity of replacing it with an Indian Health Centre."[80] This was precisely
what the minister and his bureaucrats wanted to hear and the policy
his predecessors had pursued for fifteen years. Unfortunately for the
department, the task force had made no such recommendation. In fact,
chairman Laroche, in his report, had unilaterally altered many of the
task force's recommendations. The original task force recommendation read: "The present physical entity known as the Indian hospital
to cease existing as an active treatment facility *and to be converted into
an Indian Health Centre*."[81] The change in wording, seemingly subtle,
subverted the task force's authority by giving the minister the power
to decide. More importantly for the community, the task force report's
change from *converting* to *replacing*, meant that the Indian hospital, at
once a tangible recognition of the treaty right to health care and a powerful symbol of their enduring struggle to have that right recognized,
would be lost. Recommendation #2 was also changed. In the original
task force report, the Indian Health Centre was to be under the direction and control of a board consisting of the North Battleford District
Chiefs; the board would have responsibility for all aspects of management, from policy, to budget approval, to administration. However, in
Laroche's report submitted to Health and Welfare, the board's responsibility would be "subject to the overall authority of the Government of
Canada."[82] The change in wording also affected the task force's further
Recommendation #11, that the proposed Health Centre lands, presently
hospital lands, be declared a special reserve under the Indian Act and
therefore under the control of area chiefs.

Laroche's other changes were not so subtle. Some recommendations
were removed entirely, while other revisions completely altered the
tenor and substance of the task force's most important conclusions. For
instance, the original statement on the treaty right to health is as follows
(with Laroche's deletions underlined and his altered wording in italics):

The Task Force believes that the Indian people, [*The Indian representatives
on the Task Force have expressed the view that the Indian people*] under the

Royal Proclamation of 1763, under Treaty #6 and the BNA Act, have a unique relationship to the federal government. This relationship requires the Government of Canada to accept and exercise the responsibility for the health and medical care of Indian people

There are indications that the health conditions of the Indian people have been deteriorating in recent years [*not improved as much as expected in recent years*] in spite of the present services being provided by Health and Welfare Canada.

Under the terms of Treaty #6, the federal government [*the Indian representatives strongly believe that the federal government*] is obligated to provide comprehensive health care services to Indians in the North Battleford District.[83]

In submitting his report to the minister, and before it became widely known he had substantially altered the original task force recommendations, chairman Laroche warned, "I know that the report will be controversial. It nevertheless expresses the mood of the Indians in North Battleford."[84] Even Laroche's significantly revised report was unacceptable to the bureaucrats. Preparing a counter-proposal despite the promise that the task force would be the "court of last appeal," deputy minister Bruce Rawson restated the government position: "We do not agree with the essence of the key recommendation to convert the hospital into a health centre and to grant Indians the authority to fully manage their own health services."[85]

Predictably, the four task force members (of whom only David Ahenakew and Steve Pooyak were Aboriginal) were outraged at the altered report. Minister Lalonde was at pains to explain away the fiasco. He explained that Chairman Laroche indicated some concern about the wording of the task force report and proposed changing it to make it more "palatable" to the government. Though Lalonde maintained that his officials advised Laroche to write the report as directed by the task force, Laroche himself claimed that senior bureaucrats recommended the changes.[86] Writing to task force member David Ahenakew, Lalonde apologized for the "confusion," which he claimed was the "result of good intentions and certainly not the result of a deliberate attempt to mislead."[87] Nevertheless, a telex from Lalonde's deputy minister, Rawson, to fellow bureaucrat Charles-E. Caron suggests duplicity, at best: "Personally I hope the confusion continues to mount around recommendation number one. I am sure that if the truth was known it would be quite clear and we would be in the soup."[88]

Recall, it was the Battleford chiefs' 1977 brief charting reserve conditions – homelessness, overcrowding, a lack of even rudimentary infrastructure, and the subsequent destruction of health – that prompted the task force inquiry. Although hampered by an arbitrary six-week deadline, it did not take the task force long to target a century of unfulfilled treaty promises as the fundamental problem. Recommending a renewed treaty relationship in which the Aboriginal people most affected would manage their own programs, the task force saw their work sabotaged. While bureaucratic obstruction and government intransigence marked the past fifteen years of struggle for the hospital, this was a grotesque perversion of sincere efforts to improve living conditions and health. The task force debacle was, moreover, the disturbingly logical consequence of the state's enduring assimilation project. At its core was the self-serving view that medical bureaucrats alone knew what was best for the people's health. In July, Marc Lalonde engaged independent consultant Graham Clarkson to formulate a health service plan for North Battleford. The minister promised, "I am prepared to accept any recommendations that Dr Clarkson may make after thoroughly studying this situation."[89]

Clarkson, the former executive director of the Saskatchewan Medical Care Insurance Commission and a respected health care consultant, began by interviewing all the task force members. Noting that they were "disturbed" by Laroche's report, calling his actions "inept at the best," Clarkson told Minister Lalonde, "I have no doubt that Dr Laroche is of the opinion that he acted with the interests of the Indians at heart. I also have no doubt that the Indians find it next to impossible to understand this."[90] Not surprisingly, Clarkson met considerable suspicion in North Battleford. As he put it, "Tension was high – and for good reason," not only because of Laroche's actions, but also because the government had already shut the hospital. He could not blame the people for their distrust. To demonstrate his independence to all concerned, Clarkson demanded the removal of the local IHS bureaucrat, Mr Burrows, who was increasingly distraught and unable to re-establish "sound relationships with the Indians."[91] Burrows was gone within the month.

In his recommendations, Clarkson followed closely the (original) task force report. Fundamental to his plan was Aboriginal administration of all health programs. While he agreed that the Indian hospital should remain closed, Clarkson proposed an Indian Health Centre under the authority of an executive board with representatives from each of the area reserves, a representative from each of Indian Affairs and Health and Welfare, and two non-Aboriginal community members. The centre's executive director would be appointed from among the Aboriginal members. Moreover, referring to "difficulties at the [IHS] Regional Office," Clarkson recommended that the Indian Health Centre report directly to Ottawa.[92] As Clarkson made clear, progress towards a solution of the health crisis required new, or perhaps fewer, bureaucrats at both the local and regional offices. His plan also called for a clearer focus on preventive and protective health services on the reserves, again administered by the bands and employing Aboriginal health workers.

Clarkson's study found that the long-standing local practice of contracting out medical services to a physicians' group had created unnecessary, excessive, and inappropriate hospitalization, especially of children. He noted that the volume of hospital care received by the Aboriginal community was more than three and a half times that of the non-Aboriginal community. The largest difference was for infants under one year, who were hospitalized five times more often than non-Aboriginal infants. Further, Clarkson compared just the Aboriginal population of the province, and found that the North Battleford area people were hospitalized one and a half times more often.[93] Much of the excess children's hospitalization was the consequence of poor housing and sanitation on the reserves. But calling some hospitalization "admissions of convenience," Clarkson thought it a "sad reflection on the Federal Government agency who operated the North Battleford Indian Hospital."[94] He examined the physicians' volume of practice and found that of the twenty doctors who admitted patients to either or both the Indian hospital and the Union Hospital in 1976, four had an average of 629 patients, while the other sixteen doctors collectively had 189. Clarkson could not imagine how these four doctors could spend adequate time with their patients. "Some of the doctors seemed to have little or no interest in providing medical services to the Indian community while one or two appeared to supply a remarkable volume which, to my way of thinking, would have to have been carried out all too quickly." Clarkson's plan called for the Indian Health Centre to retain two physicians on staff, under the supervision of the executive director. He quickly explained that this would not be a reversion to the designated doctor system of the past where IHS compelled patients to go to particular physicians, but rather Indian Health Centre physicians would form a nucleus whose "concern and involvement" would be working with the Aboriginal community.[95]

Organized medicine, locally and provincially, reacted negatively to Clarkson's plan and his criticisms of their work.[96] Clarkson understood the North Battleford district medical society's objections to the planned Indian Health Centre to be motivated by self-interest, specifically its impact on their incomes.[97] At a meeting with the Battlefords Union Hospital staff, IHS (properly Medical Services) director Lyall Black attempted to explain Clarkson's recommendations to a very hostile audience. He witnessed first-hand the bigotry and prejudice that Aboriginal people had long endured; as he reported, there was "little sympathy evident amongst the staff for Indian people." On the clear need for cultural orientation, Black noted the staff's confusion and surprise when he clarified that the orientation program would be necessary "for the doctors and hospital staff rather than for the Indians."[98] The Saskatchewan Medical Association's E.H. Baergen continued to oppose the Indian Health Centre in a letter to the *Canadian Medical Association Journal*. By way of "advising" any potential candidates for the staff positions at the Indian Health Centre, Baergen noted that since there was currently an adequate number of physicians practising in North Battleford, any increase would lead to friction among the medical staff of the Union Hospital, warning that "this will inevitably give rise to hard feelings against any newcomer to the centre."[99] This thinly veiled threat exposed the challenges that the Indian Health Centre posed to the medical status quo in North Battleford. Nevertheless, Clarkson's plan, accepted by the new minister of Health and Welfare, Monique Bégin, in December 1977, formed the basis for the Battlefords Indian Health Centre Inc., which opened less than two years later, while the new Battlefords Union Hospital celebrated its grand opening in June 1978.

The Indian Health Centre's board of directors stated its objectives: first "to ensure that comprehensive health services are delivered to the Indian Bands ... as a matter of Indian right under the British North America Act, Treaty Number 6 between her Majesty and the Cree Nation and the Indian Act"; and second, "to provide direction to Her Majesty in the operation of the Battlefords Indian Health Centre Inc."[100] At the Indian Health Centre's grand opening in July 1979, National Indian Brotherhood President Noel Starblanket celebrated the achievement as an example of community-based and community-controlled health care. But he also used the occasion to elaborate on the political and economic roots of ill health, in particular "coerced dependence upon paternalistic and ever-shifting federal policies ... [that] contributed to a great extent to the manifestations of social ill health now seen among us, including alcohol and drug abuse, family breakdown, suicides, accidents, and violent deaths."[101] Starblanket's remarks were especially poignant in light of the recently withdrawn federal guidelines for access to non-insured health benefits (dental care, drugs, glasses, and medical transportation). Hoping to trim budgets and stem a perceived abuse of benefits by the non-indigent, the Liberal government imposed a means test that hearkened back to the 1968 "Health Plan for Indians" a decade earlier. Protests emerged immediately with an angry march on Parliament Hill, while the St Regis Mohawk set up a $1 toll at the American border at Cornwall, Ontario, for a health fund to pay for needed medical care.[102] Experiencing its own "White Paper moment," the Department of Health and Welfare suspended the guidelines in January 1979. The government fell in June and the newly elected (albeit short-lived) Progressive Conservative government withdrew the guidelines, opting to rely on professional medical and dental judgment to determine eligibility for non-insured benefits. Starblanket praised the decision of the new health minister (and fellow platform dignitary) David Crombie. But, in language that would make any federal politician squirm, Starblanket framed the Indian Health Centre as a concrete example of self-government: "We can march with the sun to the brightness of a new and better day – through the total control of our lives and destinies – or we can retreat to the false security and darkness of government colonialist control."[103] Neither Starblanket nor the minister, in his remarks, mentioned the treaty right to health care. According to Crombie, the Health Centre was a landmark that demonstrated the government's determination "to *give* the Indian people" responsibility for their health, while confirming the willingness of the District Chiefs to "*accept* greater responsibility" for the delivery of health programs.[104] Nevertheless, the Indian Health Centre continues to stand as testament to the Aboriginal community's insistence that health services and the treaty relationship would not be severed.

Certainly, the North Battleford communities were not the only voices for change in health care delivery in the 1970s. The National Indian Brotherhood (NIB) in 1978 established a National Commission of Inquiry on Indian Health bringing together health representatives from provincial and territorial Aboriginal organizations. Taking direction from its members, not IHS or health professionals, the National Commission provided a distinctly Aboriginal perspective on health issues affecting its constituents.[105] Its 1978 brief, *Indian Control of Indian Health*, highlighted how federal policy, often formulated for political purposes and without input from Aboriginal people, lurched from crisis to crisis to the detriment of the very people it was to serve. The Indian Association of Alberta likewise characterized the federal government's approach to health care as unilateral, arbitrary, and piecemeal, while calling on the state to honour its treaty responsibilities.[106] By late 1979, taking some direction from national and provincial Aboriginal representatives, IHS developed yet another Indian Health Policy that, for the first time, acknowledged that health policy flowed from "constitutional and statutory provisions, treaties, and customary practice … and from the commitment of Indian people to preserve and enhance their culture and traditions." Not quite an affirmation of the treaty right to health, but it did move beyond the long-held claim that IHS policies stemmed from little more than a moral obligation. As a Health and Welfare bureaucrat put it, "We always thought that, as health professionals, we knew what Indians needed with respect to health care … [h]owever, not only is health status unimproved by today's standards, the situation is incompatible with both the aspirations of the Indian people and the tenets of self-determination and human rights."[107] Recognizing also the "intolerably low level of health of many Indian people, who exist under conditions rooted in poverty and community decline," the new health policy rested on three pillars: community development (socioeconomic, cultural, and spiritual); the traditional relationship with the federal government to serve as an advocate and to promote local capacity; and an active federal role in the interrelated health system.[108] An unprecedented policy direction perhaps, but old habits die hard: six months *after* announcing its policy, the government appointed a commission of inquiry to determine how Aboriginal groups should be consulted in decisions affecting health care policies and services.

The Advisory Commission, led by prominent jurist Thomas Berger, who had recently completed the Mackenzie Valley Pipeline Inquiry, advised that consultation about communities' participation in the planning, budgeting, and delivery of health programs should be the first step in their actual planning and delivery of those services. His report celebrated the achievements of the North Battleford Health Centre as a model of self-determination in health care, while also pointing to programs already developed by Aboriginal communities across the country. There were health centres, health councils, health liaison programs, initiatives in environmental health, nutrition, breast-feeding, homecare, mental and spiritual health, and midwifery programs.

All were community-based and all were chronically underfunded or funded on a piecemeal basis.[109] These initiatives, he stressed, emerged not from government policy, but often in spite of it. Berger therefore recommended that the $950,000 Cabinet had earmarked for consultation (less than 1 per cent of the IHS budget, he noted) be distributed among the provincial and territorial Indian organizations affiliated with the NIB to be used to develop the consultation process, with a separate appropriation to fund the process for the Inuit. His further recommendation – the establishment of a permanent national Indian Health Council – was not implemented.

The creation of the Battlefords Indian Health Centre to deliver health care "as a matter of Indian right," as it declared, offered a new model that reflected a changed political and medical landscape. Aboriginal self-determination in health would join similar programs to take back control of education and social services. Programs focused on preventative public health initiatives, delivered in the community, became more appropriate in the 1980s as many Aboriginal communities underwent an "epidemiological transition" with declining rates of communicable diseases and infant mortality, and an increasing incidence of chronic conditions such as diabetes and cardiovascular diseases.[110] Moreover, Canada endorsed the World Health Organization's optimistic goal of "health for all by the year 2000" and its 1978 Alma Ata declaration on primary health care as an essential first element that "requires and promotes maximum community and individual self-reliance and participation in the planning, organization, operation and control."[111] But clearly, Canada's support of primary health care in 1978 did not envision local Aboriginal control of health services. As noted, the IHS top bureaucrat had declared just the previous year "we do not agree ... to grant Indians the authority to fully manage their own health services."[112]

It was certainly no coincidence that North Battleford Indian Hospital employees, Walter Johnston and Andrew Swimmer, triggered the court challenges of the treaty right in the 1960s, much to the outrage of their employers. The court's rejection of those claims supported the state's contention that health care services are provided as a matter of policy, not legal obligation, leaving it free to change policy. Yet, the 1960s Saskatchewan Court of Appeal decisions very much reflected their times. Subsequent Supreme Court decisions, such as *Queen v Sparrow* (1990), held that the courts should interpret Aboriginal rights in a flexible manner to permit their evolution. As the Federal Court noted in reference to the medicine chest clause in 1999: "Mr Justice Angers took a proper approach in his 1935 decision in Dreaver (supra), reading the Treaty No. 6 medicine chest clause in a contemporary manner to mean a supply of all medicines, drugs and medical supplies. Certainly, it is clear that the Saskatchewan Court of Appeal took what is now a wrong approach in its literal and restrictive reading of the medicine chest clause in the 1966 decision in Johnston (supra)."[113]

It seems likely that a legal challenge today would have a different outcome. Nevertheless, the question of "insured health services" (hospital and physician services) seems resolved under the Canada Health Act (1984), in which provinces agreed to deliver care to all provincial residents, including Aboriginal people whether they lived on or off reserve, in return for federal funds, ending the often rancorous provincial-federal disputes over payment.[114] Access to non-insured health benefits remains subject to government policy, suggesting that the judgment in *Johnston*, not the 1935 *Dreaver* decision defining medicines and medical supplies as a treaty right, is the judicial last word.

The protracted struggle over the North Battleford Indian Hospital reveals the community's considerable resolve to define and defend its treaty relationship with the state. Resistance to arbitrary and shifting policies became a generation's work that ultimately contested the value of treating illness bred in poverty only to return the cured to the same conditions. The history of the North Battleford Health Centre's creation exposes an entrenched bureaucracy imbued with the increasing authority of medicine, actively working to undermine the community. State control and surveillance shifted only reluctantly and incrementally in the face of determined resistance by Aboriginal communities, and only after many years of suffering and despair. That communities might know their own health care needs came as an unwelcome challenge to a bureaucracy that consistently viewed Aboriginality as a condition to be treated and cured.

Conclusion

The history of "separate beds" for Aboriginal people complicates our understanding of twentieth-century health care in Canada. Indian hospitals stood alongside their more modern white counterparts, putting racial segregation at the core of the nascent welfare state. The Indian Health Service (IHS), removed from Indian Affairs and attached to the national health bureaucracy, acknowledged that Aboriginal people would be included in schemes for postwar health care, if only to keep them excluded. Underfunded, poorly staffed, and racially segregated institutions isolated the putative threat posed by Aboriginal people, while Canada consciously defined national health as liberal white citizenship. First Nations communities that saw hospitals as a first step towards better health found instead that the state's commitment ended with hospitalization while reserve poverty continued unabated. Separate bureaucratic silos of Indian Affairs, responsible for reserve sanitation and housing, and Indian Health Service, in charge of health care, encouraged this "vertical" or disease- or treatment-specific approach to health services and all but ensured continued poor health. Medicare only made matters worse. Accomplishing what the 1969 White Paper could not, national hospital and health insurance finally provided the federal government with a golden opportunity to jettison its legal responsibilities for Aboriginal people's health. For more than twenty years communities wrestled with an entrenched bureaucracy that sought to undermine their efforts to improve health through an integrated approach based on a measure of self-government. While most Canadians celebrated Medicare, Aboriginal communities faced arbitrary and often punitive health policies that exacerbated persistent socio-economic inequities to maintain health disparities based on race.

The meanings of Indian hospitals are inextricably linked to the larger story of health care in modern Canada. As tuberculosis retreated in the 1930s, the migration of First Nations to towns and cities reawakened fears of infection. The concerns of medical experts transformed the "Indian problem" into a threat to the public health. In urging the federal government to take responsibility, the Canadian Tuberculosis Association (CTA) encouraged the state to confine Aboriginal people in institutions well segregated from white patients. As the voice of sanatorium directors and provincial health bureaucrats, the CTA constructed the problem of "Indian tuberculosis" and devised its solution in racially segregated institutions financed by the federal state. While the first Indian Health Service hospital at Fort Qu'Appelle in 1936 was intended to provide a maternity ward to further the BCG vaccine trial on First Nations infants, the "remarkable economy" of the institution that operated at half the cost of sanatoria quickly recommended it as an ideal prototype. That model of maternity/general hospitals that also treated tuberculosis – an "unholy combination" according to one physician – underscores the baleful role of Indian hospitals as institutions of segregation and confinement.

First Nations communities initially greeted Indian hospitals as the harbinger of a brighter future where the state acknowledged its treaty obligations to better health care. But the promise rang increasingly hollow in the coercive and dangerously underfunded institutions. Shipped from their homes like spoiled cargo, patients often found themselves isolated by culture and language, unable to understand their situation, their treatments, or their prognosis. Those who challenged IHS control, like the Siksika at their Blackfoot Hospital, paid a heavy price. Overwhelmingly paternalistic, the IHS readily resorted to degrees of compulsion "for their own good," from body casts and straitjackets to the Indian Health Regulations, which essentially criminalized the ill. The promise of opportunities for medical training and employment in Indian hospitals likewise proved illusory. IHS mirrored broader social and economic inequities through rigid racialized and gendered medical hierarchies that left Aboriginal workers the least trained and worst paid. That Aboriginal employees (and patients) were often "graduates" of residential schools not only highlights the pervasive role of state institutions; it also exposes the state's hand in producing its own workforce. Nevertheless, as cultural brokers and interpreters, First Nations employees could mitigate the atmosphere of coercion and confinement that characterized the hospitals.

Blunt and unequivocal in his 1946 announcement, the minister of health rationalized the IHS and its hospitals as a humanitarian measure to protect the Canadian public. Aboriginal peoples' interests were subsumed in the medical bureaucracy's slippery understanding of humanitarianism. Constructed as objects of Ottawa's benevolence, Aboriginal people had little say in their own health care. Meanwhile, their bodies were readily exploited for research and teaching. As for postwar Canadians, Indian hospitals seemed to confirm that theirs was a vigilant yet compassionate state. As promises of a comprehensive welfare state quickly faded, Canadians could be assured that the most vulnerable were not forgotten. As the minister promised, the IHS established Indian hospitals in redundant military facilities and renovated residential schools. Meanwhile, the same bureaucracy's National Health Grants funded an unprecedented increase in hospital construction and expansion, adding thirty new institutions each year in the decade after 1948 and increasing the number of hospital beds by two-thirds. Indian hospitals had the added benefit of assuring Canadians that their new community hospitals would remain white, at least initially.

The logic of Indian hospitals for the 1940s combined enlightened self-interest, the rising social and political authority of medicine, and broad anxieties about the "Indian problem." But the 1960s saw profound transformations in national health. Massive investments in hospital infrastructure led to escalating operating costs, which yielded the national hospital insurance program and, with much political wrangling, health insurance in 1968. With the federal government sharing costs with the provinces, the seemingly redundant Indian hospitals could be "quietly closed." Responsibility for Aboriginal health care (and welfare) now shifted to the provinces. But the jurisdictional disputes that accompanied Medicare exposed Aboriginal people to the excesses of aggrieved provincial administrations and local hospital boards, which dismissed them as interlopers and less worthy of care. More ominous still was the understanding that Medicare would enable the federal government to fulfil its assimilationist goal and abandon its legal and treaty obligations.

Medicare's threat – or promise – to accomplish that aim was most clearly articulated in the protracted struggle over the North Battleford Indian Hospital. That bitter dispute exposed an obdurate and calculating bureaucracy that relentlessly undercut First Nations' efforts to address the links between ill health and the poverty that led to it. The effort to sever the legal and treaty relationship through the "equality" of Medicare continued for more than a decade after the White Paper's withdrawal, despite clear evidence that curative medical services had little impact on community health status. Medicare, not the medicine chest, would determine the state's role in health care.

To most Canadians, then as now, this was as it should be. The liberal democratic principles of individual political and legal equality imbued both the White Paper and Medicare. But Prime Minister Trudeau, who eventually admitted it was shortsighted, abandoned the White Paper within the year, saying, "we had perhaps the prejudices of small 'l' liberals and white men at that who thought that equality meant the same law for everybody."[1] Yet, shifting policies in the 1960s for hospital and health care insurance, and their implications for collective rights based on treaties and self-government, were not easily assailed. In the 1960s the court rejected First Nations attempts to assert a treaty right to health care, while the IHS bureaucracy directed them to discuss treaty issues with Indian Affairs. Nevertheless, dividing the authority between Indian Affairs, which was responsible for matters such as water quality, sanitation, and housing, and Health and Welfare, in charge of health services, did little to alleviate public health problems. Medicare threatened to exacerbate the problem by cutting the links between the roots of illness and health care services, not to mention the treaty relationship itself. Amid the socially and politically disruptive demands from Aboriginal people and Quebecers in the 1960s for collective rather than individual rights, the seemingly apolitical Medicare program bestowed a veneer of national unity that may account for its iconic status.[2] A cherished social program for a Canada that embraced liberal notions of social and political equality as the basis for good health, Medicare damaged the aspirations of many First Nations. Canadians remain eminently satisfied with Medicare, proudly proclaiming its values of equity, fairness, and solidarity as "intimately tied to their understanding of citizenship."[3] But Aboriginal citizenship was always incomplete and contingent. Denied the most basic right of the franchise before 1960, First Nations faced serial projects aimed at terminating their rights after. Medicare bestowed its benefits unevenly: "Aboriginal status" remains one of the key social determinants of health that includes other primary factors such as income, education, housing, and employment.[4]

The 1979 Indian Health Policy continues as the federal government's guiding statement on health care. Drafted in response to the determined resistance by First Nations to the state's continued attempts to shift responsibilities to the provinces, the policy pledged to preserve the federal government's "special relationship" with Aboriginal people. It employs the language of self-determination in its laudable goal "to achieve an increasing level of health in Indian communities, generated and maintained by the Indian communities themselves."[5] With a stronger federal commitment, the broken-down Indian hospitals, once powerful symbols in the long struggle for effective health care, were replaced by health clinics to provide primary care in communities. To address the problem of chronically understaffed hospitals in northern regions, IHS partnered with university medical schools to provide qualified personnel, who in turn benefited from the expanded opportunities for teaching and research. Nevertheless, significant disparities in health status persist between Aboriginal and non-Aboriginal Canadians. As T. Kue Young concluded in his study of the Anishinaabe of northwestern Ontario and the Sioux Lookout Indian Hospital, real change in health status required resources dedicated to community authority and control of health care, not highly specialized medical services.[6] In 1988, as Young's book went to press, five men from Sandy Lake First Nation went on a hunger strike at the Indian hospital to draw attention to years of worsening health care and deteriorating relations between First Nations communities and the Department of Health and Welfare.[7]

A decade after its inception, the broader promise of the 1979 Indian Health Policy, to address health care in communities, was abandoned for an exclusive focus on federal transfers to First Nations for some aspects of health care delivery. As minister of health Jake Epp told the Assembly of First Nations health transfer conference in 1987, "We, in Health and Welfare, and many others in the health field, are convinced that the future health of the Indian people rests in your hands, not in ours ... God bless you all." Author Dara Culhane Speck wondered if the minister's statement was a threat or a promise.[8] Critics suggested that the transfer policy merely offloaded the responsibility for health care to communities without actually sharing any power to develop or control programs. Was health transfer another "hidden agenda" of termination like the White Paper? The Assembly of First Nations argued that until First Nations had actual control over resources and economic development, communities would simply be "administering their own misery."[9] The policy's "non-enrichment" clause froze funding at levels in place at the time of transfer, with no provision for on-reserve population increases or shifting community needs. Other critics noted that the transfer program failed to address the wider social, economic, and environmental sources of ill health, while reinforcing a medical model of health that maintained colonial relations of power over Aboriginal people.[10] Tellingly, non-insured health benefits were excluded from the transfer program, which led to suspicions that the benefits might be withdrawn, and they would certainly be administered by government criteria.[11] A recent study concluded that the transfer policy was less concerned with self-determination than with cutting costs; it does little more than meet the Indian Act's original commitment to health – to control the spread of disease and provide sanitary conditions.[12]

In its brief to the Royal Commission on Aboriginal Peoples round-table on health issues in 1993, the Federation of Saskatchewan Indian Nations (FSIN) asked how the transfer policy would affect the treaty right to health care. If First Nations assumed the government's authority for health care, did that mean that treaty groups had absolved the state of its treaty responsibility? The FSIN brief, presented by Alma Favel-King in her capacity as the Executive Director of Health and Social Development portfolio, reflected the concerns of all treaty communities to define and protect the right to health care. But Favel-King had also been involved in the bitter twenty-year-long struggle over closing the North Battleford Indian Hospital two decades earlier. Better than most, she understood how health care policy was beholden to political caprice and bureaucratic interference. Echoing Chief Swimmer, the activist community had then argued the government's eyes "needed to be opened" to the clear link between ill health and IHS's arbitrary management of care. Although the Constitution Act (1982) reaffirmed existing treaty and Aboriginal rights, the interpretation of the treaty right to health care continues to be contested. As Favel-King told the Royal Commission, with the Aboriginal right to self-government and treaty rights clearly defined, together with adequate resources, First Nations could plan housing, sanitation, training, and community development to deal with ill health, family violence, and addictions, "in fact, all issues with a direct impact on the health status of First Nations people."[13] Until health policy was built on those acknowledged rights, she argued, health care remained vulnerable to the shifting political winds.[14]

It is only in the new century that "separate beds" has come to connote community management and control of some health care programs. With a fairly clear understanding of the health transfer's limitations, communities have embraced the opportunity for self-empowerment by managing nursing services, community health and addictions programs, prenatal nutrition, and mental health care.[15] In 2004, as part of the transfer process, the Touchwood and File Hills Qu'Appelle Tribal Councils took control of the sixty-eight-year-old Fort Qu'Appelle Indian Hospital and replaced it with the All Nations Healing Hospital, across the railroad tracks on Treaty Four reserve lands. The facility provides acute health care, community health programs, Indigenous ceremonies, and clinical counselling services in a holistic approach to health care to the whole community. The 1988 hunger strike at the Sioux Lookout Indian Hospital ended after the federal government agreed to permit the community to determine their own health needs and assert some control of the health delivery system.[16] After years of planning, the four parties – First Nations, federal, provincial, and municipal governments – agreed to amalgamate the resources of the Indian and provincial hospitals. In 2010 the sixty-bed Sioux Lookout Meno Ya Win Health Centre opened for First Nations and non-Aboriginal residents, offering acute and long-term care, mental health and addiction services, as well as community-based and Indigenous healing services.[17] Unlike earlier attempts, this "integration" has been accomplished, at least to some extent, on First Nations' terms. The inclusion of Indigenous healing with biomedical services reminds us of fundamentally different, though not incompatible, definitions of health and healing.

The history of Indian hospitals and health care policy since the 1920s reveals the limits of Canada's liberal democracy. Colonized in the interests of nineteenth-century state formation, Aboriginal people were marginalized in the construction of the welfare state. Lines of segregation and isolation, tended by the power of the state, and rationalized in the language of medical humanitarianism, did not negate Canada's liberal democratic values. In fact they were integral to the formation of national health as normal white citizenship. More than a half-century of contradictory and arbitrary policies that served the interests of the non-Aboriginal population left a destructive legacy in Aboriginal communities and beyond. Health disparities – constructed not found – have come to be seen as normal or inevitable. It is a measure of the strength and resolve of Aboriginal communities that the federal government finally was compelled to acknowledge its commitments to health care. It is with similar resolve that communities embark on, or more properly return to, the management of their health care. Whether the health transfer truly represents a new departure that will translate into better health or if the rhetoric of self-government masks yet another attempt to offload responsibility for health care remains an open question.

Notes

Introduction

1 *Edmonton Journal*, 27 August 1946.
2 The hospital began admitting patients in January 1946, before the official opening.
3 "Indian hospital" will be used throughout to reflect historical usage and the specific character of the institutions. In reference to communities, I use the national names preferred by contemporary First Nations, and where that is neither intended nor possible, I use First Nations or Aboriginal (Inuit and First Nations, or "status Indians" recognized by the state as coming under the authority of the Indian Act). The Metis are now defined as Aboriginal by the Constitution Act (1982), but in the period under study the federal government did not recognize any responsibility for their health care. Metis people's encounters with provincial hospitals would likely have been marked by the same community prejudices encountered by First Nations people, and they received no IHS support. That history remains to be written and is not treated here.
4 Mary-Ellen Kelm, *Colonizing Bodies: Aboriginal Health and Healing in British Columbia, 1900–1950* (Vancouver: University of British Columbia Press, 1998); Maureen Lux, *Medicine That Walks: Disease, Medicine and Canadian Plains Native People, 1880–1940* (Toronto: University of Toronto Press, 2001).
5 Amna Khalid and Ryan Johnson, "Introduction," in *Public Health in the British Empire: Intermediaries, Subordinates, and the Practice of Public Health, 1850–1960*, ed. Ryan Johnson and Amna Khalid (New York: Routledge, 2012), 20.
6 Waltraud Ernst, "Beyond East and West: From the History of Colonial Medicine to a Social History of Medicine(s) in South Asia," *Social History of Medicine* 20 (December 2007): 509–10, 513.

7 James Waldram, D. Ann Herring, and T. Kue Young, *Aboriginal Health in Canada: Historical, Cultural, and Epidemiological Perspectives*, 2nd ed. (Toronto: University of Toronto Press, 2006), 142.

8 For an overview of Aboriginal medical traditions see ibid., chapter 5; for the prairies, Lux, *Medicine That Walks*, chapter 2.

9 The responsibility for health care is not clearly defined in the Constitution Act (1982), where "Indians and Lands reserved for Indians" are the exclusive legislative authority of the federal government, while health and social services are provincial responsibilities. The Indian Act (1876) grants the Governor-in-Council the authority to make regulations to prevent, mitigate, and control the spread of diseases; to provide medical treatment and health services for Indians; to provide compulsory hospitalization and treatment for infectious diseases among Indians. Indian Act (R.S., c I-6, s 73).

10 Minister Brooke Claxton, Special Joint Committee of the Senate and the House of Commons Appointed to Examine and Consider the Indian Act, *Minutes of Proceedings and Evidence* No. 3 (6 June 1946), 65.

11 John L. Tobias, "Protection, Civilization, Assimilation: An Outline History of Canada's Indian Policy," *Western Canadian Journal of Anthropology* 6, no. 2 (1976): 13–30.

12 Ian McKay, "The Liberal Order Framework: A Prospectus for a Reconnaissance of Canadian History," *Canadian Historical Review* 81, no. 4 (December 2000): 625.

13 Uday S. Mehta, "Liberal Strategies of Exclusion," in *Tensions of Empire: Colonial Cultures in a Bourgeois World*, ed. Frederick Cooper and Ann Laura Stoler (Berkeley: University of California Press, 1997), 61.

14 Ian McKay, "Canada as a Long Liberal Revolution," in *Debating the Canadian Liberal Revolution*, ed. Jean-Francois Constant and Michel Ducharme (Toronto: University of Toronto Press, 2009), 351.

15 Quoted in Carolyn Strange and Alison Bashford, eds, *Isolation: Places and Practices of Exclusion* (London: Routledge, 2003), 5.

16 Adele Perry, "Women, Racialized People, and the Making of the Liberal Order in Northern North America," in *Debating the Canadian Liberal Revolution*, ed. Jean-Francois Constant and Michel Ducharme (Toronto: University of Toronto Press, 2009), 285.

17 Ian McKay, "Canada as a Long Liberal Revolution," 397.

18 McKay, "The Liberal Order Framework," 637.

19 See especially P.H. Bryce, *The Story of a National Crime: Being an Appeal for Justice to the Indians of Canada* (Ottawa: James Hope and Sons, 1922); John Milloy, *A National Crime: The Canadian Government and the Residential*

School System, 1879–1986 (Winnipeg: University of Manitoba Press, 1999); J.R. Miller, *Shingwauk's Vision* (Toronto: University of Toronto Press, 1996).

20 P.H. Bryce, *Report on the Indian Schools of Manitoba and the North-West Territories* (Ottawa: Government Printing Bureau, 1907), 18, RG10 (Records of the Department of Indian Affairs), v 4037, file 317,021, Library and Archives Canada (LAC); Bryce found that of the 1,537 school children, 35 per cent were either sick or dead, while 69 per cent of the children who had attended File Hills school in Saskatchewan were dead.

21 Bryce to Pedley, 5 Nov 1909, RG10 v 3957, file 140,754–1, LAC.

22 Brian Titley, *A Narrow Vision: Duncan Campbell Scott and the Administration of Indian Affairs in Canada* (Vancouver: University of British Columbia Press, 1986), 88.

23 Alison Bashford and Carolyn Strange, "Isolation and Exclusion in the Modern World," in Strange and Bashford, *Isolation*; Renisa Mawani, "Legal Geographies of Aboriginal Segregation in British Columbia," in Strange and Bashford, *Isolation*; Norbert Finzsch and Robert Jütte, eds, *Institutions of Confinement: Hospitals, Asylums, and Prisons in Western Europe and North America, 1500–1950* (Cambridge: Cambridge University Press, 1996); Michel Foucault, *Discipline and Punish: The Birth of the Prison*, trans. A. Sheridan, 2nd ed. (New York: Vintage, 1995); *Madness and Civilization: A History of Insanity in the Age of Reason* (New York: Vintage, 1984).

24 Colin Jones and Roy Porter, eds, "Introduction" to *Reassessing Foucault: Power, Medicine and the Body* (London: Routledge, 1994), 1–2.

25 David Arnold, "Medicine and Colonialism," in *Companion Encyclopedia of the History of Medicine*, ed. W.F. Bynum and Roy Porter (London: Routledge, 1993), 2:1411; see also David Arnold, ed., *Imperial Medicine and Indigenous Societies* (Manchester: Manchester University Press, 1988); Roy MacLeod and Milton Lewis, eds, *Disease, Medicine, and Empire* (London: Routledge, 1988); Randall M. Packard, *White Plague, Black Labor: Tuberculosis and the Political Economy of Health and Disease in South Africa* (Berkeley: University of California Press, 1989); Megan Vaughan, *Curing Their Ills: Colonial Power and African Illness* (Palo Alto, CA: Stanford University Press, 1991).

26 Strange and Bashford, *Isolation*, 3.

27 Robert Menzies and Ted Palys, "Turbulent Spirits: Aboriginal Patients in the British Columbia Psychiatric System, 1879–1950," in *Mental Health and Canadian Society: Historical Perspectives*, ed. James E. Moran and David Wright (Montreal and Kingston: McGill-Queen's University Press, 2006), 166.

28 Tuberculosis today is understood as an infectious disease caused by *Mycobacterium tuberculosis*. Spread through droplet infection, it most

commonly affects the lungs but can involve almost any organ of the body. Symptoms include fatigue, lethargy, and weight loss, progressing to coughing of sputum and blood and shortness of breath. It has a variable incubation period, and factors such as the quality of nutrition and crowding determine whether the disease develops. William D. Johnston, "Tuberculosis," in Kenneth Kiple, ed., *The Cambridge World History of Human Diseases* (Cambridge: Cambridge University Press, 1993), 1059–68.

29 Mary-Ellen Kelm, "Diagnosing the Discursive Indian: Medicine, Gender, and the 'Dying Race,'" *Ethnohistory* 52, no. 2 (2005): 373, 378.

30 Stewart to Premier Bracken, 14 November 1934, RG29 (Department of National Health and Welfare), v 1225, file 311-T7-16, LAC; quoted in "House of Commons Discusses Estimates for Indian Affairs Branch," *Bulletin of the Canadian Tuberculosis Association* 15, no. 4 (June 1937): 4; D.A. Stewart, *The Social Ramifications of Tuberculosis* (Winnipeg: Veterans Press, n.d.), 6, RG10–30-A-1, box 10, Archives of Ontario.

31 Warwick Anderson, *The Cultivation of Whiteness: Science, Health and Racial Destiny in Australia* (New York: Basic Books, 2003), 97.

32 The causes for tuberculosis decline in the Western world are not clear, but improvements in personal hygiene, increased prosperity, and improved sanitation, housing, and workplaces all had an impact; for Britain see Linda Bryder, *Below the Magic Mountain* (Oxford: Clarendon Press, 1988), 2; F.B. Smith, *The Retreat of Tuberculosis, 1850–1950* (London: Croom Helm, 1988), 1; Thomas McKeown, *The Modern Rise of Population* (London: Edward Arnold, 1976), 92; for the United States see Rene and Jean Dubos, *The White Plague: Tuberculosis, Man and Society* (Boston: Little, Brown, 1952), 185. G.J. Wherrett, the executive secretary of the CTA, wrote the CTA's celebratory history, *The Miracle of the Empty Beds: A History of Tuberculosis in Canada* (Toronto: University of Toronto Press, 1977).

33 Foucault, *Discipline and Punish*, 82.

34 Strange and Bashford, *Isolation*, 2; Strange and Bashford, "Cultures of Confinement," in Strange and Bashford, *Isolation*, 135.

35 G.D. Stanley, "Early Days at the Muskoka San," *Calgary Historical Bulletin* 18 (May 1953): 18–19.

36 Katherine Ott, *Fevered Lives: Tuberculosis in American Culture since 1870* (Cambridge: Harvard University Press, 1996), 1.

37 Quoted in C. Stuart Houston, *R.G. Ferguson: Crusader against Tuberculosis* (Toronto: Dundurn Press, 1991), 51.

38 Kelm, *Colonizing Bodies*, 122; Lux, *Medicine That Walks*, 197, 215; Houston, *R.G. Ferguson*, 92.

39 Bryder, *Below the Magic Mountain*; Smith, *Retreat of Tuberculosis*; Sheila
    Rothman, *Living in the Shadow of Death: Tuberculosis and the Social Experience
    of Illness in American History* (New York: Basic Books, 1994); Barbara Bates,
    Bargaining for Life: A Social History of Tuberculosis, 1876–1938 (Philadelphia:
    University of Pennsylvania Press, 1992); Georgina Feldberg, *Disease and
    Class: Tuberculosis and the Shaping of Modern North American Society* (New
    Brunswick, NJ: Rutgers University Press, 1995); Katherine McCuaig,
    *The Weariness, the Fever, and the Fret: The Campaign against Tuberculosis in
    Canada, 1900–1950* (Montreal and Kingston: McGill-Queen's University
    Press, 1999); Amy Fairchild and Gerald Oppenheimer, "Public Health
    Nihilism vs Pragmatism: History, Politics and the Control of Tuberculosis,"
    American Journal of Public Health 88, no. 7 (1998): 1105–17.
40 Smith, *Retreat of Tuberculosis*, 244–5.
41 Strange and Bashford, "Cultures of Confinement," in Strange and
    Bashford, *Isolation*, 135.
42 A.L. Paine and Earl Hershfield, "Tuberculosis: Past, Present and Future,"
    Canadian Family Physician 25 (1979): 55–9.
43 Wherrett, *Miracle of the Empty Beds*, 41.
44 Dr Wherrett, "Back to Work after a Bout of Tuberculosis," *Canada at Work*
    (broadcast N-537, 5 December 1954), 3, MG28, I75, Canadian Tuberculosis
    Association, v 21, file 10, LAC.
45 Ibid., 4.
46 Jordan Goodman, Anthony McElligott, and Lara Marks, eds, *Useful Bodies:
    Humans in the Service of Medical Science in the Twentieth Century* (Baltimore:
    Johns Hopkins University Press, 2003), 12.
47 Donna Dryden, Elva Taylor, Rona Beer, Ron Bergman, and Margaret
    Cogill, *The Camsell Mosaic: The Charles Camsell Hospital, 1945–1985*
    (Edmonton: Charles Camsell History Committee, 1985), 7, 98–100.
48 On these transformations in Canada see, for example, David Gagan and
    Rosemary Gagan, *For Patients of Moderate Means: A Social History of the
    Voluntary Public General Hospital in Canada, 1890–1950* (Montreal and
    Kingston: McGill-Queen's University Press, 2002); for the United States,
    see Charles Rosenberg, *The Care of Strangers: The Rise of America's Hospital
    System* (New York: Basic Books, 1987); David Rosner, *A Once Charitable
    Enterprise: Hospitals and Health Care in Brooklyn and New York, 1885–1915*
    (New York: Cambridge University Press, 1982).
49 James Wishart, "Class Difference and the Reformation of Ontario Public
    Hospitals, 1900–1935," *Labour/Le Travail* 48 (2001): 27–61; Mark Cortiula,
    "Social Class and Health Care in a Community Institution: The Case of
    Hamilton City Hospital," *Canadian Bulletin of Medical History* 6 (1989):

133–45; Gagan and Gagan, *For Patients of Moderate Means*, 39–40; for an American example see Vanessa Northington Gamble, *Making a Place for Ourselves: The Black Hospital Movement, 1920–1945* (New York: Oxford University Press, 1995).

50 The impact of this investment is at times elided by histories of postwar health policy that tend to focus on the failures of the federal Liberal government to make good on its wartime promises of health insurance and a comprehensive program of social security. Alvin Finkel, "Paradise Postponed: A Re-examination of the Green Book Proposals of 1945," *Journal of the Canadian Historical Association* 4 (1993): 120–42; Alvin Finkel, *Our Lives: Canada after 1945* (Toronto: James Lorimer, 1997), 18–20; P.E. Bryden, "The Liberal Party and the Achievement of National Medicare," *Canadian Bulletin of Medical History* 26, no. 2 (2009): 315–32.

51 Malcolm Taylor, "The Canadian Health Care System: After Medicare," in *Health and Canadian Society: Sociological Perspectives*, 2nd ed., ed. David Coburn, Carl D'Arcy, George Torrance, and Peter New (Toronto: Fitzhenry and Whiteside, 1987), 74.

52 "Fort Alexander Reserve," 1 July 1957, RG29, v 2913, file 851-A501 pt. 3, LAC.

53 B.L. Van Der Berg, MD, to Wood, 9 August 1958; "Investigation Drinking Water Supplies, Fort Alexander Reserve," July 1958, RG29, v 2931, file 851-X200, pt. 3, LAC.

54 W.J. Wood, IHS, to M.R. Elliot, Public Health, Winnipeg, 19 September 1958, RG29, v 2931, file 851-X200, pt. 3, LAC.

55 M.V. Peever, Field Nurse, to Moore, 10 October 1958, RG29, v 2931, file 851-X200, pt. 3, LAC.

56 "Investigation Drinking Water Supplies, Fort Alexander Reserve," July 1958, RG29, v 2931, file 851-X200, pt. 3, LAC.

57 "Fort Alexander Reserve," 1 July 1957, RG29, v 2913, file 851-A501 pt. 3, LAC.

58 Ibid.

59 While one monthly adult ration provided 2,500 calories, Indian Affairs used a diminishing scale so that four adult rations provided only slightly more than twice as much food as a single ration. Rations consisted of flour, rolled oats, baking powder, sugar, lard, beans, rice or potatoes, cheese, meat or fish, salt, and matches. "Fort Alexander Reserve," 1 July 1957, RG29, v 2913, file 851-A501 pt. 3, LAC.

60 Ian Mosby, "Administering Colonial Science: Nutrition Research and Human Biomedical Experimentation in Aboriginal Communities and Residential Schools, 1942–1952," *Histoire Sociale/Social History* 46, no. 91 (May 2013): 152.

61 "Fort Alexander Reserve," 1 July 1957, RG29, v 2913, file 851-A501 pt. 3, LAC.

62 "Fort Alexander Indian Hospital," n.d. (visited 25 February 1960) RG29, v 2931, file 851–1-X200, pt. 4, LAC.

63 See for instance Natalia Ilyniak, "Mercury Poisoning in Grassy Narrows: Environmental Injustice, Colonialism, and Capitalist Expansion in Canada," *McGill Sociological Review* 4 (February 2014): 43–66.

64 For the sake of consistency I will use Indian Health Service (IHS) to refer to the bureaucracy responsible for health care. Known as Indian Health Service when it was housed in the Department of Indian Affairs, it retained the name when health services were transferred to National Health and Welfare in 1945. Reflecting an increasing interest in the north, the name was changed to the Indian and Northern Health Service (INHS) in 1955. In 1962 another government reorganization saw the elimination of INHS and the creation of the Medical Services Branch (MSB), an amalgamation of seven former independent services – Civil Aviation, Civil Service Health, Northern Health, Quarantine, Immigration, Sick Mariners, and the largest, Indian Health Service; in 2000 it was renamed the First Nations and Inuit Health Branch (FNIHB).

65 For a time in the 1950s, Inuit patients were kept at the federal government's Parc Savard Immigration Hospital in Quebec City.

66 P.E. Moore, "No Longer Captain: A History of Tuberculosis and Its Control amongst Canadian Indians," *Canadian Medical Association Journal* 84 (May 1961): 1012–16; Wherrett, *Miracle of the Empty Beds*; former staff at the largest hospital collected reminiscences from patients and staff (Dryden et al., *Camsell Mosaic*). It was a premature celebration. Recent scholarship judges the history of tuberculosis as "a story of medical failure." Alimuddin Zumla and Matthew Gundy, "Epilogue: Politics, Science, and the 'New' Tuberculosis," in *The Return of the White Plague: Global Poverty and the "New" Tuberculosis*, ed. Matthew Gundy and Alimuddin Zumla (London: Verso, 2003), 237.

67 Myra Rutherdale, "Nursing in the North and Writing for the South: The Work and Travels of Amy Wilson," and Laurie Meijer Drees, "Training Aboriginal Nurses: The Indian Health Services in Northwestern Canada," in *Caregiving on the Periphery: Historical Perspectives on Nursing and Midwifery in Canada*, ed. Myra Rutherdale (Montreal and Kingston: McGill-Queen's University Press, 2010); Kathryn McPherson, "Nursing and Colonization: The Work of Indian Health Service Nurses in Manitoba, 1945–1970," in *Women, Health, and Nation: Canada and the United States since 1945*, ed. Georgina Feldberg, Molly Ladd Taylor, Alison Li, and Kathryn McPherson (Montreal and Kingston: McGill-Queen's University Press, 2003); by 1960 IHS operated thirty clinics, thirty-seven nursing stations, and eighty-three health centres.

68 T. Kue Young, *Health Care and Cultural Change: The Indian Experience in the Central Subarctic* (Toronto: University of Toronto Press, 1988).

69 Pat Sandiford Grygier, *A Long Way from Home: The Tuberculosis Epidemic among the Inuit* (Montreal and Kingston: McGill-Queen's University Press, 1994); Laurie Meijer Drees, "The Nanaimo and Charles Camsell Indian Hospitals: First Nations' Narratives of Health Care, 1945 to 1965," *Histoire Sociale/Social History* 43, no. 85 (2010): 165–91; these narratives are reprinted in Meijer Drees's *Healing Histories: Stories from Canada's Indian Hospitals* (Edmonton: University of Alberta Press, 2013).

70 Adele Perry develops the notion in relation to nineteenth-century state formation that treats the project of marginalizing Aboriginal people and the building of a white settler society as separate and discrete processes; the fiction's power rests on the assumption that settler domination was inevitable. *On the Edge of Empire: Gender, Race and the Making of British Columbia, 1849–1871* (Toronto: University of Toronto Press, 2001), 19.

Chapter One

1 See especially P.H. Bryce, *The Story of a National Crime: Being an Appeal for Justice to the Indians of Canada* (Ottawa: James Hope and Sons, 1922); John Milloy, *A National Crime: The Canadian Government and the Residential School System, 1879–1986* (Winnipeg: University of Manitoba Press, 1999); J.R. Miller, *Shingwauk's Vision* (Toronto: University of Toronto Press, 1996).

2 D.C. Scott, "Notes on Dr. Bryce's Report with Suggestions for Further Action," 7 March 1910, RG10 v 3957, file 140754-1, LAC.

3 In his *The Story of a National Crime: Being an Appeal for Justice to the Indians of Canada* Bryce blamed Scott for undermining his efforts to improve the schools, and for refusing to include responsibility for Aboriginal health in the newly created federal Department of Health in 1919. He reserved his most bitter attacks for the administration that failed to appoint him the health department's first deputy minister.

4 James Wishart, "Class Difference and the Reformation of Ontario Public Hospitals, 1900–1935," *Labour/Le Travail* 48 (2001): 27–61; Mark Cortiula, "Social Class and Health Care in a Community Institution: The Case of Hamilton City Hospital," *Canadian Bulletin of Medical History* 6 (1989): 133–45; for an American example see Vanessa Northington Gamble, *Making a Place for Ourselves: The Black Hospital Movement, 1920–1945* (New York: Oxford University Press, 1995); on hospital transformation see David Gagan and Rosemary Gagan, *For Patients of Moderate Means: A Social History of the Voluntary Public General Hospital in Canada, 1890–1950*

(Montreal and Kingston: McGill-Queen's University Press, 2002); for the United States see Charles Rosenberg, *The Care of Strangers: The Rise of America's Hospital System* (New York: Basic Books, 1987); David Rosner, *A Once Charitable Enterprise: Hospitals and Health Care in Brooklyn and New York, 1885–1915* (New York: Cambridge University Press, 1982).

5　See Constance Backhouse, *Colour-Coded: A Legal History of Racism in Canada, 1900–1950* (Toronto: University of Toronto Press, 1999). Scientist and broadcaster David Suzuki recalls in his autobiography that in Prince Rupert, British Columbia, in the 1940s Aboriginal people were not allowed to stay in most hotels, were refused service in restaurants, and were forced to sit in designated sections of movie theatres. *The Autobiography* (Vancouver: Greystone Books, 2006), 14. George Manuel, noted activist and chief of the National Indian Brotherhood by 1970, recalled the segregated movie theatres in the Kamloops of his youth in *The Fourth World* (New York: Free Press, 1974), 101. Violet Clark from Ahousaht First Nation recalled for historian Laurie Meijer Drees an incident in the 1950s when she and other Aboriginal hospital employees and a white doctor were refused service in a Duncan, British Columbia, restaurant until they sat in the back at a table separate from their white dining companion. *Healing Histories* (Edmonton: University of Alberta Press, 2013), 185.

6　Gagan and Gagan, *For Patients of Moderate Means*, 166–7.

7　Andrew Lam, Esther Fung, et al., Chinese Christian Youth Conference Committee, 5 April 1946, to W.H. Hatfield, Director Division of TB Control; JB Peters to Deputy Provincial Health Officer, 3 September 1946, GR 129, box 2, file 5, British Columbia Archives (hereafter BCA).

8　Memorandum, Forget, Accountant, 26 February 1917, RG29 v 2728, file 811-2 part 1 LAC; Mary-Ellen Kelm, *Colonizing Bodies: Aboriginal Health and Healing in British Columbia, 1900–1950* (Vancouver: University of British Columbia Press, 1998), 136–7; E. Martin, BC Minister of Health, to J.W. Monteith, Minister of National Health, 25 October 1961: "At one time it was a practice in some hospitals in BC to maintain Indian wards to which Indian patients were assigned exclusively." GR679, box 5, file 10, BCA.

9　W.H. Carter to Thomas Murphy, 4 February 1933, RG 29, v 2775, file 822-1-X200, part 1; ibid., H. McGill to Dr Bissett, 24 March 1938, part 2, LAC; J.D. Adamson to J. McEachern, 15 July 1939, RG 29, v 2590, file 800-1-D297, part 1, LAC.

10　Ken Coates, *Best Left as Indians; Native-White Relations in the Yukon Territory, 1840–1973* (Montreal and Kingston: McGill-Queen's University Press, 1991), 95.

11 Stanton to Chairman, 27 March 1950, RG 22, v 878, file 41-5-9, LAC. Unlike most administrators, Stanton was made to justify his policy in order to receive the newly established National Health Grants.

12 G.J. Wherrett, "Tuberculosis in Canada," Royal Commission on Health Services (Ottawa: Queen's Printer, 1965), 62.

13 J. Barnes to Dr H.A. Proctor, IHS, 30 September 1948; Barnes and J.D. Heaslip, MD, to chairman and members, Calgary Hospitals Board, 12 January 1949, RG 29, v 2936, file 851-1-X400, part 1, LAC. Alberta introduced hospital insurance in July 1950, but the municipally administered plan covered less than 75 per cent of the population by 1953; by 1954 only 38 per cent of all hospital income came from the provincial government. Malcolm Taylor, *Health Insurance and Canadian Public Policy*, 2nd ed. (Montreal and Kingston: McGill-Queen's University Press, 1987), 169–70.

14 Barnes and J.D. Heaslip, MD, to chairman and members, Calgary Hospitals Board, 12 January 1949, RG 29, v 2936, file 851-1-X400, part 1, LAC.

15 Ibid., Moore to Barnes, 1 April 1949.

16 Ibid., Stone to Director IHS, 5 January 1950

17 Lindsay Granshaw, "The Hospital," in *Companion Encyclopedia of the History of Medicine*, ed. W.F. Bynam and Roy Porter (London: Routledge, 1993), 2:1193.

18 Maureen Lux, *Medicine That Walks: Disease, Medicine and Canadian Plains Native People, 1880–1940* (Toronto: University of Toronto Press, 2001), 200–1.

19 F.A. Corbett to Graham, 7 December 1920, RG10, v 4092, file 546898, LAC.

20 Quoted in Elizabeth Churchill, "Tsuu T'ina: A History of a First Nations Community, 1890–1940" (PhD diss., University of Calgary, 2000), 396.

21 Ibid., 393–4.

22 Quoted in ibid., 413.

23 McGill Papers, M742, box 4, file 36, "Correspondence, 1928–41," Glenbow Archives Institute (GAI).

24 Baker Memorial Sanatorium, 1917–1937, file 73.315/37, box 2, Public Archives of Alberta (PAA); *Calgary the Denver of Canada* (Calgary: Calgary Herald Print, 1895), 5.

25 Sarah Carter, *Aboriginal People and Colonizers of Western Canada* (Toronto: University of Toronto Press, 1999), 76.

26 Diamond Jenness, *The Sarcee Indians of Alberta* Bulletin no. 90 (Canada: National Museum of Canada, 1938).

27 R.F. Battle, Regional Supervisor to Director, Indian Affairs Branch, 8 December 1955, RG 29, v 2936, file 851-1-X400, part 1, LAC.

28 In the 1920s small nursing stations, called "hospitals," were built on the Stoney (Iyarhe Nakoda) and Peigan (Piikani) reserves near Calgary; in

1928 the Catholic Blood Hospital managed by the Grey Nuns was rebuilt on the southern edge of the reserve at the nearby village of Cardston, across the street from the local municipal hospital. It is not clear if band funds or the DIA paid for these institutions.

29 Canada, House of Commons (CHC), Sessional Papers, 1911, 187; the fate of the Blackfoot Hospital is treated in chapter 5.

30 G.H. Gooderham, "Twenty-five Years as an Indian Agent to the Blackfoot Band," January 1972, M3947, GAI; "The Hospital," M4738, box 1, file 3, GAI.

31 Sally Mae Weaver, "Health, Culture and Dilemma: A Study of the Non-Conservative Iroquois, Six Nations Reserve, Ontario" (PhD diss., University of Toronto, 1967), 146–7.

32 S.L. Macdonald to Secretary DIA, 31 July 1923, RG 29, v 2795, file 831-1-D353 part 1, LAC.

33 Ibid., Joseph Guy, OMI to DC Scott, 1 December 1924; S.L. Macdonald to D.C. Scott, 15 April 1926.

34 Right Rev George Exton Lloyd, Bishop Diocese of Saskatchewan, to DC Scott, 30 July 1926, RG 29, v 2795, file 831-1-D353 part 1, LAC.

35 Author interview with Andrew and Rosabel (Ryder) Gordon, Pasqua First Nation, 14 July 2000; Gordon's father, Andrew Gordon Sr led the delegation that included First World War veterans Abel Watech and Harry Ball; Petition 30 October 1923, RG10, v 4093, file 600,023 LAC.

36 Scott to Graham, 1 December 1925; Graham to Scott, 1 February 1926, RG10, v 4084, file 495,800 LAC.

37 H.W. Hill, "The Epidemiology of Tuberculosis amongst British Columbia Interior Indians," 31, MG28, Canadian Tuberculosis Association, I75, II (a) file 33, "Indians – BC," LAC; "Conference on Tuberculosis among Indians in Canada, Ottawa, 1937," 37, MG28, I75, file II (a), LAC.

38 Canada, House of Commons, *Annual Report of the Department of Indian Affairs* 1928, 7–8.

39 Kelm, *Colonizing Bodies*, 120.

40 "Conference on Tuberculosis among Indians in Canada, Ottawa, 23 June 1937," 1.

41 J.G. Wherrett, *The Miracle of the Empty Beds* (Toronto: University of Toronto Press, 1977), 109; Wherrett puts the meeting in 1925.

42 Obituary, "Ervin Lockwood Stone," *Canadian Medical Association Journal* 98 (2 March 1968): 473.

43 T. Kue Young, *Health Care and Cultural Change: The Indian Experience in the Central Subarctic* (Toronto: University of Toronto Press, 1988), 86.

44 E.L. Stone, "Canadian Indian Medical Services," *Canadian Medical Association Journal* (July 1935): 82–5.

45 McGill to Indian agents, 14 January 1937, RG 29, v 1225, file 311-T7–16, LAC.

46 Norquay to Stone, 28 September 1937, RG 29 v 2915, file 851-1-A671 part 1(a), LAC.

47 F.R. Conroy, LLB, Barrister and Solicitor North Battleford, 20 September 1937, to DIA, Ottawa, and Department of Public Health, Regina; Director of Indian Affairs to S.L. Macdonald, Indian Agent, 23 October 1937, RG 29, v 2795, file 831-1-D353 part 1, LAC; "Appeals in Vain to Get Hospital Care for Child," *Saskatoon Star Phoenix*, 24 September 1937.

48 The Prince Albert Sanatorium, opened in 1930, admitted its first Aboriginal patient in 1935. Mary was admitted along with three other school children in 1937; the following year Prince Albert took in fifty-six Aboriginal patients, half of them schoolchildren. Increasing Aboriginal admissions reflected the declining need for sanatorium beds by the non-Aboriginal population. Saskatchewan Lung Association Files, A638, file IX.73a, Saskatchewan Archives Board (hereafter SAB).

49 D.A. Stewart, "The Red Man and the White Plague" (1936), 4, Lung Association, A638 file VII.27, SAB.

50 D.A. Stewart, Sanatorium Board of Manitoba, to R.A. Wardle, 22 January 1934, A638 file VII.27, SAB.

51 E.L.M. Thorpe, *The Social Histories of Smallpox and Tuberculosis in Canada: Culture, Evolution and Disease* (Winnipeg: University of Manitoba Anthropology Papers No. 30, 1989), 98, 106. Thorpe, a nurse by training, worked in hospitals in Britain and in British colonies in the Middle East and Far East during the Second World War. She established a psychiatric hospital in Jamaica in the 1950s, and eventually arrived in Manitoba as a consultant to the Sanatorium Board's efforts to decommission its sanatoria in the 1960s. At age sixty-five she undertook graduate studies in anthropology and used her many personal connections to Sanatorium Board personnel to critically assess the supposed racial explanations for disease in Aboriginal communities.

52 Wherrett, *Miracle of the Empty Beds*, 62.

53 Donna Dryden et al., *The Camsell Mosaic* (Edmonton: Charles Camsell History Committee, 1985), 133; Bruce Norton, "Northern Manitoba Treaty Party, 1949," *Manitoba History* 39 (Spring 2000): 15–24.

54 Thorpe, *Social Histories of Smallpox and Tuberculosis in Canada*, 106.

55 This refers to Bruce Curtis's observations of the historical practice of census making in Canada. He argues that the census was not taken, it was made. Bruce Curtis, *The Politics of Population: State Formation, Statistics, and the Census of Canada, 1840–1875* (Toronto: University of Toronto Press, 2001), 34.

56 Stewart, "The Red Man and the White Plague," 4.

57 John D. O'Neil, "Aboriginal Health Policy for the Next Century" in *The Path to Healing: Report of the National Round Table on Aboriginal Health and Social Issues* (Ottawa: Royal Commission on Aboriginal Peoples, 1993), 34.

58 R.G. Ferguson, *Tuberculosis among the Indians of the Great Canadian Plains* (Reprint, London: Adlard and Son, 1928); R.G. Ferguson and A.B. Simes, "BCG Vaccination of Indian Infants in Saskatchewan," *Tubercle* 30, no. 1 (1949): 5–11.

59 Simes to Stone, 20 March 1934; Privy Council Minute, 6 August 1934, RG29, v 2819, file 831-1-X328, LAC.

60 See M.K. Lux, "Perfect Subjects: Race, Tuberculosis and the Qu'Appelle BCG Vaccine Trial," *Canadian Bulletin of Medical History* 15 (1998): 277–96. Of the vaccinated group, 39 of 306 children died in the first year, and 38 of 303 controls died within the first year. Ferguson and Simes, "BCG Vaccination," 5.

61 McGill to deputy minister, Mines and Resources, 28 April 1938, RG22, v 1207, file 675/3 part 1, LAC.

62 Crerar, erstwhile leader of the failed Progressive Party and an articulate voice for western and Manitoba interests, returned to Parliament in 1935 as a Liberal in Mackenzie King's cabinet as minister of Indian Affairs until 1936. When the department became a branch of Mines and Resources, he assumed the new portfolio until his appointment to the Senate in 1945, where he served until his ninetieth birthday in 1966. RG29, v 3391, file 811-2-Crerar, LAC.

63 Minister to Governor General in Council, 1 December 1936, RG29, v 3391, file 811-2-Crerar, LAC.

64 MacInnes to Waite, 2 February 1937, RG29, v 3391, file 811–2-Crerar, LAC.

65 Wherrett, *Miracle of the Empty Beds*, 110, 112–13.

66 "House of Commons Discusses Estimates for Indian Affairs Branch," quoted in *Bulletin of the Canadian Tuberculosis Association* 15, no. 4 (1937): 3–4.

67 Stewart to Premier Bracken, 14 November 1934, RG 29, v 1225, file 311-T7-16, LAC.

68 "Conference on Tuberculosis among Indians in Canada, Ottawa, 23 June 1937," 11, MG28, I75, II (a), file 36, LAC.

69 Ibid., 13, 57–8, 73, 89.

70 Memorandum, E.L. Stone to Director, 29 June 1937, MG28, I75, II (a), file 36, LAC.

71 "Conference on Tuberculosis," 14; "preventoria" were intended to prevent, not treat illness, and to provide a middle-class home life for children of the tubercular indigent. Cynthia Connolly, *Saving Sickly Children: The Tuberculosis Preventorium in American Life, 1909–1970* (New Brunswick, NJ: Rutgers University Press, 2008), 2.

72 Memorandum, E.L. Stone to Director, 29 June 1937, MG28, I75, II (a), file 36, LAC.

73 "Outline of Tuberculosis Control for the Indian Population of Canada, 1937," MG28, I75, II (a), file 31 LAC.

74 E.L. Ross and A.L. Paine, "A Tuberculosis Survey of Manitoba Indians," *Canadian Medical Association Journal* 4 (Aug 1939): 180–4.

75 McGill, Director Indian Affairs to Deputy Minister, Mines and Resources, 28 April 1938, RG22, v 1207, file 675/3 part 1, LAC.

76 The Sanatorium Board of Manitoba subsequently agreed to manage tuberculosis treatment for Indian Health Service in return for per diem payments from the federal government. RG29, v 2590, file 800-1-D297, part 1, LAC.

77 "Hospitals Developed for Canadian Indians," *New York Times*, 7 January 1940.

78 Sinnott to Crerar, 2 May 1940, RG29, v 3391, file 811-2-Crerar, LAC.

79 J.D. Adamson to McEachern, 15 July 1939, RG 29, v 2590, file 800-1-D297, part 1, LAC. Sectarian voluntary hospitals were particularly vulnerable to financial distress during the Depression. Unlike municipal or city hospitals they could not turn to taxpayers for increased grants; neither could they increase rates charged to paying patients while other hospitals kept rates unchanged. In order to stave off financial ruin in the 1930s, Edmonton General Hospital, also owned by the Grey Nuns, converted its pediatric and maternity wards to tuberculosis wards to take advantage of provincial funds for tuberculosis treatment for the indigent. Pauline Paul, "A History of the Edmonton General Hospital: 1895–1970" (PhD diss., University of Alberta, 1994), 378–9.

80 McGill, "Memorandum for the Deputy Minister," 15 September 1939, RG 29, v 2590, file 800-1-D297, part 1, LAC.

81 Northwood to P.E. Moore, 3 April 1940, RG 29, v 2590, file 800-1-D297, part 1, LAC.

82 William D. Johnston, "Tuberculosis," in *The Cambridge World History of Human Diseases*, ed. Kenneth Kiple (Cambridge: Cambridge University Press, 1993), 1065. Other forms of collapse therapy included thoracoplasty (the surgical removal of several ribs to collapse the lung) and phrenic nerve crush (to paralyse the diaphragm).

83 "Report of the Resident Physician of Dynevor Indian Hospital," 31 December 1940, RG 29, v 2590, file 800-1-D297, part 1, LAC.

84 "Report of the Dynevor Indian Hospital for the Year 1945." Of the remaining patients, 27 per cent were deemed well enough to work, 22 per cent were "at school," and 9 per cent were "at home." RG 29, v 2591, file 800-1-D297, part 2, LAC.

85 Katherine McCuaig, *The Weariness, the Fever, and the Fret: The Campaign against Tuberculosis in Canada, 1900–1950* (Montreal and Kingston: McGill-Queen's University Press, 1999), 71–2; Darlene Zdunich, "Tuberculosis and World War One Veterans" (MA thesis, University of Calgary, 1984), 102.

86 Report, 31 December 1940, RG 29, v 2590, file 800-1-D297, part 1, LAC.

87 Report, 1945, RG 29, v 2591, file 800-1-D297, part 2, LAC.

88 "Meeting of the Indian Advisory Committee, March 10, 1938," MG28, I75, II (a), file 31, "Indians," LAC.

89 "Coqualeetza" is the Sto:lo word for place of cleansing or purification. "The Coqualeetza Story, 1886–1956," RG29, v 2596, file 800-1-D528, part 1 LAC.

90 Ibid., 8.

91 Moore to deputy minister, 7 June 1950, RG 29, v 2596, file 800-1-D528, part 1, LAC.

92 Charlotte Gray, "Profile: Percy Moore," *Canadian Medical Association Journal* 126 (15 February 1982): 416.

93 Wherrett produced comparable statistics for the previous ten years. Advisory Committee for the Control and Prevention of Tuberculosis among the Indians, "Proceedings of Meeting, 30 and 31 May 1945," 9 MG28, I75, II(a), file 36, LAC.

94 Ibid., 21.

95 Ibid., 31.

96 Ibid., 15, 28–9.

97 Ibid., 22.

98 Ibid., 24–5.

99 Ibid., 25.

100 Ibid., 129.

101 Ibid., 12.

102 Ibid., 118.

103 Ibid., 96.

104 Wherrett to Moore, 28 August 1946, MG28, I75, II(a), file 32, LAC.

105 "Proceedings of Meeting," 54.

106 Ibid., 62.

107 G.J. Wherrett, "Arctic Survey 1: Survey of Health Conditions and Medical and Hospital Services in the North West Territories," *Canadian Journal of Economics and Political Science* 11, no. 1 (1945): 48–60.

108 "Proceedings of Meeting," 86.

109 Ibid., 176.

110 Ibid., 162, 165.

111 Ibid., 206.

112 Department of Indian Affairs, "Regulations for the Medical Services, 1934," 22a, http://scaa.sk.ca/ourlegacy/solr?query=ID%3A32158&start=0&rows=10&mode=view&pos=0&page=1 (accessed February 2012).

113 "Proceedings of Meeting," 205.

114 Ibid., 210.

115 Moore to Curran, legal advisor, 14 May 1946, RG10 v 6811, file 470-2-3, part 11, LAC.

Chapter Two

1 Minister Brooke Claxton, Special Joint Committee of the Senate and the House of Commons Appointed to Examine and Consider the Indian Act, *Minutes of Proceedings and Evidence No. 3* (6 June 1946), 65.

2 G.J. Wherrett, *The Miracle of the Empty Beds: A History of Tuberculosis in Canada* (Toronto: University of Toronto Press, 1977).

3 John Tobias, "Protection, Civilization, Assimilation: An Outline History of Canada's Indian Policy," in *The Prairie West: Historical Readings*, 2nd ed., ed. R. Douglas Francis and Howard Palmer (Edmonton: University of Alberta Press, 1992), 219.

4 Sally Weaver, *Making Canadian Indian Policy: The Hidden Agenda, 1968–1970* (Toronto: University of Toronto Press, 1981), 46.

5 John Dent, "New Deal for Indians Is Planned by MP," *Saturday Night*, 30 March 1946.

6 See RG10, v 6811, file 470-3-6, part 1, LAC.

7 Hugh Shewell, *Enough to Keep Them Alive: Indian Welfare in Canada, 1873–1965* (Toronto: University of Toronto Press, 2004), 206.

8 Tobias, "Protection, Civilization, Assimilation," 220; Noel Dyck, *What Is the Indian "Problem": Tutelage and Resistance in Canadian Indian Administration* (St John's, NL: Institute of Social and Economic Research, 1991), 105.

9 Alvin Finkel, "Paradise Postponed: A Re-examination of the Green Book Proposals of 1945," *Journal of the Canadian Historical Association* 4, no. 1 (1993): 120–42.

10 Claxton, *Minutes of Proceedings*, 65.

11 K.S. Coates and W.R. Morrison, *The Alaska Highway in World War II: The U.S. Army of Occupation in Canada's Northwest* (Toronto: University of Toronto Press, 1992); Shelagh D. Grant, *Sovereignty or Security? Government Policy in the Canadian North, 1936–1950* (Vancouver: UBC Press, 1988), 123.

12 Donna Dryden, Elva Taylor, Rona Beer, Ron Bergman, and Margaret Cogill, *The Camsell Mosaic: The Charles Camsell Hospital, 1945–1985* (Edmonton: Charles Camsell History Committee, 1985), 8–9.

13 Mayor Fry to MacKenzie, 4 October 1945; Petition to Prime Minister, 13 October 1945, RG29, v 2592, file 800-1-D479, part 1, LAC.

14 H. Darling, RCMP 'K' Division, 26 November 1945, RG29, v 2592, file 800-1-D479, part 1, LAC.

15 J. Allison Glen to Mayor, 24 October 1945, RG29, v 2592, file 800-1-D479, part 1, LAC.

16 "Statement by the Hon Brooke Claxton" (n.d., likely November 1945) RG29, v 2592, file 800-1-D479, part 1, LAC.

17 Moore to deputy minister, 17 July 1946, RG 29, vol. 2592, file 800-1-D479, part 1, LAC.

18 Charles Camsell, *Son of the North* (Toronto: Ryerson, 1954).

19 Grant Dexter, *Dr. Charles Camsell* (Winnipeg: Winnipeg Free Press, 1958), 5.

20 Camsell, *Son of the North*, 44.

21 Dryden et al., *Camsell Mosaic*, xv.

22 Bill Waiser, "Camsell, Charles," in *Oxford Companion to Canadian History*, ed. Gerald Hallowell (Toronto: Oxford University Press, 2004), 99.

23 Mary Jane Logan McCallum, "Labour, Modernity and the Canadian State: A History of Aboriginal Women and Work in the Mid-Twentieth Century" (PhD diss., University of Manitoba, 2008), 85.

24 Grant, *Sovereignty or Security?* 317n10.

25 Dryden et al., *Camsell Mosaic*, xvi.

26 Stone to medical director, 12 June 1946, RG29, v 2592, file 800-1-D479, part 1, LAC.

27 Stone to Moore, 2 March 1946, RG29, v 2592, file 800-1-D479, part 1, LAC.

28 B.F. Wilson to H.E. Horne, business manager, 30 April 1954, RG29, v 2797, file 831-1-D479, part 4, LAC.

29 Moore to Falconer, 27 February 1950, RG29, v 2797, file 831-1-D479, part 2, LAC.

30 Moore, "Kitchen Floor CCIH," 23 January 1949; Moore to deputy minister, 6 February 1950, RG29, v 2797, file 831-1-D479, part 2, LAC.

31 Stone to Moore, 9 May 1946, RG29 v. 2796 file 831-1-D479, part 1; v 2797, file 831-1-D479, part 4, LAC.

32 Rutledge to McGivern, 11 April 1946, RG29, v 2769, file 822-1-D479, LAC.

33 Dryden et al., *Camsell Mosaic*, 15

34 Stone to Moore, 2 March 1946, RG29, v 2592, file 800-1-D479, part 1, LAC.

35 Dryden et al., *Camsell Mosaic*, 22; the forms and extent of patient discipline will be examined in a subsequent chapter.

36 See various letters, February and March 1946, RG29, v 2592, file 800-1-D479, part 1, LAC; administrative assistant Pat Blanchfield recalled that it was a "regular occurrence for him to write a blistering letter of

resignation" which she filed, rather than mailed, apparently much to Meltzer's relief. Dryden et al., *Camsell Mosaic*, 17.

37 Meltzer to Moore, 8 February 1947, RG29 v 2796 file 831-1-D479, part 1, LAC.

38 Meltzer to Moore, 28 March 1947, RG29 v 2796 file 831-1-D479, part 1, LAC.

39 Stone to Moore, 27 November 1946, RG29, v 2592, file 800-1-D479, part 1, LAC.

40 Moore to Meltzer, 3 October 1946, RG29, v 2592, file 800-1-D479, part 1, LAC.

41 Meltzer to Moore, 16 January 1947; Meltzer to Moore, 8 February 1947, RG29, v 2796 file 831-1-D479, part 1, LAC.

42 Deputy Minister National Health Cameron to the Minister, 4 February 1950, v 2769, file 822-1-D479, part 1, LAC.

43 H.A. Proctor to personnel division, 19 July 1949, RG29, v 3405, file 823-1-D579, LAC.

44 Indian Association of Alberta, Minutes of Annual Meeting, 24–5 June 1949, RG29, v 2959, file 851-3-Indian Association of Alberta, part 1, LAC.

45 Falconer to the Director, 10 March 1958, RG29, v 2959, file 851-3-Indian Association of Alberta, part 1, LAC.

46 Meltzer to Moore, 15 February 1954, RG29, v 2769, file 822-1-D479, part 2, LAC.

47 Charles Camsell Hospital records, Accession 73.315, box 2, file 33, Central Alberta (Baker) Sanatorium, Public Archives of Alberta (PAA).

48 Falconer to Director, 10 December 1957, RG29, v 2876 file 851-1-17, part 1, LAC.

49 "Admission Register, December 1956 to July 1958, Camsell Hospital." Despite the dates on the inside cover, the Admission Register recorded personal information and diagnoses only from January 1957 to February 1958; after that date no diagnoses are given and the recording of names is desultory, despite exhortations in the margins to "Please fill in this page!" The Register included diagnoses for 1,539 patients admitted in thirteen months, 204 for some form of tuberculosis and 1,335 for all other causes. Of the 951 children admitted, 92 were newborns, RG29, v 3635, LAC.

50 Falconer to Moore, 10 December 1957, RG29 v 2876, file 851-1-17, part 1, LAC.

51 Falconer to Moore, 18 December 1957, RG29 v 2876, file 851-1-17, part 1, LAC.

52 Matas to Falconer, 31 January 1958, RG29 v 2876, file 851-1-17, part 1, LAC.

53 Falconer to Moore, 18 December 1957, RG29 v 2876, file 851-1-17, part 1, LAC.

54 Quoted in Laurie Meijer Drees, "Indian Hospitals and Aboriginal Nurses: Canada and Alaska," *Canadian Bulletin of Medical History* 27, no. 1 (2010): 153.

55 Falconer to Moore, 28 January 1954; J.D. Blake to Moore, 5 May 1955, RG29 v 2926, file 851-1-D479, part 1, LAC.

56 Falconer to Moore, 18 December 1957, RG29 v 2876, file 851-1-17, part 1, LAC.

57 Moore to Regional Superintendent, Foothills, 15 July 1957; Moore to Regional Superintendent, Foothills, 20 January 1958, RG29 v 2876, file 851-1-17, part 1, LAC.

58 Moore to Regional Superintendent, Foothills, 29 November 1957, RG29 v 2876, file 851-1-17, part 1, LAC.

59 Moore to Regional Superintendent, Foothills, 20 January 1958, RG29 v 2876, file 851-1-17, part 1, LAC. For example, at this time Calgary hospitals agreed to charge IHS a per diem rate of $12.75, R.F. Battle, Regional Supervisor to Director, Indian Affairs Branch, 8 December 1955, RG 29, v 2936, file 851-1-X400, part 1, LAC.

60 Moore to Regional Superintendent, Foothills, 29 November 1957, RG29 v 2876, file 851-1-17, part 1, LAC.

61 Moore to Meltzer and Stone, 14 March 1946, RG29 v 2592, file 800-1-D479, part 1, LAC.

62 The extensive collection, consisting of hundreds of graphic and gruesome images, carefully cross-indexed by disease and patient name, was deposited at Library and Archives Canada only in 2003 by the hospital's historical society (RG29, R227-240-4-E, files 3726-32, LAC); the tuberculosis specimens were eventually destroyed (Dryden et al., *Camsell Mosaic*, 20).

63 Moore, "Memorandum to all Regional and Zone Superintendents," 11 July 1956, RG29, v 2620, file 800-2-1, LAC.

64 David Woods, "The Canadian Council on Hospital Accreditation in Canada," *Canadian Medical Association Journal* 110 (6 April 1974): 851.

65 Quoted in ibid., 852.

66 D.R. Campbell to Regional Superintendent, 5 October 1956, RG29, v 2620, file 800-2-1, LAC.

67 IHS labour problems are examined in detail in the next chapter.

68 Dr Blake to the Director, 7 November 1955, RG29, v 2620, file 800-2-1, LAC.

69 Six years later when little had changed, the Council deferred accreditation status for the hospital "pending further consideration of the hazard which exists in the physical plant." Canadian Council on Hospital Accreditation, 27 September 1963, RG29 v 2620, file 800-2-D479, part 1, LAC.

70 "List of Canadian Hospitals Approved for Advanced Graduate Training by the Royal College of Physicians and Surgeons," *Canadian Medical Association Journal* 78 (April 1958): 520.

71 Effective chemotherapy included the introduction of streptomycin in 1944, para-amino-salicylic acid (PAS) in 1946, and isoniazid (INH) in 1952. Katherine Ott, in *Fevered Lives: Tuberculosis in American Culture since 1870*

(Cambridge: Harvard University Press, 1996), states, "The surgical era of tuberculosis was brief. It began in the early 1900s … it ended in the 1940s with the slow rise to dominance of chemotherapy" (153); the Canadian experience was different.

72 Stone to Moore, 27 November 1946, RG29, v 2592, file 800-1-D479, part 1, LAC.

73 Dryden et al., *Camsell Mosaic*, 23.

74 Falconer to Moore, 28 January 1954, RG29 v 2926, file 851-1-D479, part 1, LAC.

75 Meltzer to Moore 15 February 1954, RG29 v 2769, file 822-1-D479, part 2, LAC.

76 Falconer to Moore, 28 November 1953, RG29, v 2797, file 831-1-D479, part 4, LAC.

77 Meltzer to Moore, 12 August 1954; Meltzer to Moore, 9 April 1957, RG29 v 2769, file 822-1-D479, part 2, LAC.

78 Indeed, Meltzer performed all chest surgeries and interpreted all chest X-rays (more than one thousand monthly) well into the 1960s; his surgical privileges were finally restricted in 1977 because he was seventy-one years old. B. Brett to L.M. Black, director general, 3 May 1977, RG29 v 2769, file 822-1-D479, part 4, LAC.

79 Meltzer to Moore, 15 February 1954, RG29 v 2769, file 822-1-D479, part 2, LAC; general and orthopaedic made up the remaining 32 per cent of surgeries.

80 Meltzer to Moore, 15 February 1954, RG29 v 2769, file 822-1-D479, part 2, LAC.

81 Dryden et al., *Camsell Mosaic*, 23.

82 H. Meltzer, "Results of Thoracoplasty," *Journal of Thoracic Surgery* (St Louis) 11, no. 1 (October 1941): 84–94.

83 Meltzer to Moore, 9 November 1954, RG29 v 2926, file 851-1-D479, part 1, LAC.

84 "Report on the Pembine Therapy Conference, Pembine, Wisconsin, 1953," Sanatorium Board of Manitoba, file G15, Archives of Manitoba (AM).

85 Author interview with Dave Melting Tallow, Siksika, Alberta, 9 August 2010.

86 Katherine McCuaig notes that the antibiotic era actually encouraged the surgical treatment of pulmonary tuberculosis. *The Weariness, the Fever, and the Fret: The Campaign against Tuberculosis in Canada, 1900–1950* (Montreal: McGill-Queen's University Press, 1999), 197.

87 Author interview with Roy Little Chief, Strathmore, Alberta, 8 August 2010.

88 IHS also managed its own hospitals in the province at Norway House, Fisher River, and Fort Alexander Indian Hospitals.

89 In 1955, for instance, the Sanatorium Board's income from IHS was $833,971.20; 93 per cent went for treatment in the segregated sanatoria, the remaining 7 per cent went to surveys and limited treatment in the provincial Manitoba Sanatorium (formerly Ninette). "Federal Funding of TB treatment and Control for Indians in Manitoba as Conducted by the Sanatorium Board of Manitoba," Sanatorium Board of Manitoba, file 29, T-5-7-15, Archives of Manitoba (AM).

90 Obituary, "Arthur Henry Povah," *Winnipeg Free Press*, 8 August 2001. Povah's career trajectory was not uncommon for physicians who contracted tuberculosis.

91 "Brandon Sanatorium Committee Minutes, 1947–1965," January 1953, Sanatorium Board of Manitoba, file P7102, AM.

92 "Brandon Sanatorium Committee Minutes, 1947–1965," March 1956: "We are now able to do four pulmonary resections per week." Sanatorium Board of Manitoba, file P7102, AM.

93 "Board Report Assiniboine Hospital, 3 February 1959," Sanatorium Board of Manitoba, file P7102, AM.

94 E.L. Ross, "Report on the Pembine Therapy Conference, Pembine, Wisconsin, 1952," 15, Sanatorium Board of Manitoba, file G15, AM.

95 E.L. Ross, "Report on the Pembine Therapy Conference, Pembine, Wisconsin, 1956," 16, Sanatorium Board of Manitoba, file G15, AM.

96 Dr P.E. Baldry, "Chest Diseases in Canada: A Report by the 1959 Scholar of the Chest and Heart Association" (typescript), Canadian Tuberculosis Association, MG28 I75, file 16, LAC.

97 Clarice Beaton, Prince Albert San, 1 January 1953, file A638 Lung Association, file VIII.66, "Lady Superintendent," Saskatchewan Archives Board (SAB).

98 Mountain Sanatorium, Weekly Report of Bed Compliment, 25 January 1957, RG29, v 2876, file 851-1-17, part 1, LAC; Pat Grygier, *A Long Way from Home: The Tuberculosis Epidemic among the Inuit* (Montreal and Kingston: McGill-Queen's University Press, 1994), xxi; "Dr. Karan's Report," 3 March 1958, CTA, MG28 I75, IIa, file 38, LAC.

99 "Annual Report Manitoba Sanatorium," March 1958, Sanatorium Board of Manitoba, file G13, AM.

100 David B. Stewart, *Holy Ground: The Story of the Manitoba Sanatorium at Ninette* (Killarney, MB: J.A. Victor David Museum, 1999), 111.

101 Wood to Dr Jeffrey, 5 October 1956, RG29, v 2876, file 851-1-17, part 1, LAC.

102 Rath to Orr, 30 November 1956, RG29, v 2934, file 851-1-X300, part 1, LAC.

103 Annual Report Medical Services, General Superintendent's Report 1965, Saskatchewan Lung Association files, A638, file IX.117, SAB.

104 A.L. Paine, "Supervision of Out-patient Tuberculosis Chemotherapy in Patients of Native Extraction" (typescript), February 1967, Sanatorium Board of Manitoba, file G15, AM.

105 Cameron to Minister Waldo Monteith, n.d. (likely March 1961), RG 29, vol. 2936, file 851-1-X400, part 1, LAC.

106 "Federal Funding of TB Treatment and Control for Indians in Manitoba as Conducted by the Sanatorium Board of Manitoba," Sanatorium Board of Manitoba, file 29, T-5-7-15, AM; 76 per cent of the sum went for treatment in the Manitoba Sanatorium. By 1975, when tuberculosis treatment became an insured service under Manitoba Health Services Commission, Sanatorium Board income from federal sources fell to $53,629.43 for "preventive services."

107 Paine, "Supervision of Out-patient Tuberculosis Chemotherapy in Patients of Native Extraction."

108 Stewart, *Holy Ground*, 116.

109 As cited in the previous chapter, Dr Stone noted: "It would be hard to prove that the Residential Schools, as a group, are not agencies for the spread of tuberculosis." Memorandum, Dr E.L. Stone to Director, 29 June 1937, MG28, I75, II (a), file 36, LAC.

Chapter Three

1 Minister Brooke Claxton, Special Joint Committee of the Senate and the House of Commons Appointed to Examine and Consider the Indian Act, *Minutes of Proceedings and Evidence No. 3*, 6 June 1946, 69.

2 Stone to medical director, 12 June 1946, RG29, v 2592, file 800-1-D479, part 1, LAC; emphasis in the original.

3 Aboriginal Nurses Association of Canada, *Twice as Good: A History of Aboriginal Nurses* (Ottawa: Aboriginal Nurses Association of Canada, 2007).

4 Mary Jane Logan McCallum, "Labour, Modernity and the Canadian State: A History of Aboriginal Women and Work in the Mid-Twentieth Century" (PhD diss., University of Manitoba, 2008), 244.

5 Laurie Meijer Drees, "Indian Hospitals and Aboriginal Nurses: Canada and Alaska," *Canadian Bulletin of Medical History* 27, no. 1 (2010): 156.

6 Aboriginal Nurses Association, *Twice as Good*.

7 Laurie Meijer Drees, "Training Aboriginal Nurses: The Indian Health Services in Northwestern Canada, 1939–75," in *Caregiving on the Periphery: Historical Perspectives on Nursing and Midwifery in Canada*, ed. Myra Rutherdale (Montreal and Kingston: McGill-Queen's University Press, 2010), 188.

8 Ryan Johnson and Amna Khalid, eds, *Public Health in the British Empire: Intermediaries, Subordinates and the Practice of Public Health, 1850–1960* (New York, London: Routledge, 2012).

9 McCallum "Labour, Modernity and the Canadian State," 246.

10 "Advisory Committee for the Control and Prevention of Tuberculosis among the Indians, Proceedings of Meeting, 30 and 31 May 1945," 162, 165, MG28, 175, IIa, file 36, LAC.

11 McCallum, "Labour, Modernity and the Canadian State," 255.

12 IHS Directorate report, 1960, as quoted in Meijer Drees, "Training Aboriginal Nurses," 197.

13 IHS policy was to pay some (male) patients $2.00 per day, in this case for translation for Inuit patients in the Clearwater Lake Indian Hospital in Manitoba. Moore to S.L. Carey, 15 March 1962, RG29, v 2590, file 800-1-D279, part 1, LAC.

14 Minnie Aodla Freeman, *Life among the Qallunaat* (Edmonton: Hurtig, 1978), 174.

15 Ibid., 176.

16 Ibid., 178.

17 Ibid., 189.

18 Ibid., 43.

19 Ibid., 56.

20 Maureen Lux, *Medicine That Walks: Disease, Medicine and Canadian Plains Native People, 1880–1940* (Toronto: University of Toronto Press, 2001), 218–20.

21 Author interview with Grace Anderson, Winnipeg, Manitoba, 20 February 2013

22 "Minutes of Committee Meeting, 23 October 1945," Clearwater Lake Hospital Committee minutes 1945–1965, P7101, Sanatorium Board of Manitoba Records, Archives of Manitoba.

23 Author interview with Grace Anderson, Winnipeg, Manitoba, 20 February 2013.

24 "A Review of the Historical Development, Objectives and Principles of the Indian and Northern Health Services," May 1967, accession PR1991.443, box 1, file 16, PAA.

25 The "invisibility" of Aboriginal women workers is treated in McCallum, "Labour, Modernity and the Canadian State"; Shula Marks also notes the invisibility of South African ward aides and attendants in *Divided Sisterhood: Race, Class and Gender in the South African Nursing Profession* (Johannesburg: University of Witwatersand University Press, 1994), 62.

26 Author interview with Frank Malloway Sr, Chilliwack, BC, 29 July 2010.

27 Author interview with Agnes Cyr, Echo Lodge, Fort Qu'Appelle, SK, 17 July 2009.

28 Manitoba Association of Registered Nurses, "Report – Labour Relations Committee," 1947, RG29, v 3405, file 823-1-X253, LAC.
29 Ken Coates, *Best Left as Indians: Native-White Relations in the Yukon Territory, 1840–1973* (Montreal and Kingston: McGill-Queen's University Press, 1991), 102.
30 "Resolution re Treatment of Tuberculosis and Venereal Disease in Natives in the Prince Rupert Health Unit," June 1944, RG29, v 2598, file 800-1-D579, part 1, LAC.
31 Crerar to Ralston, 5 September 1944, RG29, v 2598, file 800-1-D579, part 1, LAC.
32 "Formal Opening of Finely-Equipped Hospital at Miller Bay for TB Cases," Prince Rupert *Evening Empire*, 17 September 1946.
33 W.S. Barclay to Moore, 21 July 1944, RG29, v 2598, file 800-1-D579, part 1, LAC.
34 Ibid.
35 Campbell to Director, 17 January 1949, RG29, v 3405, file 823-1-D579, LAC.
36 Rutledge to Moore, 26 November 1946, RG29, v 3405 file 823-1-D353, part 1, LAC.
37 J.D. Galbraith to Moore, 27 February 1951, RG29, v 3405, file 823-1-D579, LAC.
38 Galbraith to Director, 13 March 1951; Galbraith to Director, 16 August 1951, RG29, v 3405, file 823-1-D579, LAC.
39 Galbraith to Rutledge, 9 October 1947, RG29, v 2598, file 800-1-D579, LAC.
40 Acting superintendent Burgess to Moore, 6 June 1950, RG29, v 2803, file 831-1-D579 part 5, LAC.
41 Martin to E.P. Applewaithe, MP, 22 September 1951, RG29, v 2803, file 831-1-D579 part 5, LAC.
42 Galbraith to Moore, 12 January 1953, RG29, v 3405, file 823-1-D579, LAC.
43 Quoted in Katherine Ott, *Fevered Lives: Tuberculosis in American Culture since 1870* (Cambridge: Harvard University Press, 1996), 150.
44 Alison Bashford and Carolyn Strange, "Cultures of Confinement," in *Isolation: Places and Practices of Exclusion*, ed. Bashford and Strange (London: Routledge, 2003), 133.
45 Kathryn McPherson, *Bedside Matters: The Transformation of Canadian Nursing, 1900–1990* (Toronto: Oxford University Press, 1996), 240.
46 Dr G.R. Howell, "Enquiry into Ward B Morale," 30 March 1954, RG29, v 2598, file 800-1-D579, part 1, LAC.
47 Marion Ballantine, RN, to Paul Martin, 14 November 1954, RG29, v 2598, file 800-1-D579, part 1, LAC; infectious hepatitis, or hepatitis A, is transmitted in food and water contaminated with infected fecal matter.
48 G.R. Howell, Grace Harris, RN, Sara Wyman, Social Worker, "A Study of Ward Morale in a Tuberculosis Hospital from the Miller Bay Indian Hospital," November 1954, RG29, v 2598, file 800-1-D579, part 1, LAC.

49 Marion Ballantine, RN, to Paul Martin, 14 November 1954, RG29, v 2598, file 800-1-D579, part 1, LAC.

50 Eric Preston, "Observations – Miller Bay Indian Hospital," 6 June 1956, RG29, v 2598, file 800-1-D579, part 1, LAC.

51 McPherson, *Bedside Matters*, 222

52 Rutledge to Moore, 26 November 1946, RG29, v 3405, file 823-1-D353, part 1, LAC.

53 Barclay to Zone superintendent, 7 February 1958, RG29, v 3405, file 823-1-D579, LAC.

54 Barclay to Director, 23 April 1958, RG29, v 3405, file 823-1-D579, LAC.

55 Barclay to Moore, 23 April 1958; Moore to Barclay, 5 May 1958, RG29, v 3405, file 823-1-D579, LAC.

56 "General Application for Authority," 22 April 1959, RG29, v 3405, file 823-1-D579, LAC.

57 "Director's Newsletter" (no date, likely Fall 1960), RG29 v 2598, file 800-1-D579, part 2, LAC.

58 Moore to Personnel Division, 25 May 1950, RG29, v 3405, file 823-1-X328, LAC.

59 Fyfe to Moore, 29 November 1952, RG29, v 3405, file 823-1-X328, LAC.

60 Moore to Personnel Division, 25 May 1950, RG29, v 3405, file 823-1-D353, part 1, LAC.

61 HA Proctor, "Nursing Establishment North Battleford," 10 August 1949, RG29, v 3405, file 823-1-D353, part 1, LAC.

62 Fyfe to Moore, 29 November 1952, RG29, v 3405, file 823-1-X328, LAC.

63 Moore to Falconer, 17 February, 1953, RG29, v 3405, file 823-1-X328, LAC.

64 David Gagan and Rosemary Gagan, *For Patients of Moderate Means* (Montreal and Kingston: McGill-Queen's University Press, 2002), 89; expenditures by Indian Health Services alone rose from about $2.5 million in the 1945–6 fiscal year to $10 million in 1950–1. Department of National Health and Welfare, *Annual Report*, 1945–6 and 1950–1.

65 Morton to Dr Head, 11 May 1955, RG29, v 3405, file 823-1-D353, part 1, LAC.

66 Head to Moore, 18 May 1955, RG29, v 3405, file 823-1-D353, part 1, LAC.

67 Dr Chou to Regional Superintendent, 17 October 1957, RG29, v 3405, file 823-1-D353, part 1, LAC.

68 Matron's Report, 14 November 1957, RG29, v 3405, file 823-1-D353, part 1, LAC.

69 Orford to Moore, 11 March 1958, RG29, v 3405, file 823-1-D353, part 1, LAC.

70 Moore to personnel officer, 29 April 1958, RG29, v 3405, file 823-1-D353, part 1, LAC.

71 Orford to Director, 2 June 1965, RG29, v 3405, file 823-1-D353, part 1, LAC.

72 Moore to Dr McCutcheon, 14 July 1941, RG29, v 3399, file 822-1-D173, LAC.

73 Stone to Moore, 29 July 1946, RG29, v 2769, file 822-1-D479, part 1, LAC.

74 Stone to Moore, 15 April 1946, RG29, v 2769, file 822-1-D479, part 1, LAC.

75 P.S. Tennant, acting regional superintendent, Vancouver to Moore, 6 January 1947, RG29, v 2769, file 822-1-D579, LAC.

76 T. Kue Young, *Health Care and Cultural Change: The Indian Experience in the Central Subarctic* (Toronto: University of Toronto Press, 1988), 103.

77 Meltzer to Moore, 30 September 1948, RG29, v 2769, file 822-1-D479, part 1, LAC.

78 Rutledge to deputy minister, 12 October 1948, RG29, v 2769, file 822–1-D479, part 1, LAC.

79 Cameron to Moore, 15 October 1948, RG29, v 2769, file 822-1-D479, part 1, LAC.

80 Rutledge to Moore, 29 Dec 1949, RG29, v 2769, file 822-1-D479, part 1, LAC.

81 Galbraith to Moore, 22 March 1951, RG29, v 2769, file 822-1-D579, LAC.

82 Galbraith to Moore, 14 January 1953, RG29, v 2769, file 822-1-D579, LAC.

83 Galbraith to Moore, 8 April 1953, RG29, v 2769, file 822-1-D579, LAC.

84 Moore to Barclay, 9 March 1955, RG29, v 2769, file 822-1-D579, LAC.

85 Falconer to Moore, 27 April 1953, RG29, v 2769, file 822-1-D479, part 2, LAC.

86 Meltzer to Matas, 20 July 1964, RG29, v 2769, file 822-1-D479, part 2, LAC.

87 Falconer to Moore, 16 May 1952, RG29, v 2769, file 822-1-D479, part 2, LAC.

88 Falconer to Moore, 30 May 1958, RG29, v 2769, file 822-1-D479 part 2, LAC.

89 Falconer to Moore, June 10 1960, RG29, v 2769, file 822-1-D479 part 2, LAC.

90 Sally Mae Weaver, "Health, Culture and Dilemma: A Study of the Non-Conservative Iroquois, Six Nations Reserve, Ontario" (PhD Diss., University of Toronto, 1967), 150.

91 Ibid., 153. Weaver conducted anthropological fieldwork on the reserve in 1964 and 1965, studying the "medical acculturation" of the three thousand "non-Conservative" Six Nations community (as opposed to the 1,500 Longhouse people, or the non-Christian "Conservative" members who retained their Iroquois social and cultural beliefs).

92 Ibid., 182.

93 Wiebe to Moore, 3 June 1953, RG29, v 3399, file 822-1-D173, LAC.

94 Wiebe to Moore, 31 December 1953, RG29, v 3399, file 822-1-D173, LAC.

95 Wiebe to Moore, 27 May 1954, RG29, v 3399, file 822-1-D173, LAC; emphasis added.

96 Wiebe to Moore, 27 May 1954, RG29, v 3399, file 822-1-D173, LAC.

97 Weaver, "Health, Culture and Dilemma," 182.

98 Wiebe to Moore, 16 February 1955, RG29, v 3399, file 822-1-D173, LAC.

99 Six Nations Council Resolution, 21 June 1960. While Moore knew that this individual wrote his qualifying examinations, it was not clear that he had passed, though neither Moore nor Wiebe considered that to be an obstacle to his employment. Moore to regional superintendent, 29 October 1959, RG29, v 3399, file 822-1-D173, LAC.
100 Wiebe to Director, 11 July 1960, RG29, v 3399, file 822-1-D173, LAC.
101 Weaver, "Health, Culture and Dilemma," 170.
102 Ibid., 327–9. The complaints were also raised in the House of Commons on 12 February 1962. Canada, House of Commons *Debates*, 761.
103 Wiebe to Moore, 12 February 1962, RG29, v 2904, file 851-1-A479, part 2, LAC.
104 Moore to minister Waldo Monteith, 9 March 1962, RG29, v 2904, file 851-1-A479, part 2, LAC.
105 Weaver, "Health, Culture and Dilemma," 330.
106 The Royal Commission on Government Organization was established in 1960 to enquire into the organization of federal departments and agencies. Despite the recommendation that the ageing Coqualeetza and Charles Camsell hospitals be neither rebuilt nor extended, the latter was rebuilt in 1967. The recommendations for changes to IHS took up a scant seven pages in the five-volume report, *Royal Commission on Government Organization, Report*, vol. 3, Report 15, "Health Services" (Ottawa: Queen's Printer, 1962) 197, 200–2.
107 Meijer Drees, "Indian Hospitals and Aboriginal Nurses."
108 Moore to Regional Superintendent, 21 May, 1962, RG29, v 2769, file 822-1-D479 part 2, LAC.

Chapter Four

 1 Minnie Aodla Freeman, *Life among the Qallunaat* (Edmonton: Hurtig, 1978), 65.
 2 Kathleen Steinhauer-Anderson, quoted in Donna Dryden, Elva Taylor, Rona Beer, Ron Bergman, and Margaret Cogill, *The Camsell Mosaic: The Charles Camsell Hospital, 1945–1985* (Edmonton: Charles Camsell History Committee, 1985), 101.
 3 "Advisory Committee for the Control and Prevention of Tuberculosis among the Indians, Proceedings of Meeting, 30 and 31 May 1945," 206, MG28, 175, IIa, file 36, LAC.
 4 Katherine McCuaig, *The Weariness, the Fever and the Fret: The Campaign against Tuberculosis in Canada, 1900–1950* (Montreal and Kingston: McGill-Queen's University Press, 1999), 98; F.B. Smith, *The Retreat of Tuberculosis, 1850–1950* (London: Croom Helm, 1988).

5 I.H. Mazer to Moore, 23 January 1946, RG29, v 2876, file 851-1-17, part 1, LAC.

6 McCuaig, *The Weariness, the Fever and the Fret*, 187.

7 Ibid., 188–9.

8 C. Stuart Houston, *R.G. Ferguson: Crusader against Tuberculosis* (Toronto: Dundurn Press, 1991), 104.

9 Stewart Murray, Metropolitan Health Committee (Vancouver) to Mr H.P.J. Gunn, Administrator Children's Hospital, 17 December 1957, GR-0129, Tuberculosis Control Division, box 39, file 1, BCA (emphasis in original); tuberculin, a solution containing substances extracted from the tubercle bacillus, became by the early twentieth century a simple skin test; a positive reaction indicated exposure to the disease, not the disease itself. The Mantoux test (purified protein derivative, or PPD) continues to be used to infer exposure to the disease. Katherine Ott, *Fevered Lives: Tuberculosis in American Culture since 1870* (Cambridge: Harvard University Press, 1996), 62–3.

10 Stefan Grzybowski and Zygmunt Dunaj, "Tuberculin Survey of the Population of Manitoulin Island," *Canadian Medical Association Journal* 81 (1 September 1959): 366–8.

11 McCuaig, *The Weariness, the Fever and the Fret*, 192.

12 W.J. Wood, regional superintendent, IHS, "Survey of BCG Vaccinated Indians in Manitoba," 13 June 1955, RG29 v 2868, file 851-1-4 part 2, LAC.

13 Armand Frappier, "Report on the opportuneness, possibility and practical means of applying routine preventive BCG vaccination," 11 January 1947, RG29 v 2868, file 851-1-4, part 1a, LAC.

14 WJ Wood, regional superintendent IHS, "Survey of BCG Vaccinated Indians in Manitoba," 13 June 1955, RG29 v 2868, file 851-1-4 part 2, LAC.

15 G.D.W. Cameron to Moore, 10 October 1952, RG29 v 2868, file 851-1-4, part 2, LAC.

16 BCG vaccination (not the skin test) is widely used throughout the developing world. The deaths between the 1990s and 2003 of six vaccinated Aboriginal infants with underlying immunodeficiency disorders led to the discontinuation of routine immunization in some Canadian provinces and territories. Routine BCG vaccination continues in Aboriginal communities in Alberta, Manitoba, Northwest Territories, northern Ontario, and Nunavut; its use in Aboriginal communities in Saskatchewan was discontinued in 2011, in Quebec in 2005, and other provinces in the 1990s. Canada, Public Health Agency of Canada, *Canadian Immunization Guide* http://www.phac-aspc.gc.ca/publicat/cig-gci/p04-bcg-eng.php#clae (accessed 22 March 2015); "BCG Vaccine use in Canada – Current and Historical," http://www.phac-aspc.gc.ca/tbpc-latb/bcgvac_1206-eng.php (accessed 16 April 2013).

17 Dr M. Matas, "Tuberculosis Programs of the Medical Services, Department of National Health and Welfare," in "Proceedings of the Third National Tuberculosis Conference," *Medical Services Journal Canada* 22 (1966): 881–2.

18 Ibid., 879.

19 Dryden et al., *Camsell Mosaic*, 134.

20 The debate over tuberculin testing and the efficacy of BCG continued in the 1980s. See Raj Narian, "Need for a BCG Trial in Canada's Native Populations," *Canadian Medical Association Journal* 127 (July 1982): 101–2; and reply by T. Kue Young, "A BCG Trial in Canada's Native Populations," *Canadian Medical Association Journal* (December 1982): 1166–7; McCuaig cites a 1995 study of the life-threatening hazards of BCG use among those most likely at risk for TB, the immunocompromised patients (*The Weariness, the Fever and the Fret*, 274).

21 Harold Lerat with Linda Ungar, *Treaty Promises Indian Reality: Life on a Reserve* (Saskatoon: Purich Publishing, 2005), 142; Dryden et al., *Camsell Mosaic*, 133; P.E. Baldry, "Chest Diseases in Canada, A Report by the 1959 Scholar of the Chest and Heart Association" (typescript), Canadian Tuberculosis Association, MG28 I 75, file 16, LAC.

22 E.L.M. Thorpe, *The Social Histories of Smallpox and Tuberculosis in Canada: Culture, Evolution and Disease* (Winnipeg: University of Manitoba Anthropology Papers No. 30, 1989), 106.

23 Bruce Noton, "Northern Manitoba Treaty Party, 1949," *Manitoba History* 39 (Spring/Summer 2000), http://www.mhs.mb.ca/docs/mb_history/39/treatyparty1949.shtml (accessed 12 April 2013).

24 Ibid.

25 "Indian Clinics," files T-6-2-2 to T-6-2-14, Sanatorium Board Manitoba, Archives of Manitoba.

26 Houston, *R.G. Ferguson*, 104, 105.

27 Baldry, "Chest Diseases in Canada."

28 Ott, *Fevered Lives*, 3.

29 Ann Meekitjuk Hanson, "Finding Hope and Healing in Memories of Our Past," *Above and Beyond: Canada's Arctic Journal* (March/April 2012), http://issuu.com/arctic_journal/docs/above_and_beyond_march_april_2012 (accessed 28 May 2013).

30 Ebba Olofsson et al., "Negotiating Identities: Inuit Tuberculosis Evacuees in the 1940s–1950s," *Études/Inuit/Studies* 32, no. 2 (2008): 131.

31 Megan Vaughan makes this point in reference to mass medical campaigns in colonial Africa in *Curing Their Ills: Colonial Power and African Illness* (Palo Alto, CA: Stanford University Press, 1991), 52.

32 Dryden et al., *Camsell Mosaic*, ix, 93–130.

33　George Manuel and Michael Posluns, *The Fourth World: An Indian Reality* (New York: Free Press, 1974), 65, 100.

34　Laurie Meijer Drees, *Healing Histories* (Edmonton: University of Alberta Press, 2013), 80–1.

35　Author interview with Dave Melting Tallow, 9 August 2010, Siksika, Alberta.

36　Quoted in "More Canadian Genocide: TB Sanitariums," *Windspeaker News*, September 1998, 44.

37　See chapter 3. "Formal Opening of Finely-Equipped Hospital at Miller Bay for TB Cases," *Prince Rupert Evening Empire*, 17 September 1946.

38　W.P.B. Pugh, Indian Agent, "Quarterly Report," 8 January 1947, RG29, v 2592, file 800-1-D479, part 1, LAC.

39　"Aged Chief Swimmer Pleads with Indians to Make Use of Hospital Facilities," *Saskatoon Star Phoenix*, 1 October 1953.

40　Interview with Gordon Albert by Alma Favel-King, North Battleford, September 2011.

41　Interview with Rose Atimoyoo by Alma Favel-King, North Battleford, September 2011.

42　Chief Cornelius Bignell, Councillors Tom Henderson, Donald Lathlin, and Matthew McGillivary to E. Law, Indian Agent, 4 July 1949, RG29, v 2590, file 800-1-D279, part 1, LAC.

43　E.L. Ross to Moore, 6 September 1949, RG29, v 2590, file 800-1-D279, part 1, LAC.

44　Freeman, *Life among the Qallunaat*, 174.

45　Ibid., 175–6.

46　G.R. Howell to Moore, 7 April 1954, RG29, v 2598, file 800-1-D579, part 1 LAC.

47　Dryden et al., *Camsell Mosaic*, 29–30.

48　*Lost Songs* (director Clint Tourangeau and Elaine Moyah, National Film Board, 1999).

49　Joanne Hader, "The Effect of Tuberculosis on the Indians of Saskatchewan, 1926–1965" (MA thesis, University of Saskatchewan, 1990), 162.

50　Miriam Wright, RN, in Dryden et al., *Camsell Mosaic*, 71.

51　Dryden et al., *Camsell Mosaic*, 95; author interview with Dave Melting Tallow, 9 August 2010, Siksika, Alberta.

52　M. Matas, Charles Camsell Hospital rules, 1 April 1959, RG29, v 2593, file 800-1-D479, part 2 LAC.

53　Hader, "The Effect of Tuberculosis on the Indians of Saskatchewan, 1926–1965," 160–1; Hader's informants, interviewed in the 1980s, remained anonymous.

54　Freeman, *Life among the Qallunaat*, 176.

55　Ibid., 45–6.

56 "Eskimo Correspondence," RG85, v 314, file 1012-8, part 3, LAC.
57 Annalisa Staples and Ruth McConnell, *Soapstone and Seed Beads: Arts and Craft at the Charles Camsell Hospital* (Edmonton: Jasper Printing, 1993).
58 G.R. Howell, "Enquiry into Ward B Morale," 30 March 1954, RG29 v. 2598, file 800-1-D579, part 1, LAC.
59 Dryden et al., *Camsell Mosaic*, 200–1.
60 G.R. Howell to Barclay, 24 August 1956, RG29 v. 2598, file 800-1-D579, part 1, LAC.
61 Petition to Rt Hon. John G Diefenbaker, 4 June 1962, RG29, v 2608, file 800-1-X328 part 1, LAC.
62 See chapter 3. Historian Mary Jane McCallum notes the state's role in the procurement of its own workforce. "Labour, Modernity and the Canadian State: A History of Aboriginal Women and Work in the Mid-Twentieth Century" (PhD diss., University of Manitoba, 2008), 67.
63 Author interview with Roy Little Chief, 8 August 2010, Strathmore, Alberta.
64 Dryden et al., *Camsell Mosaic*, 101.
65 Author interview with Dave Melting Tallow, 9 August 2010, Siksika, Alberta.
66 Author interview with Frank Malloway Sr, 29 July 2010, Chilliwack, BC.
67 The policy continued with the "Sixties Scoop," or the widespread practice by social welfare authorities of removing Aboriginal children from their families and placing them in non-Aboriginal homes. See Ernie Crey and Suzanne Fournier, *Stolen from Our Embrace. The Abduction of First Nations Children and the Restoration of Aboriginal Communities* (Vancouver: Douglas and McIntyre, 1998). The Truth and Reconciliation Commission bore witness to the legacy of the residential schools as a "sincere indication and acknowledgement of the injustices and harms experienced by Aboriginal people and the need for continued healing." http://www.trc.ca/websites/trcinstitution/index.php?p=3 (accessed 16 May 2013).
68 P.E. Moore, H.D. Kruse, F.F. Tisdall, and R.S.C. Corrigan, "Medical Survey of Nutrition among the Northern Manitoba Indians," *Canadian Medical Association Journal* 54 (March 1946): 233.
69 "New Deal for Indians," *Ottawa Citizen*, 3 February 1947; "Shifting Care of Indians," *Winnipeg Tribune*, 17 January 1947; "The Indian Still Waits," *Globe and Mail*, 14 May 1947.
70 Ian Mosby, "Administering Colonial Science: Nutrition Research and Human Biomedical Experimentation in Aboriginal Communities and Residential Schools, 1942–1952," *Histoire Sociale/Social History* 46 (May 2013): 148.
71 Meijer Drees, *Healing Histories*, 175.
72 Ibid., xxviii, 182, 202; author interviews with Dave Melting Tallow, 9 August 2010, and Frank Malloway Sr, 29 July 2010.

73 See Maureen Lux, *Medicine That Walks: Disease, Medicine and Canadian Plains Native People, 1880–1940* (Toronto: University of Toronto Press, 2001), 180.

74 Maureen Lux, "Perfect Subjects: Race, Tuberculosis, and the Qu'Appelle BCG Vaccine Trial," *Canadian Bulletin for Medical History* 15 (1998): 277–95; David S. Jones, *Rationalizing Epidemics: Meaning and Uses of American Indian Mortality since 1600* (Cambridge, MA: Harvard University Press, 2004), 195–220.

75 Barclay to Moore, 2 December 1947, RG29, v 2868, file 851-1-4 part 1a, LAC; Houston, *R.G. Ferguson*, 60.

76 Barnett to Stark, 20 May 1966, Saskatchewan Lung Association files, A638, VIII.157, SAB.

77 Barclay to the Director, 2 December 1947; Falconer to Barclay, 5 December 1947, RG29, v 2868, file 851-1-4 part 1a, LAC.

78 Freeman, *Life among the Qallunaat*, 175–6.

79 Dryden et al., *Camsell Mosaic*, 235.

80 Pat Sandiford Grygier, *A Long Way from Home* (Montreal and Kingston: McGill-Queen's University Press, 1994), 115.

81 Current definitions of informed consent are not applied here. Focus on the ethics of medical research and human experimentation, begun in the wake of the atrocities of the Second World War, continued in the mid-1960s, prompted by exposés of unethical medical research. H.K. Beecher, "Ethics and Clinical Research," *New England Journal of Medicine* 274 (1966): 1354–60.

82 See chapter 2. Moore to Meltzer and Stone, 14 March 1946, RG29, v 2592, file 800-1-D479, part 1, LAC.

83 "Submission to the Policy Review Committee on the Future of Charles Camsell Hospital," second draft, 15 May 1976, RG29 v 3379 file 800-1-D479, LAC.

84 John Robert Lymer and Arthur James Anderson, "An Evaluation of Several Orally Administered Para-aminosalicylic Acid Preparations," *Canadian Pharmaceutical Journal* (September 1957): 160–2.

85 A Cold War arm of the military established in 1947, the Defense Research Board operated its own facilities and also provided grants to universities and industry for research in areas of particular interest to Canada such as the Arctic. *The Canadian Encyclopedia*, http://www.thecanadianencyclopedia.ca/en/article/defence-research/#h3_jump_0 (accessed 19 May 2013).

86 Allan M. Edwards and Gordon C. Gray, "Observations on Juvenile Hypothyroidism in Native Races of Northern Canada," *Canadian Medical Association Journal* 84 (20 May 1961): 1116–24.

87 Edwards to Gray, 27 December 1962; Moore to Gray, 16 January 1963, RG29, v 2769, file 822-1-D479, part 2, LAC.

88 Informed consent became a national controversy in the 1970s when CBC
    Radio broadcast the stories of Aboriginal women who charged they
    were sexually sterilized in hospital without their knowledge or consent.
    Publicly, the minister of health defended the hospitals and claimed the
    public broadcaster was irresponsible; consent forms had been duly
    signed. Privately, however, it became clear to department officials that
    there were problems with the Inuktitut translations. Bureaucrats asked
    nine Inuk women "with above average education" to read the form
    consenting to sterilization; two thought it meant to have an abortion, five
    thought it meant to have an operation and have no more babies, and two
    could not discern what the message was about. It was clear to bureaucrats
    that "the form needs a bit of re-drafting to ensure that people are fully
    aware of what they are agreeing to." A.D. Hunt to M.L. Webb, 1 June
    1973, RG29, v 2870, file 851-1-5 part 3b, LAC.
89 Laurie Meijer Drees, "The Nanaimo and Charles Camsell Indian Hospitals:
    First Nations' Narratives of Health Care, 1945 to 1965," *Histoire Sociale/
    Social History* 43, no. 85 (2010): 165–91; reprinted in her *Healing Histories*
    (Edmonton: University of Alberta Press, 2013).
90 Robin Brownlie and Mary-Ellen Kelm, "Desperately Seeking Absolution:
    Native Agency as Colonialist Alibi?" *Canadian Historical Review* 75, no. 4
    (1994): 543–56.
91 E. McPherson to Indian Affairs, 5 February 1946, RG29, v 2931, file 851-1-
    X200 part 1B, LAC ("George Hamilton" was not his real name).
92 See RG29, v 2931, file 851-1-X200 part 1B, LAC.
93 L.M. (Leo) Manning Report on Parc Savard visit, 22–5 February 1952,
    RG29, v 2947, file 851-2-2, part 1, LAC.
94 J.E. Labreque to H.D. Reid, 6 May 1955; Labreque to Director, 6 August
    1956; contract with Maheu and Maheu Co. Pest Control, 14 March 1956;
    Labreque to WH Frost, 7 June 1957, RG29, v 2587, file 800-1-D117, part 3B,
    LAC.
95 P.E. Baldry, "Chest Diseases in Canada: A Report of the 1959 Scholar of the
    Chest and Heart Association," CTA, MG28 I 75, III, LAC.
96 G. Kinneard, MD, Director Regional Health Services Branch, to Dr F.B.
    Roth, Deputy Minister Health, 20 February 1953, R999 file I.70, SAB.
97 J.E. Hiltz, "Compulsory Treatment of Tuberculosis," *Canadian Medical
    Association Journal* 71 (December 1954): 569–71.
98 "Circular Letter to All Superintendents," Indian Health Regulations (sec.
    72 Indian Act, Order in Council, P.C. 193-1129), 17 July 1953, RG29 v 2936,
    file 851-1-X400, part 2a, LAC. The Regulations targeted all infectious
    disease, but made special mention of tuberculosis and venereal disease.

99 Sharon Helen Venne, *Indian Acts and Amendments 1868–1975: An Indexed Collection* (Saskatoon: Native Law Centre University of Saskatchewan, 1981), 337.

100 Indian Health Regulations, 1.

101 Indian Health Regulations, sections 6, 18, 8.

102 Derek G. Smith, "The Emergence of 'Eskimo Status': An Examination of the Eskimo Disk List System and Its Social Consequences, 1925–1970," in *Anthropology, Public Policy, and Native Peoples in Canada,* ed. Noel Dyck and James Waldram (Montreal and Kingston: McGill-Queen's University Press, 1993), 50.

103 Author interview with Dave Melting Tallow, 9 August 2010, Siksika, Alberta.

104 Zone Superintendent, Nanaimo, to Regional Superintendent, 15 December 1959, RG29 v 2876, file 851-1-17 part 1, LAC; "Advisory Committee for the Control and Prevention of Tuberculosis among the Indians, Proceedings of Meeting, 30 and 31 May 1945," 210, MG28, 175, II(a), file 36, LAC.

105 Kathleen Steinhauer, quoted in Meijer Drees, *Healing Histories,* 174.

106 K.R. Brown, superintendent, Blood Indian Agency, to Regional Supervisor, 30 October 1958, RG29 v 2798, file 831-1-D479, part 6, LAC; M. Matas, Charles Camsell Hospital rules, 1 April 1959, RG29, v 2593, file 800-1-D479, part 2 LAC.

107 In a reversal of positions from the 1950s, when the Saskatchewan Anti-TB League's medical superintendent hoped to use the public health act to detain Metis patients in sanatorium in 1969, the provincial public health director opposed the notion: "I would not like to think that selected patients should be brought before a magistrate and sentenced to a stay in a sanatorium. This would have to be done for everybody and I am sure that you could not agree to this as a measure in the control of tuberculosis. As I have said before, we can legislate and organize for the generality of patients but there is the occasion when we have to admit defeat in some instances of extreme cases." Barnett to Walker, 7 February 1969; Walker to Barnett, 14 February 1969, Saskatchewan Lung Association files, A638 file VIII.25, SAB.

108 G.R. Howell to W.S. Barclay, 5 June 1956, "Report on Hospital Progress," RG29 v 2598 file 800-1-D579 part 1, LAC.

109 Falconer to Moore, 10 December 1957, RG29 v 2876, file 851-1-17 part 1, LAC.

110 See "Sanatorium Admissions and Discharges," Saskatchewan Lung Association files, A638, file IX.73a, SAB. In northern Saskatchewan, the Prince Albert Sanatorium with 276 beds admitted only 2 Aboriginal patients in 1935; during the 1940s it admitted an average of 44 Aboriginal patients per year, but an average of 120 Aboriginal patients from 1951 to 1955.

111 T.J. Orford, regional superintendent, to G.D. Barnett, 13 October 1961, Saskatchewan Lung Association files, A638, file VIII.48, SAB.

112 M. Matas, "Tuberculosis Programs of the Medical Services, Department of National Health and Welfare," in "Proceedings of the Third National Tuberculosis Conference" *Medical Services Journal Canada* 22 (1966): 882.

113 The 1996 Royal Commission on Aboriginal Peoples devotes a complete section to relocations, highlighting the experiences of thirteen different communities relocated to ease government's administrative needs, or to make way for resource development. http://www.collectionscanada. gc.ca/webarchives/20071115053257/http://www.ainc-inac.gc.ca/ch/ rcap/sg/sgmm_e.html (accessed 24 May 2013).

114 Pat Sandiford Grygier, *A Long Way from Home* (Montreal: McGill-Queen's University Press, 1994).

115 J.M. Ridge to P.E. Moore, 28 October 1945, RG29, v 2590, file 800-1-D279, part 1, LAC.

116 *Lost Songs*, dir. Clint Tourangeau and Elaine Moyah, National Film Board, 1999.

117 Freeman, *Life among the Qallunaat*, 45.

118 Grygier, *A Long Way from Home*, 126.

119 Resident Physician's Report, February, June 1951, "Dynevor Indian Hospital Committee minutes, 1942–1957," Sanatorium Board of Manitoba files, P7096, Archives of Manitoba.

120 "It seems strange to hear people speaking of competition in the treatment field of tuberculosis when only a few years ago the hue and cry across Canada was for the federal government to provide more facilities for tuberculous Indians." P.E. Moore to G.D. Barnett, 2 April 1963, Saskatchewan Lung Association files, A638, file VIII.47, SAB.

121 "Saskatchewan Sanatoria Admissions and Discharges," Lung Association files, A638, file IX.73a, SAB.

122 C.B. Ross to Moore, 31 October 1955, RG29, v 2926, file 851-1-X100, part 1A, LAC.

123 J.S. Willis to medical superintendent, 21 March 1955, RG29, v 2926, file 851-1-X100, part 1A, LAC.

124 Report to the Board on Clearwater Lake Hospital, July 1962; Minutes of Medical Advisory Committee, 11 September 1962, RG29, v 2590, file 800-1-D279, part 1, LAC.

125 Clearwater Lake Hospital committee, minutes October 1962, Manitoba Sanatorium Board files, P7101, Archives of Manitoba.

126 Grygier recounts the experiences of Inuit patients delivered to the wrong communities, and others "lost" in the IHS system. *A Long Way from Home*,

121–8; see also Ebba Olofsson, "Negotiating Identities: Inuit Tuberculosis Evacuees in the 1940s to 1950s," *Études/Inuit/Studies* 32, no. 2 (2008): 127–49.

127 Memorandum, director DIA, 25 February 1947, RG29, v 2783, file 830-1-D479, part 1, LAC.

128 Northwood to Moore, 3 April 1940, RG 29, v 2590, file 800-1-D297, part 1, LAC.

129 E.L. Stone to director, 19 December 1946, RG29, v 2783, file 830-1-D479, part 1, LAC.

130 Falconer to Stone, 28 January 1947, RG29, v 2783, file 830-1-D479, part 1, LAC.

131 Hoey to Dr Moore, 25 February 1947, RG29, v 2783, file 830-1-D479, part 1, LAC.

132 Gooderham to Indian Affairs, 18 August 1947, RG29, v 2796, file 831-1-D479, part 1, LAC.

133 Dryden et al., *Camsell Mosaic*, 66. Former students at the Edmonton residential school, at a healing ceremony at the school site in 2004, recalled being paid to dig the graves and are still haunted by the experience of seeing the caskets being put in the ground without ceremony or markings. Carl Carter (Sweetgrass) "Journey Continues to Heal School Trauma," *Windspeaker* 11, no. 10 (2004).

134 J.G. McGilp, Regional Supervisor, to G.D. Barnett, 27 April, 1964, Saskatchewan Lung Association files, A638, file VIII.47, SAB.

135 T.J. Orford to G.D. Barnett, 13 April 1964, Saskatchewan Lung Association files, A638, file VIII.47, SAB.

136 In 1988 the government of the Northwest Territories initiated its Medical Patient Search Project to trace patients who went missing since the 1940s. *Summary: Final Report* (Department of Health Government of Northwest Territories, April 1991). A cairn in memory of ninety-eight Aboriginal people who died at the Camsell Hospital and were buried at the Edmonton Residential school, was designed and erected by former Camsell staff and dedicated in 1990. "St. Albert Cemeteries," file 991.03.01.06, St Albert Museum and Archives. In 2010 a cairn was erected memorializing the 300 Aboriginal patients who were buried in unmarked graves in the Belmont Hillside Cemetery near Manitoba's Ninette Sanatorium. *Winnipeg Free Press*, 3 August 2010.

137 Meltzer to Moore, 19 February 1946, RG29 v 2592, file 800-1-D479 part 1, LAC.

138 Minutes, Patients' Committee, 19 March 1956, RG29 v 2598, file 800-1-D579 part 1, LAC.

139 Dryden et al., *Camsell Mosaic*, 194–5.

140 Dryden et al., *Camsell Mosaic*, 66. Resident Physician's Report, February 1951, "Dynevor Indian Hospital Committee minutes, 1942–1957," Sanatorium Board of Manitoba files, P7096, AM.

141 *The Longer Trail*, dir. Fergus McDonell, produced by Julian Biggs, 30 min., National Film Board, 1956.

142 *No Longer Vanishing*, dir. Grant McLean, produced by Tom Daly, 27 min. 31 sec., National Film Board, 1955. In the training course for its Indian placement officers, Indian Affairs showed both films. Mary Jane Logan McCallum, "Labour, Modernity and the Canadian State: A History of Aboriginal Women and Work in the Mid-Twentieth Century" (PhD diss., University of Manitoba, 2008), 133.

143 Freeman, *Life among the Qallunaat*, 65.

Chapter Five

1 G.D.W. Cameron to Minister Waldo Monteith, 15 March 1961, RG 29, vol. 2936, file 851-1-X400, part 1, LAC (original emphasis).

2 J.R. Miller, *Skyscrapers Hide the Heavens: A History of Indian-White Relations in Canada*, rev. ed. (Toronto: University of Toronto Press, 1989), 222.

3 Cameron to Minister, 15 March 1961, RG 29, vol. 2936, file 851-1-X400, part 1, LAC.

4 The other was the Lady Willingdon Hospital at Six Nations in Ontario.

5 "The Hospital"; "Twenty-five Years as an Indian Agent to the Blackfoot Band," January 1972, 7, M4738, Gooderham fonds, box 1, file 3, Glenbow-Alberta Institute Archives (GAI).

6 For an overview of medical traditions in plains Aboriginal cultures see Lux, *Medicine That Walks* (Toronto: University of Toronto Press, 2001) chapter 2, and Waldram et al., *Aboriginal Health in Canada* (Toronto: University of Toronto Press, 2006) chapter 5.

7 John Milloy, *A National Crime: The Canadian Government and the Residential School System, 1879–1986* (Winnipeg: University of Manitoba Press, 1999), 77–107.

8 G.H. Gooderham, "The Blackfoot Hospital and Its Progress" 18 February 1926, RG29 v 2592, file 800-1-D443, part 1, LAC.

9 Carlotta Hacker, *The Indomitable Lady Doctors* (Toronto: Clarke, Irwin, 1974), 185–92. Windsor remained at the Blackfoot Hospital until her retirement in 1948.

10 Lux, *Medicine That Walks*, 176–7.

11 Kennedy to Graham, 7 April 1923, RG10, v 1542, LAC.

12 "Contestants in first baby show held on the Blackfoot (Siksika) reserve, 1926," PA-32-1, GAI.

13 G.H. Gooderham, "The Blackfoot Hospital and Its Progress," 18 February 1926, RG29 v 2592 file 800-1-D443, part 1, LAC.

14 Gooderham to the Secretary, 27 April 1935, RG29 v 2796, file 800-1-D443, LAC.

15 "White Attitudes towards Indians," 30 June 1938, Hanks Fonds, M8458–29, GAI.

16 Agent Monthly Report, November 1934, RG29 v 2796, file 800-1-D443, LAC. A new wing for staff quarters had freed space for beds while the building's verandas were closed in and heated with stoves, adding space for thirty more beds.

17 Gooderham to Dr E.L. Stone, 13 February 1935, RG29 v 2796, file 800-1-D443, LAC.

18 Riou to Baker, 29 November 1937, Baker Memorial Sanatorium, GR1973.0315, file 35, Provincial Archives of Alberta (PAA).

19 Dr Windsor to Gooderham, n.d. (1935), RG29 v 2796, file 800-1-D443, LAC.

20 Gooderham to H.W. McGill, 12 February 1935, RG29 v 2796, file 800-1-D443, LAC.

21 Gooderham to Dr E.L. Stone, 13 February 1935, RG29 v 2796, file 800-1-D443, LAC.

22 Hospital Accounts, Baker Memorial Sanatorium, GR1973.0315, file 25, PAA; G.J. Wherrett, *The Miracle of the Empty Beds: A History of Tuberculosis in Canada* (Toronto: University of Toronto Press, 1977), 183.

23 Gooderham to Dr E.L. Stone, 13 February 1935, RG29 v 2796, file 800-1-D443, LAC.

24 L. Hanks and J. Hanks, *Tribe under Trust: A Study of the Blackfoot Reserve of Alberta* (Toronto: University of Toronto Press, 1950), 49. To compare with the nearby Kainai reserve, using 1935 figures (the last year that detailed accounts were published), the Siksika numbered 783 and the DIA spent just $6,512, mostly for wages and maintenance for Gooderham and his clerk. All other costs were paid by the trust fund. At the Kainai reserve, with a population of 1,317, the DIA spent $51,117 ($33,653 for reserve operations, plus $17,463 for the Blood Hospital). *Sessional Papers* 1936, Canada, House of Commons, 15–16.

25 W.L. Falconer to Director, 27 May 1942, RG29 v. 2936 file 851-1-X400 part 1, LAC.

26 E.L. Stone to Superintendent, 19 June 1946, RG29 v 2592 file 800-1-D443, part 1, LAC.

27 Stone to Director, 11 February 1949, RG29 v 2796 file 831-1-D426, part 1, LAC.

28 W.P.B. Pugh, Agent, 12 February 1947, RG29 v 2592, file 800-1-D443, part 1, LAC.

29 Moore to Pugh, 20 March 1947, RG29 v 2592, file 800-1-D443, part 1, LAC.

30 Paul Martin to J. Allison Glen, 21 March 1947; Martin to Glen, 6 May 1947, RG29, v 2592 file 800-1-D443, part 1, LAC.

31 Director to Deputy Minister, 23 April, 1947, RG29, v 2592 file 800-1-D443, part 1, LAC.

32 Alvin Finkel, "Paradise Postponed: A Re-examination of the Green Book Proposals of 1945," *Journal of the Canadian Historical Association* 4 (1993): 120–42. Much opposition came from provincial premiers, who objected to the federal Liberals' centralizing tendencies such as national health insurance that required provinces to yield tax revenues and undercut provincial autonomy. P.E. Bryden, "The Liberal Party and the Achievement of National Medicare," *Canadian Bulletin of Medical History* 26, no. 2 (2009): 315–32.

33 As noted, between 1945 and 1954 hospital expenditures in Canada increased 275 per cent. D. Gagan and R. Gagan, *For Patients of Moderate Means* (Montreal and Kingston: McGill-Queen's University Press, 2002), 89.

34 Malcolm Taylor, *Health Insurance and Canadian Public Policy*, 2nd ed. (Montreal and Kingston: McGill-Queen's University Press, 1987), 163–4.

35 Pugh to Gooderham, Regional Supervisor, 15 January 1954, RG29 v 2592 file 800-1-D443, part 1, LAC.

36 Moore to Jones, 23 February 1954, RG29 v 2592 file 800-1-D443, part 1, LAC.

37 H.M. Jones to Moore, 1 February 1954, RG29 v 2592 file 800-1-D443, part 1, LAC.

38 Moore to Col. Jones, 12 July 1954, RG29 v 2592 file 800-1-D443, part 1, LAC.

39 Blackfoot Band Council Resolution, 21 September 1954, RG29 v 2592 file 800-1-D443, part 1, LAC.

40 Falconer to Moore, 28 October 1954; E.A. Gardner, Chief Architect, to Moore, 29 March 1955; G. Borthwick to Moore, 30 March 1955, RG29 v 2592 file 800-1-D443, part 1, LAC.

41 J.R. Wild to R.F. Battle, 21 June 1956, RG29 v 2592 file 800-1-D443, part 1, LAC.

42 Moore to Wild, 6 September 1956; Moore to Falconer, 8 February 1957; Battle to Falconer, 14 March 1957; Falconer to Moore, 19 March 1957; Moore to Jones, 8 August 1957, RG29 v 2592 file 800-1-D443, part 1, LAC.

43 Jones to Moore, 6 May 1958, RG29 v 2592 file 800-1-D443, part 1, LAC.

44 Moore, "Memorandum of Meeting with Blackfoot Delegation," 22 May 1958; J.C.L. Bouchard to IHS, 16 October 1958, "Blackfoot Indian Hospital – Occupancy and Staff," December 1957, RG29 v 2592 file 800-1-D443, part 1, LAC.

45 Author interview with Roy Little Chief, 8 August 2010, Siksika, Alberta.

46 B. Griffiths, "Poverty Threatens Blackfoot Tribe," *Calgary Herald*, 5 December 1958, 1, 6.

47 A few examples: "Eskimo Boy Flown Here to Save Injured Eye" (1949); "Plane Carries Sick Woman 1,590 Miles" (1961); "Eskimo Flown 1,800 Miles to Hospital in Edmonton" (1960), quoted in Donna Dryden, Elva Taylor, Rona Beer, Ron Bergman, and Margaret Cogill, *The Camsell Mosaic: The Charles Camsell Hospital, 1945–1985* (Edmonton: Charles Camsell History Committee, 1985), 154–7.

48 As a training centre for medical bureaucrats, in the previous ten years the hospital had produced three regional superintendents, two assistant regional superintendents, seven zone-hospital superintendents, three assistant zone superintendents, three directors of nursing, and a senior administrative officer at head office. "Notes on the Proposed New Charles Camsell Hospital," 23 November 1961, RG29, v 2798, file 831-1-D479, part 8, LAC.

49 Dryden et al., *Camsell Mosaic*, 68. The camaraderie was maintained through staff reunions, and by 1985 former staff formed the Camsell Hospital History Committee and published their highly nostalgic and celebratory history, *The Camsell Mosaic*.

50 RG29 v 2620, file 800-2-D479 part 1, LAC.

51 The other members of "Project Group 12" that compiled the recommendations included four physicians and two laymen. McCreary to Glassco, 31 January 1962, RG29, v 2798, file 831-1-D479, part 8, LAC.

52 *Royal Commission on Government Organization, Report*, vol. 3, Report 15, "Health Services" (Ottawa: Queen's Printer, 1962), 196, 201–2.

53 "Notes on the Proposed New Charles Camsell Hospital," 23 November 1961, RG29, v 2798, file 831-1-D479, part 8, LAC.

54 Moore to Fortier, 15 December 1961, RG29, v 2798, file 831-1-D479, part 8, LAC.

55 "Notes on the Proposed New Charles Camsell Hospital," 23 November 1961, RG29, v 2798, file 831-1-D479, part 8, LAC.

56 Moore to Fortier, 15 December 1961, RG29, v 2798, file 831-1-D479, part 8, LAC.

57 Cabinet meeting, 27 December 1963, RG2, Privy Council Office, series A-5-a, v 6254, LAC.

58 Dryden et al., *Camsell Mosaic*, 49.

59 "Transcript CFRN News Report, 29 December 1977," RG29, v 2595, file 800-1-D479 part 8(c), LAC.

60 "Official Opening Ceremonies of the Charles Camsell Hospital, Edmonton, 10 October 1967," RG29, v 2593, file 800-1-D479, part 2, LAC. Though the minister did not attend, deputy minister Dr John Crawford read his remarks.

61 Not all hospitals were to close, however. In 1965 Cabinet decided to rebuild the Peguis reserve's Fisher River Indian Hospital, where Moore got his start in IHS. It would be rebuilt at Hodgson, Manitoba, on the southern edge of the reserve and intended to serve the non-Aboriginal community as well. In 1964 Moore had approached the chief and Council with the proposal; they agreed to provide the reserve lands and also agreed that it would be named the Percy E. Moore Hospital. It finally opened in 1973. Benita E. Cohen, "The Development of Health Services in Peguis First Nation: A Descriptive Case Study" (MSc thesis, University of Manitoba, 1994), 89, 95.

62 J. Donovan Ross to R.G. Armstrong, Bassano Municipal Hospital, 16 June 1961; Ross to Mr Caldwell, Cardston Municipal Hospital, 17 July 1961, RG 29, v 2936, file 851-1-X400, part 1, LAC.

63 "Memorandum," 27 September 1961, RG 29, v 2936, file 851-1-X400, part 1, LAC. (original emphasis).

64 Aleck Ostry, "The Foundations of National Public Hospital Insurance," in *Making Medicare: New Perspectives on the History of Medicare in Canada*, ed. Gregory Marchildon (Toronto: University of Toronto Press, 2012), 34.

65 J.D. Wallace to P.E. Moore, 8 June 1961, RG 29, v 2936, file 851-1-x400, part 1, LAC.

66 The four communities – Samson Cree Nation, Ermineskin Cree Nation, Louis Bull First Nation, and Montana First Nation – comprise what was once known as the Hobbema Indian Agency. A crossroads more than a community in the 1950s, Hobbema is located approximately 90 kilometres south of Edmonton.

67 "Memorandum," 27 September 1961, RG 29, v 2936, file 851-1-X400, part 1, LAC.

68 Press release, Wetaskiwin General Hospital, 19 December 1961, RG 29 v 3378, file 800-1-D426, LAC.

69 Stone to Director, 20 April 1950, NA RG29 v 2796, file 831-1-D426, part 1, LAC.

70 Stone to Director, 11 February 1949, NA RG29 v 2796, file 831-1-D426, part 1, LAC.

71 E.L. Stone to Superintendent, Hobbema Indian Agency, 14 February 1951. Stone retired from IHS later that year and bureaucrats pushed to have the hospital named for him, but he declined the honour. Stone to Director, 30 July 1951, RG 29 v 3378, file 800-1-D426, LAC.

72 Alberta's hospital insurance, established in 1950, was a municipally administered and financed plan with provincial subsidies that provided less than 40 per cent of hospital income; Indian reserves were not considered municipalities. Taylor, *Health Insurance and Canadian Public Policy*, 170.

73 T.J. Orford, Zone Superintendent, Alberta, to W.L. Falconer, 3 July 1956; Orford to Kirkby, 6 July 1956, RG 29 v 3378, file 800-1-D426, LAC.

74 Orford to Regional Superintendent, 18 September 1956, RG 29 v 3378, file 800-1-D426, LAC.

75 Davies to Regional Superintendent, 22 January 1962; Davies to Regional Superintendent, 27 April 1962, RG 29 v 3378, file 800-1-D426, LAC.

76 Clippings from *Wetaskiwin Times* and Ponoka's *Western Weekly Supplement*, Falconer to J.D. Campbell, Hospitals Division, Edmonton, 22 August 1962, RG 29 v 3378, file 800-1-D426, LAC.

77 J.W. Monteith, Minister, to Harry Moore, 28 August 1962, RG 29 v 3378, file 800-1-D426, LAC.

78 Matas to Regional Superintendent, 11 March 1963; meeting held in the Office of the Provincial Minister of Health, 1 April 1963, RG 29 v 3378, file 800-1-D426, LAC.

79 Meeting held in the Office of the Provincial Minister of Health, 1 April 1963, RG 29 v 3378, file 800-1-D426, LAC.

80 "General Information 1 January 1963 to 30 June 1963," RG 29 v 3378, file 800-1-D426, LAC.

81 Moore to Deputy Minister, 22 March 1963, Charles Camsell Hospital records, 1991.0443, box 13, Provincial Archives of Alberta (PAA).

82 Quoted in Taylor, *Health Insurance and Canadian Public Policy*, 339.

83 Ibid., 340.

84 Saskatchewan's medical care insurance plan was funded through premiums and through increases in income tax, corporate tax, and retail sales tax. Taylor, *Health Insurance and Canadian Public Policy*, 288.

85 Moore to Deputy Minister, 22 March 1963, Charles Camsell Hospital records, 1991.0443, box 13, PAA.

86 Byron King Plant, "The Politics of Indian Administration: A Revisionist History of Intrastate Relations in Mid-Century British Columbia" (PhD diss., University of Saskatchewan, 2009), 83–4, 90.

87 George Manuel and Michael Posluns, *The Fourth World: An Indian Reality* (New York: Free Press, 1974), 106.

88 "Health Services to Indians," *Alberta Medical Bulletin* 33, no. 3 (August 1968): 107.

89 The popular term "medicare," originally a shortened form for The Medical Care Act (1966), since became conflated with The Hospital Insurance and Diagnostic Services Act (1957) to become "Medicare," though the two were not fused until the Canada Health Act (1984). Gregory Marchildon, "Canadian Medicare: Why History Matters," in Marchildon, *Making Medicare*, 5.

90 The Medical Care Act (1966) was implemented in July 1968 with British Columbia and Saskatchewan immediately qualifying; five more provinces including Alberta joined in 1969, and all other provinces enrolled by 1971.
91 Cam Traynor, "Manning against Medicare," *Alberta History* 43 (Winter 1995): 10, 11.
92 Taylor, *Health Insurance and Canadian Public Policy*, 376.
93 Rhoda Vold, secretary Asker ALCW to DIA, 8 October 1966, RG29 v 3378, file 800-1-D426, LAC.
94 Branch Policy Development Group, Minutes of Meeting, 21 August 1969, RG29, v 2936, file 851-1-X400 part 3 (a), LAC.
95 The province's payment per patient per day (per diem rate) was $40, but the Hospital Commission paid the principle and interest on capital debt (for the hospital's expansion) and then deducted those charges from the per diem rate, reducing it to just $17, RG29, v 2936, file 851-1-X400 part 3(a), LAC.
96 J.D. Henderson, Minister of Health, to R.B. Wardle, Wetaskiwin Hospital, 5 February 1970, RG29, v 2936, file 851-1-X400 part 3(a), LAC.
97 John Munro to Chief Threefingers, 14 May 1971, RG29, v 2936, file 851-1-X400 part 3(a), LAC.
98 O.J. Rath to Director, 16 March 1961, RG29 v 2936, file 851-1X400 part 1; HA Proctor, Gleichen Hospital, 10 August 1965, RG29, v 2936, file 851-1-X400, part 2(b), LAC.
99 W.B. Brittain to Director, 17 February 1961, RG29 v 2936, file 851-1X400 part 1, LAC.
100 Sally Weaver, *Making Canadian Indian Policy: The Hidden Agenda, 1968–70* (Toronto: University of Toronto Press, 1981), 25.
101 For example, see Moore to Rath, 21 March 1956; Wiebe to Wong, 17 December 1969; Munro to Coueslan, 10 February 1971, RG 29, v 3390, file 811-2-Broadview Union Hospital.
102 O.J. Rath to Director, 16 March 1961, RG 29, v 2936, file 851-1-x400, part 1, LAC.
103 Regional Director, memorandum, "Amendments to the Medical Services Program," 26 February 1968, RG29, v 2936, file 851-1-X400, part 2(b), LAC.
104 Rath to Director General, 29 April 1968, RG29, v 2936, file 851-1-x400 part 2(b), LAC.
105 "Health Services for Indians," 26 April 1968, RG29, v 2936, file 851-1-x400 part 2(b), LAC.
106 As Weaver makes clear, Trudeau's ideological opposition to "special status" or collective rights was formulated in response to Quebec nationalism. *Making Indian Policy*, 54–5.

107 "Health Plans Rile Indians: Services Linked to Need," *Calgary Herald*, 27 April 1968, 1.

108 Ross to Hon. Allan MacEachen, 14 March 1968, RG29, v 2936, file 851-1-x400 part 2(b), LAC.

109 Munro to Robert Thompson, MP, 31 October 1968, RG29, v 2936, file 851-1-x400 part 2(b), LAC.

110 Harold Cardinal to All Chiefs and Band Councils, 13 June 1969, RG29, v 2936, file 851-1-X400, part 3(a), LAC.

111 Munro to Cardinal, 6 May 1969, RG29, v 2936, file 851-1-X400, part 3(a), LAC.

112 H.B. Hawthorn, *A Survey of the Contemporary Indians of Canada: Economic, Political, Educational Needs and Policies*, 2 vols. (Ottawa: Queen's Printer, 1966–7), as quoted in Weaver, *Making Canadian Indian Policy*, 21.

113 Indian Chiefs of Alberta, *Citizens Plus*, 195. http://ejournals.library.ualberta. ca/index.php/aps/article/view/11690 (accessed 6 October 2013). The treaty right to care will be examined in greater detail in the next chapter.

114 Other counter-proposals to the White Paper included Union of British Columbia Chiefs' *A Declaration of Indian Rights* (1970); Manitoba Indian Brotherhood's *Wahbung: Our Tomorrows* (1971); Association of Iroquois and Allied Indians' *Position Paper* (1971). Weaver, *Making Indian Policy*, 188–9.

115 Indian Association of Alberta, "To Whom It May Concern," 22 July 1969, RG29, v 2936, file 851-1-X400, part 3(a), LAC.

116 "Minutes of a meeting to discuss Federal/Provincial responsibility for Hospital Services to Treaty Indians," 13 December 1972, RG29, v 2936, file 851-1-X400, part 4, LAC.

117 General Meeting of the Blood Hospital Committee, 15 February 1973, RG29, v 2936, file 851-1-X400, part 4, LAC.

118 Webb, Assistant Deputy Minister, to Rath, Regional Director, 8 November 1972, RG29, v 2609, file 800-1-X431, LAC.

119 See various letters, RG29, v 2609, file 800-1-X431, LAC.

120 O.J. Rath, Regional Director, to Acting Assistant Deputy Minister, 10 November 1972, RG 29, v 2936, file 851-1-X400, part 3, LAC.

121 T. Brown to J. Thorpe, 9 May 1974, RG29, v 3378 file 800-1-D443, part 2, LAC; "Hospital Soon to Be Retired after 70 Years of Service," *Windspeaker*, 1 January 1999. The heritage designation states: "The building's only decorative details are a stylized pediment above the main façade and a decorative raised brick panel and date stone over the main entrance. The designation is confined to the footprint of the building." http://www.historicplaces.ca/en/rep-reg/ place-lieu.aspx?id=9737 (accessed 8 October 2013).

122 Director to L.M. Black, 11 October 1978, RG29, v 2595, file 800-1-D429 part 10, LAC.

123 Memo, Rawson, Deputy Minister to the Minister, 14 September 1972, RG29, v 1604 – Charles Camsell Hospital Role Study, LAC.

124 "Report on the Future of Charles Camsell Hospital," 21 November 1975, RG29, v 3379, file 800-1-D479, LAC.

125 Memo, Rawson, Deputy Minister to the Minister, 14 September 1972, RG29, v 1604 – Charles Camsell Hospital Role Study; "Submission to the Policy Review Committee," 15 May 1976. In the fiscal year 1975–6 the operating expenses were $8.4 million and revenue $4.4 million. RG29, v 3379, file 800-1-D479, LAC.

126 Rawson to Sam Raddi, Committee for the Original Peoples Entitlement; Eric Tagoona, Inuit Tapirisat; George Erasmus, Indian Brotherhood of NWT; Joe Dion, Indian Association Alberta, 7 November 1978, RG29, v 2595, file 800-1-D479, part 8(c), LAC; Miniely to Monique Bégin and Hugh Faulkner, 14 November 1978, RG29, v 2595, file 800-1-D479, part 10, LAC.

127 News release, "New Indian Health Program Unveiled," June 1980, RG29, v 3379, file 800-1-D479, LAC.

128 It had been used as a location for B-movies; reputed to be haunted, it attracts the occasional intrepid ghost hunter. "Derelict Hospital a Project Going Nowhere," *Edmonton Journal*, 29 May, 2010, 8 November 2012, http://blogs.edmontonjournal.com/tag/camsell-hospital/ (accessed 25 September 2013).

129 Roy Romanow, *Building on Values: The Future of Health Care in Canada* (Final Report on the Royal Commission on the Future of Health Care in Canada, 2002), xvi, http://publications.gc.ca/site/eng/237274/publication.html.

130 Hospital Committee Meeting, 14 February 1973, RG29, v 2936, file 851-1-X400, part 4, LAC.

Chapter Six

1 Arthur J. Ray, Jim Miller, and Frank Tough, *Bounty and Benevolence: A History of Saskatchewan Treaties* (Montreal: McGill-Queen's University Press, 2000), 214.

2 See ibid.

3 Peter Erasmus, *Buffalo Days and Nights* (Calgary: Fifth House, 1999), 253; Alexander Morris, *The Treaties of Canada with the Indians of Manitoba and the North-West Territories* (1880; reprint Saskatoon: Fifth House, 1991), 185, 214–15.

4 Morris, *Treaties of Canada*, 355.

5 James Waldram, D. Ann Herring, and T. Kue Young, *Aboriginal Health in Canada*, 2nd ed. (Toronto: University of Toronto Press, 2006), 176–7; Yvonne Boyer, *Aboriginal Health: A Constitutional Rights Analysis* (Ottawa: National Aboriginal Health Organization and Native Law Centre, University of Saskatchewan, 2003), 20.

6 *Dreaver v The King* (1935), 20, copy in RG22 v 844, file 6-29-1 (3), LAC.

7 North Battleford, established in 1905 by the Canadian Northern Railway, left Battleford, the former Territorial capital, isolated on the south side of the North Saskatchewan River; the two towns are referred to collectively as "The Battlefords."

8 P.W. Head, *Annual Report*, 22 January 1945, RG29 v 2591, file 800-1-D353, part 1, LAC; there were approximately 2,500 people in the Battleford Agency, 700 in the Onion Lake Agency, and 1,000 in the Carlton Agency.

9 There were twenty-nine patients in the sanatorium. Memorandum for the Deputy Minister, 15 February 1945, RG29, v 2591, file 800-1-D353, part 1, LAC. Opened in 1930, the provincial Prince Albert Sanatorium admitted fifty-six Aboriginal patients by 1939, half of them schoolchildren. Aboriginal admissions reflected the declining need for sanatorium beds by the white population. Saskatchewan Lung Association Files, A638, file IX.73a, Saskatchewan Archives Board (SAB).

10 O.J. Rath, Regional Superintendent to Zone Superintendent, 12 December 1956, RG29, v 2591, file 800-1-D353, part 1, LAC.

11 "Ailing Chief Swimmer Reflects on Changes His People Had Known," *Saskatoon Star Phoenix*, 28 April 1953.

12 Corrigan to Director, 23 February 1956, RG29, v 2591, file 800-1-D353 part 1, LAC.

13 Petition to Indian Health Service, 8 March 1962, RG29, v 2591, file 800-1-D353, part 1, LAC.

14 Orford to Director, 15 March 1962, RG29, v 2591, file 800-1-D353 part 1, LAC.

15 Orford to Director, 18 April 1962, RG29, v 2591, file 800-1-D353 part 1, LAC.

16 Moore to Orford, 4 May 1962, RG29, v 2591, file 800-1-D353 part 1, LAC.

17 A.H. Fry to Regional Superintendent, 17 April 1962, RG29, v 2591, file 800-1-D353 part 1, LAC.

18 Orford to Director, 16 July 1964, RG29, v 2916, file 851-1-A67 part 3(a), LAC.

19 Ed Melynchuk, "Observations while Acting Administrator North Battleford Indian Hospital, June to August 1965," RG29, v 2591, file 800-1-D353 part 1, LAC.

20 Proctor to Regional Supervisor, 12 May 1965, RG29, v 2591, file 800-1-D353 part 1, LAC; Orford was medical superintendent at the hospital in 1957 when an infant died through neglect and understaffing (see chapter 3).

21 Sidney Fineday to Proctor, 21 July 1965, RG29, v 2591, file 800-1-D353 part 1, LAC.

22 Orford to Director, 9 August 1965, RG29, v 2591, file 800-1-D353 part 1, LAC; within two years, only Aboriginal representatives sat on the Advisory Board.

23 Orford to Director, 24 August 1965, RG29, v 2591, file 800-1-D353 part 1, LAC.

24 "Board Charges Medical Bias against Indians," *Toronto Telegram*, 19 August 1965, RG 29, v 2591, file 800-1-D353, part 2, LAC.

25 Proctor, Director, to Orford, 18 October 1965, RG29, v 2591, file 800-1-D353, part 2, LAC; Percy Moore retired in 1965, replaced as director by his long-serving assistant Dr H.A. Proctor.

26 Proctor to Deputy Minister, 21 October 1965, RG29, v 2591, file 800-1-D353, part 2, LAC.

27 "Report of the Meeting of the Lay Advisory Board, 27 November 1966," RG29, v 2591, file 800-1-D353, part 2, LAC.

28 Webb to Zone Director, 17 February 1967, RG29, v 2591, file 800-1-D353, part 2, LAC.

29 In 1962 all the North Battleford Indian Hospital's Aboriginal employees were served with "Loss of Benefit" notices, a form letter informing them that they were considered to have sufficient private resources to pay insurance premiums and they would no longer receive medical care through IHS. RG29, v 2916, file 851-1-A67, part 3(a), LAC.

30 Director to J. Williams, 10 March 1965, RG29, v 2591, file 800-1-D353 part 1, LAC.

31 Favel to G.D.W. Cameron, 9 March 1965; Cameron to Favel, 18 March 1965, RG29, v 2916, file 851-1-A67, part 3(a), LAC.

32 *Regina v Walter Johnston*, J.M. Policha, JHC, 12 May 1965, copy in RG29, v 2916, file 851-1-A67, part 3(a), LAC.

33 Proctor to Orford, 14 May 1965, RG29, v 2916, file 851-1-A67, part 3(a), LAC.

34 Orford to Proctor, 14 May 1965, RG29, v 2916, file 851-1-A67, part 3(a), LAC.

35 Cameron to Minister, 18 May 1965, RG29, v 2916, file 851-1-A67, part 3(a), LAC.

36 La Marsh to Nicholson, 19 May 1965, RG29, v 2916, file 851-1-A67, part 3(a), LAC.

37 Battle to Deputy Minister, 21 May 1965, RG22, v 844, file 6–29–1 (3) LAC.

38 Orford to Director, 25 May 1965; Orford to Zone Superintendents, 17 May 1965, RG29, v 2916, file 851-1-A67, part 3(a), LAC.

39 Steuart to Nicholson, 25 May 1965, RG29, v 2916, file 851-1-A67, part 3(a), LAC.

40 R.E. Williams to Assistant Deputy Minister, Indian Affairs, 7 October 1965, RG22, v 844, file 6–29–1 (3), LAC.

41 R.F. Battle, Assistant Deputy Minister (Indian Affairs), to Deputy Minister, 21 May 1965, RG22, v 844, file 6–29–1 (3), LAC.

42 First elected in 1935 as the Liberal member for Gravelbourg in the Saskatchewan legislature and a failed contender for the party leadership in

1945, Culliton was appointed to the Court of Appeal in 1951 and became Chief Justice in 1962. "Culliton, Edward Milton," *Encyclopedia of Saskatchewan*, http://esask.uregina.ca/entry/culliton_edward_milton_1906-91.html (accessed 10 February 2012).

43 Alexander Morris, *The Treaties of Canada with the Indians of Manitoba and the North-West Territories* (1880; reprint Saskatoon: Fifth House, 1991).

44 Ibid., 184, 214–15.

45 Diamond Jenness, *The Indians of Canada*, 7th ed. (1932 reprint; Toronto: University of Toronto Press, 1977); the seventh edition has been reprinted nine times, most recently in 2003.

46 Ibid., 264.

47 Heidi Bohaker and Franca Iacovetta, "Making Aboriginal People 'Immigrants Too': A Comparison of Citizenship Programs for Newcomers and Indigenous Peoples in Postwar Canada, 1940s–1960s," *Canadian Historical Review* 90, no. 3 (September 2009): 427–61.

48 Peter Alan Barkwell, "The Medicine Chest Clause in Treaty No. 6," *Canadian Native Law Reporter* 4 (1981): 16–17.

49 "Memorandum for Prairie Region," 1 April 1969, RG29, v 2591, file 800-1-D353, part 2, LAC; actually called the Federation of Saskatchewan Indians, established in 1940s.

50 M.P.D. Waldron to Director, 20 May 1970, RG29, v 2591, file 800-1-D353, part 3, LAC.

51 Lay Advisory Board Meeting, 30 April 1970, RG29, v 2591, file 800-1-D353, part 3, LAC.

52 See Harold Cardinal, *The Unjust Society: The Tragedy of Canada's Indians* (Edmonton: Hurtig, 1969); J.R. Miller, *Skyscrapers Hide the Heavens: A History of Indian-White Relations in Canada*, rev. ed. (Toronto: University of Toronto Press, 1989), 231. A formal retraction of the White Paper did not come until March 1971. Sally Weaver, *Making Canadian Indian Policy: The Hidden Agenda, 1968–70* (Toronto: University of Toronto Press, 1981), 187.

53 Quoted in ibid., 185.

54 R.J. Mulligan, "Memorandum," 15 June 1970, RG29, v 2591, file 800-1-D353, part 3, LAC.

55 Special Joint Meeting, 5 January 1971, RG29, v 2591, file 800-1-D353, part 3, LAC.

56 F.H. Hicks, Memorandum, 16 June 1971, RG29, v 2591, file 800-1-D353, part 3, LAC.

57 Ibid.

58 C.A. Bentley to Ken Butler, 19 May 1977, RG29, v 2592, file 800-1-D353, part 5, LAC.

59 Minutes of the Lay Advisory Board Meeting, 30 July 1971, RG29, v 2591, file 800-1-D353, part 3, LAC.

60 *Saskatchewan Indian* 3, no. 3 (1972): 5.

61 Assistant Deputy Minister to Dr M. LeClair, Deputy Minister, National Health, n.d., (November 1971), RG29, v 2591, file 800-1-D353, part 3, LAC.

62 Transcript of tape recorded meeting, 22 November 1971, RG29, v 2591, file 800-1-D353, part 3, LAC.

63 Quoted in Peter Alan Barkwell, "The Medicine Chest Clause in Treaty No. 6," *Canadian Native Law Reporter* 4 (1981): 18.

64 Following the ruling in *Johnston*, the Manitoba Queen's Bench Court ruled in 1969 in *The Manitoba Hospital Commission v Klein and Spence* that Mrs Spence, a Treaty Indian from Peguis, could not claim a right to free hospital care under the "medicine chest" clause. W.M. Weekes, Director, Legal Services, to M.L. Webb, 13 March 1973, RG22, v 1207, file 851-1-X300, LAC.

65 "Chief David Ahenakew," in *Saskatchewan Indian*, August 1972; Director, Legal Services, to Webb, 13 March 1973, RG29, v 2934, file 851-1-X300, part 2, LAC.

66 Transcript of tape recorded meeting, 22 November 1971; "Background Information for the Meeting," 22 November 1971, RG29, v 2591, file 800-1-D353, part 3, LAC.

67 Advisory Board Meeting, 6 December 1971, RG29, v 2591, file 800-1-D353, part 3, LAC.

68 Advisory Board Meeting, 8 February 1972, RG29, v 2728, file 811-2, part 2, LAC.

69 Webb to Le Clair, 23 February 1972, RG29, v 2728, file 811-2, part 2, LAC.

70 W.M. Weekes to M.L. Webb, "Legal Interpretation of Medicine Chest Clause in Treaty 6," 13 March 1973, RG22, v 1207, file 851-1-X300, LAC.

71 Lalonde to Joseph Weenie, 31 July 1973, RG29 v 3378, file 800-1-D443, part 2, LAC.

72 Memorandum, Brian Brett, 24 November 1976, RG29, v 2592, file 800-1-D353, part 4, LAC.

73 The North Battleford District Chiefs, "Proposal for a Study Regarding the Closure of the Indian Hospital in North Battleford, Saskatchewan," RG29, v 2592, file 800-1-D353, part 4, LAC.

74 Rawson to Pooyak, 9 December 1976, RG29, v 2592, file 800-1-D353, part 4, LAC.

75 North Battleford District Chiefs, "Hospital Services for Indians in the North Battleford District," March 1977, RG29, v 2592, file 800-1-D353, part 5, LAC.

76 The nine reserves were Thunderchild, Little Pine, Onion Lake, Moosomin, Mosquito, Saulteaux, Red Pheasant, Poundmaker, and Sweetgrass.

77 North Battleford District Chiefs, "Hospital Services for Indians in the North Battleford District," March 1977, 11, RG29, v 2592, file 800-1-D353, part 5, LAC.
78 Lyle Black, Director to Dr K. Butler, 6 May 1977, RG29, v. 2592, file 800-1-D353, part 5, LAC.
79 "Report of the Task Force on the Provision of Health Services to Indians in North Battleford, 30 June 1977," p. 10, RG29, v 2592, file 800-1-D353, part 5, LAC.
80 "Report of the Task Force in the Provision of Health Services to Indians in North Battleford, 30 June 1977," p. 1, RG29, v. 2592, file 800-1-D353, part 5, LAC.
81 "Comparison Noting the Differences between the Original Task Force Report on North Battleford and the Report Presented to the Department by Dr Laroche," p. 3, RG29, v 2592, file 800-1-D353, part 6, LAC. Emphasis added.
82 Ibid.
83 "Comparison Noting the Differences between the Original Task Force Report on North Battleford and the Report Presented to the Department by Dr Laroche," p. 1, RG29, v 2592, file 800-1-D353, part 6, LAC.
84 Laroche, "Memorandum for Mr Bruce Rawson," 30 June 1977, RG29, v 2592, file 800-1-D353, part 5, LAC.
85 Rawson to the minister, 19 July 1977, RG29, v 2592, file 800-1-D353, part 6, LAC.
86 Lalonde to Steuart, 17 August 1977; Laroche to Lalonde, 9 September 1977, RG29, v 2592, file 800-1-D353, part 6, LAC.
87 Lalonde to Ahenakew, 14 September 1977, RG29, v 2592, file 800-1-D353, part 6, LAC.
88 Rawson to Caron, 27 July 1977, RG29, v 2592, file 800-1-D353, part 6, LAC.
89 Lalonde to Steuart, 17 August 1977, RG29, v 2592, file 800-1-D353, part 6, LAC.
90 Clarkson to Lalonde, 6 August 1977, RG29, v 2592, file 800-1-D353, part 6, LAC.
91 Graham Clarkson, "A Functional Health Plan for the Indians in the North Battleford Area," December 1977, 1; Clarkson to Black, 8 October 1977, RG29, v 2592, file 800-1-D353, part 6, LAC.
92 Clarkson, "A Functional Health Plan," 39.
93 Ibid., 13.
94 Ibid., 16.
95 Ibid., 24.
96 Dr M.K. Sas to Bégin, 17 Mar 1978; E.H. Baergen to Bégin, 28 March 1978; Dr C.M. Furniss to Bégin, 4 April 1978, RG29, v 2917, file 851-1-A671, part 6, LAC.

97 Clarkson to Murphy, 10 April 1978, RG29, v 2917, file 851-1-A671, part 6, LAC.

98 Black, "Visit to North Battleford 1–3 February 1978," RG29, v 2917, file 851-1-A671, part 6, LAC.

99 "Openings for Physicians in North Battleford, Sask," *Canadian Medical Association Journal* 120 (3 February 1979): 270–1.

100 Battlefords Indian Health Centre Inc., *30 Years Later: July 1979–July 2009*, commemorative booklet.

101 Noel Starblanket, "The Dawn of a New Era," quoted in Hon. Thomas Berger, *Report of Advisory Commission on Indian and Inuit Health Consultation* (Ottawa, February 1980), Appendix 4.

102 T. Kue Young, *Health Care and Cultural Change: The Indian Experience in the Central Subarctic* (Toronto: University of Toronto Press, 1988), 93; Anne Gilmore, "Indian Health Care: What the Dispute Is All About," *Canadian Medical Association Journal* 121 (7 July 1979): 87–94.

103 Starblanket, "The Dawn of a New Era," quoted in Berger, *Report of Advisory Commission on Indian and Inuit Health Consultation*.

104 Battlefords Indian Health Centre Inc., *30 Years Later: July 1979–July 2009*, commemorative booklet (emphasis added).

105 Berger, *Report of Advisory Commission*, 17.

106 "Indian Health Care: A Treaty Right," Indian Association of Alberta, January 1979, 16, RG29 v 2959, file 851-3-Indian Association Alberta, part 2, LAC.

107 Health and Welfare Policy Paper, quoted in Berger, *Report of Advisory Commission*, 17.

108 "Indian Health Policy," quoted in Berger, *Report of Advisory Commission*, Appendix 2.

109 Edward T. Jackson, "A Working Inventory of Community-Based Initiatives in the Health Field Being Undertaken by the Indians and Inuit Peoples," in Berger, *Report of Advisory Commission*, Appendix 6.

110 Young, *Health Care and Cultural Change*, 125.

111 World Health Organization, *Alma Ata: Primary Health Care* (Geneva: World Health Organization, 1978), 16.

112 Rawson to the minister, 19 July 1977, RG29, v 2592, file 800-1-D353, part 6, LAC.

113 *Wuskwi Sipihk Cree Nation v Canada (Minister of National Health and Welfare)*, *Canadian Native Law Reporter* 4 (1999): 293.

114 Constance MacIntosh, "Envisioning the Future of Aboriginal Health under the Health Transfer Process," *Health Law Journal* (Special Edition 2008): 86, http://papers.ssrn.com/sol3/papers.cfm?abstract_id=2101674 (accessed 10 February 2014).

Conclusion

1 Quoted in Sally Weaver, *Making Canadian Indian Policy: The Hidden Agenda, 1968–70* (Toronto: University of Toronto Press, 1981), 185.

2 This status might also be explained by the fact that though Medicare has its historians, we await its history. Gregory Marchildon suggests that the lack of a general history stems from the value-laden and policy-heavy nature of Medicare. Marchildon, *Making Medicare: New Perspectives on the History of Medicare in Canada* (Toronto: University of Toronto Press, 2012). Gerald W. Boychuk's comparative view argues that public health insurance in Canada fostered national unity and has come to be seen as a right of citizenship. Boychuk, *National Health Insurance in the United States and Canada: Race, Territory and the Roots of Difference* (Washington: Georgetown University Press, 2008), 142–3. Two studies stress a progressive view of Medicare as seemingly inevitable: Malcolm Taylor, *Health Insurance and Canadian Public Policy: The Seven Decisions That Created the Canadian Health Insurance System and Their Outcomes*, 2nd ed. (Montreal and Kingston: McGill-Queen's University Press, 1987), and C. Stuart Houston and Merle Massie, *36 Steps on the Road to Medicare: How Saskatchewan Led the Way* (Montreal and Kingston: McGill-Queen's University Press, 2013). In a larger work on the history of social policy Alvin Finkel devotes a chapter to the compromises that resulted in Medicare in *Social Policy and Practice in Canada: A History* (Waterloo, ON: Wilfrid Laurier University Press, 2006).

3 That national satisfaction swells not least in comparison with American health care, though the program only covers about 60 per cent of health care costs. Roy Romanow, *Building on Values: The Future of Health Care in Canada: Final Report on the Royal Commission on the Future of Health Care in Canada* (2002), xvi, 34, http://publications.gc.ca/site/eng/237274/publication.html.

4 Juha Mikkonen and Dennis Raphael, *The Social Determinants of Health: The Canadian Facts* (Toronto: York University School of Health Policy and Management, 2010), http://www.thecanadianfacts.org/The_Canadian_Facts.pdf (accessed 8 February 2014).

5 "Government of Canada Indian Health Policy," in Hon. Thomas Berger, *Report of Advisory Commission on Indian and Inuit Health Consultation* (Ottawa, February 1980), Appendix 2.

6 T. Kue Young, *Health Care and Cultural Change: The Indian Experience in the Central Subarctic* (Toronto: University of Toronto Press, 1988), 110, 134. The Sioux Lookout Indian Hospital, built by the federal government in 1949, sat alongside the Sioux Lookout General Hospital.

7 Scott-McKay-Bain Health Panel, *From Here to There: Steps along the Way: Achieving Health for All in the Sioux Lookout Zone* (June 1989), http://www. slmhc.on.ca/assets/files/From_Here_to_There_-_Steps_Along_the_Way. pdf (accessed 1 December 2013).

8 Quoted in Dana Culhane Speck, "The Indian Health Transfer Policy: A Step in the Right Direction, or Revenge of the Hidden Agenda?" *Native Studies Review* 5, no. 1 (1989): 189.

9 Ibid., 206.

10 John D. O'Neil, "Aboriginal Health Policy for the Next Century," *The Path to Healing: Report of the National Round Table on Aboriginal Health and Social Issues*, Royal Commission on Aboriginal Peoples (Ottawa: Canada Communications Group, 1993), 43.

11 Culhane Speck, "The Indian Health Transfer Policy," 200. A decade later some trial transfers of non-insured health benefits began.

12 Kristen M. Jacklin and Wayne Warry, "The Indian Health Transfer Policy in Canada: Toward Self-Determination or Cost Containment?" in Arachu Castro and Merrill Singer, eds, *Unhealthy Health Policy: A Critical Anthropological Examination* (Walnut Creek, CA: Alta Mira Press, 2004), 230.

13 Alma Favel-King, "The Treaty Right to Health," *The Path to Healing: Report of the National Round Table on Aboriginal Health and Social Issues*, Royal Commission on Aboriginal Peoples (Ottawa: Canada Communications Group, 1993), 123, 128.

14 The Battlefords Tribal Council (representing Mosquito, Little Pine, Sweetgrass, and Lucky Man First Nations) signed a transfer agreement in 1993. "Battlefords Tribal Council Signs Historic Health Service Agreement," *Saskatchewan Indian* 22, no. 6 (July 1993): 2.

15 By 2008 more than 80 per cent of 599 eligible First Nations communities had entered into some form of transfer agreement, though only three Alberta communities participated because of concerns that it would affect claimed treaty rights to health services. Constance MacIntosh, "Envisioning the Future of Aboriginal Health under the Health Transfer Process," *Health Law Journal* (Special Edition 2008): 73, http://papers.ssrn. com/sol3/papers.cfm?abstract_id=2101674 (accessed 10 February 2014).

16 Scott-McKay-Bain Health Panel, *From Here to There*.

17 "Meno Ya Win" is an Anishinaabe term that connotes health, wellness, well-being, and individual spiritual, mental, emotional, and physical wholeness (http://www.slmhc.on.ca/history) (accessed 3 December 2013).

Bibliography

PRIMARY SOURCES

Archival Collections

- Archives of Manitoba
  Records of the Sanatorium Board of Manitoba
- Archives of Ontario
  Public Health Nursing, Record Group 10–30
- British Columbia Archives
  Tuberculosis Control Division GR 129
- Glenbow Alberta Archives
  Gooderham Family Papers
  Dr H.W. McGill Papers
- Library and Archives Canada
  Department of Indian Affairs, Record Group 10
  Department of National Health and Welfare, Record Group 29
  Canadian Tuberculosis Association, MG28 I75
- Prince Rupert City and Regional Archives
  Wrathall Collection
- Public Archives of Alberta
  Charles Camsell Hospital
  Central Alberta (Baker) Sanatorium
- St Albert Museum and Archives
  St Albert Cemeteries
- Saskatchewan Archives Board
  Saskatchewan Lung Association Files, A638

Oral Interviews

- Gordon Albert, North Battleford, Saskatchewan
- Grace Anderson, Winnipeg, Manitoba
- Rose Atimoyoo, North Battleford, Saskatchewan
- Agnes Cyr, Echo Lodge, Fort Qu'Appelle, Saskatchewan
- Andrew and Rosabel (Ryder) Gordon, Pasqua First Nation
- Roy Little Chief, Strathmore, Alberta
- Frank Malloway Sr, Chilliwack, British Columbia
- Hazel McArthur (née Wolf), Stoughton, Saskatchewan
- Dave Melting Tallow, Siksika, Alberta

Newspapers

- Aboriginal Multi-Media Society *Windspeaker*
- *Calgary Herald*
- *Edmonton Journal*
- *Ottawa Citizen*
- *Prince Rupert Evening Empire*
- *Saskatchewan Indian*
- *Saskatoon Star Phoenix*
- *Toronto Globe and Mail*
- *Winnipeg Free Press*
- *Winnipeg Tribune*

Published Primary Documents

Baergen, E.H. "Openings for Physicians in North Battleford, Sask." *Canadian Medical Association Journal* 120 (3 February 1979): 270–1.

Battlefords Indian Health Centre Inc. *30 Years Later: July 1979–July 2009.* Commemorative booklet.

Beecher, H.K. "Ethics and Clinical Research." *New England Journal of Medicine* 274 (1966): 1354–60.

Berger, Hon. Thomas. *Report of Advisory Commission on Indian and Inuit Health Consultation.* Ottawa, February 1980.

Bryce, P.H. *Report on the Indian Schools of Manitoba and the North-West Territories.* Ottawa: Government Printing Bureau, 1907.

– *The Story of a National Crime: Being an Appeal for Justice to the Indians of Canada.* Ottawa: James Hope and Sons, 1922.

Calgary: The Denver of Canada. Calgary: Calgary Herald Print, 1895.

Canada. *Building on Values: The Future of Health Care in Canada: Final Report on the Royal Commission on the Future of Health Care in Canada* (2002).

– House of Commons. *Sessional Papers.*

– House of Commons. Special Joint Committee of the Senate and the House of Commons Appointed to Examine and Consider the Indian Act. *Minutes of Proceedings and Evidence No. 3.*

– Public Health Agency of Canada, "BCG Vaccine use in Canada – Current and Historical." http://www.phac-aspc.gc.ca/tbpc-latb/bcgvac_1206-eng.php. Accessed 16 April 2013.

– Royal Commission on Government Organization. *Report* vol. 3, Report 15 "Health Services." Ottawa: Queen's Printer, 1962.

– Royal Commission on Aboriginal Peoples 1996. http://www.collectionscanada.gc.ca/webarchives/20071115053257/http://www.ainc-inac.gc.ca/ch/rcap/sg/sgmm_e.html. Accessed 24 May 2013.

– Truth and Reconciliation Commission. http://www.trc.ca/websites/trcinstitution/index.php?p=3. Accessed 16 May 2013.

Camsell, Charles. *Son of the North.* Toronto: Ryerson, 1954.

Cardinal, Harold. *The Unjust Society: The Tragedy of Canada's Indians.* Edmonton: Hurtig, 1969.

Dent, John. "New Deal for Indians Is Planned by MP." *Saturday Night*, 30 March 1946.

Edwards, Allan M., and Gordon C. Gray. "Observations on Juvenile Hypothyroidism in Native Races of Northern Canada." *Canadian Medical Association Journal* 84 (20 May 1961): 1116–24.

Erasmus, Peter. *Buffalo Days and Nights.* Calgary: Fifth House, 1999.

"Ervin Lockwood Stone" *Canadian Medical Association Journal* 98 (2 March 1968): 473.

Ferguson, R.G. *Tuberculosis among the Indians of the Great Canadian Plains.* Reprint. London: Adlard and Son, 1928.

Ferguson, R.G., and A.B. Simes. "BCG Vaccination of Indian Infants in Saskatchewan" *Tubercle* 30, no. 1 (1949): 5–11.

Freeman, Minnie Aodla. *Life among the Qallunaat.* Edmonton: Hurtig, 1978.

Gilmore, Anne. "Indian Health Care: What the Dispute Is All About." *Canadian Medical Association Journal* 121 (7 July 1979): 87–94.

Government of Northwest Territories. Department of Health. *Medical Patient Search Project Summary: Final Report.* April 1991.

Grzybowski, Stefan, and Zygmunt Dunaj. "Tuberculin Survey of the Population of Manitoulin Island." *Canadian Medical Association Journal* 81 (1 September 1959): 366–8.

"Health Services to Indians." *Alberta Medical Bulletin* 33, no. 3 (August 1968): 107–8.

Hiltz, J.E. "Compulsory Treatment of Tuberculosis." *Canadian Medical Association Journal* 71 (December 1954): 569–71.

"Hospitals Developed for Canadian Indians." *New York Times*, 7 January 1940.

"House of Commons Discusses Estimates for Indian Affairs Branch." *Bulletin of the Canadian Tuberculosis Association* 15, no. 4 (1937): 3–4.

Indian Chiefs of Alberta, *Citizens Plus*. http://ejournals.library.ualberta.ca/index.php/aps/article/view/11690. Accessed 6 October 2013.

Jenness, Diamond. *The Indians of Canada*, 7th ed. 1932. Reprint. Toronto: University of Toronto Press, 1977.

– *The Sarcee Indians of Alberta*. Bulletin no. 90. Ottawa: National Museum of Canada, 1938.

"List of Canadian Hospitals Approved for Advanced Graduate Training by the Royal College of Physicians and Surgeons." *Canadian Medical Association Journal* 78 (April 1958): 520.

Lymer, John Robert, and Arthur James Anderson. "An Evaluation of Several Orally Administered Para-aminosalicylic Acid Preparations." *Canadian Pharmaceutical Journal* (September 1957): 160–2.

Matas, M. "Tuberculosis Programs of the Medical Services, Department of National Health and Welfare." In "Proceedings of the Third National Tuberculosis Conference," *Medical Services Journal Canada* 22 (1966): 878–83.

Meltzer, H. "Results of Thoracoplasty." *Journal of Thoracic Surgery* (St Louis) 11, no. 1 (October 1941): 84–94.

Moore, P.E. "No Longer Captain: A History of Tuberculosis and Its Control amongst Canadian Indians." *Canadian Medical Association Journal* 84 (May 1961): 1012–16.

Moore, P.E., H.D. Kruse, F.F. Tisdall, and R.S.C. Corrigan. "Medical Survey of Nutrition among the Northern Manitoba Indians." *Canadian Medical Association Journal* 54 (March 1946): 223–33.

Morris, Alexander. *The Treaties of Canada with the Indians of Manitoba and the North-West Territories*. 1880. Reprint. Saskatoon: Fifth House, 1991.

Ross, E.L., and A.L. Paine. "A Tuberculosis Survey of Manitoba Indians." *Canadian Medical Association Journal* 4 (August 1939): 180–4.

Scott-McKay-Bain Health Panel. *From Here to There: Steps along the Way: Achieving Health for All in the Sioux Lookout Zone* (June 1989). http://www.slmhc.on.ca/assets/files/From_Here_to_There_-_Steps_Along_the_Way.pdf. Accessed 1 December 2013.

Stanley, G.D. "Early Days at the Muskoka San." *Calgary Historical Bulletin* 18 (May 1953): 17–20.

Stone, E.L. "Canadian Indian Medical Services." *Canadian Medical Association Journal* (July 1935): 82–5.

Wherrett, G.J. "Arctic Survey 1: Survey of Health Conditions and Medical and Hospital Services in the North West Territories." *Canadian Journal of Economics and Political Science* 11, no. 1 (1945): 48–60.

– "Tuberculosis in Canada." *Royal Commission on Health Services*. Ottawa: Queen's Printer, 1965.

World Health Organization. *Alma Ata: Primary Health Care*. Geneva: World Health Organization, 1978.

Film

The Longer Trail. Directed by Fergus McDonell. 30 min. National Film Board, 1956.

Lost Songs. Directed by Clint Alberta. 24 min. 04 sec. National Film Board, 1999.

No Longer Vanishing. Directed by Grant McLean. 27 min. 31 sec. National Film Board, 1955.

SECONDARY SOURCES

Aboriginal Nurses Association of Canada. *Twice as Good: A History of Aboriginal Nurses*. Ottawa: Aboriginal Nurses Association of Canada, 2007.

Anderson, Warwick. *The Cultivation of Whiteness: Science, Health and Racial Destiny in Australia*. New York: Basic Books, 2003.

Arnold, David. "Medicine and Colonialism." In *Companion Encyclopedia of the History of Medicine*, vol. 2, edited by W.F. Bynum and Roy Porter, 1393–416. London: Routledge, 1993.

– ed. *Imperial Medicine and Indigenous Societies*. Manchester: Manchester University Press, 1988.

Backhouse, Constance. *Colour-Coded: A Legal History of Racism in Canada, 1900–1950*. Toronto: University of Toronto Press, 1999.

Barkwell, Peter Alan. "The Medicine Chest Clause in Treaty No. 6." *Canadian Native Law Reporter* 4 (1981): 1–23.

Bashford, Alison, and Carolyn Strange. "Cultures of Confinement." In *Isolation: Places and Practices of Exclusion*, edited by Carolyn Strange and Alison Bashford. London: Routledge, 2003.

– "Isolation and Exclusion in the Modern World." In *Isolation: Places and Practices of Exclusion*, edited by Carolyn Strange and Alison Bashford. London: Routledge, 2003.

Bates, Barbara. *Bargaining for Life: A Social History of Tuberculosis, 1876–1938*. Philadelphia: University of Pennsylvania Press, 1992.

Bohaker, Heidi, and Franca Iacovetta. "Making Aboriginal People 'Immigrants Too': A Comparison of Citizenship Programs for Newcomers and

Indigenous Peoples in Postwar Canada, 1940s–1960s." *Canadian Historical Review* 90, no. 3 (2009): 427–61.

Boychuk, Gerald W. *National Health Insurance in the United States and Canada: Race, Territory and the Roots of Difference*. Washington, DC: Georgetown University Press, 2008.

Boyer, Yvonne. *Aboriginal Health: A Constitutional Rights Analysis*. Ottawa: National Aboriginal Health Organization and Native Law Centre, University of Saskatchewan, 2003.

Brownlie, Robin, and Mary-Ellen Kelm. "Desperately Seeking Absolution: Native Agency as Colonialist Alibi?" *Canadian Historical Review* 75, no. 4 (1994): 543–56.

Bryden, P.E. "The Liberal Party and the Achievement of National Medicare." *Canadian Bulletin of Medical History* 26, no. 2 (2009): 315–32.

Bryder, Linda. *Below the Magic Mountain*. Oxford: Clarendon Press, 1988.

Carter, Sarah. *Aboriginal People and Colonizers of Western Canada*. Toronto: University of Toronto Press, 1999.

Coates, Ken. *Best Left as Indians: Native-White Relations in the Yukon Territory, 1840–1973*. Montreal and Kingston: McGill-Queen's University Press, 1991.

Coates, K.S., and W.R. Morrison. *The Alaska Highway in World War II: The U.S. Army of Occupation in Canada's Northwest*. Toronto: University of Toronto Press, 1992.

Connolly, Cynthia. *Saving Sickly Children: The Tuberculosis Preventorium in American Life, 1909–1970*. New Brunswick, NJ: Rutgers University Press, 2008.

Cortiula, Mark. "Social Class and Health Care in a Community Institution: The Case of Hamilton City Hospital." *Canadian Bulletin of Medical History* 6 (1989): 133–45.

Crey, Ernie, and Suzanne Fournier. *Stolen from Our Embrace. The Abduction of First Nations Children and the Restoration of Aboriginal Communities*. Vancouver: Douglas and McIntyre, 1998.

Culhane Speck, Dana. "The Indian Health Transfer Policy: A Step in the Right Direction, or Revenge of the Hidden Agenda?" *Native Studies Review* 5, no. 1 (1989): 187–213.

"Culliton, Edward Milton." *Encyclopedia of Saskatchewan*. http://esask.uregina.ca/entry/culliton_edward_milton_1906-91.html. Accessed 10 February 2012.

Curtis, Bruce. *The Politics of Population: State Formation, Statistics, and the Census of Canada, 1840–1875*. Toronto: University of Toronto Press, 2001.

Dexter, Grant. *Dr. Charles Camsell*. Winnipeg: Winnipeg Free Press, 1958.

Dryden, Donna, Elva Taylor, Rona Beer, Ron Bergman, Margaret Cogill. *The Camsell Mosaic: The Charles Camsell Hospital, 1945–1985*. Edmonton: Charles Camsell History Committee, 1985.

Dubos, Rene, and Jean Dubos. *The White Plague: Tuberculosis, Man and Society*. Boston: Little, Brown, 1952.

Dyck, Noel. *What Is the Indian "Problem": Tutelage and Resistance in Canadian Indian Administration*. St John's, NL: Institute of Social and Economic Research, 1991.

Ernst, Waltraud. "Beyond East and West. From the History of Colonial Medicine to a Social History of Medicine(s) in South Asia." *Social History of Medicine* 20 (December 2007): 505–24.

Fairchild, Amy, and Gerald Oppenheimer. "Public Health Nihilism vs Pragmatism: History, Politics and the Control of Tuberculosis." *American Journal of Public Health* 88, no. 7 (1998): 1105–17.

Favel-King, Alma. "The Treaty Right to Health." *The Path to Healing: Report of the National Round Table on Aboriginal Health and Social Issues*. Royal Commission on Aboriginal Peoples. Ottawa: Canada Communications Group, 1993.

Feldberg, Georgina. *Disease and Class: Tuberculosis and the Shaping of Modern North American Society*. New Brunswick, NJ: Rutgers University Press, 1995.

Finkel, Alvin. *Our Lives: Canada after 1945*. Toronto: James Lorimer, 1997.

– "Paradise Postponed: A Re-examination of the Green Book Proposals of 1945." *Journal of the Canadian Historical Association* 4, no. 1 (1993): 120–42.

– *Social Policy and Practice in Canada: A History*. Waterloo, ON: Wilfrid Laurier University Press, 2006.

Finzsch, Norbert, and Robert Jütte, eds. *Institutions of Confinement: Hospitals, Asylums, and Prisons in Western Europe and North America, 1500–1950*. Cambridge: Cambridge University Press, 1996.

Foucault, Michel. *Discipline and Punish: The Birth of the Prison*. Trans. A. Sheridan. 2nd ed. New York: Vintage, 1995.

– *Madness and Civilization: A History of Insanity in the Age of Reason*. New York: Vintage, 1984.

Gagan, David, and Rosemary Gagan. *For Patients of Moderate Means: A Social History of the Voluntary Public General Hospital in Canada, 1890–1950*. Montreal and Kingston: McGill-Queen's University Press, 2002.

Goodman, Jordan, Anthony McElligott, and Lara Marks, eds. *Useful Bodies: Humans in the Service of Medical Science in the Twentieth Century*. Baltimore: Johns Hopkins University Press, 2003.

Grant, Shelagh D. *Sovereignty or Security? Government Policy in the Canadian North, 1936–1950*. Vancouver: UBC Press, 1988.

Gray, Charlotte. "Profile: Percy Moore." *Canadian Medical Association Journal* 126 (15 February 1982): 416.

Granshaw, Lindsay. "The Hospital." In *Companion Encyclopaedia of the History of Medicine*, vol. 2, edited by W.F. Bynam and Roy Porter, 1180–203. London: Routledge, 1993.

Grygier, Pat Sandiford. *A Long Way from Home: The Tuberculosis Epidemic among the Inuit*. Montreal and Kingston: McGill-Queen's University Press, 1994.

Hacker, Carlotta. *The Indomitable Lady Doctors*. Toronto: Clarke, Irwin, 1974.

Hanks, Lucien, and Jane Richardson Hanks. *Tribe under Trust: A Study of the Blackfoot Reserve of Alberta*. Toronto: University of Toronto Press 1950.

Hanson, Ann Meekitjuk. "Finding Hope and Healing in Memories of Our Past." *Above and Beyond: Canada's Arctic Journal*, March/April 2012. http://issuu.com/arctic_journal/docs/above_and_beyond_march_april_2012. Accessed 28 May 2013.

Houston, C. Stuart. *R.G. Ferguson: Crusader against Tuberculosis*. Toronto: Dundurn Press, 1991.

Houston, C. Stuart, and Merle Massie. *36 Steps on the Road to Medicare: How Saskatchewan Led the Way*. Montreal and Kingston: McGill-Queen's University Press, 2013.

Ilyniak, Natalia. "Mercury Poisoning in Grassy Narrows: Environmental Injustice, Colonialism, and Capitalist Expansion in Canada." *McGill Sociological Review* 4 (February 2014): 43–66.

Jacklin, Kristen M., and Wayne Warry. "The Indian Health Transfer Policy in Canada: Toward Self-Determination or Cost Containment?" In *Unhealthy Health Policy: A Critical Anthropological Examination*, edited by Arachu Castro and Merrill Singer. Walnut Creek, CA: Alta Mira Press, 2004.

Johnson, Ryan, and Amna Khalid, eds. *Public Health in the British Empire: Intermediaries, Subordinates, and the Practice of Public Health, 1850–1960*. New York: Routledge, 2012.

Johnston, William D. "Tuberculosis." In *The Cambridge World History of Human Diseases*, edited by Kenneth Kiple, 1059–68. Cambridge: Cambridge University Press, 1993.

Jones, Colin, and Roy Porter, eds. *Reassessing Foucault: Power, Medicine and the Body*. London: Routledge, 1994.

Jones, David S. *Rationalizing Epidemics: Meaning and Uses of American Indian Mortality since 1600*. Cambridge: Harvard University Press, 2004.

Kelm, Mary-Ellen. *Colonizing Bodies: Aboriginal Health and Healing in British Columbia, 1900–1950*. Vancouver: University of British Columbia Press, 1998.

– "Diagnosing the Discursive Indian: Medicine, Gender, and the 'Dying Race.'" *Ethnohistory* 52, no. 2 (2005): 371–406.

Lerat, Harold, with Linda Ungar. *Treaty Promises Indian Reality: Life on a Reserve*. Saskatoon: Purich, 2005.

Lux, Maureen. *Medicine That Walks: Disease, Medicine and Canadian Plains Native People, 1880–1940*. Toronto: University of Toronto Press, 2001.

– "Perfect Subjects: Race, Tuberculosis and the Qu'Appelle BCG Vaccine Trial." *Canadian Bulletin of Medical History* 15 (1998): 277–96.

MacIntosh, Constance. "Envisioning the Future of Aboriginal Health under the Health Transfer Process." *Health Law Journal* (Special Edition 2008): 67–100. http://papers.ssrn.com/sol3/papers.cfm?abstract_id=2101674. Accessed 10 February 2014.

MacLeod, Roy, and Milton Lewis, eds. *Disease, Medicine, and Empire*. London: Routledge, 1988.

Manuel, George, and Michael Posluns. *The Fourth World: An Indian Reality*. New York: Free Press, 1974.

Marchildon, Gregory. "Canadian Medicare: Why History Matters." In *Making Medicare: New Perspectives on the History of Medicare in Canada*, edited by Gregory Marchildon. Toronto: University of Toronto Press, 2012.

Marks, Shula. *Divided Sisterhood: Race, Class and Gender in the South African Nursing Profession*. Johannesburg: University of Witwatersand University Press, 1994.

Mawani, Renisa. "Legal Geographies of Aboriginal Segregation in British Columbia." In *Isolation: Places and Practices of Exclusion*, edited by Carolyn Strange and Alison Bashford. London: Routledge, 2003.

McCuaig, Katherine. *The Weariness, the Fever, and the Fret: The Campaign against Tuberculosis in Canada, 1900–1950*. Montreal and Kingston: McGill-Queen's University Press, 1999.

McKay, Ian. "Canada as a Long Liberal Revolution." In *Debating the Canadian Liberal Revolution*, edited by Jean-François Constant and Michel Ducharme. Toronto: University of Toronto Press, 2009.

– "The Liberal Order Framework: A Prospectus for a Reconnaissance of Canadian History." *Canadian Historical Review* 81, no. 4 (December 2000): 625.

McKeown, Thomas. *The Modern Rise of Population*. London: Edward Arnold, 1976.

McPherson, Kathryn. *Bedside Matters: The Transformation of Canadian Nursing, 1900–1990*. Toronto: Oxford University Press, 1996.

– "Nursing and Colonization: The Work of Indian Health Service Nurses in Manitoba." In *Women, Health and Nation: Canada and the United States since 1945*, edited by Georgina Feldberg, Molly Ladd Taylor, Allison Li, and Kathryn McPherson. Montreal and Kingston: McGill-Queen's University Press, 2003.

Mehta, Uday S. "Liberal Strategies of Exclusion." In *Tensions of Empire: Colonial Cultures in a Bourgeois World*, edited by Frederick Cooper and Ann Laura Stoler. Berkeley: University of California Press, 1997.

Meijer Drees, Laurie. *Healing Histories: Stories from Canada's Indian Hospitals*. Edmonton: University of Alberta Press, 2013.

- "Indian Hospitals and Aboriginal Nurses: Canada and Alaska." *Canadian Bulletin of Medical History* 27, no. 1 (2010): 139–61.
- "The Nanaimo and Charles Camsell Indian Hospitals: First Nations' Narratives of Health Care, 1945 to 1965." *Histoire Sociale/Social History* 43, no. 85 (2010): 165–91.
- "Training Aboriginal Nurses: The Indian Health Services in Northwestern Canada, 1939–75." In *Caregiving on the Periphery: Historical Perspectives on Nursing and Midwifery in Canada*, edited by Myra Rutherdale. Montreal and Kingston: McGill-Queen's University Press, 2010.
Menzies, Robert, and Ted Palys. "Turbulent Spirits: Aboriginal Patients in the British Columbia Psychiatric System, 1879–1950." In *Mental Health and Canadian Society: Historical Perspectives*, edited by James E. Moran and David Wright. Montreal and Kingston: McGill-Queen's University Press, 2006.
Miller, J.R. *Shingwauk's Vision: A History of Native Residential Schools*. Toronto: University of Toronto Press, 1996.
- *Skyscrapers Hide the Heavens: A History of Indian-White Relations in Canada*. Rev ed. Toronto: University of Toronto Press, 1989.
Mikkonen, Juha, and Dennis Raphael. *The Social Determinants of Health: The Canadian Facts*. Toronto: York University School of Health Policy and Management, 2010. http://www.thecanadianfacts.org/The_Canadian_Facts.pdf. Accessed 8 February 2014.
Milloy, John. *A National Crime: The Canadian Government and the Residential School System, 1879–1986*. Winnipeg: University of Manitoba Press, 1999.
Mosby, Ian. "Administering Colonial Science: Nutrition Research and Human Biomedical Experimentation in Aboriginal Communities and Residential Schools, 1942–1952." *Histoire Sociale/Social History* 46, no. 91 (May 2013): 145–72.
Narian, Raj. "Need for a BCG Trial in Canada's Native Populations." *Canadian Medical Association Journal* 127 (15 July 1982): 101–2.
Northington Gamble, Vanessa. *Making a Place for Ourselves: The Black Hospital Movement, 1920–1945*. New York: Oxford University Press, 1995.
Noton, Bruce. "Northern Manitoba Treaty Party, 1949." *Manitoba History* 39 (Spring/Summer 2000). http://www.mhs.mb.ca/docs/mb_history/39/treatyparty1949.shtml. Accessed 12 April 2013.
Olofsson, Ebba, et al. "Negotiating Identities: Inuit Tuberculosis Evacuees in the 1940s–1950s." *Études/Inuit/Studies* 32, no. 2 (2008): 127–49.
O'Neil, John D. "Aboriginal Health Policy for the Next Century." *The Path to Healing: Report of the National Round Table on Aboriginal Health and Social Issues*. Royal Commission on Aboriginal Peoples. Ottawa: Canada Communications Group, 1993.

Ostry, Aleck. "The Foundations of National Public Hospital Insurance." In *Making Medicare: New Perspectives on the History of Medicare in Canada*, edited by Gregory Marchildon. Toronto: University of Toronto Press, 2012.

Ott, Katherine. *Fevered Lives: Tuberculosis in American Culture since 1870.* Cambridge, MA: Harvard University Press, 1996.

Packard, Randall M. *White Plague, Black Labor: Tuberculosis and the Political Economy of Health and Disease in South Africa.* Berkeley: University of California Press, 1989.

Paine, A.L., and Earl Hershfield. "Tuberculosis: Past, Present and Future." *Canadian Family Physician* 25 (1979): 55–9.

Perry, Adele. *On the Edge of Empire: Gender, Race and the Making of British Columbia, 1849–1871.* Toronto: University of Toronto Press, 2001.

– "Women, Racialized People, and the Making of the Liberal Order in Northern North America." In *Debating the Canadian Liberal Revolution*, edited by Jean-François Constant and Michel Ducharme. Toronto: University of Toronto Press, 2009.

Ray, Arthur J., J.R. Miller, and Frank Tough. *Bounty and Benevolence: A History of Saskatchewan Treaties.* Montreal: McGill-Queen's University Press, 2000.

Rosenberg, Charles. *The Care of Strangers: The Rise of America's Hospital System.* New York: Basic Books, 1987.

Rosner, David. *A Once Charitable Enterprise: Hospitals and Health Care in Brooklyn and New York, 1885–1915.* New York: Cambridge University Press, 1982.

Rothman, Sheila. *Living in the Shadow of Death: Tuberculosis and the Social Experience of Illness in American History.* New York: Basic Books, 1994.

Rutherdale, Myra. "Nursing in the North and Writing for the South: The Work and Travels of Amy Wilson." In *Caregiving on the Periphery: Historical Perspectives on Nursing and Midwifery in Canada*, edited by Myra Rutherdale. Montreal and Kingston: McGill-Queen's University Press, 2010.

Shewell, Hugh. *Enough to Keep Them Alive: Indian Welfare in Canada, 1873–1965.* Toronto: University of Toronto Press, 2004.

Smith, Derek G. "The Emergence of 'Eskimo Status': An Examination of the Eskimo Disk List System and Its Social Consequences, 1925–1970." In *Anthropology, Public Policy, and Native Peoples in Canada*, edited by Noel Dyck and James Waldram. Montreal and Kingston: McGill-Queen's University Press, 1993.

Smith, F.B. *The Retreat of Tuberculosis, 1850–1950.* London: Croom Helm, 1988.

Staples, Annalisa, and Ruth McConnell. *Soapstone and Seed Beads: Arts and Craft at the Charles Camsell Hospital.* Edmonton: Jasper Printing, 1993.

Strange, Carolyn, and Alison Bashford. *Isolation: Places and Practices of Exclusion.* London: Routledge, 2003.

Stewart, David B. *Holy Ground: The Story of the Manitoba Sanatorium at Ninette.* Killarney, MB: J.A. Victor David Museum, 1999.

Suzuki, David. *The Autobiography.* Vancouver: Greystone Books, 2006.

Taylor, Malcolm. "The Canadian Health Care System: After Medicare." In *Health and Canadian Society: Sociological Perspectives,* edited by David Coburn, Carl D'Arcy, George Torrance, and Peter New. 2nd ed. Toronto: Fitzhenry and Whiteside, 1987.

– *Health Insurance and Canadian Public Policy: The Seven Decisions That Created the Canadian Health Insurance System and Their Outcomes.* 2nd ed. Kingston and Montreal: McGill-Queen's University Press, 1987.

Thorpe, E.L.M. *The Social Histories of Smallpox and Tuberculosis in Canada: Culture, Evolution and Disease.* Winnipeg: University of Manitoba Anthropology Papers No. 30, 1989.

Titley, Brian. *A Narrow Vision: Duncan Campbell Scott and the Administration of Indian Affairs in Canada.* Vancouver: University of British Columbia Press, 1986.

Tobias, John L. "Protection, Civilization, Assimilation: An Outline History of Canada's Indian Policy." *Western Canadian Journal of Anthropology* 6, no. 2 (1976): 13–30.

Traynor, Cam. "Manning against Medicare." *Alberta History* 43 (1995): 7–19.

Vaughan, Megan. *Curing Their Ills: Colonial Power and African Illness.* Palo Alto, CA: Stanford University Press, 1991.

Venne, Sharon Helen. *Indian Acts and Amendments 1868–1975: An Indexed Collection.* Saskatoon: Native Law Centre, University of Saskatchewan, 1981.

Waiser, W.A. "Camsell, Charles." In *Oxford Companion to Canadian History,* edited by Gerald Hallowell. Toronto: Oxford University Press, 2004.

Waldram, James, D. Ann Herring, and T. Kue Young. *Aboriginal Health in Canada: Historical, Cultural, and Epidemiological Perspectives.* 2nd ed. Toronto: University of Toronto Press, 2006.

Weaver, Sally. *Making Canadian Indian Policy: The Hidden Agenda, 1968–70.* Toronto: University of Toronto Press, 1981.

Wherrett, George Jasper. *The Miracle of the Empty Beds: A History of Tuberculosis in Canada.* Toronto: University of Toronto Press, 1977.

Wishart, James. "Class Difference and the Reformation of Ontario Public Hospitals, 1900–1935." *Labour/Le Travail* 48 (2001): 27–61.

Woods, David. "The Canadian Council on Hospital Accreditation in Canada." *Canadian Medical Association Journal* 110 (6 April 1974): 851–5.

Young, T. Kue. "A BCG Trial in Canada's Native Populations." *Canadian Medical Association Journal* 127 (December 1982): 1166–7.

– *Health Care and Cultural Change: The Indian Experience in the Central Subarctic.* Toronto: University of Toronto Press, 1988.

Zumla, Alimuddin, and Matthew Gundy. "Epilogue: Politics, Science, and the 'New' Tuberculosis." In *The Return of the White Plague: Global Poverty and the "New" Tuberculosis*, edited by Matthew Gundy and Alimuddin Zumla. London: Verso, 2003.

Theses and Dissertations

Churchill, Elizabeth. "Tsuu T'ina: A History of a First Nations Community, 1890-1940." PhD diss., University of Calgary, 2000.

Cohen, Benita E. "The Development of Health Services in Peguis First Nation: A Descriptive Case Study." MSc thesis, University of Manitoba, 1994.

Hader, Joanne. "The Effect of Tuberculosis on the Indians of Saskatchewan, 1926–1965." MA thesis, University of Saskatchewan, 1990.

McCallum, Mary Jane Logan. "Labour, Modernity and the Canadian State: A History of Aboriginal Women and Work in the Mid-Twentieth Century." PhD diss., University of Manitoba, 2008.

Paul, Pauline. "A History of the Edmonton General Hospital: 1895–1970." PhD diss., University of Alberta, 1994.

Plant, Byron King. "The Politics of Indian Administration: A Revisionist History of Intrastate Relations in Mid-Century British Columbia." PhD diss., University of Saskatchewan, 2009.

Weaver, Sally Mae. "Health, Culture and Dilemma: A Study of the Non-Conservative Iroquois, Six Nations Reserve, Ontario." PhD diss., University of Toronto, 1967.

Zdunich, Darlene. "Tuberculosis and World War One Veterans." MA thesis, University of Calgary, 1984.

Index